RUTH HAMILTON

The Judge's Daughter
&
The Reading Room

PAN BOOKS

The Judge's Daughter first published 2007 Pan Books
The Reading Room first published 2009 by Pan Books

This omnibus first published 2011 by Pan Books
an imprint of Pan Macmillan, a division of Macmillan Publishers Limited
Pan Macmillan, 20 New Wharf Road, London N1 9RR
Basingstoke and Oxford
Associated companies throughout the world
www.panmacmillan.com

ISBN 978-0-330-54565-5

Copyright © Ruth Hamilton 2007, 2009

1 3 5 7 9 8 6 4 2

A CIP catalogue record for this book is available from
the British Library.

Printed in the UK by CPI Mackays, Chatham ME5 8TD

The Judge's Daughter

In loving memory of Lydia Carroll

Thanks to my grandson, Christopher,
for making me smile on dark days

Also:
My two sons for unswerving support
Their partners Sue and Liz for the same

Imogen Taylor and Trisha Jackson from
Pan Macmillan for faith and help

Sam and Fudge, older but no wiser Labradors
Oscar (ring-necked parakeet) for eating my words
– literally

Last, but never least, the readership

2004

Long after the man had finished pacing and calculating, his footfalls seemed to echo round the house, bouncing off walls that had heard no sound in many a year. He scratched an ear, shook his head, talked to himself for a few moments before going back to work all over again. He measured room after room, the instrument in his hand clicking with every metre he covered. There had to be something wrong with the new-fangled digital equipment. Three times, he had measured Briarswood; three times, the result had been ridiculous enough for a Walt Disney cartoon.

'According to this, the place should have fallen down years ago,' he muttered. But there were no huge cracks, no faults, no gaping wounds in the plasterwork or in the exterior stone and brick fascia. A place of this size had to have twelve-foot underpinnings – it needed a solid base. And nowhere on the architect's aged plan did a flatbed foundation get a mention. Anyway, why stabilize the back of the house and leave the front to chance and nature? The rear part was correct, each storey matching the one below right down to the basement, yet the front remained a mystery.

In a huge bay window, he paused and wondered, not for the first time, whether modern science represented any real improvement in his job. Sighing, he put away the newer tool of his trade and drew from a pocket that good old standby – a metal measure encased in bright orange plastic. He would start again. This time, he began in attics, moving down to bathrooms and sleeping quarters, finally tackling ground floor and cellar. The answer was the same. The cellar was smaller than the rest of the house and this fact presented something of an enigma for prospective purchasers. As surveyor, he had to hand in a sensible report and there was nothing sensible about Briarswood.

He sat on an abandoned kitchen chair and wrote down the bare bones of his findings. Never a fanciful man, he shivered and looked up, expecting to blame an open door for creating the draught, but he was still alone. The house was dark and reeked of emptiness. Could a place express loneliness? Could a house complain about solitude and neglect? A tap dripped. Jaundice-yellow emulsion was peeling itself away from walls. He wrote about slight roof damage, ancient rainwater goods and some broken tiling in a bathroom. He reported the need for damp-proofing, a suspicion about wall ties in a gable, a decaying perimeter fence in the rear garden. Lastly, he remarked on the impossible: the footings were smaller than the building. There was no dry rot, no wet rot, no decaying timber. But there was something amiss with the specifications.

Outside, he stared into a thousand eyes created by ornate leaded windows, many of whose panes were the imperfect products of primitive glassmakers. Normally, the faceted diamond effect would have pleased him, but this place reminded him of long-ago textbooks in which, as a child, he had studied magnified diagrams of insect eyes. Like a mature bluebottle, the large house owned a plethora of aspects through which it viewed the world.

It seemed alive, yet dead. And he needed a double whisky, his dinner, his family, his newspaper.

As he climbed back into the car, he felt as if the house were continuing to watch and analyse him. It was just the sinking sun, he told himself impatiently. He wasn't one for ghosts and ghouls, but even he had to admit that there was something strange about Briarswood. Almost laughing at himself, he pushed the gearstick into first and drew away. Did the house need an exorcist rather than a property surveyor?

At the gate, he braked and looked for traffic. Ah, well. He would commit the peculiarities to paper tonight, would hand in the work, then move on to the next project. No mention need be made of icy tingling in his spine, of hairs on arms standing to attention, of the feeling that he had been followed for two hours. It was just another house, a residence built of sandstone and imitation string courses designed to allow the house a relationship with Tudor mansions. 'I get dafter with age,' he mumbled. Nothing ever went bump in the night; most certainly not at four o'clock in the afternoon. The sun disappeared behind scudding cloud and every eye in the windows was suddenly closed.

Shadows appeared. Staring into his rear-view mirror, the man studied Briarswood. There was no one in the place, yet he imagined movement and felt sadness soaking through the building's fabric and right into his bones. 'Well, I wouldn't put my name down for a seance in there,' he told his notebook, which he had placed on the passenger seat. In a career that spanned some twenty years, he had never surveyed a property so creepy and odd. No wonder it had remained empty, he mused as the sun reappeared and woke the windows once more.

There had been rumours, stories of families leaving the place in a hurry, hints about disappearing objects and noises in the night. Lancashire had long been awash with such tales, many of which were aired and embellished by folk who had taken too much ale. The whole thing was crazy and he needed to pull his ideas together and stop talking to himself before going home.

But he found himself shivering anew until he turned out of the driveway and accelerated towards Wigan Road. Someone would have to get to the bottom of the equation, and he thanked God that his part in the business was now over.

Chapter One

1964

It was a tin of Barker's Lavender Polish this time. He picked it up, stared at it for several seconds, turned and left the shop with the container clasped tightly against his chest. As always, he looked like a man on a mission, not exactly in a hurry, but with no time for dawdling.

'Mr Grimshaw?' Eva Hargreaves moved very quickly for a woman of twenty stones and fifty years. 'Come on, Fred, you've not paid.' But he was yards ahead and the ironmonger dared not leave her business untended. The old chap wasn't in his right mind just now, and his daughter would bring the money. She always coughed up, did poor Agnes. Aye, she suffered in more ways than one, had done for years. Some folk endured very bad luck and some got away with murder. It was an eternal mystery and people cleverer than Eva would never find an answer to it. All the same, the theft was a damned nuisance and no mistake, but Glenys Timpson was entering the shop and would be waiting for her firewood, so the shopkeeper returned to her rightful place.

Glenys tutted when Eva came in. 'He wants putting away in the asylum,' she said, sour mouth even more down-turned than usual. 'Doesn't know what he's doing. There's no rhyme and no reason to his carryings-on. That Agnes Makepeace wants to stop at home and see to him. God knows he looked after her for long enough.'

Eva Hargreaves didn't want to lose a customer, yet she chose to reply. 'Agnes's husband isn't paid over-well by them in yon big house. Family needs her cleaning money. Her pop will get better – he's better already; it were only a small stroke. She's gone from the house nobbut three hours a day, and she looks after her grandparents for the other twenty-one hours. The old fellow walks in the night as well, you know. It's nobody's fault. Agnes has always done her best, and I dare say she'll carry on the same road.'

The customer sniffed. 'Two lots of firewood, Eva. I've company expected at the weekend, so I'll be want-ing a parlour fire.' She inhaled again. 'For his own good, he wants putting somewhere safe. Mark my words, he'll be under a bus any day now. What price a little job in the pub when that happens, eh? She should know her duty – and not just to her kin, but to us as well.'

'It were only a tin of polish.' The shopkeeper placed two wired bundles of kindling on her counter. 'And he's miles better than he was. Takes time, getting over a stroke.'

'Happen it were only a tin of polish, but he'd not get away with it in town, would he? Then if the court says he's insane, which he is – a few raisins short of an Eccles cake if you ask me – he'll definitely get put away. Agnes'd be best doing it the right road, through her own doctor. No use sitting about waiting for a disaster. It wants sorting out now, before he goes from bad to bloody ridiculous.'

Eva offered no comment. She knew Agnes Make-peace and couldn't imagine her parting with the man she called Pop. Agnes was well aware of her duty and would see her elders through to the bitterest of ends. 'Anything else?' she asked her customer.

'Nay, just the firewood.' Glenys stalked to the door, then turned as an afterthought processed itself before pouring from her lips. 'Were he in his pyjama top?' she asked.

'Yes.' Eva was rearranging bottles of Lanry bleach. Fred Grimshaw was in his pyjama bottoms, too, though they were almost covered by a pair of tattered, unclean overalls.

'Nowt good'll come of it,' pronounced the redoubtable Glenys before striding homeward.

Eva sat on her stool for a few moments. She was getting too tired for this lark and her weight didn't help. Poor old Fred Grimshaw – what was he up to this time? Should she close her shop and dash along to the pub for Agnes? No, he'd be long gone by now. For a man with health problems, he could shift at a fair rate of knots. 'He is getting better,' she reminded herself through clenched teeth. 'And he deserves to get better, bless him. There's no man finer than Fred Grimshaw.'

She found herself praying to a God who would surely have mercy on a poorly gentleman, because Fred had been just that – one of Nature's better creatures. Then she stood up to measure paraffin into a container. Life had to go on; customers wanted their goods and homes needed to be heated, even in summer once the sun went down. Like Agnes Makepeace, Eva Hargreaves was completely powerless. Fred had likely gone missing again and there was nothing to be done.

Fred Grimshaw had never been late for work in his life. Even during this war, he still stuck to his tools, turning out ammunition instead of wrought-iron gates. His skills were required. All those railings wanted melting down and the place was full of women these days. Hard workers, all right, but they chattered a lot when his back was turned. A foreman needed eyes in the back of his head, that was a fact.

He stood outside the factory and blinked. Entwistle Motors? Ah, that must be a government thing, a way of hiding what really went on inside those sheds. Hitler was planning an invasion and he and his army needed to be confused. Entwistle Motors. Unimpressed by the new name, Fred entered his little kingdom.

Where was the furnace? Where was his lathe? The women had all gone home, curlers rattling beneath turbans made from headscarves. It wasn't home time. Bullets didn't make themselves, did they? How the hell could he carry on with no equipment and no workforce? Was he supposed to supply the army on his own?

He dropped the tin of polish and it rolled away across a flagged floor. The place was full of motor vehicles, some in one piece, others with their intestines spread out across floor and benches. His jaw dropped. How could things change overnight like this? Only yesterday, he had stood here making casings for bullets – he even remembered bandaging his thumb after he'd . . . There was no bandage on his thumb. He had made another mistake and another headache threatened.

Sam Entwistle raised himself out of a pit. 'Fred?' The unhappy wanderer was here once more, body intact, head nineteen years or more late. 'Come on, old lad. Let's be getting you home, shall we? Don't start upsetting yourself.'

Fred blinked. 'I've done it again, haven't I?'

'You have. Your mind's playing tricks because of your stroke. And I can't keep taking time off to drive you home, can I? These here apprentices get up to all sorts while I'm off the scene.' He shouted across to his second-in-command. 'Keep an eye on that crowd of buggers while I run Fred home.' Sam sighed. Fred was known far and wide as a man of opinions, a man who liked to speak his mind and shame the devil. He had even been labelled cantankerous and loud, yet he had been reduced to this in one cruel, fell swoop. 'Come on, Fred.'

Meek as a kitten, Fred allowed himself to be placed in the passenger seat of Sam Entwistle's van. 'I'm not right,' he said softly when Sam was seated beside him. 'I'm half here, half there and half no-bloody-where.'

'That's three halves.'

'I know. See what I mean?'

The fact that Fred had insight into his own condition was the biggest cruelty, Sam mused as he turned the vehicle into Derby Street. Yet there was hope, because this was not senile dementia – it was the aftermath of a bleed and the man would come good. 'See, Fred, you weren't well at all. You were a fighter, and you survived. Look – you've got your talking back and you can shift on your feet better than most your age. Another few months and you'll be right as rain in the memory department. It'll stop. I promise you – this carrying-on will stop.'

The passenger nodded. 'I blinking well hope so, son. I wait for our Agnes to come home from school – she's been working for years and she's married. I do daft things like this – going to work, getting on buses and throwing stuff out – I'm bloody puddled half the time.'

'But the other two halves of the time, you're all right. Takes a while, old son. My dad had a stroke and he never walked again. Be patient. You're doing all right, believe me.'

Fred was cross with himself. He knew full well what had happened – hadn't it all been explained in the hospital? A stroke meant all kinds of things and he could walk and talk well, could behave properly for most of the time. 'In me pyjamas again,' he pronounced morosely.

'At least you're not naked and frightening the horses.' Sam pulled up at Fred's front door. 'Now, listen to me. Find something to do with your hands – make toys or furniture or whatever you feel like. Your head's got a broken wire in – like a telephone that doesn't carry the message. There's things you've got to relearn, you see. And you're one of the lucky ones – you're not flat on your back or in a wheelchair. Get busy. Keep yourself occupied, that's my motto. It's the only way to stay out of the graveyard, old lad.'

Fred entered the house and inhaled deeply. It smelled of death. His good old girl was on her way out. He'd been married to Sadie forever, and she was leaving him. He should have been looking after her. He should have been looking at the card propped next to the clock, a white background bearing the numbers 1964 in large black print. Agnes had put that there to remind him of the year. There was a list somewhere – the Prime Minister and other stuff that didn't matter. Tory or Labour, they were all the bloody same, in it for what they could get out of it. He smiled wryly; some things were impossible to forget. Somewhere inside himself, Fred remained as angry and positive as ever.

Sadie was on morphine now. She didn't laugh any more, didn't talk to him; she just lay there till a nurse came to clean her up and try to get some fluids into her. Cancer. He hated that word. It meant crab, and crabs owned sharp claws. 'Sadie,' he whispered sadly.

His wife needed to die. That was another bit of sense he had retained – the ability to judge when a person had taken enough. And his Sadie had taken well more than enough.

She was in the downstairs front room. Denis and a neighbour had brought the bed down; Fred slept alone in a contraption that felt like an ex-army cot, just canvas stretched over a metal frame. 'But I'm alive,' he accused himself. 'And I have to learn . . .' Learn what? How to be a human being, how to get from morning till night? Hadn't he been doing that for over seventy years? Did he have to go back to Peter and Paul's nursery, start all over again?

Agnes would be home from school soon. No, that was wrong – she would be home from work. He had to behave himself, must make sure that he didn't . . . Tin of polish. Had he paid for it? Where was it, anyway? He was stupid. Then he remembered Sam Entwistle pushing something into a pocket of the decaying overalls and he plunged his hand inside. It was there. 'I remembered,' he breathed. He could go and pay for it, could complete the errand. They could call him daft if they wanted, but he was going to show them.

After looking in on his wife, he set forth to pay his debt to Eva Hargreaves. At the same time, he would buy a notebook. 'I'll write everything down,' he said to himself. 'That road, I'll have half a chance of remembering to be normal.'

Normal. What the blinking heck did that mean and who had decided? Normal was having no weak blood vessels in the brain, no cancer, a full memory. He could see the war all right – his war, the war to end all wars. Jimmy Macker blown into a thousand pieces, flesh and bone everywhere, corpses stacked beneath mud in

11

endless miles of trenches. But he couldn't remember the current days, weeks and months; was not *normal*.

Jimmy MacKenzie, usually known as Macker. Aye, he could see him now, cheeky grin, stolen silver cigarette case twinned with a silver matchbox, both taken from a body in a trench. That daft smile had been blown away with the rest of Jimmy and with a million others, all ploughed in now, all gone from mud to dust. *Alice in Wonderland*. He had read that to Agnes a few weeks – no – a few years back. Cheshire cat. The grin remained when tail, body and whiskers disappeared. Macker's grin had lodged itself into Fred's mind, clear as crystal . . . Poor Macker.

But what had Fred eaten for breakfast? Did it matter? Was breakfast important enough to be remembered? Yes, he would write everything in a notebook. Eva sold notebooks and pencils, didn't she? It was the only way to learn. He could copy the date from the newspaper at the top of a page. He would make a note of every damned thing he did, ate and said. Sadie needed him. She didn't talk, but he felt sure she knew when he was there. He must spend more time with his wife and less time wandering about in pyjamas. There was probably a law about pyjamas in the street. Blessed government – they all wanted shooting.

Glenys Timpson was cleaning her windows again. Oh, he remembered her all right. She stoned her steps and cleaned her outside paintwork several times a week, because she couldn't bear to miss anything. She was a curtain-twitcher and a gossip. That hatchet face was not something that could be forgotten.

'Fred Grimshaw?' There was an edge of flint to her tone.

He stopped, but offered no greeting.

'You pinched a tin of polish from Eva's shop before. I were there. I watched you pocket it and run.'

'And I'm going back to pay for it.' He was glad she had reminded him, as he still needed to acquire his memory notebook and the polish was not at the front of his mind any more.

'You should stop in the house,' she snapped.

He took a step closer to the woman. 'So should you. That scraggy neck's grown inches with you poking your head into everybody's doings. Mind your own business.' Another dim memory resurrected itself. 'You could try keeping your lads sober for a kick-off.' He marched away, head held high, the mantra 'Pay for polish' repeating in his head. But there was triumph in his heart, because he had remembered that nosy neighbour. One of these days, she'd end up flat on her face and with no one to help her up.

Glenys Timpson, who declared under her breath that she had never been so insulted in all her born days, retreated into her domain. Eva was right – the old man was getting better. Or worse, she mused, depending on a person's point of view. Some folk thought they were a cut above their neighbours and that there Agnes Makepeace was one of that breed. Aye, well – pride came before every fall.

Her lads weren't drunkards. They liked a drink – especially Harry, who was an amateur boxer – but they didn't go overboard unless it was a special occasion. Perhaps special occasions were becoming more frequent, but she wasn't having her lads tainted with the reputation of drunkards. She set the table angrily, throwing cutlery into place. Some folk didn't know when to keep their mouths shut. Some folk wanted teaching a lesson. It was time to have a word with Mrs Agnes Makepeace.

13

Fred entered the shop.

'Hello, love,' Eva began. She liked the man, had always had time for him and his loudly expressed opinions on most subjects. She could tell from his expression that he knew he had done something wrong and was struggling to remember the sin.

He held up a hand. 'I need help,' he said bluntly. 'Seems some of my memory got muddled while I was in the infirmary. I could do with a notebook and a pencil to help me make lists of stuff. My brain's got more holes than the cabbage strainer.'

Eva nodded. 'I've some coloured pencils. You could write about different things in separate colours. You could use both ends of the book as well – important business at the front and details at the back.'

'Good idea,' he said. 'And you can take pay for that tin of polish.' He had remembered the polish. This was a red-letter day, and he would mark it on the page in scarlet. 'Funny how you remember things,' he said. 'It's not the things themselves that come back right away – it's a smell or a sound or some bit of detail. Like Jimmy Macker's smile. I'll never forget his smile.'

Eva took money from his hand, counted it out, placed it in the till. 'Fred?'

'What?'

'Did you use that polish at all?'

He frowned. 'I don't think so.'

'Do you know whether your Agnes needs polish?'

He had no idea.

She looked at the tin. 'Tell you what – seeing as it's you, I'll take it back. That'll save you money and it'll save your Agnes worrying over where her new tin of Barker's came from. And you'll get your book and pencils for the same price as the polish.'

14

'Fair enough.' With his coloured pencils and his stiff-backed notebook, Fred went home. He intended to sit next to his dying wife and write the date in red at the top of the first page. Nothing was impossible. For the sake of his Sadie and his beloved granddaughter, Fred Grimshaw would carry on. There was life in the old dog yet.

The drain was blocked again.

Agnes, who had come to the end of her shortened tether, flung mop and bucket across the floor. Ernie Ramsden, nicknamed Ramrod by his staff, was too stingy to send for a plumber, so he would deal with this himself. He would uncover the outside drain, piece his rods together and riddle about until he had shifted the offending item. Derby Street was about to smell like a sewage works again, and the problem would return within days, but why should she worry? It was his pub, his stink, so he could get on with it, while she would clean elsewhere in the building.

In the bar, she picked up polish and duster and began to work on the tables. Ramsden came in. 'Have you done the men's already?' he asked.

'Blocked,' she answered tersely. If he wanted to go poking about in ancient drains, that was his privilege.

'Are you sure?'

Agnes shrugged. 'There's stuff all over the floor and nothing goes down. When I flushed, the place flooded. The women's isn't much better. So yes, it's happened again. You need a plumber.'

'Brewery wouldn't stand for that,' replied the landlord.

'And if something isn't done, your customers won't

15

stand for it, either. They won't be able to stand, because they'll be overcome by fumes. Every time you lift the pavement cover, folk start crossing over to the other side of the road. You're becoming a health hazard. Will the corporation not help with this mess before people start ending up in hospital?'

Ernie Ramsden shook his head. 'Nay. Trouble is, the blockage is here, under the pub. Not the town's property.'

Agnes stopped polishing. Several months, she'd worked here. It was part time and it was driving her part mad. But there was little she could do about it, because the hours suited her. Looking after aged grand-parents meant that she couldn't take a full time job, so she came here every day and, at least once a week, needed her wellington boots so that she could wade through excrement and lavatory paper. 'Up to you,' she said before resuming her attack on a circular table. 'I can't do any more.'

Ernie stood for a few moments and watched Agnes at work. She was a corker, all right. Denis Makepeace was a lucky fellow, because his wife was built like a perfect sculpture – rounded, ripe and strong. She was a good worker, too. She did her job, invited and offered few confidences, then rushed home to see to her elders. 'How's the family?' he asked.

'All right,' came the dismissive response.

The landlord sighed before retreating to his living quarters.

They were a long way from all right, mused Agnes as she placed a pile of ashtrays on the counter. Nan was dying of cancer, while Pop, who had been the old lady's chief carer, was fighting for the right to return from a world all his own. Only last week, he had been marched home by a bus conductor, a female whose vehicle had remained stationary for at least ten minutes at the top of Noble Street. Agnes could still hear the woman's shrill voice. 'Can you not keep him in? He's no right to be on a public vehicle in his dressing gown and carpet slippers. Said he were on his way to catch the train to Southport – and his train ticket were nobbut a label off a condensed milk tin. I can't be leaving the bus to bring him home all the while.'

Agnes swallowed hard while she wondered what Pop had got up to today. She'd locked the front door, but he needed to get out into the yard for the lavatory, so the back door was on the latch. Into the open drain beneath the tippler, he had thrown his lower denture, a week's worth of newspapers, one brown shoe and, she suspected, an antimacassar taken from the front room. It was probably Pop's fault that the area's drains were getting blocked. No, it couldn't be him. The stoppage was the sole property of Ernie Ramsden and the Dog and Ferret.

'I'll just have a go meself,' muttered Ernie as he struggled past with his rods. He was always having a go himself and he knew that the problem was way beyond the reach of his rods.

Agnes prayed that she had left no matches in the house. Pop needed to be separated from anything combustible or sharp. Knives were wrapped in sacking on the top shelf of her wardrobe. What a way to live. If she'd been one for visitors, she would have needed to excuse herself in order to fetch an implement with which to cut cake. But few people came to the Makepeace house. Denis's work took him away from home for many hours – and who wanted to sit with a poor old woman and a mad old man?

The familiar scent of human excrement insinuated its way into the pub. Almost automatically, Agnes took a small amount of cotton wool from her apron pocket and stuffed half into each nostril. The men's lavs were bad enough, but this smell was unbearable. Ramsden, fearful that the brewery might close him down, was trying with little success to keep the men's facilities in working condition, but he was losing the battle.

Voices floated through the open door. 'At it again, Ernie?' 'Somebody been passing bricks down yer lav?' 'Let us know when you strike gold, eh? Carry on this road and you'll hit Australia.'

She sat down for a few minutes. Even the mills were better than this, but she couldn't abandon the people who had reared her, could she? Agnes's mother had died two hours after giving birth to her only child, while the father was listed as unknown. Sadie and Fred Grimshaw, having cared for their own daughter, had been presented with her newborn baby girl and had simply continued with life. They had been firm, but kind, and Agnes owed her life to them.

A red-faced Ernie entered the arena. 'I reckon yon drain's collapsed,' he announced.

'Then you'll have to close down and tell the brewery,' she replied. She and Denis would struggle to manage. Pop could do a lot of damage in three hours, so Agnes needed to bite the bullet and quit. It wasn't going to be easy, but it had to be faced; she would soon need to stay at home all the time. Even five minutes was time enough for Pop to create disaster, and Nan was becoming too ill to be left to the poor old chap's mercies.

Ernie poured himself a double Irish. 'You're right,' he admitted gloomily. 'End of the road, Agnes.' He drained the glass. 'What'll you do? Mind, I'll take you on again like a shot if the brewery lets me carry on. You're the best cleaner I've ever had.'

She bit her lip and pondered. It seemed as if every other building on Derby Street was a pub. The Dog and Ferret, never truly popular, had lost more customers because of the drains, and its owners could well close it down or renovate it before putting someone younger in charge. There were too many pubs, and she disliked them, hated the smells, was afraid of what drinking did to people. She had taken enough. 'Nan's dying,' she said after a few moments. 'I was meaning to give notice soon, because she needs nursing round the clock. I won't have her spending her last days in hospital. I promised her she'd stop at home no matter what.'

'And is the owld chap still a bit daft?'

Everyone knew Fred, though few remembered the dedicated worker who had toiled for forty-odd years in the town's foundry. He had been a big man, but age had withered him and he was shorter, thinner and extremely frail. No, she told herself firmly – Pop was getting better. 'He's old,' she snapped. 'He's had a bit of a stroke – that's his only sin. None of us can fight the years – he's been a hard worker in his time.'

'I didn't mean to offend,' he said.

Agnes placed her box of tools on a table. 'I'm going.' She straightened and took one last look around her place of work. She would miss the thinking time more than anything, this island of relative solitude alongside which she had been allowed to moor herself for a few hours each day. At home, she had to face the reality that was Nan, the burden that was Pop, the same four walls day in and day out. If only that judge fellow weren't so selfish, Denis would be working regular

19

hours for decent pay, but the judge represented rules in more ways than one. He interpreted the law of the land during working hours, then set regulations to suit himself and only himself when he got home. Judge Spencer was a tyrant, she supposed.

'I'll miss you, lass.' Ernie's expression said it all. He would probably lose his livelihood within days.

'They'll find you another pub,' she told him.

'I'm no spring chicken.' He left her and returned to his living quarters.

Agnes put on her coat and stepped outside. She removed the cotton wool from her nostrils and crossed the road, anxious to be away from the stench of human waste. Managing on Denis's income was not going to be easy. It would mean less meat, more vegetables and no new clothes for some time. She was twenty years old and she owned nothing, no record player, no transistor radio, no decent shoes. Denis, her husband of twelve months, was in possession of a weak chest and was unfit for anything approaching hard labour. Nan was dying; Pop ... Pop was walking down Noble Street with a package in his hands. 'Pop?' she cried. Oh, no. What had he done this time and who would be knocking at the door?

He turned, frowned because she had grown again. No, she hadn't. It would go in the notebook – Agnes was a woman and no longer went to school. Denis was her husband – that, too, would be recorded. Denis Makepeace, bad chest, huge heart.

'Where've you been?' she asked.

He had been sorting out his life, but the details were vague. 'Coloured pencils,' he told her. 'And a little book to help me remember.'

She grinned, recalled him swinging her in the air,

20

running round the duck pond with her, laughing at Laurel and Hardy at the local cinema. The Grimshaws had been good parents and Agnes had lacked for nothing during childhood. They could have abandoned her to an orphanage or to adoption, but they had given her a happy life and now she had to care for them. 'Oh, Pop.' She smiled. 'I hope you've been up to no mischief.'

'Me?' He was a picture of innocence. 'I can't remember,' he admitted eventually, 'but I think I went to work again. I'm worse in a morning, you know. By afternoon, I can nearly remember my own name.'

'The year's on the mantelpiece.'

'Aye.'

'I put it there for a reason.'

'Aye.'

'And if you say aye again, I'll clout you.'

'Aye.'

They walked down Noble Street until they reached Glenys Timpson's house. She was out in an instant, seeming to propel herself with the speed of a bullet from a gun. Thin arms folded themselves against a flat bosom. 'He's been thieving again.' Triumph shone in her eyes as she nodded in Fred's direction. 'Not fit to be out.'

Agnes stared at the irate creature. 'Mrs Timpson,' she began after an uncomfortable pause. 'Your sons, Harry, Bert and Jack – have I got their names right?'

The woman jerked her head in agreement.

'You'd best keep them in, missus.' Agnes moved closer to her adversary. 'I've heard talk. They'll have to start watching their step.'

'Eh?' Like many of her generation, Glenys wore a scarf turban-fashion, curlers peeping out from the edges.

She raised her eyebrows until they all but disappeared under pink and blue plastic rollers. 'You what? What are you incinerating?' She frowned, knowing that the word she had delivered was slightly inappropriate.

The younger woman lowered her voice until it became almost a whisper. 'Selling jewellery round the pubs. Probably from that safe job in Manchester. Remember? Wasn't your Harry in the army during his service? Perhaps he learned about explosives and a safe might be easy for him. He hangs around in the wrong company.'

'What are you saying?'

'I'm saying keep your mouth shut about Pop, or I'll open mine about a few cheap brooches and bracelets. I'm saying mind your own business. Pop forgets things. Your sons are just plain bad.'

Glenys fell against the front door, a hand over her heart.

'Don't forget – my husband works for a High Court judge.' Noting that the street's biggest gossip had gone into shock, Agnes took Pop's arm and marched him homeward. As she walked, she shook from head to foot, but she remained as straight as she could manage, because she didn't want Glenys Timpson to see how scared she was. At twenty, Agnes was female head of a household and it wasn't easy, especially with a man like Pop causing bother from time to time.

Gratefully, she closed her front door.

'Were that true?' Pop asked. 'Have her sons been stealing?'

Agnes studied her grandfather. 'You remembered that all right. Yes, it's true. She's so busy watching other folks' comings and goings that she misses what's under her nose. They've been chucked out of the Dog and

Ferret twice for trying to sell things. I've heard they're not welcome in the Lion and all. Now, I'll go and look at Nan.'

Sadie Grimshaw was curled into a position that was almost foetal. Her granddaughter cleaned bed and body, listened to shallow breathing and found herself praying for the poor woman to be released. This wasn't Nan, hadn't been Nan for weeks. It was a skeleton with yellowing flesh barely managing to cover bones, a curled-up creature with no life in it. Life had dealt some cruel blows to Sadie, who had suffered many miscarriages, whose only surviving child had died after Agnes's birth, who had raised Agnes and worked hard all her life.

Pop came in. 'She's in a terrible state,' he whispered.

'She needs to be in hospital – they could control the pain better.' The old lady was now too weak to groan or cry.

'They'd finish her off and she wants to be at home. We promised her, pet. Even if she doesn't talk, I reckon she knows where she is.'

Not for the first time today, Agnes realized that her old Pop was on his way back. Since the stroke, he had acted in a way Nan might have described as 'yonderly', a term invented to describe someone who was present in body, but not in mind. 'Would it be a bad thing if the hospital gave her a helping hand?' whispered Agnes.

He shrugged and asked if she knew where his baccy and pipe were. So his thoughts were still skipping slightly, though he seemed capable of concentrating for several seconds, at least. And he had remembered Glenys Timpson's sons for about two minutes, so that was a good sign. 'Behind the clock,' she answered.

Fred disappeared, came back almost immediately with the postcard that marked the year. 'What's this?'

'The year. Your pipe's behind the clock.'

'Right.' Off he went once more.

Agnes held a withered claw that had once been a hand, a hand that had fed and clothed her, a hand belonging to the only mother she had ever known. 'Please, please go,' she wept.

The front door opened and Nurse Ingram stepped into the room. She studied the scene for a few seconds, then stood behind Agnes, squeezing the young woman's shoulder in a way that was meant to be supportive and encouraging. 'Let me get the ambulance, love,' she begged.

'I promised she'd die here.' The words were fractured by sobs.

'I know that. But we want what's best for her, don't we?'

Agnes nodded.

After a pause of several seconds, the nurse spoke again. 'Get me a bowl of water while I wash her face.'

'I just did that.'

The nurse walked a few paces and stood eye to eye with Agnes. 'Get me a bowl of water and a towel. Go on. It's what I need.'

Agnes looked into the sorrow-filled eyes of a person she had come to know and trust in recent weeks. Although no words were spoken, she heard what the woman was not permitted to say. Unsteadily, she rose to her feet and dried her eyes. 'Thank you,' she said.

'She'll be all right,' said the nurse. 'Just let me see to her.'

Agnes filled the bowl and ordered Pop to follow her.

24

They re-entered the front room just as the nurse stamped a heavy foot onto a phial.

'I get clumsier all the time. Second piece of equipment I've lost today,' announced Alice Ingram, her eyes fixed on Agnes's face. 'She's going now. Stay with her.'

'Where's she going?' asked Fred.

'To Jesus,' Agnes replied.

So it came about that Sadie Grimshaw left her body and went to meet her Maker. The only evidence that she had been awarded an assisted passage was ground into a pegged rug beside the bed. With Fred on one side and her granddaughter on the other, Sadie breathed her last. Free from pain and all other earthly shackles, she floated away on a cloud of morphine, her ravaged features relaxed for the first time in months.

Nurse Alice Ingram wiped the patient's face. 'I'll get the doctor to sign the certificate,' she said, her voice shaky. She had done the right thing. Sadie would not have survived the journey to the infirmary, she told herself repeatedly. 'I'll lay her out myself.'

Fred looked at Agnes. 'Is that it? Has she gone?'

Agnes nodded.

His chin dropped and he stared at his dead wife. 'I'll have to pull myself together now, Sadie,' he said. 'I'm all our Agnes has left, aren't I?'

He left the room.

'How can I thank you?' Agnes asked.

'By saying nowt. I've done wrong, but it was right in my book.'

'And in mine. I know you're not supposed to . . . But sometimes, it can be a kindness.'

In the back living room, Pop was weeping quietly in the fireside rocker. Agnes squatted down and took his hand. 'It was time. Every day was worse than the one before. That wasn't Nan any more. She needed to go.'

He smiled through his grief. 'Your mam wasn't a bad girl, you know. And when she died, me and Sadie got you. Eeh, you were lovely. You kept us going, gave us something to fight for. Losing our Eileen were the worst thing that ever happened to me and my Sadie. But she wasn't bad, your mam. She didn't mess with all kinds of men.'

Agnes patted his hand. He could go back twenty years, but he struggled to remember yesterday. 'Is Sadie all right now?' he asked.

She swallowed hard. 'Nan died a few minutes ago.' This had been a long day. Nan was gone, the job was gone and Pop was on his way back.

He stared hard into the blue depths of his beloved little girl's eyes. 'I'm not that daft, lass. I know she's dead. I were there when she went. Nay, that'll stick.' Red-letter day. Why had this been a red-letter day? It was black now, dark, clouded over, miserable. He had pencils and a notebook; he had returned the polish; his wife was dead. This had become a black-letter day and he had to keep going for Agnes. It had always been for Agnes, because Agnes deserved the best. 'I wish we could have got you educated, love. You're cleverer than your friends, but you work in a mill.'

'No, I left the mill and went to clean the pub, but the pub's closing.'

'Closing time already?'

'Closing for good, Pop.' Like Nan, the Dog and Ferret was about to become just another piece of local history.

*

They waited for the hearse. Denis, who had been given a day off, was smart in his dark suit and white shirt. He paced about, uncomfortable in new shoes. Outside on the cobbles, Judge Spencer's Bentley gleamed in morning sunlight weakened by layers of dust and smoke from nearby mills. The judge had lent his precious motor so that Sadie's family could travel in style to church and graveyard.

Denis kept a keen eye on his calm wife. Agnes took things in her stride, but this stride had been a mile long, because she had adored her grandmother. She had no job, little money and the old man to care for. If only Denis had enjoyed health good enough for a proper job, things would have been different, but he was a manservant on low wages and he hated to see his beloved wife so poor. Her navy suit was clean and pressed, but shabby shoes told the world how impoverished Agnes was. The new shoes had been for him and should have been for her. His love was so strong that it hurt, especially now. 'All right, pet?' he asked for the third time. The judge had paid for Denis's shoes – they were part of the uniform.

She smiled at him. Here she sat, surrounded by Nan's furniture, Nan's rugs, Nan's memories expressed in photographs on the mantel. Every pot and pan in the place was Nan's, but that lovely woman was dead and Agnes felt numb and chilled right through to her bones. How could a person be cold on a nice June morning? Could she carry on here without the woman who had formed and nurtured her? Could she live among Nan's little treasures, those constant reminders of better days?

Pop was quiet. He was scribbling again in his little book, brow furrowed as he struggled with spelling, never one of his strong points. Since the death of Sadie, the notebook had been his constant companion. Every meal, every walk, every memory got space on the page. He was going to bury his beloved today, and each move would be recorded.

Denis sighed. He knew full well that Fred would make notes through the requiem and at the graveside, but that was the old fellow's way of coping. If the system worked, it must be employed. Agnes hadn't wept properly yet; Denis hoped that this would be her day for tears.

A sudden commotion in the street caused all three occupants of the room to move towards the front door. Hearses were quiet vehicles, but tyres screeched and someone ran quickly down towards Deane Road. They stood and watched as police dragged Harry Timpson into a car. His mother, turban dangling loose from curlered hair, was screaming and pulling at the nearest officer. 'Leave him,' she yelled. 'He's done nowt.'

The drama was over in seconds. As the police car drove off towards town, the hearse entered the other end of the street, moving slowly towards Sadie's house. It stopped and two men stepped out to collect the floral tributes and place them on the coffin.

Agnes felt a hand on her arm. She turned and saw a dishevelled Glenys Timpson with a bunch of flowers that had seen better days. The woman was weeping. 'For your nan. Sadie, God rest her,' she sobbed. Then, for the first time within living memory, Glenys apologized. 'They've took him away,' she added. 'He'll be in jail. Seems you were right.'

Agnes offered a weak smile. 'It's a bad day for all of us,' she said softly. 'I'll see you later.'

Fred and his granddaughter occupied the rear seat of the Bentley while Denis drove. Without the chauffeur's cap, he looked like any other car owner, but the vehicle had to be returned and garaged by this evening.

There was a large crowd outside the church of Saints Peter and Paul. Sadie Grimshaw had been loved, because she had been a caring, generous woman. The people parted and lined the path they had created while coffin and chief mourners entered the cool interior of the porch, then the large congregation of neighbours and friends filed quietly into the church. Catholics blessed themselves after dipping fingers in small fonts of water, Protestants split again into two types – those who tried to copy genuflection and the Sign of the Cross, and those who sat at the back.

It was in here that Agnes allowed everything to become real. In the arms of her loving husband, she poured out the grief she had contained for days made busy with arrangements, with the cashing of policies and the choosing of hymns. It was a long Mass and, at the end of it, a drained Agnes was helped outside by Fred and Denis. Her eyes moved away from the coffin for a moment and she saw Glenys Timpson, whose son had been arrested just an hour ago. This street gossip, although living through one of her own darker hours, had come to pay tribute to Sadie Grimshaw.

Glenys smiled through her tears.

Agnes leaned towards her. 'I didn't say anything to the police,' she whispered.

'I know you didn't, love.'

The cortège drove through the town into Tonge Cemetery, past the Protestant graves and to the Catholic side in which Fred and Sadie had bought their little bit of England. A gaping hole was blessed by the priest before Sadie's coffin was moved for the last time. It was done.

Fred had stopped his writing. He threw soil into the grave, mouthed a few indistinguishable words, then stepped away to make room for Agnes and Denis. The sun shone brilliantly, and happy birds flitted about in trees and bushes. 'We can go now,' said Fred. 'She'd want us to have a nice cup of tea and a butty.'

People came and went all day. The Noble Street house was filled with neighbours and friends; the priest came, as did a Methodist preacher and two nuns from the Catholic school.

When daylight began to dwindle, Denis took Judge Spencer's car back to its rightful owner. Sadie's chair was now occupied by Agnes, just as it had been all through the illness. Fred scribbled and dozed, Agnes stared into the fire and wondered about her future. Was it time to think about going for a proper job? Pop would recover completely before long, so Agnes would be free to choose the course of her own future. Her friends would be coming back to sit with her soon and she would discuss the matter with them. Lucy and Mags had got Agnes through this day.

No matter what, it would be lonely without Nan. But Nan would be up in heaven and expecting Agnes to do her best. And Nan always got her own way in the end.

Chapter Two

Helen Spencer, a spinster in her thirties, lived a monotonous life in a grand, colourless house that belonged to her father.

Judge Zachary Spencer was a mean-spirited man whose years in the courts had served only to make him bitter about his fellows, and age had not mellowed him. He listened to advocates, heard testimony, sat on his grand courtroom throne and said very little. Murderers, fraudsters and thieves were part and parcel of his daily grind, and he expected little of his daughter when he arrived home. She was not a son; she was, therefore, one of the more bitter disappointments in his self-absorbed life.

Control was something he prized above all things, so, apart from the booming works of Wagner and some of Beethoven's louder compositions, he enjoyed an uneventful life cocooned by domestic legislation invented and imposed by himself. He seldom spoke except to bark an order and made no attempt to conceal from his daughter the contempt he felt for the merely female. Servants had disappeared over the years, and the household was held together rather tenuously by one Kate Moores, who owned an admirable ability to ignore her employer.

Helen was lonely to the point of desperation, though she had been careful to hide her discontent with life.

Quietly resentful, she attended church, worked in the Bolton Central Library and, during breaks for coffee and tea, found herself virtually incapable of enjoying conversation with colleagues, so lunchtimes were spent in a quiet, sedate cafe away from crowds and noise. She feared people and did not trust her own ability to cope in any social situation. Of late, she had begun to quarrel with herself. The steady rock to which she had clung was suddenly embedded in quicksand, and self-control was becoming a luxury.

Why? was a question she asked herself repeatedly. Had her mother survived, would life have been different, better? Would siblings have cheered her, or had she been born different from the norm? Father didn't help, of course, all noisy music and imperious shouts, but surely other people survived such trials?

An avid reader, she screamed inwardly with Miss Catherine Earnshaw, allowed Heathcliff to break her heart, wept over Jane Eyre and her blinded master, allowed Dickens to place her in the company of Miss Havisham presiding over an uneaten and decayed wedding breakfast. Helen also laughed when she read, though she seldom even smiled in real life. Fiction had always been a place in which she might hide, a retreat from a stale, unattractive life.

Until now. He had slid noiselessly into her pale existence, had made her giggle and told her stories of his childhood, of his life at home, of his wife. His wife. Helen poured milk into her tea and stared blindly through the window. Today he was not here, because he was burying his wife's grandmother. Denis Makepeace was a quiet man, self-educated, willing and worthy of trust. Father had lent him the car and the good man was grateful for that. Like Helen, he had to make do with leavings from the top table. He was a servant and she was a woman. Both were treated by Zachary Spencer as peripheral characters – no, as part of a backdrop created to serve only the judge, who was the main figure on the canvas. Judge Spencer was Henry VIII all over again; Helen and Denis were two of the crowd to whom he occasionally threw a bone.

Helen Spencer, having never been in love, owned no yardstick against which she might measure her feelings for Denis. Love was in books; it had never figured on the pages of reality. Was the quickening of her heart a symptom, were the shameful dreams created by genuine affection for him or by the nagging frustrations of a lone, untouched female? Her cheeks were heated as she sipped her tea, and she wondered whether other women endured such night torments. Of course, she was younger and more beautiful when asleep. Awake, she was plain, ordinary and colourless. No one looked at her. She stamped books, collected fines, kept the reference section in order. Over the years, Helen had become part of the library, although she was not worth reading, so she remained on the shelf.

The mirror over the mantel told its familiar story – brown hair, hazel eyes, pale skin, nothing remarkable about the face. She was neither fat nor thin, yet her body had no real shape and she had never sought to embellish her physical self. Would she actually use the frivolous purchases she had made and could she change herself gradually in order to avoid comments from her father and work fellows? Suddenly giddy and young, she was about to embark on an adventure usually enjoyed by females half her age.

She took herself off to the privacy of her bedroom where, once seated on the bed, she began to unwrap the evidence of her folly. Silk slid through her fingers, soft, smooth undergarments in many shades – including black. Patent leather shoes and matching handbag were placed carefully in a wardrobe beneath a hanger bearing a fine wool suit in emerald green. Blouses and skirts remained in their packages, because she had more interesting objects to investigate.

Across the surface of the dressing table, Helen set out her stall. The girl in the department store had been patient and friendly, had shown the nervous customer how to attain a daytime 'natural' look, how to make herself up for the evenings. Evenings? Where on earth would she go and with whom? The Halle Orchestra in Manchester, perhaps? Concerts in the Free Trade Hall, a single ticket to the theatre, a lone seat in the cinema? There was nowhere to go, because she was nobody; perhaps, if she became a somebody, things might begin to happen.

Darnley's Liquid Satin foundation, compressed powder, four lipsticks, half a dozen eye shadows, an eyebrow pencil, mascara – did she dare? A small phial of Chanel No. 5 had taken a fortnight's wages, while the rest of the articles had cost a king's ransom. Did she dare? Would she ever obtain the courage required?

There was an anger in Helen, a deep resentment that, since childhood, had been forbidden to show its face at the surface. It had bubbled up recently in reaction to a small event, a comment made by a child in the library. The little girl had remarked to her mother that the lady had an unhappy face, and this same unhappy-faced lady had gone that very lunchtime for a make-up demonstration in a store. Perhaps she could not change her soul – no one had the power to alter the past – but she might make some attempt to reshape her future. Yet she had cleansed herself after the event, had removed from her face all evidence of the effort made by the gentle girl who had tried to help.

Now, she unveiled cleanser, moisturizer, a tiny pot of cream for delicate areas around the eyes. Pearl nail polishes in pink and white were lined up in front of other bottles and boxes. Like a man playing soldiers, Helen assembled her troops in preparation for battle. It would have to be done gradually, but she intended to make the most of her minimal assets. Other women wore make-up and perfume, so why should she be the exception?

The car purred its way into the drive and she leapt up. Father was away in London for a few days, yet Denis had been ordered to garage the vehicle after the funeral. Father did not trust the people of Noble Street to treat his precious Bentley with the reverence it warranted.

She peeped round the edge of a curtain and watched Denis. He was an excellent man, a reader, an interesting teller of tales. He was the one who had awoken her inner self, who had reminded her that she was a woman with real needs and desires. She could not have him; he belonged with another woman, but he might, perhaps, bring her out of herself and help her across stepping stones between her own silent world and normality. Denis listened. She had never been a great talker, but he encouraged her to speak out. One of Nature's gentlemen, Denis Makepeace was Helen's only friend.

Feeling very daring, she dabbed a small amount of perfume behind her ears before going downstairs. Apart from the ticking of clocks, the house was silent, Wagner-free and peaceful. She stepped out of a side door and made for the garage.

Denis was inspecting paintwork when she arrived. He looked up and smiled at her, trying hard to squash the small surge of panic that visited his chest. Miss Spencer was becoming dependent on him. At first, their conversations had been brief and infrequent, but lately he had come to realize that the woman waited for him. She had no life. Her father was a cold fish and her job was dull, but what was she expecting from a chauffeur-cum-handyman?

'How did it go?' she asked.

'All right.' He drew a soft cloth over the car's bonnet. 'Fred wrote in his memory book all through the service. Agnes cried. It's about time she cried. She took it too well.'

He was right, of course. People should show their feelings. 'Did her friends come?'

'Oh, yes. She had a good natter with them afterwards and they were very kind to Fred. Most folk treat him as if he has some kind of dementia, but he hasn't. He's getting better. Lucy and Mags talked to him as a normal person – he responds to that. Pity more folk don't understand that he's not on the slippery slope.' She was standing too near and was wearing perfume. This gauche woman had no experience with men and was behaving like a teenager. No, he was over-reacting, he reassured himself. He was just a servant and she knew he was married.

'Do you have time to look at my car?' she asked. 'It may be dirty petrol – I let the tank get very low yesterday – but it's not running smoothly.'

Would he take a look? This was happening too often – a drawer in her bedroom beginning to stick, the need for another shelf in her little dressing room, a squeaking floorboard. Helen Spencer presented as a good person, but she was isolated to the point of desperation. He feared her, feared himself, too – wasn't pity said to be akin to love?

He fiddled with the innards of the Morris Minor, drove it round the paddock, declared it to be as fit as a flea. 'It's running well,' he said after two circuits. 'Whatever was wrong must have cleared up. I've cleaned the plugs just in case.'

'Thank you.'

He closed the garage doors and declared his intention to go for the bus.

'I'll take you home.'

The calculated nonchalance in her tone startled him anew. Had her father been in residence, Helen Spencer would never have made such an offer. 'I'll be fine on the bus,' he answered. 'I'm used to it.'

'No, I insist. You must be tired after such a long day.'

God, what should he do? If Miss Spencer ran him home, he would have to ask her in for a cup of tea – to expect her to leave immediately would be churlish. Lucy Walsh and Mags Bradshaw would still be there, and Helen Spencer was no good with folk – hadn't she already confessed as much? Agnes might notice how she looked at him, how she hung on every word – he didn't know how to reply.

'Let me do this,' she was saying now. 'And I shan't intrude, not on the day of the funeral.'

Meek as a kitten, he got into the passenger seat of the Morris. Her hands on the steering wheel were the hands of a lady – long fingers, slender wrists. She played the piano – he had heard her during her afternoons off. Helen Spencer's music was not angry – the pieces she played sounded peaceful and melodic. He was out of his depth and he could feel the glow in his cheeks. She didn't even know that she was sending out signals, but he recognized them plainly enough. He was sitting next to a female animal anxious to breed before its time ran out. His collar was suddenly tight and he pushed a finger between it and his throat. There had to be a way out of this situation, yet he could not reject her, since she had made no definite move in his direction. It was coming. Helen Spencer was losing her balance and he would be expected to catch her when she fell.

'You look smart,' she said before starting the engine. He cut a fine figure. He was nearer in age to her than he was to his young wife. Agnes was twenty, Helen thirty-two, Denis twenty-nine. Father would hate it, of course, but divorce was becoming more commonplace these days. She chided herself inwardly. An honourable woman, she would make no attempt to spoil Denis's marriage. Would she? Her heart quickened and drummed in her ears. She was changing. The change was not connected to cosmetics or black underwear – she was losing her grip on the life she had made for herself.

She pulled onto Wigan Road and drove slowly towards one of the poorer ends of town. 'Perhaps you should move,' she suggested. 'There are cottages in Skirlaugh Fall and it would be easier for you, especially in winter. You'd need no buses.'

'We're settled where we are, Miss Spencer.'

'Helen. I've told you to call me Helen – except when Father is within earshot, of course. Wouldn't a change of address suit your wife and Mr Grimshaw?'

'I might think about it. Thanks.' He needed to change his job. He needed a change because Miss Helen Spencer needed a change, and he dared not figure in her calculations. She had never walked out with a man and Denis could not afford to be a participant in her delayed adolescence.

'Look at those girls.' She pointed to a small group at a bus stop. 'Father says they are asking for trouble by dressing like that. Miniskirts? I have a winter scarf broader than those. No wonder there's an increase in attacks on young women.'

Denis found no reply.

'What do you think?' she asked.

'People should dress the way they want to dress.'

'Does your wife wear such things?'

'No. She covers her knees.'

'Glad to hear it.'

Discomfort now bordered on pain, because Denis was acutely aware of Helen Spencer's dilemma. The judge was a pain in the backside, arrogant, stubborn, selfish and domineering. He treated Denis as an article, one of life's inanimate necessities. His daughter was guilty of not being a son, of not being bright enough for what he considered a true career. She was substandard in all departments, and he had no time to waste on her. Helen Spencer had never known love. 'Have you ever thought of leaving home?' Denis asked.

She turned briefly to look at him. 'I have money enough for a small house, yes, but I have never lived alone. It's a large step to take.'

Denis kept his thoughts to himself. Aloneness and loneliness were not the same. Living with her father, she was lonely; a person could be isolated in a city teeming with folk. She would be alone if she got out of her father's house, but loneliness would not necessarily be the result.

'I suppose I am afraid of change,' she said.

'We all are. Agnes is frightened of life without her grandma. Things alter even if you stay in one place – life happens no matter where we are.'

'Yes, I suppose so.'

He knew why she stayed at Lambert House. She stayed because she would automatically inherit property, land and money once her father died. If she angered him by moving on, he might very well cut her off without a penny. But some prices were too high to pay, thought Denis as the car pulled into Noble Street. The woman should clear off and start again; needed interests, hobbies and a place where she could be herself.

'I am grateful to you,' she said as she stopped the car. 'No one ever spent time with me before – unless nannies and governesses count. I scarcely remember my mother, and you know how Father is.'

'Yes.' He didn't need the gratitude, didn't want it. She was hungry and he dared not be the one to feed her. 'I still think you should find a life for yourself. Your father could last for a long time yet. Start going out; join – oh, I don't know. They have reading groups and poetry meetings at the library, don't they? And there's your music.' He sighed. 'Sorry, I shouldn't interfere.'

She placed a hand on his arm. 'You are a good friend. Thank you.'

He stood on the narrow pavement and watched as she drove away. It was silly, but his arm glowed from the touch of her hand. It was all nonsense. He loved Agnes, and that was all he needed to know.

The place was in chaos. Agnes, whose two friends had returned long after the main funeral party was over, was in the front room with Mags and Lucy. They were all shouting, and the reason for that was a great deal of noise coming from the back of the house.

Agnes smiled at her husband.

'What the blinking heck's going on?' he asked loudly.

She shrugged. 'Denis, Pop has started his new job.'

'Eh?'

'He's manufacturing.'

'Manufacturing? The neighbours will go crazy.'

'You tell him that. We've tried while we did some washing up, but he's got a bee in his bonnet and a hammer in his hand.'

Denis sighed and walked through to the back of the house. Fred was knocking bits of wood together. 'Fred?'

'Aye?'

'What are you up to?'

Fred stopped clattering for a moment. 'I'm going into doll's houses,' he pronounced.

Denis bit back a flippant remark about doll's houses being a tight squeeze for a grown man.

'Battery packs,' the old man continued, 'so there'll be lighting in every room. I can make furniture, paper the walls and carpet floors. Bathroom fittings'll have to be bought in from a toymaker, but I can do most of it by myself.'

Denis cast an eye over the scene. There was sawdust everywhere and tools were spread about the floor along with bits of wood, nails, screws and sandpaper. 'Agnes won't like it,' he said.

'I have to be useful. If I do more, I'll remember more.'

'Well, do it outside in the shed. We'll get a light put in. You can't mess the house up like this, Fred – we eat in here. You'll be having splinters in your dinner.'

Fred shook his head sadly. 'Shed's full. This is just the prototype. At the graveside, I promised my Sadie I'd start being useful as soon as I got home. I couldn't, because folk were brewing up and eating butties, but I started when most of them had gone. I shall be earning money.'

Denis sat at the table and scratched his head. What a day. Poor old Sadie gone to her rest, Helen Spencer clarting about like a kid, now Fred wrecking a house to make a house. Sometimes, life was a trial. 'You'd best clean up, old son, before Agnes starts on you. You know she's house-proud. Come on, I'll give you a hand.'

Fred was having none of it. He was experiencing difficulty with a gable end and a window, and he would clear the stuff away when he was good and ready, not before. 'They have to be strong,' he insisted. 'Little girls can be as destructive as boys. My hinges have to be childproof. And I've the wiring to work out.'

It was no good. Denis knew his grandfather-in-law and there was no point in pushing the old chap when he didn't want to be moved. Also, it was good to see him having a go at something, because he'd done very little since the stroke. 'I'll make a cuppa,' he said resignedly. He had no wish to enter into conversation with the mothers' meeting – a term he used for occasions when Agnes and her two best friends came together – so he would stay here and drink tea with Fred.

Fred laid out his plans on the table, explained several designs and how they would be priced. 'That lot up Heaton way with more money than sense will snap these up,' he declared. 'And I shall make some to specifications wanted by the buyer, so we've got to advertise.'

Denis warmed the pot. Agnes had lost her job, Judge Spencer was a skinflint and extra money was needed – but Fred? Was he up to this kind of thing? He turned and watched the old man working on his first roof. Fred was muttering about covering it with some kind of plastic with a pattern that looked like tiles. So far, so good. It had four walls, a roof and gaps for windows. Perhaps Fred was on to something? He was certainly making a mess, whatever the outcome.

'Denis?'

'What?'

'I can do it, you know.'

The younger man grinned. He nursed a strong suspicion that Fred Grimshaw could and would do it. Ah, well. Time would tell.

Lucy Walsh was describing her wedding outfit. She had just declared her intention to wear a minidress with knee-high white boots, and her mother wasn't pleased. 'It's my wedding,' she said, her pretty face creased by a frown. 'Mam says I'll look common. But if a girl ever deserves her own way, surely her wedding's the place to start?'

Agnes had stayed out of this discussion so far. She agreed with Lucy's mother, but she dared not say so. Mags, too, was keeping her counsel. The only one of the three to have remained completely solo, she was chief bridesmaid and had no intention of becoming a critic.

Lucy described the cake, the flowers, the invitations.

Like Agnes, she was marrying someone older than herself, a lawyer with good prospects and a very nice house. Agnes glanced at Mags, then decided to hang herself out to dry. This was the day on which she had buried her grandmother – surely she could make herself strong enough to put her foot through Lucy's mini?

'Lucy?'

'What?'

'George's colleagues will be there.'

'So what?'

Agnes raised her shoulders. 'I know minis are all the rage, but I can't see a load of crusty old lawyers approving of them.'

Lucy sighed heavily. 'I want to be fashionable.'

Mags took a sip of cold tea. She and Agnes – who was matron of honour – were already dismayed by Lucy's decision to dress them in watered black silk with dark red roses at the waists. But their clothes would cover their knees, at least. Lucy, always centre-stage and stunning, wanted to shock her audience. She had clearly begun to look upon her wedding as a stage production rather than a religious ceremony. The congregation would become an audience and Lucy would be the star turn on a stage rather than a bride at the altar.

Agnes took another huge stride into her friend's limelight. 'That Empire line dress – white watered silk – would look great with our black, wouldn't it, Mags? It's the same silk, but white. That's my opinion – for what it's worth.'

Mags nodded, though her lips remained closed.

'Lucy, don't wear the mini,' Agnes begged. 'It might look stunning, but every time you bend down some lecherous old lawyer will see your knickers. When they go home, they'll laugh at you.'

'If I wear any knickers.' Lucy swallowed cold tea and a facsimile of injured pride. 'All right,' she said resignedly and with an air of acute injury. Then she burst out laughing. 'Your faces!' she howled. 'Honestly, you looked like a couple of spectators at a public hanging. Did you really think I was going to walk up the aisle in knee-high boots and a lace mini?'

Mags, who had been swallowing her own cold tea, spluttered and coughed. Agnes hit her on the back till her airway cleared, then sat down again. 'Lucy, you'll be the death of us.'

The bride-to-be grinned broadly. 'Your nan would have laughed herself sick over that, Agnes. Remember? How she used to have those giggling fits? That's how we've got to think of her now. Her spirit, her silliness and how young she always was where it mattered.' Lucy tapped her skull with a finger. 'In here, Sadie never grew old.'

Agnes wiped a tear from her eye. 'Yes, she was funny. Except for the last few months, and they weren't amusing at all. But,' she jerked a thumb in the direction of the next room, 'look what she's left us to cope with. Wherever she is, she's smiling.'

The door burst inward to allow a red-faced Fred and a wooden item into the arena. 'See?' he said triumphantly. 'I've done half already.'

Agnes glanced at her friends. 'Well, half a house is better than none.'

When Pop had retreated, Agnes sat for a while and remembered her beloved grandmother. Denis looked in, saw her expression, noticed that the other two were quiet, and decided to leave well alone. Fred started to clear away his mess. Even his tidying was noisy, thought Agnes as she gazed into the near distance. But his half-house had seemed half-decent, so perhaps he was on to something profitable.

'I'm going to miss you, Nan,' she told the ceiling. But she had been missing Nan for months already. Only the body had been there at the end, and the body hadn't functioned. Should she have stayed at home instead of cleaning for a few shillings a week? To that question, she was never going to find an answer.

'You'll not find her up yon.' Lucy pointed to the upper half of the room. 'She's more likely to be making mischief with your granddad in the kitchen.'

Agnes lowered her eyes and looked at Lucy. Lucy Walsh, Mags Bradshaw and herself had been inseparable since nursery class. Mags, who had grown into a plain, quiet and dignified adult, had been a shy and frightened child. Lucy, on the other hand, remained capable of starting a riot in an empty room. She was the one who had guarded and guided Mags, and Agnes was the cement that had held the three of them together through their passage into adulthood. The vow had been that come boyfriends, husbands or children, Thursday nights would always be girls' nights. 'Thanks for being here,' said Agnes softly.

'Where else would we be?' Lucy began to stack cups and saucers. 'All for one and one for all, isn't it?' She moved quickly, had always been the first to dress, to clear up, to organize. Slim, dark and beautiful, she was sure of herself in mind and in body. 'We couldn't have let you go through it on your own,' she said when her task was completed. 'Anyway, your nan made the best jam cakes in the business. Didn't she, Mags?'

'She made the best of everything.' Mags stood up and prepared to carry the dishes away. 'Can't have been easy when her daughter died so young. But Sadie's generation never moaned. They just got on with what needed doing and that was that.' She left the room.

'What are we going to do about Mags?' Lucy whispered.

'Nothing.'

'What do you mean? There has to be someone who'll see beyond her quietness.'

'Some people don't need to be married.'

Lucy changed tactics. 'All right, so what are we going to do about you? Will you fill that form in? Isn't it time you pulled yourself together, Makepeace? The job in the pub was supposed to be a stop-gap – you've no excuse now. Your Pop will get better in time—'

'And the kitchen will be in bits—'

'So what? It's only a bloody kitchen. At least he's doing something. It's what you've always wanted and now's the time to do it.'

Agnes thought about Pop and wondered if he would manage. The hours of work would be long and varied, there would be exams, rules, a uniform . . .

'Well?'

Agnes sighed resignedly. 'For goodness' sake, Lucy. We buried Nan today. Does all the clearing up have to be done now?'

'You're the fastidious one,' replied Lucy. 'Get it done. You've always wanted to be a nurse and now's as good a time as any. You knew the mill was just for money till you got married, then the pub job came along and it fitted for a while. But are you going to be just a married woman? All that went out at the end of the war. Women work. They get decent jobs and keep house at the same time. What would your nan say?'

'She'd make me go for it.'

Lucy picked up her bag and gloves. 'Right, madam. I

47

want that form filled in or I wear a mini wedding dress. I mean it. George would be delighted – he says my legs go up all the way to Glasgow – so think on.'

After her friends had left, Agnes thought on. She peered into the kitchen, saw that Denis had been dragged into the business of house-building, took the form from the front room bureau. 'Bloody hell,' she cursed quietly. 'They want to know everything I've ever done. What have I done?' How might she fill all the naked spaces on the application form?

She had doffed spools at a mule, back soaked in sweat, feet aching, head banging because of noise and heat. She had cleaned lavatories, had cared for Pop and Nan, had even helped Nurse Ingram to see the old lady into the next world. Lucy and Mags, both legal secretaries, were pushing her towards a career, but what about Pops? With Nan dead, he was going to be at a loose end, and his mind was not yet fully healed.

Agnes stared through the window, saw a car edging its way past the house. She knew little about motors, as few in these parts owned vehicles, but the driver seemed familiar. Was it Miss Spencer? Why did she suddenly speed up after gazing into the house? Even Judge Spencer's Bentley caused discomfort to passengers when it moved at a snail's pace over cobbles – his daughter's smaller car might actually be shaken to bits. Oh well, it had been an odd day, an unhappy day, and Miss Helen Spencer was probably taking a short cut to somewhere or other.

'Agnes?' A hand touched her left shoulder.

'Miss Spencer just drove past.'

Denis felt the heat in his face. He coughed quietly. 'She brought me home.'

'Yes, you said. I wonder why she's still out there?'

He shrugged with deliberate nonchalance. 'No idea. She did seem concerned – asked about you.'

'Nothing like her dad, then.'

'No.' Helen Spencer bore not the slightest resemblance to her parent. She had a soft centre. She played Chopin and something called the Moonlight sonata – was that Beethoven? She had needs. Beautiful hands, desperate needs.

'Denis?'

'What?'

'Lucy threatened to get married in a crocheted mini.'

He relaxed. For now, the subject was changed. Yet the subject remained behind the wheel of a Morris with clean plugs and excellent timing. Denis shifted himself. There was sawdust to sweep, there were tools waiting to be tidied. 'I love you,' he advised his wife.

Agnes nodded. 'Make sure you pick up all the nails. And I pray to God that Pop hasn't got to the painting stage.' Doll's houses, indeed. Whatever next?

Imitating the process of osmosis, Helen Spencer was seeping via some invisible semi-permeable membrane right through the defences of Denis Makepeace. She booked her time off from the library, making sure that her holidays coincided with her father's absence on circuit business. While the judge covered his territory, she set up a stall on her own tiny piece of England. The campaign of which she was scarcely aware was plotted in her dressing room and completed in her bedroom.

She was now two people. There was the librarian – severe hair, sensible shoes, tweeds with kick-pleated skirts; there was also the strangely innocent siren. Transformation proved an interesting process. Her face was an almost blank canvas onto which she painted today's self. Eye shadows and liners emphasized her best features, and her skin glowed with brilliance borrowed from Max Factor. As the days wore on, Helen's confidence grew, bolstered by scaffolding acquired in department stores and chemist shops. She was finally a woman and he was watching her. When he watched, she tingled with anticipation, often blushing when suddenly aware of the full extent of her sins. She wanted him.

Denis, plodding through chores, pretended not to watch. But he was fully conscious of the dangerous game over which he had no control. There were no rules, no linesmen, no flags raised when play got out of hand. He washed the Bentley in which he had driven his employer to Trinity Street Station, pruned hedges, mended a gate, watered lawns. From open windows in the music room floated the accompaniment to his labours, as did a pair of muslin curtains through which he caught an occasional glimpse of the entertainer. For him, she had made herself beautiful; for him, she played brilliantly, windows flung wide, heart on a platter for the taking.

He had begun a frantic but futile search through the *Bolton Evening News*, eyes ripping down the jobs column in search of an occupation that might be managed by a man with a weak chest. Thus far, he had found nothing suitable and his main emotion had become that of dread. She had made up her mind. A poem about a fly invited into the parlour of a spider dashed through his head. He had to resist her because he was a decent man and he loved Agnes, yet he continued to harbour very mixed feelings. Helen Spencer needed someone and she had chosen him. 'Because I'm here, that's all,' he announced softly. 'Anybody would do for her, the state she's in.' And a married man should not stray, he told himself regularly. Even so, the pity he felt for the judge's spinster daughter remained.

He was flattered by the attentions of such a woman and that was normal – all men responded to this kind of courtship. Helen Spencer was gifted, knowledgeable, educated and, when encouraged, interesting. 'And rich,' he grumbled. She wasn't ugly, wasn't beautiful, but she certainly looked better in her new guise.

Denis continued to rake gravel on the driveway. The judge insisted on ordered pebbles and smooth grass with stripes rolled across its surface. He was a boring old bugger, and his daughter was delivering a pretty piece of Chopin – well, Denis thought it was Chopin. The gauze-like curtains parted anew, allowing him a brief glimpse of a handsome woman in a satin gown, probably something called a peignoir. 'Playing in her underwear now,' he muttered. There were no jobs in the papers. He was married to Agnes. Curtains came and went while Denis listened to a grand mixture of birdsong and nocturne.

She summoned him. He stood, face turned away from the house, heavy-duty rake clenched fiercely in his hands. He wanted to run, but his feet were welded to loose chippings. Ridiculous. He had to go inside, needed to tell her that he loved Agnes and only Agnes.

'Denis?'

Helen Spencer was not in her right mind just now. Running out of time, out of hope and patience, bored to death, in love, in this miserable house, she had set her sights on one of the few men within her limited orbit. What would happen when he told her he didn't want her? Would she fall apart, and would he feel guilty? Beautiful hands. She played like an angel, chose pieces that haunted, poured all her loneliness and despair onto piano keys.

'Denis?'

With excruciating slowness, he turned to face her, saw her standing in a frame of cloudy white muslin. On leaden feet, Denis Makepeace walked towards inevitability.

'Denis?' Her tone was quieter.

'What?'

'You enjoyed my playing?'

His heart was fluttering like a bird in a chimney, all fear and darkness and no points of reference. 'Yes, but I've a lot to do. Judge Spencer left a list and—'

'Have a rest.' She draped herself across a small sofa. Denis could imagine her practising such moves in bedroom mirrors. 'I like you.' Underneath the panstick, her cheeks glowed. 'I have grown fond of you.'

He opened his mouth, but no words emerged.

'You are a fine man. Even my father says so, and he hates just about everyone, as you probably know by now.'

Denis pulled at his collar, which was already open. 'I'm chauffeur and handyman, Miss Spencer.'

'Helen.'

'I work outside except for the odd mending job in the house. The judge would go mad if he knew I was taking time off to chatter. Sorry.' He turned to leave, but she went after him. The seconds that followed were a blur, but she managed to catch him, arms clasping tightly round his neck, tears hovering on the edges of blatantly false eyelashes. 'I think I've fallen in love with you,' she whispered.

His body, suddenly detached from brain and heart, responded automatically to soft skin, heady perfume and sad eyes. But he pushed her aside. 'No,' he said. 'No, Miss Spencer. This can't happen. You know it and I'm sure of it. You're a well-read woman, so you must know about infatuation. I was infatuated with Barbara Holt in my class when I was ten, but I got over it.'

She nodded. 'I am not ten years old.'

'Yes. But infatuation's nothing to do with age.'

Helen began to cry. Through loud sobs, she poured out a jumble of words relating to her ugliness, her loneliness, her love for Denis.

'You aren't ugly,' he told her. 'But I'm married and I love my wife. You're fishing in the wrong waters, Miss Spencer. You should be going for salmon or rainbow trout, not for plain tench.' He strode out of the house, picked up the rake and continued to work. But unsteady hands made a poor job of straightening shingle, so he went off to mend a fence. As he drove home a nail, he wondered whether his fences could ever be truly mended after today's tragic scene.

Eva Hargreaves stepped tentatively into the house. Even after knocking loudly and shouting at the top of her range, she had been unable to make herself heard. Into a brief silence, she called again. 'Agnes?'

Fred, hair full of sawdust, hands clutching hammer and nails, appeared in the kitchen doorway. 'How do?' he said politely, eyes blinking to rid lashes of wood shavings. 'She's gone into town – something to do with being a nurse.'

'Oh. Right.' Eva didn't blame Agnes for absenting herself from the factory that had once been her home. 'I've shut the shop.'

'You what?' The hammer landed at his feet, just half

53

an inch away from his toes. 'Shut the shop?' Eva never shut her shop. She was open from seven in the morning till nine at night, no excuses, no rest, food eaten at the counter, a stool the only perch she allowed herself. 'What's up?' he asked.

Eva dropped into an armchair. 'I've had enough,' she answered wearily. 'Everybody's beck and call, firewood, paraffin, nails, buckets – I shall be kicking the bucket meself if I don't slow down.'

'Nay, lass – you're not cut out for retirement.' Fred made some effort to shake dust from tattered overalls before joining Eva in the front room. 'You'd go daft in six months. And remember – I'm experienced in daft. Daft's making bullets for a war that's twenty years over and—'

'But you're all right now.'

'Aye, happen I am, but it's only through fettling with these doll's houses. I might branch out into railways – stations, trees and all that – but Eva, you've never been idle since your husband died.'

'I know.'

'What'll you do?'

She raised her shoulders in a gesture of near-despair. 'Little bungalow up Harwood, read some books, get a dog and walk it.'

'You'll not cope.'

'I'll cope. Other folk cope—'

'Yes, but . . . but you're—'

'That's why I'm here.' Eva took as deep a breath as cruel corsets would allow. 'Help me, Fred. If I get some help, I might just hang on a bit longer.'

'I've had a stroke, lass—'

'And you're turning this place into a right pigsty, aren't you? Yon shed's not big enough, but my air raid

54

shelter is. They put it there in case of a bombing with a shopload of customers, so it's time it got used. Make you a good workshop, that would. Fred, you could serve a few customers while I rested – just a few hours a day.'

He leaned back and closed his eyes. If Eva would pay him, he could get better wood – he might even acquire nails in her shop for no price at all. And it was true – he was spoiling Sadie's house, making life difficult for his granddaughter. 'Is there electric in the air raid shelter?' he asked. 'Only I need to see what I'm doing.'

'There is now.'

'Let me think on it.'

While he was thinking, the back door opened.

'Bugger,' said Fred softly.

Eva squashed a grin.

'I'll be left out with the bins come Thursday,' groaned the old man. 'The dust cart'll take me away, just you wait and see.'

Agnes arrived in the doorway, arms tightly folded, lips clamped together, her expression promising some very bad weather. 'Hello, Mrs Hargreaves.' Agnes's eyes never left her grandfather's face. 'What the heck have you been doing, Pop? We can't live like this – I've a meal to make and baking to do.'

Fred scratched his head. 'We've been thinking,' he replied eventually. 'Me and Eva, I mean. She wants help in her shop and I could do with her air raid shelter.'

Agnes nodded. 'Yes, you'll need somewhere to hide if I find the place in this state again. Oh, and I could do with a kitchen table without a lathe stuck to it. Are you up to serving in a shop, though?'

He rose to his feet. 'Yes, I am up to serving in a shop and running me own business at the same time. There's still a bit of life in me, you know. And I would have tidied up, but—'

'But you didn't.' Agnes shook her head. 'He'll fill your shelter and spill into the house,' she told the ironmonger. 'He's all talk and screwdriver when it comes to straightening up after himself. Yes, you can have him, Mrs Hargreaves.' She grinned at her beloved Pop. 'You're well and that's all that matters. I love you, you old goat.'

An unhappy Denis had accidentally unleashed a woman of great passion and uncertain temperament. Freed from restraint, she followed him, played music for him, courted him. She would hear no argument. She wanted her way all the time and considered no one's feelings but her own.

'I'm a fool,' he told the pigswill bin as he emptied scraps into its depths. The daily, a woman from Skirlaugh Fall, was in the house and Denis was panicking. He had stepped out of his league all the way up to Lambert House, Skirlaugh Rise, and he had almost betrayed a beloved wife. Mrs Moores, the daily, had taken to looking at him sideways and Denis was sure that the whole village knew of his supposed crimes. 'I'm sorry, Agnes,' he breathed, his head leaning on cool stone. What was he going to do? What on earth could anyone do?

A light step bade him turn and he looked right into the angry eyes of his mistress.

'There you are,' snapped Helen. 'I want you to mend my bookcase upstairs.'

He placed the bucket on the ground. 'This has to stop,' he said.

'Why?'

Denis inhaled as deeply as he could. 'You're different. Everyone can see that you're different. They'll know. Your dad will find out, Agnes will find out.' There was a kind of madness in her eyes, a brightness that went beyond mere happiness or excitement. She didn't care about being discovered. 'It has to stop,' he said again.

'You have regrets.' Her tone was accusatory.

'Of course I do. I'm married. I love my wife. Your father's a judge with a lot of power. This should not be happening. I want things back the way they were. And that's just the start of the list.'

Helen Spencer nodded, turned on her heel and walked back into the house. Fury quickened her step as she ran up the stairs and into her bedroom. She dropped face down onto a chaise longue, balled fists beating pink velvet upholstery, mouth opened in a scream she managed to strangle at birth. He didn't love her. If an odd-job man could not love her . . . What was happening to her? Why did she occasionally lose herself and where had self-control gone for a holiday?

She had to have him, had to keep him for herself. He could get a divorce. Father would not approve, but Father seldom approved of anything. If Agnes Make-peace knew the full extent of her husband's supposedly bad behaviour, perhaps she would leave Denis. 'But I would be named,' she said aloud. Did it matter? Was any price too high when it came to the love of her life? She was unbalanced, yet she retained sufficient intelligence to allow insight into her own disorder. This was a clear route to madness.

She turned over, closed her eyes and imagined how he would be as a lover. He would treat her like precious porcelain, would be amazed and pleased by her responses. But no. He had no intention of indulging in an animal act, a business performed by any beast in field or stable yard. He was a good man in a world inhabited by the bad.

What could she do? Angrily, she rose and began to pace the floor, back and forth, hands rubbing together, forehead creased by a deep frown, ears on alert just in case he deigned to climb the stairs to mend her bookcase. Mother's money. Helen placed herself at the dressing table. She had come into a small inheritance at the age of twenty-one, and it had languished in a bank for all these years. Her own house. If she bought a place, he could visit her there ... but would she have any power if she moved out? His job was here, her father was his employer and she, daughter of the house, held some sway during her father's absences.

It was hopeless and she wanted to die if she could not have Denis. The library? She didn't care about her job any more, could take it or leave it. Mrs Moores knew what was going on, but that didn't bother Helen. Why should she care what a skivvy thought? And what was wrong with a few fashionable clothes and a bit of make-up?

He was walking across the lawn. Through narrowed eyes, Helen took in every single detail. Denis was carrying a canvas bag, a pair of work boots joined by laces hanging from a shoulder. 'He's leaving,' she whispered. 'He's walking out. And I am supposed to sit here like Little Miss Muffet.' She left the room and ran downstairs.

From the drawing room window, Kate Moores watched the scene as it unfolded before eyes that had seen too much in recent days. Helen Spencer had finally gone off her rocker. Kate knew Denis Makepeace well enough to realize that he had been used by Madam. She also knew Madam, had often seen damped-down fury in pale hazel eyes. Lipstick and high heels? The reason for those articles was only too clear – Miss Helen Spencer had decided to indulge in sins of the flesh.

The view from the window was not pleasant. Denis was almost motionless while his companion stamped and ranted until she collapsed on the grass. 'Go,' urged Kate quietly. 'Get out now, lad, while the going's good.' He should stay away from Helen Spencer. Anyone who wanted the ordinary life should keep a fair distance from that woman. Kate dusted quickly. 'She was a sneaky kid and she's no better now she's grown.'

Applying beeswax to a side table, Kate Moores continued to pray inwardly. If Denis left today, he would get no reference; if he stayed, he would get no peace. The clock chimed, and Kate knew that her working day was almost over. She was also fully aware of Helen Spencer's quiet power, of her persuasive tongue. Only the judge had remained unmoved by his daughter's clever ways. 'Go home, Denis,' Kate begged inwardly. 'Dear God, make him go home.'

But he didn't go home. Helen Spencer returned to the house and ran upstairs once more, while Denis sat on a bench near the rockery. Kate dragged her coat from a hook in the laundry room, decided that the day was too warm to merit outdoor clothing, and left the house by the kitchen door, coat draped over an arm. As she rounded the corner, she met Denis on his way back. Dragging him along the side of the building, Kate tutted at him. 'You should have gone,' she said. 'What's the matter with you?'

He swallowed audibly. 'I don't know.'

'Well, I do. My Auntie Vi looked after Miss Spencer

for years back in the days when they had servants – before they closed off half the house.' She nodded furiously. 'From the age of about three, Miss Spencer had a way of getting her own road. Not where her dad's concerned – she gave up on him when she was a baby. Happen that's why she bends other folk to do her will – I'm not a head doctor, so I can't work it out. Get gone before it's too late, son.'

'She said she'll go and see Agnes. Nothing's happened, but she's going to pretend I've been to bed with her. She'll tell my wife.'

Kate Moores puffed up her cheeks and blew noisily. 'Will she heck as like. Come what may, she protects herself. That quiet woman in the dowdy clothes is just what she wants us to see – inside, she's all for number one. You're just another thing she wants. She'll do nowt that'll pain herself.'

He sighed. 'She's round the bloody twist and it's my fault.'

'No, it's not. Now, listen to me, Denis. Although she can't see it, she's her dad all over again – selfish, nasty, ill-tempered. I'll bet a year's wages she started it. Am I right?'

He nodded. 'It's my fault as much as hers – I should have told her to bugger off right from the start. I haven't even kissed her. I'm fed up.'

'And a bit flattered because she's Miss Spencer?'

'Aye, perhaps I was. Not now, though. She's dangerous.'

Kate gripped the young man's arm. 'Find yourself another job. This is just the start, Denis. You're like a fish on a hook – the more you struggle, the more she digs in. Look at me. There's none down the bottom

know about this.' Her head bent in the direction of Skirlaugh Fall, the dip in which lay the village of her birth. 'I'll say nowt. But the longer you hang about round here, the more chance you have of getting caught out. You're a sitting duck, son. Bugger off home.'

Kate Moores was putting his own thoughts into words. He knew all the dangers, yet he feared that Helen would abide by her threat and tell Agnes a pack of lies if he left his job at Lambert House. 'He's bound to see the change in her when he gets home,' he said. 'She's walking about like a fourteen-year-old with a crush on some daft lad.'

Kate nodded in agreement. The judge said little except when giving orders, though he noticed everything and meted out punishments when life did not suit him. 'He'll hit the roof. I'd not like to be at the receiving end. All the lawyers hate him, you know. Prosecution or defence, they can't abide him.'

'If she's so clever, why can't she see sense?' Denis asked. 'She knows I don't want her and that I love Agnes – so why doesn't she leave me alone?'

Kate pondered a while before replying. 'Auntie Vi told me a few tales before she died. Too many for me to start telling now – my Albert'll be wanting feeding. But when she was a little lass, Helen Spencer stole and lied and played the angel all the while – butter wouldn't melt. She's sly and I'm going home. So think on. Remember – she's made in the image of her dad, not her mam, God rest that good soul.'

'I just don't know what to do. No matter what, I'm the one in trouble. Who'd believe me, Kate?'

'I would.'

'But everyone else?'

'Like I said, just think on before you do anything. And make sure the anything you do is not done with her.'

Denis thought on until it was time to go home. He toyed with his meal, found great difficulty in looking his wife in the eye, tried to feign interest when Fred rattled on about Eva and the shop. The thinking continued through evening and into the night, sleep punctuated by nightmares populated by silk and muslin and Chopin. This could not go on, yet Denis had not the slightest idea of how to make it stop.

'Are you all right?' asked Agnes sleepily.

'Yes. Go back to sleep, love.' There was nothing to be done. Unless ... Unless he could pluck up the courage to tell the judge.

Chapter Three

Talk to the judge? Denis struggled to remember a proper conversation with Zachary Spencer, realizing that there had been little true communication since the interview for his job. He tried to imagine himself asking for his employer's help in the current situation, and dismissed the idea before it had even taken root. But he shuddered at the thought of what might happen when the man returned in a few days to find his spinster daughter glowing with make-up and desire. Perhaps she would revert to normal?

'Denis?' Agnes was giving him one of her more searching looks.

'What?'

'There's folk in Africa would kill for that boiled egg.'

He finished his breakfast quickly, aware that his wife was troubled, knowing that he had to present himself at Lambert House within the hour, fearing the next move of a woman he now considered unbalanced. He could not hide from Agnes forever – she could read him like an open book.

'What's wrong?' Agnes asked. 'You've been like a cat on hot bricks since last week. Is the job too much? Could you not take it a bit easier if you're off-colour?'

Denis shrugged. 'I'm tired, love. It must be the heat. I'll do my best to slow down a bit.'

He left. While dusting, reading, shopping and washing,

she was worrying about Denis. It wasn't just his chest, not this time. He was walking about like a man with the whole world weighing him down and Agnes was troubled.

'We've always talked about stuff,' she advised the sink. Marriage was based on three things – love, trust and friendship. Those elements needed to run seamlessly through daily life, but Denis was holding something back. It wasn't like him. Any troubles, however small, had always been shared. Denis had got her through the months after Pop's stroke when she had worked at the pub. He had agreed happily about the nursing, had offered his support no matter what. If they had to eat less while she studied, that problem would be shared. The slightest thought was always meted out between the two of them so that a solution might be found before thought became difficulty. There was something wrong with Denis.

Agnes sat down. Pop was bringing in a wage, so things were not as bad as they might have been. Except. What a big word that was. Was it his job? Or was he trying to shield his wife from some terrible truth about his health? There wasn't another woman. 'I'd have known if it was that,' she whispered. 'But the lad's suffering.' If anything happened to Denis, she would be unable to continue alive.

She would deal with this tonight, after Pop had gone to bed. Whatever it took, Agnes Makepeace was going to get to the bottom of her husband's unhappiness.

Someone hammered on the front door and she ran to open it. A very flustered Glenys Timpson burst into tears as soon as she saw Agnes. 'It wasn't him,' she wailed repeatedly. 'He wouldn't. He was selling stuff, but . . . but he never did the shop. Oh, Agnes . . .' Loud wailing drowned the rest of her words.

Agnes produced tea and biscuits, waiting until Glenys had calmed before asking, 'Who and what? Slow down a bit, Glenys – I don't know what you're on about.'

'They've done something called referring him to Crown Court. He was handling stolen goods, but he never did the burglary and he won't say who did. He thinks he'll get beaten up or worse if he tells. There's some nasty folk about. He could get killed by the Manchester mafia.'

'This is Harry?'

The visitor nodded. 'Will you have a word with your Denis?'

'Eh? What for?'

'He can have a word with the judge. Even if he's not the judge on my Harry's case, he might say something to another judge.'

Agnes processed the odd request. 'So you want me to have a word with Denis about having a word with the judge about having a word with somebody else?'

'Summat on them lines, aye. I don't want Harry going down for years, do I? He's been in trouble afore, so it's not a first offence. I could lose him for good.'

'Were Jack and Bert involved?' Agnes asked.

'I don't know. I'd be lying if I said no and lying if I said yes. But they're not the ones in trouble. That Judge Spencer might listen to your Denis. You're the only chance I've got.'

Agnes shook her head. The judge never listened to anyone on the domestic front. 'It wouldn't make any difference, honestly. The judge is away at the moment, but he's not an approachable man, Glenys. And they're paid a lot of money so that they can't be bribed.'

'I'm not talking about bribery. Just a word in his ear. It won't do any harm to try.'

'He has to be impartial, love. You know the saying – justice must be done and must be seen to be done. The court'll look at it from the jeweller's point of view – his shop was wrecked and his stock was stolen.' She reached out and took the older woman's hand. 'I know it's horrible, love, but maybe your Harry will learn his lesson. Sometimes, it's the only way they do learn.'

Glenys closed her eyes and leaned back. 'He'll learn, all right. Last time, he learned just about every crime there is and how to break the law in a big way. Borstal near finished him. Prison'll only make him a lot worse. I'm frightened to bloody death. If he gets put away, it'll kill me and that's the top and tail of it.'

Agnes studied the woman in front of her. Glenys Timpson was near the edge of her chair and almost at the rim of reason. 'Glenys. Look at me. Go home, wash your hands and face, then come back. It's a nice day and we'll have a leisurely walk. We'll go up Skirlaugh Rise and see Denis while the judge is away. His daughter's off work at the moment. She might listen, but I can't promise that Judge Spencer will listen to her. It's worth a try, I suppose.'

Glenys awarded Agnes a weak smile. 'Thanks, love. Then at least I'll know I did everything I could. Even if it doesn't work, I'll have tried.' She left the house at top speed to prepare herself for the outing.

Agnes was not hopeful. The daughter was a pale, lifeless creature, while the judge was about as movable as the Rock of Gibraltar. Still, having made the offer to

Glenys, she knew that she had to carry it through. And it was a lovely day for a walk.

As Fred put it when speaking to his granddaughter, he and Eva Hargreaves got on 'like tongue and groove' from the very beginning. With no need for a timetable, they ran the shop between them, Fred disappearing into his shelter when he felt that Eva was up to scratch. A large woman, she needed frequent rests and was enjoying her business for the first time in years. She looked forward to Fred's arrival every morning, was pleased to have his company, was glad that he took to shop work like a duck to water.

'It's done me good, has this,' he told her one afternoon as they sat drinking tea outside the shop doorway. The pavement, covered in buckets, mops, brooms and other paraphernalia, was not exactly picnic territory, but both were content to bask in the sun during a lull in trade. 'I remember nearly everything now,' he said. 'Thanks, Eva. You've done me a lot of good, giving me this chance. There's not many that would take me on, the state I was in. I'm happy. You've made me happy. I'm grateful.'

'You're welcome.' She smoothed her apron. 'I saw your Agnes stepping out with Glenys about ten minutes ago. I wonder where they've gone?'

Fred nodded and took another gulp of stewed tea. 'Never holds a grudge, our Agnes. That battleaxe took to coming round after Sadie died, even made me a few meals. Not a bad cook, either – does a smashing corned beef hash. Everybody has a good side and Agnes always winkles it out. She's a grand lass.'

'She is.'

He studied his enamel mug for a moment. 'I might be holding them back, you know. Agnes and Denis, I mean. I don't like feeling as if I'm holding them back.'

'How come?'

'Well, they've been offered a peppercorn cottage in Skirlaugh Fall, just a stride away from his work. It's lovely up there – fresh air, good place to rear kiddies, plenty of places to play. It's dirty round these parts and Denis could do without breathing all these damned fumes. They stay because they think I can't manage by myself.'

'That's because you can't manage. When did you last cook a decent dinner, eh?' She grinned at him. 'You need them. Agnes feels she should look after you because you looked after her when her mam died. Just be glad you have a family that cares.'

'I don't want to be a burden,' he answered.

'It'll get sorted out.' Eva went into the shop to serve two newly arrived customers. A seed of an idea had planted itself in her brain, but she needed time to think about it, time on her own. She doled out paraffin and coal bricks, weighed some tacks, found a spanner for a man who needed to move a bed frame. The solution would arrive, she felt sure.

Fred wandered through the shop on his way to the air raid shelter. His doll's houses were coming on a treat and word was spreading. If he carried on this way, he would be hiring an assistant before the year was out. It was time to put an advert in the *Bolton Evening News*. Eva believed he deserved success after the work he had put into the enterprise.

Fred settled in his new workshop, proud eyes surveying shelves and cupboards – a place for everything and everything in its place. Agnes would be pleased when she saw this. Sadie would have been thrilled to bits. All he needed was a bit of advertising, and Eva had promised to see to that. He took a swig of cold tea before carpeting his tiny bedrooms. For the first time in months, Fred Grimshaw was a contented man.

It was a long walk and its duration gave Glenys the opportunity to unburden herself. She talked about her dead husband, about Eva Hargreaves, also a widow, with whom she had shared grief over premature deaths. 'We both married lads younger than ourselves and both lost them early. Very good to me and my boys, was Eva. Which is why I near flayed our Harry for breaking into her shop. He were only a kid, but I should have seen it then, Agnes. Three lads and I needed eyes in the back of my head – I still do. They've been trouble, but I love them all to bits. What the hell am I going to say to Miss Spencer if she sees me?'

Agnes didn't know. She'd come into contact with Helen Spencer in the big library, had even managed a bit of conversation with her once, but the woman seemed too quiet and shy to have any influence with her dad. 'You can only do your best – like you said earlier. Harry will have to take his chances, but your conscience will be clear.'

'Aye, let's hope so.'

During a quieter spell, Agnes wondered about the level of ferocity displayed by many women when one of their offspring was in trouble. It was clear that Glenys would rather do the time for Harry. 'I wonder if I'll be like you when I have a child?' she asked eventually.

'Like me?'

'Yes. Going to any lengths to help your son.'

'You will,' said Glenys with certainty. 'You'll be a good mam, Agnes Makepeace.'

'I hope so.'

They were in Skirlaugh Fall, a small village built in a cleft between moors. Glenys paused for a rest. 'I'll bet these places get flooded in heavy rain,' she pronounced, her eyes fastened to the big house at the top of Skirlaugh Rise. 'I mean, water runs downhill, doesn't it? They'll need wellies in their back kitchens if a storm comes.'

Agnes smiled. Her companion was trying to take her own mind off the task in hand. 'Denis has been offered one of the cottages,' she said. 'Small, but lovely – and look at that scenery.'

'Will you take it?'

'I would if Pop decided to come, but he's embedded down yonder.' She inclined her head in the direction of the town. 'He thinks Bolton'll come to bits if he's not there to supervise matters. And I'd have to travel to the infirmary every day, so I suppose we'll be stopping in Noble Street. Till they pull it all down, of course.'

Glenys grabbed Agnes's arm. 'This Manchester job were a big one. They'll need a whipping boy, and my Harry's been picked. It weren't him. I'd know. I always know. He were in on it, but he didn't blow that shop to bits.'

'And he knows who did?'

'Aye, he does, only he'd sooner be alive in prison than join his dad in Tonge Cemetery. His mouth's shut tighter than a prison door.'

When the two women walked through the gates of Lambert House, they scanned the front for a sign of Denis, but he was nowhere to be seen. 'Let's split up,' Agnes suggested. 'You look round the back, while I go over yonder.' She pointed to a nearby cluster of trees. 'I know Denis said something about thinning out branches, so he could be in the copse.'

'What's that when it's at home?'

Agnes grinned ruefully. 'Judge Spencer doesn't have anything ordinary like a wood or an orchard – he has to have a copse. I think Denis might be working in there, but he could be round the back, so you go and have a look.'

Glenys decided on a straight swap. 'I'll go in the corpse—'

Agnes laughed. 'Copse.'

'You know what I mean. I don't want to be poking about round the back of the house. At least you have Denis as an excuse – let me go to the woods.'

So it came about that Glenys Timpson unwittingly embarked on a course of action that would have repercussions for many years to come. Feeling relatively safe, she opted for the copse. Surely she would be all right in there? Surely no one would see her? She didn't mind being spotted by Denis, but the thought of being accused of trespass with a view to house-breaking was frightening. She was still on Spencer land, but the trees would hide her.

She entered the wooded area and looked for Denis Makepeace. He was a grand lad and he would help her. It occurred to her that she had never before been in a wood, had seldom seen dense foliage. It was dark and eerily beautiful, all dappled shadow and birdsong. 'Lovely,' she breathed softly. 'Scary, but lovely.' Birds rattled branches and a ladybird landed on a leaf. She might have been a thousand miles away from the centre of Bolton, because this place was truly beautiful.

Round the back of Lambert House, Agnes came into contact with Kate Moores, who was taking sheets from a washing line. 'I'm Denis's wife,' she told the red-faced female. 'Give me those. This weather's too hot for housework, isn't it? All I want to do is sleep, and I was hoping the walk up here would do me good. But this heat's turned me into a withered lettuce.'

Kate allowed Agnes to take some of the burden. 'I don't know where he is,' she lied. 'He's been doing all sorts today.' At the kitchen table, she studied Denis's wife. Why was she here? Did this young woman suspect that her husband was being pursued by Madam? And where the hell was Madam, anyway? 'I don't fancy ironing,' she added lamely. The washing had been baked dry by a relentless sun.

'It'll all want damping,' agreed Agnes.

'Have you come about anything in particular?' The daily set a kettle to boil, her face turned away from the visitor.

'Just fancied the walk. I might have enjoyed it if there'd been a bit of a breeze.' Agnes looked round the kitchen. It was bigger than the whole ground floor of the Noble Street house. 'Do you have to clean the whole place by yourself?'

Kate turned. 'No. Most of it's shut off. I don't know why he hangs on to it – they use four rooms at the most. A girl comes in sometimes to do the silver and a few other odd jobs.'

'What's the judge like to work for?'

'He's straight from hell,' came the swift answer. 'Never has a good word for anybody, never says much at all.'

'Oh.'

'I think your Denis is the only person he likes. But I'm guessing there and all. I've never heard him saying anything nasty about Denis, any road. But you really can't tell – he's shut faster than the cat's backside, is old Spencer.'

Agnes laughed out loud.

'Hey, you'd not find it funny if you worked here, lass. When was the last time you coped with oysters and bloody avocado? Smoked salmon has to be thin enough to see through. He likes his caviar chilled and on a bed of crushed ice – any melting and I'm for the high jump. Napkins have to be starched just right – too much or too little and I get the third degree. I reckon his wife died on purpose to get away from him. I'd sooner be in heaven than in this house, but we need his money.'

'Not a nice man, then?' Agnes smiled.

'He wants a bloody good hiding, and that's the truth of the matter. He'll be back in a few days, so expect rain.'

'I wouldn't mind a bit of rain.' Agnes added milk to her cup. 'I'll look for Denis in a minute,' she said.

Feeling reasonably safe, Kate chattered on about ironing shirts just right, about polishing antiques and trying to clean the drapes round a four-poster. The trouble was, you could never tell with folk these days. Denis's wife seemed calm enough, but there was no way to be sure. Kate clung fiercely to hope. When everything else failed, hope was all that remained.

A woman was weeping.

Glenys secreted herself behind a wide tree and listened. Denis was speaking now. 'I've told you to leave me alone. What do you want from me? No, I'll take that back – I'm pretty sure of the answer. Have you no pride?'

The sobbing continued.

'I've enjoyed listening to your music this summer. But that's all there is to it. I'm married. You know I'm married – you've always known. I'll tell you what I think, shall I?'

'No.' The reply was almost strangled at birth.

'I think you need to see a doctor. This isn't normal behaviour. Running after a married bloke who hasn't had a proper education – that's not right, is it? What would your father say? What will he do when he gets home and finds you in this state? If I did anything wrong, I'm sorry. If I led you on, I apologize. I can hardly look Agnes in the eye – and what have I done? Nothing. Or, in the language I'm more used to, bugger all.'

Glenys remained frozen, though the heat of the day had penetrated dense branches and leaves. Her mind was far from still, though. Harry was her son and she loved him. No matter what, she loved her boys. Could she make use of this situation?

'I can't help loving you,' said Helen Spencer. It had to be Helen Spencer, thought Glenys. Who else round here talked through a gobful of plums? She listened while the invisible female ranted on about touching Denis's arm in her car on the day of the funeral, about him hovering near a window while she played the piano. 'You didn't exactly push me away or avoid me, did you?'

'I like music,' he said, his voice louder. 'Do I have to stop liking music? Look, get back to the house, for goodness' sake. Mrs Moores must be wondering what the hell's going on. Before you know it, we'll be the talk of the Fall and nothing's happened!'

Glenys held on to her courage and stepped forward. 'Hello, Denis,' she said, her voice sounding different, high-pitched and unsteady. 'Hello, Miss Spencer.'

'Who are you?' Helen's hand was suddenly at the base of her throat and her cheeks became ruddy. 'You are trespassing.'

'I'm with Agnes,' replied Glenys. 'Nice day, so we thought we'd have a walk and see how Denis is going on. I'm their neighbour.' She was here for her son and nothing else mattered. Whatever it took, she would have her say and to hell with the consequences. 'You all right, Denis?' she asked.

'It's hot,' came the reply.

It was hot, thought Glenys. In more ways than one, this was a situation near boiling point. She felt sure that she could feel steam rising from ground protected from direct sunlight, but still subjected to high temperature. Tropical jungles probably smelled the same. 'I'm Glenys Timpson and I'm here about our Harry,' she said boldly, voice strengthened by determination. 'Harry Timpson. He's up before a judge soon and I wanted to have a word with you, Miss Spencer.'

'Not a concern of mine,' replied Helen.

No trace of tears remained on Helen Spencer's face, and Glenys wondered whether the woman should be on the stage. 'I want you to talk to your father. Tell him our Harry's not a bad lad and he blew no safes in Manchester. Your dad might be the judge or one of his mates could be – I don't know.'

Helen waited for more, but nothing was forthcoming. 'Due process,' she said eventually. 'I have no say in any judgement made in court. Your son will have to take his chances along with anyone else who has broken the law.'

Glenys inhaled deeply. 'Aye, and you'll be forced to take yours if I know Agnes Grimshaw-as-was. She holds no prisoners, you know. It won't be a cell – you'll be six feet under if she gets her own road.'

'I'm not afraid of her.' Helen Spencer's voice trembled.

'Then you're daft,' spat Glenys. 'Agnes's nan used to say that their Agnes could start a war in a chip shop. She's put me and the rest of the neighbours in our places a time or two. A fighter, is Agnes. Well, just you listen to me, Miss Spencer. I stood there behind yon tree and I heard it all. Denis has no need to feel guilty, 'cos he's done nowt. But you? Huh!' The 'huh' arrived seasoned with more than a sprinkling of contempt. 'Your dad wouldn't be right pleased if he knew, eh?'

Helen blinked several times. If Father found out about her behaviour, it would be out in the open and . . . and Denis still wouldn't want her. Even if Agnes left him, he had no interest in his employer's daughter. Why bring it all out if she couldn't get what she wanted? On the other hand, why not bring it out into the open? She had nothing further to lose . . .

'I'm waiting,' snapped Glenys.

Helen sniffed. 'I shall think about it,' she said.

'Aye, you do that.' Glenys drew herself to full height. 'The name's Harold Timpson and he's up for a burglary in Manchester. He's frightened of saying who blew the safe, but he never did it, not in a million years. So, unless you want muck raking all over your name, think on and talk to your dad.' Glenys could not meet Denis's gaze. She was threatening him, too, but no other course of action was available, so what was she supposed to do? Three decades of the rosary and hope for the best? Not likely – she hadn't come this far to end up on her knees.

Helen looked from one to the other, acutely conscious of her own misbehaviour, painfully aware that she had laid herself open to blackmail. She was expected to talk to her father, a man who had never listened to a mere woman in his life. 'I'll do what I can,' she said stiffly before walking away.

Denis closed his eyes and leaned back against the bole of a substantial oak. 'God, Glenys,' he breathed. 'What next, eh? What the bloody hell next?'

She placed a hand on his arm. 'You know, lad, as I'll say nowt to your Agnes, but happen you might have to in the end. I'd cut my own throat before I'd hurt your family now. How the hell did all that lot come about? What's Spencer's daughter doing sniffing round you?'

'No idea,' he replied wearily. 'I liked this job well enough till she came over all peculiar. I reckon she's desperate to get away from her dad and start a family of her own. I was the nearest.'

'And you're wed.'

'I know.'

'And she's a few slates short of a full roof.'

'Or several straws short of a thatch, as my old dad used to say, God rest him. What a pickle.'

Glenys told him how lucky he had been, how she had changed places with Agnes. 'She was going to come to this here copse, but I didn't want to be seen mooching about round the back of the house. If Agnes had heard what I heard . . .'

'I wish she had,' said Denis. 'Then she'd know what's

77

really gone on. If she finds out some other way . . .
Mind you, there's nothing to find out. I've never looked
at another woman – Agnes'll know that.'

Glenys nodded thoughtfully. 'Keep your mouth shut
for now, Denis. Let Miss Silver-spoon talk to her dad
before you have a word with Agnes. And when you do,
I'll back you up. But while there's a chance of our
Harry getting help, hold your tongue.'

Hold his tongue? He had no choice in the matter.
How the heck was he going to explain this predicament
to his wife? Who would believe that Miss Helen Spencer
had made the only moves? 'Let's go and find Agnes,' he
said. 'I think I've had enough for today.'

Helen peeled off the layers and placed them in a small
heap on the bed. Father would be back tomorrow. Judge
Zachary Spencer's return was imminent and his daughter had to . . . Had to what? Ah, yes. She had to become
dowdy again. The exercise had been a failure, anyway,
because Denis wasn't interested. No one was interested.
She needed to return to her former self, unlovable, sad,
the spinster and librarian.

In her dressing room, she rinsed Lux Flakes from
underwear, wondering whether or when she would
wear such luxurious items again. Bubbles disappeared
down the drain, taking with them every drop of hope,
every fleck of excitement. After cold cream had wiped
off her make-up, Helen sat on her dressing stool and
stared at the mirror's reflection until it disappeared into
an almost amorphous lump of matter, a shapeless item
in flat glass.

Then she heard them talking. Noiselessly, she posi-
tioned herself near the window, curtains concealing her

from the happy people below. Denis was talking to the woman who had been in the copse. Was she Glenys? Denis and Glenys – how droll. But Denis was not the property of the older female. No. Denis was with a person of some beauty, owner of chestnut tresses, dark-lashed eyes and a pretty smile. 'I've seen her in the library,' mouthed Helen silently. She returned to her seat, her solitary position, her loneliness. She could still hear them chattering below. They were members and she was not. No matter what she did, she would never be able to join their exclusive club, because she was different, unloved and unlovable.

'I am no one,' she said just before the tears came. It was as if she had been parked in the margins of life, a shadow, a fleeting thing that would never be noticed. She hated who she was, what she had become. But above and beyond that, she despised her father, the one who had made and shaped her into an unattractive and self-absorbed creature with no idea of how to behave, of how to relate to others. It would be back to work, back to the little cafe where she ate her lunches, to filing systems, reference section, nice little love stories for nice little old ladies. In twenty years, she would become one of those old ladies, but she would never be nice because she was bitter to the core.

Kate Moores tapped on the bedroom door and announced her intention to go home.

'Very well,' Helen answered.

'I've left you some salad,' said the disembodied daily. 'Miss Spencer? Are you all right?'

Of course she was all right. In a few years, she might be chief librarian, bespectacled, respected, bored to tears. 'Thank you, I am very well.'

Footsteps faded, a door closed, gravel shifted under

the weight of the retreating Mrs Moores. The sigh that left Helen's body shuddered its way past quietening sobs. Six o'clock. What did normal people do at six o'clock? They probably ate in family groups, then talked, listened to the radio, played with their children. Occasionally, there would be an outing to a public house, a visit to relatives or to the cinema. There was television, of course, with its grim news programmes and silly games. The clock was ticking her life away. She did not want to watch TV, didn't relish the idea of an evening with her radio. She was losing her grip. Was she losing her mind?

'I want a family,' she informed the creature in her mirror. She wanted what most people had, needed to be ordinary, settled. But would she know how to behave at close quarters with others? Could she imagine herself as a wife and mother? And would any man fill the void left by the gentle, handsome creature known as Denis Makepeace? 'Infatuation,' she snapped. 'A childish fad, no more.' What on earth did she know of love, of normality?

The salad did not tempt Helen that night. Unfed and incomplete, she curled up on her virgin bed and cried herself to sleep. Tomorrow, she would think; tomorrow was the only certainty, and she had to content herself with that knowledge.

While Helen Spencer lay alone and disappointed, Agnes went about the business of getting to the bottom of her husband's misery. She talked and questioned and complained until he finally caved in. While he answered, she listened intently. 'I've no need to talk to Glenys,' she said when the tale had been told. 'I know you, Denis

Makepeace, and I trust you. Poor Miss Spencer. I suppose she just wants to fit in like anybody else.'

He should never have doubted his wife, should have confided in her from the very start. 'So, if she comes to you with tales of abuse, you won't listen to her.'

'Of course I won't. But if you think about the life she's had with that misery of a dad, it's understandable. Anyway, isn't it all a bit the other way round? Did you say Glenys threatened to tell me if Miss Spencer doesn't try to help their Harry?'

Denis nodded thoughtfully. 'She's not right, you know.'

'Glenys?'

'Don't be daft. Mind, thinking about Glenys, you may have something there. No. Helen Spencer. Sometimes, she has a wildness about her. She's very . . .'

'Intense?'

'Yes. Desperate. One minute she wants to tell the world that she loves me, then the next – oh, I don't know. Anyway, the old man's home tomorrow, so that'll cool her down a bit. And she'll be going back to her job soon enough. But I find myself half waiting for her to do something peculiar like drinking paint or ripping her hair out. She stares at me. Her eyes bore right through me – I feel as if she can read my mind.'

'Only a couple of paragraphs, then, so don't worry.' Agnes grinned, then shook her head pensively. 'So she threatened to tell me herself, then changed her mind. And when Glenys said she'd tell me, Miss Spencer ran off?'

Denis nodded.

'Doesn't know what she wants, does she?'

'No. I suppose this will sound daft, love, but it's as if she doesn't know who she is, who she ought to be, who she wants to be. I remember girls – and boys – very like her when I was at school: ready to grow up, but still kids. Oh, well. Where's our Pop?'

'Sorting out his batteries. He's putting torch bulbs in all his ceilings. Central heating next, I shouldn't wonder.'

'Shall I walk up and fetch him home?'

'No. Let me have you all to myself for a few minutes, Denis.' She kissed him. 'If we were all like you, we'd do.'

Denis, relieved of the larger burden, still managed to feel a pang of guilt. He remembered the music, the elegance of Helen's hands, the sadness in her eyes. Perhaps he had encouraged her on a level that lay just below full consciousness. But he hadn't done anything wrong and life, as the saying went, had to go on.

Glenys put in a sudden, belated appearance. 'I knew you'd come,' Denis said as soon as she stepped into the house. 'I knew you wouldn't leave me in a state.'

Glenys, flustered beyond measure, blurted out the tale. 'I said I wouldn't say anything, Agnes, but then I thought on and here I am.'

Agnes grinned. The arrival of her neighbour had not been completely unexpected. 'He told me,' she said. 'Don't worry – for your Harry's sake, I'll pretend I know nothing, then we'll see if Miss Spencer will have a word with her dad.'

'Might as well talk to the fireback,' muttered Denis before going to make hot cocoa.

Agnes studied her neighbour, the gossip, eyes and ears of the street, she who had always made everyone's business her own. Glenys had altered. Her face was thinner, there was more silver in her hair and her skin was lined. This was going to be a good friend.

82

'It's a hard life, all right,' Glenys was saying now. 'If he goes to jail, it'll kill me.'

It wouldn't kill her. Agnes, having grown up among strong women whose husbands were at war, recognized the steely quality that had kept machines turning and a country fed for six long years. Glenys would not die if her Harry went to prison; she would do what all females did in such circumstances – she would work and wait. 'We'll look after you, Glenys. Remember that.'

'Aye, I know you will, lass. Where is he with that cocoa? My throat's like the bottom of a parrot's cage.'

Sleep eluded Helen for the whole of the night. When she did drift for a few minutes, she was back in the copse with Glenys and Denis, whose rhyming names were no longer a source of amusement. Father was in the woods as well, his voice drowning hers, his presence crushing the very air from her lungs. There was another dream too, one she did not care to remember just yet. It was nasty and she was glad to be free of it. These days, it recurred more often and sleep had ceased to be a hiding place. There was noise in the second dream. And terror . . .

Awake, she stared into blackness and tried to curb her imagination, failing completely to control the circular motion of her thoughts. If people knew how she felt about Denis, Agnes Makepeace might leave her husband, but would he turn to Helen? If no one found out, might she persuade him to love her in secret? 'Why did I declare myself?' she asked the ceiling. 'What is happening to me?' Women in books didn't go around opening their hearts to all and sundry. Elizabeth Bennet, Jane Eyre – all the great heroines played their cards close to their hearts, never, ever wearing them on sleeves of transparent silken robes. 'I am sitting at my own wedding feast with no groom,' she whispered. 'Dickensian, over-dramatic and downright stupid. I should be shot, then I'd be released from everyone's misery.'

Sleep. She needed rest. Father had a cure for sleeplessness and Helen, desperate for some peace, descended the stairs and entered the sanctum of Judge Zachary Spencer in search of help. Rows of leather-bound books occupied polished mahogany shelves. His desk and blotter were pristine, no sign of work, no notes, no splashes of ink. The room displayed no character; it was a reflection of his severity and conservatism. Had he ever owned an imagination, had he suffered at all, had he loved her mother?

She removed a bottle of brandy from a cupboard, hoped he hadn't measured the contents. Instead of taking one of his sparkling crystal glasses, Helen went into the kitchen and chose a less ostentatious water tumbler before returning to her room.

The first mouthful made her cough, burning her throat like hot ashes. But the second went down easily and she felt calmer and almost carefree. Denis Makepeace? Why had she worried about a man so much lower than herself? Her father was a judge in the High Courts, for goodness' sake. She would find someone else, someone worthy of her attentions. Her body, limp from the effects of alcohol, began to relax. With the tumbler still in her hand, Helen fell asleep on the chaise. Everything would be all right. All she needed was a good night's rest.

If she had any nightmares, she did not remember them. Morning found her very well except for a slight headache that disappeared after several cups of tea and a light breakfast. But, when Denis arrived to do his job, her heart lurched in her chest as soon as she caught sight of him. Brandy was good for sleeplessness, but it did nothing to eradicate the cause of discomfort. It dealt with symptoms, not with cause. 'Like aspirin,' she muttered as she stood at her window. Denis looked handsome in his uniform. Shortly, he would leave to pick up Father from Trinity Street, and the house would once again be filled by the noise and bluster that always accompanied Judge Zachary Spencer. It was, thought Helen, time for a hair of the dog. A very little would suffice, as she sought waking peace rather than unconsciousness.

She ascended the stairs and prepared for the return of her only parent. He would dominate the house, would ignore her, would act the part of monarch again.

Brandy made it all much easier to bear.

Chapter Four

Lucy looked wonderful in her watered silk wedding dress. She would have looked gorgeous in a potato sack, Agnes thought as she took up her position as matron of honour. The bride turned just before preparing to leave the porch and enter the church. 'The old dragon's here,' she whispered, 'with his dragoness. I should have put garlic flowers in our bouquets. Grab a crucifix and don't look him in the eye.'

Agnes swallowed. Judge Zachary Spencer had begun his illustrious career in the chambers of Henshaw & Taylor, and he had apparently decided to grace the occasion with his surly presence. Helen Spencer, his 'dragoness', was the last person Agnes wished to see today, but the groom's side was wall-to-wall lawyers and it couldn't be helped. George's father was head of chambers and he had probably invited all his colleagues. Agnes drew back her shoulders, raised her chin and walked with Mags behind Lucy and her father. Aware that she looked her best, she intended to show Miss Helen Spencer that Denis was married to a fine specimen. She cast a sideways glance at the judge's daughter, who looked decent but unimaginative in a colourless suit that had probably cost an arm, a leg and a full dining room suite.

Helen watched the service, teeth biting down on lower lip, hands clenched around bag, gloves and hymn book, face deliberately cleansed of all expression. She could and would get through this. A half-bottle of Napoleon was secreted in a pocket of her bag hard against a quarter of Mint Imperials to shift the scent of alcohol from her breath. Father was huffing and puffing beside her. Father had no time for Catholics, foreigners, vagrants, criminals and daughters. The Latin Mass probably infuriated the bigoted old buffoon, and Helen was mildly pleased about that. He shifted his weight, sighed repeatedly and joined in none of the prayers.

During the hymn 'Love Divine', he bent his head and whispered to her. 'Chap over there, third row from the front – friend of the groom – you could do a lot worse.'

Helen followed his nod until her eyes alighted on a gaunt man with thinning hair and a very stiff collar. 'James Taylor,' mumbled the judge. 'Good man, big future. Time you settled.'

Icy fingers curled around her heart. She had seen Denis looking smart in his suit, had devoured the vision that was his wife and was now expected to pay full attention to a man with a neck thinner than Denis's wrist. She was exaggerating, she told herself sharply. James Taylor was probably no oil painting from the front; from the rear, he resembled an anxious-looking character from a Victorian novel, all starved and on the lookout for its next meal.

It was her turn to sigh. Why was she pretending to have a choice? There was no queue of suitors, no line of men waiting to meet the daughter of Judge Spencer. She remembered Charlotte Lucas from *Pride and Prejudice*, who had married a buffoon of a clergyman just to be safe in a comfortable home. Elizabeth Bennet was maid of honour in Helen's own story. Helen, halfway down the church and nowhere in anyone's opinion, was the plain and sensible woman who would have to settle for a Mr Collins. 'Just to be safe,' she whispered. Was that all there was going to be? Safety and a man uglier than sin?

'Did you say something?' asked her father.

Surprised beyond measure, she shook her head. When had he last been interested in any words emerging from her mouth? When had he last deigned to notice her? Noticed now, she felt threatened and decided that she could go through life more easily without the attention of her father. She wanted to run, but dared not follow so base an instinct. She did not want to be here, did not want to be anywhere, but she must endure.

The judge coughed his way through the nuptial Mass and proxy papal blessing. The whole thing was a bloody nonsense. Henshaw Senior refused to handle divorce because of his religious beliefs. Fortunately, his son, who was bridegroom, seemed more willing to accept lucrative cases. Divorce was about to become big business and sense needed to be employed when it came to litigation.

James Taylor, of a landed family, was a good prospect for Helen. He was already a senior partner and he showed great promise in spite of his lack of style. She was drab, as was he, and she would do well to marry him. If the union crumbled, any settlement would be large. 'Called to the bar before he hit thirty.' The words slid from a corner of his mouth towards his daughter. 'About your age, too.'

She suffered a renewed desire to run, but this time she felt like screaming while dashing from the church. As 'Love Divine' faded into the ether, Helen's first free-floating panic attack crashed into her chest like a ten-ton lorry. Oxygen suddenly became a luxury, and she grasped each breath, lungs stiffening, throat as dry as bone. She dropped bag, gloves and hymn book, sinking onto the pew bench just in time. Her heart was going too fast. Sweat gathered on forehead and upper lip, and she longed for brandy. Brandy was the answer. If she could take a drink, she would be all right. As soon as everyone else was seated, the judge, who had given his only child a withering look, forgot about her. She had sat down a second too early, that was all, and few had noticed, he hoped.

With a lace-edged handkerchief, Helen dried her face. Why had she suddenly become so frightened? It was like being in a darkened room with a wild animal, no chance of knowing where it was, just blind fear and a strong desire to be elsewhere. Was this her heart, would she die young? Her mother had died a premature death caused by a heart attack after some kind of accident. Would Helen suffer a similar fate? It didn't matter. The moment she ceased to fear death, her pulse slowed and she breathed evenly. If she died, it would be a release from the torture named life.

It was over. Bride and groom emerged from a side room in which they had signed legal documents attached to marriage. The main party left the church to the strains of a pleasant piece of Bach, then the congregation peeled itself row by row out of the pews.

Avoiding photographs at all costs, Helen stayed in the school playground, treating herself to a few drops of brandy before sucking on the necessary mint. 'Ah, there you are,' said a disembodied voice.

'Yes,' she replied, embarrassment staining her cheeks. Was there to be no peace at all today?

'I've seen you in the library,' added the owner of the

89

voice. 'I'm James Taylor. Your father suggested that I seek you out, as he will be in older company. You are Helen Spencer, I take it?'

'Yes.' Her vocabulary had shrunk, it seemed.

'Nice wedding.'

'Yes, it was. The bride looked lovely.' Agnes Makepeace had looked lovely, too.

'George is a lucky man. Shall we?' He crooked an arm.

Tentatively, she placed a very light hand on his sleeve and allowed him to lead her back to the large gathering at the church gates. He was definitely not a thing of beauty. Had she allowed herself to wear some of her new clothes and make-up, she would have outshone him with comparatively little effort. But Helen had come as her father's companion, and no one competed with Judge Zachary Spencer. The king of the beasts demanded pride of place. Pride among a pride, she pondered giddily, because most lawyers were bigger than their boots. The collective noun for lawyers should be 'pride' – and pride, as everyone knew, came just before a fall. She hoped with all her heart that the fall would be soon and that she could be there to witness the undoing of the super-king – her father.

A woman among the spectators was mouthing at Helen. It was Glenys Timpson, and the silent message was, 'Don't forget.'

'Are you coming to the reception?' James Taylor asked.

She nodded. Her father was studying her and she knew that she could not run away. The reception was to provide the setting for the mating ritual ordered by the judge. By the end of the month, she must be engaged. A winter wedding needed to be followed closely by pregnancy and trouble-free birth. Perhaps a grandson would placate Father, though he would doubtless have preferred a Spencer to a Taylor. That fact might well result in hyphenated surnames and she could not imagine herself sleeping in the same continent as her intended appendage, with or without hyphenation.

James drove her to the centre of Bolton, where the party was to be held. In a large ground floor room of the Pack Horse, tables formed three sides of a square, and Helen decided that the bride and groom must have been in on the plot, as she was seated next to James Taylor. From the rear, he had worn the air of a bird of prey; from the front, he was no less startling, as his nose resembled the beak of an eagle and he had a habit of staring unblinkingly at his companion. Any minute now, she would be snatched up and carried in talons back to his eyrie. Determined not to be cowed, she attacked her food with all the enthusiasm she could muster. It tasted like cardboard, but wine improved her palate.

He told her of cases in which he had triumphed, boasted about his prowess in court, declared himself to be quite the orator. His long-term intention was not the bar; he wanted to take his seat among the Conservative Party in Westminster. Before the meal was over, Helen had the full picture of his life, including attitudes to the work-shy, immigrants, miscreants and golf. The last saved a man's sanity after days spent in court. If rain stopped play, he joined his fellow damp players for a game of chess at the nineteenth. Did she play chess or golf? Oh, what a shame, but he would teach her both – it would be an honour. Golf would keep her physically fit, while chess would hone her brain to perfection. She hated him. Hating him was easy, but escaping him in this claustrophobic environment might prove difficult.

When the cake was cut, and speeches had been delivered, Helen excused herself and went to a powder room on the first floor, a quieter area well away from the wedding feast. In a cubicle, she gulped down another dose of her chosen medicine, remembering the Mint Imperial before emerging to stare at herself in an enormous mirror in the outer area of the women's rest room. 'What a mess,' she said aloud. In fawn and brown, she resembled a sixth-former from some Catholic grammar school run by over-protective nuns. She was not pretty, would never be pretty, yet she knew she could look better than this, though not in the company of the pride of the pride.

A cistern flushed, then a young woman emerged from the second stall.

'Sorry,' said Helen. 'Talking to myself again – I am the only audience that will tolerate me.'

Mags Bradshaw grinned ruefully. 'Did you come here to escape the madding crowd?'

Helen nodded.

'So did I. There's only so much beauty and happiness that can be digested in one day. I think my cup runneth over and I needeth a break.'

Helen found herself smiling. 'I'm Helen Spencer.'

'Mags Bradshaw, friend of the bride for my sins. As you can tell from the silly clothes, I am also bridesmaid.'

'Yes. You and Agnes Makepeace, isn't it?'

'She was matron of honour, because she has bagged her man. I am now the only singleton in the pack, and no sign of a man on the horizon.'

'I have had one thrust upon me.' Helen wondered why she was speaking so freely, remembering after a second or two that this was a side-effect of her brandy. 'In the middle of a hymn, my father announced that I am to be sold to a balding eagle. Aforementioned balding eagle has been pecking away at me since we left the church. Any idea of how I might get away? These birds of prey are terribly persistent and I have no wish to be swallowed whole.'

Mags pointed to a green door. 'Fire escape? We could go and watch Donald Duck at the children's matinee. Or what about a manhunt? If we sit for long enough on the town hall steps, someone will pick us up. We'd do better there than here. I work with lawyers and they are a dry lot. Let's go and be discovered by a pair of lusty youths. We could repair to some nearby tavern and talk about football and stuff.'

Helen considered that. 'A balding eagle could find us. The eyesight of the species is legendary.'

'True.' Mags sat on a pink stool. 'Being unbeautiful isn't easy.'

'I know.'

'Lucy always says that my beauty lies within. I bet no one ever says that to Marilyn Monroe.'

Helen voiced the opinion that it was easy to hate Marilyn Monroe. 'Beautiful women have a special knowledge that precludes the need for actual brains. They always seem to know exactly what to do and say – it must be something that arrives with maturation and admiration. One minute, they are sitting at the back of the class with runny noses. The next they are at the Palais de Danse picking up every youth without spots.'

Mags agreed that the whole thing was sick-making. 'I had a boyfriend for six months. Then I found out he was only in it for the chips. My parents own a fish and chip shop and he got a free supper every time he took me out. A piece of bad cod put paid to that adventure, I'm afraid. Nearly put paid to him as well – terrible case of food poisoning.' She sighed. 'Alas, he survived. There is no true justice in this world.'

'So you are a friend of Agnes?'

'Yes.'

'Her husband works for my father.'

Mags nodded. 'Denis needs an easy job – he had TB when he was a child and it left a few scars. Even then, he and his family were well loved. Three mills set up a fund to send him off to Switzerland. He couldn't go till the war was over, so his lungs never fully recovered. He's lucky with his wife, though. Agnes has never been one for frills and flounces – and she adores him.'

'Good. He works hard. My father appreciates him.'

Mags raised an eyebrow and smiled broadly. 'Really?'

'Father approves of anyone who fights the odds, but there is no real affection in him.'

'Your mam died?'

Helen dusted a hair from her shoulder. 'I scarcely remember my mother, but I believe my birth was her undoing. She became unsteady and prone to accidents. Childbirth weakened her heart.'

'Sad.'

Emboldened by alcohol, Helen continued to open up to the stranger. 'I used to think he blamed me for her death, but nothing is as easy as that with him. He doesn't like women. I am a woman. Quod erat demonstrandum, as the theorem states. It's as if I'm not there. Or I wasn't until today.'

'Balding eagle?'

'Exactly.' Helen applied lipstick. 'We still haven't an answer. Where do we hide?'

'Give me five minutes.' Mags disappeared into the corridor.

Helen sat on the pink-padded stool and stared unseeing at the mirror. What on earth was she thinking of? First, she had tried in vain to have an affair with Agnes Makepeace's husband; second, she was currently engaged in conversation with one of that woman's closest friends. A nip of brandy put paid to misgivings. She was a thirty-two-year-old adult and she could do what she damned well pleased.

Mags returned, a key brandished in one hand. 'I got us a room for the day,' she crowed in triumph. 'Two beds, two chairs and our very own bottle of champagne.'

'But my father—'

'Your father can bugger off. If anyone questions you, I was taken ill and you were kind enough to cater for my needs. It's nearly true. I am allergic to lawyers and I need champagne. You can pour, thereby providing me with the medication I require.'

Helen blinked. Could all lies be turned into truth? Could she marry a man she had disliked on sight, could she go through a hyphenated life with a smile on her face? 'I won't marry him.' The announcement surprised her – she hadn't meant to say the words out loud.

'You tell 'em, matey. We've a similar article at work. He *is* articled – a mere clerk. He's as fat as two boars and the beer gut enters a room five minutes before the rest of him. He breathes.'

Helen giggled. 'Everyone breathes.'

'It's his main occupation. You can hear him from the other end of the building. Near me, he breathes more heavily and, to top it all, I get the impression that he expects me to be grateful for his attentions. Come on. We can manage an hour away from the chaos, but I'll have to go back eventually. Lucy and I have been friends since school.'

They drank the champagne, then laid themselves flat on the two beds. Helen, who had never before mixed her drinks, was decidedly befuddled, though she managed to remain alert while Mags told tales from a childhood she had shared with the bride and the matron of honour.

Then, while Mags Bradshaw snored gently, Helen considered her own childhood. It had not been normal, and she found herself resenting three girls who had played with skipping ropes, bats and balls, pieces of slate as hopscotch markers. They had been injured in the rubble of bomb sites, had gone to Saturday matinees armed with liquorice allsorts and sherbet dabs, had been dragged home by a constable after stealing apples from an orchard.

Helen's own childhood? A series of nannies, then a governess followed by some years in a select school for the privileged. Dance and music lessons while Father was in court, silence when he was at home. She had never been to the roller rink, to public parks, to the wild and wonderful moors. For her, Rivington Pike had been the name of a place; to Mags, Lucy and Agnes, the pike was for rolling eggs at Easter, for sliding down on an old tray in snow, for picnics on summer days.

'I hate him,' Helen advised the ceiling, which suddenly refused to keep still. 'It's not an earthquake,' she added, a barely contained mirth accompanying her words. But it wasn't just mirth – she felt like sobbing. The feelings were justified this time, though. The thing that had happened to her in church had been unattached to any particular fear and she hoped it would never return. She liked Mags Bradshaw. Would she be allowed to like Mags? Would she ever be allowed to choose anything or anyone?

Mags woke with a start and tried to work out where she was. Someone was talking. That someone lay in the other bed, and Mags remembered the strange turn of events that had led to her current situation. Downstairs, people were dancing and talking, celebrating Lucy's marriage to George Henshaw. She had to go.

'I hate him,' said the woman in the other bed.

Was she referring to her dad or to the balding eagle, Mags wondered.

'Nowhere to go, nowhere to go.' The words were accompanied by a few quiet sobs.

Mags sat up. 'Oh, my God,' she moaned. 'Remind me that champagne's off-limits for me, will you?'

But Helen continued to mumble, and Mags realized that the woman was now asleep, but still speaking.

As quietly as she could, Mags repaired damage to make-up, straightened her skirt, walked to the door. She had just spent an hour or so in the company of a very strange woman. No one loved Helen Spencer. She had travelled thus far without encouragement or affection. But Lucy and Agnes were downstairs and this was an important day.

Before leaving the room, Mags found hotel notepaper and scribbled a message for Helen. *Had to go back to the party, hope you are OK, Mags Bradshaw.* She placed it on the bedside cabinet and crept to the door. A strange feeling of guilt accompanied her all the way back to the reception. Helen Spencer was not fit to be left alone. Although Mags did not understand why, she continued to feel uneasy for the remainder of the day.

'Where've you been?' Agnes pulled Mags into a corner. 'You missed Pop having a go at the twist. He got stuck between Eva and the groom's mother – said he thought he'd need a bloody doctor to cut him out. Mind, he looked quite happy wedged between two pairs of enormous bosoms. So, where did you get to?'

'I found Helen Spencer in a bit of a state. So I put her in a room and sat with her till she fell asleep. It's her dad. He's found her some lawyer to marry and she's not best pleased.'

Agnes blinked rapidly. Had Miss Spencer mentioned anything about her misplaced affection for Denis? Probably not – Mags owned a face that gave away inner feelings, and she was looking her companion in the eye.

'Agnes?'

'What?'

'Have you ever met anyone really desperate?'

'My grandfather when he loses his rag with one of his blinking doll's houses. Lucy till she found the right wedding shoes. Oh, and you now. What's happened?'

Mags shook her head. 'I don't know. But she shouldn't be on her own. I feel as if she might do something horrible. She's living life right on the edge, Agnes. He never talks to her.' She nodded in the direction of Judge Spencer, who was holding court across the room. 'Now, he says she's got to marry somebody who looks like a starving hawk. I've never in my life met anyone so completely miserable. She's given up.'

'Stop worrying about other people and start thinking about yourself.'

'What's to think about? I look like the back of a bus stuck in mud.'

'You don't. You've lovely hair and—'

'Oh, shut up, Aggie. I know what I look like. Helen Spencer's the same – plain and resigned to spending the rest of her life as half a person. She looked at me and knew that I was in a similar boat. It takes one to know one.'

Agnes sighed and shook her head. If Mags would only add some colour to the thick, mouse-coloured waves, she would look so much better. Green eyes begged for blonde highlights, but Mags, who hated artifice, seemed determined not to make the best of herself. 'Right, you.' Agnes folded her arms. 'You are coming with me to the hairdresser's and I'll get you sorted out. Nothing drastic – don't worry. It's time somebody took you in hand, because you do nothing to help yourself.'

Mags blew out her cheeks. 'He'll breathe even louder!' She was referring to the articled clerk at her place of employment. 'It's bad enough now – if I go glamorous, he'll blow a fuse. I can't be doing with clerk articles puffing around my chair. And my nose will still be the same.'

'There's nothing wrong with your nose. God, are you determined to become a carbon copy of Helen Spencer? In ten years, you'll be exactly like her, dowdy and dull. If necessary, I'll get Lucy in on the act,' Agnes threatened. 'The minute she comes back from Paris, I'll beg her to help me frogmarch you to Bolton.'

'All right, I give in. But nothing spectacular – are you listening?'

'I'm listening. I'm always bloody listening. You're worse than the *Billy Cotton Band Show*, all noise and no sense. Mags, put your future in my hands. By the way – where's your locket?'

'Locket?'

'The one given to you by George – your bridesmaid's gift.'

'Bugger.'

'Let's be refined just for today. Buggery is off the menu.'

'I've left it upstairs. God, Lucy will kill me.' Mags left the scene at speed.

Helen was still unconscious, though the mumbling had ceased. After retrieving the silver locket from a dressing table, Mags stood over the sleeping woman. Agnes's words echoed through the whole building – if Mags wasn't careful, she might end up like the tormented and lonely soul in this characterless room. Mags swallowed. Agnes was probably right. In fact, Agnes had only skirted the edges of the problem.

On the landing, she fastened the locket round her neck, smiling as she remembered George's speech. For a lawyer, he was very funny. He had spoken of a queue of women wanting to marry him, of Lucy winning hands down because she told the muckiest jokes.

'Right,' breathed the bridesmaid. 'Might as well hang for the full sheep.' She had saved for long enough. It was time to bite the bullet and endure the knife. And the chisel. She swallowed hard. Margaret Marie Bradshaw was going to have a new nose.

Denis was relieved when Helen did her disappearing act, perturbed when Mags followed her. All through the service, he had imagined Helen's eyes boring into the back of his head like a pair of red-hot pokers. He hoped with all his heart that the judge's daughter would keep her mouth shut about a situation that existed only in her head. She was ill. Beyond a shadow of doubt, Helen Spencer was a sick woman, a time bomb preparing to explode.

But Mags was a sensible girl. Of the trio, Lucy Walsh had always been the fun, Mags Bradshaw the brains, Agnes a mixture of both. Of said trio, Agnes was the best by a mile and he didn't want her life made difficult by lies which would result in pity from her lifelong friends. Lucy would probably have dragged the screaming cat out of the bag; Mags, on the other hand, would always weigh pros and cons before wading in at the shallow end. He had to stop worrying.

The worry abated for about five minutes, then returned in the form of Fred, who had recently been rescued from the clutches of two inebriated and larger than life women.

'I were nearer death then than in any bloody trench,' cursed Fred, a grin widening his mouth. 'Stuck between two fine ladies – what a way to go, eh, Denis?'

Denis feigned displeasure. 'You're old enough to stop chasing the girls.' One of the 'girls' appeared behind Fred. 'Hello, Eva. Can't you keep him out of trouble?'

'No.' She lowered her bulk into a chair that looked too frail to bear such weight. 'I thought about locking him in my shed for the day, but he would have got out one road or another. I didn't know you could dance, Fred.'

'That weren't dancing,' came the swift response. 'That were hopping – you were stood on my other foot. It felt as if the coalman had dropped all his bags at once. Denis?'

'What?'

'Can we have a word?'

'I've never known you have less than five hundred words, but feel free.'

Fred placed himself in the chair next to Eva's. 'I want to ask you about Agnes,' he said.

'What about her?'

The older man inhaled deeply. 'I want to know how she'd feel if I got married again.'

'Married again,' echoed Eva.

Denis scratched his head. Was marriage infectious? Was this a germ picked up by Fred at the church this morning? 'Who'd have you?' he jested.

The 'She would' and the 'I would' arrived simultaneously.

Denis glanced from one to the other several times. 'Oh, I see,' was the best he could achieve.

'I've been thinking,' Fred said. 'I spend more time in Eva's place than I do in ours and we get on a treat – don't we, lass?'

The 'lass' nodded. 'House on fire,' she agreed.

This was a pantomime, thought Denis. Or perhaps a Laurel and Hardy film with a slightly altered cast. Fred, recently bereaved, stroke victim and doll's house builder, wanted to marry a shed. Was it right for a man to marry just for a damp-proof area in which he might work for a few years?

'We're suited,' chimed the chorus of two.

'Eva, you're a good twenty years younger than Fred.' Denis could think of nothing else to say.

'Companionship, mainly,' said Eva.

'And good meat and tatie pies,' added Fred. 'She's a better cook than our Agnes.'

Denis took a quick sip of beer. So, he was marrying

a shed and some pies. Oh, well – better two reasons than one, he supposed. And Eva was well respected by all who knew her. But how would Agnes feel? He had no idea whatsoever.

'There's a lot of reasons for getting wed.' Fred was clearly reading his son-in-law's thoughts. 'Eva here's been on her own for a fair while and she gets fed up.'

'Fed up,' she agreed.

'I know my Sadie's not long gone, but she thought a lot of Eva, and me and Eva think a lot of you and our Agnes. That's why we're going to clear a path for you. You'd be better off up Skirlaugh Fall with fresh air for that chest of yours. I'm holding you back.'

'Back,' chirped Eva.

Denis wished he hadn't drunk three pints plus champagne for toasts. He didn't want to be released to live in Skirlaugh Fall, right on the doorstep of a woman who was plainly suffering some kind of breakdown, a female who had set her sights on him. And how would Agnes react when she heard that Fred intended to remarry before Sadie was cold in her grave?

'What do you think?' Fred was staring hard at Denis. 'Will our Agnes throw a fit?'

'I don't know.'

'He doesn't know,' agreed Eva.

'It makes sense, though,' argued Fred. 'I am at one end of life, you and Agnes are at the other. Eva might be a few years younger than me, but we can keep each other company and run that shop. I can't have you two looking after me all the while, can I? Me and Eva will look after each other.'

Denis waited for the echo, but nothing came. 'I'll talk to her.'

'You talk to her.' Eva patted her rigid curls. 'Let us know what she says, like. We don't want to go upsetting her, but at our time of life, we can't be hanging about.'

'No,' agreed Fred. 'We can't hang about.'

This double act worked both ways, Denis realized. They were good people, lonely people who had found each other in spite of the odds against such a match. They talked in harmony, danced with difficulty and ran an excellent business between them. The doll's houses, recently advertised in the *Bolton Evening News*, promised to bring in a decent income – Fred was taking orders for Christmas and would soon have to close the book, as he had a full schedule for the foreseeable future.

'He's thinking,' said Eva, pointing at Denis.

'He is,' replied Fred. 'And it's a strain, because his brain cell's had a couple of pints – it's in danger of running out of steam.'

Denis found himself incapable of suppressing his mirth. 'I'll talk to you two later,' he threatened. 'And don't be getting into any mischief before the ink's dry on your marriage certificate, or Agnes will have your guts for garters and your bones for soup.'

Fred bowed comically at his intended before leading her to the dance floor for a sedate waltz. Denis watched. Eva had been an important ingredient in the recovery of a sick and confused man. She had given him space in her home, in her shop and in her heart. Fred could have done a lot worse. All that remained now was telling Agnes, and Denis had been selected to soften the blow.

It wasn't a blow, he told himself as he saw the couple laughing on the dance floor. It was a blessing. He would make sure that Agnes felt the same way. But Skirlaugh Fall? He shivered. Where was that bloody woman?

The judge arrived at Denis's side. 'Have you seen my daughter?'

'Erm . . . she left about an hour ago.'

'Her coat is on her chair.' The judge pointed to a table. 'She must be in the building, then.'

'I suppose she must,' agreed Denis.

Zachary Spencer lit a fat cigar. 'Find her,' he ordered before returning to continue a lecture on the anomalies of the British system of justice.

Denis gulped a large draught of air. He found Mags and asked the necessary questions. On leaden feet, the judge's servant made his way to the room booked for Helen Spencer. At the top of the stairs, he breathed deeply again. His master had issued an order and it must be obeyed. 'Three bags full, sir,' he muttered, touching the neb of an absent cap before knocking.

There was no reply. He knocked again, then entered the room. She was flat out on the bed, a half-bottle of brandy in one hand. The lid had not been replaced and she had a damp patch on her blouse. God, she was drinking. Because he had enjoyed her music and her conversation, she had turned to the bottle.

He shook her gently. 'Miss Spencer?'

Helen opened an eye. 'Denis? Where am I?'

'You're at a wedding. Pack Horse, Bolton. Your dad's downstairs looking for you.' She stank like a distillery. 'Can you stand up?'

'Of course I can.' She swung her legs over the edge of the bed, then fell backwards. 'Oops-a-daisy,' she said before righting herself.

Denis's mind shot into top gear. 'Listen to me. Listen!' He removed the brandy and screwed on its cap. 'You had better sober up. I don't need to tell you what

105

your father's like about appearances – and disappear-ances, come to that.'

'Where's that young woman?'

'Mags? She's where she should be – with the wedding party. Look at me.' He had considered sending for Mags or bringing her to the room, but he knew Helen's vagaries too well. It was better to make sure that as few people as possible from his regular circle came into contact with Miss Spencer. 'Look at me,' he repeated.

She obeyed. 'You are so handsome.'

'And you, Miss Spencer, are drunk.' He picked up the phone and ordered black, strong coffee. 'Your story is this. A man bumped into you and spilled brandy all over your clothes, so you came up here to try to get yourself cleaned up. Do you understand?'

'Very handsome.'

Denis sighed. He had travelled from one comedic scenario to another, but this one was definitely a piece of black humour. 'Your father will ask questions.'

'He got me a balding eagle, you know.'

'What?'

'I am supposed to be courted by a man with little hair and a lot of nose. You must have noticed. His name's Pinocchio.'

Ah, so here was a second case of wedding fever, though this bride-to-be was not quite as happy as Eva. 'You must get downstairs before your father decides to have the whole hotel searched. Remember the brandy story.'

While she attempted to tidy herself, Denis received coffee delivered by a young man in braided uniform. He forced Helen to drink two cups, then began the business of persuading her to leave the room.

She studied him, following his every move. 'I expect

you think I'm a lunatic and a drunk,' she said eventually, words slightly blurred by the earlier bout of drinking. 'I'm neither. The brandy is a crutch to get me through occasions like this one – it isn't easy for a spinster to stand and watch others fulfilling their dreams.'

'We have to go soon.'

'Because he said so?' There was no need for a name.

'Yes. Like it or not, he's your dad and my boss. I hope you didn't say anything to Mags Bradshaw about . . .' About what?

'Of course I didn't. As for your neighbour at the church gate begging me to intercede on behalf of her son – what was I supposed to do about that? Does she know what an absolute monster my father is? When I was five years old, he locked me in my room for three whole days, food delivered on a tray, lectures delivered every evening. My crime?' She laughed mirthlessly. 'I stole a brooch of my mother's. I wanted something she had worn, something that would remind me that I was normal, that I had once had a mother.'

Denis dragged a weary hand through his hair.

'What does Glenys Timpson expect me to achieve for her son? Acquittal? A short sentence? A tap on the hand and advice to behave himself in the future? No one knows the life I have had with that man. He isn't normal.'

He began to wonder what 'normal' was. Agnes was probably the closest he could get to an embodied definition of the adjective. 'We'd better go.' At least her speech was improving. 'Remember – you came up here after someone spilled a drink on you.'

Helen shook her head. 'Mags booked this room for me and for herself. Like me, she is wallpaper. In a decade, she will be me. I just hope she doesn't fall in love as heavily as I did.'

'It wasn't love,' he protested. 'It was your loneliness and my liking for your piano playing.'

'I'm sorry,' she said quietly. 'But when a person falls in love, he or she has no choice in the object of their affections. You are a handsome man and I know you have feelings for me.'

He did have feelings for her. He pitied Helen Spencer, sympathized with her situation, wished with all his heart that he could do something to improve her lot. But Helen's predicament was not a matter in which he could intervene. He sat on a dressing stool. 'I love my Agnes so much it hurts,' he told her. 'I wouldn't swap her for a bank vault full of gold. You have been a friend to me, and your father is cold and unfeeling – I have to work for him, so I know that much. But I can't get you away from him.'

Helen gazed into her coffee cup. 'The balding eagle could,' she said.

Denis shrugged. 'All I can tell you is this – marry for love, not for money, not to please your father. Marriage is hard even if there's love in it. You have to make room for your partner's faults and needs. We're going to be a bit poorer while Agnes studies nursing – but we'll get there. We might have a few rows, but love sorts all that out. More important, Agnes is my best friend in the world. You have to find a friend you can love.'

'I love you,' she whispered, 'and I am a fool for telling you that.'

'We're friends and we'll get over it,' he replied.

'But not loving friends?'

'No.'

'I'm a silly woman?'

She was a frightened woman – Denis knew that. The prospect of living at Lambert House until her father's death was a terrifying one. Her only chances of escape thus far were to marry in accordance with her father's wishes, or to accept her daily escape into the dry and dusty embrace of the town library. 'Not silly.' No, she was more than silly – this poor woman teetered on the brink of reason. 'You did one daft thing. That doesn't make you altogether daft. Now. Go downstairs and I'll follow in a few minutes. Your dad sent me for you, but we don't want to set other tongues wagging, do we?'

She wanted tongues to wag like flags in a hurricane. She wanted to re-enter that big room on Denis's arm, wanted to fling abuse in her father's face, wanted the world to see that she had a man. But she had no man. Denis was immovable and she had to accept that. All her life, she had been accepting; all her life, she had been denied and ignored.

'Go,' he urged.

She went. As she walked down the corridor towards the stairs, she felt that she had left behind all hope. Even Pandora's box had contained some of that element, but she, Helen Spencer, was denied that one last straw. It wasn't fair, never had been fair. 'Abandon all hope ye who enter here,' she murmured under her breath before rejoining the party.

After explaining her absence to the judge, she found herself in the company of James Taylor, who stuck to her like an incubus. He must have had bad acne in his youth, she mused as she watched his mouth opening and closing. So busy was she studying the craters in his skin that she was surprised when his lips stopped moving.

After a moment or two, he asked, 'What do you think?'

Helen blinked. 'Sorry. I am too concerned about the way I must smell – brandy all over my clothes, I'm afraid. What did you say?'

He repeated a request that she would accompany him to a concert in Manchester.

'I'm afraid I can't go,' she said. 'I have been away from work for a while and will have to catch up. We have to list missing books and try to retrieve fines from those who have kept them. Another time, perhaps.'

He frowned, causing two pock marks above his nose to join in a miniature imitation of the Grand Canyon. 'Just one evening? Surely you can manage that?'

The man had a temper, she decided. Denied his wishes, he became another like Father, turned into a man who did not take rejection well. 'I must keep myself available,' she told him. 'It's like a massive audit and we all have to pull our weight.' She needed brandy.

'I shall telephone you,' he promised.

Feeling threatened, Helen declared her need to talk to a friend. She found Mags Bradshaw temporarily alone at the edge of the dance floor. 'Help me,' Helen begged. 'The balding eagle is back.'

Mags patted the chair next to hers. 'Sit down.' She giggled. The champagne had gone to her head, but this poor woman had taken in more than bubbles. 'How are you now?'

'Still running. Seated, but running.'

Mags told Helen of her plan for her nose. 'Agnes is determined to do something about me, but I am going to do something for myself. Harley Street. I've saved up. This is our secret, Helen. I am not telling anyone but you.'

110

Helen felt strangely pleased. As far as she could recall, no one had ever trusted her with a special confidence. She repaid the compliment. 'He asked me out. I made an excuse about working overtime. He's staring now – don't look just yet, but have a glance in a moment.'

Mags laughed again. 'I've seen better-looking road accidents,' she declared. 'Mind, I'm no raving beauty myself, so I should keep my mouth well and truly shut.'

'You've good hair and eyes,' said Helen.

'Have to get highlights – Agnes has spoken.'

'And your nose? What will happen to that?'

Mags shrugged. 'They use a hammer and chisel, I believe.'

'No!'

'Not a lump hammer, not a big chisel. But it's the same as a sculptor working with marble. For about three weeks, I'll look as if I've been in a boxing ring – black eyes and a nose like rising dough. Work has granted me extended leave – they let me save last year's holidays – so I'm doing what I always said I wouldn't: I'm trying to join the beautiful set.'

Helen wondered whether plastic surgery might improve her lot in life, but she did not air her thoughts. For the first time ever, she longed for her father to order her to accompany him home. Although she was enjoying the company of a potential friend, James Taylor stared constantly and the desire to scream and run was returning.

'Are you all right?' Mags asked.

'I'll go to the powder room.' Helen rose to her feet. 'He can't follow me there, can he?'

Mags blew out her cheeks. 'I have to talk to Agnes – see you later.'

Abandoned by Mags, Helen saw James Taylor embarking on a beeline in her direction, so she picked up her bag and fled the scene. This time, she remained on the same floor, locking herself in a cubicle before taking a few sips of brandy.

Cisterns flushed, taps ran, women chattered. 'He's a boring old bugger.'

'All judges are boring.'

A third voice chipped in. 'And that stuff about bringing back hanging – God, I wouldn't want to stand trial with that sitting on the bench in his flea-bitten wig. I bet he still has his bit of black cloth and I'll bet further he wishes he could use it.'

Helen fought a fit of giggles. She was separated only by a thin door from the wives of lawyers who had to contend regularly with the vagaries of Judge Zachary Spencer.

'My Peter gets in a terrible mood if Spencer's in court. He's always dishing out homilies on moral standards – but what about his own? Have you heard about his latest? A dancer. According to gossip in chambers, she can't possibly know her two times table, but she must have some good moves, eh?'

Helen's giggles subsided and she listened intently.

'They were seen in Chester last week. In a restaurant whispering sweet nothings, by all accounts. They say she looks like her clothes have been sprayed on. So how can he sit there telling criminals to stop sinning? Bloody old hypocrite.'

'His daughter looks like she's had a hard life. Librarian, isn't she?'

'Yes. I feel sorry for her. I feel sorry for anybody who has to live with that miserable monster. She's the one with the life sentence, isn't she? I wonder why she doesn't clear off and leave him to his mistresses? He could be charged with running a house of ill-repute if he brought home more than one at a time. You know how he'd look his best?'

'No,' chorused the rest.

'Six feet under with a nice headstone.'

The laughter rose, then died of its own accord. 'There'll be no real justice in Britain while that man lives,' said the one who had recommended a graveyard. 'According to Charlie Fairbanks, Spencer treats women criminals like aliens – he thinks only men should have the luxury of sinning. If a man steals a car, he gets his dues. A woman gets branded by his red-hot tongue. He's one of those who think women belong in kitchens and bedrooms. We're just another utility in his book.'

Helen swallowed. No, it wasn't just her. Other women hated him, too, while men didn't have a great deal of time for him either. How she wished she could have made a recording of the conversation. Hated and berated, the judge went through life crippling most in his path. Except for the dancer and her ilk. Jesus Christ, what a two-faced barbarian he was. Women? How many had there been in thirty years, she wondered.

Helen stood, flushed the lavatory and emerged to wash her hands.

Half a dozen women froze when they saw her. 'Miss Spencer?' said the nearest. 'Sorry about that. If we'd known you were there—'

'If you'd known I was there, your opinions would have remained the same.'

Bangles clattered on wrists while bags were grabbed.

'Don't worry,' Helen told her companions. 'I live with him and I know what he is. My sole regret is that I don't have the courage to tell him what I heard in here today. He's a bad man. None of us can choose our parents.'

A chorus of apologies echoed round the room after the women had rushed away. Helen dried her hands. A dancer? A dancer who was merely the latest in a long string of women? Yet his daughter was ashamed of admitting her feelings for a fine man who worked as hard as his disability allowed?

She sat on a stool for a long time. Women came, used the facilities, left. Some bothered to speak to her; others, seeing the expression on her face, or knowing who she was, left in clouds of perfume and heavy silence. Active hatred for her surviving parent was flooding her veins and increasing the rate of her heart. 'Why my mother and not him?' she asked of her reflection during a lull in traffic. 'It should have been him. I want him gone from my life.'

She fantasized for a few moments on the idea of a house all to herself, of an existence containing music, laughter and, above all, friends. There was Mags Bradshaw for a start. Helen could not imagine entertaining Mags while the judge was in the house. Even fellow school pupils had not visited Lambert House. A sad child, Helen Spencer had attracted few companions and, because of her father, had brought no one home.

But there was nothing she could do; there had never been an escape and she must continue, as always, to live in the shadow of her parent's sins. To do that, she would need her brandy.

Chapter Five

The wedding celebrations drifted to a halt as the sun began its descent across a flawless sky. Lucy and George left in a flurry of confetti and good wishes, a flustered Mags retrieving the bridal bouquet when Lucy tossed it over a shoulder. Mags, who had imbibed several glasses of champagne, held on to the flowers tightly – were they an omen foretelling the success of her planned hammer and chisel job?

Helen watched impassively as the bedecked Rolls-Royce pulled away towards Manchester Road and the airport. Mags didn't like the look of Helen Spencer. The woman appeared shocked, white-faced, and her fingers trembled. The others probably didn't notice, but Mags, even after so short an acquaintance, knew enough to feel concern for the librarian. Drinking was a terrible thing. It had taken an uncle and a great-uncle from Mags Bradshaw's family, and she didn't want Helen to suffer the same fate. Not that her dad would miss her, she mused as she joined with the rest and waved at the disappearing Rolls. He had a face like a clock stopped at midnight, two deep furrows above his nose announcing the time. The man was not smiling even now. He stood out among the happy throng and Mags, who knew what he was, shivered at the thought of such a father. Her own upbringing, while far from perfect, had been full of love. Love, batter, marrowfat peas and mounds of chips were Mags's foundation, and she pitied anyone who had not experienced the first on the list. Love was everything. It made even cod more palatable.

The judge frogmarched his daughter to the Bentley and prepared to motor homeward. Never the world's greatest driver, he missed Denis, but this was Denis's day off, and the man had to get his family back to that hovel in Noble Street. Denis Makepeace ought to take the cottage and be grateful, but he was fastened, via his wife, to her grandfather. It was nonsense. The cottages had two bedrooms, so there was space enough if she wanted to hang on to ancient emotional baggage. People were a mystery to Judge Spencer, as he did not make room for emotion.

Agnes, Denis, Eva and Fred walked to the station and climbed aboard the Derby Street bus. They sat on the lower deck, each tired and deep in thought, waiting for the stop nearest to Noble Street. Eva fiddled nervously with gloves and handbag; Fred stared through a window, outwardly absorbed in sights he had seen for seventy years.

As they walked to the shop after leaving the bus, Fred mouthed a message at Denis, a clear enough instruction regarding the approach to Agnes. Denis sighed. He had rescued Helen; now he had to contend with Agnes, who was sober, at least. Didn't Fred know his granddaughter well enough to approach her himself?

'Aren't you coming home, Pop?' Agnes asked.

'No. Me and Eva are going to have a drop of cocoa and Navy rum. We've things to talk about.' He winked at Denis. 'I won't be long. Go on – get yourselves sat down and have a rest.'

Agnes remained where she was, arms folded under her chest, a foot tapping the ground. The old couple disappeared into the shop before she spoke. 'What's going on, Denis? I know there's something brewing – I've felt it all day. I didn't arrive here with yesterday's Fleetwood catch, you know.'

He sighed again, wishing that his wife could be slightly less sensitive to atmosphere. 'I have to talk to you, but I'd rather we did it at home. Come on, shift yourself.'

She tapped the foot again. 'Is Miss Spencer still after your body? Has she asked you to elope with her?'

Denis forced a smile. 'As good as, yes – but that's nothing to do with what I have to say. Sad woman, that. The drink loosens her tongue – I've heard more words out of her this last couple of weeks than she's spoken in years. But there's nowt I can do about her.'

Agnes gritted her teeth during the short walk to the house. Secrets were things to be investigated, considered, dealt with. As soon as they were both inside, she spoke. 'Well? Come on, out with it.'

'Sit down,' he said.

'Why? Am I going to fall over with shock? Have you done something terrible?'

'I've done nothing,' he answered. 'Apart from trying to separate Helen Spencer from her brandy bottle. She's got that many sheets in the wind, she looks like Nelson's little trip to Trafalgar. No. It's not her this time. It's your granddad.'

'Oh?' Her face blanched. 'He's not ill again, is he? He looked well enough today, showing me up all over the Pack Horse. Don't tell me he's sick, Denis. I can't face any more, not after Nan.'

'He's not ill.'

'Good. What, then?'

'He's engaged.'

117

Agnes flopped into an armchair. 'He's what? He's seventy-bloody-two, Denis. He's not long recovered from a stroke and Nan's death – engaged? Don't talk so daft – he's having you on. Who's he engaged to? Helen Spencer and her brandy bottle? Or did he pick up a floozy outside Yates's Wine Lodge while I wasn't looking?'

Denis shook his head. 'No. He's engaged to Eva Hargreaves and her back yard air raid shelter. And tatie pies.'

'You what?'

'You heard me, Agnes. He's engaged to Eva. They're both happy, and he asked me to tell you about it. I suppose he doesn't want any scenes. He thought you might be upset because of your nan, you see. It's a bit quick after her death, and he's well aware of that. He's doing what he thinks best all round.'

Agnes tried to be upset, but could not manage it. She had watched her beloved grandfather blossoming in the company of Eva, had been relieved to hear his jokes and listen to tales about customers for firewood, customers for doll's houses, the price of paraffin and coal bricks going up. The old man was alive again, was laughing, remembering, was almost in charge of his own day-to-day existence. God love him, he was one hundred per cent better since starting to work with Eva.

'Agnes?'

'I'm thinking.'

He left her to it and went to make cocoa. She needed leaving alone when thinking deeply – that was one of the many traits they shared. Although there were few secrets in the marriage, each kept thoughts and feelings inside until ready to communicate. Denis knew that this was common sense, so he was willing to wait as long as necessary.

But he didn't need to wait.

She took the mug, enjoyed a sip of hot chocolate, then spoke. 'He does right,' she said. 'From that very first day with the notebooks – the day Nan died and we had that bit of bother with Glenys – Eva's been helping. She went out of her road to make sure Pop had a purpose in life, first with his notes in different colours, then with the shelter for his houses. Trusting him to work in the shop did him good, too, gave him a bit of responsibility and dignity. No, I'm all right about it. Run up and tell them it's OK – these new shoes are killing me. If I don't separate them from my feet, I'll have to separate my feet from the rest of me.'

While Agnes soaked her battered toes, Denis ran up to the shop to tell Fred that he didn't need a white flag to get back in the house.

Agnes leaned back and closed her eyes. It had been a funny sort of day. Nice – the wedding had been lovely – but Mags getting friendly with Helen Spencer had seemed rather strange, as had the information that Helen was on her way to alcoholism. Agnes hadn't mentioned Denis's predicament, but she hoped that Mags would not get too close to that sad woman. What if Helen Spencer had told Mags that she loved Denis? Oh, bugger.

Now, here she sat with her feet in hot water and her grandfather on his way to the altar. She raised her eyes to the ceiling. 'You always liked Eva, Nan. She'll look after him and he'll look after her. That doesn't mean he wouldn't want you back. You were the love of his life. We just need him to be safe and happy.'

Denis returned. 'He'll be back in half an hour,' he said.

Agnes stared at him with mock severity in her gaze. 'Just one thing, Makepeace.'

'Oh, aye? What's that, then?'

'I am not being a bloody bridesmaid or an anything of honour at Pop's wedding. I've had enough of watered silk and new shoes to last me a lifetime. I shall go to the church in me pinny.'

'All right.' He grinned. 'Better still, you can be the pretty little ring-bearer with a satin cushion and some rose petals. Hey!' he yelled when a missile hit him in the chest.

'There's your satin cushion,' she told him.

He tossed the weapon back to her. 'All right. Have it your own way, as per bloody usual.'

When he arrived home, Fred was the receiver of another of Agnes's famous 'looks'. This time, having achieved an air of patience layered over anger, she looked like a headmistress in the process of punishing a naughty child. 'I'm disgusted with you,' she began.

Denis fled to the scullery and stifled laughter with a tea towel.

'Seventy-two,' she went on. 'Seventy-two and still running after women. It's like living with a teenager, honestly. I mean, most folk grow old gracefully; you are doing it disgracefully. Thank goodness you've got a decent suit, you dirty old man.'

Fred beamed. He knew his Agnes of old. 'Second childhood?' he suggested tentatively. 'That does happen to old folk.'

'If it were second childhood, you'd be chewing

crayons. This is second adolescence. Chasing the girls, indeed.'

Fred sat down. 'Well, I was lucky for a while, because they outran me. Every bloody one of them was faster than me. But it'd take a mad bull to make Eva run – that's why I caught her. She just stood there. It's not my fault that she can't get any steam up.'

Agnes rose, removed dripping feet from the bowl, bent over and hugged one of her favourite men. 'Be happy,' she whispered. 'That's an order.'

'I will, lass. And it's no reflection on Sadie. If you look at it one road, I must have had a happy marriage – otherwise, I wouldn't try it again, eh? It's a compliment to a very good wife.' He dried a tear. 'And Eva can cook proper.'

She slapped his hand.

'Well, she can. She can do more with a potato than anyone else I've ever known.'

'She can stuff a pound of King Edwards in your gob and shut you up, then. That way, she'd be of service to the nation. The queen would give her an OBE for outstanding achievement as a peacemaker.'

Fred laughed. 'We'll look after each other, babe. You and Denis can take that nice little cottage without thinking about me. There's a bus. You'll still get to your training from up yon. Think of his chest, love. Up Skirlaugh, Denis would breathe better.'

In the scullery, Denis stood still as stone. Move nearer to madness? Be on hand every time the judge fancied a little ride out? Stand by helplessly and watch the decline of a woman for whom he had felt respect, a woman he had liked? But Skirlaugh Fall was pretty, and Agnes, who had always wanted a garden, deserved pretty.

He washed cocoa mugs and decided to let Nature take its course. In the absence of any other solution, it was the best he could do.

Zachary Spencer drifted into the kerb for a third time. 'Something wrong with the steering,' he said, also for the third time.

Helen, in the back of the car, replayed in her head all she had heard in the ladies' room. It wasn't just her. Even those who had to bow to his superiority in court disliked him. Their wives made fun of him; his daughter despised him; Denis Makepeace tolerated him for the sake of a pitifully small income.

'What did you think of James Taylor?' asked the judge.

He expected an answer? This was an unusual day. 'I scarcely know him.'

'Get to know him. He's a high flyer.'

She fought the need to cite as a mitigating circumstance an inbuilt fear of heights.

'Good barrister, good chap, has his sights set on government. Several of the Inns of Court have expressed an interest in him. Like me, he will go the whole hog – no pussyfooting around for that young man. Well thought of in the Masonic Lodge, too.'

Mixed metaphors. She wondered whether he used those in court. A hog and a cat's paw were hardly partners. Unless the cat was partial to bacon, of course. A giggle rose and she coughed it to one side.

'Did he ask you out?'

'Yes.'

He sighed impatiently. 'And?'

'He will telephone me.'

'Good. You should snap him up like a bargain. You'd want for nothing if you married him. Get yourself settled.'

Helen seethed. For some unknown reason, the balance of power had shifted slightly today. No, that was untrue, because she did recognize the reason: a catalyst had suddenly been poured into the mix. The chattering women had made her feel stronger, because, from this afternoon, she had not been alone. Would there be a hung parliament in Lambert House? Was she going to start arguing her own case from the back benches?

'You will go out with him,' ordered the driver.

As usual, she offered no reply.

'Did you hear me?'

'Yes.'

'Develop the friendship and let it take its course.'

Seething inwardly, Helen forced herself to imagine donating her virginity to a man whose face resembled the surface of the moon, whose nose was the upper half of a question mark, whose body was thin to the point of emaciation. Denis rushed unbidden into her thoughts. He had a frail chest, but his physique was excellent. Tanned from hours of working outdoors, his muscles had developed normally. That was the difference, then. Denis was normal, while James Taylor was a joke.

The rest of the journey was accomplished in complete silence, a fact that made Helen more comfortable, because silence was her father's preferred environment. It was hers, too, as she had been raised in a vacuum created by the selfish male who was biologically responsible for her existence. This was not a father; this was a mere robot with grandiose ideas and a liking for loud, dictatorial music, the kind of noise that had been much loved by Adolf Hitler.

He parked the Bentley, removed the keys and marched into his domain. She waited for a few seconds. When leaving the wedding, he had opened the rear door for her, had closed it after she had sat down. There was no one here for him to impress, so he reverted to type. He was a pig. No, she had met pigs, and they had been noisy, but pleasant.

She got out of the car, closed her door and walked inside, making straight for the staircase and her own room. Halfway up the flight, she paused. His eyes were boring into her spine. He ordered her into the study, then preceded her into it. Oh, no. Helen felt ill-prepared for further lectures on the virtues of James Taylor.

Her father was seated behind his desk, fingers steepled below his chin. 'Sit,' he said.

Feeling like one of his clerks, a mere minion provided to serve his every whim, she sat. He was ugly from a distance; close up, he was hideous. His face was lined, and none of Nature's tracks could be blamed on laughter, as he seldom smiled. She could not imagine him indulging in a good belly laugh when anecdotes were shared at his place of work. This was the face of a disappointed man, a man of ill-temper and personal indulgence. He was flabby, ill-defined, a glutton, a drinker. Helen swallowed. She, too, was a drinker, though she had yet to serve out her apprenticeship.

'There is a matter we must discuss,' he began.

Discuss? He would hold forth; she would be allowed little space for opinion or comment.

'I have remarried,' he stated baldly. 'My wife is currently collecting her belongings with a view to setting up home here, with me.'

A clock chimed. Outside, blackbirds fussed their way through evensong. Helen's spine was suddenly rigid. He had married without a word to her, his sole relative? Her flesh crawled. The thought of him touching a woman – any woman – was almost as repulsive as her earlier musings on the subject of James Taylor. Married? Living here? With me, not with us, he had said. Helen was anxious not to react, yet she could not quite manage to hold her fire in these circumstances. 'The dancer?' In spite of better judgement, she allowed her lip to curl.

The judge's face became a pleasant shade of purple. 'What?' he roared.

She was betraying nobody when she spoke again. 'The ladies' lavatories were alight with the news. It seems your colleagues cannot contain such secrets.' Her heart was banging like a steam hammer.

'The lavatories?' he roared. 'Today?'

She nodded.

'You should not listen to such drivel.'

'Contained in a stall, I had no option.' She could feel her moment travelling through her body. It was now; she could say much if she so chose. 'They were all agog about your many indiscretions – their words, not mine. I confess I was quite shocked when they spoke, but I heard a great deal.' The man was squirming, and she had a sudden urge to cheer.

He shifted his weight in the chair yet again. 'It's all nonsense,' he blustered. 'What else? What else was said?'

It had arrived. Her time was now and she must use it well. 'They were laughing at you and saying that their husbands often do the same. You are not popular among lawyers – that was the gist. At that point, I forced myself to put in an appearance and the gossip ceased.' Married? She could not believe it. He was going to bring home a wife?

'Who were these people?' The judge's skin had returned to its normal condition – grey and moist.

'I have no idea. They were married to the lawyers at the wedding – friends of the bridegroom.'

'Describe their clothing,' was the next order.

'There is no point,' Helen replied. 'I heard voices, but I could not attach any one voice to any one outfit. As I said, they stopped talking when I joined them at the washbasins. They know I am your daughter.'

Zachary Spencer banged both fists on his desk. 'I owe you no explanations,' he spat. 'As you just said, you are my daughter, no more than that. Yes, I have searched for a wife. I want a son.'

He wanted a son? God would surely need to come to the aid of any male child who might be raised in the image of such a man.

'To answer your earlier question – yes, Louisa has been a dancer, though she is also a qualified legal secretary. You might feel happier in another house – there is your mother's money to be used for that purpose.'

Helen simply stared at him.

'We shall need our privacy.'

She stood up and gathered all her strength around her, building a cage of anger and grief. 'This is a large house. I shall open up some of the far rooms, install a kitchen and live there until I choose to leave.' The glove had been cast onto the desk, and she waited for him to rise to her challenge. Never before had she denied or defied him. His discomfort was a joy she could scarcely contain. 'I can win the battle, but not the war,' her inner voice said.

Only his laboured breathing and the ticking of the clock pierced the ensuing silence. Unused to discussion,

Zachary found himself almost speechless. Helen's mother had possessed a backbone – it appeared that her daughter had inherited some of that wilfulness.

'Is that all, Father?' she asked.

The judge blinked. 'For the moment, yes. Louisa will arrive in a week or so. Perhaps you should remain here for a while – you can make yourself useful to her.'

Helen nodded. Her staying had to appear to be his idea, otherwise he would have failed to get his way. Had she owned a gun, she could have shot him quite cheerfully in that moment. 'Oh, another thing, Father. There is a young man named Harry Timpson – some nonsense about a jewel robbery in Manchester. He was involved, though just on the fringes of the crime. His mother is an acquaintance of mine – a great reader.' The lies slid glibly from her newly loosened tongue. 'She is not in good health. A long custodial sentence might well mean that she would never see her son again. You know the importance of sons in a family – he is the oldest.'

Colour rose in his cheeks once more.

Helen continued to stare in fascination. She had mentioned Harry Timpson not because she cared for him or his mother, not because she sought to conceal her silliness about Denis, but because she could. She owned an ounce of power and intended to build on it.

He cleared his throat.

Helen continued, pushing herself into an imitation of a caring daughter.

'Beard your lawyers in their own den, Father. They think you are too harsh and unfeeling. Alarm them by showing some compassion. Make fools of them. They will not speak badly of you again – I will not allow it. But you can help yourself. Change their opinion, make them worry. It will unseat those defence barristers for a while. If they are speaking so ill of you, make them uncomfortable. I should – most certainly.'

He tapped his fingers on the desk. With alarming suddenness, he finally understood that his daughter had a brain, an excellent brain. She might have made a good enough lawyer herself . . .

'I shall go now, Father. I need a bath – this blouse is saturated in brandy.'

Outside the study door, Helen found herself trembling. The palms of her hands were slick with sweat and, without thinking, she dried them on the jacket of her fifty-pound suit. He intended to father a son. That would mean . . . no. It did not bear thinking of. All the years she had served in silence, all the time she had spent in the presence of a cruel father, would come to nothing. Her reward for endurance was to have been sole ownership of this house and the large parcel of land that contained it. Her expectations would come to nothing if he sired a male child.

She sat on her bed and counted nosegays on wallpaper. She would lose the room, the corner that had been all her own. Since childhood, this had been her exclusive area, her bolt-hole. Now, she would be forced to remove herself and her furnishings to a neglected part of the house, while he moved in a dancer, a potential mother for his son. Try as she might, she could not imagine her father with a woman. He probably wanted Helen to move out in order to avoid having a witness to his silliness.

But she would not move out. Why was she staying? Because this was her setting and, like any other still life arrangement, she felt forced to remain where she had been placed more than three decades ago. She had neither the imagination nor the bravery to face a new beginning. And why should she go? Why should she move out for the sake of some cheap dancing girl?

A smile touched on her lips as she recalled her father's reaction to today's gossip. It had affected him – of that she was certain. Monarch of all he surveyed, he would perhaps look more closely now at those who worked below him, because they made fun of him. He would not like that at all. Nor would he be pleased about his daughter's refusal to move out of his house. As for her plea on behalf of Harry Timpson – that would leave him thoroughly flummoxed. Flummoxed was an expression she had borrowed from Denis. His father-in-law had been flummoxed after a bleed in his head.

Well, she could now tell Denis's neighbour that she had attempted to intervene on Harry's behalf. It would be interesting to see what happened, thought Helen. She would be in court on that day if her father was sitting; she would see whether she had had any effect on Judge Zachary Spencer. It was never too late to begin again, she advised herself. In some small areas, she must take the upper hand and manipulate him.

The biggest problem hung in the air like a low thundercloud. After thirty years as a single man, the blundering fool had married. Had she been challenged, Helen would have bet a month's salary that Louisa was under thirty, silly and impressionable. The woman was probably a fortune-hunter, too. How long would Father last with a young woman to satisfy? If he died, this house would pass to Louisa, and that was not fair.

She undressed and placed the suit on a chair in readiness for the dry cleaner. Brandy beckoned, but she refused to indulge. Her supper would be on a tray next to his – they never ate at the table – would that change?

No. Helen intended to have her own kitchen and her own life, though she would keep a close eye on those who shared her home. It was *her* home, not Louisa's. She didn't need servants, didn't require people on whom she might wipe her feet. 'I am not my father's daughter,' she told the flowers on her wallpaper. 'And I am certainly in no mood for a stepmother.'

Everything was about to change, and there wasn't anything to be done about that fact. But she had bearded him in his den, had pretended to support him. In truth, Helen Spencer's hatred for her father increased tenfold that evening. Had she possessed the smallest amount of courage, she would have packed up and left the house. But she needed to stay. She wanted to watch him closely. Helen Spencer prayed that he was sterile, even wished for his death. And guilt played no part in her musings.

Agnes Makepeace strolled through town, looking into shop windows, appearing engrossed in displays, her mind jumping about all over the place. It couldn't be true. It was true. No matter what she did, it would remain the truth.

She studied three-piece suites, clothing, shoes, even managed to feign interest in Thomas Cook's package holidays. But she did not want new dresses or foot-wear, had no interest in a week on the Costa Brava. Her life had changed with the suddenness of a lightning bolt and she was having trouble adjusting to the news. The nursing would have to lie in a pending tray, because Agnes was pregnant.

She should be pleased. The tiny life in her belly was a demonstration of the love that existed in her marriage.

They wanted children, but she needed a career. Nursing could be heavy work, though, and training in a lecture hall was only half of the course. The other half included bed-making, the lifting of patients, the laying out of the dead. She would have to give up her place, because pregnancy and heavy work were not ideal companions. Perhaps she would find a minder when the child was born, but would she be able to leave a baby? Raised by wonderful grandparents after her own mother's death, Agnes had developed a strong sense of family. A child needed a mother. Would she be granted another place next year? Would she be in a position to accept such a gift?

Feeling selfish and guilty, she rounded a corner and almost collided with Glenys Timpson. 'Sorry.' She smiled. 'I was in a world of my own.'

They drank coffee in the UCP, chatted about the forthcoming wedding between Fred and Eva. 'She'll look after him,' said Glenys. 'She's all right, is Eva Hargreaves. Speaking of all right, you don't look so clever yourself.'

'Bit of a summer cold,' replied Agnes. She could not yet confide in her neighbour, because Denis had not heard the news.

'When do you start your nursing?'

'September.'

'Good. That'll give you a proper job. I always wanted a proper job myself, but with three lads I had no chance. It's their turn to feed me now. I've done my share. So have you, love, but in a different direction. You looked after Sadie and Fred – grab your freedom while you can. You'll make a smashing nurse.'

Another pang of guilt stabbed at Agnes's chest. She had probably been looking forward to doing something for herself, for her own sake exclusively. But there would be no time, because babies required attention.

Glenys changed the subject. 'I went in the library and spoke to yon Miss Spencer. She's had a word with her dad. He didn't say much, but she planted the seed, said I wasn't well and I needed my eldest. Now, we just have to wait and see.'

'She tried, then.'

'She did. Give her her due, Agnes, she had a go. Our Harry's like a dog with two tails. I mean, he could still go down, because he's pleading guilty to receiving and handling, but not guilty to blowing up the jewellery shop. Seems there's enough evidence for him to be cleared of that, but he's admitting the rest. Fingers crossed, eh? Let's just hope the judge goes easy on him.'

'Fingers crossed, Glenys.'

They went their separate ways, Agnes to the Co-op, Glenys to meet her son at his solicitor's office.

When her purchases had been made, Agnes decided to walk home. The doctor had told her to keep active as long as she was fit, and she might as well take her exercise before she got a bump as big as Brazil. The timing of her pregnancy was not ideal, but God had dictated that she should have her first child in 1965. It would be a spring baby, a child born with all the blossom that was noticeable by its absence in Noble Street.

Oh, well. The decision had made itself. Agnes and Denis would be moving to Skirlaugh Fall, because a child would enjoy that blossom.

Louisa arrived in a cloud of perfume and fuss. She left Denis to bring in her expensive luggage while she greeted her husband. 'Darling Zach,' she exclaimed in a lightweight voice. 'How I have missed you.' After a pause, she spoke again. 'This place could do with brightening up a little.'

Helen, who had just arrived home from work, hid on the landing and listened to the canoodling. Father was whispering, while his wife giggled in a silly, childish way. 'She'll never fit in,' whispered Helen. Lambert House needed brightening up? For that to happen, its owner would need to put a great deal of space between himself and his home.

The reed-like voice made its way up the stairwell. 'But I must meet your daughter, Zach. We shall be like sisters.'

The judge muttered something about that being highly unlikely before positioning himself in the hall. 'Helen?'

The twin syllables sounded strange, as he had seldom spoken her name. Like a woodlouse, she was alive, an uninvited guest, usually invisible. Helen didn't know what to do. She crept hastily to a bathroom and locked herself inside. This was, she told herself sharply, very childish behaviour, yet she dreaded meeting the wonderful Louisa.

He was on the landing. 'Helen?'

'In the bath,' she lied.

'Oh. Very well. Louisa is anxious to meet you. We'll be in the main drawing room.' Heavy footfalls marked his retreat. He was angry. The speed of his movements betrayed inner fury.

Helen leaned on the door. Hurt and helpless, she felt much as she had just before declaring herself to Denis, upset and confused. The only time she felt sane was for an hour or two after a drink – and she needed a larger dose these days. It happened quickly, then, the dependence on alcohol. Within a matter of weeks, her capacity for brandy had grown.

Softly, she opened the door, went into her bedroom, gulped some of the precious amber fluid. A mouthwash at the handbasin should chase away any fumes, she decided.

The staircase seemed to have shrunk, because she reached the hall in seconds. The judge and his wife were side by side on a sofa. Through the open door to the drawing room, Helen watched her father smiling. The whole world was standing on its head. He had listened to his daughter, had married, was smiling. Perhaps he would change; perhaps he would sire a son, then Helen would be out in the cold.

He rose to his feet, clearly embarrassed by the situation. 'Louisa, this is my daughter.'

Louisa leapt up. 'Hello!' she chirped.

Helen nodded and attempted a pleasant smile. Louisa was small, dark and beautifully turned out. This was a woman to whom she needed to become close, because the eleventh commandment was 'know thine enemy and guard him well'. She held out a hand and Louisa shook it warmly. 'You're a librarian, aren't you?'

'For my sins, yes.'

'I'm a big reader,' announced the young wife.

'So am I,' said Helen. 'I like Trollope and Galsworthy. You?'

Louisa reeled off a list of authors, some who produced trash, others who loitered on the hem of literature. This was not a stupid woman.

Zachary was pouring himself a drink. 'Louisa?' he asked.

She asked for a sweet sherry.

'Helen?' The name sounded rusty. He would need to practise it.

'Brandy for me, Father.' Helen placed herself next to her stepmother. He could sit elsewhere, as the sofa would not accommodate two women and his considerable bulk.

'When do you eat?' Louisa asked. 'I am famished after the journey.'

Helen became engrossed in a pattern on the rug. Her father cleared his throat. 'My daughter and I work strange hours. We usually eat separately. Mrs Moores makes up trays and we eat when we can.'

The new wife declared that this would not do, that they must be a family and eat together in the dining room. There were several changes to be made, it seemed. She wanted a horse, a dog and a proper dinner in the evening. 'Breakfasts on trays are all very well, Zach. But we must be civilized. Each evening, we shall eat together and talk about the day. That's the normal thing to do, I think.'

Helen finished her brandy, then excused herself, saying that she had a very important letter to write. Outside the rear door, she found Denis sweeping a path. He tried to smile. 'Well, he's gone and done it, then.'

'He has. Says he wants a son. If he gets one, I'll be left absolutely nothing but a bad temper.' She sat on a low wall. 'I don't know what's happened to me lately, Denis. Life seems to have got away from me – not that I ever had a life.'

'You're warm and fed,' he replied. 'Where I come from, that counts as a life. And, if you don't mind me saying, you should knock the drink on the head before it gets hold of you. I've seen too much of that in my time. I've known folk to starve their kids to feed the habit.'

She shrugged. 'Before brandy, I seldom spoke to anyone. With brandy, I talk to the wall – for want of better company, of course.'

Denis paused and leaned on his broom. 'She seems decent enough.'

'For a dancer, yes. But she isn't stepmother material.'

'No, you're right there. When he told me he had a new wife, I expected all peroxide and lipstick, but she's not loud. As for being your stepmother – I reckon she's younger than you. Oh, well. You'll just have to put up with it. You can't change anything.'

'Indeed, it's put up with that or a barrister with no hair and a hooked nose. Father's found me a bride-groom and told me to leave home. I'm not leaving. You are going to move me to the east wing. I'm not living with them, but I'm not leaving Lambert House. It's mine.'

A chill travelled the length of his spine. From the sound of Helen Spencer, she would stop at little to get what she considered her due.

She jumped down from the wall. 'Letters to write. See you tomorrow,' she said as she re-entered the house.

Denis finished his work. It was a rum do, all right. The old bugger had gone and got himself wed with never a word to anyone. His wife was about the same age as his daughter, and his daughter was going off her rocker via brandy and too much time spent on her own. Denis felt sorry for Helen, but he knew he had to keep his distance. He shouldn't be having conversations with her. She was like a boil ready to burst, and he wanted to be out of reach when she did finally explode. He would keep looking for another job.

He travelled home on buses, eager to tell Agnes. She would be amazed at the judge's behaviour, of that he felt sure. But when he reached Noble Street, he found his beloved doubled over the slop stone, her face as white as the blouse she wore. 'Agnes?'

'It's supposed to be mornings,' she groaned.

'You what?'

'Morning sickness. Not morning, noon and night sickness. Oh, Denis. I wanted to meet you with a smile and a nice meal, but I can't be anywhere near food.' She inhaled through her mouth in an attempt to quell the nausea. 'I'm not going to be Nurse Makepeace, love. I'm going to be a mother. Hello, Daddy.' She was in the very early stages, but her stomach was already a mess.

Denis's mouth hung open. He snapped it shut and picked up his wife. 'Don't you dare vomit on me,' he warned. Tears streamed down his face, but he was laughing at the same time. 'Lie down.' He placed her on the sofa. 'I'll make my own tea.'

She fell asleep almost immediately.

He sat and watched her, a silly smile on his face. He was going to be a dad. Agnes would be the best mother in the world. Noble Street was not a good place in which to rear a child. Fred would soon be settled in Eva's house. There was nothing standing in the way. Except for . . . Except for his employer's daughter, who spoke to him as a friend, who wanted him as a lover. He longed for the days when she had seldom addressed him, because she was not a safe friend to have. But other matters had to come first, and at the top of his list was a pregnant wife.

The *Bolton Evening News* poked its way through the letterbox and landed on the doormat. Normally, he would have peeled away the pages until he found the jobs column, but there was no need, as the decision had been made. They would move to Skirlaugh Fall as soon as Fred had left this house. God must take care of the rest.

'I feel as if I've just escaped from the lunatic asylum.' Kate Moores hung up her raincoat and threw herself onto a sofa. 'Albert?'

Albert, who was semi-retired and taking his rest, opened one eye. 'What?'

'It's him – lord and bloody master. He's fetched a woman home, says she's his wife. No warning, mind. No meal ordered for her, nothing prepared, just one of them fate accomplishes.'

'Fait accompli,' grumbled Albert, who had read a few books in his time. 'What's she like, then, this new madam?'

Kate shrugged and lit a Woodbine. 'Smallish, darkish, prettyish and dressed to kill. Why has he waited this long, eh? Yon daughter of his could have done with a replacement mother when she were little, but she's thirty-odd now. Bit late in the day for him to be starting all over again.'

'First wife were never happy,' said Albert. 'Bonny lass, too good for him. I never could fathom what she saw in Spencer – she'd half of Lancashire chasing her for a date.' He went to put the kettle on. The conversation continued, as the lower storey of the house consisted of just living room and kitchen, so residents were never more than a few feet apart. 'How's Miss taken it?' he asked.

'That's another thing – dry as a bone, she was, till a few weeks back. Then she goes all daft, starts playing the piano with the window open, wears next to nowt and makes eyes at poor Denis. Lipstick and all. I'm telling you, nowt good'll come of that caper.'

'How did she take it?' he repeated.

'She ran out to Denis, of course. He's looked a bit easier since his missus come up with that neighbour – I think Mrs Makepeace sorted the bother. Any road, Miss Helen met the new wife – Louisa – then rushed outside to mither Denis again. She never used to have two words to grind together, now she can't shut up with him. She'll have took it badly, I'd say. She's a lot to lose and I don't trust her. She's sly.'

Albert returned with the tea. 'True – she has got a lot to lose. If he starts breeding again, she could be out on her ear come the day.'

Kate took a few sips of Black and Greens. 'I've not told you the best. His flaming lordship comes up to me just as I'm putting me coat on, tells me to find more servants on account of Mrs Spencer wanting the house nice. What am I supposed to do? Go to the village post office and order three maids and a partridge in a pear tree? I told him. Advertise in the paper, I said. He wanted locals, but he can find his own. I've not time for it and my energy's drained as it is. I wish I could afford to give up and let them get on with it. And I'll have to answer to the new upstart.'

Albert shook his head sadly. 'There's not many will want to work for that queer fellow. Denis Makepeace would have a better job and all but for his chest. The new Mrs Spencer's going to have her work cut out if she wants to live the high life.'

Kate agreed. 'Place is like a morgue till he starts with his music.'

'Do you think Miss will leave home, love?'

'Nay.' Kate poured some spillage from the saucer into her cup. 'Nay, she's opening up the other end of the house to get away from him and the new woman. Says she wants no servants and she'll do for herself.'

'It's him somebody should do for.' Albert shook open his paper. 'Anything tasty for tea, Kate?'

'I pinched a bit of ham and some eggs. Give me a minute and I'll get cracking.' She laughed. 'Cracking eggs, eh?' She paused for thought. 'You know, I've never heard anybody laugh in that house for years. I don't think I've seen a smile, either. Oh, well.' She stood up. 'Fried or scrambled?'

'Just get cracking,' said Albert. 'If the yolks break, scrambled. If not, fried.'

While Kate cooked the meal, she decided there was a lot in what Albert had said. Life was like eggs – to be taken as it came. See a problem, mend a problem, live and let live. He was deep, was her Albert, and she was a lucky woman. Kate didn't envy the new Mrs Spencer one little bit. The judge was just a big load of ear hole. And his daughter was going as cracked as Kate's stolen eggs.

The new Mrs Spencer sat on Helen's bed. Determined to make the best of things, she had decided to be a friend to her husband's daughter. 'We'll go shopping in Chester,' she said. 'I know Chester. Lovely shops, good clothes. I'll get you dressed to the nines in no time. You need brightening up a bit.'

Like the house, thought Helen. She worked hard to dislike Louisa, but it wasn't going to be easy. The new wife wasn't brainy, wasn't stupid, was astute enough to aim for peace in this fragmented household. The house was to be opened up. Helen should stay where she was. 'This has been your room for a while, hasn't it? Well, don't move on my account. If Zach wants to shift you, I'll fix him.'

'I would like a suite of my own,' said Helen. 'This one room and the dressing room – hardly enough for a grown woman.'

Louisa clapped her hands. 'What fun. All right, let's plan your move. We'll make you a boudoir, nice colours, plenty of space and light. Your own sitting room with a television, some bookcases, pretty rugs, nice pictures on the walls. The whole place could do with a bit of colour.'

Even the voice ceased to grate after a while. Did this woman know that she had been purchased as a breeding machine? Had she realized that she must produce a son for the great man in order to fulfil her function at Lambert House?

Louisa was suddenly serious. 'He says he's found a man for you.'

Helen frowned. 'Yes. He's found me a pock-marked beanpole with a face like the backside of a cow and a high opinion of himself.'

Louisa doubled over with glee. 'Oh, stop it. My God, I can see him – you should write a book, Helen. Have you never thought of writing? I mean, you're surrounded by books at work – you must know what people want to read. I'd love to write, but I haven't the brains or the patience. The way you described that poor bloke – hey, I hope he doesn't turn up here. I wouldn't be able to face him without laughing myself sick.'

'We met at a wedding,' Helen told her. 'I spent most of the reception – once the meal was over – hiding in lavatories and bedrooms. He even sat next to me at the table – talked with his mouth full, went on and on about himself. He seems to think he's God's finest gift to the world.'

Louisa laughed again. 'Put your foot down. I suppose you know how to handle your father.'

'I don't.' Though she was learning . . .

'He's a bully,' said Louisa. 'Like all bullies, he backs down if you stand up to him. It took me months to agree to marry him, and I did that only once I knew I could handle his moods. He can be very kind, you know. Zach's been good to me.'

Helen gritted her teeth. He could be kind, she supposed, if he wanted something. How would Louisa fare now that he had married her? Tempted to ask what on earth Louisa saw in such a man, Helen changed the subject. 'You're a legal secretary?'

'Yes. And I teach ballet and tap. I wanted to go into dance professionally, but I never made the grade. And I married young, but – anyway, it didn't work. Since then, I've done a few pantomimes, but more teaching than anything else. I'd like to open a school in Bolton, but Zach isn't keen.'

Helen walked to the window. No, Zach would not be keen, because the wife of a judge should not labour for money. How well did this young woman know the creature she had married?

'I'll get my way,' said the voice from the bed.

Perhaps she would. It promised to be an interesting episode, and Helen would watch it as closely as possible. Could this person really manage Father? Or would the honeymoon period come to a halt when he reverted to type? Something akin to pity for Louisa entered Helen's thoughts. She wasn't quite the expected floozy, was a decent enough soul. 'Let's get some coffee,' Helen suggested. Life promised to be improved by this newcomer. At last, there was someone to talk to. Things promised to go swimmingly. Until Louisa bore a son, at least . . .

Chapter Six

Excitement reigned during the next 'mothers' meeting' after Lucy came home from her honeymoon.

Repeated bouts of sickness had kept Agnes away from Mags: she couldn't visit the Bradshaws because of the smell of fish and chips; Mags had stayed away from Noble Street since her friend's closest companion had become a bowl over which she could hang her head while lying on the sofa. Agnes had managed, just about, to hang on to the contents of her stomach for the very small wedding of Fred and Eva, but had become increasingly fearful of leaving the house. She was not yet three months pregnant, and she had been warned that these symptoms might continue up to week sixteen.

'Have you chosen any names?' Lucy asked.

Agnes shook her head. 'At the moment, it doesn't answer to Bloody Nuisance. Denis calls it Bertie – no idea why – and it doesn't respond to that, either. The Bloody Nuisance was my idea, because I can't seem to keep down more than a cup of tea and a biscuit without starting World War Three. I'm living on dry cream crackers and arrowroot biscuits – can't walk past a bakery without coming over all unnecessary.'

'You be careful,' Mags warned. 'Don't be going all dehydrated on us. We don't want to arrive and find you curled like a crisp.'

'Desiccated, more like.' Agnes laughed. 'I knew

there'd be pain at the end, but I hadn't catered for this.'

'Tell me about the wedding,' Lucy begged.

The other two girls painted a vivid picture of Eva Hargreaves in full sail and powder blue. It had been a small wedding, they agreed, but the bride had made up for that, as she had practically filled the centre aisle by herself. They described her hat – a strange collection of netting, sequins and small feathers – Fred's new and squeaky shoes, the choice of hymns, one of which – 'Fight the Good Fight' – had been rejected by a very amused priest, and the post-nuptial feast of pasties and ale in a local hostelry. 'It wasn't anything like your do,' concluded Agnes. 'There was a game of darts in one corner, some old men fighting over dominoes next to the window, and the wedding in the middle. On top of all that, the brewery delivered and they had to fetch an ambulance when one of the brewer's men hurt his back.'

'Lively, then,' said Lucy.

'Lively?' Mags hooted with laughter. 'After four pints and a glass of bubbly wine, Mr Grimshaw had to be practically carried home by his new wife and Denis. He had no visible means of support apart from them.'

'Denis wants danger money if Pop ever marries again. It was good fun, though. Tell us about Paris.'

Lucy waxed enthusiastic about the city, which she had enjoyed hugely. 'But one thing I hadn't thought of – it's full of French people.'

'It would be,' said Agnes. 'It's in France.'

'They say the English have stiff upper lips.' Lucy was getting into her hilarious stride. 'You could park a double decker bus on a Frenchman's gob, and he wouldn't flinch. And we ate horse – we didn't know till afterwards. Sorry, Agnes – it would make anyone feel sick. George dared me to eat a snail, so I had five, then he had to eat frogs' legs. Tasted like strong chicken, according to him. The *Mona Lisa*'s horrible, the Eiffel Tower's a pile of rust-coloured girders, but the rest is stunning.' Thus she dismissed that wonderful city, adding only her opinion that the Arc de Triomphe was a bit good.

Mags cleared her throat. 'I'm off to London for a month soon,' she said as casually as she could. 'Time I took a break.'

'Why?' chorused the others. 'Why London?'

'It's there, we know it's there, but do we need to go?' added Lucy.

'We should enjoy our own cities first – what's the matter with London?'

'Southerners?' offered Lucy.

'Traffic?' suggested Agnes.

Mags shrugged. 'Victoria and Albert, Science Museum, Buck House, Tate, National, St Paul's – need I go on?'

'Pickpockets,' shouted Lucy.

'Thieves and vagabonds.' Agnes grinned.

'You've been reading Dickens again.' Mags smoothed her skirt. She wanted the whole thing to be a surprise, yet she feared the pain and worried about the outcome – what if they gave her the wrong nose? What if they gave her the right nose, thereby making the rest of her face wrong?

'She's hiding something.' Lucy folded her arms.

'She is.' Agnes stared hard at Mags. 'Out with it. Is it a man? Are you sneaking off for a dirty month with a married person?' She glanced at Lucy. 'George isn't going to London, is he?'

146

'No, he isn't. If he decides to go, I'll ground him with a couple of tent pegs.'

'Denis isn't going, either. Whose husband is she pinching, Lucy?'

'It'll be your Denis's judge. That should get her into the House of Lords. By a back door, of course.'

The judge. Agnes began to tell her friends about recent events at Lambert House, thus changing the subject for a relieved Mags. 'The wife's younger than Miss Spencer. Denis says the two women get along well enough together, so that makes life a bit easier. I feel sorry for Helen Spencer, you know.'

'She drinks,' said Mags. 'It's a damned shame, because it's all her dad's fault. Did you see the article she was sitting with at Lucy's reception? That's the husband chosen by his flaming lordship. Looked like the back of a mangled tram. That's why she ran off. Then I met her in the loos and booked her a room. I found her soaked in brandy later on. The judge sent Denis to find her.'

'I know.' Agnes chewed on a nail. 'We're going to live up there. Judge Spencer will like that, because he'll have Denis on the doorstep. We're to have a phone. If the old devil can't fasten his corsets, he'll be sending for poor Denis. I'm in two minds.'

'Does he wear corsets?' Lucy's perfect eyebrows almost disappeared under her fringe.

'He did the last time I saw him stripping off.' Agnes looked from one to the other. 'Joke,' she said. 'Anybody seeing him undressed probably needs to be under the influence of a strong tranquillizer. He's a mess. I hear he's to be the judge at Harry Timpson's trial. He's a hang-'em-high type, or so I'm told. Glenys spoke to

Miss Spencer, asked her to help, but I'm not holding my breath – unless I'm going to vomit, of course.'

'When will you be normal?' Mags asked.

'She was never normal.' Lucy drained her coffee cup. 'If she'd been normal, I wouldn't have wanted anything to do with her. Normal's boring.' She looked hard at Agnes. 'Is this vomiting going to carry on all through?'

'No idea. It could be temporary, could be hyperemesis.'

'Who?'

'Stop messing about, Lucy. If I've got hyperemesis, I could damage my brain, my liver and my child. I'd spend most of the time in hospital.'

Nobody liked the sound of that. 'Can I press you to a jelly?' asked Lucy, her stern expression surviving snorts of laughter. 'Look, some folk can hang on to that when all else fails – calf's foot, fruit jelly – it slides down. And,' she smiled again, 'if it comes back up, there's nothing to it – it slides like sugar off a shiny shovel.'

Cushions flew in the company of several impolite words.

They settled back eventually. 'London, though,' pondered Agnes aloud. 'You'll not need your bucket and spade or a phrase book, will you?'

Mags shrugged. 'I might need the phrase book – they talk a load of rubbish down there. And I draw the line at jellied eels and whelks. They don't even eat proper like what we do.'

'And we talk proper and all, don't we?' Lucy jumped to her feet. 'I've a hungry lawyer and three cats to feed. Look after yourself, Agnes.' She glared at her other friend. 'Don't go marrying any cockneys – I had enough of them with the *Billy Cotton Band Show* and his

"Wakey, wakey". Load of flaming numbskulls.' She swept out, leaving a sudden silence in the house, the word 'London' thrown over her shoulder as she closed the door.

'What's going on, Mags?'

'Eh?'

'You're up to something.'

Mags sighed. 'Don't tell anybody.'

'I won't.'

'Well, you know how I've never left home for a flat of my own?'

'Yes?'

'It was so I could save up for a new nose. If I decided not to have a nose, I could put a deposit on a house or a flat. But when I was sitting with that Miss Spencer at Lucy's wedding, I thought I might end up like her. She's plain, but not ugly. If I have a new nose, I might graduate to plain. With the right clothes and a good haircut, plain can pass as OK.'

Agnes bit her lip. 'God, that's scary. They break bones and stuff, don't they? And doesn't it take a few weeks for all the swellings to go down?' She shivered. 'It'll hurt.'

'Yes.'

'Aren't you scared?'

'Yes. Aren't you scared – all biscuits and bowls?'

'Yes.'

Mags reached out and grasped her dear friend's hands. 'Then we'll be scared together. I don't know what I'll look like; you don't know what Nuisance will look like. I'm sorry about your nursing, but we have to get on with life, haven't we? We only get the one chance.'

Agnes nodded. 'But a baby's a natural thing, Mags.

149

New noses interfere with nature. You've always been against make-up and hair dye – yet here you are, going for plastic surgery in London.'

'I am not walking behind this great big conk for the rest of my life. It comes into a room ten full minutes before the rest of me. There's no getting away from a nose like this. This is a nose you have to live up to. I'd do all right as one of the three witches in *Macbeth* – no greasepaint required. And I want to go to Carnaby Street for some daft clothes, get my hair done in the West End, see all those London markets. I'm doing it, Agnes. For better or worse, I'm doing it.'

Alone, Agnes thought about Mags's parting words. For better or worse sounded about right. You had to live with a nose before you understood its significance. The same might be said for marriage – for better or for worse, a partner, once chosen, was supposed to be there for life. Mags's nose was going to be a better or worse job, and everyone would have to take time to get to know it. 'Good luck, Magsy,' she whispered. Then she went to try a bit of toast.

She was still coming to terms with her bit of toast when love's young dream – as she had nominated Fred and Eva – burst into the house. 'Hello,' she said. 'Do come in. Oh, I see. You're already in.' Agnes noticed that Eva was breathless and that Pop was a strange shade of pink. Eva stood in front of the dresser.

'Tell her,' she ordered.

'They're coming,' he announced. 'With a great big van and stuff. You'll have to help me, Agnes – I don't know what to say.'

Thus far, the toast had sat well enough. But all Agnes needed was two confused senior citizens and she would lose calories, plus moisture, all over again. The pair shifted weight from foot to foot, putting her in mind of a couple of children kept in at playtime for bad behaviour. 'What are you on about?' she asked.

'Me doll's houses,' spluttered Fred.

'Doll's houses,' came the echo.

Agnes chewed, swallowed, took a sip of tea. 'Start at the beginning and finish at the end, please.'

Fred dropped into a chair. '*Coronation Street*,' he said.

'Them as makes it,' added Eva in an attempt to make matters clear. 'I've shut the shop. Your granddad's famous.'

Agnes glared at the personification of fame – dirty overalls with an off-the-shoulder touch of fashion at one side, hair full of sawdust, eyes as wide as a frightened rabbit's. 'Granada?'

He nodded, causing a shower of fine wood shavings to abandon his person. 'Making a series called *Man at Work*. It's about retired folk doing crafts and stuff. They say my houses are in a class of their own. Somebody up Chorley New Road ordered a Tudor mansion, then, after seeing the plans, went and phoned these here Granada folk. I'm going on the telly. They're doing an OB on me.'

'Isn't that a medal?' asked Agnes with feigned ignorance.

'That has an E fastened to it,' said Fred. 'OB is outside broadcast and they cost money. They want to see me in my natural wotsername.'

'Habit,' said Eva.

'Habitat, you daft lummox.' Fred sighed. 'We've even shut the shop to come and talk to you.'

'Yes, Eva said so before,' said Agnes.

'What'll I do?' Fred looked truly frightened.

'Nothing.' Agnes placed her cup on the table. 'They ask questions, film your houses, you just give answers. You don't know what they'll ask, so you can't practise for it.'

'Can't practise,' said Eva.

Fred jumped up. 'What are we doing here?' he asked his bemused wife. 'I've carpets to fit and lights to install. Come on.' He rushed out of the house. 'Where did I put that box of doorknockers?' The final words grew fainter as he marched up the street.

'I hope this doesn't make him ill again.' Eva walked to the door. 'He's getting all worked up.'

Agnes sighed and shook her head. 'For better or worse, Eva. Just let it all happen. It'll happen anyway. Enjoy it. He'll be all right. If he isn't, send him back. You've a twelve-month guarantee for parts and labour on that item.'

Alone at last, Agnes put her feet up and waited for her stomach to rise, but her indigestive system seemed to have made up its mind to take time off for good behaviour. She kept the bowl nearby, just in case, but minutes passed without the need to leave a deposit.

'Let's hope I'm finally on parole,' she told her feet. 'Because the three of us – not including toes – have to get moving – literally. Skirlaugh Fall, here I come.'

Skirlaugh Fall was a village consisting of a group of houses that clung together for support at the bottom of Skirlaugh Rise. The big house sat on top of the Rise, as if it oversaw movements among serfs condemned to live lower down both social and geographical scales. It was a pretty place and Agnes had always loved it. She was excited. Nuisance, too, seemed impressed, though it

152

was too soon for him to start kicking and Agnes put the flutters down to wind or imagination.

On all sides, moors swept towards every compass point, so the Fall could be a bit damp, but that fact made it all the greener. It was a fresh, wholesome place that made her think of the hymn 'All Things Bright and Beautiful'. The cottage was a bit small, but no one could have everything. There was no scullery, though the kitchen, which ran the full width of the building, was big enough to double up as a second living room. 'Nice,' she told her husband. It was more than nice. It was cosy, with wonderful views, clear air and decent neighbours in the form of Kate and Albert Moores. This was a splendid place in which to raise a child. There was a school within easy reach, there was clean oxygen to breathe, and there were playgrounds in the form of lush, green fields.

Inside the cottage, they had found a welcoming bunch of orange flowers in the grate. Agnes declared this to be a thoughtful gesture, as it gave colour without heat and made the place seem homely right from the start. 'They're from Mr and Mrs Moores,' she told her husband. 'That was a friendly thing to do, very thoughtful.'

'She's all right, is Kate Moores,' he declared. 'Solid as a rock and no nonsense. Her husband works the land, but he's semi-retired these days. She's run off her feet. Wife the Second up at the house wants more servants. Most round here would kill the judge before they'd work for him, so Kate's having to look further afield. It's all new curtains and rugs up yon. Mrs Spencer's a fresh broom, but she'll not do her own sweeping.'

'They never do. Denis?'

'What?'

153

'Come in the kitchen – Mrs Moores has left us new bread and butter, some cheese and a pot of home-made strawberry jam. She's got willow pattern plates. I've always wanted some of those.'

'And I grew the strawberries.' He came to stand by his wife at the kitchen window. The mock-Tudor mansion was clearly visible from this position. 'They're getting on too well for the old bugger's liking,' he said. 'Mrs and Miss are busy footling round Manchester, Chester and Liverpool, separating him from his brass, I shouldn't wonder. He's not saying much, but he's aged about ten years these past few weeks. Mrs is there just to produce a son and heir; Miss is staying put because she won't be shifted and I can't say I blame her. But the new wife's done her a lot of good, I must say. No, I can't blame either of them.'

'Me neither,' agreed Agnes. 'It's lovely here, Denis, but I don't like being near him. If there's a devil, he'll look just like Judge Spencer.'

'Well, I can't disagree with that. Now. Where are we putting all our stuff? The van'll be here in a minute, so we'd best decide.'

'I don't care,' she sighed happily. 'I'd sit on orange boxes if necessary. Nothing matters but this baby and that view. Not Lambert House – the rest of it out there.' She wished that they didn't have a view of her husband's place of employment, but it had to be accepted. 'Denis?'

'What?'

'Can we afford a television set? Just a small one?'

He smiled. 'We might be able to manage that. You want to see your granddad flummoxed in front of the nation, don't you?'

Agnes laughed. 'Flummoxed? He'll be in his element. As soon as he gets talking, they'll have trouble shutting him up. Camera shy? Not him. He'll be like a dog with five tails and a thigh bone to chew on. Yes, I want to see him on TV, bless him. That stroke and Nan dying – he deserves a good life, what's left of it. So does Eva, come to that.'

Denis chortled. 'She's getting herself painted and decorated all the way through – even the bedroom. The back bedroom's for storage, but she was going to empty that for painting till Fred put his foot down. He said he wasn't carrying that load of stuff downstairs, not even for bloody Granada. I wouldn't mind, but the TV folk'll be setting up in the shed. The only thing that'll bring them inside is tea and Eva's scones. Honestly, the way Pop's carrying on, you'd think it was going to be a Hollywood film.'

Leaving Denis to wait for the removal men, Agnes went for a short walk. These were proud cottages, each with a well-kept front garden and decent curtains. She found the post office, which doubled as a grocery, a tiny pub and cottage industries advertising eggs or bedding plants for sale.

She placed a hand on her belly. 'We'll be all right, Nuisance. You, me and your dad can make a fine life out here, just you wait and see.'

Two women were walking towards her, and she recognized one of them. Miss Spencer was in the company of a small, dark, attractive woman. This must be Wife the Second, then. Agnes stopped and pretended to study marigolds in a cottage garden.

'Is that Mrs Makepeace?'

Agnes turned. 'Hello, Miss Spencer.'

'This is Mrs Spencer – my stepmother.' Both women giggled. 'She's not old enough to be a wicked stepmother, is she? We're playing truant – we're supposed to be interviewing staff for the house, but we escaped. Kate will keep them in order – won't she, Louisa?'

'She keeps me in order.' The judge's wife smiled. 'She has a face that could stop a tram in its tracks. Mind, she does work hard.'

Agnes bid them a polite good day, then walked on. In her soul, she was chuckling, because those two ladies were in cahoots, if she wasn't greatly mistaken. From what Denis had said, Agnes knew that Spencer wanted the house to himself and his wife, that he longed for Helen to leave, but this unexpected friendship would leave his plans in tatters. Which was exactly what the old goat deserved, Agnes believed. He was always sending for Denis. Denis was expected to have no life beyond the judge and his needs. Well, with a new baby, things would have to be different.

She walked along tracks that bordered farmland, watched cows and sheep grazing, saw a donkey resting his head on a dry stone wall. It was another world altogether. No deposits from the Industrial Revolution were visible from here. Cotton mills? What were they? Yet the houses in the village had been built for one purpose only, to accommodate weavers and spinners before cottage cotton died.

At the top of a lane, she stopped and looked at Lambert House. It was massive. She would wager that three people could live in there for months without seeing each other. There was water nearby, so the house might have been the property of a fulling miller in the days of homespun yarn, but she doubted it. The mansion had been built to look old, was a pale imitation of Hall i' th' Wood, the place in which Crompton had invented the spinning mule. That had been a waste of a life, she mused, because the rights had been virtually

dreams were nudging her to remember something, but her stepmother distracted her during the days and panic attacks were fewer.

Denis? The feelings remained, yet she managed to control herself. If she saw him, she spoke to him, but she never sought him out. There was no time. Helen's life was fully occupied with the library and with Louisian adventures. Helen smiled. The Louisian era was her favourite so far, and long should it reign.

When Mags Bradshaw returned from London, she did not go home. Having booked a room at the Pack Horse, she shut herself away and waited for the last of the bruising to subside. Over a period of days, she watched the butterfly emerging from its dark chrysalis. It was rather frightening in a sense, because she was looking at a stranger. All the time, it had been only her nose. She was no Marilyn Monroe, no Jane Russell, but she was almost pretty. Everyone in her position should have a new nose. It improved a person's outlook, her mental state, her whole life. She would never regret postponing the purchase of a house, because she had spent her money wisely on a whole new promise of adventure.

Margaret Bradshaw had new hair, new make-up, new shoes, new clothes. 'I am a reformed woman,' she said as she sat at the dressing table. It had been a painful road, and at times she had regretted the surgery, but the result was so stunning that she could not stop looking at herself. If this behaviour continued, she would become so self-absorbed that she might well imitate those she had always mocked, the look-at-me girls, the floozies, the good-time females. Although she wanted to show off to her friends, she dreaded the initial impact that would cause embarrassment at work, at home, in shops. But she would have to bite the bullet, and home was the place to begin.

After three nights, Mags made up her face, packed her bags and stood at the bus stop on Deansgate. It was time to face the world. No one stared, so that was the first hurdle cleared. The application of heavier make-up had concealed the last pale traces of multi-coloured damage. She was free. She would be able to walk into a room without her nose acting as usher. She was normal and she wanted to cry.

In the living quarters behind the shop known locally as Braddy's Chippy, Mags comforted her mother, who shed tears enough for both of them. 'You were lovely before, baby, but you are a stunner now.' It was clear that Mam had not realized how desperately Mags had hated her appearance. 'We thought you'd gone looking for work down yon,' she wailed, referring to the many days Mags had spent in London. 'We thought we'd lost you, sweetheart.'

Her dad was less emotional on the surface. He asked the usual questions about cost and pain, though he wiped a tear from his eye once he had gone back to his batter mix. Mags was beautiful. Like many fathers, he worried about the male of the species. His little girl was going to attract attention, and not all that attention would be welcome.

Work was the next hurdle. When she arrived on her first day, a receptionist looked at her quizzically, asked did she have an appointment; then, once Mags grinned, the girl leapt from her chair. 'It's you!' she yelled. She fled through the outer office and into the inner sanctum. 'It's her,' she shouted. 'Come and look.'

Animals in zoos probably got fed up, Mags decided

as secretaries, clerks and solicitors came to view. At one point, she made monkey noises and pretended to scratch her armpits before asking for coffee and a bun. 'For God's sake, bog off, will you? I feel like something in Tussaud's. Yes, I've had a nose job, yes, I had a deviated septum, so it was a good idea from a medical viewpoint, yes, I now cast a smaller shadow and no, I'm not going to tell you how it felt.' She marched to her desk, exclaimed over the heaps of post in her in tray, then carried on as usual. It would all calm down, she told herself. But she still had to face Lucy and Agnes.

An item in her tray provided her with the opportunity to plan the first meeting between her nose and her two confidantes. It was an invitation to celebrate the recent marriage between Zachary Spencer and a woman named Louisa. In handwriting at the bottom, someone – probably poor Helen Spencer – had appended a message containing the information that Lucy and Agnes would be there with their partners. Partners? Where could she get one of those within days? It was best to go alone anyway, because her nose would probably be the star, while she would play the part of a small attachment. She smiled to herself. After twenty years of being a mere appendage to a colossal proboscis, there had been no change – just a simple adjustment of parts to be played. Until people got used to her face, she would have to sit back and let the surgeon's triumph take the glory.

In her lunch hour she walked around Bolton, pretending to look at displays in shop windows while, in truth, she was looking at herself. She was an inch from pretty. When she passed some painters working on the frontage of Woolworth's, Mags Bradshaw was in receipt of her first ever wolf whistle. There had been times when she had almost used her savings on a deposit for a place of her own. That whistle told her that she had spent her money well. Now, all she had to do was find a truly stunning dress, because she wanted no complaints from this new, upstart nose. With a spring in her step, Mags Bradshaw began her search for suitable trappings.

Agnes answered the door. It was the twins, as Denis had begun to describe Miss and Mrs Spencer. 'Come in,' she said tentatively.

Louisa Spencer was an extremely pleasant woman with a high-pitched voice to which Agnes became attuned within minutes. Whatever the woman was – gold-digger or just plain silly – she had a genuine affection for and interest in her fellows. 'Was that your grandfather on TV last night? The doll's house man?'

Agnes laughed. 'It was.'

'You ask her.' Louisa was speaking to Helen. 'Go on.'

'Would he come to the party?' Helen asked. 'It would be nice to have someone famous – apart from my father, of course.'

'He's more notorious than famous,' said Louisa cheerfully. 'What a wonderful man your granddad is. He had Helen and me in pleats. I thought he'd never stop talking – I wanted him not to stop. He should have his own TV show. I laughed and laughed.'

'Me, too,' said Agnes. 'Though I'm used to it. He and Nan raised me – my mam died when I was born.'

'He's very witty.' Louisa laughed again. 'He treated the interviewer like an apprentice and I swear he could talk for ever. Those houses are extraordinary. He has actually made some real houses to scale, hasn't he?'

'He keeps busy.' Agnes smoothed her apron. 'Would you like some tea? It's ordinary Indian, I'm afraid.'

Louisa blew out her cheeks. 'Thank God for that. I'm not that keen on perfumed stuff. And I'm common – I take milk and sugar. Yes, I'd love a cuppa.'

While Agnes busied herself in the kitchen, Helen looked at Denis's home. It was small, but beautiful. Agnes was beautiful, too, but bigger than she used to be. A sharp pang of jealousy pierced Helen's chest, but its duration was short. She could manage without him. She had taken no brandy for days. Louisa, her friend and her prop, had shown her another way of life, had lent some of her own pragmatism to a woman whose life, thus far, had been filled by unattainable dreams. The nightmares continued, but every day was good and exciting and different from its predecessors.

Agnes brought in the tray.

'You're expecting,' announced Louisa.

'Yes.' Agnes poured. 'That's why we finally came up here. It's better for children and easier for Denis. Pop married Eva – she was the one who appeared on the programme by accident. Mind, she's a big woman, and she seems to get everywhere, so I'm not surprised. When Pop married, we didn't need to stay in Noble Street, so here we are.' She handed out cups and saucers.

'Will he come to the party?' asked Louisa. 'We haven't many older people on the list, and I'm sure he'd pick up some business. Not that he needs to. Didn't he say they were thinking of selling the shop?'

Agnes nodded. 'Eva says she'll do his soft furnishings. He's got so many orders, he'll have to take on a man to help. God help that man. Pop's talking about buying Bamber Cottage, so we'll have him near us again. But they could change their minds – they often do. Eva's not one for quick decisions. She's not one for anything quick, come to that. Pop says she's built for endurance, not for speed.'

'But will they come?' Louisa begged. 'He has to come. I never had a doll's house as a child – perhaps I'll order one now.'

'He'll cause trouble. I mean, think about how he made that interviewer look daft. I can't see him fitting in with Judge Spencer and a load of lawyers.'

Louisa frowned. 'My husband isn't what people believe him to be. He may be a tough judge, but he's all right.'

Helen almost choked on her next sip of tea. All right? He was far from that. But Louisa had a knack of seeing the best in just about anyone. Helen envied her that. In spite of a past about which she would say little, Louisa Spencer looked on life as a glass half full rather than half empty. Above all, she was lively, unafraid and funny.

'I liked the bit where the man asked your granddad about material for the roofs.'

Agnes laughed. 'I know. When he said he'd stripped a church roof and cut all the slates into smithereens, I think they believed him for a minute. It's all wood and paint.'

'And electric lights. Very clever.' Louisa returned her cup to its saucer. 'Make him come.'

'I can't make him do anything. Nobody has ever been able to make him do anything – even Nan had a fifty per cent success rate at best. As for stopping him, you'd have a job. You should have seen my kitchen till he married Eva and her air raid shelter. Murder, it was.

Sawdust in the jam, chippings in my pastry, paint all over the ironing.'

'Then he definitely has to come.' Louisa stood, and Helen copied the movement.

In that split second, Agnes forgave Helen Spencer for chasing her husband. She had needed someone like Louisa, a pattern to follow, a friend – almost a sister. Louisa seemed to be a steadying influence, and that had to be a good thing.

'Promise you'll invite him,' Louisa pleaded.

'I promise.' Agnes suffered a temporary mental picture of two old men in a corner. Like Kate's Albert, Fred Grimshaw would tug at his collar, complain about the heat, hate the food, wish he could be normal in overalls. Perhaps they could keep one another company at the dreaded event.

'Goodbye,' chorused the two women as they left the house.

Agnes sank into a chair for a rest – the dishes could wait for half an hour. Pregnancy still failed to suit her, though the vomiting had stopped. She was tired all the time. Everything was an effort and she had to force herself to keep going. Nan would have shifted her, would have urged her on, but there was no more Nan.

She drifted into sleep, her mind filled with dreams of Pop making a doll's house in the middle of Judge Spencer's living room, of the judge bawling and his wig slipping. Miss Spencer had her arms round Denis's neck and he was bending to kiss her. Albert had stripped all the way down to vest and pants. Eva ate most of the food, leaving just a few scraps for a large dog.

Agnes woke with a start. What a stupid dream that had been. Everyone knew that judges didn't wear their daft wigs at home . . .

Chapter Seven

Zachary Spencer sat on the end of an oversized, custom-made bed. In his opinion, which was correct at all times, the situation within his own household had gone too far. Louisa, an excellent wife with many plus points on her check sheet, had upset the balance. The subject had to be addressed. It should have been dealt with earlier, but he had allowed things to slide because he needed to please Louisa. Now, he was going to put his foot down. A bride was required to learn her place in a household, and the shape and size of that position was the responsibility of the husband. There should be laws on statute books, then the whole business could be made clear from the start.

He fastened his waistcoat and waited for his wife to return. Where was she? She was at the other side of the house in her stepdaughter's rooms, was preparing Helen for this evening's party, was with her best friend. The fact that the atmosphere had changed shortly before Louisa's arrival had not escaped him, but his wife's support had allowed Helen to open up further, and he did not like the latter's attitude. Overtly supportive of and pleasant to her father, Helen was becoming talkative, was even daring to express opinions. While she invariably agreed with the few words he spoke at table, she continued to hold in her eyes an expression of challenge, as if she were taunting him and fooling him. He was nobody's fool. Fools did not become judges; judges seldom became fools unless senility overcame them after long service in the name of the Crown.

Inwardly, he seethed. He could not identify the game Helen was playing, but he had glimpsed the edge of her cleverness, had realized too late that she was bright as well as unpredictable. Her mother had been clever, yet not clever enough to conceal from her husband the fact that she disagreed with his politics and his attitudes. Helen had the brains to wear a thin gilding of good metal over her true self. She was brilliant, had inherited her father's brains and her mother's wilfulness. As time wore on, the veneer covering Helen's true core was beginning to erode. The result had to be dealt with immediately.

It was getting late. He glanced at a clock, imagined the two of them together in Helen's suite, all laughter and smiles. It was not natural. Most daughters would leave home if a parent brought home a new partner, but Helen was not a bolter. He had asked her to leave; she had stayed, had spent a great deal of money on creating her own apartment within his house, was even stealing the attention of his wife. It had to stop, he told himself for the thousandth time.

He fastened his shoes, pulled on a jacket, continued to wait. Unused to waiting, he tapped an impatient foot on the carpet. Louisa should be here with him. She was a good wife – that fact was undeniable. Always pleasant, always accepting of his attentions, never angry, she catered to his whims, yet stuck to Helen like glue.

She came in. 'Darling, you look smart,' she announced.

'Thank you. You were away a long time.'

'Helen's nervous,' she replied. 'She hasn't had much

of a social life, and I had to calm her. That's the problem with a girl who has been without a mother – she has no pattern to follow.'

He was surrounded by clever women.

'Let me fix your tie.' She stood over him and straightened the offending item. 'There. You'll be the best-dressed man in the room.'

'So I should be – this suit is hand-made by craftsmen.'

'Yes, dear.'

'I don't know why we need to have this damned party,' he complained. 'I can think of a thousand ways to spend an evening fruitfully, but this is not one of them. Damned fools coming into my house, eating my food, drinking my—'

'You'll enjoy it,' she promised.

'Will I?' His house would be full of lawyers, yet he could not be himself among his own colleagues, because Helen had put a stop to that. Had she really heard that gossip in the Pack Horse, or had it been an opening salvo, a warning shot to his stern? Whatever she had sought to achieve, she had been successful. 'Louisa?'

'Yes?'

'You spend too much time with my daughter.'

'Do I?' She sat at the dressing table. 'It is much better this way, my love. Imagine how hard life might have been had she hated me. I am fortunate. She likes me and I enjoy her company. Helen is very knowledgeable and interesting, you know.'

Life, he thought, would have been a great deal easier had Helen flounced out of the house in temper.

'I like your daughter, Zach. And she fills some of the hours during your absences. What am I expected to do? Sit at one end of the house while she is at the other? And she goes to work, so we are scarcely constant companions. We are the same age and we complement each other well. She needed help and I enjoy her companionship. She is coming out of her shell, probably for the first time in her life. Your daughter is lonely.'

He seethed. Presented by the defence, the argument for Helen's case was solid. In court, it would stand up to the most skilful cross-questioning from the best prosecutor on the planet. Louisa was talking sense and he felt like a boxer who had been knocked out in the first round. Yet he continued to cling to the ropes, refused to lie down for the count. 'She's devious,' he said.

'All women are devious, sweetheart. We are what men have made us.'

'Nonsense.'

'Yes.' She spun round on the stool. 'I'm sure you are right. I shall try to spend more time with you in the future, but you will need to be here. I can't go travelling from court to court, can I?'

He had lost. The jury would definitely come down on the side of the defence – there would be no sentence to impose. Sliding into his other simile, he was in the corner of the ring and the fight was lost. 'We shall have to go down shortly,' he said almost resignedly.

'Yes, dear. The food looks wonderful.'

'Good.' He looked at his watch again.

Louisa smiled brightly. 'Before we do go, I want you to know that you are going to be a father again.'

He simply nodded, though his eyes blazed with pleasure. That would be a nail in Helen's coffin. As soon as he had his son, the will would be changed. Of course, he would have to leave her something, but the boy would inherit the bulk. 'I am delighted to hear that,' he said. 'But should you be organizing an event in your condition? Don't you want to stay up here and rest? I can explain your absence if necessary.'

Louisa shook her head. 'No. I am well. Explain nothing, Zach. I always think it's tempting fate to announce a pregnancy too early. Let's keep this to ourselves for the time being. No one needs to know – except us and the doctor. This is our special secret.' A smile hovered on her lips. She could manage the man. Like many of his gender, he was a fool when it came to the machinations of females.

He kissed her on the cheek, then left the room.

When he had gone, Louisa stared at her reflection. The desire to scream had been with her for a while, but she would never indulge it. Zach was her safety and her future. The life she had left behind could be allowed no significance, because she had gained what she had sought – security and wealth. This was not a play in three acts, though; this was a charade she would need to perform well until the day he died. He was thirty years older than she was. All she required was patience, humour and one other important element – the distraction embodied by his daughter.

Scars from the past ached, and she pressed a palm into her right side. The disfigurement of her lower body was officially attributed to surgery. Before she had learned to compose herself and take silent charge, she had spoken her mind, had been battered and stabbed by a man who had supposedly loved her. Aware that she now lived with another man of uncertain temperament, she had laid her plans well. No longer a secretary, no longer the dancer, she was determined to make the best of Zachary Spencer. He was an unpleasant man. She would cope.

The door crashed inward. 'Denis? Are you there?' Kate drew breath before repeating the call.

Denis descended the stairs. 'I think I'm there,' he said. 'I was there when I looked a minute ago, but I'm here now, aren't I? Shall I go back there, then I'll be there?'

Kate tried to frown, but failed. 'Listen, you daft lummox. I can't do nothing with him. He's dug his heels in and won't fettle. It's like the horse and the water – he won't shift.'

Denis did not need the name of the 'him'. 'What's the matter?'

'Says he's not going, says he's no intention of wearing a suit, says the shirt I bought him's too tight at the neck. I'm going to kill him if he doesn't shape. Will you come and deal with him?'

'What can I do that you can't? You're his wife – I'm only a neighbour.'

Kate nodded several times. 'He'll listen to you. You're a man.'

'That still doesn't tell me what to do, though, does it? Shall I anaesthetize him? Knock him out? Fetch an ambulance? I know how he feels. I'd sooner sit knitting fog than spend three or four hours up yon. Send Agnes. She'll shift him. She's even shifted her granddad a few times, and that's like moving the Isle of Man.' He shouted up the stairwell. 'Agnes? Go and dress Albert, will you?'

Agnes appeared at the top of the flight. 'I've had trouble enough fastening my own frock – it fitted last week when I bought it. Anyway, I can't dress a man. It wouldn't be right.'

'I've got him into the trousers,' said Kate. 'You'll not see him naked. I wouldn't let that happen to my worst enemy. There's enough shocks in life without seeing my Albert in his birthday suit. Bad enough me having to put up with it. Just finish him off, Agnes,' she begged.

'What with?' asked Denis. 'Arsenic?'

Kate folded her arms. 'If necessary, yes. We can prop him up on a chair in a corner and say he's not well. We can order the gravestone tomorrow and I'll lay on a ham tea for the funeral. Stubborn as a mule, he is.'

Agnes sat on the top stair. 'Why don't we all go somewhere else? Please? I don't know which knife to use for what.'

'You don't need to,' said Kate. 'You'll be eating stood up. It's a buffet. Bits of stupid things on bits of stupid biscuits to start with, then salads and all kinds of meat – for God's sake, help me.'

Agnes rose to her feet. She was grinning broadly, because she was looking at herself and Denis in forty years' time. Kate and Albert were happy. They had celebrated their ruby anniversary and they were still happy. Until it came to suits. Dressing up was not Albert's idea of fun, and Denis was much the same. 'All right,' she said resignedly. 'But I'm promising nothing.'

'Fair enough.' Kate sank into a chair. 'I'm exhausted and we still haven't had the kick-off.'

After knocking, Agnes entered the cottage next door. Albert, in vest and trousers, was hiding behind the *Bolton Evening News*. 'Hey, you,' she began. 'Stand up, get rid of the reading matter and put your clothes on. You're driving Kate out of her mind.'

He folded the paper. 'Then she's not far to travel, has she?'

'If your wife's crackers, you've sent her that way. Now, get dressed or Denis'll do it for you. You've got five minutes. No use fighting it, Albert.'

He glared at her. 'I didn't ask for no bloody party, did I? I'm all right with me telly and the wireless. From the start, I told her I didn't want to go.'

'You'd let her go on her own, then? Four minutes and twenty seconds, you've got now.'

'She works there – she's used to it.'

Agnes sat down. 'Right. Remember my grandfather – he was on the telly with his houses?'

He nodded.

'He'll be there. Like you, he'll moan every inch of the way. Like you, he'll not want to go. And we have to put up with him all night, because he'll be sleeping over with his wife in our house.'

'What's that got to do with the price of fish?'

'Well, he's thinking of buying Bamber Cottage. If and when he does, he'll be looking for an apprentice.'

'And?'

'And you can apply. Get in first, get to know him and Eva, and you'll be working out of the weather and with my Pop.'

'I can't be an apprentice at my age.'

'You can. If Pop likes you, that is. He won't even meet you if you carry on sitting on the shelf like cheese at fourpence. What's up with you, anyway? Grown man, won't get dressed, carrying on like a five-year-old in a tantrum. Ridiculous.' She tapped a foot. 'Come on – the baby'll be due at this rate. Just do as you're told, because you are outnumbered.'

179

Sighing dramatically, Albert did as he was bidden. She tidied his collar, straightened the tie, examined his shoes. 'Right,' she said. 'You'll pass as human as long as you stay in the shade.'

The four friends made their reluctant way to the big house. Given a choice, each of them would have been otherwise engaged, but the judge had spoken. Or his wife had spoken. Whatever, they had to go.

Helen trembled, but the brandy remained in its container. She didn't need it, because Louisa would be there, and Louisa would look after her. James Taylor, the balding eagle, had also been invited to the party, but Helen had been prepared for him. Louisa had the answers; Louisa was Helen's prop.

'Tell him to bugger off,' Louisa had said. 'You're out of his league now. Time you started sticking up for yourself. You don't want him, you don't need him – just say so.'

From her bedroom window, Helen watched caterers carrying in the last of the food and drink. She didn't know how many people were coming, but she wasn't looking forward to the event. James Taylor had telephoned several times. Telephones were easier than face-to-face meetings. She had to get rid of him tonight, and he would probably run to Father with his tale of woe.

She sat down and thought about her stepmother. Married young to a man who had turned into a murderous monster, Louisa had escaped with her life, without a spleen and with one savable kidney. After four weeks in hospital, she had gone home, had sat, had made her decision. She had recently married a man who was worth divorcing. 'Only the very rich and the very poor can afford divorce,' she had advised Helen. 'The very rich don't miss a few thousand, while the poor have nothing to lose.'

She was wise. Zachary Spencer did not figure in his wife's emotions – he was just a piece of scaffolding designed to support her. If the marriage failed, there would be a decent settlement. As delicately as possible, Helen had asked about the intimate side of the marriage, had received the reply, 'I close my eyes and think of Gregory Peck.' Louisa was brave. She probably recognized Helen's vulnerability because it echoed her own past. 'But she is more Charlotte Lucas than I am,' Helen whispered. Austen's Charlotte had married a fool; Louisa had fastened herself to a bank balance; the fictional character and the living woman had both married for safety.

Was James Taylor to be Helen's safety? She thought not. As Louisa had said, if Helen didn't want him, he should be advised to bugger off. A smile tilted the corners of Helen's mouth. She would have loved to own the guts to scream those two words into a crowded room, but she would never get that far. Denis. A part of her still wanted and needed him. He continued to occupy her dreams, but she could never have him. Soon, Denis would be a father; Helen Spencer would probably be the eternal virgin.

The dreams about Denis came less frequently these days, but the other nightmare remained. She always woke in a sweat, always tried to piece together what she had seen while asleep, always failed. It was a noisy scenario, terrifying and intense. And she could remember no details. Louisa made up for the dreams, because Louisa had both feet planted squarely on terra firma. But Helen wished the night terrors would abate.

She stood and looked in the mirror. Underneath a deceptively simple dove grey dress, she wore the silk underwear she had bought during her silly phase. Her hair had been styled by Louisa, who had also applied cosmetics in muted tones. Helen knew that she had never looked as pretty as she did this evening, yet she feared company. An outer shell of acceptability would never completely shore up an injured soul. She did not possess Louisa's strength of character and she probably never would.

Cars began to arrive. Her father and stepmother would greet the guests, but Louisa had asked Helen to be present. 'This is your home, too. Let people know who you are.' Her home? According to her father, she deserved nothing, simply because she had failed to be male.

She touched up her lipstick, checked her hose for ladders, picked up a glittering evening bag. But she drank no brandy.

Dressed in their best, Eva and Fred were taking the opportunity to have a second look at Bamber Cottage. Detached, it stood in a large garden that would easily house a shed big enough for Fred's business. The house itself was not oversized; between them, they would be able to keep it in decent order. 'It's that quiet, I'll not know what to do with meself,' said Eva. 'No buses, one little shop, the same people every day.'

'If you don't want it, we won't have it,' Fred told her. 'It's your shop that'll be paying for it, so the decision's yours, too.'

'We'd live longer up here,' she said. 'And Agnes is near.'

'She is. She's near and she's bossy.'

Eva laughed. 'She can see straight past you, if that's what you mean. And I'm not going through what she went through – sawdust and paint. You get that shed built before we come. There's no room for your trankle-ments in the house – I don't want to see even one screwdriver. Do you hear?'

'Yes, miss.'

'And I'll want a proper washing line.' In her head, she carried a wonderful picture of snow-white sheets blowing freely against a background of greenery. 'I've never had country-aired clothes. We can plant flowers, too. Is there room for a greenhouse as well? I could grow me own tomatoes.'

Fred smiled. She had made up her mind and they both knew it.

The owner asked whether their mortgage was arranged. Eva, in a moment of pure pleasure, held her head high and her stomach as far in as she could manage without girders. 'We won't be having one of those,' she replied. 'We are already owners of property.'

The owners of property made their offer on the spot and it was accepted. They wandered off in the direction of Skirlaugh Rise, saw the house at the top and paused for thought. 'I'll never get there,' Eva moaned. 'It's too steep. By the time I get to that house, everybody else will be on their way home.'

'Take it slowly,' Fred advised. 'You'll get used to walking more once we live here. And we won't be going to Lambert House every day, will we?' Cars were passing them. 'Shall I thumb a lift?'

Eva shook her head. She was a big woman and there probably wasn't enough room in a normal-sized vehicle. 'No, we'll walk it. If it takes me till Christmas, I'll get there.' At snails' pace, the couple began the ascent to the top of the Rise. Fred wanted to kick himself – if he'd had an ounce of sense, he would have catered for this situation. When they were halfway up, they paused for a rest, though Eva, who was still forced to bear her own weight, got no benefit from stopping.

By the time they reached the front door of Lambert House, she was in a state of total disarray, face damped by sweat, skin reddened from exertion, ankles swollen like a pair of balloons.

Agnes flew to her side and ushered her into a downstairs bathroom. 'Sit,' she ordered, pointing to a wicker chair. She bathed the poor woman's face in cold water, pressed a damp towel against her neck, did her best to straighten Eva's powder blue wedding suit. It took over half an hour to achieve a condition in which Eva was sufficiently composed to join the party.

By that time, war had broken out.

At first, it was easy to keep away from the dreaded man. Helen, as deputy hostess, circulated and made the best she could of her conversational abilities. All the time, she could feel his eyes boring into her flesh, but she kept travelling about the room, since a moving target was reputed to be more difficult to hit. While she had improved in appearance, he had not. He was ungainly, ugly, disgusting. She could not embrace Louisa's theory of thinking about a film star – if this man touched her, she would scream.

The scream was meant to be silent, but it was far from that. When he stopped her for the third time, she eyed him sternly. 'Leave me alone,' she said quietly.

He blinked and swallowed, the protruding Adam's

apple moving like a buried mole beneath a stretch of sun-deadened lawn. Her flesh crawled with a million invisible ants and she stepped away from him. Unfortunately, she reversed into a waitress bearing platters. Food was spattered everywhere and she felt the colour rising in her cheeks. He had done this; why would he not leave her be?

The silliness happened then. She felt very much as she had during the Denis episode – detached from herself, yet deeply disturbed. Anger rose within her. It was a fury too hot to be contained and too strong for the current small crisis. The room disappeared and became silent. She was alone with the balding eagle. He had a great future, terrible skin and a horrible nose. He wanted her to be his biddable wife – grateful, obedient, unquestioning. He wanted to be her father all over again – another great dictator.

As her hand came up to slap his face into eternity, the waitress stopped scrabbling about on the floor, retreating to a safer area. The room became truly silent. Helen's slap, fuelled by emotions for which she would never account, reverberated around the large area. She was alone with him. Echoes from the bad dream bounced around in the caverns of her brain. Helen wasn't anywhere. She simply existed. As did James Taylor.

The man with the great future staggered back, a hand to his reddened cheek.

'Leave me alone,' she shouted. 'I don't want you near me, don't even like you.'

Louisa dashed to Helen's side, but although she tugged on her arm, she remained unnoticed.

'Father chose you for me. He thought I would be grateful. Now, bugger off out of my house and out of my life. My father never got one thing right in his life, but you are the ugliest of the man's mistakes.'

The mist began to clear. As if waking from sleep, Helen looked around at all the people in the room. Something had just happened. A burst of applause drifted through from the hallway where several lawyers had gathered to snort and chortle like honking geese. Why were they clapping? What had she missed?

Zachary arrived at her other side. 'Go to your room,' he snapped.

Helen began to laugh. She wasn't five years old, wasn't a child to be punished. 'No,' she answered clearly. By this time, she knew where she was. Something had happened, and she was at the core of it. What would people think? Did she care?

The gloves were off. Zachary Spencer, feet covered in caviar and face aglow with dismay, did not know what to do. Another ripple of offstage applause disturbed him even further. Who were those invisible chaps? Did they not realize that they were in the house of a judge?

James Taylor turned on his heel and left.

Louisa came to the rescue. 'Helen, there is food on your dress. Come with me and let's see what can be done.'

All the way upstairs, Helen whispered, 'Something happened. What happened? What did I do?' Yet she could only rejoice at the memory of her father's expression of confusion.

In the bedroom she shared with Helen's father, Louisa led her stepdaughter through recent events. 'You told him to bugger off, but you did it very loudly. Some sort of small riot exploded in the hall – your father's enemies were pleased. You blamed your father.'

Helen swallowed. 'I did what?'

'You said he had encouraged Taylor to court you. And you were very loud about the whole business.'

Helen's hands flew up to cover her face. What was happening to her? First, she had pursued the odd-job man; second, she had disgraced herself and her father in front of company. 'My secret world is breaking through,' she muttered. Part of her continued triumphant, yet the idea of being out of control made her panic. It was an attack of panic that had triggered the episode . . .

'What?'

'When I was a child, I lived in my head. That was the secret world. I used to act in front of the mirror and speak my lines out loud. I'm doing it now as an adult and without the mirror. Am I crazy?'

Louisa stared at her friend. She probably was slightly insane after a lifetime spent in the company of a cold father, no mother to soften the impact. 'You're tired,' she replied eventually. 'This event is probably too big for you and I apologize.'

'The room disappeared. The whole party melted away. There was just me and that horrible man. Father will force me to leave now.'

'Don't worry about that, petal. I can manage him, especially now – I'm pregnant.'

Helen blinked several times. This was the moment in which she should begin to hate Louisa and her child. Helen might live in the house for the rest of her life, but a son would inherit everything. 'It has to be a boy,' Helen said.

'I know.'

'Girls get locked in their room. Girls don't count.'

Louisa knew about that, too.

Whatever the situation, Helen could not manage to

hate this woman. For the first time, there was meaning to life, there was fun, there was conversation. 'We'll look after each other, Louisa.'

The pact was made there and then. No matter what happened in the future, Helen and Louisa were a team. There were two of them; there was only one of him. That special cleverness known only to women would need to be employed. Without any word on the subject, each knew that the other disliked Zachary Spencer. United by near-contempt, they intended to thrive in his shadow.

Louisa approached her husband. 'She is raving,' she said. 'If her temperature gets any worse, we must send for the doctor. She scarcely knows what happened, bless her. The fever made her act out of character, my love.'

Bless her? He could have killed her quite cheerfully. 'Did you hear what she said about me? Did you?'

Louisa nodded.

'I cannot allow her to stay under my roof when she slanders me in that fashion.'

His wife walked away and asked the string quartet to stop playing. Then she raised her voice and spoke to the gathering. 'Miss Spencer is not well,' she said. 'She has a fever, so I shall look in on her from time to time. She begs you all to forgive her bad behaviour, but she was not herself this evening. Carry on,' she told the musicians.

Albert and Fred, in a corner as predicted, complained to each other. How much longer would they be forced to listen to the wailing of cats? 'And this bloody collar's strangling me, as well,' moaned Albert.

Fred sympathized. 'They call that music? I'd sooner

'But that's not why I became . . . upset. I seem to have had some sort of episode – I think I've had one or two before. Were you there tonight?'

'No. I arrived late, but I heard about it.'

'I think I forgot where I was and gave James Taylor both barrels. Now, I can remember some of what I said, but I scarcely understood what had happened while I was downstairs. And I insulted my father. He is not a man who takes insults. Louisa is a good woman – she helped me up the stairs and said she'll take care of everything, including him.'

'Hardly a wicked stepmother, then?'

'The opposite. She's kind to me. I feel I have let her down, too. She so desperately wanted this party to be a success. I ruined it for her.'

Mags took Helen's hand. 'Please don't be offended – are you drinking?'

'No. I have scarcely touched a drop since Louisa came. She's fun. I don't want to lose her. He'll send me away, make me live elsewhere. You don't know him . . .' The nightmare knew him. How could she not have realized that the dream contained her father? She remembered few details of the almost nightly torment, yet she knew he was part of the plot.

Mags didn't know what to say. It was suddenly apparent that her own solution to life's problems had proved an easy option; a new nose was not the answer for Helen Spencer. A new nose was easy. It was money and pain, no more. Helen's difficulties were more radical. How might a person acquire a new soul, a centre of self cleaned of scars from the past? How could anyone help in this case?

'I am so miserable, Mags.'

'I know.'

'He's quite nasty without being angry. Once he loses his temper, my father becomes one of Earth's elemental Forces – I swear the sky darkens. He may even be one of the four horsemen come to warn us of the end of the world.'

'Leave home.'

Helen shook her head. She was her father's daughter, and she recognized in herself the stubbornness displayed by him when he was cornered. He was going to have to force her out. Louisa would fight Helen's corner. But why should Louisa be upset, especially in her condition? 'I haven't the backbone to start all over again, Mags. In truth, I don't feel steady enough to live the isolated life.'

'These turns you have – what form do they take?' Mags chided herself inwardly – she sounded like a bloody doctor.

Helen shrugged. 'I am – well – I imagine myself in love with a married man. At the worst point in that scenario, I chased him, told him I loved him – I was all over the place. Tonight? Oh, I don't know.' Tonight had been much, much worse, because a piece of the bad dream had broken through. 'There was a noise,' she whispered. The noise had been a part of the dream. 'I don't know,' she repeated.

'Yes, you do,' Mags urged gently. 'Tell me. The noise was a waitress dropping plates and trays. Why did you turn on the balding eagle?'

After taking a deep breath, Helen relived all she remembered of her real world. She spoke of phone calls, of persistence, of politeness. 'After half a dozen refusals, any man should accept that a woman isn't interested. Tonight was his big chance – or so he believed.'

'And?'

'And he collared me. I avoided him successfully for well over half an hour, but he would not be denied. Then it happened.'

Mags waited.

'It was as if I were alone with him after the noise happened. I knew my father had chosen him for me, because he told me so at that wedding. James Taylor almost became my father tonight. He was yet another piece of damage inflicted by a man who has never forgiven me for being female. There are many witnesses to the rest of it. I screamed at him and I think I hit him. The thought of hitting him makes me sick, because I can't stand the idea of any physical contact with him. It isn't just his appearance. Inside, he's a damaged person – it takes one to know one. He bolsters himself, brags about a big future. He is his own favourite topic and that's my father all over again.'

Mags stroked Helen's hand.

'My biggest fear is that I, too, am my father all over again. I am so angry, Mags. Anger is all that sustains me. The only time I get anywhere near happiness is when I am with Louisa. If I lose control, then I lose everything. My small amount of control is all I have and I can't afford to have it disappear.'

'Helen?'

'What?'

'You need other friends close at hand.'

'There is no one.'

'But there is someone. There's Agnes. She is the best and most loyal person you could wish to meet. She's funny, clever, supportive and just at the bottom of the Rise.'

Helen dropped her chin. How could she be a friend

to someone whose husband she had tried to seduce? She continued to want Denis, although the feelings for him no longer consumed her. 'I don't know.'

'Think about it. You could do a lot worse than Agnes Makepeace. She hasn't had it easy, you know. Her mother died when Agnes was born, so the grandparents raised her. When they got old, she looked after them. Her nan died of cancer, her granddad is a handful – she nursed him after a stroke – yet Agnes manages to see the best in life. We're all hurt, Helen. A person would need the hide of a rhino to get through this world without pain.'

'I'll think about it.'

Forced to be content with a half-promise, Mags left Helen to her own devices. Descending the staircase deep in thought, she decided that Helen was probably ill. The self-effacing librarian had been kept down for too long, and the inner woman was fighting for her place in the world. It was understandable; it was also rather unnerving, because Helen was not thinking in a straight enough line.

Agnes joined her at the bottom of the stairs. 'Is she all right? I still can't get over how brilliant you look.'

'She needs a doctor. A head doctor. That bloody father of hers has messed her up to the point where she doesn't cope with life at all. Agnes, I want you to help her.'

Agnes swallowed. 'That's all I need. Thanks a lot, mate. If she needs a psychiatrist, what the hell can I do?'

'You can listen.'

Agnes thought about that. The woman upstairs had recently made a beeline for Denis. Denis worked at Lambert House – must Lambert House claim an even bigger portion of his life? There was a baby coming,

Pop and Eva would move into the village soon, and Denis had had quite enough of Miss Helen Spencer. Agnes decided to hang for the full sheep – Denis would understand. 'She's been making passes at my husband, Mags.'

'Ah.'

'What do you mean by "ah"? She's more than three sheets to the wind, is that one. Glenys Timpson heard her trying to get off with Denis – and you want me to help the damned woman? Not on your flaming nelly.'

'Agnes—'

'Sorry, love. She was walking round in a nightdress for days, windows wide open, playing the music he loves. He's fond of her, feels sorry for her, but she wanted more. A bloody sight more.'

'She can't help it, Agnes.'

'Can't she?'

'No.'

'Well, I can help it. I can help her stay away from my husband. You're asking too much of me, Mags.'

'She's aware that she's done wrong, but she's . . . Oh, I don't know. It's like she's two different people. Something triggers her and she changes. Take tonight. She lost herself. I can't explain it, but she becomes something else and all hell lets loose in her head. It's that bugger's fault.' She inclined her head in the direction of their host. 'Helen was born a girl, and to him that's unforgivable. He's a nasty creature.'

The nasty creature led his new wife into the office. Determined to be careful because of her condition, he sat her down before beginning his homily. Helen had never shown him any respect. He had supported her, sheltered, educated and housed her, but he had never received any thanks.

'All children take their parents for granted,' came her swift response. 'Every father in the world would agree with you, darling. But you must not throw her out. She is too frail to become a wanderer. Let me deal with it.'

He carried on passing sentence. His daughter had always been wilful and difficult. She had taken poor advantage of her education and was content to follow the lazy path via the library. She never spoke to him. She made up stories about other lawyers and how they hated him.

Louisa kept a poker face during this section of the monologue. The cheers in support of Helen still echoed in her mind; this was, indeed, a much despised man.

With fat fingers gripping lapels, he strutted up and down like the great prosecuting counsel trying to convince a jury. While she was the jury, Louisa would never be won over. 'She's lonely.'

'Her own fault,' he boomed. 'There's a perfectly decent and successful man chasing her, but is she satisfied? No, she is not.'

'She's lonely for friends, not for a husband.'

'Then she should make friends. God knows she meets enough people in her silly little job.'

Louisa groaned inwardly. Were it not for the likes of Helen Spencer, literature would be available only to the precious few. It was not a silly little job – it was a vital service. He rambled on, warming to his subject with every inch of the carpet he threatened to render threadbare.

She rose to her feet. 'I have no wish to be contentious, sweetheart, but if Helen is forced to leave this house, I shall have to accompany her and stay with her until she is settled. She is unwell.'

'What?' he roared. Had he made another huge mistake? Was this one going to be like the first wife, a moaner and a bolter? Not that the first had actually left, but she had threatened . . .

'She's in a state, Zach. She doesn't know whether she's coming or going – it's a nervous condition.'

'My family doesn't have nervous conditions.' He banged a fist on the desk. 'If she has a nervous illness, it's from her witch of a mother. Does she need to go into an asylum?'

'No.' Not yet, Louisa said inwardly. But if Helen ever did need a hospital, he would be the cause of it. It would be easy to dislike him. But she remembered the keywords – safety and wealth. 'A move might well destroy her. She would have nowhere to turn.'

'If she went into a mental hospital, it might quieten my colleagues in the wake of tonight's fiasco.'

'She hates the man,' said Louisa.

'Who is she to pick and choose?'

'She's human, not an animal to be mated with a chosen sire.'

Zachary Spencer glared at his wife. She was a good wife. She had never refused him, had never rejected him. The bad apple in this house was the one upstairs. 'I am not pleased with you, Louisa,' he said.

'I know and I am sorry. But that woman is your flesh and blood. She needs help and I will not turn my back on her. I look at her and I see you. To send her away would be unbearably cruel, and that is why I would have to go with her and help her to settle.'

His shoulders sagged, reminding her of a balloon

with the air escaping. She supposed that she was seeing a fair illustration of the saying about wind being taken from sails. No longer a galleon, he dropped into his leather chair. 'As you wish,' he said behind gritted teeth. 'But one more episode and she goes. I don't care where she goes, but I will not allow a madwoman to share a house with my son.'

Louisa nodded. She was an incubator, no more than that.

After escaping from the lion's den, Louisa fled upstairs to comfort her stepdaughter with the news.

But Helen astonished her. 'I think I want to leave,' she said.

'Helen – I have just been through hell and high water to—'

'I know, and I love you for it. But there are cottages in the village. I'd still be near you. You could visit me and I could come here while he's out. If he goes away, I'll stay with you.'

The idea of being alone with Zachary Spencer was not palatable. Panic seared through Louisa's body. She had known all along that Helen needed her; she now realized that the reverse was also true. 'Think before you act,' she advised.

'I will. Yes, I definitely will.'

'He's not been a good father, Helen. Some people are not cut out for parenthood.'

'He would have been good to a son.'

'Would he?'

The two women stared at each other. Had their relationship required a further application of cement, it would have arrived in this moment. The reject and the breeding machine were completely bound together.

'Cocoa?' asked Louisa.

'Yes, please. Louisa?'

'What?'

'Thanks. You are good to me.'

Louisa smiled and left the room. Life was not going to be easy in this house. The least troublesome option would have been to allow him his way, but Louisa feared for her stepdaughter. Helen needed a friend. As long as Louisa remained alive, she would have one.

Chapter Eight

Denis, a man of even temperament, slammed the front door.

Agnes ran through from the kitchen, a journey that required no more than four paces. 'Are you all right, love?'

Was he all right? Was he heck as all right. 'Put that kettle on, Agnes. It's been a foul weather day and there'll be more to come.' He threw down his canvas work bag and dropped into a chair. Anyone who knew Denis Makepeace was of the opinion that he was not easily riled; when he did lose his patience, the results could be almost meteorological.

Agnes did as she was asked, her eyes scanning a bright blue sky with just a few cotton wool clouds decorating its surface. There had been no rain and no thunder, but there had been Judge Zachary Spencer trying to save face after that disastrous party. Never a pleasant man, he had probably given her beloved husband one hell of a time. Poor Denis deserved better than this.

He took the tea. 'Thanks,' he sighed. 'Let me have ten minutes, then I'll tell you. My brain's all over the place.' He shook his head. 'Sometimes, I wonder whether there's any sanity left in this world.'

His head spun. Helen had paced through the day like a caged tiger, back and forth across lawns, round the outside of the house, in and out of the copse. She had popped up all over the place. Sometimes, he had wondered whether an identical twin had escaped from one of the attics. Officially, she had a summer cold and could not get in to work. In truth, she was a mixture of fear and fury, was every inch the caged wild animal.

Wife the Second was in a state, too. She had spent her day running between the judge and his daughter, clearly attempting to negotiate a treaty with more clauses than Utrecht. 'Bloody madhouse,' whispered Denis between sips of strong tea. 'They want their flaming daft heads knocking together.' But he couldn't be the one to do it. No one emerged unscathed from a confrontation with Judge Zachary Spencer.

It seemed that Helen Spencer had threatened to rent one of the Skirlaugh Fall cottages, an event that would surely unseat her dad. He probably wanted her well out of the way while he prepared his kingdom for a son and heir; the village was not far enough. The judge didn't want her on his doorstep, couldn't stand the idea of close neighbours accusing him of throwing his daughter out of Lambert House. Pride came before a fall? Had that been the case, the judge should have no intact bones in his whole body, because he had pride enough for ten.

The most panic-stricken of them all had been Louisa. On the odd occasion when Denis had got close to her, he had seen terror in her face. She was frightened of being alone with the old man. The judge's daughter had clearly proved to be a distraction for Louisa, and she dreaded losing the balm provided by this unexpected friendship. Denis, caught in the middle of hostilities, had washed cars, swept paths, weeded gardens. No one had spoken directly to him. Helen was possibly seeking to reinstate the necessary distance between employer and employee, a move for which Denis would be grateful beyond measure. As the day had matured, so had she. The walking had stopped and she had returned to the house.

Agnes sat down. 'Well?'

He sighed heavily. 'Just after dinner – lunch to that lot up yon – I was passing his office window with my wheelbarrow. The window was wide open. The boss was yelling like a madman. He was screaming at Helen, asking her why she wanted him to go easy on Harry Timpson. She gave him an answer, all right. She said, "Because I can" – just came out with it. I don't think she's even scared of you finding out about what never happened – she's well past that now. So she's doing it for devilment. Come to think, she's well past everything. She doesn't care – opens her gob without thinking first.'

Kate knocked and entered. 'Blood and stomach pills,' was her opening salvo, 'they want shooting, the lot of 'em. Miss Helen's riding high, told him he's made her ill, even invited him to bugger off and die. I'm surprised, because it looked like she was going out of her way to be nice to him for a while. Mrs Spencer can't cope – she'll be losing the kiddy if this carries on. I feel like packing it in, Denis. How was your day?'

'The same,' he answered.

Kate complained of untouched meals returning to the kitchen, said she had enough to feed Albert and herself for three days. She continued to moan, citing the noisiness and stupidity of her employers. 'It's a lunatic asylum, that's what. Miss Helen's off her rocker, her

enough. Stay. Eat his food, use his furniture, let him pay all the bills.'

There followed a long pause before Helen responded. 'If he wants me not to move down the hill to sit on his doorstep like a boil on his nose, he must do one thing.' The one thing was no longer anything to do with Glenys Timpson or the Makepeaces – she was beyond such trivia – but simply to prove her power. 'I want a featherweight sentence for Harry Timpson.' The Timpson man had become a loaded gun for Helen. She needed to prove that she could encroach on her father's territory and even get her own way.

'Then you'll need to stay until after the trial.'

'Yes.'

With that, Louisa was forced to be content. Unhappily, she now faced the prospect of persuading her husband to go easy on a criminal. But she would try. If it meant that Helen would stay, Louisa would attempt the apparently impossible.

It was mayhem. Agnes, standing in the middle of it all, remembered reading about people throwing up their hands in despair, but it was too hot and she couldn't spare the energy. 'It's not a big house, Pop,' she said for the third time.

'Not a big house, love,' echoed Eva.

'I know it's detached and I know there's land, but you'd never get this lot in ten big sheds. I mean, what do you want with half a dozen paraffin heaters? Haven't you sold them on as stock, anyway? What are you planning?'

Fred sighed. 'The new owner of this here shop's

already minted. He won't miss a few heaters. I'll have to warm the shed, won't I? I can't risk good wood going dampish.'

Eva and Agnes stared at each other with near-despair in their eyes. Fred was in one of his squirrel moods and wanted to keep more than he could house. 'I'm going to see Glenys,' snapped Agnes. 'Because if I stay here, I'll wrap these bloody heaters round his neck.' She left the scene. Fred was stubborn, but so was she – it was best for them to be apart for the immediate future.

Glenys opened her door. 'Hello, love,' she said. 'You look like you need a wipe down with a damp cloth.' They sat in the kitchen. 'How's it going?'

Agnes told her ex-neighbour about developments at Lambert House, about Helen's continuing strangeness, about Wife the Second walking about with a face like ten wet Sundays. 'She's not happy.'

'Neither am I.'

Both knew the source of Glenys's unease, but the subject had been aired so often in recent months that it was beyond resurrection.

'It'll be all right,' said Agnes.

'I bloody well hope so.'

They sat with their cups, Agnes musing over her little job at Lambert House, Glenys praying silently for a son who probably didn't deserve to remain free.

'Kate Moores is good company,' offered Agnes to break the quiet.

'And the job gets you out. Are them two moving today?' She jerked her head in the direction of Eva's shop. 'I've seen some comings and goings. I'll miss them, you know.'

'Yes, it's today. That's why I'm here – I've escaped

from the shop. They're trying to get a whale to fit into a sardine tin. The stuff for his shed's already gone, but nobody will ever get past the vestibule in Bamber Cottage if he takes all he wants to take. I mean, who needs four clothes horses?'

'I wouldn't say no.' Glenys poured more tea. 'Have they not measured the house, then measured their furniture?'

'Have they heck as like. He's going off half-cocked as usual. And we can't blame his stroke – he's always been like this. Eva just agrees with everything he says, so she's as daft as he is. They'll never get up the stairs to bed tonight. Fully furnished? They'll be bursting at the seams and Denis will have to sort it all out.'

'I wish I could live up yon,' ventured Glenys.

'Stop where you are, that's my advice. You'd end up working at Lambert House – they can't get enough staff – and that would be a sure and certain way to insanity. I'm only there twice a week and that's plenty.' She replayed in her mind the slamming of doors, the grim atmosphere, the expression on Kate's face whenever the judge came home. 'None of them is happy. Miss Spencer has a face like a squeezed orange most days – nothing left in it, just a dry shell. Denis reckons she's heading straight for the mental hospital. I think he's right – she's not the same two days running. She talks to me, then ignores me. There's something very wrong with her.'

'That's a shame,' said Glenys. 'My Harry thinks the sun shines out of her, but we'd best wait for verdict and sentence, eh?'

Agnes agreed, then left to continue in her role as ignored supervisor.

Fred glanced at her. 'I'm taking two of them heaters.'

213

The tone was rebellious, putting her in mind of a young schoolboy after a telling-off. 'You never know – we could get a bad winter,' he added.

'Aye, a bad winter,' repeated Eva.

Agnes was past caring. They could leave their furniture on the front lawn if necessary, because he wouldn't listen to reason and, as ever, he needed to learn the hard way. 'I'm going for the bus,' she said, 'because I'm doing no good here. I'll get a bit of shopping in town, then I'll see you up yonder later on. God help Skirlaugh Fall. You'll be parking half your furniture with the neighbours and they won't be best pleased.'

Gratefully, Agnes sank into a seat on the Derby Street bus. Normally, she would have walked the short distance, but heat, pregnancy and Pop were against her. His furniture was stacked against the front of the shop, and it would shortly be stacked yet again all over the garden of Bamber Cottage, but she had tried her best.

After alighting from the bus, Agnes made her way towards the main shopping centre. Rounding a corner, she came face to face with a familiar figure, and she stopped in her tracks. She had taken a job in order to meet and help this woman but had scarcely seen her in the house, and now here was Helen Spencer, out of context and turning pink. 'It's warm,' Agnes said, inwardly kicking herself for stating the blatantly obvious.

'It is.'

'I was just going for a cup of tea,' lied Agnes. 'Would you like to join me?'

So Helen found herself in the company of a not-quite-rival. Already aware that she had never stood a chance with Denis, she now drank tea with his beautiful, pregnant wife.

'You are working at the house occasionally,' she said.

Agnes nodded. 'Mostly sitting down jobs. It's just to keep me occupied till Nuisance is born.' She patted her abdomen. 'I can't do much, but the work gets me out of the house a couple of times a week.'

Helen asked Agnes where she had been.

When the tale had been told, both women were laughing. 'What's going to happen?' Helen asked. 'And how will they cope?'

Agnes shook her head. 'I did my best, but my best wasn't good enough. They're bringing enough blankets to keep the Russian army warm and I never saw so many plates and cups.'

'And the shed?'

'That's for making his doll's houses in.' Agnes noticed that Helen's laughter was shrill, too loud. It came from a woman who probably cried just as easily. Did Helen Spencer live on the cusp, somewhere between hysteria and silent sadness? Did she swing from one to the other easily, because the two extremes were close neighbours? 'I'll have to be getting back. Somebody's going to have to make sense of the mess.'

Helen declared that she had finished for today, as the library was closed this afternoon. 'I'll give you a lift,' she said.

The lift developed into more cups of tea at Agnes's house, followed by the inevitable assault on Bamber Cottage and its soon-to-be occupants. For the first time, Helen had a glimpse of a normal family with its banter, small arguments and jokes. On her part, Agnes realized that Helen Spencer was a clever and humorous woman who was not insane. She was probably emotionally unstable, but she was not out of her mind.

By five o'clock, everyone was exhausted. Between

215

items of furniture, a small corridor to the kitchen had been achieved, but Eva was not built for small corridors. Agnes, hands on hips, stood in the kitchen doorway. 'You'll have to choose,' she advised her grandfather. 'It's you and Eva, or all the furniture. Get a tent. The weather's good, so you'll be all right in the back garden.'

Eva glanced from Fred to Agnes, then to Miss Spencer. Denis arrived, providing a fourth resting place for Eva's eyes. 'We don't know what to do,' she wailed. 'I can't get nowhere.'

'House is too small,' grumbled Fred.

'It's the same size as it always was.' Denis kept an eye on Helen Spencer. He still felt uncomfortable in her presence, but Agnes had stated her intention of helping the woman, so he had to accept that decision.

At the end of more lengthy discussions, Helen provided an answer. 'This won't do,' she declared unnecessarily. 'It won't go away, will it? There's far too much furniture to fit into a place of this size. You need to decide quickly what stays and what goes.'

Fred didn't want to part with anything of Eva's, but even he was forced to see sense in the end. 'Aye, we'll have to do something. We'll not fit a size nine foot into a size seven shoe.'

Agnes set the kettle to boil yet again. She felt as if she had been running a cafe all day. From the cluttered kitchen, she listened to Helen Spencer laying down the law. The woman was enjoying herself. All she wanted was to feel needed, to be part of a family, to be loved and respected. Agnes dashed a tear from her cheek; she had been lucky. Like Helen, she had lost a mother. Unlike Helen, she had been raised by grandparents in a caring environment. Money wasn't up to much, she thought as she poured tea. Money could not buy happiness for Miss Helen Spencer.

When the great plan had been finalized, Helen and Denis left together in order to begin the first phase. In Helen's car, they drove out to a farm and persuaded the tenant to bring horse and flat cart into the village. As they drove back to Bamber Cottage, Helen spoke. 'I'm sorry for what I put you through, Denis. Your wife's a lovely woman.'

'It's all right.'

She nodded. He had a generous nature and she was grateful for it. 'There's something wrong with me,' she continued. 'It's not madness. Sometimes, I lose control, but there's a reason. I have to find the reason.'

'I see.'

She smiled. 'No, you don't. I have a memory that I can't reach. It must be something that happened before I got to the age of reason. Whatever it was, it terrified me and has remained all through life. It's not diminished by the years, yet I seem no nearer to remembering what it is. I get panic attacks. They come from nowhere, yet there's something ... There's a big happening lodged somewhere in my brain and I can't get a hold on it.'

'Then how do you know it's there?'

'Because it's bigger than me, bigger than him, bigger than Lambert House.' She had no need to name the 'him'. 'Louisa has brought it back. Until Louisa, I thought I was just a quiet, uninteresting sort of person. But since she has been with us, I have come to realize that there is more to it than just that. There was a woman in my life thirty years ago.'

'Your mother?'

Helen nodded. 'And now, we have her replacement.

She's a trigger. And I like her. I like her very much. She may be a gold-digger, but she's not harsh, not unkind, not completely selfish. Louisa noticed me and is pleased to have me there. My mother was probably glad to have me there. So Louisa has taken me back to a place and a time where I was safe and happy. Because of that, the memory of whatever it was is digging at me, prompting me. I thank God for Louisa.'

'She probably reminds you of the mother you lost.'

'It's not so simple, but it is something like that, yes.'

With that, Denis had to be content.

They reached Bamber Cottage to find Agnes and Fred in another heated exchange. Helen looked at Denis and he looked at her. In that moment, both realized that the recent past could be laid to rest. They were good friends, and both felt comfortable about it.

Agnes was in full flood. 'I know what you're saying – I'm not deaf and I'm not daft. You've told me so often that it's probably printed through me like a stick of Blackpool rock. Eva makes your curtains. Yes, she needs her sewing machine and no, it can't stay down here. The spare bedroom can still be a bedroom – we can put the Singer in a corner.'

'That means she'll have to go upstairs to work. She can't do stairs all the while.'

'I can.'

Fred and Agnes turned and stared at Eva. Not since the wedding had she disagreed with her husband. She was of the generation that recognized the superiority of mankind over womankind, but she was putting her foot down with all her twenty stones behind it.

'Put it upstairs,' Eva said.

'Bloody women,' Fred cursed.

There followed an uneasy couple of hours during

which Fred and Eva were separated from half their worldly goods. Although Fred fought right down to the last picture of the Sacred Heart, he was forced to see sense. When the cart pulled away, the Grimshaws had a house in which it would be possible to live and move in a normal fashion.

Eva made the final cup of tea.

'Are them cellars dry?' asked Fred.

'Very,' replied Helen. 'The boiler's down there. It's a big one, because it heats a big house. Stop worrying, please, Mr Grimshaw. If you find you need something, it will be no trouble to have the item returned to you.'

Fred gulped a mouthful of hot tea. He studied Miss Helen Spencer. 'You're all right, you are,' was his stated opinion. 'Feel free to drop in for a cuppa whenever you've a mind.' He looked at Denis and Agnes. 'See? Not all rich folk are toffee-nosed.'

Helen Spencer went home a happier woman. Knowing that Louisa, the Makepeaces and the Grimshaws were her friends, she felt almost capable of coping.

Agnes phoned her two friends from the newly installed telephone in her cottage. Only if she canvassed their opinions could she make any changes to arrangements. 'Isn't she crackers?' was Lucy's typically direct response.

'She's lonely.' The line crackled while Agnes waited. 'Are you there, Lucy?'

'I'm here. Look, don't tell her it's a regular thing. If we don't get on, we can go back to the way it was before.'

Mags too agreed to the temporary admittance of Helen Spencer to their Thursday meetings. Agnes replaced the receiver, wondering whether she had done the right thing. She, Lucy and Mags had a long history and shared common ground, but Miss Spencer was very much the outsider. Would their evenings be spoiled? 'Somebody has to help her,' she told herself out loud. Agnes was no psychologist and no expert in any field connected to the behaviour of her fellows, but she knew need when it hit her in the face. Helen Spencer was needful and Agnes was there to help.

When Thursday arrived, she made a few scones and cakes, found Mags's favourite parkin at the shop, put crisps in a bowl for Lucy. Unsure of Helen's preferences, she threw together a few thinly cut sandwiches, removed the crusts and hoped for the best.

Lucy arrived in fine fettle. She and her new husband were selling their bungalow and buying a barn just a few miles from Agnes's house. 'It's huge,' she crowed. 'We can have visitors to stay and there's loads of land.' She paused. 'Where's Helen Wotsername?'

'Coming.'

'Remember the fit she threw at the party? Everybody in the legal community talked about it for weeks.'

'Then they'll be leaving some other poor soul out of the gossip while they deal with her.'

'What's the matter, Agnes?' Lucy sank into a chair. 'It seems ages since I saw you and you're in a mood.'

Agnes told the tale of the move to Bamber Cottage. 'It was hell,' she concluded. 'Hot day, pregnant, Pop on one of his hobby horses, Eva too big to get past the furniture – it was a farce. Helen Spencer sorted it.'

'Ah.'

Agnes dropped into the chair opposite her friend's. 'There's a terrible sadness in her. She spoke to Denis and he says she thinks it's something that happened, but she was too young to remember it. What's more, she seems to believe it was something too bad for a young child to cope with, so it's in a parcel at the back of her head.'

'Well, let's hope it's not in the lost property department at the post office.'

'It's not funny, Lucy. She's got a terrible life.'

Mags arrived. The other two were repeating their approval of her new face when Helen knocked.

'Come in,' said Agnes. 'Denis is at the pub with Pop. I don't know who to feel sorry for – Denis or the landlord.'

They settled into seats, picked at food, drank tea.

'I'm grateful to you,' Agnes told Helen. 'Goodness knows what we would have done without you.'

'Oh, it's nothing. We've huge cellars and Father's wines take up a very small part. I thought your grandfather was very amusing.'

Agnes snorted. 'You can say that when you've lived with him for twenty years. I love him to bits, but he would make a saint swear. Nan could manage him – she just gave him a certain look when he went too far. I've borrowed Nan's selection of looks, but he doesn't take much notice of me. Thank God he's over the stroke. If it wasn't for his funny walk, you'd hardly know he'd suffered. Now, everybody else suffers. Since he was on that Granada programme, he's decided he's in charge. Honestly, he couldn't run a bath, let alone a business. Thank God again for Eva's acumen – and Pop's near enough to us now, of course.'

A small silence hung over the room.

'I know,' said Mags eventually. 'It's a lovely evening – why don't we go for a walk?'

They left the house in two pairs, Lucy with Agnes,

Mags with Helen. At the top of the main street, Agnes got one of her ideas. She pointed to the pub. 'Let's go in.'

Helen looked at Mags. 'I've never been in a pub before.'

'Time you got educated, then,' Mags answered before grabbing her companion's arm and following the other two into the Farmer's Arms. 'You'll enjoy it,' Mags promised.

Denis and Pop were playing darts. The pub was about half full, and many of its occupants became silent on seeing Helen Spencer in their midst. Agnes marched up to her husband and her grandfather. 'Three teams,' she said. 'Two in each. You and Denis, me and Lucy, Helen and Mags. Lowest scorers buy the drinks.'

'I never played darts before, either,' Helen whispered to Mags.

'Just pretend the board's your dad. Don't kill any customers and watch Denis – he's silent but deadly when it comes to darts.'

It was a hilarious evening. Nobody died and Helen managed to hit the board on most occasions. There was a small contretemps when Fred was accused of overstepping the line before throwing, but all ended well. Mags and Helen, the losers, bought the drinks, then they all crowded round a table and argued about the game.

'I haven't had much experience,' said Mags.

'I've had none,' added Helen.

Fred guffawed and declared that darts was a game just for men. Agnes battered him about the head with his cap, Fred complained of ill-treatment by his own granddaughter, Lucy pretended to smile. There was in Lucy a reluctance to accept Helen Spencer, Agnes thought. Helen was older than the others, was quieter and less easily drawn into fun. But Agnes liked her. In spite of the Denis business, in spite of her reticence, the woman was all right in Agnes's book.

The women left the men to their drinking, Lucy driving Mags homeward as soon as they reached the Makepeace cottage. It was sad, Agnes thought, that Lucy could not even try to accept the new addition to their group. After waving off her friends, Agnes took Helen into the house. 'That's the last time I play darts in heat like this,' she declared.

Helen smiled in agreement. She felt strangely comfortable in the company of Denis's wife. She had expected Mags Bradshaw to be a closer friend, but there was in Agnes a dependable and supportive nature that was much admired by Helen. Agnes knew how to join in, where and when to have fun, how to speak up for herself. There was no fear in Mrs Makepeace, but there was respect for all around her.

'Do you like living here?' Helen asked.

'I do. We both do. I don't know how we'll go on with Pop so near – he's a caution. I love him dearly, but he can stretch my patience from here to Manchester and back. It's even worse since his stroke. I always knew we'd get him well again, because he'd the devil in his eyes even when he was flat out and unable to speak. He's the same, but different. Everything has to be done now and in a great hurry.'

'That's because he's looked Death in the face,' said Helen.

'Maybe.' Agnes sighed. 'If he carries on as he is, he'll die a rich man. There's a long queue for his houses and he's branching out into bigger things, Lord help us.'

'Oh? What's he doing?'

'Play houses for back gardens – Wendy houses, I

think they're called. Eva just says yes to everything he suggests. Meanwhile, the grass at the back of his house is dying, because he has bigger pieces of wood for the outside houses and he covers them in tarpaulin.'

'Oh, dear.'

'Yes. Eva's not been married to him for more than a few weeks and she's under his thumb already.'

Helen nodded thoughtfully. 'He must have a big thumb.'

Agnes laughed heartily. 'He likes large women. Nan was big till near the end. He says a big woman's the best hot water bottle available to man.'

Helen stared through the window at a darkening sky. 'You are so lucky, Agnes.'

'I know.'

'You love people.'

'Not all people.'

'But you approach them with an open mind and heart. I am ... closed down, I suppose.'

'Your father.' This, from Agnes, was not a question.

'Yes. Lately, though, I have changed. In a sense, I appear to have woken up, yet in another I seem to be grabbing a childhood I never had. Control slips away from me at times.'

'Yes, I saw that at the party.'

Helen told the tale of the wedding reception, including the part played by Denis. 'I've stopped drinking,' she said. 'The expression on your husband's face on seeing me drunk would have stopped a bull smashing a gate.'

Agnes could almost taste the woman's misery. She wanted to jump up and shake her, wanted to drag her away from Lambert House and the man who had spoiled her life, but it wasn't her place. 'I'm always here, Helen,' she said. 'When it gets too much, come to me. Don't suffer by yourself, because you do have friends.'

Helen turned her head slowly and faced Agnes. 'There's Louisa. Louisa is the reason I am staying.'

'She married him with her eyes open,' said Agnes.

Helen nodded. 'The sighted make as many mistakes as the blind. She knows now that she is just an incubator. He wants a son.'

'Yes, Denis said.'

'Once he has his son, Louisa will be of no further use.'

Agnes wished that her visitor would cry, but it was clear that some of the hurt went beyond tears. No one liked Judge Spencer, and his daughter had travelled past dislike and was walking alongside hatred where her father was concerned. 'I'm sorry.'

'I've lived for over thirty years with my father, Agnes. Yet it's as if I was born again just recently. There's something . . .'

'What?'

'Just something. Tell me, Agnes – what's your earliest memory?'

Agnes pondered. 'I remember sitting outside the house – presumably in a pram. And being held over a tin bath in front of the fire while my hair was rinsed – I remember that. Don't know how old I was.'

Helen bit her lip. 'I have a not-quite memory. It's similar to a dream that's forgotten the instant you wake. Sometimes, I grab the edge of it, but it unravels like a badly knitted sleeve as soon as I try to concentrate. There was noise. I do know there was a great deal of unusual noise.'

'And then?'

'Nothing.' Helen looked down at her folded hands. 'Like Louisa, you make me feel better. Almost normal.'

'You are normal.'

'Am I? Is it normal to imagine yourself in love with a married man? Or to stand in the middle of a social gathering and decry the host – my own father? Is it normal for all those people at the party to disappear from my sight and slip beyond hearing while I have a tantrum worthy of a two-year-old?'

'You are not mad,' Agnes insisted. 'You are damaged. I know he's a tartar. I've seen and heard him for myself. Kate Moores, too, knows that life hasn't been easy for you – so does my Denis. Helen, look at me. I'll be here, Denis'll be here, Kate and Albert will be here – even my Pop and Eva will be here. You know where to run.'

'Thank you.' At last, the tears flowed.

Agnes, hanging on tightly to the tense body of Miss Helen Spencer, wondered whether she had bitten off more than she could chew. This lady had more than a chip on her shoulder – she carried a whole yard of lumber. What on earth had happened to reduce Helen to this? Why had she no friends and why didn't her father love her? And could Agnes be what Helen needed? Was a special doctor required?

Helen straightened. 'Thank you,' she said. 'I like you.'

'And I like you. Look after that stepmother of yours, but come to us if it all gets too much. We'll be here. We may not have much, but you're welcome any time.'

When Helen had left, Agnes sat very still in a chair by the window. Dusk was falling fast, but she didn't bother with any lighting. In her heart, she walked every weary and unwilling step of Helen Spencer's homeward journey. 'I'll do what I can,' she swore aloud. 'I'll try to make a difference.' Nan had always said that life was about making a difference, preferably for the better. Wisdom from the mouths of the uneducated was often raw and special. 'I'll try, Nan,' she repeated. Helen Spencer needed saving. She deserved to be saved.

Denis arrived home with Fred in tow and began to make cocoa. Pop was enthusing about his Wendy houses while Denis was quieter than usual. He left the older man to heat milk while he sat with Agnes. When he asked why she had been sitting in the dark, she replied, 'Helen Spencer lives in darkness, love. She thinks she's mad, but I think she isn't.'

'When did you pass doctor exams, sweetheart?'

She shrugged. 'She's not mad, Denis. I need to do something and I'll start with Kate.'

'You what?'

'There has to be somebody still alive who knew the judge and his first wife. They had more servants then. Whatever's in her head wants finding. Until she can get it out, she'll not cope. While she's not coping, she'll give her dad loads of excuses to lock her up. She'll not get better till she gets to the bottom of whatever it is.'

Denis swallowed. 'He won't go that far, will he? Locking her up, I mean. Madness in the family would reflect on him.'

But Agnes suspected that Judge Spencer would go to any lengths to rid himself of his difficult daughter. It would be relatively easy to lie, to say that Helen had gone abroad for a rest cure or was on an extended holiday in Europe. 'Judge Spencer will find a way to get what he wants. You know that, Denis.'

Fred entered. 'Nowt wrong with that lass except for the man who fathered her. She's nowhere near mad. I

227

know what happened at the wedding and at the house party – I'm not as deaf or as daft as some folk want to believe. Helen Spencer's a gradely lass. You do right, our Agnes. Find out what you can, but don't get wore out. I don't want owt happening to that great-grand-child of mine.'

The back door rattled. Sighing, Agnes went into the kitchen. The miscreant had visited three times in one week, and Agnes was in several minds. 'Stay sitting down, or you'll be knocked over,' she ordered her menfolk before opening the door.

Louisa Spencer's puppy, Oscar, shot in like a furry missile from a powerful cannon. He jumped first on Fred, then on Denis, before launching himself at the woman of the house. A long-haired Alsatian, Oscar had a happy temperament and a bottomless appetite. He knew already that women meant food, so he concen-trated on the female of this malleable species.

'Going to be a big bugger,' commented Fred after managing to save his cocoa. 'Feet like dinner plates.'

Denis simply laughed. When he was working, the dog was a companion, following him from garden to garden, task to task. Unfortunately, the animal knew little of the differences between weeds and legal resi-dents of a garden, so Denis's life had taken on a new interest.

'Here.' Agnes threw a bone and the dog pounced on it. He settled in front of an empty grate and began to gnaw.

'He likes you,' Fred told Agnes.

'He likes her because she's soft,' Denis said. 'He hates the judge. The feeling's mutual – Judge Spencer would shoot the poor dog if he could get away with it.

Found a hair on his jacket on Tuesday. It had come off that tatty wig, I bet, but he insisted it was Oscar's fault. As far as I can see, Oscar has no white hair.'

'Animals have good taste,' Fred declared. 'No decent dog ever liked a bad human. Yon Oscar likely had the judge summed up in ten minutes flat.' He took a sip of cocoa. 'Hitler had dogs like that one,' he mumbled sleepily.

'Go home before you drop off,' advised Denis. 'Eva will be wondering where you are.'

Fred stood up, said his goodbyes and left the house.

Denis and Agnes stared at the dog. 'He'll have to go home,' Agnes said. 'If Louisa misses him, she might get upset.'

Denis found a length of rope and tied it to the puppy's collar. 'I'll come,' said Agnes. 'It's best if I exercise while I still can.'

They set off with dog and bone in the direction of Skirlaugh Rise. Oscar carried his meal proudly, wore the air of the triumphant hunter bringing back his kill. When they neared the house, the dog stopped, placed his bone on the ground and growled deep in his throat. A plume of smoke rising from a small circle of red advertised the judge's presence. He was having a final cigar before bedtime. Denis urged the dog onward, but Oscar refused to move until his mistress's husband had returned to the house.

'Oscar really doesn't like him, does he?' whispered Agnes.

'Hates the bloody sight of him, love. And he isn't on his own. Come on, let's get rid of Spencer's latest victim.' They put the pup in his kennel, tied the frayed tether to a ring in the floor, then walked home.

'We're all living in her nightmare,' said Denis when they were halfway between Rise and Fall.

Agnes gripped her husband's arm. Sometimes, he was very wise. She was grateful for that.

Chapter Nine

Agnes Makepeace was exhausted to the core. Her waist was thickening and her patience was shrivelling at a similar pace. Summer continued into September, which wasn't right in Agnes's book. Leaves had scarcely started to crisp and, apart from a slight nip in the air at dawn, the hot weather lingered. She spoke to Nuisance. 'No more summers with you attached, anyway. After a few more proddings by doctors and a bit of hard work on my part, you are out of there. You'd best look lively and get yourself a job in the pits, because you've been hard work up to now. It's payback time, mate.'

Had she bitten off more than she could chew? She had travelled the length and breadth of Skirlaugh Fall, which, though small, contained a couple of hundred people who might do well if gossip should become an Olympic sport. She knew who had slept with whom, could now nominate at least three people who were 'bad with their nerves', was custodian of confidences involving intricate surgical procedures performed on several men and women from here to the horizon. Oh, and there were a lot of folk suffering from piles. It had all been interesting, but not as productive as she had hoped.

The questions relating to the Spencers had been hidden within conversation – or so she trusted. The judge was clever; if he believed that Agnes was working to help the daughter for whom he had no love, repercussions might occur. Agnes had a husband and a baby to protect; should they become threatened, poor Helen would be on her own. Well, not quite on her own, but Louisa, too, was in a position of compromise. Agnes answered her own question. 'I have bitten off more than I can chew. Let's hope I never have to swallow any of it. Bloody man.'

One last chance lay with a married couple named Longsight, who lived in the larger village of Harwood. They had worked for the Spencers many years ago, so they had become the final target. What was Agnes seeking? She had no idea. Yet the feeling that Helen had suffered some kind of abuse in childhood remained strong. It had to be more than neglect. The neglect of a child was unforgivable, but Helen's unreachable memory was of one specific incident. The woman remembered well the occasions on which she had been deprived of space and company, could chatter away about days spent in her bedroom, yet the nightmare continued and Agnes was here to discover the eye of the storm. Or perhaps not – the eye of a storm was quiet and relatively peaceful. Whatever it was that made Helen so agitated was not in the eye – it was spinning around the edges in the company of a million particles of frantic dust. And the storm was no act of God; this was a tornado created by a man who was used to being king in his own arena. Judge Zachary Spencer had probably wounded his only child so badly that she could not allow herself to remember the incident. That was mental trauma, Agnes believed.

On the bus ride to Harwood, she wondered why she was doing this. Perhaps the discovery of the truth would injure Helen even further. Perhaps all this should be left to time and chance, because it was no one's business. Yet Helen was frail. It would do no harm for someone to be around when the memory came back. That someone should know as many of the facts as she could. That someone was going to be Agnes.

Denis's spine stiffened.

'So, you've given up your job? How on earth will you manage with no library books to stamp?' The judge's voice crashed through an open window. 'For God's sake, woman.'

Helen must have responded and the judge was quick to shout again. 'Louisa doesn't need you. If she required nursing, I'd hire somebody with nursing skills, not a woman who knows how to catalogue the reference section or find a stupid romantic novel for some elderly spinster. What will you do all day? James Taylor has left Bolton after your ill-treatment of him, so you won't be wasting his time any longer. He should sue for slander, as should I.'

A door crashed home. Denis tried to relax, but fury made his muscles taut. Now that the silly business was over, Denis considered Helen to be a friend, and a friend of his wife, too. That mean-minded and lily-livered Spencer needed his eye wiped, and Agnes was doing her best. There was something radically wrong in this household. Denis had begun to agree with Agnes that an event in Helen's childhood had shaped her and almost finished her. He shivered. Zachary Spencer was a fish cold enough to have perpetrated the worst of crimes; he was also sufficiently intelligent to clean up after himself. A bad but clever man was a dangerous enemy.

Oscar arrived and began to claw at a flower bed. Denis grinned. While Louisa was still suffering the nausea experienced by Agnes for just a few weeks, the dog had sought refuge with him. 'Leave the lobelia alone,' Denis advised, 'or I'll clobber you with my rake.' He wouldn't, though. Unlike Judge Spencer, he was incapable of damaging other people or animals.

Oscar fetched a stick and Denis threw it. Every job took twice as long these days, yet Denis would not have parted with the daft pup for all the tea in Asia. The dog returned, dropped his prize and panted hopefully.

Helen arrived and took over the job of throwing.

'Are you all right?' Denis asked. 'I heard.'

She shook her head. 'I keep telling myself that he can't hurt me any more, that I'm an adult and capable of answering back. Sometimes, I do answer back. Today I'm not up to it.' She fastened a lead to Oscar's collar. 'I'll walk him,' she said. 'Otherwise, we'll be throwing sticks and balls all day.'

Denis knew her probable destination. 'Here's my key. If Agnes is out, let yourself in and make a brew. There's a bone in the kitchen for Oscar.' He watched as she stumbled away behind Oscar, who dictated the pace of mobility. 'Find something, Agnes,' he begged inwardly. Somebody had to help Miss Helen Spencer, and that somebody could not be a member of her own family. Saddened, he returned to his weeding. The lobelia was safe. Were Helen and Agnes safe?

Agnes emerged almost unsatisfied from the Longsight house in Harwood. She could see the couple now, eyes darting away from her face, each looking at the other, a damped-down terror weakening their voices. They knew something. The judge had been a fair but firm boss, there had never been any trouble, the first Mrs Spencer had been a nice, pretty sort of woman. Helen was a difficult child sometimes, but she had improved with age. Yes, everyone had been sad when Mrs Spencer died; yes, Miss Helen had been upset for quite a long time and yes, there had been a big funeral.

The last hope sat in Agnes's handbag, a scrap of paper on which was written a name. This person was the one who had cared for Miss Helen during her early years. She was retired now and lived in a Blackpool rest home. Blackpool. It might as well have been the moon, because the chances of Agnes's getting to Blackpool were remote. She was pregnant, she suffered from the heat and Denis had little time for day trips and no money to afford such luxuries.

On the way home, she called in on Pop and Eva. The latter was making tea for 'them two'. 'Them two' were Fred Grimshaw and Albert Moores, who now held the grand position of superannuated apprentice. Agnes carried mugs to the shed.

'It's not seasoned,' Fred was yelling.

'Course it is. I got it from Jackson's Lumber and Jackson said it's well seasoned. Shall I fetch salt and pepper then you can give it another go?'

Agnes grinned. Had Pop met his Waterloo? Oh, how she hoped he had.

'Don't talk so daft.' Fred grabbed his tea. 'Hello, love.' Without pausing, he continued, 'I know seasoned wood like I know the back of my hand. This isn't for a doll's house – it's for a kiddies' play house. It'll likely be out in all weathers.'

Albert also knew his wood and he said so.

'My name has been built on things that don't fall to bits,' yelled Fred.

Agnes smiled. 'But his first chimneys were crooked.'

Fred glared at his granddaughter. 'That was deliberate,' he insisted. 'It was for that poem thingy – crooked man, crooked mile.'

'Rubbish,' she said sweetly.

Fred sank onto one of the work benches. 'Nearest and dearest?' he asked of no one in particular. 'I know what I'm talking about, but I can't get sense and I can't get good wood. Albert?'

'What?'

'Who's the boss?'

'You are, master.'

'Then take that bloody wood back and get summat as'll stand up to rain for a week or three. Then get down to the ironmongers in Bromley Cross and buy me a new drill – this one couldn't get through butter.'

'Yes, master.' Albert stalked out of the shed.

Agnes sat next to her grandfather. 'Go easy on him, Pop. He's a good man and a good worker.'

'I know. Worth his weight in gold – and he can take a joke.' He looked at her face. 'You're hot again. Any luck?'

She told him of the morning's events.

'Then you go to Blackpool.'

'How? When?'

Fred tapped the side of his nose. 'Leave all that to me,' he said darkly. 'I have ways of making things happen. Now, get you gone. Miss Spencer's in your house with yon daft dog. If you don't shape, he'll have eaten the sofa by the time you reach home.'

Agnes kissed him. 'You're a terrible man, but I love you.'

Eva arrived, a school bell in her hands. 'Oh,' she muttered.

'What's that for?' Agnes pointed to the instrument.

'It's for the end of the round,' replied Eva. 'When they get too loud, I send them back to their corners for a rub down with a wet cloth. Without this here bell, the authorities would be evacuating Skirlaugh Fall.'

Agnes went home with the distinct feeling that there was more to Eva than met the eye. As there was already quite a lot of Eva, this new version promised to be a remarkable phenomenon.

Helen was dozing in a chair, while Oscar, in his element, was crunching bone to reach the marrow. As soon as he saw Agnes, he dropped his prize and went to greet her.

Helen woke to joyous yapping. 'Sorry,' she said. 'I don't get much sleep these days.' The truth was that she was afraid of sleeping, because sleep brought dreams she could never piece together once she woke. 'Shall I make tea?'

'Yes, please.' Agnes reunited puppy and bone. 'Stay,' she ordered, though she expected little or no obedience from the young Alsatian. He needed training, and his owner was not well enough to spend time with him. She listened to sounds from the kitchen, the clatter of cup in saucer, the rattle of the spoon in the caddy, the decanting of milk from bottle to jug. This was what Helen needed – the ordinary, everyday things in life.

'Shall I pour?' Helen asked when she returned with the tray.

'Please. I'm hot.'

'Where have you been?'

'Oh – here and there – visiting, looking at shops.'

'You bought nothing?'

'No.'

'I'm trying to train him to walk to heel.' With a look of hopelessness on her face, Helen waved a hand at Oscar. 'He's going to be too big soon. We can't have a huge, frisky dog. Louisa loves him dearly, but he tires her and, like you, she is in no condition to be directing a determined self-guiding missile. He drags me from pillar to post.'

Oscar, tongue lolling, smiled at his womenfolk. They were talking about him and they wanted to slow him down, but the world was so exciting – all those sights and sounds, the wonderful smells, the inbuilt knowledge that he was born to annoy smaller creatures. He wagged hopefully, depending on his charm. Soon he would chase rabbits again.

'Any more dreams?' Agnes kept her tone in everyday mode.

'Yes, but I can't catch them.'

'Still no idea of what it might be?'

Helen shook her head. There was noise, a high-pitched sound followed by several crashes. After the crashes, she invariably woke and reached for pen and paper. But there was never anything to write, because she could not grasp the centre of the dream.

'Still writing?' asked Agnes.

'Yes. It seems to be a circular effort, since I appear to have begun in the middle. I suppose once I have written the middle, I should know the beginning.'

'And the end?'

The end was like the dream, full of noise and fear.

The end might come after the middle, or after the beginning – Helen wasn't sure. 'I thought I'd lived the dull life until I started to write about school. I expect most authors' early books lean towards personal experience. All of Austen's did, and she had a life as narrow as the ribbons she applied to her dresses when she needed something to look new. I think writing helps. Even if it's never published, it will be out of me. It's therapy.'

Agnes understood perfectly. For Helen, the writing was like going to confession or seeing a doctor. It was balm for the soul; it was also a search for truth, and Helen had to walk through a minefield to reach even the edge of that commodity.

'Like Austen, I write what I know. I didn't realize how much I had absorbed, because I have always kept it to myself.'

'You're a people-watcher.'

'Probably.'

Having said goodbye to Agnes, Helen left, the daft dog pulling her at considerable speed in the direction of Skirlaugh Rise. She tried to rein him in, failed, found herself chuckling as she was dragged along the lane.

'I am glad you have something to laugh about.'

Helen's flesh seemed to crawl. She looked through a gap in the hedge, saw her father's unwelcome sneer. 'The dog is silly,' she replied defensively.

'It'll have to go once the child's born.' He stared hard at her. What was she up to? Her attitudes ranged from the compliant to the argumentative with no visible warning of any impending change.

'I shall keep him in my apartment,' she replied. Father would not get rid of Oscar. She would not allow that. The power she owned was connected to . . . it was connected to . . . To what? The end of the book, the end of the dream? He was afraid of her. Why should he fear his own daughter?

'Keep the damned thing away from me,' he ordered before storming off in the direction of the house.

As soon as she was on home ground, Helen released Oscar and he dashed into the copse to annoy wildlife. She followed and leaned against the very tree behind which Glenys Timpson had concealed herself. 'Did I love Denis?' she asked herself in a whisper. 'Or was I merely imagining that I might have found someone who could take me away from here?'

Dappled light caressed the ground. A few leaves had followed the norm and were beginning to carpet the ground. It was a lazy day. She sat on damp moss, breathed the scent of earth, watched the pup as he leapt insanely from tree to tree. He was dragging a bough through a gap, was growling and panting as he fought to move the heavy object.

The world changed. Something in the sound made by the large branch cut into her head like a warm knife through butter. She was elsewhere. There was not much light, but there was noise and movement. Someone panted. Was that a scream? 'Come away.' The voice was female. There was not enough light. Backwards. She was pulled backwards into . . . Into the copse.

The dog, head leaning to the left, one ear cocked and the other remaining in Alsatian puppy mode, was panting in her face. His breath stank of marrowbone. 'I was dragged backwards,' she told him. 'There wasn't much light. Someone pulled me away from . . .'

Oscar grinned broadly before turning to display his huge find. He could not carry the whole piece home, so he began the business of stripping branches from the main stem. A happy woodsman, he became absorbed in the task.

Where? When? Who had said the words? She remembered half-light, a hefty tug, dragging, that panting sound. Had she been pulled away from something? Was she the something that was dragged? Quickly, she grabbed the dog and fastened lead to collar. She had to get home; there was the writing to be done.

Agnes picked up the receiver. 'Hello?'

'It's me – Lucy. Your granddad wants me to drive you to Blackpool. Will this Sunday do? Denis doesn't work Sundays, does he?'

'Erm – not usually, no.' Agnes feared that Lucy would not be happy if she knew the reason for the trip. 'I have to visit a nursing home,' she said.

'Oh?'

'I may have a lead on something I've been researching.'

There followed a short silence before Lucy spoke again. 'Mags tells me you've been trying to find out about Helen Spencer's childhood. May I ask why?'

'You can ask, but I don't know the answer.'

A long sigh preceded the words, 'Can't she do her own research?'

'No. She can't.'

'Why?'

How to explain that Miss Spencer was not crazy? How might Agnes convey her own feelings about this matter?

'The woman's had all the good things in life—'

241

'She's had no mother, Lucy. And her father is terrible to her. There's something she needs to remember, but I want to filter it and tell her gently. She's delicate.'

'She's crackers.'

'That isn't true. Lucy, don't bother yourself – we'll get a lift from someone eventually.'

'We'll do it. I'm sorry, Agnes, but you are on a hiding to nothing. George thinks the whole Spencer family is crazy.'

'Hmm. All two of them? Three if you count the new wife, I suppose. Why are you so much against Helen Spencer?'

Lucy sniffed. 'Madness frightens me.'

'Then don't drive us to Blackpool.'

'We are driving you to Blackpool and you are driving me mad.'

'Then you'll be in good company – sanity has never appealed to me. Much better to be happily mad than sanely unhappy.'

At last, Lucy giggled. 'How about unhappily mad? See you about ten on Sunday morning. 'Bye.'

Agnes sat down, a duster in her right hand. Absently, she cleaned the top of a small table as she thought about Sunday. Mabel Turnbull, the lady in the nursing home, was the last chance. According to the Longsights, she had been Helen's nanny, so she might be in a position to clarify some of the goings-on. A day out would do everyone good, she told herself. George and Lucy need not come into the nursing home – they could return to the Golden Mile for half an hour. Denis would be there. As long as Denis was there, Agnes could manage just about anything.

The man in question entered the house. He was laughing.

'What's funny?' she asked.

'That bloody dog dragging Helen all over my lawn.'

'The judge won't be pleased.'

Denis shook his head. 'He's never pleased unless he's punishing some poor bugger. You stay where you are – I'll brew up and see to the cooking.'

Agnes had always known that she had been lucky in love. During this seemingly eternal pregnancy, she had indeed been blessed. Her man thought nothing of doing a full day's work, only to come home and start all over again. His excuse was simple and beautiful – he hated a woman with swollen ankles. The truth remained that he loved and respected his wife. It was a pity that more men did not put family first.

'Are we having this liver?' he called.

'You are and Nuisance is. I am a mere third party – I just have to process the nasty stuff.' She sighed dramatically. 'Never mind, I'll get my own back when he's born.'

She hadn't realized that she could write, yet once she started her fingers flew over typewriter keys in a vain attempt to keep up with the speed of her thoughts. Sometimes, her poor typing skills were a good thing, as they slowed her down and made her consider what she was creating. There was an urgency in her, as if she believed her time to be limited, though there was no binding deadline to the unsolicited script.

Helen Spencer forced herself to stop. She leaned back in her chair and stared through the window at gathering dusk. Days were growing shorter. Autumn and winter would be bearable, she reminded herself, because the dog could be her excuse to leave Lambert

House several times a day. Should she have kept the job in the library?

He was out a lot these days. Summer recess stretched across several weeks and, unless there was a massive crime, Father could be around whenever he pleased. However, he seemed to prefer his Manchester club, often staying there for several nights in succession. Lodge meetings took up more of his time, and he played chess or bridge in town once a week.

Helen and Louisa were coping well with his neglect. They needed only each other, and both enjoyed being apart for a few hours each day. A rhythm developed and life became good as long as the head of the household was absent. The two women read, Helen wrote, Louisa was having a stab at tapestry work. The house hiccuped along under the watchful eye of Kate Moores, who supervised the comings and goings of three newly hired dailies. It was not a bad life. Helen knew that she ought to have been grateful, yet she continued to simmer and to suffer spells during which she was mentally removed from her environment. It was the dream. It was all tied up in that nightmare.

She left her desk and walked through the house towards Louisa's room. Life ticked on. As long as he wasn't in it, there was a degree of transient freedom.

Louisa opened her eyes. 'He phoned,' she announced. 'He's bought a yacht and he wants me to sail with him. I've told him I get seasick on a boating lake, but would he listen?'

'He never listens.'

Judge Spencer's wife nodded. 'He's getting sailing lessons. I'm going near no ships until this child is born. I've put my foot down.'

'Good for you.' Helen sat down and continued to

read aloud from *Great Expectations* while Louisa dozed. A yacht? She tried to imagine her father at the helm, failed miserably. He wasn't an outdoors type of person. Perhaps the sea was going to be his next conquest. A second Canute, he might well expect time and tide to work to his schedule. Never mind. With any luck, he would sink and drown. And *Great Expectations* deserved Helen's full attention.

Agnes replaced the receiver and looked at her husband. 'Miss Turnbull isn't in full possession of her faculties – that's what the matron said, anyway.'

Denis folded his newspaper. 'Who the hell's Miss Turnbull?'

'The nanny from thirty years ago. Blackpool – in a rest home.'

'Oh.'

She bit down hard on her lip. 'I might have to just give up. Lucy doesn't want anything to do with it, anyway – I wish Pop hadn't asked her to take us.'

'That doesn't sound like Lucy – she's usually game for anything.' Denis sighed. 'What's the matter with everybody these days? It's murder up at the house, Fred and Albert are always arguing—'

'No. They're being crusty old men. If you separated them, they'd wither a lot faster. People are just being themselves, that's all. The only one who needs help is Helen, and it's starting to look as if I can't do much for her. If the old lady's off her head, there's no point in me being car sick all the way to Blackpool, is there?'

'I suppose not.'

'And Lucy doesn't want to help Helen. Like you, I can't understand that.'

The phone rang a second time. Agnes, still unused to living alongside the instrument, jumped. She took the call, replied in a short series of yeses and nos, returned the receiver to its cradle. Triumphantly, she turned to Denis. 'There is something. That was Lucy's George. It all gets mysteriouser and mysteriouser. He told me to stay away from Miss Turnbull for my own good.'

'Eh?'

'Those were his exact words, love. "Stay away for your own good. There's nothing in Blackpool for you, and you need to be safe."'

'Bloody hell.'

'Bloody hell is right. George said the judge pays the rest home fees. He said he shouldn't be telling me that, but he had to say it because I'm Lucy's best friend. He said, "Look, Agnes, you're a clever enough woman. He pays the fees. Follow that train of thought and see where it leads. I can't say any more, because I am breaking contract by discussing a fellow lawyer's client." Those were his exact words, more or less, Denis. He's breaking some law or other to keep me safe. How can I follow that train? And should it be the Blackpool train out of Trinity Street?'

'No. George is a good lawyer and he's looking out for you.'

'Follow that train,' Agnes whispered.

Denis went to make a pot of tea. Judge Spencer was a rich man, but he didn't throw his money at the needy. He didn't like the needy; he believed that poor people were one of life's less savoury necessities, since they kept the wheels of manufacturing turning and cleaned up after the rich. The poor were often criminals, too. He was very harsh on penniless breakers of the law.

Agnes stood in the kitchen doorway. 'Don't pour a

cup for me, love. I've drunk enough tea just lately to refloat the *Titanic*.'

Denis went with her into the living room. 'Have you followed the train?'

She nodded.

'So have I. The matron said the old girl's doolally, right?'

'Yes.'

'He probably doesn't know she's gone senile. That's hush money, Agnes.'

'That's what I was thinking.'

'And George's firm – or George's friend's firm – handles the fees, I'll bet. No, I'll go further than that. I'd wager a pound to a penny that Miss Turnbull's been kept by Spencer since she left Lambert House. There has to be a reason for that. Another thing – what if the judge told the rest home to contact him if she got any visitors?'

A shiver ran the full length of Agnes's spine. 'Dear God,' she murmured. Then her face brightened slightly before she added, 'I don't think I gave the matron my name. I just said Nan had known Miss Turnbull and that Nan had died. She said nothing would register with the old lady and I rang off. I hope I didn't give my name.'

'I didn't hear you say who you are. Sit tight and try not to worry. But, Agnes . . .'

'What?'

The pause lengthened slightly before Denis spoke again. 'Miss Turnbull might have been paid to keep quiet because she could remember what Helen Spencer has forgotten. For all we know, the whole business could be tied up in the one knot.'

Agnes agreed.

'We don't need Lucy,' said Denis. 'I'll go to Blackpool and give a false name, see if I can get through to the old lady.'

'No, you won't.' Agnes shook her head vehemently. 'Unless you want to wear specs and a false moustache – and even then I'd say no.'

Denis sighed. 'Who wears the trousers in this house? No, don't answer that, because I know what you'll say. We wear one leg each – eh?'

'Too damned right, mate.'

'Mate is about correct,' he grumbled. 'Bloody stalemate or checkmate or whatever chess players say. We can't help her, sweetheart. At least you'll always know you did your best.'

But Agnes was far from satisfied. 'I'm taking her to Manchester.'

'Eh? Who?'

'Helen. I'm going to get her hypnotized.'

Denis almost choked on his tea. 'My leg of the trousers is planted, Agnes. You're having a baby. You've seen what happens to her when she nearly remembers. If one of those quacks can take her back to wherever she was when whatever it was happened, you could end up with a full-blown nervous breakdown in the middle of Manchester. Even I wouldn't take that on. You're not making yourself ill, and that's an end to it. There's nothing more to be said.'

Agnes, like Denis, knew when to concede defeat. He was right. There was no way of predicting what might happen if and when Helen remembered. 'All right,' she said.

'Promise me?'

'I don't need to. It was just a thought.'

'Right.'

They sat in silence until someone tapped at the door. Denis opened it to admit Lucy. 'Has he told you?' was Lucy's immediate question.

'George? Yes, he has,' Agnes replied.

Lucy sank into a chair. 'Thank God. Listen, both of you, and listen hard. Put as much space as you can between yourselves and the Spencers. Denis, you can help with the barn – we need to do a lot to make it fit to live in. When it's done, George will get you work in the fresh air. You have to leave the job.'

Denis stared steadily at the visitor.

Lucy turned her attention to Agnes. 'You, too. Let them clean their own bloody silver – you should be training for something better.'

'The judge pays half the rent on this house,' said Denis.

'I want to stay near Helen and Louisa,' added Agnes.

Lucy leapt to her feet. 'All I can say is this – a letter was witnessed thirty years ago. It's lodged with another firm, and we can only imagine the contents. The woman who wrote it is in that Blackpool home – that's why I didn't want to get involved. When the lady dies, Helen Spencer won't need to remember, because we think – we believe – that the whole mess is sealed in that envelope. The lawyer who witnessed it is dead – he went to pieces shortly after reading the contents. The woman asked him to check it to make sure she'd made her point clear. It's bad. It's sealed with wax and tied up with string, but we all know it's there.'

Agnes swallowed hard.

'Lawyers gossip, too,' said Lucy. 'And that judge is a much-hated man, so George and I have been on tenterhooks lately. When it happens, it'll be like World War Three, believe me.'

Denis stared through the window. Much as he would have loved to leave Lambert House a few weeks ago, he now needed to stay. Helen was a friend and someone needed to keep an eye on her ill-tempered father. Skirlaugh Fall was a good place; they had decent neighbours and Fred nearby. 'We'll let you know as soon as possible,' he told the visitor. 'I'm due back at work now. Thanks for coming, Lucy.'

Alone, Agnes and Lucy stared into separate near distances. Agnes, her eyes on the fireplace, was racking her brain for an idea that might enable her to help without putting herself in danger. Lucy, who had already said too much, looked through the front window. 'Pretty here,' she remarked eventually.

'Yes, it's lovely.'

'It's a big barn, Agnes, with a cottage at the back. It's every bit as nice as Skirlaugh Fall.'

'I know.'

'Will you leave?'

For answer, Agnes shrugged her shoulders.

'It's not a good idea to get too close to that family. You'll be dragged in when the day comes. Helen Spencer is unstable.'

'I know.'

'Then why stay?'

Agnes sighed deeply before replying. 'If you or Mags were in trouble, I'd swim to Timbuktu to help. Helen's become a friend.'

'Does that stop you listening to a longer-standing one? We've been together for ever, Agnes. If you only knew the whispering that's gone on in legal circles for thirty years, you'd buy a gun and lock yourself in.'

Slowly, Agnes turned and looked Lucy full in the face. 'He killed someone, didn't he?'

Lucy's face was stained by a sudden blush. 'There are crimes other than murder – serious ones.'

'Rape?'

'Agnes, leave it alone. The guy who handled all this became ill – he was getting on in years. But he never again spoke to Spencer, who was a leading barrister at the time. It all smells worse than the Tuesday fish market. Mabel Turnbull has senile dementia and can't talk in straight lines any more. Even so, her bills are paid. There has to be a reason.'

Agnes nodded thoughtfully. 'How come the judge has never heard about this letter? He seems to be the only one in ignorance.'

'Lawyers do gossip, as I said before, but no one cares enough to warn him. And it's thirty-year-old news. For all we know, this Miss Turnbull could live to be a hundred and the judge might die tomorrow. Whispers started up again when I told George about Blackpool. This time, Agnes, you had better ignore that stubbornness you inherited from Pop. You've a child to think about – and a husband. George has gone out on a limb for you and Denis, so think about George as well. If that limb snaps, my man will never work again.'

'So, if the rest home told the judge that Mabel Turnbull had had visitors ... Well, it doesn't bear thinking about. Even senile folk can often remember what happened decades earlier. Tell George not to worry.'

Lucy pleaded again, begging Agnes to walk away from Skirlaugh Fall with Denis. There would be work, a cottage and George nearby. It made sense, she insisted. Events from thirty years ago could catch up with the Spencers at any time, and Agnes should put herself away from the fallout area. 'Talk to Denis,' she insisted.

'I will.'

'Safety first, last and always. There's a wicked genius in Lambert House. When a clever mind turns bad, a psychopath is born. Think about him. He worries about no one but himself and he loves no one but himself. That's one dangerous man and his daughter could be cut from the same cloth.'

'No,' said Agnes. 'She isn't.'

Lucy picked up her bag. 'Don't be too sure of that. Even if she is sane, she's an emotional wreck. Don't be pulled down the plughole with her.'

When Lucy had left, a weary Agnes laid herself flat out on the sofa, her head spinning. A part of her wanted to pack up straight away and walk the three or four miles to Lucy's barn; the rest of Agnes needed to remain where it was, near Pop, near Helen, near Louisa. And the decision could not be made while Denis was at work. Tormented by dreams that were probably pale echoes of Helen Spencer's nightmare, Agnes slept.

She woke screaming. Trying to hang on to the tail end of the dream, Helen Spencer jumped from her bed and ran all the way across the long landing until she arrived at her old room. There was a small bed in a corner. Dolls sat on a shelf, fairytale books beside them. She was small. She could not reach the shelves, but adults could. 'Come away,' said the voice. There was urgency in the tone. 'Come away now.'

Helen blinked. Her mouth opened again and the child yelled at the top of its lungs. *I am not a child. This is all wrong.* The man came in, a woman behind him. They were from the other time, yet they stayed. She stared at her father. He was old. The woman was the wrong woman and the screaming would not stop.

He went out of the room. The child sat on a rug. The rug was made in the shape of a teddy bear. She wanted her . . . she wanted her mother. The woman was touching her. 'Helen, please stop this – he's getting the doctor.' But Helen heard another voice, the one that urged her to come away. It had happened. It was terrible. The child carried on screaming.

Louisa turned to the doctor the moment he arrived. 'Help her,' she pleaded. 'Can't you knock her out? She'll be all right after a sleep.'

Dragging. Banging. Someone else's scream. Two screams now.

A needle. Sharp. Silence.

By the time the ambulance arrived, Helen Spencer was unconscious. She was lifted onto a stretcher and carried down the long, winding staircase. Louisa, terrified, could only stand and watch while her best friend was removed from the house. Having pleaded with her husband and with the doctor, she knew that she had no chance of keeping Helen at home. She turned, saw triumph in her husband's eyes. 'She won't be away long,' she said.

Zach Spencer looked at his wife. 'She's crazy like her mother was,' he crowed. 'She'll be away for as long as it takes. If she doesn't buck up, she could be gone for the rest of her life.'

Louisa fled the tragic scene. Helen was not insane – he was. Pressing her hands against her belly, Louisa worried about the unborn child. Zachary Spencer had unseated his daughter – what would he do to her sibling? 'All I wanted was to be safe,' she told her abdomen.

'This isn't a safe place.' Nowhere was safe. Wherever she went, he would find her. He knew police, private detectives, lawyers by the score. There was no escape.

What about poor Helen? She had always known that there was no way to avoid the nightly torments – it was plain that something had upset the balance of her soul rather than her mind. Would she remember in hospital? Would the doctors help?

Louisa forced herself to return to her husband. The plan was a frail one, but it was the only idea she owned. 'Sweetheart?'

'Sweetheart' was looking very pleased with himself.

'Yes?' His lip curled. Louisa was no longer pretty; pregnancy did not suit her – she had a bloated face with dark patches near the eyes.

She inhaled deeply. 'It may be a good thing,' she ventured.

'What?'

'The hospital may get to the bottom of it all.'

He frowned. 'Ah. Yes, they might well do that.' Turnbull and Helen, the two biggest threats, had almost seemed to disappear in recent years. They knew nothing, surely?

Louisa continued. 'She dreams almost every night, Zach. It seems to be something from childhood, and she gets nearer to remembering it every day. Can you recall her being hurt?'

'No.'

'Are you sure?' Was Louisa sure? Was she now threatening Helen's very existence? Because she knew with blinding certainty that her stepdaughter's buried secrets involved this man. Might he hurt Helen all over again? Was he capable of killing her?

Zachary Spencer shifted weight from foot to foot.

He was unused to fear, was happy only when in full control of everyone around him. There was a danger that he had just painted himself into a corner. 'I'll get her home,' he declared. 'You are used to her and you probably need the companionship. I shall be sitting soon, when the courts reopen.' The mad should be left to their madness, he told himself firmly. Helen was insane, but psychiatry had advanced and she might very well respond to treatment. Was he in danger? No, no. Mabel Turnbull had seen nothing, his daughter had seen nothing. Or was he mistaken? He had kept Mabel Turnbull sweet just in case, but he had never considered his daughter to be a threat. Adults did not remember events that had taken place when they were twenty-eight months of age.

Louisa left him to his musings. As she walked away, the child kicked. It was as if the poor mite knew that trouble lay ahead. She closed her door and leaned against it for support. The beatings she had received from her first husband had been nothing compared to this. Even the stabbing and the surgery had left mere physical scars. Helen had been right. Judge Zachary Spencer was not a safe place for anyone. His daughter was now paying her dues and, at some stage, Louisa's turn would surely arrive.

Agnes refused to be moved. She stood at the desk in the ward sister's office, feet planted firmly, face set in a scowl. 'I'll wait,' she said. 'I've plenty of time today.'

'A first assessment can take several hours.' The crisply ironed female glanced at Agnes's abdomen. 'You should be taking better care of yourself in your condition.'

The unwelcome visitor seated herself in the corridor, took flask and box from her shopping bag, and began to eat her lunch. She wasn't going anywhere. The sister's eyes were still on her – even the eyes seemed fixed by starch – but Agnes munched stoically on her sandwich. She was not hungry, yet she refused to be beaten by a woman too big for any boots. Helen was here and Agnes had no intention of leaving before seeing her.

The woman in question emerged from her office. 'Follow me.'

Was it possible for vocal cords to be starched? 'Thank you.' Agnes repacked her lunch in its original place of residence. There followed a journey slowed by the unlocking and locking of doors. The fact that she was inside a mental hospital was underlined by the nurse's behaviour. In this place, those who failed to cope with life were condemned to exist. It was all cream and green, with fat radiators punctuating walls.

'She's in there.' The blue-and-white-clad woman walked away, turning as she reached yet another locked door. 'I'll come back for you shortly. Try not to tire her. If you have any trouble, press the red button.'

Agnes swallowed. Thus far, she had managed well enough, but now she was about to face grim reality. Helen was in that room. She had been hauled from her house by two big men, placed in an ambulance and driven to Manchester. She had not been certified. Had she been declared unfit for human company, Agnes would definitely have been turned away.

She turned the door knob. 'Here goes,' she whispered softly.

There were bars at a high window. A bed with a white quilt sat next to a nasty little locker that carried the scars of past assaults. Paint failed to hide completely scratch marks on a wall. Helen sat in a green chair, hands folded in her lap, eyes down-turned, lips slightly apart.

'Helen?' The eyes looked dim. 'Are you drugged?'

'Yes, I think so.'

Agnes sat on the bed. 'What happened? Denis ran home this morning to tell me about the ambulance arriving in the night. Louisa had a word with him. She wasn't well enough to visit you, so I took her place.'

'I'm glad you came. Thank you.'

'Has your father been?'

Helen smiled ruefully. 'No.'

'What happened?' Agnes asked again.

'The dream. This time, I woke screaming – please don't ask me why. I was little Helen all over again – dolls in my room, a teddy bear rug, fairytale books. I could hear and see him and Louisa, but I also heard another woman's voice telling me to come away.'

'Your mother?'

Helen shook her head. 'No. A servant of some kind. This time, I must have got very near to the truth, because I woke in terror. A doctor gave me an injection, I believe. Then I was brought here. I'm a voluntary patient, but, if I try to leave, I'll be certified for a month while they test me. I can't win, so I have bowed to the powers and promised not to attempt to escape. With so many locked doors, it would be a useless effort, anyway.'

Helen was a prisoner. Agnes held the woman's trembling hands. It was all she could do; no one on God's earth could change the minds of doctors.

'I've been assessed once,' Helen said. 'So far, so good. I think I passed my scholarship all over again. They looked very confused, as if they didn't know what to do with me. A peculiar set of people, I must say. If they are the ones who decide whether the rest of us are sane, God help the world. As for therapy – what good are they doing by shutting me in here without company or reading matter?'

Agnes smiled. 'They're watching us,' she said, her voice deliberately loud and clear. 'We are animals in a zoo, you and I. There's a camera in the corner, some sort of microphone, too, I expect. We are under scrutiny.' She rose and walked towards the corner. 'Hello, doctors,' she said. 'I am Agnes Makepeace. There's nothing wrong with this woman, but her father needs locking up. He's a vicious, nasty piece of near-human detritus. Save a room for him.'

'Good afternoon.'

Agnes froze, then turned slowly. Zachary Spencer, face stained a dark red, stood in the doorway. 'You are coming home,' he told his daughter.

'Am I?'

'Yes. They say there is nothing the matter with you.' His eyes remained on Agnes. 'I wish I could say the same for your friend. Meet me at the main entrance. Do you require a lift, Mrs Makepeace?'

'No, thank you.'

'Very well.' He turned on his heel and left.

Agnes crossed the room and perched on the edge of the bed. 'Jesus,' she said. 'He heard me.'

'Yes, he did.'

'Will he sack Denis? Only Denis has been offered another job, so we can escape if necessary.'

'Don't go. Please, don't go.'

'He'll punish Denis. He might even stop paying some of our rent. Helen, your father is one scary man.'

'He's afraid.' Helen's tone was quiet. 'I may be on

the receiving end of those little yellow pills, but I know why he's here. He wants to pull me out before doctors get to the bottom of me.' She stared hard at her visitor. Nothing must happen to Agnes, Denis, Louisa. Four friends, she had now. To the list of three, she added the name of Mags Bradshaw. Friends meant strength and support. 'He'll do nothing to you,' she said. 'He'll do nothing to Denis. Don't move away, please. I have his measure now.'

'And the dreams?' Agnes asked.

'Will be dealt with. I don't need to be in hospital to get help. I can visit a psychiatrist privately – Father need never know.'

Inwardly, Agnes shook. The judge knew her opinion of him. Denis worked for the judge. Helen lived with him, as did Louisa. Louisa's pregnancy was proving difficult. Inner instinct dictated that Agnes and Denis should leave Skirlaugh Fall and go to live near Lucy. The stubborn streak, along with concern for Helen, urged Agnes to remain exactly where she was. Then there was Pop. How would Pop manage without her and Denis?

As if reading her ally's thoughts, Helen asked, 'Did you know that your grandfather is commissioned to make a scale model of our house? It's to be a present for Louisa after her child is born. She never had a doll's house as a child. It will take months to make, but Father insisted and he's paying a good price.'

'Oh.' Agnes could find no sensible remark with which to punctuate the pause.

'He gathers all around him like a farmer bringing home the harvest. He pays Denis, he pays some of your rent, he pays the staff. Now, he goes for your grand-father. We exist only at the edge of his vision –

especially if we are female.' She sighed. 'Don't walk out on me just yet, Agnes, because you are a piece of my harvest.'

Agnes gazed at the floor. 'I can't help being afraid. He's so high and mighty, and I said what I said and he heard me and—'

'So did the microphone.' Helen strode to the corner and spoke to the box near the ceiling. 'You know I'm not mad,' she said clearly. 'My father is the cause of my temporary disarray. Keep your drugs and your electric cables for him. I am going home. Home is another word for hell. Goodbye.'

As if on cue, a nurse arrived with a sheet of yellow paper on a clipboard. 'You are released,' she said. 'Follow me.'

Helen laughed mirthlessly. 'I'll never be released, Nurse Jenkinson. Not until the day someone signs his death certificate.' On this note of high drama, Helen walked out of the room, Agnes hot on her heels. A key chain clattered, doors were unlocked, locked, unlocked, locked again in a seemingly endless walk to the outside. A woman screamed. Echoes of other doors slamming in other corridors flooded the air. Cream and green were the colours of the day, while the scent was pine disinfectant with a faint whiff of carbolic.

'God help all who stay here,' said Helen as they reached fresher air and open space. 'Come with me, Agnes – don't leave me alone with him.'

'You won't be alone – Denis is driving.' Agnes waved a hand at the Bentley. 'See?'

'Then you will cause more speculation by refusing a lift from your own husband. See? Whatever you do, my father enters the equation. So come along – let's go home.'

The drive started in complete silence. Helen, next to her father in the rear seat, saw nothing of the landscape throughout the journey. Agnes and Denis, in the front of the car, made mindless small talk about Pop, Eva and little domestic issues, but the conversation was strained. Agnes, dropped off at the cottage, thanked the judge with all the politeness she could muster.

Inside, she collapsed onto a sofa. How many times had she berated Pop for failing to hold his tongue? What had she done? That foolhardy business with the camera had given Judge Spencer further food for thought. 'Don't let him take it out on Helen or Louisa,' she begged God.

It was a long day. When Denis finally came home, he stood over his wife, one hand running repeatedly through his hair. 'He wants to know who you've been talking to,' he said.

'No comment.'

'Agnes, he demands to be told how you formed such a distorted view of him. We'd better clear off – we'll be safer with George and Lucy.'

'No.'

'What do you mean, no? He's boiling over in his study right now. Helen's shut herself in her flat, won't talk to anyone – even Louisa. He's banging about like a bull at a gate – why did you do it?'

'I didn't know he was there – what are you up to?' Denis had picked up the phone. 'Denis?'

'I'm phoning George.'

'No. We stay for now. He daren't touch me.'

Denis shook his head and walked into the kitchen. Much as he wanted to remain in the village, he needed his family to be safe. The phone rang. He answered it. 'Ah. Hello, sir. Right. Thank you very much.'

Denis replaced the receiver and spoke to his wife. 'He forgives you because of your condition and because he knows his daughter was out of sorts when she expressed her opinion of him.'

'Load of tripe,' was Agnes's reply.

'Very likely. We're keeping our options open, love. One more day like this one and we leave the village. All right?'

She nodded.

'I mean it, Agnes – I'm not messing about.'

'I know. He won't do anything to us, Denis. He's already in trouble up to his double chin. Helen is the only one in real danger. Please, love, let's wait a while.'

With that, Denis chose to be satisfied for the time being.

Chapter Ten

Stella Small, a woman of over six feet in height, saw private patients in a room that matched her name. For her own part, she had lived at peace with her surname, although, while growing at a rate of knots in childhood, she had needed to adjust her attitude at an early age. Having overcome her own giant status and silly name, she had equipped herself to help others through a life whose stone-punctuated and mud-spattered alleys marked Stella's clients in ways that went above and beyond feet and inches.

'I'm Helen Spencer.'

'Ah. Yes. Do sit down. My name is Stella and yes, I am Dr Small. If you are anxious or depressed, you will not wish to joke about my name. If, however, you are enjoying a good day, feel free to smile and we can get the business of my size out of the way.'

Helen chose to smile. 'You were recommended by my GP. Father had me locked away in a mental hospital for about sixteen hours, then decided that I had recovered. He fears my memory.'

'Right.' The doctor scanned Helen's notes, adjusted her spectacles to achieve better vision, then sighed heavily. 'These doctors can't write legibly. You are unhappy?'

Helen nodded.

'Which is not the same as depressed. But you have

had some panic attacks and have behaved unconventionally from time to time.' She closed the file. 'Happily, I am able to do two things at once and, while appearing to read your notes, I have been counting the number of times you have blinked. You are not neurotic.'

'Good.'

'Tell me everything.'

Helen would never be able to explain why, but her whole life poured from her lips within half an hour. The doctor did not prompt, was not worried by short silences and, when Helen had finished, stood and walked to the window. 'When I pour tea into a cup, the tea takes on the shape of the cup.'

'Yes?'

'But you have no shape. You cannot measure yourself – no comments about my height, thanks – and you pour all over the place. There's no mould, you see, no cup to give you shape.'

'But that doesn't mean I am insane.'

Stella Small shook her head. The spectacles left her nose and dangled on a piece of braid just above her breasts. 'I must get some new glasses,' she remarked. 'No, you are not insane, but your father may be. You have had no love and no parents – that is his fault. Those dreams – that lost memory – he is a part of that.'

Helen waited for more.

'The brain is a clever beast. It will allow you to remember when remembering will do less harm than it might just now. Meanwhile, get out of your father's life.'

'But Louisa—'

'Will have to take her chances with the rest of us.' The doctor returned to her chair. 'Emotional retardation is completely divorced from intellect. You are a clever woman, but you have been through adolescence in your early thirties. You even chose a man who was safe, a man who would never carry you off on a white steed. Miss Spencer, you have only recently reached maturity. You don't need me or drugs or a straitjacket. You need a removal van and a fresh start. I repeat – get out of your father's life as soon as possible. You have my telephone number. If you need me again, I shall be here.'

A few minutes later, Helen found herself wandering aimlessly through the bustling streets of Bolton on a market day. She bought tomatoes, lettuce, cucumber and a large box of Milk Tray for her stepmother. The doctor's words echoed – 'Get out of your father's life.'

She sat on a bench and opened the chocolates. Louisa did not like coffee creams, so Helen rooted them out and chewed thoughtfully. Why should she do the moving? He was the miscreant, the sinner, the bad apple. 'Get out of his life?' she whispered. Oh, no. It would be far better if he got out of hers. How did a person get rid of a father? What plan might be employed to shift him from Skirlaugh Rise?

After finishing the coffee creams, Helen walked towards her car. There had to be a way. Because she was going nowhere, while he, the big man, should go to the devil in whose company he belonged.

Life settled into a routine of sorts after a while. Agnes continued to work part time at Lambert House, though she chose to be there only when the judge was absent. Through Denis, she was able to predict Zachary

Spencer's schedule, thus enabling her to appear at Kate's kitchen door when the chances of the man's putting in an appearance were minimal.

Louisa continued unwell while Helen, Agnes and Kate competed in an effort to find something she would eat, but the judge's wife seemed to have slipped into a state in which she cared little for herself. When reminded and bullied, she ate for the sake of her unborn child. Helen and Agnes watched the slow deterioration with concern – Louisa, the bright spark, the giggler, was no longer resident at Lambert House; in her place, a pale, listless creature lingered, all hope gone, the light in her pretty eyes extinguished, her lust for life diminished.

Under a cloud of gloom, the other three women sat in Kate's domain, a kitchen vast enough to house a whole family, beds included. 'I can do no more,' Kate grumbled. 'Scrambled eggs, beef tea, nice soups – I've tried the lot.'

Helen stared into her coffee cup. 'I warned her. It was already too late – they were married – but I told her what would happen.'

Kate nodded wisely. Forced by circumstance, Helen had found it necessary to include Kate Moores in her list of friends, because Kate needed to be aware of Louisa's needs and difficulties. The older woman blew on her coffee. 'She's not carrying well,' she pronounced. 'God help her if owt happens to that kiddy, because he's hung his hat on having a healthy lad.' She glanced at Helen. 'Your dad's a bad bugger.'

'I know.'

'We all know,' said Agnes. 'But the main problem for now is keeping Louisa in one piece. Like me, she'll be two pieces in a few months and she'll need to be strong to give birth and mind the baby.'

Kate stared into the near distance. 'You should beggar off, Miss Helen. Get gone and take her with you, because she's not the woman he brought home. You've that bit of money your mam left – get some out of the bank and use it.'

Helen half smiled. 'Where could we hide from him? No, he would seek us out even if we went to Mexico. Judges have long arms.'

Agnes blinked a few times. 'Look, if you could just get her away for a few weeks, it might make all the difference to her attitude and her health. Tell him you're definitely taking her away. He'll hardly notice anyway – too busy trying to learn to drive that damned boat.'

'Yacht,' said Helen. 'If you call it a boat, he goes purple.'

'We're serious, Miss Helen.' Kate patted her hairnet, pushing a stray strand of iron-grey hair into the mesh. 'Just go.'

'He'll bully you if I just disappear. I can't do that to you, Agnes and Denis.'

Kate snorted. 'I'm not frightened of that great lummox. I reckon if it came to the shove, my Albert and Agnes's granddad could give him a good hiding.'

'Never thump a judge.' Helen looked at her hands. She hadn't played the piano in weeks, hadn't written a syllable, had given up trying to read to Louisa, whose sole aim in life seemed to be constant sleep. 'If anyone hits him, he'll send that person down for twenty years. I've served thirty-two years of my sentence and—'

'Then give yourself time off for good behaviour.' Kate refilled Helen's cup. 'A month or two could make a big change to that poor girl up yon.' She pointed to the ceiling. 'Take a chance. Don't tell anyone where

267

you're going, then, if we are asked, we won't be lying if we say we've no idea.'

Agnes gazed steadily at Helen. There was something different about her, something new. 'The dream?' she asked.

'Gone,' was the reply. 'The whole situation has righted itself.'

Both women knew that Helen Spencer had spoken the truth. She was calm – almost cold. There was a new set to her shoulders – the slight roundness had disappeared, while her eyes no longer betrayed sleeplessness or troubled nights.

'Did that head doctor help?' Kate asked.

'Partly, yes. The pills from the hospital helped me to sleep at night. But Dr Small wasn't the whole answer. That came from a totally unexpected source.'

The housekeeper and Agnes waited, but no further information was forthcoming. Helen, her mouth set in a determined line, made up her mind there and then. 'I shall take Louisa to the sea and I shall tell him where we are. If it's for the good of her health and for the sake of his child, he will have to agree. Before you ask – yes, I am still afraid of him. But because of ... oh, never mind ... I am now in an even better position to stand my ground.'

Kate snorted. 'Good luck. You're going to need it.'

'If I am sure of your safety,' Helen told Agnes, 'then I can be stronger. We must all cease to show fear of him – keep it hidden, keep him guessing. If we can do that, he will leave us alone. He needs to be in charge, needs to translate fear into respect. His weakness is that he needs to believe himself to be respected in spite of ... in spite of all he has done.'

Agnes swallowed hard. It had happened. The dreams were no longer necessary, because Helen had the truth at last. From where, though? Had she travelled all the way in her sleep, had she woken with the full story in her head? Or had Mabel Turnbull died? To whom had that letter been addressed? 'I'll come with you,' she decided aloud. 'Denis won't mind. If I pay for my own food, then—'

'No.' Helen's face was alight with joy. 'No, you'll pay for nothing, my friend. I'll be so glad of your company – and a holiday will do you good. Denis will be glad for you, I'm sure.'

So it was decided that Kate would stand guard on the home front while Helen and Agnes looked after Louisa. Destinations were discussed before Agnes began the walk homeward. How cool Helen had been, how sure of herself. She was a new woman, remoulded and ready to take on the world. But would she really manage her father?

In the cottage, Agnes removed her coat and picked up the phone. As she had expected, Mabel Turnbull had died two weeks earlier. The letter, she concluded, was now in the possession of Helen. When asked by the matron for her name, Agnes terminated the call. It was over. Helen knew what her father had done and appeared to be dealing with it.

Denis agreed right away that a holiday would do Agnes good. 'But don't go too far,' he warned. 'I might get there for a weekend if it's not at the other end of the country.'

Agnes tried to imagine the scene at Helen's house, judge in his chair, defendant standing on the carpet, his face reddening, hers white with nerves. But it had to be done. Louisa's life was in danger, as was that of the child she carried. Away from Lambert House, there was a chance that she might thrive once more.

Had Agnes taken her imaginings to the ends of the earth, she could not possibly have pictured the reality of that meeting between father and daughter. When Helen had said her piece, Zachary Spencer, shaking from head to foot, could find no immediate reply.

'What's the matter, Father?' she asked. 'Did Oscar run off with your tongue? Don't worry – Denis and Fred will look after the dog while we're away. Oh, and remember my warning – it includes the dog. Miss Mabel Turnbull was brighter than you thought. In all honesty, I can't remember her face, but the letter convinced me that she had been a part of the household all those years ago. So.' She straightened her spine even further. 'So, I, too, have written a letter. It contains Miss Turnbull's letter to me and the whole bundle is in very safe hands. That letter could ruin you for ever – we both know that.'

He gulped noisily, reached for his brandy. The letter would be with George Henshaw, of course. Had anyone other than Helen read it?

'If I die, that envelope gets opened. Miss Turnbull's letter, too.'

So, Helen had been the sole reader. After clearing his throat, he finally spoke. 'Miss Turnbull was a nervous woman. She saw trouble where there was none.'

'Really? That explains how clearly her story resembles the dream that haunted me for months. I was there.'

'You were not three years of age when Mabel Turnbull ceased to be your nanny. She acted as housekeeper after that.'

'Yes, and after you had relieved her of her virginity.'

The judge took another hefty mouthful of brandy. 'That is neither here nor there. What else was in her letter? Not that anyone would believe her, of course.'

'Then why have you paid for her upkeep since she left? Why did you pay the fees at the home when she got old?'

He lowered his chin and said nothing. For the first time in his adult life, he was losing an argument. His daughter was the only person who had defeated him. He needed to know the contents of Mabel Turnbull's letter, but he realized that he dared not ask. 'Where will you go?'

'Somewhere between Blackpool and Morecambe – not too far away, as Louisa is unfit for long journeys. We shall travel in my car. You will continue here as usual, I suppose.'

'Don't tell me what I will do,' he snarled.

Helen clung to the edge of her courage. 'There was a name in that letter, Father. There were several, but I recognized one of them immediately. Need I go on?'

He hurled the brandy globe into the grate. 'Travel where the hell you like – summer is gone, anyway, so you have missed the best of the weather.'

She had never seen the best of the weather, because she had lived her whole life in the long, dark shadow of this man. Helen did not react to the smashing of the glass. 'Bracing winds might be just what Louisa needs. She did not enjoy the heat. A few weeks on the coast will do her the world of good.'

'Leave my office, please.'

She walked to the door, placed a light hand on the knob, turned to look at him. 'Isn't knowledge a wonderful thing, Father? It's power. All these years, you have presided over my life like some ugly ogre, ill-tempered, unpredictable, devoid of all decent human emotion. It's my turn now.' She opened the door. 'Go to hell,' she ended clearly. 'I am a match for you, because your blood runs in my veins, too.'

The trembling began as soon as she reached the main hall. Even now, she was terrified of him, because she knew that he was capable of acting beyond the reach of reason. It was all in the letter from Miss Turnbull, a message written decades earlier when the woman's mind had been young and clear. Judge Zachary Spencer was a self-created law. He embodied the book of rules, amended the contents to suit himself, assumed that he was beyond the reach of other mere mortals.

Helen closed the door of her apartment and sank to the floor. What was she going to do? Not about Louisa, not about the immediate future, but in the long term. Her father knew the true law of the land and might even escape the spectre of Miss Mabel Turnbull. But there were names in the letter. He had been a womanizer all his life and Miss Turnbull had watched the comings and goings in Lambert House for years before leaving. When his first wife's body had barely cooled, he had begun to share his bed with anyone who became available. After that, he had, for the most part, amused himself well away from the house.

The rest of the message? She shuddered anew. Two facts had emerged, one of them terrifying, the other a mixed blessing. There was a great deal to be absorbed and she could take her time over it while away by the sea. Helen now held her father's fate in her hands;

she was judge, prosecution and jury. His defence? There was none. Those twin facts from the nanny's letter were burned into Helen's brain like brands on the skin of farm animals; from two pieces of knowledge, she had gleaned insight into herself. She was her father all over again and she was the only person qualified to mete out his sentence. Judge Zachary Spencer was a marked man. And he knew it.

Lucy Henshaw, who still worked part time for her husband, looked up as a large shadow touched her desk. Irritated already by the complicated documents in her hands, she sighed heavily. People who wanted to play at litigation were silly and made a lot of work, so— It was Judge Spencer. 'Yes?' she asked.

'I need to talk to your husband.'

'He isn't here.'

He frowned. 'Then I shall wait.'

Lucy shrugged. She knew the probable reason for the man's visit – he would be looking for two letters, one written by his daughter, the other a legacy from Mabel Turnbull. Lucy knew nothing of their contents; neither did her husband, but the firm was responsible for the safekeeping of Helen Spencer's property. 'Please yourself, sir, but he won't be back for hours.'

Yet another woman was standing in his way – well, sitting in his way.

'Do you wish to make an appointment?' she asked sweetly. 'Or shall I get another of the partners?'

'No.'

'Is that a no to both suggestions?'

'Yes.' He walked out of the office, slamming the door in his wake. Lucy picked up her phone. George was having a word with builders at the barn, where, according to him, the telephone was just about the only item in working order.

'George?'

'Yes?'

'The judge has been and gone.'

'Ah.'

'Is it lodged with the bank?'

'It is indeed. What was his mood?'

Lucy laughed, though there was no glee in the sound. 'The same as ever, love. Bright, breezy, cheerful – need I go on?'

'No. Tell me – what are we going to do about this damned fireplace?'

They talked about modifications to their new home, then Lucy returned to the original subject. 'Does this mean that Agnes is safe, George?'

'Safe as houses and a great deal safer than our barn.'

'Good.' She returned to her work, which embodied a silly quarrel about two feet of land at the rear of a pair of semis. Agnes was safe. Nothing else mattered. Two feet of land certainly failed to enter the equation.

They stayed outside Morecambe, Blackpool's poorer twin. It was quieter than Blackpool, with fewer shops and vehicles, but the sea was there, the air was clean and their accommodation, a rented semi-detached house, was comfortable. The only cloud on an otherwise clear horizon lay in the knowledge that Judge Spencer's yacht was moored well within driving distance. 'He won't come,' said Helen repeatedly.

Agnes kept a close eye on both her companions. Louisa, still quiet at the start of their holiday, was beginning to eat more regularly, while Helen was a strange mixture of calm and alertness. It was all tied up with the death of Mabel Turnbull – of that Agnes was certain. But she asked no questions, because the judge's daughter needed as much rest as anyone.

After three days, Louisa showed signs of her old self. As it was raining, she insisted on games of Monopoly and cards, even showing elation when she won. Away from her husband, she started to thrive, often cheating at dominoes and palming cards when she thought no one was watching. They were watching, each glancing at the other with relief in her eyes.

He came. Agnes saw the expression on Louisa's face when he kissed her on the cheek. It was as if a darkness had fallen over the woman's skin, a stain applied by the very man to whom she had entrusted her life.

Denis, who was on driving duty, followed his master into the house. If there was going to be any argument, he wanted to be there to protect his wife. The judge had damned and cursed his daughter for days, so there could well be a battle in the house.

Denis found the women seated in three chairs at a dining table across whose surface were scattered playing cards and dominoes. The judge had taken up a position of superiority near the fireplace, chest and stomach pushed outwards, hands clasped behind his back. There was a deafening silence in the room.

The big man cleared his throat. 'Are you improving, Louisa?'

'Yes, thank you, dear.'

Helen shook her head so slightly that the movement was scarcely noticeable.

'The air will do you good,' pronounced the embodiment of authority.

'We are all well, Father,' said Helen.

The judge did not look at his daughter. 'We have done a little sailing, Denis and I. It's quite easy once one grasps the basics. Denis?'

Denis hated the yacht. 'Yes, not as difficult as I thought.'

'We'll make a sailor of you yet,' promised Spencer.

There followed another silence. Helen folded her arms and stared hard at her father. 'We are better here than at Lambert House,' she said. 'There's been a dreadful atmosphere there just lately.'

The judge shifted his weight from foot to foot. Had she spoken to Louisa, to Denis's wife? Were these two women aware of the preposterous meanderings of Mabel Turnbull? What an ungrateful wretch that woman had been. He had kept her for years, had made sure that her dotage had been comfortable. Women were all the same – even when dead, they continued a torment.

'We shall be eating soon.' Helen's tone was soft. 'Unfortunately, we cannot ask you to stay, because we have not catered for company.' She glanced at Louisa, whose downcast eyes and sad expression spoke volumes about inner misery. 'Louisa needs to eat at regular intervals. In Morecambe, she will get well.'

He glowered. She was ordering him out of the house, was in charge of his every move. He needed those letters. A plan, half-formed thus far, was taking shape in his mind. There was always a way, he told himself. His treatment of Harry Timpson, which would be lenient, was going to pay off soundly. He could use a man capable of breaking and entering a well-locked jewellery store.

'Please go,' said Helen.

'You haven't won yet, madam,' mumbled her father.

Helen's cheeks glowed with anger. She wanted a blunt instrument and a chance to use it, needed to pound away at him until he died. The death sentence was still on the statute book in her personal legal system, and she was the only one qualified to apply it in this instance. The room was fading. She had promised herself that this would never happen again, but here it came, prompted by no dream, no sound, no warning. 'I know what you did,' she cried. 'I know all of it.'

He staggered back. 'Quiet, woman!'

But she saw him and only him. There was a long staircase, darkness, dragging, crashing. A woman bade her come away, but this time, she did not come away. 'Eileen Grimshaw,' she whispered.

He made for the door.

'How much did you pay to be rid of her? What contribution did you make to the upkeep of your other daughter?' Helen blinked, cleared her mind and focused on the present. 'Agnes, I am so sorry.'

Agnes had slid down in her chair. 'No,' she whispered.

It was too late. Helen, knowing that she was doing damage, had no way of taking back what she had said. At least she remembered the episode this time, but that was no compensation for the harm she had done to her half-sister. 'Meet your daughter, Father. I intended not to tell you until after the birth,' she said to Agnes.

Agnes shot out of her chair, reached the judge in two strides, raked her nails down both sides of his face. Denis grabbed his wife and pulled her away into a corner. 'Stop it, love,' he begged. 'Come on, this is doing you no good at all.'

'My mother died,' she screamed. 'And my Pop and

277

Nan were left to bring me up. They were poor. You left them poor. God, I'd rather have anyone but you as a father.' Did Pop know? Surely not. Surely, he would not be making a scaled-down copy of Lambert House if he knew that the customer was the one who had fathered his granddaughter? Silly little thoughts tumbled about in her mind, a million questions seasoned by fury and loathing.

Helen was sobbing. 'I wanted to protect you, Agnes. I've known about this for only just over a week.' She raised her head. 'And I know the rest, Father. There's enough there to send you to prison for life. Remember that. Remember and leave us alone.'

The judge wiped his bleeding face on a snowy hand-kerchief. 'Let's go, Denis,' he muttered.

But Denis held on to his wife. He placed her in the chair she had just vacated, strode across the floor and punched Zachary Spencer on the nose. The man fell back, his head striking a wall. Dazed, he struggled to his feet, eyes watering, face creased by fear.

Denis threw the keys on the floor. 'Drive yourself home,' he wheezed. 'Stay away from me and mine, or, God help me, I'll not be responsible for my own actions. Scarred lungs or not, I'll beat the living shit out of you.'

The unwanted guest opened his mouth as if to speak, snapped it closed almost immediately. His cheeks continued to bleed, as did his nose. He retrieved the keys before continuing to mop his bloodied countenance. Unfit to drive, he stumbled from the house and sat in his car. She had won. The damned woman had won – unless he could retrieve the letters. If he could get his hands on those, Helen might be disposed of quite easily via the mental hospital – who would listen to her there?

Who would listen? The doctors would. No matter what, he was almost cornered, but he could, at least, make an effort to retrieve those papers from Henshaw & Taylor. Harry Timpson was his best chance. God, he hoped his face would heal before the session.

Inside the house, Agnes rocked back and forth in her chair. The baby, too, was mobile, as if the shock had affected the space in which he or she lived. She could not believe it, would not believe it. His skin was under her nails and his blood ran in her cold veins. Nan and Pop had laboured all those years to provide for a child whose father was one of the richest men in Lancashire. 'I have to wash my hands.' Agnes fled.

Denis's breathing righted itself after a few minutes. He was angrier than he had ever been in his whole life. That thing was Agnes's father. His knuckles ached from the blow he had delivered to the nose of a High Court judge. The job was gone. Agnes had to be cared for, as did the unborn child. Agnes needed more than money. He followed her path to the bathroom.

She was staring at herself in the mirrored front of a small cabinet over the basin. 'I don't look like him.'

'No, you are beautiful.'

Agnes turned. 'I hope my mother went with someone else as well as him. I hope my dad's out there some-where sweeping up or weaving sheets. I'd rather be the daughter of a criminal...' She was the daughter of a criminal – Helen had just said so. Helen was her sister. 'I always wanted not to be an only child,' she said. 'But him? Why him? Why did my mother go with a brute like that one?'

'We'll never know, sweetheart.'

'Rape?' she asked.

'No way of finding out.'

'Nan and Pop always said my mam wasn't cheap, that she seldom went out of the house and seemed to have no boyfriend.'

Denis nodded.

'We have to look after Helen now, Denis. She's family. What will Pop say?' She sank onto the toilet seat. 'Pop doesn't deserve this.'

'He doesn't need to know. Remember the stroke? News like this would put his blood pressure at the top of Everest. You know what he's like, love. He gets himself worked up even when he's having fun – imagine what this could do to him.'

She nodded.

'I've got a feeling I lost my job today.'

Agnes stared into the near distance. 'Lucy was right. We should have kept away when she told us to.' She lifted hands reddened by scrubbing. 'I've nearly worn the nail brush out,' she said. 'But I can't rub him out. I'll never be able to rub him out, because he's in me.' She swallowed hard. 'I came from that pig.'

'So did Helen.'

'She's used to it.'

Denis perched on the edge of the bath. 'We haven't read the letter. I'm not saying that Helen is lying deliberately, but she does get confused.'

Agnes shook her head. 'Not any more, she doesn't. What she gets now is angry. She has his temper.'

'You don't, though. You're nothing like him.'

'No, but I am carrying his grandchild.'

'Agnes, you can't be sure of that.'

But she was sure. She continued sure for the rest of the day, even after questioning Helen very closely. 'It fits,' Helen informed her firmly. 'Miss Turnbull had nothing to gain by nominating your mother as one of his conquests. She herself was another victim, though she can't have borne a child or she would have mentioned it in an effort to secure some inheritance for it. No, she was simply recording the facts – it has to be true.'

Evening found them in the living room, all thoughts of board games abandoned. Louisa, who had eaten a good meal, was the first to speak. 'He's not hurting this baby,' she declared. 'I'm going to eat everything that gets put in front of me, because the child must be strong.'

Helen nodded. 'What do we do about you and Denis?' she asked her newly acquired sister. 'The half of your rent will be paid – I'll see to that.' She raised a hand to stop any argument. 'I'll see to it,' she repeated.

'I'll help with George's barn,' said Denis.

Agnes had little to say. Stunned, she merely sat, hardly hearing the conversation. She thought about her poor mother, knew that Eileen had gone right through a pregnancy with no husband and little financial support. Pregnancy was not much fun, but Eileen had been forced to endure it without the comfort of a partner. Agnes thanked God for Denis, for Pop and for Nan.

Denis, too, seemed lost in thought. He was chewing his nails – a habit he had lost in his teens. He had clouted a judge.

Helen was the one who brought sense to the situation. 'Look, none of this is new. Life is much the same as it was yesterday, except that we now have a little more knowledge. That can be said of any day – we learn as we grow. He didn't suddenly become your father, Agnes. Denis – you've never liked him. Louisa – you've lived with your mistake for months – what's changed? I have a sister and a brother-in-law – I shall be an aunt in the spring. We can't let him win. There is more to that letter than your mother's name, Agnes – a great deal more. But that's my problem – you all have enough of your own. Let's have our holiday. Denis – you phone George and tell him you'll take the job. Go by bus to work, or borrow my car. Agnes – just learn to live with it. Sorry to sound harsh, but nothing matters beyond your own family.'

'You're my family,' Agnes whispered.

Helen smiled. 'So it would seem. Louisa, do your best. You are the one who is forced to be close to him. For the baby, play your part. We'll rethink after the birth.'

No one slept well that night. But each realized that Helen was right – life had to continue alongside him and in spite of him. Helen rested better than the others. Her anger was too deep to be allowed near the surface, so she lay sleepless, though not in pain. Retribution had not yet begun . . .

He did not remember the journey, partly because he had been unfit to drive, mostly because his mind was filled by the dreadful scene in the house he had visited. What had that damned Turnbull woman written and what had she seen? Yes, he had known her in the biblical sense, but had the quiet, compliant woman been a witness to something he had sought to hide? That letter had to be retrieved from the offices in town.

Kate Moores was just leaving. She saw him, but asked no questions about his scarred face. It seemed that she was yet another member of his daughter's coven. How much did Helen know and what had she told the other witches?

Eileen Grimshaw. He threw his hat in the general direction of the coat stand. She had been about as much fun as a burning orphanage. He remembered her tears, recalled her coming to his office to speak of her pregnancy. He had dragged her outside, had told her to keep her mouth shut, as he would deny everything. Who would take the word of a mill girl over that of a rising lawyer? She must have come here, to the house, must have told her tale of woe to Mabel Turnbull. Mabel Turnbull had seen fit to record the incident along with . . . The big man shivered.

He dropped into a chair. Bolton was the biggest town in England, yet the Makepeace woman had found her way to Skirlaugh Fall and into his house. Her grandfather's surname had not registered – it was not a common name, but there were too many Grimshaws in Lancashire to merit undue concern. In truth, he had forgotten about Eileen Grimshaw until today.

His face hurt from twin track marks made by an illegitimate daughter, while his nose, victim of his son-in-law's punch, throbbed with every beat of his heart. He had lost Denis. He realized that the loss of Denis was no small matter, because Denis had always listened, and seldom replied. He was a good gardener, an excellent driver and a man on whom the judge had come to depend.

He needed to find another chauffeur-cum-handyman, someone biddable, grateful and good-tempered. The nose continued to throb – even Denis Makepeace's patience did not last forever. The assaults would have to be ignored – Zachary knew he was in no position to have his assailants arrested. Helen had ensured their freedom from prosecution. She was a clever woman, had probably been a clever child – he should have noticed her. Clever women were a commodity much resented by him – they were unnecessary. But, had he kept her on his side, she might have turned into an asset rather than an adversary.

In the bathroom, he bathed his face, flinching when applying ointment to marks bequeathed by Mrs Agnes Makepeace. His hand stopped in mid-air. She was his daughter; she was carrying his grandchild. Louisa's chances of giving birth to a healthy son were not looking good. That wife of Denis's was a fine specimen – nothing like her downtrodden mother.

'Bloody hell,' he mumbled. 'Fine pickle, this is.' He felt his nose, assumed that it was not broken, went to bed. He lay there for half the night, his mind on one single track – he tried to imagine what was in the Turnbull letter. Helen had judged the contents to be enough to send him to jail – but no, that could not be right. No one had seen. He remained absolutely sure that there had been no witnesses to . . . It was better not to think about that particular event. Nothing could be proved, anyway. Yet he wanted to see both letters, needed to know the lies contained in those pages.

When he slept, he groaned and moaned his way through a dream that was new to him. A long staircase, noises, dragging. What was that? Had he heard the closing of a door? Had the sedatives failed? No, he was imagining the sound. The staircase grew longer. The nearer he got to the bottom, the more stairs it collected. He had to get there soon – had to move the evidence. That door again. No, no, they were fast asleep.

Morning found him in physical pain from yesterday's attacks. His mind, too, was disturbed by the troubled night. Women. This was all the fault of the female of the species, the mothers, wives, sisters and daughters inflicted by God as a punishment on mankind. It wasn't fair. And he had lost Denis.

October was passing. With enormous reluctance, Helen, Agnes and Louisa packed. Denis, who had visited most weekends, carried the baggage out to the car. It was time to go home.

Louisa, leaning for moral support on her stepdaughter, was returning to a man she had not seen since the day Helen had routed him. He had telephoned, had asked about the well-being of his wife and child, but he had not dared to come again to Morecambe. Louisa, in better health, had finally begun to bloom, but she showed signs of wilting when they left the house for the last time.

'Stay with us,' Agnes begged. 'We've got a spare room and you're welcome to it.'

'I can't.'

'I'll look after her,' said Helen. 'She will live with me in my apartment. There's nothing he can do, you see. I'd have fleeced him of all his money by now if I'd chosen to blackmail him. But I want him exactly where he is while I work out what to do with him.'

Agnes shivered. The weather was cold, but not as icy as the tone of Helen Spencer's voice. 'Don't do anything daft, Helen,' she begged.

'I won't.'

Agnes did not believe that. Helen seemed to have achieved a state in which she was calm to the point of madness – if such a thing were possible. The woman had a goal in life, and that goal was probably the destruction of Zachary Spencer. Agnes's own anger remained, but that was a healthy reaction, she believed, since she had only recently found out the name of the person who had impregnated and abandoned her own mother. Perhaps anger cooled over a period of months or years; perhaps she, too, would arrive at a place in which she wanted revenge. But she doubted that. The facts had to be accepted and dealt with – the rewriting of history was an impossibility.

'Agnes?'

She looked at her sister. 'What?'

'Don't worry.'

'I'll try.'

Helen climbed into the front passenger seat while Denis took the wheel. She was calm. But her main goal in life for now was to get past the two births – it was suddenly important that the expected children should be delivered in safety. Louisa, who had become a dear friend, must be guarded at all times; Agnes, Helen's new-found sister, should also be made secure. The babies were the priority for the time being. After the births, open season could begin.

Denis started the car. 'Are we set?' he asked.

'In stone,' replied Helen.

Louisa was weeping softly in the back of the car.

'Don't cry,' begged Agnes. 'Helen will look after you. Once she's made her mind up about something, there's no budging her. He's never hit you, has he?'

'His blows don't show on the surface.' Helen settled back in her seat. 'He's careful like that.' But so was she. Helen was, after all, her father's daughter.

The judge was away. Helen and Louisa settled into the apartment. Their prepared story was to be that Louisa needed a female at hand, because certain symptoms had begun to appear, and a man would not understand. He would fall for that, or so Helen believed. She could not imagine her father wanting to discuss the complicated arrangements of a woman's reproductive system.

Oscar had returned from his holiday with Fred and Denis, who had taken turns to mind him. The dog, who was twice the size he had been a month ago, yapped joyfully when he greeted them. Slightly older and wiser, he knew what he had to do. He had to be here; these women needed him.

They had been back for three days when Kate Moores knocked at their door. 'There's a young fellow to see you,' she told Helen. 'Wants to see you on your own. I'll sit with the missus while you go.'

Helen descended the back staircase slowly. Where was Father? And which young man had he sent to perpetrate some kind of revenge? No, no, he would not dare . . . Would he?

The young man stood in Kate's kitchen, flat cap squashed in nervous hands, a slight slick of sweat glistening on a handsome face. 'Miss Helen Spencer?' he asked timidly.

'For my sins, yes. But you have the advantage of me, because I don't know you at all. Or do I?'

'Harry Timpson, Miss Spencer. My mam asked you to help me and you did.' He moved forward, words tumbling from his lips. 'You've turned my life round. I couldn't have done prison again. It would have killed my mam. Your dad gave me probation – I expected a good three years. But I never blew the safe – I just took the jewellery to sell. Anyway, the long and short is this – I'm not the same person, honest. I have to behave now.'

'Please, it was nothing—'

'It was everything. I mean, I've no job and no money,

but I can walk about and meet my mates – as long as I don't break the law. Which is why—' He stopped abruptly.

Helen set the kettle to boil. 'Milk and sugar?' she asked.

He nodded, but remained silent.

She placed the pot on the table, asked him to sit, poured the tea. 'What's bothering you, Harry? May I call you Harry?'

'Aye, it's my name.'

'Well, Harry?'

He took a mouthful of tea. 'I'd be better off with whisky,' he managed.

'Shall I get some?'

'No.' Harry inhaled deeply. 'I'm in a bit of a pickle, as my mother would put it.'

'Oh?'

'Aye.' He drank more of the scalding tea, wiped his mouth on the back of a hand. 'There's this man,' he began lamely.

She decided to allow him to proceed at his own pace.

'He's asked me to do summat. It's a break-in at a lawyer's.'

Helen nodded. He scarcely needed to utter another syllable, but she let him continue.

'I'm to look for files under two names.' Harry bowed his head. 'I'm on probation. If I get caught, my feet won't touch the floor, because nobody would believe the name of the man who told me to do this. He's promised me a job, a proper job, if I do the robbery. He's high up, you see. I'd get years inside and he'd get away with it.'

'The names?' she asked.

He shook his head slowly.

'Do they begin with S and T?'

'Yes.'

'Then I know who has asked you to do that dreadful deed.' She stood up and paced about for a few minutes. 'The man who broke the safe in Manchester – do you know him?'

Harry nodded.

'I'll pay him to do this job in your place. Don't tell me his name – I have no need of it. I shall give him one thousand pounds.'

Harry swallowed. 'Eh?'

'One thousand. But wait until next Friday. Tell my— Tell your employer that it will be next Friday.' She needed time, needed to plant something in those offices – the safe-breaker should not leave empty-handed.

Harry's eyes were bright with a mixture of tears and adoration. She had saved him once and she was about to save him a second time. 'I don't know how to thank you,' he mumbled.

The boot was on a different foot, mused Helen after her grateful visitor had left. Her father was wasting his time by getting the offices raided, because both documents were sealed in an impenetrable vault below the pavement at a Bolton bank. There would be something to be found, though. She intended to hand another sealed letter to Lucy Henshaw. The contents could be quite amusing – she might write *Fooled you, Daddy* – no, she would not do that, because Harry Timpson needed to be in the clear.

A little note reminding George to confirm that her letters were in the bank would suffice. She had already received confirmation, but she could pretend that the letter had gone astray in the post. Life was interesting, she reminded herself as she returned to her rooms.

Revenge was sweet, but it needed to be served cold. There would be something for the burglar to find and, if he were arrested, no one would believe that a judge's daughter had initiated the crime. 'It works both ways, Father,' whispered Helen into the quiet of the hall. 'I can play the game, too.'

'What did he want?' Louisa asked when Helen returned.

'My father is thinking of giving him a job,' she said.

Kate was not pleased. 'I felt safer when Denis was here,' she grumbled.

'We all did.' Louisa went to lie on a sofa. Her back ached, her feet were swollen – and she had another five months to endure.

'That's right, you have a sleep,' advised Kate. 'I'll go and get on with me baking.'

Helen gazed into the flames. It seemed that Father had played right into her hands by asking for Harry Timpson's help. Harry was Helen's man. He was grateful to her and only to her. Harry would be an asset – she would make sure of that.

'What are you cooking up now?' asked a sleepy Louisa.

'Nothing of any consequence. Go to sleep. We'll need our wits about us when Father gets home. If he comes home.' Perhaps he was afraid. Perhaps he would move into his club for good.

'He'll come home,' sighed Louisa.

Helen made no effort to reply. Her father had no home, though his place in hell was booked and waiting. Nothing mattered now, because Helen held the biggest weapon available – she knew his darkest secrets. Let him come, let him go – she had the upper hand and would hold on tightly to the bitterest of ends.

Chapter Eleven

The thousand pounds, filtered through several minor representatives of the Lancashire bad boys, would never be traced back to Helen. When the story of the crime broke, it was given suitable prominence in local newspapers, but the reason for the burglary remained unclear. Several items of no particular import were stolen, and the job was generally believed to be the work of drunken amateurs.

Almost two weeks after the break-in, Judge Zachary Spencer returned to his own domain. He accepted the explanation for his wife's disappearance into Helen's part of the house; then, after a few days had passed, he sent Kate to fetch his daughter. Stalemate had been reached and he needed to clarify matters as quickly as possible.

She sat in a chair opposite his, noticed that his nose advertised his continued dependence on alcohol, thanked God that she had nipped her own problem in the bud. 'Here I am,' she said unnecessarily. 'What can I do for you, Father?'

He closed his eyes for a weary second. 'Look. I don't know what Mabel Turnbull wrote about me, but, whether it's right or wrong, it could do harm to this family.'

Helen nodded her head in agreement. 'It's my insurance policy,' she told him. 'To be used only in the direst of circumstances.'

'Quite. Thus far, we think alike.'

'Yes. Thus far and no further.'

She was more than a match for him now. He studied the set of her mouth, the erect shoulders, the quiet confidence in her face. 'Does anyone else know?' he asked.

'Agnes knows she is my sister – you were there at the time. I'm so glad the scars on your face healed, by the way. Beyond that, I have kept my counsel. There is no point in showing my hand before all betting has ceased. We are the only two players – you will have to take my word for that, since you have no other option. Even her grandfather does not know that you are the reason for Agnes's existence. Thus it will remain unless or until circumstances alter.'

'Good.'

'So now, we negotiate, Father. First, we want Denis back. Harry Timpson is a good worker – thank you for giving him that chance – but we are all used to Denis. I suggest you crawl on your belly and beg Denis to return – even on a part time basis if necessary.'

He blinked rapidly. 'He hit me.'

'Yes, he did.'

'But yours was the weight behind the blow.'

'Yes, it was.'

A short silence ensued. 'I shall give them the deeds to their house – the landlord will sell to me if I offer the right price. The grandfather, too, must be compensated—'

'No. Mr Grimshaw will be kept in the dark about Agnes's situation. He's had one stroke – a second could kill him. He is secure now, thanks to his second wife and his business.'

'I see. Any more conditions?'

'Leave Louisa with me until her confinement – as I told you already, there are complications best dealt with by the females of the species. After the child is born, she will make her own choices and decisions. Father, you have ruled for too long – I think it's time for another Regency period. You and I can be courteous in company, at least. As long as we understand each other, we'll cope. My documents will remain in a bank vault.'

'Ah.'

Helen tried not to smile – the burglary had been a waste of time, energy and money, yet she considered her thousand pounds to have been well spent. She watched while he processed the information, noticed that he did not flinch. 'We have each met our Waterloo,' she said sweetly, 'though I hold the bigger guns. Get Denis back.' After delivering the order for a second time, she left the room.

Judge Zachary Spencer walked to the window and gazed out on the land between Skirlaugh Rise and Skirlaugh Fall. He had to go down there now and prostrate himself before his illegitimate daughter and her husband. Unused to backing down, he watched Harry Timpson as he dragged a wash leather across the bonnet of the Bentley. Harry Timpson was a big man, but he was not suitable for manual work and held no driving licence. 'Bloody women,' cursed the judge as he turned and poured himself a drink. Two daughters, he had now. And he was in thrall to both.

After a large brandy, he decided to get the visit over. It promised not to be easy, yet it had to be done, because Miss Helen Spencer had spoken.

*

293

It was love at not quite first sight. Mags, who had been visiting Agnes, had been brought up to Lambert House in order to see Helen and Louisa. Full of stories about her new social life and about men who wanted to take her out and buy her gifts, Mags Bradshaw was rendered almost speechless by the sight of Harry Timpson. He was a seasoned if petty criminal; she was a legal secretary, but she fell hard.

She had seen him before, of course. He belonged in Noble Street, had lived for years a few houses along from Agnes, but Cupid had never loaded his bow until now. Harry was handsome, quieter than she remembered, polite to the point of shyness and she intended to ignore him.

Nevertheless, reasons for visiting Lambert House suddenly multiplied. She brought new-laid eggs to a village where they were always available, knew that she was carrying the proverbial coals to Newcastle. She bought baby clothes, blankets, a shawl for Louisa's expected baby. Sometimes, he wasn't there. Helen, who had been watching the situation with a degree of glee, decided to step in as ringmaster. She collared Harry one wet afternoon, brought him into the kitchen for a hot drink. Dripping wet, he huddled over the cup, steam rising from his person as he leaned towards the fire. Kate was elsewhere in the house, so Helen embarked on her matchmaking. 'Mags Bradshaw's looking well,' she began.

He nodded, causing a small shower of water to tumble from thick, dark locks. As ever, he hung on to every word uttered by his saviour and mentor. He adored Miss Spencer and it showed. 'She looks different,' he replied eventually.

'Pretty,' said Helen.

'Yes.'

'And she likes you.'

'Oh.' He swallowed the rest of his tea. 'I like her. She always stops and talks to me as if I'm an equal.'

'You are an equal.'

Harry laughed. 'What – me? The only qualification I've got is a life-saving certificate from the swimming baths. I had to sink to the bottom in my pyjamas, pick up a brick and save it from drowning. Oh, and I won the flat race at school once. I could have won again, only Bernard Short cheated. He used to copy my sums as well.'

Helen smiled. 'I notice that you're good with figures.'

'What? Oh, yes – I've always been like that, so Bernard Short got ten out of ten every time. Until the teacher moved him, then he fell flat on his face, but not flat in the flat race.'

Helen stood up and poured more tea. 'Then we'll send you to night school at the technical college. You can become an accountant.'

'But—'

'Leave butting to goats. And ask Mags Bradshaw to go to the cinema with you.'

'Eh?'

'You heard me, Harry. Mags could get any man she wants, but she's taken a liking to you. Look after her. She needs someone steady.'

He laughed joylessly. 'Steady? Aye, steady as a broken rock before I stopped drinking. It was the drink that got me in hot water, you see. I was always drunk when I went on the rob.'

'I gave up drinking, too,' she said. 'Take her out.'

He whistled softly. 'Are you sure?'

'Have I ever lied to you?'

'No. You're the best thing that's ever happened to me – apart from Mam. Mam was stuck with me, had to help me, but you chose.'

'I had my reasons.'

'I don't care.' He would have gone to the ends of the earth for Helen Spencer. 'You got me one last chance and I won't forget it. Mind you, I'm not so sure about working for your dad – sorry.'

'You're working for me, Harry.'

'OK.'

'And you're going to ask Mags out.'

Harry coughed. 'I'd feel daft.'

Helen sighed. 'You can't get all the way through life without feeling daft. It's daft to expect to get through without feeling daft.'

He understood her perfectly. He would always understand her perfectly.

By the time Judge Zachary Spencer arrived at the Make-peace cottage, its residents were already fully conversant with the plot. On the telephone, Helen had mithered, as had Louisa, until Denis had finally agreed to give the old swine a hearing. As for the deeds to the house – he would accept those without a quibble. Agnes had never received anything from her biological father – their child would get something, at least, in the form of a small, stone-built dwelling.

Agnes opened the door. She had not expected to feel embarrassed, yet she did. This was her dad. She didn't like him and would probably never like him, but he was related to her. 'Come in,' she said softly. He did not look at her as he walked into the house.

Zachary Spencer had always been a good public

speaker, which quality had taken him all the way to the top of the legal tree, but he had never been competent in a small setting. He needed to preach, to be heard by as many as possible; he needed the right setting and a big audience – here, he had neither.

Denis stood in front of the fire, his stance reminiscent of Judge Spencer's attitude on the day of reckoning in Morecambe, the day when Agnes and Denis had both injured him. 'Well?'

'The past,' began the judge, 'must be laid to rest. We have all been at fault. When the child is born, I shall set up a fund.' He waited for thanks, but received none.

Agnes was seated, hands folded in her lap. Her father, acutely aware that both his daughters were strong women, glanced sideways at her. 'I am sorry,' he said, his voice strained by the necessary apology. 'I was in the wrong.'

The Makepeaces nodded.

'Denis, I want you to come back to the house as chauffeur and handyman. Harry Timpson is a good enough sort, but he doesn't drive. He's learning, but he hasn't passed his test yet.'

Prepared by the Spencer women, who had dripped on him like water on stone, Denis made his reply. 'I have another job, sir, with a friend who is renovating a barn.'

'Ah.'

'I can't just walk out on him. Will you take a seat?'

The judge sat. 'There's a lot of that going on these days,' he offered in an effort to punctuate the weighty silence. 'Barns and so forth being made into houses. Sensible idea, I suppose. Though crops will always need storage . . .' His voice died.

'Yes.'

Two robins fought on a bush outside the front window. Robins, mused Agnes, were aggressive little buggers. Two angry robins outside, two inside. And who was she? Jenny Wren? Her supposed father spoke not to her, but to the man of the house. She didn't count, didn't matter, was only a woman. 'If my baby is female, will you still set up an account?'

At last, he looked at her. But his expression betrayed the impression that he had been interrupted from an unexpected source. 'Of course I will.'

Agnes leaned her head to one side. 'You know, Judge Spencer, you should have lived in Victorian times when women stayed at home and had vapours; when their dads could throw them out for no reason. Or maybe you'd be best off in one of those Eastern countries where wives and daughters stay several paces behind the men. You've used and abused women all your life, haven't you? Oh, and I'd better remind you – we have the vote these days.'

He simmered, but dared not explode.

'We sit on juries, some of us are doctors – even lawyers. Ah, but you know all about that, don't you?'

'Mrs Makepeace, I am here to make peace.'

Denis did not smile; neither did his wife. Their surname often brought forth puns and silly jokes.

'I'll do three days,' said Denis, anxious for the meeting to close. 'Thursday, Friday and Saturday, I'll help George.'

'George Henshaw?' The older man's face reddened. They were all in it together, of course.

'Yes,' replied Denis. 'That's the chap.'

The judge looked at his watch, remembered an appointment, made his excuses and left. Denis saw him off the premises, then dropped into a chair next to his wife. 'Well, Helen's certainly got him sorted out,' he observed. 'I wonder what else is in that letter? Being your dad isn't enough to reduce him to the state he's in. There's more, isn't there, love?'

There must be a lot more. Agnes wondered yet again about Judge Spencer's past misdeeds, tried to imagine anything bad enough to make the stubborn old man submit. 'It has to be either rape, massive theft, or murder,' she concluded out loud. 'For him, rape would scarcely be enough. It has to be worse than rape.' She shivered. The days were becoming shorter and colder, although pregnancy was easier in weather like this.

'Are you all right, love?' he asked.

'Something walked across my grave, Denis. It's bad enough thinking he might have raped my mam – but murder?'

'He didn't murder her. She died in bed, didn't she?'

Agnes nodded. He hadn't murdered Eileen Grimshaw, but he had taken the life from her, had probably removed her will to live. 'People kill people without actually murdering them,' she said softly. 'If someone stamps hard enough on your soul, you can die many times over.'

'Stop it, Agnes.'

'I'll be all right in a minute.'

Denis hoped so. For over twenty years, his wife had existed in the 'father unknown' category of life. That was difficult enough for anyone, but, for Agnes, the discovery of her father's identity had brought no relief. She was pregnant and tormented. She knew that the blood of Zachary Spencer ran through her own veins. She knew that her child would carry that same blood, albeit to a more diluted degree. 'Agnes?'

'What?'

'I have to go back to the house – you know that. They don't feel safe. Even Helen can't make them feel completely safe. Kate needs me there, too.'

'I know. They explained it enough times.'

'We have to get on with it.'

'I know that as well. It's just that . . .' She couldn't express how she felt, though a terrible feeling of dread had descended on her. Denis should not go back, yet he must. Her reluctance was all a part of being pregnant, she supposed.

'Just that what?' he asked.

'Nothing,' she said. 'It was nothing. Put the kettle on.'

The No Poultry Allowed party was the brainchild of Helen Spencer. 'I don't mean a political party,' she said in response to her half-sister's quizzical expression. 'Christmas evening. We'll all have eaten turkey, chicken or goose at lunchtime, so I vote we have anything except poultry. My father will be at his club with all the other lonely bachelors and widowers. So Louisa and I decided to have a bit of a gathering.'

They were with Louisa in Helen's apartment. She was looking well, was eating everything in her path and was even managing the odd quip. 'The rooster will be absent,' she remarked. 'He can crow in Manchester where we can't hear him.'

There had been little crowing from that source, thought Agnes as she accepted a cup of coffee. This was now Helen's house, with Helen's rules and Helen's style. The main rooms remained unaffected, but the flat used by her and Louisa was modern, all G-plan and teak, glass inserts in tables, rooms divided by open bookshelves, a light, airy feel to the place.

'Mags is head over heels,' Louisa remarked. 'And that young man of hers is doing very well at the college – his tutor says he's a natural accountant.'

Helen almost choked in her tea. 'There's nothing natural about accountants,' she spluttered. 'They're like lawyers – focused to the point of obsession. But he sailed through second year exams at the test, and he's only been there three months.' She was pleased with herself; she had found what her father might have begrudgingly termed a primitive genius. 'I'm glad for Mags,' she added.

'What about you, though?' Louisa asked.

Helen looked at her young stepmother. 'I have a different role to play. There can be no room for marriage in my life, Louisa. Like an accountant, I am completely focused.'

Sometimes, Helen frightened Agnes. A bright and amusing woman who had acquired her self-certainty almost at the cost of her sanity, Helen Spencer was an enigma. When she spoke of her father, her eyes seemed to darken, while the corners of her mouth dipped, as if she tasted something unpalatable. The calm she displayed was a cloak. It hid a turmoil too deep to be allowed space at the surface, yet it burned white-hot in her bones. To a mere onlooker, she was considerate, happy with immediate friends, capable of delivering a joke. Yet often, when companions spoke among themselves, she retreated into her shell, brow furrowing as she visited her own centre.

'Marriage is good,' Louisa said. 'I am so happy. Look at the daughter I acquired, look how she takes care of me.'

Agnes shook her head. Louisa wasn't married at all. She saw her husband a few times a month and spent the rest of her time with Helen and Oscar, who had calmed slightly now that his second lot of teeth had broken through. The new furniture had been bought only after his chewing phase had ended. He was a good dog. While the women talked, he lay at their feet, sometimes asleep, often glancing from one to another as if trying to understand their conversations.

'I have a list,' Helen announced.

'She likes lists,' said Louisa. 'Her whole life is planned in a locked drawer – isn't it, Helen?'

The dog scratched an ear.

'Not all of it, no,' Helen replied. 'But I shall be cooking on Christmas Day, so that's a big list. Kate will rest. She's on the guest list—'

'Another list.' Louisa laughed.

'Yes.' Undismayed, Helen continued. 'And we shall eat in the kitchen – I'm not keen on the dining room.'

The dog woofed.

'Yes, you'll get the leftovers.' Helen patted his head. 'This will be our last child-free Christmas – let's make the most of it.'

Agnes was certain that Helen Spencer was looking forward to the births of the two babies. Gone were the days when she feared being ousted by the new addition to her household, while the arrival of her niece or nephew was anticipated with pleasure displayed in the form of concern for Agnes and gifts for the nursery. But what was she up to this time? 'Are you sure he won't be here?'

'Our father who will never be in heaven?' Helen, who had stopped going to church, had got into the habit of referring to her father in biblical terms that were not far short of heresy. He would be Lazarus without resurrection, a shaven Samson, the stunned Goliath, Moses minus tablets, Judas at the feast – but not at this feast. 'He won't be here.'

'Are you really sure?'

Helen shrugged. 'We haven't done Christmas for years. When I was little, someone would stay in the house to give me my presents – a servant, a nanny – anyone who would agree to do it for a bit of money. Since I grew up, I have spent all my Christmases alone.'

A tear pricked Agnes's right eye. Christmas had always been magical for her. Stocking filled with tiny toys and nuts, always a surprise in the toe. One year, the surprise had been a little silver ring – she had outgrown it years ago. Downstairs, there would be a doll, or a toy sewing machine, several books. Dinner was chicken, as turkey could never be afforded. Her father would have had a good dinner, she supposed. But not with Helen, never with his own daughter. 'I had lovely Christmases, Helen. I wish you'd been there then. There wasn't a lot of money—'

'But there was love,' Helen finished for her.

'Yes.'

'Mr and Mrs Grimshaw will come, I hope. And Mags with Harry. We'll be merry if it kills us. Of course, we can't play cards, because my stepmother cheats.'

Louisa clouted Helen with a newspaper. 'I came up in the school of hard knocks.'

'As did I,' Helen said. 'Money, but no love. This party is for all of us, so that I can show my gratitude to those who have helped turn my life around. The loyal toast will be the Queen, the Duke of Lancaster and Mabel Turnbull. She knew loyalty.'

Agnes shivered. There was no point in asking Helen

to reveal in its entirety the document she had read, because such a request would receive no more than a polite refusal. The automatic response had been delivered many times – Helen remained as secretive as ever. 'Do we bring anything?' she asked.

'Just yourselves.' Helen smiled at her sister. She, too, wished that those long-ago Christmases could have been spent with Agnes. 'I wonder how many of us there are and whether we are all female,' she said, almost as if speaking to herself. 'There could be dozens of little Spencers spread across the northern circuit. He's a rake, but I am the shovel that will dispose of him.'

A heavy silence rested on the shoulders of Agnes and Louisa.

Helen laughed. 'Don't look so glum. I am speaking metaphorically, of course.'

Agnes was not sure, would never be sure. She changed the subject. 'Your doll's house is almost ready,' she told Louisa. 'Even the cellars are included. He's charging your husband a fortune for it, says it will allow him to charge less when it comes to ordinary folk.'

Louisa shook her head. The doll's house was not for her – it was for the proud owner of the house on which it had been modelled. 'It will be kept in the hall,' she said, 'so that everyone can see what a wonderful home the judge has.'

'He never has visitors,' said Agnes. 'It's for himself.'

'Isn't everything?' Helen stood and walked to the door. 'I declare this meeting of the NPA party closed. Unless there's any other business?'

Louisa raised a deliberately hesitant hand. 'Please, miss?'

'Yes?'

'Will somebody get Oscar off my foot? The toes have gone dead – he's cut off my circulation.'

Helen whistled and the dog dashed to her side.

'Thanks.' Louisa stretched her legs and counted her feet. 'I seem to have two,' she said.

'Don't brag,' quipped Helen. 'You'll soon have four.' She left the room.

'It's a big thing, isn't it?' Agnes asked. 'The thought of producing another human being, I mean. I'm not talking about the pain – it's the afterwards that frightens me. If a child is good and successful, they get the credit. If not, the blame is ours.'

Louisa was staring into the fire. 'I won't raise a child,' she said quietly.

'No. He'll get nannies and nurses, I suppose. The judge, I mean.'

After several seconds, Louisa replied. 'Yes. That's how it will be.' She leaned her head against the wing of her chair and dozed.

Agnes waited until Louisa was asleep, then crept from the room. Across the landing, Helen was seated at a bureau in her bedroom, head down, right shoulder moving. She was probably continuing with her book. Agnes left the author to the necessary privacy and silence.

Helen put down her pen, listened as her sister walked out of the apartment, looked down at the list she had made. Louisa was right – her stepdaughter was a maker of lists. The page she currently worked on was one no one must see. Its subject was retribution . . .

Christmas Day was fine, but cold. The party, due to begin at seven in the evening, was delayed slightly by

Helen's over-ambition in the area of cookery. Her philosophy was simple – if a person could read, he or she could cook. It did not run to plan. Six o'clock found her on the phone to her new sister. She refused to allow Agnes to fetch Kate, because Kate cooked frequently in the kitchen of Lambert House, and this was one of Kate's few holidays.

'What the heck have you done?' Agnes asked.

'Crème caramel is my first problem. It's in a bain marie and it's as stiff as the bread board.'

'Oh. Did you put water in your caramel?'

'What?'

'It's probably stuck. You've got melted sugar acting as glue. Start again.'

'There isn't time.'

'Cheese and biscuits?'

'That's the last course. We still need a pudding.'

'I've an apple pie, half a trifle and some mince tarts,' said Agnes.

'Bring them. Bring everything. Bring hammer and chisel for this crème caramel. Bring the fire brigade and bring Denis. I am in a mess.'

Agnes replaced the receiver and turned to her husband. 'Helen's in a mess.'

'Ah.'

'What do you mean, "Ah"?'

'She's bound to be in a mess. Her doings with ovens stop at warming up what Kate leaves. I thought she was taking too much on. Game pie? When she told me she was making that, I decided I wasn't game enough for her pie. Too ambitious, she is.'

'She needs us. Come on, shape yourself.'

He shaped himself and both entered the kitchen of Lambert House within half an hour. It was a war zone.

The table was littered with eggshells and implements; the floor was in a similar state. Helen was nowhere to be seen. Denis sighed. 'She's got herself in a right pickle this time, Agnes.'

The woman in question crawled out from beneath the large table. 'I've lost an onion,' she pronounced.

'Does she know her onions?' Denis asked.

Agnes shook her head. 'Probably not. She's likely lost a cauliflower. Perhaps she calls a cauliflower an onion—'

'A spade a lawnmower?' asked Denis helpfully.

The mistress of the house struggled to her feet. 'Shut up, both of you. My consommé is lumpy, the beef's still rare enough to be saying moo and you've got the pudding, I hope.'

'Yes.' Agnes placed a basket on the table. 'Right – stock cubes?'

Helen waved in the direction of a cupboard.

'I'll do imitation French onion soup – if you can find the onion. Denis – clean up and sort out the puddings.' She glared at Helen. 'You can just bugger off. Where's the game pie?'

'In the pigswill bucket.'

'Good. So it's pretend French onion soup, roast beef with Yorkshires and veg, then leftovers for pudding, followed by cheese.' Agnes cast an eye over Helen. 'You haven't managed to ruin the cheese, by any chance?'

'The cheese is fine,' said Helen before stalking out of the arena.

Agnes and Denis looked at each other and burst out laughing. It was one of those rare and precious moments in life when laughter takes over, when the body becomes too weak to fight hilarity. They cobbled together a meal of sorts, each working hard not to surrender to mirth all over again. It was an image worth remembering, thought Agnes. With flour on her nose and in her hair, Miss Helen Spencer had looked every inch the angry housewife. It had been fun.

The party started well. Eva, suitably impressed by her first taste of 'foreign' food, sipped politely from her soup spoon. Agnes, who had made the soup from half a dozen stock cubes and three onions, almost suffocated on her own spoonful. Helen pretended to glare at her. 'Careful,' she warned. 'You'll choke.'

Denis proved the worst. His silliness took him further than his wife was willing to travel. 'Helen?' he said.

'Yes?'

'You're a good cook. This is lovely soup.' The word 'soup' emerged slightly crippled, because Agnes kicked him under the table. With the air of an injured angel, he continued to enjoy his strange food. 'Are we having that game pie?' he asked, his face framed in innocence.

Agnes kicked him again.

'I decided on beef,' replied Helen.

'Good.' Fred Grimshaw slurped another mouthful of French onion. 'If I see another turkey butty, I'll scream.'

Agnes laid down her spoon. She had taken enough of her Oxo cube and onion. 'Shall I check the beef and Yorkshires, or will you, Helen?'

'Thank you. You do it.'

Agnes escaped to the far end of the room. Lucy and George, too polite to say much, were looking at each other in bewilderment. Mags and Harry had eyes only for each other, while Louisa, determined to eat anything and everything in sight, scooped up her soup without comment. It was Kate who broke the silence. 'This is nobbut Oxo with an onion in it,' she exclaimed.

Thus ended the charade. 'Out of the mouths of babes and servants,' Agnes muttered from the safer end of the room.

The story was told by Helen, who was prompted all the way by Denis. Kate hid her face in her napkin, her shaking back betraying uncontrollable glee.

George stood and pushed thumbs under his lapels, voice imitating that of the judge at whose table he was dining. 'The defendant must stand,' he ordered.

Helen stood.

'Before I pass sentence, may I say how dim a view I take of plagiarism. You have stolen the work of another woman and have passed it off as your own.'

'Yes, m'lud.' Helen's tone was suitably subdued.

'Have you anything to say before sentence is passed?'

'Yes, m'lud.'

'Very well.'

Helen inhaled deeply. 'I do not know my onions, m'lud. Nor do I know my bain marie from my elbow, if your lordship will permit so bold a statement. I am but a poor serving girl with no brain, no hope and no pudding.'

George smiled at Lucy, composed himself and carried on holding court. 'Your sentence will be three years in the Cordon Bleu Prison, Paris – which is in France.'

'Yes, m'lud.'

'This is one of the worst cases I have tried. Yes, it has been very trying. Compensation will be made to every person who has suffered as a result of your French onion soup and you will pay all costs pertaining to this case. Mrs Agnes Makepeace will no doubt take her own measures via litigation. All rise.'

They rose.

'This court is closed.'

They sat.

A shadow in the doorway became flesh. Judge Zachary Spencer walked into the kitchen. 'Very funny, Mr Henshaw,' he said.

Oscar, who had been sitting hopefully by the table, shot out of the room. He didn't like the big man. Nobody liked the big man.

George blushed, but made no reply. Lucy spoke in his defence. 'It was just a bit of fun.'

'Quite.' Judge Spencer looked at all the people in the room. A mixed bunch, they represented most levels of society, and they had been having fun at his expense. He had paid for the food; he was also the subject of mimicry. It occurred to him that he was the outsider, that he was condemned to look at life through tinted glass. He was alone, had always been alone.

His daughter – the real one – had managed to carve out a niche for herself. She sat among Henshaws, Makepeaces and others, seemed at ease with them and with herself. Well, she had been at ease before noticing her father. Now, she was staring at him with naked loathing in her eyes. He ignored her, walked into the kitchen, kissed his wife on the cheek, then left the room.

Silence reigned, the quiet interrupted only by the over-enthusiastic slamming of the vast front door. 'He's gone,' breathed Lucy. She no longer feared that Helen might be untrustworthy; Lucy realized at last the poor woman was the product of a brute and that Helen deserved better.

'I wonder what he wanted?' asked Louisa.

'A good kick up the backside.' Fred answered for

everyone present. 'Is that blinking beef ready yet? We're all dying of hunger.'

He drove at a furious rate in the direction of Manchester. After travelling so far just to visit his wife, he had found her ensconced with all kinds of idiots in the kitchen. In the kitchen? What on earth was Helen thinking of? There were servants at the feast, there was George Henshaw trying to be clever with his impertinent imitation of the man who owned the very table at which he was eating. 'Preposterous,' he spat.

The club was tedious. This year, only a handful of geriatric widowers and bachelors were in residence, most of them deaf, some in their delinquent dotage. There was no one to listen to tales of interesting cases, no one who was capable of enjoying a sermon on the legal system. He was bored.

Oh, well. There was nothing else for it – he would have to take an evening meal in the company of his peers. The conversation would involve symptoms of illnesses, requests for mustard, loud comments on the cardboard consistency of the meat. Some old beggar would break wind at table. Waiters would decide to ignore it, but Zachary Spencer would hear all, see all and say nothing.

At Lambert House, people were having fun. Zach did not believe in fun, as it wasted time that might be better spent in the furthering of one's career, yet he had a strong suspicion that he had been missing something. His daughter had looked happy. The other one, basting meat at the cooker, had ignored him. Happy? How happy would Helen be when a son turned up to deprive her of her inheritance?

He parked the car and entered the club. It smelled of old people, stale food and spilt drink. His own home had been taken from him by Helen, who had invited his other so-called daughter to share in the spoils. Well, it wasn't over yet. Soon, a son would be born.

Fred was rubbish at charades. Incapable of acting without speaking, he was sacked in the first round, thereby depriving his team of several points. He said it wasn't fair, he hadn't been ready and he'd never heard of the book whose title he had been trying to convey to team mates. 'What the hell's wuthering?' he asked. 'I can't wuther. Did she mean wither, that there Brontë woman? Or did she mean weather?'

'Or whether, or whither?' added George helpfully.

Fred glared at him. 'Shut up,' he ordered. 'For a lawyer, you're no bloody use at all. No wonder the court system costs too much. Where do you think you're going?' he asked Lucy, who was another member of his team.

'I'm just wuthering off to the bathroom,' she replied.

Fred retreated to his chair and grumbled softly about young people not being as they used to be. There was no respect any more and people were getting too big for their clogs.

Oscar, who had enjoyed many leftovers from the hastily prepared feast, stretched out on the rug in front of the drawing room fire. As the rug had been the stage, charades was abandoned while Helen and Agnes experimented with mulled wine. Fred poured himself a whisky, declaring that he had had enough of being a guinea pig for mulling, wuthering and culinary disaster, so they could leave him out of the mixture.

Agnes, who was being disturbed by the movements of Nuisance, sat aside from the rest of the party. If Nuisance was going to practise cartwheels, she would need to be near the door in order to reach the bathroom when required. She watched her family – this was her family now. Pop, whom she had loved for a lifetime, continued to argue about wutherings and mullings. He was doing well in business, was content with his second wife, and was always at his most satisfied when involved in a dispute. He was involved at this moment, so he was as happy as a dog with two tails.

Eva, hoping that no one was watching, was fiddling with a tiny gold-coloured safety pin in an effort to fasten her blouse – a button had shot off into her food, an accident caused by hilarity during the meal. Once her blouse was fastened, Eva dozed by the fire. Pop was old, but happy; Eva was older because of her weight and all those years spent making a living at the top of Noble Street. They were a special breed and, Agnes hoped, not a dying one.

Helen, her new-found sister who had been the grey, listless librarian, was very much alive this evening. She had ousted her father, had humiliated him in front of many of the people here tonight. Only Pop and Eva remained unaware of the relationship between Helen and Agnes.

Lucy and George were still blissful. It was a good marriage, Agnes believed. No longer resistant to the approaches of Helen Spencer, Lucy had enjoyed herself this evening. George was quieter, because he was the one who had been caught by the judge while imitating him, yet even he seemed to know that Zachary Spencer's days were numbered. What would happen, Agnes wondered. When would Helen reveal the ace she held so close to her chest?

Mags, who had grown into her new nose, stared lovingly into the handsome face of Glenys Timpson's oldest lad. Agnes smiled to herself. Harry had always been a source of trouble to his mother, yet he had settled into his studies and showed great promise – which fact, Agnes thought, was sufficient to verify the saying about every dog having his day.

The canine dog was certainly having his day. Replete and exhausted by the effort of over-eating, Oscar lay at Eva's feet. They seemed to be indulging in synchronized snoring – the company was suddenly silent as each person became aware of the comic scene.

Oscar rolled over and broke the rhythm. 'Shame, that,' muttered Fred. 'I were going to accompany them two on me comb and paper.'

Kate and Albert laughed. They were the best neighbours in the world and Agnes was glad to know them.

Denis was joking with George. The scars left on Denis's lungs had not been too troublesome this winter, so that was another worry gone.

Only Louisa remained. Agnes cast an eye over the young woman who had married a man twice her age in order to secure a safe future for herself. But she had gained a good friend in her stepdaughter and motherhood would surely bring its own reward. Yet her husband remained in the house even though he was absent. It was as if he stained everything he touched, because each person here had been affected by him to a greater or lesser degree.

The thoughts came full circle. Agnes found herself

gazing at Helen yet again. Laughing and joking, she seemed to fool most people, though Agnes was not convinced by the act. Helen's anger was so deep that it had cooled all the way down to ice. She had a plan of some kind and it was tied up in the letters held by a Bolton bank under the instruction of George Henshaw. The judge seldom came home; he was threatened by his daughter and chose to keep a distance between himself and his own house.

Helen arrived at Agnes's side. 'You're quiet.'

'I'm tired – Nuisance is learning to dance.'

'He'll be born walking, then.'

'Probably. Helen?'

'What? Oh, not again, Agnes. Stop worrying. Nothing will happen. He'll simply disappear one day and we'll have peace.'

'Disappear?'

'Yes. Retire abroad – whatever.'

'And Louisa?'

Helen shrugged. 'Will stay with me.'

'The baby?'

'We haven't got there yet. Can't you just enjoy Christmas, Agnes? You're surrounded by friends and family, yet you still worry about Father. Forget him. He is a man of no importance.'

With that, Agnes had to be satisfied.

Chapter Twelve

As the date of Louisa's confinement drew near, Judge Spencer began to spend more time at Lambert House. Louisa, who was in better health, appointed herself peacekeeper during this stressful time. Helen, living in her own apartment, saw little of her father; Louisa, in search of a more tranquil household, divided her time between the two adversaries. She was a poor go-between, as she determinedly avoided conversations involving any controversy, and she realized that the relationship between father and daughter was not easily redeemable. She continued to eat well, using the latter part of her pregnancy as a cocoon inside which she was safe. But she dreaded the afterwards. The real trouble would begin once the baby had been delivered. For now, she was cushioned by her passenger, and she chose not to think too clearly about the birth and its aftermath.

Helen kept to herself, emerging only to visit Agnes. Mags and Lucy came each Thursday to the Makepeace cottage, and Helen was now part of the group. The subject of Helen's letter and the accompanying document from the deceased nanny had ceased to wear out telephone lines between the houses of Agnes, Mags and Lucy; the matter was no longer raised in the presence of Helen Spencer, and it seemed to die a natural death as the confinement of Agnes drew near.

'It's going to be a whopper,' declared Lucy, who, still slim as a reed, was munching on a chocolate bar.

'I hate you.' Agnes looked down, tried to see her feet, failed. She raised one leg to display a slightly swollen ankle. 'Ah, there you are,' she told the foot. 'But there should be two of you.'

Helen ate a sandwich. 'Louisa looks like a galleon in full sail. I'd swear she was carrying twins, but the doctors say not. It seems she's storing fluids. If she gets any bigger, we could rent her out as a petrol tanker.'

'Better a commercial vehicle than an object that stays in and waits,' Agnes grumbled. 'I'm a thing now – not a person. I'm just a building that's been placed around this child.' She patted her belly. 'I'm going to have a raffle when it's born. The winner gets the baby, three dozen nappies, a Silver Cross – second hand – and a good supply of clothing.'

'Green Shield stamps?' asked Lucy.

'Definitely not. I'm saving up for a coffee percolator.' Agnes winced. 'I didn't like that.'

'What?' asked Mags.

'Pain in my back.'

Helen sat up straight in her chair. She had read a book about labour and considered herself something of an expert. 'It can start there,' she advised cheerfully. 'The coccyx moves.'

'Does it?' Agnes shifted her weight. 'I'm not due. The coccyx can stay where it is or it'll be raffled off along with the rest.'

The three women stared hard at their friend.

'Stop it!' she yelled. 'Unless you paid to come in, you are not to look at the exhibits. Also, this zoo is closed until the spring. We are hibernating. Now, bugger off and let me get some sleep.'

317

Helen remained when the others had left. She declared her intention to stay until Denis got home. The book was in the car. A person who could read could deliver a child; a person who could read had failed to deliver a simple crème caramel . . . 'Any more pain?'

'No. The only discomfort I'm feeling comes from the expression on your face. I'm not due for a couple of weeks. Even if it does start, it can take days. God – can we not talk about something else?'

Helen grinned. 'Yes, we can. Your grandfather's work is on display in the main hall at Lambert House. It is brilliant, though. He did the immediate garden, and the house lifts off, section by section, until you reach the cellars. Father said – to Louisa, of course – that Mr Grimshaw can bring people in to look at his handiwork. The TV people are to be involved again, along with several newspapers. Your grandfather is a star.'

Agnes groaned.

'Are you all right?'

'No, I'm not all right. He's bad enough without being a bloody star. It'll all go to his head. He'll get himself excited, then he'll start going too fast for his own good. Poor Eva and Albert will bear the brunt. There'll be no living with him.'

'Oh, dear. Sorry.'

'Not your fault. He will push himself until he has another stroke, but that's his nature. Or he may prove too stubborn to have another attack – he could outlive us all. He will certainly brag about his house in your house.'

'Never mind.'

'Exactly.'

Helen smoothed her skirt. 'Our father who isn't in heaven is talking of retirement. According to Louisa, he intends to spend much of his time on the yacht. I never saw her more pleased, because she won't take a baby to sea. We may survive despite him.'

Agnes looked at her visitor. She knew full well that Helen's brain seldom rested, that her thoughts were predominantly about her father and the damage he had done throughout his life. More specifically, there was one occasion in particular that had resurrected itself and Helen brooded about whatever it was. There was no point in asking; Agnes had stopped wasting time in that area months earlier. 'Denis will be home soon. Go back and make sure that Louisa is OK.'

'You're due before she is.'

'I know that, Helen, but babies are not trains – they don't run to a timetable.'

'Nor do trains. All right, all right, I shall go. Phone me if you need me. Promise?'

'Promise.'

Helen bent and planted a kiss on her sister's head. These babies would thrive in safety. Whatever it took, Helen Spencer would make sure of that.

'Helen, why don't you find yourself a nice man? Has there been no one since—'

'Since the balding eagle? No.'

'I was going to say since Denis.'

'Ah.' Helen blushed. 'Denis was one of my crazy times. I suppose I went through my teenage at thirty-two. No. My energies are directed elsewhere. Into writing, for a start.'

'For a start? I thought you'd stopped.'

Helen sighed. 'My dear, disabuse yourself of the mistaken concept that an author writes only with a pen or a typewriter. Every waking moment is spent writing. In here.' She tapped her head. 'It's a collection box.

When it gets full, I shall empty it, discard the dross and polish the good stuff.'

'But no man?'

'No.'

It was more than writing, mused Agnes when Helen had left. She was concentrating on something, and the something was a worry. Denis, too, had remarked on the preoccupation of Miss Helen Spencer. She was up to no good. But the room was warm and sleep beckoned. With her hands folded on the ever-increasing mound of her belly, Agnes slept the sleep of the very pregnant.

Denis came out of the pub. He was two quid better off after a game of dominoes and was looking forward to a brisk walk homeward. When he reached the bottom of the lane that led up to Skirlaugh Rise, he stopped. 'Judge Spencer? What are you doing here?'

'Waiting for you.'

'Ah.' What did the old beggar want at this time of night? 'I'm on my way home,' said Denis.

'I know. Just give me five minutes. It's about my daughter.'

Denis cleared his throat. 'Oh? Which one?'

'Helen.'

'Right. What do you want from me?'

Much as he hated to beg, Zachary knew that he had no alternative. 'Talk to her. Ask her whether she would thrive if she made public the contents of Mabel Turnbull's meanderings. Ask whether her expected sibling would thrive on the exposure of such lies. I just want . . .' What did he want?

'Yes?' asked Denis.

'I want things back to normal – family meals and so forth – the way Louisa had it when we were first married. My daughter hates me, but something must be done before my son is born.'

Denis did not ask how the judge would feel should the son turn out to be yet another daughter. 'I don't carry that much weight with Miss Helen, sir.'

'You carried enough to strike me a few months ago. Try. I want my house in some sort of order.' He placed a hand on Denis's arm. 'Tell me – how is Agnes?'

Denis blinked. Was the old bugger softening in his old age? 'She's OK, thanks. Getting a bit fed up with the weight and the swollen ankles, drinks a lot of bitter lemon – she's uncomfortable.'

'Give her my best wishes.' With that last unnerving request, the man disappeared into the blackness of the Rise. 'Blood and stomach pills,' mumbled Denis, 'he has to be going off his rocker.' Perhaps insanity ran in the family? Or was the judge genuinely interested in improving the lives of all around him? Probably not. He was more likely to be making an attempt to make his own existence more bearable.

Denis entered the house. His wife was asleep in a chair, feet propped on a padded footstool, hands folded across her swollen abdomen. Give her Judge Spencer's best wishes? Not likely – he wanted to keep her blood pressure at an acceptable level. He kissed her. 'Cocoa?'

Agnes opened an eye. 'Bitter lemon, please.'

'You don't like bitter lemon. You've always hated bitter lemon.'

She yawned. 'Tell that to the passenger on the lower deck. It's all his fault.'

Denis made his cocoa while Agnes chattered on about the visit of Mags, Lucy and Helen, complaining

321

loudly about Lucy, who could eat sweets and chocolates with obvious impunity. 'I haven't had chocolate in six months,' she moaned.

'Have some cocoa – that's chocolate.'

But no, she had to have her bitter lemon. They sat in front of the fire like an old married couple, each too tired to talk or move. Agnes knew that this was a precious time, that the marriage would change once there were three of them. 'I love you, kid,' she told her husband. 'I'm saying it now before the dynamics get bewildered, before I become all nappies and feeds and walks with a pram.'

Denis grinned. She would be the best mam in the world. And he couldn't wait to be a dad.

He woke sweating again. As far as he could remember, Zachary had never suffered from nightmares. Even after . . . after that business many years ago, he had slept the sleep of the just.

He switched on a lamp and struggled into a sitting position. The room was cool, yet his skin seemed to be heated by the fires of hell. Some medics were of the opinion that everyone had dreams and that they were often forgotten, but Zachary had not been aware of dreaming. Until now. Until now, when his daughter occupied the witness stand, the judge's seat and every space along the jury's benches. Almost every night during his sleep, she appeared and screamed out his sins for the world to hear. Journalists dashed in all directions, each needing to be the first to break the story of a corrupt judge.

When he poured the brandy, decanter and glass

shook in uncertain hands. He could do nothing, because Helen had protected herself. Even were she to die of natural causes, the documents would be opened. Brandy burned in his throat, dragging into his digestive tract any vestige of heat that had been present in his sweat-slicked body. The shivering began, so he staggered to a wardrobe, found an extra blanket and placed it on his bed. Denis Makepeace? Forced to beg the help of one of his two manservants, he hated his daughter all the more. He should have made an ally of her, because she was proving to be a formidable enemy. Women were stealing positions of authority, were called to the bar, were becoming hospital consultants and managers of industry. He should have noticed, should have encouraged her.

It was too late for that. But it was never too late to paper over cracks. He, Louisa, Helen and the expected child should cobble together an outwardly happy picture of domesticity. Denis, nearer in age to Helen, might just be able to plead the cause on his master's behalf. But even Denis had little time for his employer. He did his duty and no more, was always keen to return to his wife or to his other job. It all boiled down to those damned letters in the vault of some damned bank, contents to be revealed in the event of Helen's demise.

Retirement beckoned. Many judges continued into their dotage, but this judge was standing – or sitting – on rocky ground. He had his yacht and could disappear whenever he chose, but first, he had to be here for the birth of Louisa's child. Another brandy slipped down into his stomach and he leaned back against the pillows. He needed sleep, dreaded the dream, hoped that the brandy would preclude it. It wasn't fair. Life had never been fair. Pitying himself for his gross misfortunes, Judge Spencer fell asleep for a second time. And the dream came again.

For the sake of Louisa, Helen agreed to the terms put forward via Denis. An uneasy truce ensued, with all three Spencers eating together in the main dining room when the judge was at home. When he was away, the two women returned to Helen's apartment to experiment with Helen's faith in reading as a basis for cookery. She improved, though meals created by Kate Moores remained superior to Helen's efforts.

A rhythm developed. Breakfast was taken in Helen's part of the house, as was lunch; then, if the judge was at home, a later meal was served at the dining table downstairs. The women read, watched television, became addicted to *The Archers* on the radio. While Louisa napped, Helen dealt with Oscar. It was the happiest time in Helen's life thus far. She had her family at last – Louisa, Agnes and the dog.

The dog, walked by Helen every day, always made a beeline for the Makepeace cottage. He had three homes, and he made determined use of every one of them. Agnes and Fred usually kept scraps for him; he was having an excellent life – as long as he stayed away from the big man.

On the day of the second visit by Granada, Helen and Oscar returned, with Agnes, to a house of turmoil. Cameras and boom microphones took up most of the space. Kate, who was still running around like a cat on hot bricks, had polished to within an inch of its life anything that failed to move – the hall sparkled. In its centre sat a large table on which was displayed Fred's latest work of art. Even his granddaughter gasped in wonderment when she saw the model. Pop was gifted. If he could learn to keep quiet, he would go far.

But he didn't keep quiet. Fred delivered a lecture on life's never being over until the lid settled on the coffin; he berated all who retired to idleness and argued with the interviewer that tiredness and ill-health were no excuse for inactivity. 'Everybody should be doing,' he said fiercely. 'There's no excuse for sitting and doing nowt.'

'But what about disability?' asked the poor newsman.

'I'm disabled. I've had a stroke and was as daft as a brush for a while. No excuse. You have to keep at it.'

Agnes hid her face in one of Denis's handkerchiefs. She knew her Pop inside out, knew he wasn't one to change his mind even when in the wrong.

When cameras and microphones were switched off, the interviewer collared Agnes. 'How do you put up with him?' he asked.

'I don't. I sold him to the highest bidder and she sold her shop to afford him. He's a kind man in his way. He just wants to encourage folk to be useful.'

'Yes, and he'll have several of them depressed. Some people really can't do anything. But his work is brilliant. He'll be doing models of all the big houses soon.'

'He won't. He's booked up for two years. So if you want a house for your daughter, you'll have to wait.'

The man grinned. 'I ordered mine months ago. I could tell then that he was unusual.' He walked away.

Unusual? Fred was a one-off, a treasure, a pest and a wonderful man. He was now tackling the judge, who had come home to bask in the reflected glory of Fred's model of Lambert House. 'You can't retire,' said Fred. 'Judges don't retire – they die with their wigs on.'

Judge Spencer was not used to such bluntness. 'I've served my country,' he answered stiffly.

'Aye, so have I, but that's no excuse. Will you go travelling on yon yacht?'

'Probably.'

Fred was quietened by that single word. 'That's all right, then. You're doing summat different – sailing. If you can afford it, you do it, lad.' Thus spoke the father of Eileen Grimshaw, mother to Agnes, victim of Judge Spencer. Having granted permission to retire, Fred went off to irritate others. Helen grinned broadly. Her father was taking advice from his chauffeur, the grandfather of an illegitimate daughter and from his one and only recognized child. At table, he often asked Helen's opinion. It was a charade, but it would do for now, she supposed. Louisa was better, there were just a couple of months to go, and all was well thus far.

Agnes tugged at Helen's sleeve. 'Did you hear Pop talking to your dad?'

'I did. Our father's being kept in his rightful place, exactly where I can see him.' She shook her head. 'Agnes, stop looking at me like that. I don't know what will happen in the future any more than you do. Leave him to me. He'll get what's coming to him.'

Agnes sat and gazed again at Pop's handiwork. She wished Nan could have seen it, though she would not have denied Eva the opportunity to wear her wedding outfit for a third time. Eva was as proud as Punch of her husband. There was no one like Fred in her book. There was no one like Pop, full stop, thought Agnes.

Denis joined her. 'Are you all right?'

'Eh?'

He pointed to the floor beneath her chair. 'I think your waters just broke.'

'Oh.'

Denis pushed a hand through his hair. That 'Oh' was typical of Agnes. She took life as it came, didn't seem to panic, wasn't one for the vapours. He grabbed Helen. 'Please get your car. Agnes is going into labour and I don't want to put a wet wife into your dad's Bentley. We can collect her bag on the way to Townleys.'

Helen gasped. 'It's not due yet, is it?'

'No, but this is Agnes we're dealing with. She's got a lot of her granddad in her, so she doesn't work to any timetable. Please hurry.'

Agnes was bundled into the car and driven to the cottage to wait while Denis got her case. She sat in the back seat and sucked a mint.

'Any pain?' asked Helen anxiously.

'No.'

'Are you sure?'

'Yes. When the pain starts, you'll be the third to know. Me first, then Denis, then you. OK?'

Helen shook her head. She wished she could boast such pragmatism, but she never would. According to Father, Helen's mother had been difficult; Eileen Grimshaw had probably been compliant, though there was little of that quality in Agnes. Agnes just got on with life, Helen supposed, as Denis jumped back into the driving seat.

They reached the hospital within twenty minutes, Agnes complaining not of pain, but of dampness. 'I can't remember the last time I wet my knickers,' she complained as she was led towards Maternity.

When Agnes had been taken away for examination,

Denis and Helen sat nervously under a poster about inoculations. There was clearly a lot of complicated stuff involved in the production and rearing of a child. 'Denis?'

'What?'

'Have you thought about names?'

'Oh. Yes, we have. A boy will be David and a girl Sally.' He drummed his fingers on a knee. 'They've been a long time.'

'They've been three minutes, Denis.'

'Oh.'

Agnes returned eventually. She wore a nightdress, a dressing gown and a disappointed air. 'Can't go home because the waters have gone. Can't get on with it – nothing's happening. The baby is happy where it is and we just have to wait.'

'You can go home,' Denis advised Helen. 'Tell Fred and Eva what's happening.'

'What's not happening.' Agnes's tone was gloomy. 'And get me some bitter lemon, please. And keep Pop away from here – he'll be telling everybody how to do their job and I won't cope with him.'

Helen left.

Agnes paced up and down the corridor until her husband thought her in danger of wearing out the tiles. She counted doors, posters, other pregnant walkers, teacups and saucers on a trolley. Finally, she counted her blessings. There were girls here with no company, no husband, mother or father. Denis intended to be present throughout – she was very lucky.

By evening, the corridor was packed as tightly as a children's matinee at the Odeon. Eva had arrived in full sail – including wedding outfit, as she had not had time to change – with Fred in tow. Helen sat with Lucy and

Mags; Harry Timpson came to keep Mags company. He was followed closely by Albert and Kate Moores, who wanted to know if Agnes needed anything. When George put in an appearance, Agnes had gone off the idea of a quorum. 'Will you all beggar off home?' she pleaded.

A midwife arrived to take Agnes's blood pressure. 'There's ten of you,' she exclaimed. Agnes, who had taken to counting anything and everything in order to relieve boredom, put the midwife right. 'There are twelve if you include parents and lower deck passenger.'

Agnes sat while the monitor did its work, was told that the reading was acceptable, then she waded in. 'Will you get rid of this lot? I'm beginning to feel like a spectator sport at Olympic level. There should be two of us, three if you count Nuisance – but no more. Evacuate this corridor, please, or I am going home.'

The midwife did better than that by removing the patient from the scene. 'She's going on a ward until labour starts,' she explained to the audience. 'We won't move her to the labour room until she's further on. Please go home – we haven't room for a crowd.'

Agnes didn't move further on until the next morning, when she was delivered of a healthy boy weighing almost nine pounds. When he was handed to her, she nodded and spoke to him. 'I've a bone to pick with you,' she said before giving him to his dad.

Denis wiped away a tear as he passed the child over to the team for cleaning and checking. 'You did well,' he told his wife. 'No swearing, no screaming.'

'I couldn't let him win the last round, could I?' She took a cup and drank from it. 'Yuk,' she exclaimed. 'What's this rubbish?'

329

'Bitter lemon.' He took it away. 'I did warn you – you've never liked bitter lemon.'

Agnes smiled at all around her. She had a son, a wonderful husband and a nurse bending over her. 'Your dad phoned,' said the latter.

'I haven't got a dad.'

'Oh. Right.' The young woman left the bedside.

Exhausted, Agnes leaned on her pillows. Judge Spencer had no claim on her son, no proof that he was the grandfather. If he thought he was going to get his sticky paws on David Makepeace, he had another think coming. Helen would sort him out, she told herself. Helen had him by the scruff of the neck, didn't she?

Denis returned. 'I'll come in tomorrow,' he promised. 'Oh – the midwife said well done, because if our lad had gone full term he would have been an eleven-pounder.'

Agnes winced. It had been like launching a battleship, but if the pregnancy had gone full term it would have been the *Queen Mary*, plus all hands on and below decks. 'It's over,' she said unnecessarily. 'And I'm not doing it again, so enjoy your little lad.' She lowered her voice. 'My father phoned.'

'Eh?'

She nodded. 'Tell Helen to get him to back off. And bring me a quarter of Keiller's butterscotch and some proper lemonade.'

'Right.'

'I love you, Denis Makepeace. Fetch me that noisy child while I learn how to feed him.'

Denis handed over the baby, kissed his wife and left the hospital. Helen was waiting at the door. 'Is she all right?'

'Course she is – you know our Agnes.'

'And the baby?'

'Screaming fit to bust – she's going to try feeding him. Are you giving me a lift?'

She nodded and led him to the car. On the way back to the village, Denis told her about the phone call. 'Said he was her dad.'

Helen grimaced. He couldn't do anything and wouldn't do anything. The bombshell under the Midland Bank was for emergencies only, but, if necessary, Helen would use it now. 'Don't worry. He daren't move a muscle without asking me first.' She smiled. 'I'm going to be a good aunt. I shall teach him to read, take him to the zoo and to the seaside. I could help him play the piano, get him taught to swim, buy him books.'

'Hang on.' Denis laughed. 'Let's change his nappy first, eh?'

Agnes had heard all about post-natal depression, but she didn't agree with it. A lot of new-fangled illnesses didn't make sense, and that was one of them. She loved being a mother, even when it didn't quite work. David was, she supposed, an easy baby. He took his nourishment, brought up wind and soon learned to play with anything within reach. The child laughed a lot, and Agnes found herself wondering about the joke she had missed. Was he remembering stuff from before he was born? That was possible, because he was particularly amused by certain words, one of them 'nuisance'. 'You've been here before,' she told him with monotonous frequency.

With pride in every step, she pushed her second-hand Silver Cross through the village and allowed all comers to coo over him. He liked an audience; oh, God – was he going to turn out like Pop? Pop had gone all posh and was going into marketing strategies. Marketing strategies involved a big sign in his garden – *POP'S HAPPY HOUSES* – a great deal of advertising and the employment of a small sales team. He was probably going to be a millionaire and that would make him thoroughly rumbustious. Rumbustious – that had been one of Nan's words. Sometimes, when she remembered Nan, Agnes cried because the old lady had never seen her great-grandson. Perhaps that was post-natal depression? If it was, then she was in step with everyone else, so that was all right.

Denis rushed home every night from Lambert House or from Lucy and George's barn, always ready to fight about who should bath the baby, always willing to do battle with Napisan, terry towelling and water. They managed to buy a washing machine and Pop paid for a tumble dryer, so life was a great deal easier than it might have been.

Helen, Lucy and Mags visited. They, too, fought over the child and who should hold him. Agnes borrowed a stopwatch and turned the whole thing into a farce, but David adored it all. He was loved; everybody wanted him, everybody sang and read to him, so he embraced his correct place as centre of the universe and thrived.

Helen borrowed David when he was six weeks old. She took him to visit Louisa while the judge was safely out of the way. Louisa broke down in tears when she saw the little boy. 'He's gorgeous,' she declared. 'There's the son he wanted.' Her own baby had not moved in the womb all day, and the midwife was expected at any moment. 'Don't let him get near little David, Helen.'

'He has no chance. Come on, buck up.'

The midwife arrived and exclaimed over the thriving baby boy before listening to Louisa's abdomen. 'Is your case packed?' she asked.

'Yes.' Louisa was to have her child in a private hospital at the other side of Blackburn. 'Will you phone the Manse?' she asked of Helen.

'No time,' said the midwife. 'Townleys is nearer. I think we need to get this child out today.'

So Louisa was rushed by her stepdaughter into the hospital in which young David had been born. The surgeon was waiting, as was the anaesthetist. They asked questions about when Louisa had last eaten, placed her on a trolley and dashed away in the direction of the theatre.

Helen paced about like an expectant father. The real father was away in some court or other, far too busy to be in attendance at the birth of his long-awaited son. When an hour had passed, the double doors at the end of the corridor were pushed aside to reveal the surgeon. Very slowly, he walked towards Helen. She waited. The journey could have taken no more than a few seconds, yet it seemed to continue forever.

He reached her side. 'Are you related to Louisa Spencer?'

Helen nodded. 'Stepdaughter.'

He took her arm. 'I am very sorry, but she suffered a pulmonary embolism and we couldn't save her.'

She stumbled. The man steadied her and placed her in a chair. 'Deep breaths,' he advised. 'She didn't suffer.'

Helen shook from head to toe. 'Did she see her baby?'

'No.'

'Is the baby ill?'

'She's small, but there's nothing wrong apart from

low birth weight and the need for a little help with her lungs.'

A girl. Helen swallowed. Father's wrong-side-of-the-blanket daughter had birthed a son, but his second wife had failed him. 'Millicent,' she whispered. 'That was the name Louisa chose. Millicent. Millie for short.'

'Can I get anyone for you?'

Helen shook her head. Denis and Agnes would be here soon. Kate was going to mind David while they came to the hospital. 'Can I see Louisa?'

'Soon, yes. They are preparing her now.'

Alone in the well-scrubbed, green-and-cream-disinfected silence, Helen wept. She mourned a stepmother who had been a sister, cried for the motherless baby girl, sobbed because she knew that her father would never accept little Millie. Agnes and Denis did what they could, but she was still weeping when they all visited Louisa in the chapel of rest.

'God,' whispered Agnes. It could have happened to her and little David. Fiercely, she clung to her husband's arm.

'She looks pretty again,' said Helen.

'Does your father know?' Denis asked.

Helen shrugged listlessly. 'It won't matter. Meals at the table will stop, but that's all the effect Louisa's death will have on him.' A light dawned in her head. 'She'll have to be mine,' she murmured. 'Millie will have to be mine.'

They said their goodbyes to the cooling corpse, then set off in the direction of Maternity. Millie was in an incubator, small hands closed like sleeping flower heads, little chest moving with each quick breath she took.

'She's perfect,' said Helen. 'Not all creased and squashed.'

'Caesars are pretty. They don't have to fight to get out, you see.' Agnes squeezed her sister's hand. 'We'll help. Denis and I will do all we can, and I'm sure Kate will, too.'

'She's lost her mother.' Helen's tone was soft. 'She has lost a wonderful woman. And she'll never have a father, because she's just another bloody woman in the making. I have to make her life special. I shall make her life an adventure.'

Agnes and Denis were in no two minds about that. Helen had suffered and she would ensure that Louisa's baby had a childhood better than her own had been.

'He has to be told,' murmured Agnes.

Helen took a deep breath. 'I'll tell him,' she announced. 'It's my place to do that, isn't it? Then he can bury his second wife and ignore his second daughter.' She glanced at Agnes. 'His third daughter, I mean.'

Agnes grasped Helen's hand. 'I know this is horrible, love. I can't think of anything worse, but you have a daughter and a little sister all in the one package. If you can't bear to live in the house, move in with us for a while. Eva's lovely – she'd help. And you know Kate Moores would.'

'She doesn't like me. I've heard her saying I was sly as a child.'

'And now she knows why.'

Helen's eyes brimmed over. 'No, she doesn't. No one does. Mabel Turnbull and I are the only ones who know the full truth – and she's gone. No. Millie will live in her own house – our house. David will be her friend. We can rear them between us.'

In that moment, the rest of Helen Spencer's life was laid out for all to read. She would be a mother who was not a mother; she would stand between her father and Millie, would devote every waking hour to the child. Agnes dashed from her heart a stab of fear about David – was he Judge Spencer's only male descendant? Now was not the time for such selfish worries; now was the time to support Helen and this newborn girl.

A nurse came and opened a small door in the side of the incubator. 'Put your hand in,' she told Helen.

Small fingers curled around Helen's thumb. But the sudden, vice-like grip on her heart was an unexpected reaction. Her brain had already accepted responsibility for rearing the child, but this was different – this was emotion. Maternal love bloomed in a soul who had never been a mother, who would probably not give birth to a child of her own. Tears stopped flowing down her cheeks as she felt the tightening of tiny digits. Here was her goal in life, and it had nothing to do with writing books or getting the better of her father. This baby owned Helen Spencer. She would never again be the sad and lonely spinster. All the same, she grieved for her friend and close companion. Louisa had left yet another gaping hole in the fabric of life. No amount of patchwork or darning would close the gap.

He seethed. Helen stood at the other side of his desk. She had said all the right things, had expressed her sadness and her worry about the premature child, had told him that she would miss her stepmother.

The judge took a mouthful of brandy. 'Another girl, then?'

'Yes. And your lovely wife is dead.' He reminded her of Henry VIII, a man who had gone through many women in order to father a son. And then the sickly boy had reigned for a mere six years before making way for his sisters: first Mary, and then Elizabeth I, a queen with the heart of a lion, had taken the reins. 'I shall arrange the funeral,' Helen said.

'Good. I have a busy schedule.'

'When will you visit the hospital?'

'I shall leave all that to you.'

Furious, she stamped out of the room. A son would have had him resident in the hospital; a male child would have wanted for nothing. Millie, who fought for life on a daily basis, was unimportant. 'Be strong,' Helen whispered. 'Get to the right weight, then I shall bring you home. As for him – he doesn't count.'

When the post-mortem had been completed, the body of Louisa Spencer was brought home. She lay in the hall next to Fred Grimshaw's model of the house, her stepdaughter a constant companion, her husband elsewhere at sessions. When the undertaker arrived to place the lid on the casket, Helen had to be led away by Agnes. 'Why her?' she sobbed. 'Why not him, Agnes? It should have been him. If you only knew . . .'

The church was packed. Zachary Spencer, who had managed at great personal cost to squeeze his wife's funeral into a hectic list, left after throwing a few crumbs of earth into a gaping maw in the churchyard. Mourners returned to Lambert House, where Kate Moores served sandwiches and many cups of tea and coffee.

Lucy arrived at Helen's side. 'If there's anything we can do, Helen—'

'Just keep that letter safe.' Underneath the tear-stained skin, an expression of cold determination was fighting to reach the surface. 'Those documents are the future for me and Millie. I cannot emphasize enough the importance of that package.'

'George and the bank will make sure. God love you.'
Lucy fled in tears.

Harry Timpson appointed himself guardian of his saviour. He followed her constantly, made sure that visitors did not overtire her, brought her tea, gave her several clean handkerchiefs. Occasionally, he nodded and smiled at Mags, who was taking care of Agnes. Mags was now Mrs Timpson, though no one except their parents knew. Harry loved his Mags and worshipped Helen Spencer – he was a lucky man.

When everyone had eaten, Helen got Harry to silence the gathering. She stood near a window and addressed them. 'If Louisa had been here, she would have enjoyed today. That may sound silly, but she preferred the uncomplicated life, which is why we chose to have plain fare.

'There are some of you here who remember me as a child and who thought me unpleasant. I hope most of you realize by now that I was the product of a miserable excuse for a father and a dead mother. I scarcely remember her, you know. But I'll never ... I'll never forget my wonderful stepmother.' She paused for a while, a cloud seeming to pass over her features.

'When she died, Louisa had been delivered of another disappointment – a girl.'

A murmur spread across the drawing room.

'Millie is improving. She's still a bit small, but I shall be bringing her home soon. Many here have visited her; her father has not been near the hospital. So I stand here now, a spinster with no experience, and I beg your help. Millie will not be sly or bitter – she will not need to lie or steal in order to compensate for lack of love. To that end, I ask all my friends here to advise and guide me while I rear my sister.'

'He should be bloody shot at dawn,' shouted Fred from the back.

Eva thumped him and Agnes told him to be quiet, wondering how he would react were he to discover his relationship with the object of his indignation.

Helen smiled. 'I'll put that one on the list, Fred. Any further suggestions should be made anonymously on postcards and sent to my solicitor. Thank you all for coming. Louisa was special and I shall miss her for the rest of my days.'

Harry pulled her into his arms and allowed her to sob on his shoulder. That bloody judge wanted a boot up the backside; he might have helped save Harry from prison, but he was as bent as a nine-bob note. Judges shouldn't be bent – their reliability and moral strength were the reasons for their very existence. This woman in his arms was the one to whom Harry owed everything. He whispered into her hair. 'Hey – I've got a secret.'

She looked up at him. 'Oh?'

'Me and Mags got wed the same day that . . . The day the baby was born.'

'The day Louisa died.'

'Yes. It was family and witnesses only – Mags hates fuss.'

Helen nodded. 'Congratulations, Harry. Louisa would have approved of that. She would have wanted us all to go on in a fashion as near to normal as possible.'

'Don't tell anyone. We're going to have a party, but we'll wait a while now. My mam's like a dog with two tails – thinks I've landed a gradely catch.'

'So has Mags,' Helen whispered. 'You will make a brilliant accountant one of these days.'

'I'm always here for you, no matter what. Remember that. No matter what.'

339

'I'll remember,' she promised.

A fortnight later, Millicent Louisa Spencer was released into the care of her sister. She came home not in the majestic Bentley, but in a very small Morris. A beautiful nursery had been prepared, all pastel colours, teddy bears and pretty pictures on the walls. The crib was next to Helen's bed, because she intended not to allow Millie out of her sight until she had gained weight and strength.

After three days, the baby, almost a month old, met her father for the first time. He looked her over, grunted, poured a brandy.

'Would you like to hold her?' Helen asked.

'Not at the moment.'

'Her name's Millicent.'

'Yes, I believe you mentioned that.'

Helen lowered her tone. 'Not a boy, though, eh? You'll have to work fast to find another wife, you know. After all, you left all this business very late, didn't you?'

He offered no reply.

'And you could carry on forever having girls. The father dictates the gender, or so I am told. You might take four or five wives in some countries and still have only daughters.'

'Go away,' he said.

She sat down, the child clasped to her chest. 'You know what's in Mabel Turnbull's letter, don't you, Pater?'

His face was suddenly deep crimson. 'I do not.'

'You know. Had you not known, you would have kicked me out months ago. So. You are in a delicate position. And I shall rear this child. You will pay me. Then bugger off to your yacht – I hope you drown.'

340

He maintained eye contact with her, but remained silent.

'You will leave this house, not I, certainly not Millie. Try sailing round the Cape – that should shorten your life by a year or two. You've a stroke coming – your face is a dreadful colour.' Helen stood up and carried her precious bundle out of the office. She walked through the house until she reached her own area, locked herself in and gave Millie her bottle. Sometimes, her father seemed beyond the reach of reason, and when he was in such a state, she believed him capable of doing harm. In a blind rage, he might forget about letters and threats.

The baby finished her feed and was congratulated for consuming three whole ounces. Back in her crib, she slept, one hand on her face, the other clutching a blanket. This child would hang on – she had no intention of giving up on life.

Helen herself drifted in and out of sleep. Nights were fractured by Millie, who needed feeding little and often, so her guardian had to snatch rest whenever the opportunity arose. In her dream, she opened the package and read the contents to a gathering of people in the drawing room. A little girl in the corner began to cry – was that Millie?

Her eyes flew open. It was strange how often sense arrived during sleep. The letters would hurt Millie. He knew that. With her heart beating wildly, Helen Spencer leaned over the sleeping child. Father was not a stupid man. He was rash, but not deficient. Even if he had not already spotted his oldest daughter's Achilles heel, it would come to him. The whole family would suffer once the secret became public. 'We are still vulnerable,' she told the baby.

Had she been the only one involved, Helen could have carried the burden of truth, but Millie had her whole life ahead of her and the sheet needed to be clean. Why on earth should a small child suffer because of the sins of her father? 'I have to talk to someone,' Helen whispered. The weight was suddenly too great for one person to bear; it needed to be shared. There was just one name on Helen's list of possibles. It had to be done and it had to be done today.

Pop was fuller than ever of his own importance. Granada Television had taken his plans for Lambert House, framed them, and placed them on a wall between studios. Anyone might have believed that his name was lit up in Piccadilly Circus, thought Agnes. She was pleased for him, yet worried about him. Fred Grimshaw needed an aim in life, but he also needed to take things at a slower pace. He and Eva had taken David in his pram for a walk through Skirlaugh Fall. Here was an opportunity for vacuuming without waking the baby, but Agnes simply sat and flicked through a magazine. House-proud was one thing; obsessive was another.

Helen arrived. It occurred to Agnes that she had simply swapped one baby for another, but she smiled and greeted her visitors gladly. Helen needed help and Agnes had made a promise.

Oscar bounded in first. He did three circuits of the living room, then a lap of honour at a slower pace.

'He misses Louisa,' said Helen. 'Even though she seldom fed him or took him out, he knew who his mistress was.' She sat down.

Agnes noted the expression on Helen's face and waited for her to speak again. To fill the gap, she went into the kitchen to fetch coffee and biscuits. Oscar, hearing the noise of dishes and cutlery, performed another circuit of the room in the hope of winning a treat. He accepted a few morsels, then went to claim his customary place on the hearthrug in the living room.

Agnes placed a tray on the coffee table. 'Well?' she asked.

'Let me sort my head out. I'll tell you in a minute.'

They drank coffee while Millie slept.

Suddenly, Helen leapt to her feet. 'I'll be back,' she promised.

Agnes scratched her head. 'You were going to tell me something—'

'Yes. I'll be back.' She rushed out of the house, leaving Agnes standing in her doorway and staring stupidly at the disappearing woman, baby and dog. Perhaps she would do the vacuuming after all.

Chapter Thirteen

Agnes answered the phone. 'Lucy? Whatever's the matter?'

Breathlessly, Lucy tripped over the words. 'She's gone wild-eyed again – Helen Spencer, I mean. George went to the bank with her – he's nominated second key-holder for the box. She's bringing her letters to you. Agnes, she's got Louisa's baby with her – she isn't fit to mind the dog. I thought I'd better let you know. I thought she'd got over all the nonsense.'

Agnes dropped into a chair. 'She was here earlier on, said she wanted to talk to me, then disappeared in a rush.' Poor Helen Spencer seemed to have crammed a whole life into the past few months. She had travelled through teenage fixation, had attempted to grow up and cope with her father, was now in charge of a baby girl. But to remove from a vault items she considered beyond value? There was something afoot once more. Helen had been wrong with Denis, wrong at Lucy's wedding, wrong at the Lambert House party. Was she off the tracks once more? 'Thanks for letting me know.'

'Be ready, love – she's off her head again. I'd better go – don't want anyone to overhear me. Be careful.'

Agnes replaced the receiver and waited. She knew all about waiting, realized that it could become an active occupation – she'd studied it before going into proper labour with David. But she didn't feel like counting flowers on the wallpaper, so she brought in her washing from the line and was engaged in folding nappies when Helen arrived. She was, indeed, wild-eyed.

'Sit down.' Agnes took the baby. 'What's the matter, Helen?'

Helen remained silent for a while. She remembered the therapist's words – 'get out of your father's life' – but would it not be better to get him to leave? What must be done to make him go?

'Helen? I asked you a question. What's up?'

'I don't know. Well, I do know, but I could be mistaken. Millie has taken away my insurance.'

'Ah.' After waiting again, Agnes asked, 'How?'

'By being born.'

'Right.'

'It could ruin her life.'

'I see.' Agnes couldn't see, but she decided to agree with everything while Helen was in this state.

'Read them and hide them.' She placed a package on a small table.

Agnes swallowed hard.

'They're possibly useless now. That letter of Mabel Turnbull's could ruin Millie's chances in life. If I went public with that stuff, my sister could be pointed at and bullied. It wouldn't be fair. I have to manufacture a different plan.'

Agnes followed her to the door. 'Take the edge off for me,' she begged. Denis had gone to the yacht with Judge Spencer and would not be back until quite late. 'Tell me what it's about. I want to hear it before I read it.'

Helen looked at Agnes as if Agnes were the crazy one. 'The murder, of course. Hadn't you worked it out? He killed my mother. After killing her, he carried on womanizing instead of remarrying. When he got older and ugly, no one wanted him. Until Louisa, who had her reasons.'

Agnes closed her gaping mouth with an audible clash of incisors. A judge who sentenced lesser mortals was a murderer himself? 'Are you all right to look after Millie?' was all she managed to say.

'What? Of course I am. And if anyone tries to take her away from me – ever – I shall follow the same path as my father. She's mine and I'll kill anyone who makes a move on her.'

As if the threat might be an immediate one, Agnes stepped back.

Helen looked her half-sister up and down, ordered her not to be upset, reclaimed Millie and left the house.

The car drove off. Agnes stared at the sealed envelope. It was a huge brown packet with an old-fashioned seal set in red wax. Although the seal was already broken, she was wary of opening so fierce-looking a bundle. It was a legal thing: it contained the thoughts, memories and feelings of a nanny who was dead. 'Nothing to do with me,' she mumbled nervously. Her Catholic upbringing had taught her that the confessional was sacred, that no secrets could be divulged by the priest – wasn't the law similar? No, because this was Helen's property and she had opted to share it. Even so, it didn't seem right.

David woke and demanded attention. When he was fed, loved, cleaned and bedded, Oscar arrived. Agnes played with the dog in her back garden, but she stayed near the door. David had to be minded, as did that flaming package. She half wished that someone would come along and steal it, but she knew she would be unable to live with that.

The phone sounded again, its shrill bell almost making Agnes jump out of her skin. 'Ah, Lucy,' she said nervously.

'What happened?' asked the disembodied voice.

'Nothing.'

'Did she come?'

'Yes.'

'Have you read it? What did it say? I won't tell anyone, honestly.'

Agnes took a couple of deep breaths. 'I've no idea. It's still sitting on the table where she left it. Denis is at the yacht, so he'll be late, and I don't feel like looking at it while I'm by myself.'

'I'll come.'

'No, Lucy. It wouldn't be right. Remember hearing about the old lawyer who checked Mabel's letter for spelling mistakes? Remember how everyone thought that was what made him ill? The fewer people who handle this, the better. Sorry.' Agnes could not repeat the words of Helen Spencer, would not tell anyone about the supposed murder. Denis would be the sole exception.

Lucy was not pleased. After replacing the receiver, Agnes stared at it for several seconds, as if expecting Lucy to continue berating her even after the connection had been severed. The packet was still on the table. It was only seven o'clock. Oscar was demolishing a small dinner of chicken skin and dog biscuit. One minute past seven. The man who had fathered her was a murderer. The murderer was a judge. That thought had consumed ten more seconds. Her bones felt cold; having a murderer for a father was truly chilling.

Pop entered the arena. He was still full of Granada and his blueprints for Lambert House, which items were now on display in a corridor leading to the *Coronation Street* studio. Eva came in behind him, and said she would go quietly upstairs to see the baby. Nothing Eva did was quiet, so Agnes was forced to bring down the disturbed and crying David. She was grateful, because the moment of the grand opening had been postponed yet again.

She made tea. Pop played with his great-grandson while Eva waited for *Coronation Street* to begin.

'All them stars'll be looking at my blueprints,' bragged Pop. 'I'll be getting orders from them next – they've plenty of money.'

The baby slept while Eva watched a fight between two women near a viaduct on an imaginary street. Some people came along and separated the warring females; Agnes made more tea during the advertisements. After the break, there was louder shouting, some smoking and a bit of a story about two young girls wanting the same unkempt and totally undesirable man with red hair and bad skin.

The music played. Eva, who seemed to think that the programme was fact rather than fiction, waxed on about Ena Sharples being rude and Annie Walker being too big for her slippers. 'She wants shifting,' she declared. 'They should put her in a posh pub over in Cheshire, bring her down a peg or three. She pretends she's posh, but she's not.'

Pop snored. 'Well.' Agnes plumped up her cushion. 'That's both babies asleep.'

Eva smiled. 'What's happened, love? I've known you since you were knee-high to a cotton spool and I can tell when summat's up.'

Agnes sighed and shook her head. 'Just stuff, Eva.

Stuff I can't talk about, because it's someone else's secret.' That wasn't true. She would have to talk to Denis, because she couldn't go through this business all by herself. 'It'll rinse out with the whites, as Nan used to say. I never realized how wise she was till she'd gone. She was always at the back of me, always showed me what to do.'

Eva's eyes narrowed. 'She did a good job, lass. You're the most sensible one I know out of your generation. Look at Mags Bradshaw – all that pain for a new nose, head over heels for a wrong 'un, married in secret, party next week. And that there Lucy carries on like a bloody teenager – skirts halfway up her bum, false eyelashes thicker than your yard brush.'

Agnes laughed in spite of her tension. Eva had a way of summing people up in a couple of sentences. 'Perhaps I'm too sensible?'

'Nay.' Eva heaved her bulk out of the chair. 'Eeh, love, if I put any more weight on, we'll be needing a tin opener to get me off the furniture. Fred?' The final word was shouted. David woke, Agnes grabbed him from her grandfather's arms, and Eva went about the business of shifting her husband.

'Come on,' she chided.

'I'll be there in a minute.' The voice was sleepy.

'There in a minute? Last time I gave you a minute, you nodded off in the shed with a hammer in one hand, nails in the other. Come on. Now.'

He stood up, rubbed his eyes and glared at Eva. 'All right, boss,' he said before a yawn overcame him.

Eva ushered him out of the house, leaving Agnes alone once more with twin burdens – one a small child, the other a quantity she wished could remain unknown.

It was ten minutes past eight and, though the days were getting longer, the light was diminishing fast. Denis had to be home soon.

With the baby settled once more, Agnes picked up the envelope and weighed it in her hand. It looked heavy, but it wasn't. Its contents were going to be heavy, though. Where was Denis when she needed him most? He hated the yacht, only went aboard if the judge had too small a crew to help with his latest toy. The big man was talking about retirement. Well, if he thought Denis would traipse around the seven seas with a murderer he had another think coming.

She looked inside. There were two smaller envelopes, one off-white and flimsy, the other buff-coloured and brand new. 'Come home, Denis,' she mouthed. 'I can't do this.' The washing was folded and the house was clean. She should start ironing. The trouble with being a housewife was that most jobs were automatic and didn't prevent the mind from working. She had books. But she couldn't imagine concentrating on the written word while she was in her current state.

The phone sounded again and she picked it up quickly in case it woke the baby. It was Helen. No, she hadn't read the letters. She was waiting for Denis. Helen didn't want Denis to read the letters. 'We have no secrets,' Agnes said. 'Don't you trust him?'

She did trust him, but Agnes was her sister and this needed to be kept in the family for now.

'Then come and take the damned things away, Helen. Anyway, he's my family. You've told me already that your dad killed your mother – I expect he killed mine, too, though not as directly. I'm sorry – it's me and Denis or neither of us. Whether I read this lot or not, my husband will know what you told me earlier.'

Helen expressed the fear that Denis might walk out of the job if he knew the full truth. 'Neither Millie nor I will feel safe if Denis isn't here for half the week.'

It was stalemate. In the end, Helen had to grant permission for Denis to see the letters, because, no matter what, Agnes would tell him what she already knew. 'As I just said, I'll be telling him about the murder anyway. We lead a shared life, Helen. It's the only way to stay married.'

At last, he came home. Still on tenterhooks, Agnes served his meal and waited until he had finished and the table was cleared. They drank coffee in the living room, Denis describing his time in Morecambe Bay, Agnes listening while he went through seasickness and his employer's attitude to the crew. After five or so minutes, Denis finally noticed his wife's silence. 'What's going on?' he asked.

She nodded in the direction of the offending item. 'Helen dragged George to the bank and pulled the letters from the vault. She brought them here for me to read. Denis?'

'What?'

Agnes swallowed. 'She says he killed the first Mrs Spencer – Helen's mam. The proof's in that package. I couldn't read it on my own.'

He placed his cup and saucer on the windowsill. 'Killed her? By making her life a misery? Aye, I've heard people saying she died on purpose just to get away from him.'

Agnes shook her head. 'No. Murder. Real, actual murder.'

A heavy silence hung over the room while they both stared at Helen Spencer's property. 'How long's it been here?' Denis asked.

'Hours. Helen phoned, because she thought I'd have read them. Lucy phoned and asked what was in them. Pop and Eva came – that killed half an hour or so. I'm worried about Millie in case Helen isn't up to the job. It's not easy work.'

'No.' He stood up. 'Shall I read it out?'

Agnes closed her eyes for a moment. 'No. Read a sheet, then hand it to me. I don't think I want to hear the words from you. This is none of our doing, so it's best if the words stay flat on the page.'

He opened the main envelope and removed the contents. 'Right,' he said, 'that's the first incision.'

It took over an hour. Agnes wept, while Denis determinedly held back his own tears. At the end, he folded everything and placed both letters, each in its separate envelope, back inside the outer cover. 'I don't want that stuff in my house,' he said gruffly.

'Neither do I.'

'Why did she bring it?' he asked.

Agnes had an insubstantial answer. 'Millie's father is a killer. Helen holds those letters over him like the sword of Damocles. But if she is forced to reveal their contents, she will be tainting Millie's life for ever. Millie would have to go through school in the company of people who might be aware of her family's skeletons. Helen knows her father will be thinking along the same lines, so I suppose she just wanted someone else to have seen the contents. She said Millie has taken away her insurance policy. Denis, she's running round like a blindfolded cat, all confusion and desperation.'

Denis sat quietly for a few seconds. 'I could take it out of her hands now. I could carry Mabel Turnbull's letter to a police station and get the bloody business over and done with.'

'But you won't.'

'No. It could destroy Helen, too. She'd be so worried about the baby that she'd lose her marbles again. What a mess.'

'She wants you to promise not to give up working part time for her dad. She'd be scared if you left.'

Agnes could not get to sleep that night. She tossed and turned alongside her husband, tried to relax, failed miserably. In the end, she abandoned the attempt and, at three in the morning, she reread the close, tiny handwriting of Mabel Turnbull. It was no less shocking the second time, but Agnes needed to make an effort to digest it fully.

With a cup of tea at her elbow, she started again.

My name is Mabel Anne Turnbull. I was employed by Mr and Mrs Spencer in 1932, when their daughter (Helen) was a few months old. Mr Spencer was away quite often. His work took him all over the place and he stayed at his club a lot. He seemed to be keener on his friends and colleagues than on his family and was anxious to be invited to join the Freemasons. He was one of the youngest ever lawyers to be called to the bar and was always determined to become a judge. His wife was frail. I was left to look after her and Helen during his absences.

I am ashamed to say that I was one of the many women to be seduced by Zachary Spencer. He was very attractive and charming and he gave me a job in his household. My head was turned – I was a silly girl. From the day I began working at Lambert House, my sympathies and loyalties were with Mrs Spencer and her young daughter, Helen. I made it plain to my employer that there would be no further intimacy between us and he was unconcerned, as he had many lady friends all over the country. He came home from time to time, but not on a regular basis, as he was far too selfish to consider the needs of anyone but himself.

Not that he was any use when he was there. Mrs Spencer had a bad heart, but he yelled at her a lot and got her worked up. She gave as good as she got sometimes, but would be ill afterwards. He kept screaming at her because she hadn't managed to give him a son and was too ill to try again. Sometimes, I wanted to hit him. He ignored Miss Helen most of the time. She was all right at first, because she had her mummy as well as me to play with, but her father made her feel unhappy when he shouted. I loathed and despised Zachary Spencer and my feelings towards him remain the same, but I swear I am telling the truth rather than seeking vengeance.

It got worse. He was bad when he drank and he drank too much. I used to keep Miss Helen upstairs a lot of the time because she was safer away from him and his noise. But there wasn't much I could do for her poor mother. She stood up to him and got weaker all the time.

The weakness took the form of turns – like fainting fits – and she would lie very still and hardly breathing. There were tablets to put under her tongue. She always had them with her and I always carried some just to be safe. I begged her to stop facing up to him, but she wouldn't listen. If her health had been good, she would have divorced him, I'm sure. He was and is a cruel man. He hates his daughter and she likely hates him, with good reason on her part.

Things went on the same with him away a lot and his wife not well. We had some nice times when there were just the three of us. Helen seemed shy and frightened, but that was his fault, because she was all right with her mother and me. (After her mother died, she got naughty, but that was understandable.)

His absences became less frequent. Most people in normal families would have been glad, but we weren't, because we dreaded him being back full time and we were better off without him. He stayed for longer periods at the house. The mistress, Miss Helen and I kept out of his way whenever possible, but there was no way of avoiding him altogether.

He started telling the mistress to get out of his house because she was useless. I remember her laughing at him – not amused laughing, more sneering. She said she would leave Lambert House in a box and he said that could be arranged. I could hear from the top of the stairs – they were really screaming at one another.

When I got to bed that night, my cocoa was already waiting for me. Old Mrs Battersby, who slept in an attic, was the live-in cook in those days and she was very good to me and to Miss Helen and she always made my cocoa before going up to her own room under the eaves at the other side of the house. I drank my cocoa and must have fallen asleep straight away. The next thing I knew, Miss Helen was tugging and pulling at me. I got out of bed and I felt very strange. Ever since, I have been sure that he must have drugged my cocoa after Mrs Battersby left it by my bed.

They were fighting again. Mrs Spencer was calling him all kinds of names and her language was very strong for a lady, but I didn't blame her. I pulled open the door a crack and he had her at the top of the stairs. He pushed her. I swear on a hill of Bibles that I saw Zachary Spencer kill his wife that night. The drugs dulled my mind, but I know what I saw.

He made her fall down the stairs. She had tumbled down before – one of her fainting fits on the stairs – the doctor knew about it and had told her to sleep on the ground floor, but she was never one for doing as she was ordered. She was weak in body but determined in mind and her husband did not like anyone who argued with him. Anyway, I saw him push her. Where the stairs turn near the bottom, she was lying like a rag doll. I think she was already dead before he went near her again. He walked downstairs and pulled her down the rest of the steps into the hall and I could hear her head banging on each of the treads.

He stood over her and told her she would be leaving in a box. I saw him bend and feel for a pulse. Then I noticed Miss Helen clinging to my nightdress. I don't know what she had seen, but I told her to come away. We went back into the bedroom. Miss Helen didn't say a word. I sat with her till she fell asleep, then I opened the door again and he was still standing over Mrs Spencer. As I closed the door, he looked up, but I didn't think he had seen me.

The ambulance came. Mrs Spencer was taken away and he went with her. He was shouting and pretending to be upset. I drank a lot of water to get the drugs out of me. The little girl slept. I sat all night in a chair and I heard him come back. The next morning, he told us his wife had suffered a heart attack and broken her neck on the stairs. He was staring at me.

I handed in my notice after the funeral. Mr Spencer begged me to stay as housekeeper for a lot more money. I did stay, but more for the sake of the child. I was frightened all the time, yet I worried about Miss Helen and stayed for her sake. But he got her a governess and I didn't have a lot to do with Miss Helen after that. From the age of three, she was given lessons and she read like an adult at a very young age. She had a good brain. The first governess said she was the cleverest child she had taught so far. But she did become very quiet and rather underhand and naughty at times. I was the only one who understood why, but I could not talk to such a small child about what had happened before her third birthday.

He continued to behave atrociously to women. I remember clearly one occasion just before the end of the war. A young girl called Eileen Grimshaw came to the house. She was pregnant and he would not help her in any way. He had thrown her out of his office and denied his involvement with her. She came to me and there was nothing I could do for her.

I left the house in 1944. He got me a good job and continued to send me money. When I was still relatively young, I became disabled with the arthritis. He still sent me money and paid for me to have residential care.

I have nothing to gain by writing this letter. I don't know how much time I have left, but I am leaving what I have written in the care of a solicitor. It is for Miss Helen Spencer, daughter of Judge Zachary Spencer and Elizabeth Spencer, deceased. He should not get away with it. A man in his high position is supposed to be decent and law-abiding. He killed his wife. Please accept this as the statement of a dying woman. I don't know when I will die, but I have to write this while my hands still work.

Helen may remember that night. She has not spoken of it as far as I know, but she may have seen some of what happened. When she became naughty, I truly believed that what she knew had affected her, but I am not a clever woman and I can't say for sure.

Miss Helen, if you read this, please know that I did all I could for you. When I became housekeeper, I saw less of you, but at least I was there. Sometimes, he would look at me and I could tell he was wondering what I knew of the night when your mother died. He was never sure of me, which is why he has kept me in comfort.

I wish you well in your life and hope you grow strong in spite of your father and his wickedness. My only regret is that I did not prevent your mother's murder. She would not have lasted long, but her death should have been natural and not assisted by the creature she had married. If he had been putting her out of her misery, I might have understood, but he killed her because she disappointed him and answered him back.

Should Miss Helen Spencer predecease me, this will be read by the lawyers into whose hands I have placed it. Sirs, Judge Zachary Spencer is a murderer and he should be tried for his crime. I swear by Almighty God that everything I have written here is the truth. My education is limited, but I am well read and I know right from wrong. Please have him arrested.

Yours sincerely, M. Turnbull (Miss)

Agnes took a sip of water. There was a ring of honesty to the letter and she did not doubt the contents for one moment. The handwriting was shaky, because the author had suffered pain in her joints, yet she had laboured, possibly over a period of days, to get the letter finished. It was the absolute truth – of that Agnes was certain. The bit about her mother had cut her to the quick.

There was no need to reread the few lines appended by Helen in the other envelope. Helen had confirmed Mabel's statement and had explained about the nightmares and the amnesia brought on by shock. But now Helen was afraid of these letters. She had depended on them for her own safety and security, but she now felt that their very existence threatened the well-being of an innocent baby girl.

Birds began to sing. Agnes drew back the curtains and watched the dawn as it started to break. This was a time of day when wakefulness could be a burden, because the person who did not sleep felt truly isolated and out of step. It would be a difficult day, since she was bound to be tired and edgy. But no – it was a George-and-Lucy day, so Denis could make his apologies, stay at home and help with the baby, because George knew that Agnes had the letters and would be in some kind of shock. Agnes and Denis needed time together, as there was a decision to be made. Should they go to the police and risk Helen's wrath? Or should they keep quiet, just as Mabel Turnbull had kept quiet?

Sometimes, there was a very hazy line between right and wrong, Agnes thought. Pure right could be a terrible thing with dreadful consequences; wrong was often the kinder choice. A man who abused his position should be punished, yet his punishment might affect the lives of people who did not deserve to be hurt. Denis wanted to go to the police. Agnes did not. The decision would be hers, because Helen Spencer was probably her half-sister. But what was the right thing? Nobody wanted Millie to become the butt of jokes and snide remarks because her father had been the infamous and murderous judge.

'Agnes?'

She turned to her husband. 'She's right, Denis. Millie could suffer if all this came out. Poor old Mabel Turnbull was wasting her time, too, it seems.'

'So we do nothing?'

Agnes nodded. 'We can only make things worse by interfering.' The charade had to continue. 'Don't go to work, sweetheart. Phone George – he'll understand.'

'Spencer should be in jail, Agnes.'

'I know.'

'And the house is like a time bomb – something has to give. She'll crack. He's made her brittle and frail. God, what is the right thing to do?'

Agnes shrugged and smiled weakly. 'The wrong thing

is sometimes the right thing. This is one of the sometimes.'

The house had been built very cleverly, each room a section that slotted onto the room beneath. Even the ground floor lifted off to show cellars with boiler, coal store, miniature wine racks and bottles. Fred was very proud of his achievement, though his delight was tinged with sadness, because the house had been made for Louisa, who had died giving birth to a daughter. 'Just like our Eileen,' he whispered as he put some finishing touches to his work. The house would belong now to little Millie, so it needed to be strong and durable. He was examining pegs and slots when the row began.

The replica of Lambert House, now in its permanent place of residence in the hall, looked wonderful. Absorbed in his work, Fred fought not to hear the raised voices of the judge and his daughter. All families had differences that needed airing from time to time, and he was wondering whether to change the carpet in one of his rooms, since the real floor covering in Lambert House's library was in a lighter colour than the one he had used. It was hard to concentrate.

The volume increased. It was a pity that folk didn't own wireless knobs, because they needed to be turned down a bit when a bloke was trying to do a job of work. The judge was yelling about his retirement and his intention to spend time at sea. His daughter was urging him to stay at sea, as he would not be welcome here. She was also advising him to leave all lifebelts at the moorings – she had quite a temper, it seemed.

If he varnished the tiny door handles, the brass would stay bright. Fred wrote that in his notebook. He was still waiting for a pair of lions couchant to arrive for the top of the front steps. He had explained on television that he had been let down by a maker of miniatures – he wasn't having folk think he did half a job. There were sets of moulds he might buy – rubber contraptions into which plaster of Paris could be poured – perhaps he could make his own garden ornaments? Trees were easy – train set manufacturers made good trees and hedges.

'This is my house!'

The old bugger was in danger of blowing a fuse, Fred thought. Like a pressure cooker, Zachary Spencer could do with a valve on the top of his head for the letting off of steam.

'You're not wanted here.'

Perhaps his daughter might benefit from similar equipment – she was more like her dad than she chose to believe.

'I shall do as I please.'

It happened then. As clear as any church bell, Helen Spencer's voice travelled through the hall to Fred's ears. 'You have three daughters. Me, you ignored to the point of neglect. Agnes was raised by grandparents and Millie will be raised by me.'

'Better if I had her adopted,' shouted the judge.

'No! Millie will stay with me.'

Fred stood as still as one of the stone lions. He blinked stupidly, then leaned for support on the huge table that bore the weight of his model. Agnes. Eileen. Sadie, God rest her. Spencer, bloody Spencer. Dear Lord, let this be a lie.

'Agnes knows,' Helen was saying now. 'She knows everything.'

Fred pulled himself together and left the house by

the front door. He would not have another stroke; he would not weaken to the point of illness. Had anyone asked him about the walk from Skirlaugh Rise to Skirlaugh Fall that day, he would not have had anything to say. Seeing and hearing little, he simply placed one foot in front of the other, all senses dulled by shock.

Without knocking, he walked into his granddaughter's cottage.

Denis, who had taken the day off to think about Helen's famous letters, stood up as soon as Fred came in. There was no need for the old man to speak, because the whole mess showed in his face. 'Fred?'

'Where's our Agnes?'

'Hanging nappies on the line.'

Fred, whose legs were threatening to buckle, dropped onto the sofa. 'How long has she known that yon bugger's her dad?'

Denis swallowed. 'Long enough.'

'I'll kill him,' snarled Fred. 'I might be old and weak, but I can wait till he's asleep and—'

'Stop it, Pop.' Agnes, washing basket balanced on a hip, stood in the doorway between living room and kitchen. 'Don't make things worse than they already are,' she said. 'There's more to it – a lot more. He's given us this house and Helen will make sure we are OK.'

'OK?' yelled Fred. 'OK? Your mam wasn't OK when she bled to death, was she? Three dead women – that's some track record for a judge, eh? And what's this house worth – a couple of hundred quid? What about your shoes and your clothes when you were growing, eh? What about the times when my Sadie had to do magic with a few bob a week?'

'Stop this, or you'll be in hospital again,' advised

Denis calmly. 'Take my word – there's stuff you don't know, stuff you're better off not knowing.'

'I know what he did to my daughter, and that's enough.' Fred stood up and walked out of the house. In Eva's fleshy arms, he wept until he felt weak, weary and dry to the core. 'Bastard,' he cursed.

'You'll make yourself ill, love.'

He pulled away from his wife. 'Nay, I won't. Ill's stuck in a trench with your best mate's blood on your face.' He pulled from a pocket Macker's stolen lighter. 'Ill's not knowing what you're doing, or having no control over what happens. Ill's cursing your officers for sending you up front, then finding the same officers as dead as the rank and file. I'm thinking, Eva. I'm thinking and I'm grieving and yes, I'm bloody furious. But I'll do nowt till I've thought on it. This time, I'm in charge. It's my bloody turn now.'

He sat in the same chair for the rest of the day, stirring only when food and drink were carried to him. Eva watched, waited, said nothing. Agnes called, but was told by her grandfather to go home. He loved her and he told her that, but he was busy thinking. The sun began its descent and Fred walked to the bathroom. He completed his toilet with a shave; then, when dusk thickened, he left the house.

Eva ran as quickly as she could to Agnes's cottage. 'He's got the big axe,' she mumbled through tears. 'And his dander's up. I know he's a noisy old bugger, but this time it's different, because he's quiet. I've never known him like this.'

'Silent?' Agnes asked.

Eva nodded.

Silent was dangerous. Agnes pushed her husband out

of the house. 'Be quick,' she said. 'He'll kill him. Make sure Helen and the baby are all right, too.'

Eva and Agnes stared at one another for what seemed like hours. The clock was on a go-slow, its hands moving reluctantly to mark each passing moment. Eva sobbed quietly; Agnes trapped nervous hands between her knees and prayed. Pop was lethal when truly angry. He had almost belted a teacher for giving Agnes the cane, and he had been very subdued and menacing on that occasion, too. 'Mark our Agnes again,' he had said softly, 'and I'll have you skinned at yon Walker's Tannery – your hide's thick enough.' Oh, God, please don't let him kill anyone, Agnes pleaded inwardly.

'How long now?' asked Eva.

'Twenty minutes.'

'Is that all?'

Agnes nodded. Denis would catch him and stop him – wouldn't he?

Fuelled by anger, Fred Grimshaw took the short cut across the fields. Denis would be hot on his heels, but nothing could stop Fred now. He remembered Macker, remembered also the lads who had fought in the second half, as he termed the later war. A country fit for heroes? A country in which a barrister, soon to become a High Court judge, could impregnate an innocent girl and get away with it? 'We didn't lay down our lives for this,' he told his inanimate companion, a weighty axe that was suddenly as light as a feather.

Denis was there before him. He was hanging around at the front of the house, so Fred took a detour through the copse and entered the building by a rear door. The place was as quiet as a graveyard. With no one to impede his progress, Fred walked through the mansion until he reached the hall. 'Sorry, Millie,' he said before delivering the first blow.

Now, the axe was suddenly heavy, but he dragged it over his shoulder and into the model until the table below, too, began to buckle.

Denis ran in and tried to stop the destruction, but Fred ignored him. Yet he saw the judge plainly enough, mouth opened wide, feet planted halfway down the stairs, hand gripping the banister rail. 'Stop this foolishness,' Zachary Spencer called, but Fred was beyond retrieval.

When his work was completely destroyed, the grandfather of Agnes Makepeace paused for breath. Then he raised the weapon once more and addressed the man on the stairs. 'This should have been planted in your head.' He nodded at the blade. 'Agnes's father? You? Our lovely Eileen made dirty by a man who was never a man? Missed the second war, didn't you? You sat at home and kept the legal wheels turning, soft job, soft chair, soft life.'

'Be quiet, man,' spat the judge.

Fred took from his pocket a handful of coins. Macker had died for this creep and for governments who still failed to make sense. Macker, twice the man that Spencer would ever be, was just a cigarette case, a lighter and a remembered smile. 'You big shit,' said Fred, his voice unnaturally low. 'Here you are, Iscariot – count them.' He cast the coins into the debris that had been the model of Lambert House. 'Judas,' he spat before walking out of the house, thirty shillings left behind for the traitor's pay.

Denis said nothing. He simply followed his grandfather-in-law down the hill to Skirlaugh Fall, made sure that he went into Bamber Cottage, then turned to go home to Agnes. Eva, who had fastened herself to Agnes's window, left and pursued her husband homeward. It was going to be a difficult night, but Eva would cope, because Eva loved her husband.

'Don't go,' Agnes begged the next morning.

Denis shook his head. 'Sorry, love. The judge will be like a tiger on fire – I can't leave Helen and the baby to his tender mercies.'

'There'll be repercussions. You're related to Pop by marriage. The man's a killer, Denis.'

But he would not be persuaded. He left the house by the front door, turned and waved to his wife and child.

Agnes felt a chill in her spine. She wanted to run after him, to plead with him to stay at home, but she knew he had made up his mind. She watched as he moved towards the big house, her heart filled by fear, her mind scarcely working.

In years to come, she would speak sometimes of the dread she felt that day. After Denis had disappeared into Skirlaugh Rise, Agnes never saw him again.

Chapter Fourteen

2004

Ian Harte stepped out of his car and locked the door. The house known as Briarswood, formerly Lambert House, was still on the books, but a keen client had emerged and it had fallen to the surveyor to discover, as cheaply as possible, why the house conformed to no law of architecture, gravity or simple common sense. The front of the building should sag, but it did not, so an explanation had become flavour of the moment. Alterations to the cellars were the probable cause of the dilemma, but proof was needed in order to furnish the prospective purchaser with a proper report.

A Mrs Agnes Makepeace was caretaker and key-holder, so he sought to discuss the matter with her, but no one responded to repeated knocking at the door of her cottage. After a couple of fruitless minutes, he moved to the house next door. A young woman answered. She was done up like someone preparing to have tea with the queen, but that was normal these days, because the long-ago weavers' homes had become the bijou residences of the up-and-coming. 'Yes?' she asked.

He cleared his throat. 'Do you know where Mrs Makepeace is?'

'Morecambe,' she replied. 'She goes once a year to remember.' The woman looked over her visitor, deciding that he seemed of decent enough professional standing before allowing him into her overstated home. The windows were dressed in knickers, as Ian Harte had come to name foolish looping draperies with lace and broderie anglaise trimming their edges. Dried flowers in terracotta cones hung each side of the fireplace, while the mandatory pot pourri acted as centre piece on a coffee table.

After an invitation to be seated, he placed himself in a cream leather chair. The room was stuffy and over-perfumed. Imitation antiques lined the walls – a bureau, a chesterfield, some deliberately distressed bookshelves that housed, among others, Barbara Cartland, Mills & Boon and, to add a little class to the establishment, a few tomes in imitation leather. *Lancashire Life* and *Ideal Home* flanked the pot pourri with a set of silver-plated coasters completing the piece. This was the stage on which actors acted day-to-day parts in their make-believe lives. The setting was a much-loved disaster, its owner proud to show it off. 'Morecambe?' he asked.

'Would you care for a cup of tea or coffee?'

He saw the desperation in her face, recognized lone-liness, opted for coffee. While she made the drinks, he sat feeling sad. Why? Because this village, once bustling with life and a sense of community, had become a waiting room for the ambitious young who clung by the skin of their teeth to the first rung of the property ladder. Gardens had been replaced by slabs on which cars could be parked, while almost every house boasted a burglar alarm colourful enough to catch the eye of any would-be thief. The residents of Skirlaugh Fall were in hiding, each holding on desperately to pos-sessions and position, every man for himself, lottery ticket in a drawer, the pub continuing to serve chicken in a basket and Black Forest gateau, post office gone, new dormer bungalows in hideous pink or yellow brick hiding in dips behind the original stone-built dwellings.

'How long have you lived here?' he asked. Had she not heard that minimalism was now in vogue, that dado rails were no longer the fashion?

'A few months. We stand to make a killing and move on pretty soon. This house isn't big enough for a family, and I am expecting our first. You were looking for Mrs Makepeace?'

'Yes.'

She poured coffee from a steel-and-glass jug, said she hoped he liked Kenya blend, offered him a bourbon cream. 'She'll be in Morecambe. That's where he died, you see.'

'Oh?' He swallowed a mouthful of biscuit. 'Who died?'

'Her husband. It must be going on forty years ago now, but my mother remembers it. They died at sea.'

'They?'

She nodded. 'Him – Mr Makepeace – and a judge who used to live at Briarswood – they were the only two on board. No crew that night, my mother said. It was all over the papers. Anyway, Mrs Makepeace never remarried. She must be sixty now, but she's still pretty.'

'So is her garden.' The Makepeace house was one of the few to have survived the invasion.

'She does it all herself. Not that I know her, you understand. We keep ourselves to ourselves. Anyway, the yacht exploded and both men died. They'd been putting some sort of fuel in the kitchen – the galley – and something went wrong. Mrs Makepeace was left with a small baby and no husband. Very sad.'

'Terrible. When will she be back?'

The woman raised her shoulders. 'No idea. I believe

she rents a house for a few weeks, but, like I said, we don't mix.'

Nobody mixed any more, because there was nowhere to go. The pubs in towns were crammed with kids, the bulk of whom appeared to be below the age of reason. Cars disappeared with monotonous regularity, many burned and exploded in an effort to destroy all evidence when petrol tanks ran dry. Life was lived these days in secure units that had once been proper homes. Keeping people out was the main aim in life as man entered the twenty-first century.

The town centre was dying, its murderers sitting in municipal offices to plan the rerouting of a river, the destruction of beautiful commercial properties, the reduction of Bolton to a town like any other, building societies, fast food, fast shopping, layered car parks. Social life was arranged these days around fortresses occupied by friends – so it was dinner parties, bridge, garden barbecues. No one borrowed a cup of sugar any more; no one took sugar any more, he thought as he dropped a sweetener into his cup.

'If you leave a card, I'll get Mrs Makepeace to phone you when she gets back.'

'No need,' he answered. 'I shall put a note through the door. Thank you for your help.' He took a last sip of coffee and decided that he didn't like Kenya blend.

Outside once more, he unlocked his car, climbed into the passenger seat and sat for a few moments outside the Makepeace house. He now knew the recent history of Briarswood and was coming close to believing in ghosts. Over several decades, the building had been rented out to various people, but no one had stayed beyond a few months. As for the construction, there was an extra wall in the cellar – that was the only explanation for the anomaly. To investigate, he needed the permission of the current owners. The owners were Helen Spencer, Millicent Spencer and Agnes Makepeace.

Briarswood was supposed to be haunted, and Ian Harte understood why tenants had quit. It was a very odd place. He remembered his last visit and had no desire to return to the house, but, as the one elected to get a builder to sort out the footings, he was forced to become involved. Because Briarswood, once Lambert House, was to become a health farm. 'Another slide into bloody stupidity,' he muttered. The country was going to the dogs and he was forced to play a part in the sin.

It would be a simple case of taking out a few bricks to ensure that the building was stable, but permission was required. He sighed, wrote his note for Mrs Makepeace, delivered it and returned to his vehicle. As he turned the key in the ignition and pulled away, he found himself wishing that someone else could take charge of this job. Briarswood was crazy, and he wanted nothing more to do with it.

Agnes gazed out to sea, her eyes fixed on the area in which her beloved husband had last drawn breath. There had been no funerals, because the yacht, reduced to matchsticks, had taken with it two people whose bodies had never been found. She recalled the inquest, remembered a man from the Lifeboat Association stating baldly that any persons on board would have ended up as fish food.

For at least two years after the accident, Agnes had been a robot. She had functioned, had fed and clothed her child, had scarcely noticed when Helen had left with Millie, Mags and Harry to live in the south of England.

'Just me and Lucy now,' she breathed. George had lasted longer than poor Denis, but a single coronary occlusion had eventually taken him away from his wife and children.

She said her goodbye to the grey water, picked up the handle of her wheeled suitcase and dragged it towards the station. Home. She was going home to an existence that held few pleasures now that David was gone. She was proud of her son. He was a consultant who specialized in childhood cancers at Great Ormond Street hospital. He was married, Agnes was a grandmother, and she lived for infrequent visits. Everyone was so busy these days, seeming to live at the speed of light, with no time for anyone or anything.

Mags, Harry and Helen were becoming distant memories. The geographical space between them was a factor, though separation had begun before they had left Lambert House. It was probably because of the accident. Harry, who had passed his driving test just before the explosion, could have been the driver, but Denis had taken the judge to Morecambe Bay and Denis had died. That was not Harry's fault, though he had shouldered a form of guilt, and, probably for that reason, he and Mags had followed Helen to Hastings.

In spite of his position in the legal world, Judge Zachary Spencer had died intestate, so all property and monies had gone by default to Helen and Millie. Helen, in typical fashion, had managed to divide everything into three parts, for herself, Millie and Agnes. Should Lambert House be sold, that money, too, would be split in a similar fashion.

But no one had wanted the house. Agnes could not understand why. She had spent nights there, had experienced nothing, yet she had been forced to listen to complaints from tenant after tenant while wild stories were told. No, they hadn't actually seen or heard anything, yet stuff moved. The furniture remained in situ, but smaller, personal items disappeared all the time, only to turn up later in improbable places. The house was dark and often chilly, they said. Agnes had never found it to be dark. One tenant pointed out that the place became lighter and warmer every time Agnes entered it, but that was foolishness, surely?

She played with a crossword, read the headlines, then fell asleep. Morecambe was miles behind her when she woke. Oh, Denis. How could the pain continue after thirty-nine years? Why did his raincoat still hang from the hall stand with that ancient brown-and-black-checked scarf? She had never let go, had never said goodbye, had remained half a woman. Perhaps the burial of a body might have made things easier to accept, though she doubted that, too. He had been her soulmate and she had lived nearly two-thirds of her life without him to keep her warm and safe.

The bus dropped her outside the house and she entered by the front door. There was no one to greet her, no human, no animal, no sound. The television filled the void and she sat, still wearing her coat, to stare at a bouncy young woman making garden features. The young woman was not wearing a bra and her hair kept falling over her face. She spoke loudly and dragged bits of grey, dried wood hither and thither, her plan to make a Chinese garden in an English suburb achieved within five heavily edited minutes.

His photograph was on the mantelpiece. Pop and Nan were there, too, along with Pop and Eva, then Albert and Kate, who had lived next door. They were all gone now, of course. Agnes had inherited Bamber

Cottage, had sold it and was living comfortably on her savings. What was this card about? She stared at the item she had picked up on her way in, fished out reading glasses and saw Ian Harte's name and telephone number with a message. He was a surveyor and he wanted to talk to her about selling Briarswood. Agnes sighed. She had changed the name and the decor, yet still no tenant had endured beyond six months. Haunted, indeed. Oh, well, she would phone the man in a day or so.

As if reading her thoughts, the instrument rang out. It was Lucy. She was going round the bend with boredom and stated her intention to visit the next day. 'Heard from Mags?' she asked.

'No,' replied Agnes.

'I'd never have believed she'd stay out of touch,' Lucy complained. 'We were all so close, weren't we?'

Agnes sighed. A lifetime ago, she had married the sweetest man in the world, and Lucy had married her George, who had been the second sweetest. Mags and her new nose had been joined in wedlock to Harry Timpson, who had become a very successful accountant. Then, suddenly, it had all gone awry. 'Morecambe was cold again,' she said.

'Isn't it time you stopped going, Agnes?'

'No. You can put flowers on George's grave, but the sea is all I have when it comes to Denis. Yes, get your old bones round here tomorrow. I'll go mad, butter some bread and open a tin of soup.'

She decided to unpack in the morning, made her way upstairs and, after the necessary preparations, climbed into a bed that had seen better days. She would never part with it. On Denis's side, the old pillow remained. She had worn out several of her own and had replaced them, but she kept his and changed its cover twice a week. For a while after he had gone, the scent of him had lingered, but he was all swallowed up now, obliterated by time and by the fact that few of the current neighbours remembered him.

'It just goes on, come what may,' she told the luminous dial of her alarm clock. The ticking and the turning of pages in a calendar continued, no matter what. She remembered the day, felt the baby in her arms and the chill travelling the length of her spine. He should not have gone to work, should have stayed at home after the previous day's troubles. But he had gone and nothing would ever bring him back.

Denis remained the same as ever, young and handsome in various frames around the house. Agnes, still straight and fairly strong, had silver in her hair and lines on her face. She was not afraid of ageing, was not afraid of death. All she feared was this continuing emptiness, the silence, the isolation. All she wanted was to be part of a family, but David was too far away and Denis was long gone.

Never mind. Lucy would be here tomorrow.

Lucy bustled in with fish and chips. 'I didn't get any mushy peas for me,' she said, 'they give me wind in the willows.'

They sat at the kitchen table, each leaving many chips uneaten. 'One portion between two next time,' said Lucy. 'Never mind – it saved you opening a tin and buttering bread.'

In the living room, they played Scrabble for a couple of hours. Lucy, who had become an addict, manufactured some improbable words. When challenged by her partner, she came up with the inevitable Chambers dictionary and proved herself right. 'Shall we go to the pub?' Agnes asked as dusk fell.

'No. It's full of thirty-year-olds with prospects.'

'And credit cards.'

'Exactly. I can't recall the last time I was in there. Remember Helen's first game of darts? I reckon they had to plaster three walls after that. Anyway, I have come with a cunning plan.'

'Ah.' A cunning plan was typical of Lucy, who still continued to be the naughty child. 'What is it this time?'

Lucy grinned. 'It's time we had another Hastings adventure. We won't tell them we're coming, eh? I can book us into a hotel and we'll get fed and watered with our own money. Then we just turn up at the house and surprise them.'

'I'm not sure that's a good idea.'

Lucy sighed heavily. 'Look, we were the three graces for long enough – brought one another up, we did.'

It was Agnes's turn to sigh. 'I just feel we're not wanted. Helen said she would do what she saw as her duty by me, then that was that. I even had the DNA done to prove that we share blood, which took ages – it's harder to prove siblinghood than parenthood. But I had to do it before accepting all that money and a share of the house. She's stubborn, but so am I. I had to hang on until DNA technology had been refined before accepting the money, but she never touched my share. She waited for the test, then made me a rich woman, and that was the end of it. If they wanted us there, we would have been invited, Lucy.'

The visitor scowled. 'Time we had it out with Mags, then. She just buggered off without so much as a by-your-leave – we hadn't done anything to deserve that, had we?'

'I suppose she knew we were surprised when she married Harry. He turned out OK and we all like him. But we're not wanted.'

'Why, though?'

'I don't know. I've told you for years that I don't know.'

But Lucy had made up her mind. Agnes, who knew that Lucy could be rather direct and indiscreet, had to agree to the plan. She wasn't going to allow Lucy to barge in and start a war – Hastings had seen enough of that in 1066. 'All right, but you'll have to behave.'

Lucy pretended to pout. 'You mean I can't wear my crocheted wedding dress and high boots? Do I have to be sensible?'

'Yes, you do.'

They parted company just before the six o'clock news. Lucy returned to her converted barn, while Agnes stared at trouble in the Middle East and decided that religion was a bad thing. Wars had been fought in the name of Jesus Christ; now people quarrelled over another prophet. Even the Jews, whose Messiah was still awaited, couldn't sit still and behave themselves for five minutes. She shook a fist at the television and turned to a cable channel. It was chewing gum for the mind, but it got her through another evening spent in the company of soup, sandwiches and silence. Broadcast sound made the house seem occupied, and she was fast becoming a fan of soaps and comedy series. But such luxuries were a poor substitute for a family. Yes, she would go to Hastings, because time, the great enemy, needed to be filled. And she must remember to phone that surveyor.

*

'What did you say?' Mags leaned over the bed and waited for an answer.

'The parcel. As soon as I go – post it.'

Mags blinked away yet more tears, wondered how much more saline she could possibly produce. 'Are you sure?' What good would it do? What was the point, after all this time? Helen was fast losing her hold on life, and Mags was her sole attendant. This stubborn patient had refused admittance to hospital and had banned all visiting nurses. The doctor who handled Helen's drugs was allowed begrudgingly to attend the bedside when the drip needed checking. All other callers were turned away from the door. Helen, having been given little choice in the early years of her life, was taking full control of the end. 'Try not to think about it,' Mags urged.

A travesty of a smile stretched parchment-thin skin. 'What else would I think about?' She often thought about Millie, although she didn't want to, as Millie had been spoiled to a point where she considered herself to be the centre of the universe. Helen's sister, who, because of the age difference, had been more like a daughter, was not here to support the woman who had guided her through life. Millie was on the point of divorcing a second husband and had no time for visits while chasing a third. 'I was not a good guardian,' said the woman in the bed.

'You did your best. No one can do more than that.'

'She's selfish.'

'So are my sons. Don't dwell on it. And yes, I shall post your parcel when the time comes.'

'Thank you.'

When Helen had succumbed once again to morphine-induced stupor, Mags crept out of the room and descended the stairs. Away from Helen, she managed not to cry, choosing instead to tackle stained bedlinen and other daily chores. The cancer had travelled at lightning speed through the poor woman's body; she had days to live and Millie didn't seem to care.

As she filled the washing machine, Mags thought about the Helen she had met almost forty years ago at Lucy and George's wedding, remembered her pain, her brief flirtation with alcohol, her vulnerability. Thought skipped ahead to Harley Street, the new nose, her own marriage to Harry Timpson. Harry had made a good job of himself, though his nerves had never been in top condition. Mags knew why. The knowing why had brought her here, to Hastings, had separated her from Agnes and Lucy, the two people who had been her constant companions through childhood, adolescence and into adulthood.

Helen had forbidden Mags to inform Agnes of her illness and imminent death. Mags, having returned to work after her sons had grown, had now retired, but caring for Helen had become a full time job. She no longer went home at night; Harry, too, slept at Helen's house. His blind loyalty to Helen Spencer would stay with him until the day she died.

Mags was bone weary. Although Helen had become slight after the ravages of disease, the task of moving and changing her was taking its toll on her carer's health. 'I'm too old for this,' Mags told the wall. 'I should be knitting for my grandchildren.' She should also be up north. Hastings was a good place, but it wasn't home. Living on the hem of the sector known as Bohemia, she had made friends among writers and artists, many of whom were interesting, some of whom were precious posers and unloved. Now in her fourth decade as a resident, Mags knew every house, every fishing boat, every spire, castle and battleground within ten miles of the town. But she still wanted to go home.

Harry appeared. 'How is she?' were his first words.

'The same.'

He banged a briefcase onto a side table. 'If she were a dog, she'd be humanely destroyed.'

'But she isn't a dog. What we did for Oscar can't possibly be done for Helen.'

'No.' He studied his wife. 'I'm going to take a few weeks off work. Let's face it – I should have retired by now. I'll help you. You look like you need a rest.'

'I can't rest. And you know why. None of us can rest while we know what's coming.' She shook her head. Harry was already on the highest permitted dose of an anti-depressant. He would probably have fared better at work, but there was no point in arguing and she was too tired, anyway, to start a discussion on a subject that was already worn thin. 'I'll make some tea,' she said.

But he was up and out of his chair before she had finished speaking. The kettle clattered and cups were banged onto a tray. Mags simply stared at the wall. It was all going to happen and she dreaded the outcome. Helen Spencer was on the brink of death and Mags, acutely aware of the promise she had made, would abide by her word. It would be a repeat of the Battle of Hastings, but nothing could be done about that.

A picture of Agnes and Lucy suddenly insinuated its way into Mags's exhausted brain. Oh, for the chance to talk to Agnes, to prepare her for what was about to happen. She sat with her head in her hands, elbows on the table, mind in turmoil. For Helen, death was going to mean an end to all troubles; for those she would leave behind . . .

'Shall I take some tea upstairs?' Harry asked.

Mags sat up straight. 'She won't drink it. I've been wetting her lips with a bit of ice. She'll be needing no more tea, love.'

He sat opposite his wife. 'Not long, then?'

'No. Could be today, tonight, tomorrow – I've no idea.'

'And Millie?'

Mags shrugged. 'Mucking about in London as far as I know. She dumped the dentist and she's chasing a stockbroker. I think she'll become one of those serial monogamists.'

Harry attempted a joke. 'I thought she was a physiotherapist.'

Mags shook her head. 'She's a bloody pest, that's for sure.'

'Aye, she is. Oh, I bought a bit of fish for a change.'

Mags pretended to frown. 'That's unusual, isn't it? Fish in a fishing port?'

'It is,' he replied. 'Especially when ninety per cent of it goes to Captain Birds Eye or some such frozen person. Do you not fancy fish?'

She closed her eyes. She fancied fish and chips Lancashire style, nice, smooth batter beaten by her dad, chips fried by her mam at Bradshaw's chippy. She fancied eating from newspaper on the moors, drinking dandelion and burdock from the bottle, wiping her hands on grass. 'I want to go home,' she said quietly. Mam and Dad weren't there any more, but she still needed to be in Lancashire with Agnes and Lucy. 'Retire, Harry. We'll go home and face the brass band.'

His face was ashen. 'I'm scared.'

'So am I.'

'I did what I did for Helen.'

'Yes.'

'But it was wrong.'

'I know. At the time, there seemed little choice.'

They drank tea in silence, then Mags went to prepare the fish for supper. She was worried about her husband, about the poor soul upstairs, was still homesick after going on forty years in the south. Someone rang the front doorbell, and she heard Harry walking down the hall. When he returned, he was not alone. Mags dropped a knife. 'Agnes,' she whispered. 'Lucy – when did you get here?'

'Yesterday,' answered Lucy. 'We've done all the compulsory things, just as we did last time we came. We've done Battle, the Shipwreck Centre and the Fishermen's Museum. I still say we would have won if King Harold hadn't been worn out after York.'

Agnes saw the expression on Mags's face. 'Mags?'

'Hello.'

'What are you doing in Helen's house? Is she all right?'

'No,' replied Harry. 'She's on her last legs.'

Mags dried her hands on a tea towel. 'She hasn't been on her legs for weeks, Harry.' She turned her attention to her two friends. 'She's got cancer. It's a nasty one. It travels express and takes no prisoners. There's nothing to be done apart from palliative care. She refused to go into hospital or into a hospice, so I look after her. Harry helps all he can.'

Agnes leaned against a wall. 'How long?' she asked.

'Any minute now.' Mags sat on a straight-backed chair. 'Helen forbade me to contact you. She said you'd suffered enough and she didn't want to put you through this.' Mags could not mention other difficulties that would surely arise in the very near future.

Agnes's jaw hung open. She could not think of anything to say.

Lucy waded in, of course. 'Agnes is her sister. She should have been told.'

For once, Mags stood up to Lucy. 'When a dying woman expresses a wish, I listen. Isn't it time you did the same – time you listened, I mean? Hear yourself, Lucy. Think about what you're saying before allowing the words out of your mouth. There – I've waited years to say that.'

It was Lucy's turn to have a slack jaw.

Agnes left the room and made for the stairs. Apart from her son, she owned but one living relative, and her sister was about to die. There was Millie, of course, but Millie was too busy crossing the pond to buy shoes on Park Avenue, or, when she was in London, chasing someone else's husband, to count. Panic fluttered in Agnes's chest. Poor Helen. She had never married, yet she had been a mother to the ungrateful Millie, had devoted her life to the child.

Lucy stared at Mags. Mags had changed. 'So, you're standing up for yourself at last, are you? I'll go and look at Helen—'

'No you won't. As you just said, they're sisters. They haven't seen one another for God alone knows how long – let Agnes have some time with Helen alone.'

'I never realized how much you dislike me,' said Lucy.

Mags smiled grimly. 'I don't dislike you. It's just that you've always been the centre of attention and it's time we all grew up. Try some sensitivity. Think about other people for a change.' Lucy put Mags in mind of Millie, who had always been precocious and spoiled. The small, neat woman who had been married to George Henshaw continued to act the clown, the beautiful, forgivable girl. It didn't work any more. Like body parts, the personality should age as gracefully as possible. Naughty children in their sixties were not charming.

When Agnes walked into Helen's bedroom, a silly, disjointed thought entered her head. She had forgotten to phone that surveyor. Helen, who had wanted to retain Briarswood for rental only, had been outvoted by her two half-sisters. Millie demanded the money, while Agnes, tired of being caretaker to an empty pile, simply needed to be rid of the house.

All thoughts of surveyors left her when she saw what time and cancer had done to Helen Spencer. Limp, grey hair hung in clumps, punctuating baldness resulting from chemotherapy. The neck was more than thin, while the shape beneath the blankets was horribly emaciated. She was awake, at least.

'Hello, love.' Agnes sat down by the bed, afraid of touching a hand that was almost transparent.

The skull on the pillows smiled. 'Hello.'

'Don't tire yourself,' Agnes begged.

'No point in saving energy,' came the reply. 'I'm on borrowed seconds now.'

Agnes swallowed.

'I'm sorry.'

'For what?'

'It's all there for you – in the book I never published. Let me die first.'

'I don't want you to die.'

'You can't choose. Is the house sold?'

'No. But a man wants to survey it properly.'

'When I'm dead. Wait, please.'

'All right.'

Helen took a deep, rasping breath. 'The haunting began before we left. Millie's toys would be moved, my watch disappeared more than once. He's there, you see.'

'Your dad?'

'And yours. Agnes – get Mags.'

Agnes descended the stairs and gave Mags the message.

'She's too weak now to deal with the morphine,' said Mags, drying her hands.

Lucy and Agnes waited in the drawing room. They listened as Harry followed his wife to Helen's bedroom, sat in silence among Helen's treasured antiques. A grandmother clock chimed the quarter-hour as Mags entered the room. 'She's gone.'

It was Lucy who cried, Lucy who said it wasn't fair. Agnes simply sat and allowed the message to be absorbed by her soul. She was glad. No one should be forced to continue alive in such condition.

'She didn't suffer,' said Mags. 'She just closed her eyes and fell asleep. You helped her, Agnes. It's as if she knew you would come. I think she was waiting, but she wouldn't let me fetch you.'

Lucy turned her face to the wall and stifled the sobs.

'The funeral will be at Skirlaugh,' Mags announced. 'I have detailed instructions – she is to be buried with her mother.'

Agnes nodded, sighed, looked down the long road she had travelled in the company of Helen. The further back she went, the narrower the track became, because the beginning had been so unreal – Helen trying to seduce Denis, Denis resisting, Helen turning on her father – on the man who was Agnes's father, too. There were those letters, there was an unpublished book, a funeral to arrange. 'We'll go home and get ready for you,' she told Mags.

'Thank you.'

Agnes and Lucy went to say their final goodbyes to Helen. The face on white linen was as pale as the pillowcase, but pain seemed to be lifting itself out of features in which it had become ingrained. 'She's all right now,' Agnes told her weeping companion. 'Don't cry. You never trusted her, anyway.'

'I did. Once all had been explained, I even liked her.'

'How fortunate for her.'

Lucy, unused to sarcasm from her friend, had nothing else to say.

They left for the north the next day. A Hastings undertaker would take the body, then it was to be transported home and delivered to a funeral parlour in Bolton. For Agnes and Lucy, the rest was vague, though they had been instructed to arrange a buffet at Briarswood. The will would be read in a Bolton office and Agnes hoped against hope that Millie would at least come to the funeral of the woman who had been a loving mother.

'What about that surveyor?' Lucy asked as the train pulled into Trinity Street Station. 'The one you forgot to ring?'

'He can wait till it's all over.' The selling of the house was no longer at the top of the list, because Helen Spencer was coming home.

Chapter Fifteen

It was over. Agnes, feeling like a limp dishcloth, returned with Lucy from the reading of the will. Lucy, pleased to have been left pearls she had always coveted, expressed her concern about deserting Agnes in her hour of need. 'I have to get home,' she grumbled. 'The decorator's going to do an estimate today. I could put him off—'

'No. Go and get it over with.'

'Phone me if you need me.' Lucy left. Agnes, glad of her own company, sat and studied the fireplace. Lucy had had an ulterior motive for wanting to stay, because Agnes was in possession of the sole copy of Helen Spencer's unpublished typescript. Lucy always wanted to be the first to know just about anything – she had been the same since childhood.

'No Millie, of course,' Agnes whispered into the silence. 'After all Helen gave up for her, she couldn't even be bothered to put in an appearance now.' It had been a very quiet funeral. The village that had known Helen no longer existed. After almost forty years, the residents of Skirlaugh Fall had forgotten the Spencer family of Lambert House, now Briarswood, Skirlaugh Rise. People came, people went, life went on. 'Just as well,' said Agnes as she removed her shoes and pushed her feet into a pair of old, well-loved slippers. 'Or we'd still be mourning Adam and Eve.'

She looked at the parcel, recalled another package left here many years earlier, remembered with clarity the day she had read how Judge Spencer, after murdering one woman, had impregnated another, her own mother. More reading to be done – more discoveries to be made, she supposed. A long time ago, Mabel, Helen's nanny, had left a letter; Helen had left several hundred thousand words.

The doorbell sounded. Agnes hauled suddenly heavy bones from their resting place, opened the door and was shocked to find Millie on the step. 'Yes?' Agnes had little time for her devious and rather decorative half-sister. She was wearing well for her age, but plastic surgery had become a necessity, clothes a fixation, make-up an absolute must-have. Her surname seemed to change with the seasons – few remembered whether she was married or to whom. This woman seemed to be as ruthless as her dead father had been; she cared only for herself.

Millie pushed her way into the house. 'I missed the reading of the will,' she said as she placed herself in front of the over-mantel mirror. A hand strayed to her throat. Did she need a little more work in that area?

Agnes closed the door. 'You aren't welcome here,' she snapped.

Millie, unused to being addressed in such fashion by Agnes, turned away from her own precious image and glared at the owner of this tiny house. 'Why is that?' she asked. 'I haven't seen you for years – what on earth has happened to make you so nasty? I'm sure I don't know what I am supposed to have done.'

'You missed the reading of the will? Bugger the will – you missed the funeral. Helen gave up her whole life for you.'

The visitor shrugged. 'No one asked her to. Anyway, what sort of life would she have had? No man wanted her. I was the only reason for her to get out of bed every morning.'

'That's not the point.' Helen had indulged the child, had made excuses for the teenager, had lost the woman who stood here now. 'Your father didn't want you. He threatened to have you adopted.'

'Good job he died when he did, then.'

'And you know about the will – half to you, half to me.'

'But you aren't a proper sister.'

Agnes lowered her chin. 'I didn't see much of Helen after she left for Hastings, but I was a better sister than you were.' She raised her head. 'What did you ever do for her – for anyone other than yourself? Go and contest the will – I don't give two hoots about the money. My grandfather – his work now sells second hand for a small fortune – left me very comfortable. And Helen made sure I was safe. Do as you please, but leave my house.'

Millie's jaw hung for a split second. 'I couldn't make the funeral – I was in hospital in San Francisco. What was I supposed to do? Get on a plane and let my wounds become infected?'

Agnes half smiled and shook her head. 'What was it this time? Liposuction? Another implant, a bit of collagen? You want to be careful – the skin of your face is stretched so tight you look like something out of Tussaud's.'

'Nonsense. I like to make the best of myself. What's wrong with that?'

'Look at that skin-bleached pop star – the one whose nose seems to be parting company with his face. You can go too far with that particular addiction. Anyway, I have something to do straight away, so leave now. Oh, and if you were going to ask yet again about the house – a surveyor is looking at it. You'll get your share.'

Millie opened her mouth to speak, thought better of it, and left the house in a cloud of expensive and rather overpowering perfume.

Agnes set the kettle to boil, then stood and leaned against the kitchen sink. Through the window, she had a clear enough view of the big house. It wasn't as easy to see as it had been forty years ago, because trees had grown thicker, but it remained visible. Briarswood had become a thorn in her side. It had been impossible to let and was even proving difficult to sell. Briarswood had been a suitable name for a thorn in her flesh, she mused for a second or two. She had just shown another spiky problem out of the house – how dared Millie turn up at this late stage?

She settled in front of the television with toast and tea. Whatever was in Helen's book would still be there tomorrow. But no programme suited her tonight, and she found herself thinking about Mags, who had already returned to Hastings with Harry. Mags knew about the house and its weirdness. She had stayed in it with Helen and Harry after the explosion that had taken Denis and the judge. It was creepy, she had said.

Agnes chewed thoughtfully. Bangles, beads, watches, cufflinks, wallets and purses had all disappeared, only to turn up an hour or a day later in rooms that had been unused. Mags didn't lie. Therefore, it was probably right to believe the stories of tenants, most of whom had left the house within a few months of failing to settle into it. Had the surveyor noticed anything odd? Was that why he needed to speak to the owners?

Her eyes strayed once again to the parcel. According to Helen, the book was her own life story, but all names had been changed. The haunting was probably mentioned in there – perhaps she should read a little of it tonight.

She finished her simple supper, checked locks and windows, picked up the package and carried it upstairs. It was unlikely to be suitable bedtime reading, but Agnes wanted Helen's view of the so-called spirits who were said to inhabit Briarswood. After preparing herself for sleep, she switched on her reading lamp before settling in bed with the large envelope. Poor Helen. Did she want Agnes to try to get the story published?

The accompanying note said nothing about selling the script. It simply drew Agnes's attention to chapter seven.

The rest is just a piece of self-pity and an account of the devil who was our father. I ask your forgiveness before you begin to read. This story will help you understand why I left the north for Hastings. It will also explain my over-lenient attitude towards Millie, who has grown into a person of whom I find it impossible to be proud. In trying to make her happy, I spoiled her beyond retrieval.

My dear Agnes, I thank you for your friendship and forbearance. I have loved receiving your letters and I love you for the time and trouble you took to keep in touch with me.

I beg you to forgive me.

Your loving sister, Helen

Forgive? Forgive what? Agnes turned immediately to chapter seven. From the start, she was riveted to the script. Oh, God, this could not be true. But it was true, it had to be true. She got no sleep that night.

Ian Harte knocked on the door of the only decent-looking cottage in the terrace. Mrs Makepeace had never got back to him, so he was making a renewed effort to solve the riddle of Briarswood. It was a valuable property, and his employers were keen to get it sold so that they could reap their statutory percentage.

The door opened to reveal a dishevelled woman who did not seem to fit with the neat house and garden. She was in dressing gown and old slippers, but it was the expression on her face that dismayed him. The woman looked ill and worn out.

'Yes?' she said.

'Ian Harte, Mrs Makepeace. I'm the one trying to do a full survey on Briarswood. You are one of the key-holders, I take it?'

'I am.'

He hesitated. 'Is this a bad time?'

'I just buried my sister.'

'Ah. I'm sorry. Would you like me to come back in a few days? I've no wish to intrude on your grief.'

It was Agnes's turn to dither. Should she wade in and get the business over and done with? Or did she need some more thinking time? 'There are complications,' she said slowly. 'My sister who died was part-owner, as is another sister. There were three of us,' she added lamely.

He gave her an encouraging smile. 'I see. Well, if you want to leave it for now, I'll—'

'Come back on Wednesday,' she said. 'Sorry to mess

you about, but I have some legal business to finish and . . . erm . . . I'm not feeling too well.'

'Is there anything I can do?'

Agnes smiled at him. He reminded her of Denis. Denis would have become a gentle, thoughtful soul – no – he had always owned those qualities. 'No, thank you. This is something I have to do by myself. Family and lawyers – I'm sure you understand.'

'Of course.' He turned, then swivelled back to face her. 'Look after yourself, Mrs Makepeace. You have my phone number.'

Lucy phoned. 'Have you read it?'

Agnes was transported backwards in time to the day when Lucy had asked the same question about testimony bequeathed by an ex-nanny. 'Some of it, yes.'

'What did it say?'

Lucy had always been so full-on, so direct and challenging. 'I can't talk about it. Lucy, please don't ask.'

'But—'

'I told you not to ask. Mags lost patience with you in Hastings – it takes a hell of a lot for Mags to lose patience. Sometimes, people need to be left alone to digest information. Not all knowledge needs to be broadcast immediately, you know. I have to come to terms with this on my own. When I am ready to talk, you will not be the first to hear – I am sorry about that. Things need to be done now in the correct order. I shall give them their airing when my own head is clear.'

'Oh. Right. Shall I stay away for a while, then?'

'Good idea. I'll call you once the show is on the road.' It would be a show, too, she thought. A three-ringed circus was about to pitch its big tops in the grounds of the village named Skirlaugh.

Agnes sat all day in her dressing gown and slippers. She drank what seemed to be a gallon of tea, ate arrowroot biscuits and half an apple. The typescript remained upstairs, because she did not want it in the same room as herself. Its current place of residence was at the bottom of a blanket box underneath one of Denis's cable-knit jumpers. Denis. Oh, Denis. At last, the tears came. There was no need to cry quietly, because this was a proper house, its walls inches thick and made of stone.

The truth of which she had just become proprietor weighed heavily. It was not something she could keep to herself, yet she scarcely knew where to begin. Was there a right way? Who would be hurt?

She dried her eyes and phoned Hastings. 'Mags?'

'Yes?'

'You were expecting me to call.'

'I was, yes.'

'Is it the truth – this chapter seven?'

'I never read it, Agnes, but I think I know what it says.'

'And Harry really did do that?'

'He did. He would have done anything for her. It's been difficult. Their relationship had a passion I never shared with him.'

A few beats of time passed. 'Did they sleep together?' Agnes asked.

'It was the price I had to pay to keep the man I loved. And, no matter what, I could not have resented Helen Spencer. I cared for her in my own way, you see.'

Agnes replaced the receiver. Everyone had paid, it

seemed. The judge was the rot in the fruit's flesh. He had caused pain to all in his path, and Helen had suffered the most. It was ten o'clock, almost time for bed. She did not want to go upstairs. Still unwashed and bedraggled, Agnes Makepeace curled herself on the sofa, head propped on cushions. She leaned over and pushed *Pride and Prejudice* into the DVD player, pretending to watch a story told in a time that was difficult, but clearcut. Jane Austen knew all about the small life, the ribbons, the gowns, the carriages. Yet she said nothing real about men, was a mere observer of their functions and a listener to their pronouncements.

Jane Austen had never attempted to climb into the mind and soul of the human male. It was plain that she knew nothing of true evil. If Wickham was the wickedest creature that writer could imagine, her life had been blessed indeed.

Agnes rose at nine o'clock, went upstairs and took a hot shower. She dressed soberly in black skirt, white blouse, grey cardigan and a small amount of make-up. It had to be done today, and Ian Harte had seemed a decent enough man. After telephoning to ask him to come today instead of on Wednesday, she busied herself with chores in an attempt to fill in time. He would help her. With unwavering certainty, she knew that she had found the best compromise.

He came, as arranged, at two o'clock. Agnes provided tea and biscuits, then sat for a few minutes arranging her thoughts into a semblance of order. It had to be done; things could not be left as they were.

'In 1965,' she began, 'my husband and Judge Zachary

Spencer died. Judge Spencer and his daughter, Helen, lived at Lambert House – Briarswood, as it's called now. There was an explosion on the judge's yacht in More-cambe Bay – something to do with fuel in the galley – and the yacht was blown to smithereens.'

'Yes, I know. It must have been a very sad time for you.'

Agnes inhaled deeply. 'It never happened.'

'I beg your—'

'It was a lie, a sham. Helen Spencer murdered her father and killed my Denis by accident. Helen's father had done away with her mother thirty years earlier – that's why she murdered him. There was written evidence of his crime and Helen had witnessed it herself, though she was very young at the time and needed her memory jogging. She wrote her life story in the form of a novel – the names are changed – and she waited until after her own death to let me know. I don't blame her for that – she had trouble enough in her life. Now, I have to bear the weight for her.'

'So – where are the bodies?' He knew the answer before the question was fully aired. 'They're in the cellar, aren't they? That's why the specifications have gone awry.'

Agnes nodded. 'It was arsenic. Denis never touched brandy, but he must have taken a drink of it on that particular evening.' Hardly surprising, she thought, after the trouble of the previous day. 'The yacht was blown up by some man from Wythenshawe – I suspect he had played a part in a robbery at a Manchester jeweller's in the previous year. Someone drove the judge's Bentley to Morecambe, Helen followed in her car and brought the driver back. The Bentley was found by police in

Morecambe. They assumed that Denis had driven the judge to his yacht. The crew of the lifeboat said no remains would be found, as the yacht was in splinters.'

'Bloody hell.' Ian Harte pushed a hand through his hair.

'My Denis hated that bloody yacht.' Agnes shook her head. 'We need the police,' she said, her voice steady. 'A wall was built in the cellar with both bodies behind it. The cellar was plastered over – Helen wrote all the details – and those two souls – one good, one evil – have haunted that place ever since.'

'More evil than good,' he said. 'I've never had faith in such things, but the house is definitely creepy.'

Agnes smiled wanly. 'Not evil when I'm there, though. If I go into the house, Denis looks after me.' It all sounded silly in broad daylight, yet she now believed in those two spirits. 'The police will have to deal with this, Mr Harte. Your client must step back for a while – the house cannot be sold just yet.'

'Quite.' He shivered. 'You want me to do this for you?'

She nodded and handed him chapter seven. 'It's all in there. I know full well what needs to be done, yet I find myself incapable of doing it.' Harry would be implicated. 'You came along at just the right time, Mr Harte.'

He lowered his chin. 'We've both been through the mill, Mrs Makepeace. I lost my mother to cancer just weeks ago, so I know what grief is. Yes, of course I'll help.' He scribbled on a scrap of paper. 'That's my home number and my mobile – call me any time. Joyce – that's my missus – is a good listener, too. Don't be alone, please.'

Agnes stood at the window and watched as Ian Harte drove away to instigate enormous trouble. When the car had disappeared, she pulled on a coat, picked up the keys to Briarswood, and left the house. She was going to say goodbye to Denis. This would probably be the last day of sanity for some time to come, and the big house was going to be out of bounds.

When she opened the front door, she smelled brandy. That was ridiculous, she told herself, because no one had lived here for many months. Dust motes floated in weak sunlight, and beautiful wood panelling seemed to scream for beeswax. She unlocked the door to the cellars and went down below ground level. With just a vague idea of the location of the bodies, she sat on an old crate and talked to Denis. 'I didn't know where you were, sweetheart. All these years, I've been going to Morecambe, but you were here all the time. He's with you, isn't he? Never mind. They'll be getting you out soon, then you can go and have a decent burial in Tonge Cemetery.'

A slight breeze brushed her cheek. Where had that come from? Agnes stood up and walked towards the front of the house. She knew she was nearer to him. The cellars were made up of load-bearing walls that carried the pattern and shape of rooms above, yet the layout was slightly confusing for Agnes, who had never before descended to this level. Some areas were plastered, some were not. Several of the judge's wines rested on wooden racks, and the remains of Pop's model of Lambert House were jumbled in a corner.

Placing her hands against one of the plastered walls, she spoke again. 'I know you're inches away from me now,' she said. 'I think you're under the judge's study. There'll be police and all sorts of people around soon, but I had to do it, had to tell. Helen meant me to release you from here. You're not resting. Before you can rest, you have to become a crime scene.' The smell of brandy came again. 'Neither are you resting,' said Agnes, her voice louder, 'and you never will, you bad bugger. Helen did the right thing. Denis – you know she never meant to kill you.'

She left the house and stood outside for a while, remembering Kate, who had run the kitchen here for years. Gardens, neglected and overgrown now, had been cared for by Denis under the watchful eye of an Alsatian named Oscar. Louisa had breathed life into the place until her pregnancy; Helen, who had once believed herself to be in love with Denis, had matured and improved greatly under Louisa's protection.

All gone now, all ground to dust, but never forgotten by Agnes. A thought struck her and she picked her mobile phone from one pocket, Ian Harte's card from another.

He answered immediately. 'Hello?'

'There are blueprints with Granada TV,' said Agnes. 'My grandfather made a model of the house and, if you look at his drawings, you'll see where the original walls of the cellar were. The judge and Denis were still alive when Pop built that huge doll's house, so that should show you where any changes were made. He did the cellars as well as the upper part of the building, you see.'

He cleared his throat. 'I don't need the plans, Mrs Makepeace – I know exactly where the . . . the problem lies. I'm with the police now,' he said softly. 'They'll be up there soon.'

'I know.' She understood what was coming. Feeling strangely peaceful, she wandered back to her cottage and telephoned her son. He needed to know what was happening and he promised to travel up as soon as possible. Agnes smiled. Denis would have been so proud of David, who fought daily battles on behalf of sick children. 'You are proud, aren't you?' she asked a photograph on the mantelpiece. He was still here, would always be here.

Cars began to arrive, one stopping outside her house, others carrying on round the corner and up Skirlaugh Rise. There would be questions, of course, then inquests, then two funerals. Agnes would go to her husband's service and burial, but her father could be put out with the council's bins for all she cared.

She opened the door. A plain clothes officer who looked far too young for such responsibility entered the house. 'Mrs Makepeace.'

'Yes, that's me.'

And so it began.

Skirlaugh was packed with reporters, photographers and television crews. Whenever Agnes left the house, she was accosted by seekers of sensational headlines. One man, who had entered her rear garden without permission, was dealt with very tersely. 'Your sort may have chased Diana to her death, but pond life has no effect on me. Bugger off before I clock you with my poker.' She brandished the brass-handled fire iron. The man stood his ground until she raised the weapon, then scrambled up the wall, almost screaming when brambles bit into his flesh.

After that small event, life moved slightly closer to normal. When she walked to the village shop, a policeman accompanied her, and she was grateful for that small service. Shopping further afield involved Lucy and her car, but they almost always managed to outwit their pursuers.

David arrived with his wife and children. The youngsters had to sleep in their parents' room, but reporters melted into the ether as soon as they noticed a man in the cottage. David Makepeace, who was kindness itself when it came to his family and his job, had little time for tabloids or broadcasting journalists. Within twenty-four hours of his arrival, Agnes had the peace she had sought.

However, the story was front page news, not only in Lancashire, but throughout the whole of Britain. The nanny's letter was mentioned, as was the illegitimate status of Agnes, second daughter to a corrupt judge. One daily tabloid gave graphic details of the state of the two bodies – it seemed that they had mummified because of airbricks at the tops of walls and the proximity of a huge, oil-fired boiler that heated the house. There was no escape. Television and radio chipped in. Pop was there once more in all his glory, a wonderful, difficult old man showing off his doll's houses and his model of the then Lambert House. Tears flowed down Agnes's cheeks as she listened to him lecturing on the subject of retirement. 'You can retire when they put the last nail in your coffin lid,' he pronounced.

Lydia, too, wiped away a tear. 'Come on, Mum,' she said. 'Turn that damned thing off. David's taking us out for a meal.'

'People will stare,' said Agnes. Then she raised her head. 'Let them,' she whispered. 'There's enough of Pop in me to tell them to bog off.' So she went with her son, daughter-in-law and grandchildren to face the world.

'I'm not leaving my cottage,' she told David. 'I'm not running away like Helen did.'

'Nor should you,' said Lydia. 'But you know where we are if it gets too much. You could have your own flat in the basement.'

Agnes managed a smile. 'No, love. My Denis was nearly forty years in a cellar – I think I'll keep my head on the surface, thanks.'

The inquest was a nightmare. The police had gathered from Helen's script and from Agnes that Harry Timpson, whose name had been changed by Helen, had been working for the Spencers in 1965, so he was summoned to answer for his actions. His name was called, but he never entered the room. The meeting was adjourned until the next day, giving the police time to force Harry to obey the order commanding him to attend both inquests.

David and Lydia, having spent two weeks in the north, had to travel back to London. They would return for Denis's funeral, but David was needed by the sick. They made Agnes promise to visit as soon as the business was over, then left with their children to drive home to Islington.

Alone again, Agnes suddenly felt more isolated than ever. It had been an exhausting time for a woman no longer in the first flush of youth. 'I'm old,' she told a contestant on Who Wants to be a Millionaire. The Sky channels offered nothing better. There was a film named What Lies Beneath – she wasn't going to look at that. So she tuned into a shopping channel to learn the virtues of foam mattresses and American hand-sewn quilts.

Denis's body would be released for burial within days. She would be able to claim the watch he had worn and his mother's rosary, which he had always carried in a pocket. 'But you'll rest soon,' she promised. 'Away from him, you'll feel better.'

The evening dragged itself along on feet of lead. Agnes picked up some unopened mail, found an offer from a trashy newspaper whose editor wanted to publish Helen's script for a six-figure sum. They could ask Millie, she thought before tossing the letter into a bin. The police held chapter seven while she owned the rest, so they could all bugger off, because Millie had been left just money and property.

Ian Harte arrived at nine o'clock. Aware that Agnes's family had left for London, he wanted to check that Mrs Makepeace was safe and well.

'They were mummified,' she told him.

'Yes.'

'Did you see my Denis?'

He shook his head. 'No one was allowed in. But a young policeman said your husband didn't look as if he had been dead for long. They'll let you see him if you like.'

Agnes looked at all the photographs in the room. 'I can see him here,' she said. 'There's no need for me to look at his body. I have a few of what they called his effects. Soon, I'll get his watch and rosary – they're enough for me.'

She was all right, Ian decided. He finished his cup of tea, said goodbye, then left for home.

It was half past nine. Agnes, having endured many half past nines and beyond, wondered why time had suddenly started to drag to the point of stopping. She could go and live in London with David and Lydia, but London was not for her. It was full of people who knew no one. She glanced through her window – did she know these people? Hardly. But she was on nodding terms with plenty of trees and pathways, and had even been known to greet a neighbour in the street. During the police enquiry, three women had taken the trouble to come to her door with home-made scones, pies and casseroles. She could and would make a life again.

It had been like a football match with a very long half-time, she supposed. That was how Pop had described the twenty-one years between the Great War and the Second – time for a butty and a cuppa, he had named the interval. Since Denis had died, Agnes's life had been on hold. For a reason she failed to understand, the burial of his body would open a new chapter for her. 'But not a chapter seven,' she said aloud. 'Never a chapter seven.'

The doorbell sounded. It was a quarter to ten. 'Who is it?' she called.

'Me.'

'Who's me?'

'Mags.'

Agnes froze. Harry would be with her. Harry was the man who had moved Denis's body down to the cellar. He had also loved Helen and had betrayed poor Mags. 'Are you alone?' she managed eventually.

'Yes. Very much so.'

Agnes opened the door. Mags, in the company of a small suitcase, stepped into the house. She placed the case on the floor, righted herself and spoke again. 'He hanged himself, Agnes.'

'What?' A hand flew of its own accord to her throat. She swallowed hard. 'Harry's dead?'

Mags nodded.

'Bloody hell. Come in – sit yourself down. Oh, my God – whatever next? Why, Mags?'

'He knew he was guilty of helping to conceal the bodies – he was accessory after the crime. And Helen was his raison d'être. I must go back for the inquest, but I had to come and tell you myself. He won't be at the court tomorrow, Agnes. The police know what's happened. I am so tired.'

They sat for over an hour in a companionable silence that was familiar to both of them. Lucy had always been the noise-maker, Mags the quiet one, Agnes the go-between. Two elderly ladies gazed at a dwindling coal fire, each knowing what would happen next, neither needing to speak. Agnes knew that Mags wanted to come home; Mags knew that Agnes needed to share her living space with someone she knew and trusted.

'Shall I put a bottle in your bed?' Agnes asked finally.

'Please.'

'When everything's done and dusted, you can choose your own wallpaper.'

Mags's eyes filled with tears. 'Next door's selling up,' she said. 'I've seen the sign and you can put in an offer for me. We can knock through and make it one big house, or we can keep things as they are. But we'll be together, won't we?'

'Course we will, kiddo. One for all—'

'And all for one. With Lucy as our beloved nuisance, eh?'

That night, both slept well.

The Reading Room

In loving memory of Laura Latimer, whose surname I borrowed for the main character herein. She comforted my mother when my dad was killed, and was one of the kindest people I have ever known. Until the end of her life, Laura fought to save the church of Sts Peter and Paul, Bolton, which place of worship was so pivotal in many lives, including my own. Sleep well, dear friend.

Also for Zelia Cheffins who died on Christmas Day 2008. She was a much-loved mother, grandmother and great-grandmother. To her granddaughter, Carol Sharpies, I send much affection. Chin up, Carol. Remember her laughter and the pleasures you shared.

One

Many people in the Lancashire village of Eagleton expressed the opinion that Enid Barker had sat at the upstairs window of 5 Fullers Walk since the old mill had been shifted forty years ago. It was further rumoured in jest that she had been pulled down with the mill, and had come back to haunt the newer development. Whatever residents thought of the matter, that grey shape sat, day in and day out, in the same position for hours at a time. Had her son not been so valued by the community, those whose imaginations ran towards the dark side might have likened her to the mummified corpse in *Psycho*, but Dave was a grand man who probably never took a cleaver into the shower in his life, so that particular piece of lunatic folklore died stillborn.

In spite of suggestions to the contrary, old Enid was very much alive. At almost seventy, she was astute, judgemental and extremely well versed in the ways of her fellow man. Because of a condition known as 'melegs', she could not walk very far. The medical reason was diabetic neuropathy, but she couldn't be bothered with words of such a size, so she stuck to 'melegs'. It was melegs that kept her upstairs, melegs that forced her to sit for most of the day, but it was her antipathy to daytime TV, which she could never manage to enjoy, that became the final clincher. Given all these circumstances, the window was the best place to be.

She enjoyed watching that lot scuttering and meandering out there. For a start, there was Valda Turnbull. Valda was wearing a new coat. She was a very fertile woman with five children already, so Enid knew what was coming and she said so. 'Dave?' she shouted. 'Come here a minute.'

He arrived at her side. 'Yes, Mam? Did you want some more toast?'

Enid shook her head. 'Now, you mark my words. Just keep an eye on that Valda. I'll bet you five quid she has another baby in less than nine months. She must be thirty-eight, so you'd think she'd have more sense. Look. New coat.'

'Eh?'

'She gives him sex for clothes. With their Molly, it was a powder blue three-piece. Terry was red high heels and a matching handbag. I think Anna-Louise was a cream-coloured coat, but you get mixed up when there's so many of them.'

Dave shook his head and groaned. Mam was becoming an embarrassment. No, that wasn't true, because she'd been an embarrassment for most of his forty-seven years, but this was interfering in the lives of all the victims who walked below. They knew she talked about them; she had talked about them when she had helped run the Reading Room. Well, at least she no longer had a big audience when delivering her vitriol. 'I got you some talking books from Isis, didn't I? I know your eyes get tired, so all you need to do is listen. You'd get more out of that than sitting here watching life pass you by.

2

There's some good stuff on that shelf if you'd only try it.'

Enid glared at him. 'This is real,' she snapped. 'Books is all lies.'

He bent his knees, puffing heavily because of the exertion, and squatted beside her. 'They talk about you. They call you the eyes and ears of the world. It's not nice, is it? For them, I mean. Going about their daily business knowing there's somebody staring down at them all the while.'

Enid sniffed. 'At my age, I can do as I like. No need to ask permission off nobody.'

Dave cringed. As a purveyor of many kinds of literature, he longed to uphold decent grammar at all costs. But Mam would not endure correction, so he had to ignore her ill-treatment of the most wonderful language on earth. He stood up and walked away.

At her age she could do as she liked? She had always done as she liked. For a kick-off, he'd no idea who his father was, and he often wondered whether she was any wiser concerning the gap on his birth certificate. How could she criticize anybody after the life she'd led? He still remembered her men friends, noises from the bedroom of their old house, sometimes money left behind the clock. But she was his mam, and he did right by her. 'I'll be going down in a minute,' he told her.

Enid sniffed again. 'Leave me a cup of tea, then go and enjoy yourself.' Her son was a great disappointment to her, and they both knew it. He was a short man, no more than five and a half feet, with a rounding belly and abbreviated legs. Every pair of trousers he bought had to be shortened, while his hair, which had started to thin in his twenties, was allowed to grow long on one side so

3

that he could comb it over. His belts always dug into him, causing the pot to seem bigger than it really was. She was ashamed of him. He looked nothing like her, and she wondered where he had come from. The fact that several candidates for paternity had been on the hustings never troubled her. Enid's memory was selective, and she accepted no blame for anything.

Dave tidied up, picking up the last slice of toast and loading it with marmalade, then taking bites between tasks. Food was his comfort, and he admitted as much to himself on a daily basis. As long as he had a book and something to eat, he was as happy as he could manage. All he had ever really wanted from life was a wife and at least one child of his own. But no one would look at him, not when it came to love and marriage. So he simply carried on with his life, eating, having the odd pint, looking after Mam and running the shop downstairs. He was determined to be of some use to the world, and that was the reason for his Reading Room.

Enid glanced at him. He knew full well that folk hereabouts called his establishment 'the old folk's home', but he didn't seem to care. People gathered in his downstairs back room to drink coffee or tea, eat snacks, and swap newspapers and opinions in a place where they felt safe and welcome. Unlike reading areas in long-deceased branch libraries, Eagleton's Reading Room was somewhere where folk could chat. Conversation was freer these days, Enid supposed, because she was no longer present in her supervisory capacity. She hated not being there; she hated the thought of him spending time with that woman, but what could she do?

Dave's thoughts matched his mother's at that moment. The back room was a happier place without Mam in attendance. Subjects ranging from politics through religion to the condition of someone recovering in hospital were discussed openly now. The atmosphere had improved a lot since Mam had got past wielding the teapot. Having her sniffing behind the sandwich counter had hardly been attractive for customers, so the whole caboodle flourished much better without her.

Dave's helper was a woman who went by the name of Philomena Gallagher. She was a strong Catholic, so she never worked Sundays or Holy Days of Obligation, events which occurred rather too frequently behind the hallowed portals that guarded her complicated and extremely demanding religion. But Philomena made great butties and scones, so her trespasses were eternally forgivable.

'Is she in today?' Enid enquired. 'Or is it the feast day of some daft bugger who chased all the snakes out of Ireland?'

He must not get annoyed with Mam. If he ever did let his temper off the leash, God alone knew what he might do, fired up as he would be by years of anger and resentment. He loved his mam. He kept reminding himself that he loved his mam, because she'd never given him away for adoption even though she hadn't had the easiest of lives. 'No. St Patrick's is in March. She's clear apart from Sunday for a while now.'

'Oh, goody.' Enid didn't like Philomena, because Philomena had taken her place downstairs. Thanks to mel-egs, Enid had been dumped in the upper storey while everybody praised the newcomer's food. Still, at least the damned woman wouldn't marry Dave, because Dave was Methodist. He was lapsed, but he was a long way from Rome. Anyway, nobody in their right mind would marry

Dave. Or so she hoped. Because she had to admit that she'd be in a pickle without him. And that was another cause of annoyance. 'I get fed up here on my own,' she complained.

'I come and make your meals, don't I?' He knew he'd been an accident, but she treated him more like a train wreck.

'I'd be better off in an old people's home.' She knew she was on safe territory with this remark, because the places in which society's vintage members were currently parked cost arms, legs, houses and bank balances. There was no welfare state any more – he couldn't afford to have her put away. 'I'm a millstone round your neck,' she complained.

Dave thought about Coleridge's ancient mariner with his albatross. No. Mam was more like the sword of Damocles, because he never knew when she would drop on him. She owned a barbed tongue, and she used it whenever she pleased. 'Here's your tea.' He placed it on a small table beside her chair.

'Out of sight, out of mind,' she snapped. 'You've no sooner cleared them stairs than you've forgotten me.'

As he walked down to the shop, he wished for the millionth time that he could forget his mother. Other men seemed to manage it well enough, though they usually had a partner with them. She'd trained him. She'd made sure nobody else wanted him – hadn't she all but kicked out every girl he'd brought home during his teenage years? He'd never been Richard Gere, but he'd had hair, at least. His childhood had been difficult, to put it mildly, because she had expected him to bring, fetch, carry, cook, shop and iron. Why couldn't he have

6

been a rebellious teenager? Because none of the gangs had wanted him, that was the undeniable reason.

Downstairs, Dave opened the door to his kingdom. Perhaps it was more like a regency, because Madam upstairs still ruled with the proverbial rod, but how he loved his little shop, even if he was treated by her upstairs as mere minder of the place. It was a lone ranger, as there wasn't another proper bookshop for miles – just chains and supermarkets – and where could a man buy a German–English dictionary these days? Not in Sainsbury's, that was certain. No. They had to use the Internet or come to a proper bookshop. He provided a service. There was somewhere to sit when the weather was cold or rainy; there was a cup of tea served with scones or sandwiches, always with a smile as the side dish. 'Hello,' he said to Philomena. She opened up every day while he gave Mam her breakfast. On holy days and Sundays, Dave did a juggling act, but he didn't mind.

She nodded at him and awarded him his first smile of the day. 'You all right, Mr Barker?'

'Fine and dandy, love.' For a Catholic, she was a nice woman. She'd nearly become a nun, but she'd escaped at the last minute. There weren't many nuns these days, Dave mused. There weren't many priests, either. The chap at St Faith's ran three churches, so some folk had to go to Mass on Saturday evenings just to pass the confession test. Missing Mass was a sin that had to be told through the grille, but dispensation had been awarded by the Vatican due to the shortage of staff on its books. So Sunday sometimes became Saturday, and Philomena's life was complicated.

He walked through to the front of his domain. With

tremendous reluctance, he had become a newsagent. Just to hang on to his precious books, Dave Barker had been forced to allow the premises to be desecrated by the *Sun* and the *News of the World*. It was a pity, but it remained a fact of life – bookshops were dying, and few people seemed to care.

Today was to be another milestone about which Dave was in two minds. He was about to become a mini Internet café. Was he making a rod for his own back? Weren't people already spending enough time glued to the TV or plugged into the ether? 'Go with the flow,' he told himself. He already had a computer – it was essential when it came to ordering stock – but did his Reading Room need that facility for its customers? Would the young start to come in? Probably not, since most seemed to receive at least a laptop as a christening gift.

Ah, well. The world was going mad, so he might as well follow the herd. Being a purist was all very well, but a man needed to earn a living. There was no money in purism, and he needed to allow himself to become contaminated by the twenty-first century. Pragmatism was the order of the day, he had decided.

'Here you are, Dave.'

He took the proffered cup. 'Thanks, Philly,' he said absently. Then he looked at her. She seemed . . . different today. Very smart – was that lipstick? Probably not. Perhaps she was going somewhere after work. She left early, because she arrived early to deal with the news-paper deliveries. He supposed she had learned about early in the convent. 'You look very nice today,' he told her.

She blushed. 'Visitor this afternoon,' she said, before fleeing back to her sandwiches and fairy cakes.

8

Dave stared into his cup. Forty-seven years old, and he still couldn't talk properly to a woman in his age and size bracket. She was shorter than he was, and she wasn't in the best shape. But she had lovely eyes, though he had better stop dreaming, because she was a holy Roman.

Number nine Fullers Walk was Pour Les Dames. Locals had taken the mickey for a while, because Maurice (pronounced Moreese) and Paul (pronounced Pole) presented as a pair of colourful gays with eccentric mannerisms and plenty to say for themselves. The joke had finally died. No longer did anyone ask how poor they were and which of them was Les, and no one had said they were both dames for ages, so they had survived the initial onslaught.

Their logo was an interesting one, as it portrayed the sign used on most women's lavatories, but with a curly mop on its head, a primitive scribble that looked as if it had been perpetrated by a pre-school child. They did good business in a large village surrounded by many rural satellites, and were often up at the crack of dawn preparing for the day's trade, as both were sticklers for hygiene.

Maurice was standing by the window. 'She's got a face like a funeral tea – everything set out in a nice, orderly fashion, but not a desirable event.'

Paul clicked his tongue. 'You're getting as bad as her at number five – Eyes and Ears. Don't let your gob join in, Mo. Before we know it, you'll be sitting upstairs staring at every poor soul that passes by.'

Maurice laughed. 'I don't think so, somehow. But look at her. She's carrying her flowers in now. I can't put my finger on it—'

'You'd better not put your finger anywhere it's no business to be.'

Maurice stamped a foot and dropped a deliberately limp wrist. 'She's bloody gorgeous, man. But her face is kind of dead. There's not one single fault, yet she seems so distant from everything and everybody. A bit like something out of Tussaud's. There's history there – just you mark my words. And history catches up with folk every time.'

Paul came to stand beside his partner. 'Hmm,' he breathed. 'Let's hope our history doesn't catch us, eh? We've all got something to hide, haven't we? But yes, I see what you mean. Lovely head of hair, so why does she bleach it? It's definitely a brunette face, that one. She'd look better with her own colour – it would frame her – so why gild the lily?'

They both laughed, as the woman in question was named Lily.

'Perhaps she's hiding grey?' suggested Maurice.

'Maybe. I don't think so, because I do her roots. If there is any grey, it's not enough to write home about.'

Maurice nodded his head knowingly. 'Exactly. I think she's concealing more than that. I mean, what's she doing round here? That accent's Somerset or Devon, isn't it? Why come up to sunny Lancashire, eh? Imagine living in Devon, all those little fishing villages, the surf pounding on the beach–'

'Hello, sailor,' said Paul in the campest of his range of tones. 'Does seem a funny thing to do, though. Fresh start, do you think?'

'She's running,' Maurice insisted. 'And she's had to run a very long way.' He turned. 'Now, we've Mrs Entwistle for a perm – even though we said we weren't doing perms any more. But if she wants to spend money having her hair assassinated, that's her prerogative.'

'Three blow-dries and two cut and blow-dry,' Paul added. 'Oh, and Sally's coming down later to do some manicures and a bikini wax, so we're booked for the morning, more or less.'

But Maurice was back at the window. 'Paul?'

'What?'

'I swear to God there's been a wedding ring on that finger.'

Paul joined him. 'Your name Hawkeye? How can you see that?'

'Next time she comes in, you have a proper look. I'll bet my Shirley Bassey outfit that she's in hiding. Including the purple boa. She's incognito, Paul.'

'Incognito? Fronting a shop?'

'Yes. Running a shop because that's what she's always done. Going blonde and travelling hundreds of miles because she had to. She's got a business head on her. Blonde, but no bimbo.'

'Your Shirley Bassey, though? Boa as well?'

Maurice nodded. 'Yes.'

'But I can't do Shirley Bassey. We'd get no bookings if I had to do Shirley Bassey. I haven't the waist for it.' At almost thirty, Paul had some difficulty when it came to the imitation of the female shape. Maurice, even though he was a couple of years older, had a smaller middle.

'I know,' said Maurice. 'I always hedge my bets, don't I?'

Paul punched his partner before returning to the task of sorting bottles and jars. As he began to count perm curlers, he heaved a sigh. Some women never learned. A perm in this day and age? Preposterous.

Maurice was still thinking about the woman next door. The unit had been empty for months, then she had arrived with all her bags and moved into the upstairs flat. Within a fortnight, she'd had all the ground floor decked out properly, and the florist business literally bloomed. Lily. It suited her. She was as pale as her natural colouring permitted, looking as if she had stayed inside for a long time.

Inside? Had she been to prison? When she came to get her hair done, she indulged in little or no conversation. Her past was not pure white – of that he felt certain. There was a sadness in her, something that cut very deep, a horrible emptiness. Was she lonely?

'Have you seen that other pair of ceramic straighteners? Another weapon to help kill hair off, I suppose.'

Maurice got on with the job. In time, he would come to know her.

Lily Latimer sat upstairs in the lotus position. Yoga had helped keep her sane, but her sanity tank had started to run low of late, as she had tired herself out with the new venture. She concentrated on her breathing and muttered her own mantra, a saying much used in Lily's life these days. 'Carpe diem.' She had to seize each day and get through it like some alcoholic on a set path punctuated by points and tiny goals. Sad, but true – it was the only way forward.

Lancashire was all right. It was as good a place as any other, and it was far enough away from the situation she wanted to avoid. Although it wasn't a case of want, was it? Absolute necessity was nearer the mark.

The people here were friendly, though the accent had presented her with some difficulty at first. 'Carpe diem.' They spoke slowly, at least. Her landlord was a different matter altogether, as he came from Liverpool. His words were delivered at a speed similar to that of water emerging from her Karcher power washer, an item designed to shift dirt, weeds, moss and any other unwanted matter that might cling to the exterior of a building. But he seemed a jolly soul, and his wife was pleasant enough. 'Carpe diem,' she repeated, a slight smile on her lips.

She was doing well. In the week to come, she had to cover two funerals and one wedding. Weddings were her real forte, as she was a qualified interior designer, but her certificates no longer counted, as they had been issued under another name. A change of identity was all very well, but a person had to ditch the good along with the bad. There could be no half measures, but she would be doing a great deal more than flowers in a few days' time. The wedding would be a triumph, word would spread, and she would be as busy as she had ever been in Taunton. Yet she must not shine too brightly, had to make sure that her work hit none of the national glossies or newspapers, because if it did, all she had achieved would be for nothing. Worse, it would be dangerous.

Lily sighed. She missed home, and she knew that it showed. These lovely people wanted to get to know her, but something in her appearance held them back. She wasn't ugly, wasn't even ordinary-looking, but something in her eyes had died. Killing Leanne and inventing Lily had hurt. Ma and Pa were dead, and she had no brothers or sisters, but she'd known some special folk at home. After a long time away, she had been welcomed back with open arms – there had even been bunting and home-made signs to tell her that she was loved, that she had been missed. How sweet freedom had tasted then. Yet how terrifying freedom could be once its implications became clear. Today was her birthday, and there was no one with whom she might share the joy of having survived for twenty-eight years.

'Carpe diem.' Without a word to anyone, she had upped and left in the middle of the night. Her house and shop were now on the market, and she had brought with her a minimum of furniture, as her exit had needed to be more than simply discreet. She felt terrible about that. Ma's furniture was still there, was to be sold with the building in which it had stood since her grandmother's day. Day. Seize it. 'Carpe diem.'

Thoughts of Gran and Grandpa sent her back more than a quarter of a century. Theirs had probably been among the first organic farms, though they might not have known what that meant. Grandpa had declared himself to be a 'natural farmer', one who disapproved of chemicals and kept their use to the barest minimum.

She remembered shows with huge horses pulling ploughs, competitions to win first place on one draw across a field. The feet on those beasts had been as big as dinner plates, and all the surrounding hair, known as feathers, had been combed to perfection. Until the plough race had started, of course. Prizes. Gran's apple pie from a secret recipe she had taken to her grave; Grandpa's tomato sausages made in his own kitchen – a proper kitchen with huge dressers and a table big enough for Henry VIII and his whole court. The parlour with its display of trophies, teapot always back and forth to the kitchen, scones with clotted cream, home-made strawberry jam, wine produced in a barn . . .

This was definitely not yoga. This was long-term memory, mind-pictures of a time when life had been sure and steady. Safety? Did she have to go all the way back to Grandpa's farm to feel a sense of security? Perhaps most people found true warmth only in childhood, when love was unconditional and all decisions came from reliable elders. It was no use wishing she could go back. No one could go back.

The phone rang. Lily stood up and grabbed the instrument from her desk. 'Hello?'

'That you, Leanne? If it is, happy birthday.'

'Hello, my lovely. Thanks for the card. No. I'm Lily. Remember that. If you forget everything else, remember my new name. Though you can call me Lee, I suppose. What's happening?'

'Sorry. We'll be with you in a few days. Are you sure about this?'

'Of course I am. But never forget – I'm Lily. Cassie will have to learn that, too. How are you, Babs?'

'OK. Glad I don't have to change my name. It'll be OK, won't it? If I keep my name? And is there enough room?'

Lily glanced round the flat. 'It's all right. Big sitting cum dining room, kitchen large enough for a breakfast table, and I've given you and the babe the big bedroom. Until I find a house for myself, we'll manage.'

'See you soon, then. I'm more or less packed.' Babs paused. 'I'm a bit scared. It's a very long way, isn't it?'

'Yes, but the natives are friendly. They won't eat you – they trapped a Manchester United fan last week, so they're not hungry. Like snakes, they eat about once a month.'

'Stop it.'

Lily said goodbye, then sat on a sofa. How many lives had been altered beyond recognition during recent years? How long was a piece of string? She picked up a pad and wrote *twine*. There'd be plenty of that needed when she did her wedding garlands. Was there enough white satin ribbon? Would the three of them manage living here together? Bridesmaids – what was the colour of their dresses? She had a piece of the material in the desk, so that was OK. The landlord of the shop and flat had been approached, and he was cool about the arrangement, didn't mind Babs and Cassie coming to live with her. The bride was wearing oyster satin ...

It was a decent enough living space. Lily was fairly sure that the landlord wouldn't object if or when the rent book went over into Babs's name if or when Lily moved out. Babs could front the shop sometimes, and that would leave more time for Lily to do her wreaths and bouquets.

She stood up and paced about. There wasn't a lot of storage for toys – she would buy some colourful plastic boxes. Cassie's dolls' house was probably the largest thing Babs would bring in her little car – that particular toy would have to go into the bedroom. It was big enough, she thought when she opened the door to survey it yet again. The whole flat had been carpeted in tough, natural-coloured sisal, and that should survive most of Cassie's spills. Poor little Cassie, not yet two years old, and having to be dragged away from home just because Leanne, now Lily, had got herself into a bit of bother. Well, more than a bit ...

It would be silly to leave that fortune in the bank. Grandpa had always said that money should earn its keep by going to work, and he had been wise. How long had he saved for that prize bull? Oh, she couldn't remember. But his money had been put to work, and Grandpa had done well.

Lily's money was . . . different. Some of it was unearned, yet she had paid for it. She supposed it was funny money, though its source had hardly been amusing. There was family money, and she was the last survivor. She would buy a house nearby.

At a front window, she stood and stared at the square FOR SALE sign across the road. It was a large, rather grand building next to the Catholic church, but she dared say that she could afford it. Babs and Cassie would stay here, while she went to dwell in splendid isolation, rattling about in a house big enough for seven or eight people. There was a tree in the front garden that looked at least a couple of hundred years old. The place was too big. Silly.

Was it, though? Investment was never a bad idea. And the house was utterly unlike anything Leanne Chalmers might have dreamed of owning. Leanne liked cottages, beams, cosiness, coal fires and Christmas trees. Lily was more elegant, surely? Perhaps she would go and look at the house tomorrow. Or she might wait until Babs arrived, because Babs usually gave a forthright opinion on any subject about which she was questioned.

She walked to the fireplace and gazed at herself in the mirror. 'Should I have brought them to live here?' she asked the face in the glass. No wonder people did not meet her eyes. 'I look quite dead,' she told the vision before her. The radiance of youth had gone, had been stolen away and left to rot beneath years of torment. Yet it was a good face, well proportioned, the sort of face painters seemed to use. Perfect? No. Without character was nearer the mark. Blonde hair and huge weight-loss were sufficient to disguise Leanne, and she scarcely knew herself.

'I offered them a home because I want Cassie. There, I've said it aloud.' So much for altruism, then. How splendid her behaviour seemed on the surface. She appeared to be rescuing someone whose ordeal had mirrored her own, whose freedom had also been curtailed – but was she really doing that? Was she? Or had this desiccated female decided to cling to a child, someone on whom she could lavish attention in return for love?

There was, she concluded, no way of knowing oneself completely. A person existed in the world and became a reflection, like this one in the glass, because humanity allowed itself to be shaped by feedback, by the reactions of others. 'In the end, we become whatever the rest choose to perceive. We believe each other's lies.'

She must go down and bury her face in freesias. They reminded her of Ma. Today, she needed to remember her mother. She needed to be grateful.

'Chas?' Eve Boswell stood in the doorway of the bedroom she shared with her husband. How far could he get in a flat as compact as this one? 'Where the bloody hell are you?' He kept disappearing. One of these days, he would disappear with half a pair of her size fives planted on his backside. She called again, but he failed to reply. She knew he hadn't gone down to the shop, because a blue light above the door to the stairs was shining brightly, proving that the alarm was still on. With thousands of pounds' worth of alcohol and tobacco on the ground floor, the place needed a good system.

A face appeared above her head, and she clasped a hand to her chest as if terrified. He was going from bad to worse, she decided. What the hell was he doing in the roof space? Another hiding place for dodgy gear? 'You are one soft bugger,' she told him.

'I'm in the loft,' he said unnecessarily. 'Seeing if the pitch is enough to give us a bit of an office and somewhere to put our Derek. He's been getting on my nerves. I heard accountants were boring and quiet, so why can't he stick to Mozart or something of that sort, music fit for an educated man? If I hear one more note of his hippy-hoppy stuff, I'm off back to Anfield.'

Eve tutted. 'I must phone the Kop and tell the team it can rest easy, because Chazzer Boswell's on his way. You'll be able to shout advice from behind the goal mouth again. Now.' She waved the shirt she was carrying. 'How many people have worn this, eh?'

'Only me,' he replied with his usual cheeky grin. 'Why?'

'Butter wouldn't melt,' she said in a stage whisper. 'Did you clean the car with it? Or have you leased it out to the bloody fire brigade?'

'Eh?'

'It's a good shirt, is this. I know because I bought it myself personally with my own money, all on my own, just me, with nobody. It was thirty quid in the sale. Have you no sense?' She tapped a foot. 'Delete the last bit, Chas. I stopped looking for sense in you years back. Liverpool's loss is Lancashire's gain, isn't it?'

He stared at her for a moment, then announced that he mustn't have any sense, because he'd married her, hadn't he? But thinking aloud was never a good idea when Eve stood within earshot. 'You're the best thing that ever happened to me, Eve,' he said by way of apology. 'Except for when LFC won them five cups and Man U got sod all.'

She wouldn't laugh. Every time a bone of contention was dug up, he made her laugh. He'd got her to marry him and to have Derek by making her laugh. There would have been another ten kids by now if she hadn't lost her equipment to cancer, because she'd never stopped bloody laughing at him except for when she'd been in hospital. Private hospital – he'd seen to that, hadn't he? Chas was the best man in the world, and she would kill him in a minute – as long as he didn't make her giggle. 'Get down here,' she ordered. 'Make yourself useful. The washing machine's vomiting again. It's a drip at the moment, but I'm expecting Niagara any time now. They'll be swimming in to buy booze downstairs.'

He smiled again. 'Another thing, love. It's not Lanca-shire – it's Greater Manchester.'

Eve was ready for that one. She'd had to be ready for ever, because Chas had a quick brain and a quicker mouth. 'You ask this lot round here – them over fifty, anyway – and they'll tell you where to shove Man-chester. Now get down here and see to that machine. I'll take the washing down to Mo and Po – they can put it in their machine when they're not doing towels.'

He climbed down the ladder. 'I hope it's not catching,' he said.

'What?'

'Wash my underpants with theirs, and I might come over peculiar.'

She hit him with the shirt. 'They're nice men.'

'Lovely,' he answered, striking a pose. 'Tell you what, though, babe. Their drag act is something else, according to our Derek. Did you know they're going on *Britain's Got Talent*?'

Eve laughed helplessly. 'Oh, God,' she moaned, holding her aching side. 'Can you imagine the look on Simon Cowell's gob when he cops a load of that? He'll have a heart attack.'

'Couldn't happen to a nicer fellow.' He thought for a moment. 'No, I take that back. Cowell speaks his mind. He could become an honorary northerner the way he talks without dressing up. There'll be enough dressing up when Mo and Po walk out with their six-inch heels and eyelashes to match. I can see that panel now – she'll be on the floor laughing herself sick, and Piers Morgan won't know whether to laugh or cry. Face like an open book, that's his problem.' He went off to stem the tide in the kitchen.

Eve made the bed and straightened the room. She'd work on him again later, she promised herself. He was sticking to his guns, because he didn't trust anyone, but she was fighting for a house. They owned the whole row of shops and flats, so he could well afford it. He didn't want anyone else living and working here, because he was always up to something. A few of those somethings had put his brother in Walton jail for three years, yet Chas was still taking chances. It had been just luck and a good following wind that had kept Chas out of prison, and he should start behaving. He was near enough to fifty to have a bit of sense, and she wasn't too many years behind him.

She put on make-up, combed her hair and prepared to go down for her shift in the shop. The first part of the day was usually quiet, and the shop staff operated behind bullet-proof glass, so she was allowed to take her turn. He was so protective of her. As a dyed-in-the-wool operator, Chas liked to think ahead. No bugger was going to burgle him or hurt his family. Set a thief to catch a thief? He went further than that. Chas, well versed in the art of redistributing the wealth of the nation, was also adept when it came to outwitting his fellows. No Scally-Scouser would outwit him. As for the Woollies – they had no chance at all.

Eve shook her head. Just because folk round here talked slowly, he thought they weren't as quick-thinking as the Scallies. But he was wrong. A bad Woolly was hard to spot, but he could do as much damage as a Scouser any day.

Anyway, none of that mattered, because her Chas was going straight from now on. She'd straighten him herself. Even if she had to use an old flat iron to do it.

Philomena Gallagher rushed home to her little stone-built weaver's cottage. It sat on the end of a row next to three of its siblings, all pretty and well kept, all owned by proud people who knew they were sitting on potential gold mines. The rich often bought a pair of such cottages, knocking them together to make a substantial semi-detached house, and the end of a terrace usually attracted a slightly higher price.

She entered an exterior porch, opened her front door and stepped straight into the parlour. Philly's Irish grandmother had christened the room parlour, and Philly carried on in the same vein. A mirror over the cast-iron grate showed a flushed face, so she ran into the kitchen to splash a bit of cold water on her cheeks. She didn't want to appear over-excited, because that was hardly a Christian thing to be.

'Why me?' she asked herself. 'Not much special about me.' Still, she had done nothing wrong, and he had spoken to her pleasantly while announcing his intended visit. A priest coming to the house while nobody was ill? It wouldn't be for money, since Philly had made her pledge and the specified amount went into that little brown envelope each week, rain or shine. But she had better not appear too excited. Nevertheless, a cake stand appeared, both layers covered in her home-made baking.

Her hair was tidy, the house was tidy, the coffee trolley was tidy. Was the garden all right? She rushed to the window and cast an eye over alyssum, lobelia and French marigolds in pretty beds surrounded by pebbles. Yes, the path was clean; yes, the paintwork outside had been wiped only yesterday. The honeysuckle round the door had been given a haircut quite recently, so there was nothing to offend the eye.

Father Walsh. His first name was Michael, but she would never dare use it. There was no respect these days, especially where young priests were concerned. They seemed to neither ask for nor expect it, so it was probably as much their fault as anyone's.

He would be here in a minute. She had better compose herself, or she would be needing a priest for the wrong reason. With her heart in overdrive, she sat and waited for Father Walsh to come. What did he want? Breathe deeply, breathe deeply. All right, then. Just breathe.

A very handsome man presented himself at the counter. He wore faded jeans, and his pale blue short-sleeved shirt was open at the throat. 'Roses, please,' he said.

'Colour?' Lily asked. 'I have red, yellow and cream.'

She didn't look directly at him. Lily didn't trust men who were overly good-looking. She knew all about the confidence they owned, the way they managed to exert power over people they considered to be mere mortals. He was probably just another god with clay feet.

'Cream, I think,' replied Adonis.

She went to select the flowers. 'Some are still in bud,' she said. 'I'll pop in a bit of plant food. Oh, make sure you take the ends off the stems. Some people crush the wood, but I've never found that to be any use. A diagonal cut is enough.'

He handed over a twenty-pound note. Lily used the till, then counted out his change.

'You're doing very well,' he commented. 'Lovely flowers.' He sniffed the roses. 'Are you from Devon?'

'Yes,' she lied.

'Then welcome to the dark satanic mills.' He extended a hand. 'I'm Michael Walsh, parish priest to St Faith's and a couple of other village churches.' He turned and glanced across the road. 'That's my presbytery on the market. I'm such a nomad, I'd do better with a caravan.'

Lily swallowed. She went from fear to astonishment in a split second. It wasn't the first time she'd seen a priest in mufti, but he looked so ... so normal. No. Hardly normal – he was muscular and very well put together. 'Catholic?' she asked.

'Indeed. You?'

She shook her head. Lily wasn't anything any more. From a family of Baptists, she had lost all faith when ... 'No.' When everything had been stamped out of her, when Leanne had begun to die, when the world had gone dark. Lily was a shell, an empty house waiting for furniture, for warmth and safety, for a comfortable chair

24

in which life might just seat itself and begin all over again. 'No,' she repeated. 'I'm not anything, really.' In that house, there should be curtains opened wide to the world. Not yet, though.

Michael Walsh stared at her. There was something wrong, something missing. She had no light in her beautiful blue eyes. A man of astute instinct, Michael lowered his tone. 'Lily, I deal with many people who are not of my faith. One thing you can be sure of in a priest is that he will use his ears, but not his mouth. Like a doctor, I keep secrets – and not just for my immediate family, my parishioners. Should you need to pray, come in and sit. Should you need to talk—'

'I'm fine, thank you.' She still could not meet his eyes. The talking had all been done. One-to-one therapy, group therapy, physiotherapy, baby-steps therapy, hypnotherapy, acupuncture, yoga.

'The offer stands.' He picked up his change and left the shop.

Lily Latimer sank into her chair. 'Hurry up, Babs,' she muttered. She could talk to Babs. Babs was the only one who could begin to understand Lily. Babs had known Leanne. It was suddenly important that the one person who knew everything should be here. Oh, how she wished that she might have stayed at home, that she could still be Leanne Chalmers, possibly the most successful and gifted interior designer in the west country.

But she had to stay away, must make the best of what remained, which was the money. She had inherited some, had earned some, was waiting for some from the sale of the property in Taunton. The rest – her funny money – should also be used. Compensation? How could any amount wind a bandage round her soul, the most damaged of her components? 'Put together enough of it, then make it work for you.' Such a clever man, Grandpa had been.

So. She might well be putting the modern, look-at-me priest out of house and home, because the Catholic church in England could no longer afford to hang on to presbyteries that stood empty for half of the time. Over the phone, she asked the estate agent for details. It needed work. It had over an acre of land with it. It was freehold, and there was an apple orchard in the grounds. She booked an appointment to view.

When the call was over, Lily smiled to herself. She came from scrumpy country, so an orchard would be lovely. He didn't need it any more, did he? And Cassie could stay with her sometimes. The smile broadened, just as it always did when she thought of the child. But she knew it didn't reach her eyes. She remembered the giggling, rosy-cheeked girl she had been. Perhaps, in the orchard across the road, she might find herself again. Perhaps . . .

Philomena was flustered. He could tell that she was excited and not a little nervous, because her breathing was shallow, while pink cheeks spoke volumes about her steadfast, old-fashioned attitude to the representatives of her religion. This was another woman who needed help and encouragement. But at least a person saw what he was getting in Philomena Gallagher. With the florist, there had been a deadly emptiness, a quality that was sometimes apparent in the terminally ill once they had come to terms with the dictates of destiny.

'Tea or coffee, Father?' she enquired.

'Tea, please. When I'm not in uniform, I'm Michael.'

She didn't like that. Nor did she approve of his

clothes, though she made no comment. 'I'll just ... er ...'
She went off into the kitchen.

While Philly just-erred, Michael looked around her
neat little house. One of these would be big enough for
him, surely? There was a second bedroom if anyone
wanted to stay, and he didn't take up a great deal of
room. Except for his books, of course. He looked at the
alcoves that flanked the fireplace. He could put some in
those, others in a bedroom.

She returned and poured tea with a hand that was
noticeably unsteady.

'None of these properties up for sale?' he asked.

'I don't think so, Father. If I hear of anyone wanting
to sell, shall I let you know?'

'Please.' He took a sip of tea.

'Is that all right for you, Father?'

'Fine, thanks.'

'More milk? Not too strong? Are you sure?'

He told her to sit down and stop worrying, knowing
that she would never achieve the latter. Philomena Gallagher might be a woman in her forties, but she still carried within her all the older mores pertaining to the
Catholic faith. As an enlightened priest with a broader
attitude, he worked hard to understand people like Philomena. They were inestimably valuable, though he wanted
to extend their horizons. He was here today to make an
effort with this woman's self-confidence. It might all backfire, but it was time to take a risk, time to enliven her if
at all possible.

She sat, hands clasped on her knee, looking for all the
world like a junior school child waiting to come face to
face with the head teacher's wrath.

'Amdram,' he said.

'Pardon, Father?'

'Amateur dramatics. We should use the school hall, bring everyone in, try to liven the place up a bit.'

Philly nodded absently.

'The community needs to come together for projects. There must be some around who'd enjoy being on the stage.'

'But I don't—'

'But you're not one of them. Don't worry about that. All I want is for you to ask Dave Barker if you might use his computer to print some flyers – I'll ask him myself, in fact. Then, if you would organize distribution throughout the parish, we might just get something going. You could perhaps consider being secretary cum treasurer. Keep people in line, so to speak. Your honesty is obvious, and I thought of you straight away.'

Philly nodded again. Why her? Why couldn't he have chosen somebody who didn't mind knocking on doors and giving out leaflets? 'Just Catholics, then?'

He laughed. 'Not on your nelly. We want all kinds of people.' He leaned forward in a conspiratorial manner. 'You see, Philomena, priesthood these days is about community service, and I thought—'

'Isn't community service something criminals do instead of jail?' She felt her cheeks burning; she had interrupted a man of God.

'They don't even have to be Christians. A shepherd looks after all his sheep – he can't choose the prettiest or the woolliest ones, can he? This isn't about religion, it's about giving people something interesting to do.' He paused. 'Will you help me?'

She nodded.

'If it gets too much, I'll find a helper for you.'

Philly had her pride. 'It won't get too much, Father. I shall do it. Of course I shall.' She'd make sure it didn't get too much. Even a priest needed showing a thing or two from time to time. Especially a priest who wore the clothes of an errant teenager.

'Settled, then?' he asked.

'Yes,' she replied. She would show him.

He looked at the slight glint of determination that entered her eyes in that moment. He had done his job, and the mouse would roar.

Life sentence. Bloody life for a kid that never even existed. And what will Madam do now with her so-called freedom? She knows I have friends on the outside, knows there's money hidden. But she's no idea about where, has she?

Starting off on 43, stuck on a landing with nonces and perverts. I don't belong here. She put me here – they both did. I've got curtains because we're special up here and none of us expect to see the outside again. Parole board? My name won't be on the list. Still, they're thinking about moving me away from the nonces, said they'll see how it goes. I suppose if I get attacked, I'll be shoved back up here.

They watch me for suicide. As if. Ways and means, Leanne. Just you wait. There's always ways and means ...

Two

Somewhere along the line, wires must have been crossed. The man from the estate agency turned a remarkable shade of purple and clapped a phone to his ear as soon as he realized that a mistake had been made. Eve adopted her 'posh' voice, though distorted vowels continued to betray her provenance. 'He'll be having a stroke if he doesn't watch out,' she told her unexpected companion. 'My mam had wallpaper that shade of yuk in the back bedroom. God, look at the colour of him. Is it aubergine?'

Lily stood in the hallway of the presbytery, a clearly agitated Eve Boswell by her side. 'Poor man,' she said.

Eve's jumpiness was soon explained. 'He doesn't know I'm here,' she said. 'My Chas, I mean. I've been trying to make him see sense, only it's like knitting fog. "I want a house," I keep on telling him. But I will get my own way in the end, 'cos I always do. A house makes sense, anyway. See, there's our Derek's music for a start, then there's—'

'So sorry, ladies.' The troubled representative of Miller and Brand clicked his mobile phone into the closed position. 'What can I say? Someone's head will roll, I can promise you that.'

Eve tutted, then discarded her posh voice. 'Ar 'ey,' she said in her best Toxteth accent. 'Don't get some poor devil the sack just on account of me and Lily. We're neighbours, aren't we, love?'

'Indeed,' answered the florist. 'Don't do anything, please. My friend from Som– from Devon should have been here to help me choose a house, and she hasn't arrived, so Eve and I will look together.'

He calmed down a little. 'Nevertheless, this is all highly unprofessional. You are interested separately – am I right?' When both women nodded, he clung to his portfolio and sighed sadly. 'Follow me,' he suggested. Hoping that world war would not break out, he led the way.

But Eve and Lily weren't going to follow anyone. Both women had stood in the hall; both had realized immediately how badly they wanted this house. No matter what the rest of it was like, the solid door with stained-glass panels, and those matching windows at the sides, were enough for them to have fallen head over heels before taking two paces. 'It's lovely,' breathed Eve. 'Needs a bit of work, like. Look at this kitchen for a start.'

Lily was looking at the kitchen. It was wonderful, because it put her in mind of Grandpa's farm. It contained an eclectic mix of items, yet they all seemed to rub along splendidly. Apart from two sets of built-in floor-to-ceiling cupboards flanking the hearth, nothing but sink and cooker was fixed. Three Welsh dressers displayed a mixture of pottery, while two old meat safes, painted cream, stood side by side just inside the rear door.

'I'd have it Shaker,' pronounced Eve. 'What would you do?'

Lily cast an eye over the old pulley line, admired a scrubbed table big enough for six or eight, glanced at the hearth and at a grate that still needed blackleading. 'I'd change very little,' she answered. 'I like it just the way it is.' She was no lover of brushed stainless steel, was not a paid-up member of the fully-fitted brigade. 'I'd open up the fireplace if it's blocked off – I might even bake bread in the coal-fired oven.' She sighed. 'It's perfect.'

Eve smiled to herself. Lily Latimer's voice had lifted slightly, and there was a faint glimmer in her eye. If this house would fetch her out of the doldrums, then she should have it. Lily's need was far greater than her own. Something on one of the fast-encroaching modern estates would do for the Boswells. There were several nice five-bedroomed detached with double garages and up-to-the-minute streamlined kitchens – there'd be no stained glass, but so what? Lily suited this house, fitted in as if she had always lived here. But Eve would play the game. If she stayed and pretended to be fighting for the property, she might just wake up her listless tenant.

There was a morning room, a study, a formal dining room, a big sitting room and a lean-to that held washer and dryer. Crucifixes and holy pictures made the place grimmer than it needed to be, but the two women were trying to look past the decor. Upstairs, no fewer than five bedrooms and two bathrooms completed the tour. Oh, no – there was another little staircase up into the roof. Lily remembered noticing the odd-shaped dormer.

It was breathtaking. The window was circular. Lily imagined waking up here, with her bedhead against the glass, knew that her white coverlet would be spotted with colours borrowed from leaded lights. There was a small shower room on this top floor, and Lily knew with undeniable certainty that she would fight to the last for this place, that the room in which she currently stood would be her own.

'Lot of money,' said Eve.

'Yes.' Lily scarcely heard the remark. It was worth every penny.

'I'll go home and talk to him,' Eve said. 'Mind, I might as well talk to the fireback for all he cares. But I will be putting in an offer. If he'll listen for once. I'll make him, I will, I will . . .' She left, her grumblings drifting back up the stairs until she was finally out of range.

Lily followed the man down to the first floor. On the landing, he stopped and looked at her. 'Would you like another look round?'

Lily nodded. 'But I can tell you now that I offer full price subject to survey and valuation. Should anything major need doing, I shall lower the offer accordingly.'

'I see. Erm . . .' He shuffled some papers. 'Mortgage?' he asked. 'Do you need help? We are in contact with all the major societies, and we have an adviser to help you find whichever deal is most suitable.'

She shook her head. 'It will be cash,' she said. 'I shall put the wheels in motion right away. Don't worry, I have the Yellow Pages, so I can find my own lawyer and surveyor.'

He blinked. It wasn't every day he sold a house of this price for cash. Was she serious, or might she be one of those time-wasters who visited houses for recreational purposes? 'Right,' he mumbled. 'If you would care to come into the office – shall we say Monday?'

'No,' she replied. 'You will need to come to me – I run a business single-handed at present, and can't just up and away whenever I like. To come and view this house, I've had to close my shop.' She handed him a card. 'That's my personal number, and the shop details are below. Thank you.'

He was being dismissed. Yet he had to make the house secure and report back to work. 'I'll ... er ... I'll be downstairs in the room at the front when you have finished. You see, I am required to secure the premises and then I have to go to an appointment—'

The front door slammed. 'Buckets of blood,' cried a male voice. 'I'll get the hang of that door if it kills me.'

Lily and her companion stared down at the top of a head owned by Father Michael Walsh. He was struggling with a pile of books and papers, and was clearly annoyed by his burden. He looked up, saw two people, and dropped everything. 'Sugar,' he said.

Lily felt the corners of her mouth beginning to twitch slightly. He had very untidy hair. 'Good afternoon, Father,' she said.

He opened his mouth, but offered no reply.

The estate agent descended the staircase. 'I'll be on my way, then,' he said, his tone apologetic. He pointed to the mess on the floor. 'I'd help you with that lot, but I'm due to show a house on Bradshaw Brow in twenty minutes.' He left the scene.

'There are rabbits in the garden,' announced Michael.

'Right.' Was he all there? What had rabbits to do with anything?

'And one of them's in trouble. But I had to go and ... There was stuff in the sacristy ... I won't be a minute.' He left scattered items on the floor and ran through to the dining room. '*Watership Down* was never like this,' was his departing remark as he made for the French windows.

Lily followed and watched him as he poked his head into a tangle of exposed roots beneath an old tree. *Watership Down* was a sad film ... His pose could never have been deemed dignified, as he was on his knees, backside in the air, T-shirt riding high and displaying a great deal of skin. She thought she heard him swear. Well, it might have been 'sugar' again, but she didn't think so. 'Are you all right?' she asked.

'No,' he said. 'The bugger bit me.'

It hadn't been sugar, then.

He pulled the animal out and shoved it in a box. 'Get the cat basket out of the utility place,' he ordered. 'I should have thought. Get it before this nightmare eats its way through the cardboard. Go on! I'm serious. The fellow's a big buck and he hates me.'

She found the requested item and carried it out to the rear garden. The scent of honeysuckle touched her nose as she passed the plastic and metal container over to him.

'No,' he said. 'Open it. Put it on the floor, woman, and open it.'

She did as she was ordered.

There followed a blur of activity which she would never in a million years have been able to describe, but the animal was finally behind bars and the priest was triumphant.

Lily looked at the angry rabbit. 'What's the matter with it?' she asked.

'Big sore on his ear. We'd been getting along famously till now – he even took carrots and stuff from me. Not bad going for a wild rabbit.'

'He's very wild now,' remarked Lily.

'Well – wouldn't you be if your freedom had been curtailed?' He watched the cloud arriving in her eyes, realized that she had seemed almost normal up to this point. He studied his prisoner. 'I am not inflicting you on that poor vet,' he told the furious creature. 'It'll be an antiseptic, then you can take your chances with the rest.' He looked at his visitor. 'We have foxes, too. There's a mum and a dad and some young ones.' He sighed. 'Until just now, I thought of myself as a watered-down Francis of Assisi – he had a way with animals. But I was sadly mistaken.' She was thawing again. 'I'll get the towels.' Suddenly, he ran away.

Lily squatted down. 'Hello, bright eyes burning like fire,' she said. The rabbit immediately became still. 'Why would we need towels?' she asked. 'Are you going in the bath?'

'Here.' Michael thrust a pair of large bath sheets into Lily's hands.

'He's gone off,' Lily told the rabbit when the priest did another of his now familiar disappearing acts.

'Here.' He was back once more. 'Put these on.' It was a pair of thick gardening gloves. 'Strategy. We need to discuss.'

What was this? Lily asked herself. A G8 conference, a meeting of heads of state? 'You first,' she suggested.

'Right, yes.' He rubbed his chin. 'Erm ... I'll get the first aid. Not for us,' he added in a tone that was meant to be reassuring. 'For him. There's a thorn stuck in his ear and he's been trapped in those roots for who knows how long, so no wonder he's in a bad mood. And gentian violet.'

'What?'

'My grandmother swore by it.' He walked away again.

The task proved far from easy. Lily held the struggling animal in two towels, her hands protected by heavy-duty gloves. Michael used tweezers to remove the thorn before soaking the ear in a bright blue dye. 'You can let him go now.'

She released Bright Eyes, watched him lolloping away, was surprised when he stopped, turned and looked at them. 'You'd think he was saying thank you,' she said. 'He looks a bit odd, doesn't he?'

Michael Walsh shook his head. 'A priest's life is often surreal, but this takes the chocolate digestive. We're not even drunk, are we? Pink elephants, purple rabbits – what's the difference?'

'Size,' was her prompt reply.

'He looks cute, though,' Michael said. 'I'm sure the lady rabbits will find him more attractive.' He turned and looked her full in the face. 'So, it is to be you, I take it? Who'll force me out of house and home?'

Lily shrugged. 'You're here only two or three nights a week. Anyway, talk to the bishop and the Pope – it's their fault.' She paused for a couple of seconds. 'Religion's dying, isn't it? They have football now – they can sing in a stadium instead.'

'Very astute,' he remarked drily.

If anyone chose to ask her, Lily would never be able to explain what happened next, why it happened, whether she wished it hadn't. 'You can have a couple of rooms upstairs,' she said. 'For nothing. Just in case there is a God, heaven, hell – all that stuff. You can tell the angels I paid my dues by sheltering a man of the cloth. Who's the bloke with the keys?'

'St Peter.'

'Have a word with him. Tell him I've paid my rent. OK?'

She was a good woman, a hurt woman, a person who had held a terrified creature and helped calm its fears. 'Thank you, Lily,' he said. 'I truly appreciate that. I've a bit of family money, and I was considering buying a cottage, but we'll see. Thanks again. Very good of you.'

Lily didn't know what else to say. She told him that she would keep him advised about the progress of her intended purchase, that she wanted the kitchen left as it was; asked who owned all the furniture. He kept smiling and trying to make eye contact with her, but she couldn't quite manage to look at him. She felt safe, because he was a priest, yet his behaviour was that of a very ordinary – no – a very extraordinary layman. He'd cared about that daft, purple-eared rabbit, had cared enough to expose hands and arms to some angry little teeth. 'There's an orchard?'

'Yes. Way down at the bottom of the garden. Greenhouse, too. I grow my own tomatoes. You could perhaps propagate some of the rarer lilies?' She was a rare lily, but a damaged one. 'Or orchids? The sort that need a special feed tube in with the rest of the bouquet?'

Lily shook her head. 'Probably not, Father. I won't have the time to spare, not with the business. Mind, I have a friend coming tomorrow. She's bringing her baby daughter, but she'll give me some help, I'm sure. But I like to sell flowers that are slightly more robust.'

'I see.' He looked at his watch. 'I've sinners to deal with,' he told her. 'Confession time.'

'Oh. Right.' She picked up her small clutch bag. 'Goodbye, then.' She walked through the beautiful panelled hall, saw his scattered papers on the floor, picked them up and placed them on a table.

'Thanks.' He stood behind her.

'Oh. Yes. See you soon, then.' Lily stepped out into the sunlight and walked down the path. Feeling like a very silly schoolgirl, she crossed the road, entered her shop and turned the sign to OPEN. He was standing at his gate, staring at her. 'Stupid,' she said aloud. 'Because you know you're safe, you've taken a liking to him.' She shouldn't take likings to new people, because she wasn't allowed to get to know anyone, was she? Thank goodness Babs would be here in about twenty-four hours.

She turned her back on the village road and started to sort out her bedding plants. These could sit outside where passers-by could see them. How quickly the months passed. In a matter of weeks, she would be buying in spring bulbs. Cassie was coming. Cassie could never take the place of the dead, but she did brighten up life. Cassie. She would soon be here.

'Dave?' Enid Barker craned her thin neck and peered into the street below. 'There's two of them been in there this afternoon. Two.' She raised her voice by several decibels. 'Can you hear me? I've seen two going in.'

He dried the last plate and placed it in the cupboard. Could he hear her? She was probably audible as far away as Salford Quays in one direction, John Lennon Airport in the other. 'Here I am,' he said after finishing his chores and walking to her side. 'I have to go back down, because Philly's gone home, and I've left Valda in charge. She's helping out for nothing, so I don't want to take advantage of her good nature.'

'Good nature?' The old woman cackled. 'You'd best watch her, son. Her nature's that generous, she'll have a thriving whorehouse running if you're not careful. She's anybody's for the price of a skirt off Bolton Market.'

He sighed resignedly. As far as he was concerned, Valda's arrangements were private, as were everyone else's. And his mother should be the last on earth to criticize anyone who chose to survive by unorthodox methods. 'Two what been where, Mother?'

She pointed to the presbytery. 'Over yon. I know Eve Boswell's likely Catholic, because most of them Scouse types are, but Lily Wotserface? I don't think she's one of them.'

'Her name's Latimer.'

'Daft name. They went across, then he came home from church with a load of papers and books—'

'Who did?'

'The priest. Oh, I wish you would listen properly. You take all the bone out of a story with all them daft questions.'

He closed his mouth, folded his arms and waited.

'Two women he had inside the house. She's never been to church across there since she came here, that Lily one. As for Mrs Boswell – she's too busy keeping an eye on her old man and his late deliveries.' She nodded. 'Oh, aye, I've seen and heard them in the night. And he keeps stuff in that garage, you know – that's why he has it alarmed.'

Dave maintained his silence.

'Well? Nowt to say for yourself?'

'I don't want to fillet your story, do I? I mustn't take the bones out, you said.'

Enid pursed her lips. 'I sometimes wonder if they gave

40

me the wrong baby. Somewhere, there might be a tall, slim lad with a sense of style and a bit of humour in him, happen some hair and all. And I got you.'

He'd wished all his life that he'd had a different mother – a mix-up at the hospital might have been a good thing in his case. The computer man was downstairs. The poor chap was surrounded by potential silver surfers who didn't know their pixels from their hard drive. 'I'm going,' was all he had to say.

'You're no fun,' she complained.

'I'll send Valda up with a cup of tea.'

'I don't want her here. She swaps sex for clothes, and she's–'

'Some old women used to sell it for cash,' he snapped before crashing out of the flat. On the landing, he held his breath for a few seconds. God, what was the matter with him? In his hands, he could almost feel her scrawny neck as she breathed her last. He wanted to kill his own mother? Sitting on the top step, Dave Barker considered his options, knew he had just two. He could stay, or he could go. There was the shop, and there was his mother. He loved the shop. As for his mother – well, he loved the shop, and she had the ability to close it. Number three was empty – could he rent just the flat? Would Chas Boswell find a tenant for a lock-up?

Dave rose to his feet. It was an effort, because weight had become an impediment, while his centre of gravity seemed to have planted new roots. Next door was too near. Africa was too near, he supposed, because her tentacles were longer than the Nile. Hatred for one's own single parent was neither usual nor pleasant, but Enid had filled every waking hour he had known. A lousy childhood had drifted into a lousy adulthood, no seams showing, just a natural progression from bad to worse. It was worse because he now understood what she was; as a child, he had simply obeyed the orders of a larger person who had not been averse to slapping his head. He remembered the belt – it had been her father's. She'd used that with relish on the legs of her only child. Then the cupboard in the hallway of their old terraced house, so dark and lonely . . .

Downstairs, he found that the IT man was currently buried beneath a crowd of pensioners.

Valda laughed when she saw the expression on Dave's face. 'He's in there somewhere, love,' she advised him. 'I promise you they haven't eaten him. You're out of snacks till tomorrow, but he's still alive.' She grinned. 'They wouldn't get far with National Health dentures, any road.'

Dave dug his way through the three-deep circle of people. They were looking at soft porn. He smiled to himself, then pushed his way out into slightly fresher air. 'He's all right,' he told Valda.

'See? I told you he was. He asked them what they wanted, and they said dirty pictures. So he did as he was told.'

'I noticed.'

Valda piled up the clean saucers in readiness for the next day. 'How's your mam?' she asked.

Dave sat down at one of his five tables. 'Evil,' he answered.

'Normal, then.' It was not a question.

'Yes.' He drew a hand across his forehead. 'I'd hate to go through life like she does – finding fault after sin after mistake. She can only see the worst, Valda. In all my life, I never heard her say either thank you or sorry.'

'Perhaps she had a hard time and it turned her?'

He nodded. 'Perhaps. But why spend the rest of your life making trouble for everybody else? Is unhappiness something that needs spreading, like margarine?'

'There's folk like that, Dave. It's as if they just can't help theirselves. Take my mother-in-law – oh, I wish you would. You could stick her in with your mother and you'd swear they were twins. She's a right one. Nice to your face, but never turn your back, or you'll end up with a knife in the middle of it.'

Dave stared at Valda. 'You're serious?'

She pursed her lips. 'She's not happy living with us, and she makes my life a misery. Shall I introduce them? Bring her round for tea, cakes and a slanging match? We'd need a referee with a strong stomach, mind.'

He thought about that. Valda was a Catholic, and Mam didn't like them. She didn't like gay people, black people, Muslim people, any kind of people. 'Is your ma-in-law a churchgoer?'

'No. Lapsed. I reckon if she went to confession, it would take her a week to say her penance on the beads. Tell you what, though. We'd be better off with all the bad apples in one barrel, eh? It would make my life easier – and yours. Imagine it. Your life with no Enid, mine with no Mary.'

Dave closed his eyes. 'Bliss,' he breathed.

Valda took her cardigan from a hanger. 'Think about it. I'll think, and all. We're not getting any younger, lad. I've kids to see to, and you've got your shop. Nothing to lose, eh?' She left him to an uncertain fate. The poor IT man was buried under pensioners, and their questions were sealing him in.

'You all right in there?' Dave called.

The man emerged. He was red in the face and decidedly the worse for wear. 'They're keen,' he complained. 'Fortunately, computers are tough these days, but I hope your software survives.' He left his card and dashed off in search of somewhere safer.

'Has he gone?' someone asked.

'Yes,' shouted Dave. 'You had him frightened halfway to death. Now, who has a child or a grandchild who's experienced in computers?'

It seemed that most of them knew someone.

'Send them round,' Dave told them. 'We'll have a rota. Now, you can all go home, because I've things to do.'

He locked the door and looked round his empty shop. This was all he had in the world. Tuesdays and Fridays, he went to the Hen and Chickens for a pint. Tuesdays and Fridays, he got an earful from his mother. It was clear that her selective memory had deleted much of her own past from the hard drive, but it was retrievable – oh, yes. Nothing was ever completely wiped. A word here, a word there, and he could make her life totally unbearable.

The times she had come home the worse for wear; the many occasions on which he had cleaned up vomit because fish and chips didn't always sit well on a bellyful of cider and spirits. Her sex life had been audible and had sometimes involved more than just herself and one other. Did she really believe that he could forget all that? How could she imagine that a child of at least average intellect would not remember at least some of what he had seen and heard?

But. Ah yes, there was *the* word. *But* if he moved out or showed signs of discontent, she could force him to buy her out. 'Maybe I should,' he said under his breath. 'Get a loan, open another kind of shop – or extend into

44

number three – live above number three.' He swallowed hard. There had to be a way. Valda's suggestion might not be as daft as it had first sounded. Two rotten eggs in one carton could be part of the answer.

He stood at the door and looked out onto a beautiful summer evening. Father Walsh was gardening, and a group of children played near the stocks on the green. Stone cottages looked particularly lovely at this time of day, when the sun was nearing its nadir. It was as if Earth's star threw out a last blaze of life before starting to dip towards the west. 'Rose-coloured specs,' he murmured. He knew he couldn't leave Eagleton. After being raised in the back streets of Bolton, he had fallen in love with the countryside. Everything he needed was here – farms, woods, shop, books, plenty to eat.

Sighing, he turned round and prepared to return to the woman upstairs. If he wasn't careful, she would win. He was eating too much, too often. He was eating the wrong stuff. The chances of living long enough to bury her were as slim as he ought to be. She might well outlive him. He wasn't far away from fifty. She was a mere twenty-two years older. 'It's about staying alive. I have to stay alive.' In order to do that, Dave Barker would need to take his future and hang on to it – otherwise, all his efforts would count for nothing.

He needed to diet; he needed to get rid of as much aggravation as possible. Kill her? Lovely dream, but not worth the probable consequences. Eat less, get out. It was time to change.

They were shutting the shop when Philomena Gallagher arrived. 'Sorry, love,' said Maurice. 'I know we say appointment not always necessary, but we're doing a gig

45

tonight. Paul needs so much make-up it takes hours and a builder's trowel. We're going to invest in an industrial paint-sprayer.'

Paul sniggered. 'Take no notice. He's always in a filthy mood when he knows he's got to wear his corsets.'

Philly didn't know where to look. She had never been in Pour Les Dames before, and she knew that the owners of the business were ... different. It was best not to think about the details of their relationship, but she couldn't help herself. Red in the face, she passed Maurice a leaflet. 'Father Walsh asked me to do this,' she explained. 'There's a group being set up in the school hall. Amateur drama.'

Paul struck a pose. 'Oh, but we're pros, sweetheart. Aren't we, ducky?' He touched Maurice's arm.

Maurice refused to laugh. Paul always went a step too far when in the presence of a bigot. He'd taken a few beatings from homophobes for it, but he still wouldn't help himself. 'Take no notice,' Maurice advised. 'We'll think about it.' He stared at the visitor. 'Who does your hair?' As always, the senior partner in the business put the shop first. This was a potential client. Furthermore, she needed help immediately, and he loved a challenge.

Philly's colour deepened. 'Nobody.' A hand flew up defensively and she placed trembling fingers on her head. 'I do it.'

Maurice nodded. 'We could help you with that,' he said. 'Given a decent style, you'd be quite pretty. It's needing shape, you see. A bit of feathering, a touch of my genius, and you'll feel brand new.'

Philly swallowed. It was a case of give and take, she supposed. But would she be able to bear these men

46

touching her head after they had . . . done whatever they did to each other? 'Right,' she answered lamely.

'Shall we say half two tomorrow? After you've finished at Dave's?'

She nodded.

'We'll put you in the book. Paul?'

'Yes, master?'

'Cut and blow for a start. We'll look at the colour next time.'

'I don't want to be blonde,' she managed after a sizeable pause. What would everybody at church think if she turned up to Mass with platinum hair?

Paul shook his head vigorously. 'Oh, no. Blonde would never suit you, darling. You'll need something a lot more subtle. Low lights with a touch of warm chestnut.' Philly flinched as he touched her hair. 'Good quality stuff, is that,' he announced. 'And plenty of it. Dave'd give a fortune for a sixth of it – wouldn't he, Mo?'

Maurice nodded. 'I dare say. Now, come on, Paul. Get the cement rendering and we'll try to make you look nearly human.'

Philly left the shop at speed.

Maurice turned the sign to CLOSED, then rounded on Paul. 'You could see she was uncomfortable. Years I've tried to drum this into you – button your gob when they don't know you. I can guarantee she'll be telling us her innermost secrets if you behave.'

'Women like a gay hairdresser.'

'Well, of course they do. With a gay, a woman isn't a sex object, is she? She opens up after a while – if you treat her right. Some of them have to be handled with care, that's all. Leave her to me. She's terrified.'

47

Paul sniffed. 'It's her hair that's bloody terrifying. We should have left her alone.'

Maurice shook his head in despair. 'Look – they talk to us and we keep their secrets. That's why we decided on separate cubicles – remember? We listen and we keep quiet. That's as important as any hair treatment or manicure. We look after the whole person – hair's incidental.'

'What are we? Psychiatrists? Vicars? Hair stylists?'

'All of the above, and don't you forget it. Now, come on. We're due at the Rose and Crown in just under two hours. I've got to wax my arms.'

'Ouch.' Paul grimaced. 'So glad I'm not an ape.'

Maurice looked him up and down. 'Rather an ape than a bitch. So, move it pronto.'

Paul knew there was only one real boss, so he moved it. Pronto.

Philly sat on a stone wall at the edge of the village green. Her face had cooled down, but her heart seemed to have remained in top gear. She should have posted the wretched flyer through the letterbox, then she wouldn't have needed to talk to them, listen to them, think about them. Some children were playing with a long skipping rope. It was good to see them outside. Philly didn't approve of computers, and she wondered why Dave had bothered. Didn't folk spend enough time locked indoors? Some of those screen games were vicious, too. It was a shame; it was a pity that human nature forced people into pushing back boundaries all the time.

Nobody worried about gays any more. Homosexuality was openly accepted – they could even go through a form of marriage if they so desired. It was all wrong. Men and women were meant to get together in order to make children. But the process of child-making had become an amusement, a pastime in which people overindulged. Like drink, it got a hold on them. Like drugs, the habit became hard to break. Now, same-sex couples almost flaunted their status. Gay pride? Well, pride always came before a fall.

A car pulled into the slip road that fronted the five shops. It stopped outside the florist's, and a small woman got out. Lily Latimer received her with open arms before lifting a child from the back seat. Squeals of childish delight fought with the sound of adult laughter while the three greeted each other.

The trio disappeared into the building, and Philly watched as Father Walsh flung down his garden fork and leapt across the road. He pulled boxes and bags out of the car and placed them inside the shop. But he didn't stay, probably decided not to interfere. He walked back to the presbytery, picked up the fork and started working again. But he glanced across the road from time to time. Was he trying to convert the florist?

Looking up, Philly saw the pair of women at the front window of the upstairs flat. The florist was pointing towards the presbytery, while the other woman, child in her arms, nodded and smiled. Was Lily Latimer going to buy the priest's house? Such a shame that it had to go, that Father Walsh was forced to go from pillar to post in order to provide services for the few. And they were a few. Mam and Grandma had talked about the walks, days when Catholics from Bolton and its satellite villages walked through the town to display their faith. The one true faith.

She stood up. The walks didn't happen any more. It was said that they had stopped in the early sixties when the first signs of rot had set in. Little girls in white dresses had been replaced by creatures whose clothes were the same as their mothers', who played with make-up given free with magazines, who wore bikini tops although they had nothing to hide. They were too . . . too aware. Innocence was now a luxury enjoyed by very few.

Philly walked into her little cottage and switched the kettle on to boil. Her movements were automatic as she put vegetables to cook in the microwave, grilled her lonely chop and a single sausage, set one place at the kitchen table. She had never expected to receive anything in life, so she had not been disappointed. But she wished with all her heart that Dave Barker had been born Catholic, because he was a nice man and would have been good company. Her single status did not exactly upset her, but the evenings were extremely lonely. She finished her meal and went to make coffee. He was a lovely man. It was a shame.

Excitement died a natural death after an hour or so, as both Babs and the child were exhausted. Cassie fell asleep in the small spare bed in her mother's room, and the two women sat down with a bottle of Crozes Hermitage.

Babs yawned. 'Oh, let me at the wine – get me a bucketful. God, that was a bloody long drive,' she said. 'And Cassie hated the hotel. She was asking for you all the time – I finally got her to call you Auntie Lily.'

'Yes, it's a long way.' Lily slid down into the comfort of an oversized armchair. 'Thanks for coming. It's been a bit stressful on my own.'

'I'll bet. Are the natives civilized?'

Lily grinned. 'Fairly. There's a dreadful old woman

next door, but she stays upstairs. Rumour has it that her son keeps her caged because she bites. On the other side, we have a pair of gay hairdressers and their lodger, Sally Byrne. She does manicures, waxing and so forth. The shop at the far end is run by our landlord – he's from Liverpool, as is his wife. Lovely rough diamonds, they are. They have a son called Derek who's an accountant.'

'And that's it?'

'No, there's a whole village of them. New estates all over the place, smaller villages dotted about – it gets quite lively sometimes. They keep threatening to build a supermarket, but the natives have managed to beat off the developers so far. It's only a matter of time, though.'

Babs stared into the near distance. 'I can't believe what we've done, Lee. Sorry – Lily. To come so far and live among strangers—'

'We had no choice. And if you want to call me Lee, that's OK. I chose Lily because if you slip up, it's near enough to be a nickname. I honestly think we had no alternative. We both need a completely clean slate.'

'Yes. Yes, I think you're right. In fact, I know it. This way, we get a chance to start again, but we can't pretend it never happened, can we? It's not going to come out of the washing machine brilliant white.'

Lily shook her head slowly. 'None of our yesterdays can be bleached away, Babs. You didn't tell anyone you were coming up here?'

'No, of course not. Being an orphan made it a bit easier, I suppose, but it was still an awful wrench.' She nodded in the direction of her bedroom. 'Thank goodness she's young enough for it not to matter. Anyway, I told everyone we were going on holiday to Cornwall, so people saw us leave. It made it a bit less stressful, though I did feel mean – I had lovely neighbours. So Cassie and I are on holiday. We just won't return, that's all. Had to leave the dolls' house. Had to leave everything but clothes.'

Lily stretched her legs in front of her. 'We'll get her a new dolls' house. It's OK here. I promise you, it'll be fine. There's no one who will connect us with what happened, and that's the main thing. We aren't front-page news any more–'

'But we may be when someone reports us missing.'

Lily had thought about that. 'You have to do one thing, Babs. I've already done it.' She sat up again and leaned forward. 'Tell the Bolton police where you are. You have the right to live wherever you like and you have the right to privacy. But yes, folk at home may well report us as having disappeared, though because I have property on the market my absence will be labelled deliberate. You're mother to a young child, so go to the cops and let them know you're both alive. If you choose not to be found, your wish will be respected. After that, it should be plain sailing.'

'Better be.' Babs stood up. 'Is it all right if I go to bed now? I'm absolutely worn out.'

On her own again, Lily watched the priest as he finished his gardening. She wondered briefly about Bright Eyes with his purple ear, hoped he was recovering from the ordeal. Father Walsh had probably brought in the luggage from the car. Or it could have been Dave Barker. Whatever, they were good people and she would settle. So would Babs. As for Cassie, she didn't care as long as she had Mummy and her auntie Leanne, who was now Lily or Lee.

It would never be completely safe, though. Even emigration might have failed to conceal the real truth behind the changes in three lives. Yet it had to be worth the effort, at least. The hardest part was being unable to concentrate sufficiently to read a book, or watch TV, or listen to the radio. The music she had loved had begun to remind her of a time she would never completely forget, and she wanted no prompting. It took a great deal of effort to run the shop, but she was managing that. 'Baby steps and carpe diem,' she whispered.

He was going inside now. If she ever needed to unburden herself, he was the man on whom she might impose. Father Michael Walsh's promise to keep quiet referred not only to Catholics, not only to Christians, but to every soul who chose to confess or disclose. Strangely, it was the rabbit that had convinced her. Any person who would do all that for an animal, who would drag in a near-stranger to help, had to be intrinsically good.

Lily found herself smiling. 'The bugger bit me.' That had been quite funny, especially coming from a man of God. She had always imagined the representatives of Rome to be strict and humourless – he was hardly either of those. With hair as untidy as that, it might be hard for him to be taken seriously. He reminded her of the chap who played Darcy to Jennifer Ehle's Elizabeth. Lily had always thought that the hair of the bloke in that serialization belonged elsewhere, since it made a bloody-minded and self-absorbed man completely childlike on the outside.

He had gone. He had gone, and she felt colder. 'Don't,' she advised herself. 'For God's sake – literally.' That said, she took herself off to bed.

'There's a kiddy next door now,' grumbled Enid Barker. 'There'll be noise – you mark my words.'

53

Dave placed breakfast on the side table from which she ate. Although she blamed melegs for her inability to reach the dining area, the real reason for her chosen position in life was her need to stay by the window. When she required the bathroom, she moved at considerable speed, shooting back to her chair within a minute of finishing her ablutions. She was a fraud – and worse.

'Is there no eggs?' she asked.

'Your cholesterol,' he answered. 'Remember? More in one egg than in a pound of liver? Three a week is your maximum.'

Enid snorted. 'Bloody doctors. What do they know?'

'Enough,' he replied smartly.

She eyed her son. He seemed to be developing a bit of backbone. Pity about his great big belly, then. He was bringing her a visitor, had announced that she needed the company. Valda Turnbull's mother-in-law was coming to tea. They were Catholics, though Mary wasn't sure what she believed in any more. 'I don't want anybody coming here,' Enid said.

'Tough. Because she's coming – end of.'

This was starting to be vaguely interesting. Dave had never answered back, had always allowed her the last word. In recent days, he'd tried coming over all clever, as if he might just be a man after all. 'I'll bolt the door,' she threatened.

'Then we'll break it down. After all, we can't leave an old diabetic who could be in a coma.'

'I'll be shouting. So you'll know I'm awake.'

Dave nodded sagely. 'If your sugar gets too low, you go quiet and confused. If it goes through the roof, you shout and get confused.'

She didn't know the truth of the matter, so she offered

no reply. She'd had hypos, but no hypers, and was not in a position to comment. Should she call his bluff, eat a quarter of butterscotch and see what happened? He was winning. Just because she had become an old and dependent woman, he was taking advantage. 'More tea,' she snapped.

He brought the pot and a milk jug. If he'd had any sense at all, he would have remembered the arsenic. 'There you are, Mother dearest.'

Sarcasm now! This game promised to become interesting, because she could close that bloody shop, and he knew it. How far was he prepared to go? 'I'm getting on that phone to Chas Boswell, to ask about Madam next door subletting.'

'The precedent's set,' Dave replied. 'Sally Byrne at the hairdressers' – she has the spare room.'

'Bloody poofs,' she snarled. 'Shouldn't be allowed.'

'True.' He poured in the milk. 'We could put them in the stocks one at a time and throw tomatoes at them. I suppose tinned ones would do. They'd get concussion and brain damage, so that would be all right, eh?'

Enid blinked. He was up to something. The proverbial worm was definitely on the turn, and she would put a stop to it. 'I can get you out of that bloody shop like that.' She clicked her fingers. 'Don't you forget it.'

Dave reined himself in. 'I've got some savings,' he advised her. 'And a clean credit rating.' His heart was working overtime. He really must diet and try to get a bit of exercise. But he failed to stop himself. 'Mam?' He took a deep breath. 'I think it's time I filed for divorce. Do what you like – I'll manage.'

She blinked again, this time very rapidly. 'You couldn't survive without me.'

He folded his arms as if trying to hold back the rising tide of fury. 'I think you'll find the shoe's on a different foot altogether.' He left her with her jaw hanging, slamming the door in his wake.

On the stairs, he sat down, his whole body trembling, head pounding as the blood coursed too quickly through his brain. It would be a stroke, he supposed – or a heart attack. It would amuse her no end if she outlived him. Would she make him buy her out? The business wasn't worth a great deal – it was more scones and goodwill than anything. What would a prospective purchaser see? A shop with below-average turnover, a place that kept two people in reasonable comfort, no more. Savings? He had less than five grand, no big deal at all.

So the shop would change into something else, and that something else would come with the sitting tenant from hell. Dave stood up and crossed his fingers. He prayed that Mam and Mary Turnbull would get on, that he would get out, that the Reading Room would endure. It was time for him to start having some of his own way.

Solitary again, but not rule 43. Wasn't me. I know the bloke who made the knife, but I daren't say a frigging word, or it'll be me with my eye out next time.

Five of us in solitary. It's no big deal, because I like being on my own; few interruptions, time to think and concentrate on what needs doing. Not easy to make stuff happen when you're locked up, but I'm owed a few favours, could get more than a handful of folk sent down if I wanted to.

Food's crap. Sit and think. All the time in the world to work it out. Yes. All the time in the world.

Three

Lily had failed to remember one vital thing about her friend, but she was reminded early on of a particular characteristic that was very much a part of Babs. She talked. She talked on any subject for any length of time, was able to discuss matters about which she had little or no knowledge, and entered conversations even if she needed to interrupt.

She hadn't always been like this. The anxiety had only surfaced after the two women had met, and was probably the result of certain events about which Babs seldom spoke, a series of traumas that had left both of them bruised in more ways than one. Lily had become quiet and withdrawn, while Babs now employed compulsive talking in an effort to distract herself to the point where she might forget some of it. For her, it was therapy, and, if it worked for Babs, Lily would endure it.

In spite of her questions about the population of Eagleton, Babs floated through her early days in the village like a duck on an extremely placid pond. Some feathers might have been ruffled by her head-on approach, but Babs's own plumage remained smooth. It was almost frightening. Like Lily, she had a west country accent; unlike Lily, she was not good at remembering the alibi on which both had supposedly worked, so she often gave Somerset as her place of origin. No one had commented so far, but it might make matters more difficult in the future.

Lily came downstairs, stopped and listened. Babs was talking to a customer. 'No, she hasn't always been quiet. She's been through a lot of—'

'Hello.' Lily bustled in and made herself busy with a bucket of pinks. The customer was Father Walsh, and he was in receipt of the dubious benefit of Babs's wisdom. 'Get Cassie out of the roses, Babs,' Lily begged. 'It's not just a matter of saving the flowers – she could prick herself on a thorn.'

Babs picked up her daughter. 'Right. I'll take you upstairs.' The reluctance in her tone was clear.

Lily eyed the priest when Babs had gone. 'Yes?' she asked.

'I'm begging,' he replied. She looked frightened. 'If you have anything left over on a Saturday – anything that won't last till Monday – could we have it for a special rate for Sunday Masses and Benediction?'

Philomena Gallagher had already made the same request, so Lily repeated her consent. 'Either free or very cheap,' she added.

'Paying your rent again just in case?'

She smiled, but her eyes remained cold. 'How's the rabbit?'

'Pale mauve,' he said. 'And he still lets me feed him.'

Lily picked up a rose from the floor. 'You've met Babs, then.' Cassie had broken the stem.

He nodded. Babs was quite a character. She was pleasant, inquisitive, nervous and damaged. But she was not

58

as traumatized as Lily appeared to be. 'Yes, it was a pleasure to talk to her at last. She's very amusing.'

'Good.' She straightened a pile of wrapping sheets on the counter. 'Anything else? Do you need a kidney, blood transfusion, flowers? No? All right, I have to see to something upstairs.' She left him in the shop.

In the living room, she collared her friend. 'Babs, I wish—'

'I'm sorry, I'm sorry. You know what I'm like. I can't help it.' She shook russet-coloured hair and smiled an apology. 'I like people. In spite of everything that's happened, I still like the beggars. It's how I am, Lee. It's how I've had to become, because . . . you know why.'

Lily sighed heavily. 'We are incognito – well, I am – for a very good reason. And you could ruin it all by letting your tongue wander off on its own without a collar and lead. Babs, I could be in danger.'

'I know.'

'My life and yours could depend on how well we manage up here.'

'I know.'

'Then there's Cassie. I won't draw any nasty pictures, but you know damned well what we could be up against in time. There could be a lot of red in those pictures—'

'I know! I do know!' Babs sat down and burst into tears. 'I shouldn't have come. I should have stayed at home, because I might just say too much and give you away. I'll go back.' She dried her face and lifted a determined chin. 'I'll go back and leave you in peace with a better chance of survival.'

'You can't. You need to be out of the way as well. So does that child. I'm afraid you're stuck here, my lovely.

And when I move across the road, you'll be in this flat with just Cassie. If I can't trust you, I can't move out. And I want to live in that house. Now, dry your eyes again and take this little girl for some fresh air.'

The smaller woman sighed, and there was a slight sob in the breath that escaped her lungs. 'All right,' she said eventually.

'Babs, I don't like upsetting you, because God knows you've had enough misery, but I can't have you running away at the mouth.'

'Collar and lead?'

Lily nodded. 'Straitjacket, if necessary. Now, pull yourself together. That was the shop bell, and I've flowers to sell.'

Back in the shop, she found a tall, attractive man in a short-sleeved shirt that just about contained his muscular body. 'Yes?' she said.

He had come to see Babs. Lily paused and processed his request. Who did Babs know up here? Was he a villager – or perhaps it was someone from one of the estates? Or could it be ... God, no. Not yet, surely? 'She's busy,' Lily managed eventually. 'Taking her little girl out.' If anyone did come after them, it wouldn't be in daylight or without disguise.

'Are you Lily?'

Fear cut through her like a knife, and she understood all about knives. 'Who wants to know?' Blood pounded in her ears. England was a relatively small country, and news travelled fast. Was this the new face of an old danger? Had she and Babs been cornered already?

'It's all right,' he said. 'I'm Peter Haywood. Sergeant. Greater Manchester Police.'

She relaxed slightly, felt the stiffness leaving her shoulders. It might be an idea to book an Indian head massage on her next visit to Pour Les Dames. 'Ah yes. I'll ... I'll go and get her.' The police were not always trustworthy, yet she had been forced to advise them of her arrival, since friends back home might well be getting her listed as missing. Was he a good cop or a bad cop?

She came back into the shop with Babs and Cassie following in her wake. 'Hello,' Babs said rather loudly. 'To what do we owe the pleasure?'

He passed her a scarf. 'You left this at the station.'

Lily glanced up at the ceiling. She was in the presence of strong chemistry and didn't know where to look. The scarf was silk and had been a gift from her to Babs when they had still lived in Taunton. Babs and the scarf were close companions – virtually inseparable. It had been forgotten on purpose; this visit had been engineered by a clever little woman who had taken a fancy to a tall, handsome stranger at least ten years her senior.

'Shall we go for a walk?' Babs asked the policeman. They left, Cassie toddling between them, Babs winking at Lily. The remarkable fact was that Babs was still on the market. In spite all that had happened, she was organizing a manhunt.

Lily watched them while they sat on a bench at the edge of the green, her mind racing. She wondered whether Babs might change her name via marriage to a man who would protect her and Cassie, but the idea did not sit comfortably in Lily's soul. Cassie was all she had. Babs was the little girl's mother, and Lily had been fighting her feelings for some time, yet the thought of parting with this near-daughter made her ill. Only one good thing had escaped Taunton, and that good thing was playing near the stocks. 'I must distance myself,' she whispered.

There was a wedding to prepare. Philomena Gallagher had promised to sit with Cassie while Lily and Babs took flowers and drapery into Bolton in order to prepare for tomorrow. They had a church and a reception hall to cover, so it promised to be a long evening. Lily folded lengths of satin that would be fashioned in swags suggested by the bride. Given free rein, Lily might have done things differently, but tomorrow belonged to the bride. The bouquet had to be taken away straight after the service, as it was to be professionally dried and framed.

Babs and Cassie were still with the policeman. He would know the whole story, since it had all been broadcast in newspapers and on TV, so he was learning nothing new. Yet Lily's skin crawled each time she thought about people hereabouts learning exactly who she was, who Babs and Cassie were. The sergeant might keep his counsel, might not. Like the purple-eared rabbit, Lily did not want to feel trapped.

She needed more ice. As she came through from the back of the shop, she looked outside again. They were still sitting on the same bench while Cassie played ball with another child. Lily smiled. Cassie couldn't catch yet, couldn't even throw properly. How fortunate the child was. Too young to worry, she simply went from day to day without a care in the world. And that was a blessing indeed.

'She's going to buy the priest's house, and good luck to her. Looks as if she's due a change of fortune. Put these on the shelf.' Eve passed a box of cigars to her husband. 'But I still want to get out of here, Chas. We had our own house in Liverpool, so why can't we have one here? I can't fit a proper Christmas tree upstairs. Last year's looked like an accident that had fallen off the bin wagon. I wouldn't care if we couldn't afford— Take that stupid look off your face and shut your gob – there's a bus coming.'

Chas sighed loudly. 'I like to keep an eye on things,' he said lamely. She'd win. She always won in the end. He was the one who was supposed to be in charge, because he could make her laugh until she changed her mind, but Eve was the home-maker, and she wasn't satisfied with the raw materials on Fullers Walk.

'Then go straight,' she suggested. 'Sell just kosher gear, and tell your special customers to bog off.'

He shook his head. Go straight? He was nearly that already. It was just a few cases here and there, bits and bobs obtained by his brother from a source on the docks. Security was now so paranoid that no one could go out-and-out criminal these days. 'I'm as straight as I can be,' he said.

'But your Robbo or one of the lads could bring stuff to our house, then we could fetch it here in the boot of our car or something.'

Or something. The trouble with women was that they didn't think things through properly. 'The less you know, the better. My eggs here are all in one basket – they need to be.'

Eve's shift was ending. Without another word to her beloved spouse, she walked out of the shop, slamming the door behind her. Chas hated sulking. If she could keep it up for a few days without succumbing to laughter, if she could stick to her decision, she might be in with a chance.

Eve stood at the front window of the flat. The woman who was staying with Lily Latimer was sitting on a bench near the green. She was in the company of an eye-pleasing piece of male furniture, and she was laughing. Babs, she was called. From the same neck of the woods as the florist, she was certainly a great deal livelier than her hostess. The child was pretty, with large eyes and a mass of blonde hair. There seemed to be no husband in the picture, but that was only too common these days.

Both adults were laughing. Lily didn't laugh very often, though. She was beautiful, yet there was something missing in her face, as if pieces of life had been taken out of her. But she'd bucked up in the priest's place, so that was definitely going to be her property. It would be interesting to see if she would come out of her shell after moving from the Walk.

Eve sat down and took from behind a cushion a pile of leaflets sent by estate agents. There were many houses for sale in the area, some old, many new. The old ones were prettier, while the new were more sensible, easier to keep and still under guarantee. There was a lot to be said for a guarantee, but Rose Cottage still sat on top of the pile, because that was where it belonged. Detached and built of thick blocks of stone, it looked as if it had been here for ever – it would probably survive Armageddon.

'I'll have to get inside that one,' Eve told the empty room. 'And there's enough outbuildings for all Chas's palaver.' It looked as if talking him round wasn't going to be easy. But Derek was away on a course, so Eve could play a trump card by sleeping in her son's room. Chas didn't like sleeping alone. Well, if he wanted company, he could always get a bloody cat.

The intercom buzzer sounded, so she picked up the phone. 'Hello?' It had to be Chas – there was no one else around to use the intercom facility.

'You win,' he said.

She wouldn't crow, wouldn't laugh, wouldn't scream with joy. 'You're no fun,' she told him. 'I was going to curl up with Daphne du Maurier in our Derek's room.'

'Is she a dyke?'

'No, she's a writer, soft lad. How much? Because it has to be Rose Cottage. It's just across the road and I like it. You'll like it. Because if you don't like it, I'll kill you.'

'What's the price, Evie?'

'Never mind the price. We're viewing it tomorrow when Derek gets home. And be nice when we get there. We can talk about the price when you've seen it and decided you'd give anything to live there.'

After a pause, he asked, 'How do you know I'd give anything to live there?'

'Because I say so.' She put down the phone and tried not to cheer. Men were easy, she reminded herself. They liked what they were told to like and they'd do almost anything for a quiet life.

The intercom sounded again. 'What?' she pretended to snap.

'Can we have beef and Yorkshires tomorrow?'

'All right.'

'With rhubarb crumble to follow?'

'Yes.'

'Custard?'

'Don't push it, Charles Boswell. I do have my limits,

65

you know.' She replaced the receiver. Rose Cottage. It was next to St Faith's, while the presbytery sat on the church's other side. Chas would be able to see his beloved shop from the front window. Derek would probably stay here, since it was time he had a pad of his own.

There was a very long rear garden, as long as the one behind the priest's house. The church would be sandwiched between Lily Latimer and the Boswells, as would the graveyard, the size of which was probably the reason for those two long plots behind presbytery and cottage. Eve rubbed her hands in glee. She had always fancied some land. There wasn't even a window box here, but she would make up for that soon enough.

With a cardigan draped across her shoulders, she went downstairs and out through the rear door. There was joy in her step as she crossed the road and looked at the facade of the house she coveted. There were roses everywhere. A very primitive example clung to the masonry outside the front door. Its flowers seemed to have just one layer of petals – was it a dog rose? She would order a book from Dave's shop. In fact, she would order several, because she wanted to grow her own herbs and vegetables as well as flowers.

There would be amateur rose specialists all over the villages. Would she dare keep chickens? Not to eat, of course, because a chicken in the oven needed to be anonymous. But there could be fresh eggs almost every day.

The windows were lovely, sashed and set in sandstone. The rest of the house was in a greyer colour, but it was beyond beautiful – it was absolutely gorgeous. The roof was slate, and probably needed attention. A little water feature sat in the front garden, just stones over which the liquid trickled. Slabs at the edge wore patches of moss, and Eve was glad that no one had cleaned them off. It was an idyll, with a huge plot at the back and civilization at the front in the form of shops and a properly laid main road.

They were still sitting there. The woman named Babs was leaning towards the man. If what Eve had read about body language was correct, she was practically giving herself to him, and who could blame her? He was such a big, handsome fellow, while Babs was a likeable soul. Ah, well. Good luck to the pair of them.

Father Walsh came past. 'Hello, Eve. What are you up to now?'

'I'm up to trying to force Chas into buying this house. I think I may be winning.'

'Oh?'

She nodded. 'He isn't ready to die yet, Father. And I don't want to be confessing to you that I murdered him.'

'Good enough reason.' He wandered off towards the church.

To think she had been afraid of leaving Liverpool. Life here was good, the people were great; even the priest was a nice man. She would never go back. There was still a slight pain in the hole where Liverpool had sat, but she couldn't manage to miss it badly any more. There was something about the villages surrounding Bolton, and that something was probably natural beauty. Movement in the land, soft, gentle slopes in velvety greens, made the area desirable. Patchwork was held together by stitches shaped out of dry stone – it was a wonderful area for picnics. Unlike West Yorkshire, Lancashire was not sudden. It had no steep climbs into the Pennines, just these lifts and falls that looked so peaceful and inviting.

'I am home,' she whispered to her inner self. Had anyone told her twenty years ago that she would be living among Woollies, she would have scoffed. Liverpool had been everything to her, and she owed this new life to Chas's brother. He had been caught; Chas had been lucky. With no record, he had been able to obtain the licence required to sell wines, spirits, beer and tobacco. 'Thanks, Robbo,' she mumbled before going home. 'Thanks for not grassing on my Chas.' Robbo seemed to have done something good after all.

'I can't just go off as and when I please,' Babs told her companion. 'Tonight, we have a babysitter, because Lee – Lily – is doing a wedding, so a woman from the village is minding Cassie.'

'Short for Cassidy?' he asked.

'Cassandra. Lily chose it.'

'Really?'

Babs nodded. 'She did a lot for me, Pete. It could all have turned out a great deal worse than it did, but she stood by me once she was fit. With the way things are now for her, Cassie's as near to a child of her own as she's going to get. Damned shame.'

Pete agreed. 'It was a terrible thing that happened to her. Must take time to get over stuff like that.'

Babs placed a hand on his arm. 'One point. She doesn't like being talked about. It makes her a bit paranoid, and very frightened. Lily trusts very few people. In fact, I am the only people she trusts, so that's just one. Don't try to get her to talk. It's all over, and she wants to leave it in the past. She needs to bury it.'

'That's her privilege,' he said. 'So. When are we going to have our first date? When I met my wife, it took me over six months to ask her out. Six months is a long time at my age, so I'm beating round no bushes.' He was quiet for a moment. 'Since she died, I've concentrated on the kids and the job, but it's time I put on my dancing shoes. What do you say?'

Babs grinned. 'I've got your mobile number. Lily will sit, but let's get this big wedding over with. I promise I will phone you.'

He stood up. 'No rest for the wicked. Back on duty in just over an hour.' He placed a hand on Cassie's head. 'Look after your mam for me, babe.' Then he kissed Babs's hand and walked back to his car.

She sat for a while, her skin tingling because he had touched her. Feeling like a teenager, she separated Cassie from her playmate and walked back across the road into the shop. Lily was placing wreaths for a funeral just inside the door. 'Hi,' said Babs.

Lily looked at her. 'Don't let Cassie near these,' she said. 'They have to be just right – funerals deserve respect.'

Babs scooped up her daughter. 'Are you in a mood?' she asked her friend.

Lily shrugged. 'It's your business, Babs, but don't go jumping into love. Falling is an accident, but jumping is asking for trouble.'

Babs stood very still and tried to hold on to her temper. It got the better of her, though she did not raise her voice. 'Lily, just because you've decided to be a recycled virgin doesn't mean I have to go all straight-lipped and sad. I like him. He likes me. It doesn't mean I'm going to jump, does it? I'm not old enough to give up, not young enough to be completely daft. Please don't look at me like that, because it makes me angry.'

'It's your business. But please, please—'

'Don't talk about you. I promise, Lee. He's a cop, so he knows enough, but he's not interested.'

'Interested in you, though?'

'Yes.'

Lily managed a half-smile. None but the hardest heart could possibly remain angry with Babs. 'Then he isn't a complete fool – he clearly has good taste. And yes, I will mind young Madam while you go out with him, so get up those stairs, put on some don't-matter clothes and wait for Philly Gallagher. What with weddings and funerals – ain't life fun?'

Babs breathed easily again. It was true that for Lily life had to be tackled in bits, or in baby steps, as she put it. No sudden changes for this girl, not yet, anyway. And none of it was Lily's fault, just as none of it was Babs's fault. Lily's head was fully furnished, but her soul remained bruised. Whatever, the Lancashire air seemed to suit her, and Babs would pray for a good outcome.

'No good clothes, babe,' Lily shouted up the stairs. 'And put a mop and bucket in the van, will you? Sewing kit as well – you never know.'

'Well, bugger me.' Enid looked up at her son as he walked in with her lunch. 'Did you see that carry-on outside? Bloody disgrace, I call it.'

He made no reply except to tell her what was on the

70

plate. 'Bacon, lettuce and tomato sandwich, and one of Philly's fruit tarts.'

Enid glanced at the ceiling. 'So you saw nowt?'

'Nothing worth writing home about, Mother dear.'

The old woman picked up her binoculars. If only she could lip-read, she'd have a much fuller story. 'Five minutes, she's been moved up here from wherever, that Babs one. And there she was, bold as brass, sat on a bench with a man. Hard-faced in my book.'

She never read books. Dave had noticed the couple, and had smiled. Little Babs and her lovely daughter were pleasant additions to Fullers Walk. He hoped they might help bring Lily Latimer out of her shell, because she'd looked very down in the dumps since arriving in the north. 'Were they actually fornicating, Mam?'

Enid blinked. Her son didn't use such words. Her son did as he was told, though he'd stepped just a whisker out of line lately. 'No. But she was throwing herself at him. Acting like a tart if you ask me.'

Dave didn't ask. He poured her tea. She moved to the dining table, groaning with each step, because melegs hurt today. He sat down opposite her, placed his elbows on the table, and rested his chin in his hands. 'You know, Mam, I've had just about enough of you.'

She paused, sandwich suspended in mid-air. Shocked, she could not manage to put her tongue in gear.

But Dave didn't stop. 'When I was a kid, you had man after man in your bed. I heard it all and saw too much for a lad of tender years. Money changed hands. Did my father pay? Did he?'

The sandwich dropped onto the table, spilling tomato seeds and shredded lettuce all over the cloth.

'And you sit here, day in, day out, making nasty remarks about folk who are just going about their business. She's not a whore. She's just a young woman, possibly a widow with a child, and she's looking for friendship – even for love. But there'll be no money left behind a clock for her. Because she's something you'll never be, and that's decent.'

The silence that followed was weighty. Enid clutched at her thin chest, a small groan emerging from thin, pale lips.

'You hit me repeatedly. You used me as a servant and you locked me in a cupboard. These days, I could go and report you to the police, but things were different when I was a kid. You are a nasty piece of work, madam. I don't care what you do – I'm not staying here. You can rot, for all I care.'

Enid closed her eyes. She didn't remember the past in quite the same way. She'd been firm, but … 'You hate me, don't you?'

'I don't like you. I despise you for what you are, and most of this village feels the same way. You're my mother, and I've tried to look after you, but I've had more than my fill. So.' He picked up the tray on which he had carried up her lunch. 'So, I am moving out.'

Her eyes flew open. 'You've nowhere to go.'

Dave smiled grimly. 'Don't fool yourself, old woman. Everybody round here knows what I have to put up with. There are plenty of spare beds in Eagleton. Someone will take me in, because they understand. They remember how you were downstairs, so they're on my side. You'd better get yourself a new slave, because this one's escaping.'

'Over my dead body,' Enid spat.

72

'That can be arranged,' he replied before leaving the flat. On the stairs, he paused for thought. What had happened lately to push him so near the edge? Why was he suddenly strong? Or perhaps strength was something he had lost, an element he used to employ during the years when he had tolerated her. Had his skin been worn so thin that his feelings had begun to show? And where was he going to sleep tonight?

Downstairs, three people were arguing over the computer, while a couple sat at one of the far tables doing the *Telegraph* crossword. Philly was brewing a new pot of tea. He beckoned, and she followed him though to the shop.

'You don't look right,' she told him.

'I'm not right.' Dave inhaled deeply. 'I've just told my mother to get lost.'

'Oh.'

'My feelings exactly. I've got to get out of here, Phil. Do you think people would talk if you took in a male lodger?'

She snapped her jaw into the closed position. 'Erm ... Father Walsh might want the spare room when the presbytery's sold.'

He nodded. 'And he's a man. But he won't need you, because Lily's giving him some rooms in the house – that'll save him being disturbed.'

'Oh,' she repeated.

'I won't beg,' he said. 'But I need somewhere. Tonight, if possible.'

Philly organized her thoughts. He was a nice man, but she had never shared a bathroom with a male. It could be embarrassing, because she often spent evenings wearing pyjamas and dressing gown ... 'All right,' she

73

said. 'Just till you find somewhere a bit more permanent.' She pondered for a moment. 'Doesn't she own half of the business?'

Dave nodded. 'Without it, she'd have only a small pension to live on. Anyway, there's a plot on.' He told Philly about Valda's mother-in-law. 'She's coming to see her soon, so they may get on OK and live together.'

'Shall I make you a brew?' she asked.

'Please.' He watched her as she walked away. There was something different about Philomena Gallagher these days – what was it? Ah yes, it was her hair. It had been cut and it shone like silk. He had better behave himself. He needed to be a model lodger.

The business of acquiring the presbytery proved to be fairly plain sailing. There were a few problems, including aged rainwater goods, a chimney that needed stabilizing and a couple of patches of damp. But the house was in good condition for its age, and Lily enjoyed measuring and planning and imagining her future. The garden was the biggest attraction, as it seemed to go on for ever, and she was always finding nooks and tables, sundials, broken benches, and paths that led nowhere in particular.

She was sitting nowhere in particular when she had her next encounter with the priest who would soon become a sitting tenant.

'Who's minding the shop?' he asked.

Lily jumped. 'For goodness' sake, you'll give someone a heart attack creeping about like that. Babs is minding the business, while Cassie's in the Reading Room with Philly Gallagher. She's teaching her to read.'

'Good,' he said, dropping to the ground beside her.

'It's time Philly had a few lessons. I'm fed up with her singing all the wrong words.'

Lily awarded him a glance designed to wither. 'I love this place. It reminds me of that children's story – *The Secret Garden*. Every time I come, I find another surprise.'

'So do I,' he answered ruefully. 'I think I sat on a nettle.'

Another withering glance crossed the small space between them. 'Put some purple stuff on it and call yourself Bugs.' At least there was no wildlife involved this time, no danger of staining her new cream blouse with gentian violet.

She had humour, then. She was different here. It was as if the main road separated one Lily from the other, and she relaxed in the wildness behind the house. Even in repose, a slight smile betrayed a deep contentment. This place would be loved and cared for. 'I'll help you with the garden,' he said.

'Just tidying,' she ordered. 'Don't change a thing. I love the wildness. My grandparents had a farm. Mixed arable and stock – it was great.' She paused. 'My grandpa worked like a dog, saved, speculated, owned bulls other farmers coveted to the point of sinfulness. It's thanks to him that I can take your home from under you, Mr Priest.'

'And did the farm have a wild bit for you?'

'It did.'

At last, the smile was completely real. In that moment, her expression was not pinned in place, was not a garment stuck on to cover nakedness. The woman loved the land, loved nature, loved Babs's child. He'd watched her trying

75

not to interfere, had known that she was fighting her feelings for Cassie. What on earth had happened?

'I had a secret garden,' she told him. 'It was walled, and only Grandpa and I had keys. Oh, that was a magic place. In the summer, I would read in there. No one ever found me. I expect they knew where I was, because no one was allowed to worry. He thought worry was a sin of self-indulgence.'

'He had faith?'

'Meeting house. He was Quaker, but not rigid. There was no standing barefoot on cold kitchen floors for morning prayers in winter.' Again, she smiled. 'My friend Josie told me that her gran's teeth were set in ice on the windowsill, yet they had to stand and pray before breakfast, even on the most vicious of days. No shoes allowed. The fire couldn't be lit until prayers were over. No, my grandfather was brilliant. I would have been named Charity or Sarah had he been a dictator, but he allowed my mother to name me Leanne.' She stopped. 'Lily is my second name.'

'Ah. You have a lot of ells in there. Leanne Lily Latimer.'

'Bloody 'ell,' she answered. Then she giggled.

Michael studied her. The giggle was slightly rusty, as if it needed oil after long neglect. 'You should laugh more often,' he advised. 'You're very pretty when you laugh.'

Something touched Lily's spine. It wasn't real, wasn't visible, yet she felt a cold finger at the small of her back. 'Pretty can be a curse,' she said softly.

'Ready to talk?' he asked.

'No.'

'When you are . . .'

'Yes. If I am ever ready, I'll let you know.'

Philly burst through the bushes, Cassie in her arms. 'Lily,' she cried. Then she noticed the priest. 'Oh. Sorry, Father. I didn't know you'd be here – I thought Lily was measuring.'

'I am,' answered Lily. 'I'm measuring how peaceful the garden is.'

An expression of confusion sat on Philly's face. 'Stay, please,' she begged when Michael stood up. 'He's asked me again.'

Lily turned to her male companion. 'Philly's been babysitting for Babs, so we've come to know each other. Dave Barker's walked out on that cantankerous mother of his, and he's asked to move in with Philly.'

He smiled. 'Is that all? I'd have done the same if you hadn't offered me a few rooms here. What's the matter?' Philly and Lily. Rhyming names, two very different women. 'Philly, for goodness' sake–'

'He's a man,' she cried, cheeks burning. 'And I'm a woman.'

'She's right so far,' Lily said. 'You can't deny any of the above, Father.'

Michael laughed. 'You're worried about what people will think? *Honi soit qui mal y pense.* That means shame on those who think evil of others. Dave Barker is one of the most decent men I know. He's survived a harridan of a mother by all accounts, though it's rather unchristian of me to judge her. There's no harm in him. And you know he loves your cooking.'

Philly's face continued pink. 'I never lived with a man.'

'Your dad?' he asked.

'Don't remember him. He died when I was small. Oh, Lily—'

'Just take one day at a time,' Lily advised. 'That's what I do.' She stood, scooped up the child and went off to demonstrate the wonders of her garden.

'Father?'

'What, Philly?'

'They will talk. And I'm not used to that, not ready for it.'

Michael placed a hand on her head and blessed her. 'Go in the love of Christ and live your life. Take no notice of gossip, I beg you.' He walked back to the house.

Philly sat and pondered. They were right – Dave was a nice man, and he deserved a chance away from his cruel and thoughtless mother. It would be all right. She would make sure that it would be all right.

Maurice was trying not to listen to Paul. As usual, the man was indulging in gossip, and he seemed to be developing a tongue far sharper than Enid Barker's was reputed to be.

'Worms always turn,' Paul announced to his captive audience, a woman from the south end of the village. 'I said to Mo – didn't I, Mo? I said she had it coming. Anyway, he no more than ups and offs and moves in with Philomena Gallagher, the holiest Roman in history.'

Maurice gave no answer to Flapgob – his nickname for Paul. Many gays were total bitches – Mo had met enough of those on the cabaret circuit – but Paul was in a class all his own. 'Do you want a spray of lacquer?' Mo asked his customer. The answer arrived in the affirmative and, as he sprayed, Mo wished the mist could be directed into the face of his partner.

'No backbone, some men,' continued Paul. 'Should have gone years since. No way would I have stayed. These high-and-low lights need doing again if you're going to keep up with them, so shall I book you in?'

Mo knew he would have to do something about Paul very soon. As senior partner, Mo had the final say, but Paul, being a gobby type, always seemed to hack into discussion and get his own way. It would soon be time to terminate Paul's contract. Sally was a dream, but she wasn't a hairdresser, and there was enough work for two stylists. Where would he find a replacement?

At that very moment, Sally dashed in from the back of the shop, thrust a bulky envelope into Mo's hands, then ran out again, a handkerchief pressed to her nose and mouth.

'Excuse me.' Mo went into the store room. He opened the package, dropped its contents, picked up an item from the floor. A grin spread itself across his face as he stared down at the article resting on his palm. With no thought for anything but the matter that was literally in hand, he dashed upstairs, where he found Sally in near-hysterics. 'Calm down,' he begged. 'Come on, you're doing yourself no good. This is wonderful news, so kindly treat it as such, madam.' He placed the positive pregnancy test on the coffee table.

Sally continued to weep. 'But they'll find out. And they'll think we're both horrible people, that you're bisexual or something. You shouldn't have listened to Paul, and I shouldn't have listened to either of you.'

Mo laughed. 'We come clean. You're pregnant, I'm the father – oh, and I happen to be your husband. What's to worry about?'

'The lie we've all lived,' she sobbed. 'Pretending I'm the lodger, while it's really him. Carrying on as if you were gay just to get more customers.'

He sat next to her on the sofa, a hand across her shoulders. It had seemed a fairly good idea at the time. Gay hairdressers did well, and he and Paul were certainly partners on the entertainment front. People had assumed that they were a couple in their private life as well, and no one had bothered to put them right. The fact was that Paul had the small bedroom, while Mo and Sally slept in the larger room. 'I'll sort it out, love,' he said.

'Then there's all my manicuring and waxing – how am I going to manage Indian head massage when my belly's halfway across the road? And he'll have to go.'

She meant Paul, of course. Mo agreed, and not just because of his partner's vicious tongue. Paul was vying for joint ownership. And, worse still, he came on to Mo in front of customers, clearly enjoying himself by displaying affection and a closeness that did not truly exist – or, if it did, that travelled in one direction only.

'He's in love with you,' Sally added.

Mo suspected that she was right. 'Can I leave you for ten minutes?' he asked.

Sally nodded. 'I'm turning the stopwatch on,' she warned.

Mo dashed through the shop like a cat with its tail on fire. Paul, who was up to his ears in Mo's customers as well as his own, failed to stop him.

Mo arrived in Lily's shop. 'Every flower you have,' he

gasped. 'No, I'll have to be sensible. Just loads of flowers. We're pregnant.'

Lily closed her mouth sharply, came round the counter and guided the hairdresser to the customers' bench. 'Breathe,' she ordered.

He breathed. 'Me and Sally,' he said eventually. 'Baby.'

Lily had heard of this sort of thing. It usually involved close friends and an implement whose primary function was to baste roasting meats, but she didn't want to start asking detailed questions. 'Are you all right?' she asked after a few seconds.

He nodded. 'I'm not gay,' he advised her. 'Paul is, I'm not. Sally and I were married last year, and Paul hated it.'

'Does he love you?'

'No idea,' Mo lied. 'He loves himself, and he loves us performing our stage act, so that false closeness was allowed to become part of our other business. For a laugh, and for improved takings, I went along with it, but Sally was always in two minds.' He paused for breath. 'Women having their hair done actually like homosexuals. They don't feel challenged or judged by a gay man, you see. But I've got to tell everybody now. It's not going to be a walk in the park, Lily.'

Lily scratched her head. 'Right.'

'A notice on the window – I'm serious, honestly. A notice saying that Sally and I are married to each other and that we expect a happy event. I don't want her thinking about abortion just for the sake of the business and the drag act.' He stood up. 'Deliver flowers in abundance to my wife immediately. Are you any good at writing?'

'Calligraphy? Yes, I did a course.' It had been in another life and under a different name, but it was the truth. 'Listen. There's no need for a notice pinned to the window, lad. How many customers at present?'

He couldn't remember. His head was full of joy, trepidation and love for little Sally, who was to be a mother. 'A few.'

'More than two?'

'Six. Five, at least. She's upstairs having the screaming ab-dabs in case people start thinking I'm ambidextrous.'

'What?'

'Bisexual.'

Lily stood in front of him and held his hands tightly. 'Maurice, the only people that really matter are children. I have none, and I'm telling you now, I'd give my eye teeth for a baby. Now, you want people to know, right?'

'Yes.'

'Then go back in there and say it. The bush telegraph will spread the news for you. By midnight, there won't be a soul in the five villages who doesn't know. Let the customers do the work for you. Go in. Face him and them. Say it, then get rid of him, because you'll need that little bedroom for a nursery.'

'I'm scared, Lily.'

'Don't be. I'll be there in five minutes with the Chelsea Flower Show in a wheelbarrow. OK?'

He left. Lily stood for a while and wondered whether she had pointed him in the right direction. If the selfish Paul decided to make a scene, it might all backfire and put poor Mo in a very bad light. 'Come on,' she told herself as she started grabbing flowers. 'Colour scheme, plenty of greenery and a big smile.'

Minutes later, in Pour Les Dames, she found half a

dozen silent customers. Paul wasn't silent, though. He was ranting and raving about how he had given up his life for Mo, how he had stood by him, how Mo had cheated on him with Sally.

Lily placed the flowers on the reception desk. 'Shut up,' she shouted. 'Mo isn't gay, and he never was. He married the woman he loves last year, and you found that a bitter pill to swallow, because no one but you should be loved. You've always wanted him, and you can't have him.'

'What do you know?' he screamed. 'Bloody southerner, moving up here and telling us all what's what.'

'But she doesn't,' said a customer whose head was covered in foil wraps. 'If Mo says he's not gay, then he's not. He might be a good hairdresser and a bit camp, but he's a married man with a kiddy on board. So leave them alone.'

Paul was genuinely upset. As long as he'd had a foot in Mo's life, he'd been in with a chance. The intention to turn Maurice had been his *raison d'être* for as long as he could remember. Their drag act was the best on the circuit, while they made a formidable team when it came to hair. 'I'll move out then,' he announced, lower lip trembling. 'But I'm not quitting Pour Les Dames. If he wants rid of me, it's two verbals, then a written warning.' He flounced out of the salon. After a few seconds, he was back. 'Plus, I'm a partner. Let him put that in his pregnancy test and smoke it.' With his nose in the air, he stamped out again.

The babbling began. One woman said she'd been under the dryer since about 1947, while a second worried that her hair would be bleached silver if the wraps didn't come off. Another customer, whose hair had not yet been touched, rushed out of the shop. With any luck, the news would be spreading already, Lily hoped.

Instinct drove Lily the rest of the way. She tore off foils, rinsed hair, began to blow-dry. The woman whose life had been spent under hot air was given a basket into which she might put her rollers. It took an hour, but everyone was very pleased with the results.

'Have you done this before, love?' asked Valda Turnbull.

'Yes,' gasped Lily. 'Let me catch my breath.' She inhaled deeply for a few seconds. 'Babs is a hairdresser. I've helped her when staff let her down on odd occasions. I'm no expert, but I cope.' She smiled when the clients gave her a standing ovation. Then she remembered the flowers. 'Bugger,' she said before gathering them up in her arms. 'I don't think Mo will mind if we don't charge for your hair today. Go and drink the health of these two people and their baby. Use your hair money.' She went upstairs.

Sally was asleep in her husband's arms. Small noises from the other bedroom betrayed the fact that Paul was packing his bags.

'Customers?' asked Mo.

'All gone. I did what I could, and I didn't charge them. Paul left after I said what needed saying. The news is spreading like an oil slick in the English Channel. It'll be OK.'

Mo's eyes were wet. 'Thanks, love.'

She understood why people thought he was gay, because he was a beautiful man. He probably looked fabulous in drag. 'Babs is a hairdresser,' she told him. 'The little I know I was taught by her.'

'Specialty?'

'Babs?'

He nodded. 'Yes. We all have a favourite area – mine's cutting.'

'So's hers, Mo. But I know she loved colouring as well.'

His mind was working overtime. If Babs could get a sitter, she could take Paul's place. Paul would not leave quietly, but he might be disturbed by the sudden arrival of a third hairdresser. Mo would have a word with Babs as soon as possible.

Lily put the flowers in three vases.

'Lovely,' said Mo.

Lily left. The nice thing about her new job was the pleasure people took from receiving a bunch of flowers. There was also the joy she got when delivering. All in all, life was beginning to improve.

I don't know what they expected me to do with the shit they delivered this lunchtime. You never know who's peed or spat in it when it comes to us in isolation.

There were all sorts on my previous landing. Paedophiles, serial killers, a nurse who killed more than he saved. Should be in the nuthouse, something called Munchausen's by proxy. Bollocks. He's just another bad bugger.

Dan came to see me last week. No prison record, though I have enough on him to put him away pronto and for a long time. So now I'm thinking in here and he's thinking out there. Two heads? I know a lot more than two people who'd kill a granny for a few quid...

Four

He would come back. She knew he'd come back, because he had nowhere else to go. Staying with Philomena Gallagher? That would never last – Philly Gallagher was a Roman, all rosary beads, prayer books, choir practice and Holy Days of Obligation. As for the rest of the village – who would want a fat, balding idiot to become part of the household? Enid smiled. He'd be back, red-faced and begging, before the week was out.

He'd taken the rest of his stuff, had used bin bags because Enid hadn't allowed him to borrow the suit-cases. After his little tantrum – and even that had been quiet – he had gone about the business of leaving in silent mode, never answering a question, refusing to react whenever she had railed at him. She was all alone now. Except for Mary Turnbull, of course. Valda's mother-in-law came in on a daily basis. She cooked and did basic cleaning; best of all, she liked a good old natter. Without realizing it, Enid was in danger of becoming dependent on another Roman, albeit a lapsed one.

Enid Barker adjusted her reading glasses. The *Daily Mail* wasn't much fun these days, since she was alone in the mornings until Mary arrived, so there was no one with whom she might discuss the contents of the paper.

Philly came up to give her her breakfast, but Enid would have nothing to do with her, and stayed put in her bedroom until she had left. Let the bloody woman interfere in her son's life if she wanted to, but there would be no blessing from this quarter. As for the idea of discussing the situation with Dave's landlady – Enid would sooner eat worms on toast.

She went to sit at the window, taking her usual commanding role in the village. And that was another thing: Philly Gallagher was going around inventing FADS, which was short for St Faith's Amateur Dramatic Society, but with the word 'saint' left out. Dave had joined. Enid tried to picture him as the hero in something Shakespearean, but she failed to manage it. They'd keep him behind the scenes where he could do least damage. If they had any sense, that was. She sniffed. Catholicism and sense didn't belong in the same sentence.

Lily Latimer was still rushing back and forth across the road at least once a day. She'd bought the priest's house, so her common sense wasn't up to the mark. A great rambling place like that for just one person? Daft. Perhaps her friend and the kiddy would move in with her, though it was widely believed that Babs meant to stay in the flat above the florist's shop. Even with three potential occupants, the house would be empty.

Babs had started going out with a man. She'd been half an hour in Lancashire, and she was already on the make. The child was blonde, which fact proved that some people had good luck, as her mother was a redhead and redheads weren't everyone's cup of arsenic. God alone knew who the father was . . .

Enid shifted uncomfortably in the chair. Her own son had called her a whore, and after all she'd done for him.

There'd be no stupid shop without her, no safety net for her well-read but ill-qualified son. He knew she wouldn't sell; he knew she needed the income. He knew other things, too. Yes, she'd had male friends, yes, some of them had been generous with their money, but what had the alternative been? Give him up for adoption and work full time? Enid had been a martyr to that kid, and this was how he repaid her generosity.

It was true that she was unable to name his father, because she had enjoyed the company of several grateful friends at the time of his conception, but she had not been a prostitute. Prostitutes did it every night, sometimes during the days as well. They were dirty and careless, often had teeth missing and were forced to sell themselves cheaply. She had brought her friends home and had never worked the streets.

A whore, indeed. What did he know about it? He was probably still a virgin, with no idea about life. Oh yes, he'd be back. But did she want him back? Could she stand the sight of his face etched so deeply with patience while he dealt with her needs? Did she need the company of a man who was wading through *War and Peace* for the second or third time? He believed himself to be a cut above his own mother, but he certainly wasn't. Had he been half a man, he would have done something about his appearance long before now.

The door flew inward to reveal a breathless Mary Turnbull. 'Enid,' gasped the newcomer.

'What? Get yourself in, woman. Are you ill?'

The grey head shook. 'No, love, I'm all right. But Sally Byrne isn't.'

Enid's ears pricked up. 'Why? What's up with her?

Isn't she the one who does hands, feet and whoops-a-daisies in the hairdressers'?'

'Aye.' Mary was still struggling to regain a degree of composure. She wasn't completely sure about the 'whoops-a-daisies', but she had a vague idea that it might be a euphemism for bikini waxing. 'Pregnant.'

'And?' The pregnancy of an unwed woman was normal in the twenty-first century; had been unremarkable for years.

'The dad is the one they call Mo. Maurice Jones.'

'Eh?'

Mary sat down. 'I've got some yellow fish and eggs for our dinner. Nice bit of haddock with a poached egg—'

'Never mind that. Isn't he queer?'

Mary shrugged her shoulders. 'Hard to tell these days. Some of them swing both ways, some are what they call gay, but they still have babies.'

Enid had read about this kind of carry-on in the newspapers. 'Should be ashamed,' she pronounced.

Mary said nothing. She'd heard something of Enid's past, so she had to be careful not to go too far.

'They use like a syringe thingy, don't they?' Enid went on. 'I suppose they look at photos of naked men, then bingo – here come the kids. They must put it in a cup or something like—'

'Oh, stop it,' said Mary. 'Or I'll never be able to have coffee in that place again when I go to get my hair done. Anyway, there's more to it. Pin your lug'oles back, kid.' She went on to tell the full tale. 'You see,' she concluded, 'with you being sat up here like this, you see it all, but you hear nowt. Time you had another go at being outside, love. I'll help you if you like.'

'I'm all right where I am, ta.' Still, perhaps Mary had a point.

'There's more,' continued Enid's new companion. 'That florist.'

'Oh aye? Her with the pretty face that manages to look like a smacked bum?'

'That's the one. Buying St Faith's presbytery—'

'I knew that.'

Mary smiled knowingly. 'Yes, but I bet you never knew that Father Walsh will be living there and all.'

Enid's jaw dropped. 'With her?'

'Yup. He's got a church house in one of the other villages, but he'll be handy for St Faith's when he needs to be if he sleeps here part of the week. Now.' She looked from side to side as if half expecting to be overheard by some invisible presence. 'I heard Valda talking to our Tom. She said the priest looks at Lily Latimer in a funny way.'

'Funny? What sort of funny?'

'Not funny ha-ha for a kick-off. More like funny isn't-she-gorgeous. And she gives him free altar flowers. And they sit talking in the back garden for hours on end. And he's going very easy on penances. If you go to confession, he'll give you five Hail Marys, not a sign of an Our Father. You could go in and say you'd set fire to the village, but you'd get just the same penance. He's not listening.'

That had been a lot of ands. 'How do you know?'

Mary snorted. 'Not first-hand, that's for sure. I've not been near since 1992, but I know folk who do go. Like my daughter-in-law.'

'What are you thinking?'

The visitor snorted again. 'Pretty young woman,

handsome young man. He might be a priest, but he's still human. They often had live-in housekeepers in the old days, but they were always ancient and ugly. She's not old, is she?'

'She's not, Mary.' There was a lot happening, and binoculars weren't enough. 'Get me that catalogue,' ordered Enid. 'I want a lightweight wheelchair if you're willing to push.'

'Course I will.' Mary fetched the catalogue, then set the kettle to boil for elevenses. 'With a wheelchair, you can sit on the village green and hear all the news. And we can do the shopping together, go down to the next block and buy your meat and veg. If we ever get that supermarket, you'll be able to go inside, up and down the aisles – they have special trolleys for the disabled.'

But Enid wasn't listening. Sally Byrne and Maurice Jones were down below. They were hugging each other. 'Come and look at this, Mary,' she called.

Mary joined her new-found friend. 'Enid?'

'What?'

'Makes no sense, me going home. I can't be doing with Valda, you know. We get on great, thee and me, eh? And there's Dave's empty room. What do you say?'

Enid nodded thoughtfully. With Mary in residence, she'd get her meals on time, wouldn't have to wait for Philly Gallagher, wouldn't be alone. As for Dave – if he wanted to come back, there'd be no room for him. 'If you like,' she replied. 'Move in when you're ready.'

Mary Turnbull relaxed. She would be away from her daughter-in-law, but near enough to see her grand-children. This place would suit her down to the ground, because the ground floor was the Reading Room, and that was a good place to hear gossip. And Enid and she were like peas in a pod: both interested in what went on in Eagleton.

She opened a box of biscuits. The future certainly looked brighter.

Paul Smith was not in the best of moods. He had loved Maurice Jones for years, and had tried to hide his feelings, but his emotions seemed to have become swamped by absolute fury since Sally's pregnancy had been revealed. Life had changed, and the changes were certainly not for the better.

For a start, there was the business of finding somewhere to live. A guest house in Edgworth was all very well for now, but it wasn't the same as having his own kitchen and bathroom. Yes, he had shared those amenities with two other people, but he had been able to eat what he wanted, when he wanted and where he wanted.

At the house known as Cherrymead, breakfast, lunch, tea and supper were served at certain times and in the dining room. There was some leeway, but not enough for a man who sometimes worked late or started the day early. He had to find a flat, so he decided to have a word with Chas Boswell. Chas was a decent sort who made no judgements about people's lifestyles, and he might have a suggestion for Paul. With fingers crossed, the ex-lodger from 9 Fullers Walk made his way up the stairs into Chas's living area.

'What the hell happened?' Chas asked in his usual direct manner. 'That's a bloody good business you and Mo have.'

Paul sat down. 'Not for much longer – I can't work in that kind of atmosphere. He married her last year, didn't he? But we said nothing, because people had always seen me and Mo as a couple. Sally went along with it, but she made fun of me a lot, and Mo – well, he's always known I loved him. But what do I matter, eh? I'm just one half of a drag act and the gifted half of a salon. What the hell do I have to offer apart from my genius?'

There was a bitchiness in Paul that Eve had noticed when he'd done her hair. He was clearly a bitter man, but Chas remained as impartial as he could. He'd learned long ago about the frailties and faults in human nature, so he wasn't going to start acting differently now. 'Right. What can I do for you, lad? I can see you're not what we might call happy.'

'I was thinking about the empty shop, Chas.'

'And?'

'I could set up my own business.'

Chas sat down in the other armchair. 'Look, Paul. With the best will in the world, I can't have two hairdressers on one parade – it couldn't possibly work. You'd have number three at daggers drawn with number nine, and you'd all suffer.'

'I wouldn't be a hairdresser.' Paul paused for a moment. 'Actually, I would, but I'd offer a mobile service to folk who want their hair done at home – people who are disabled or have kids and can't get out. A beautician, I'd be, because I can do false nails, hair extensions, facials – all kinds of things. If he thinks he's put a stop to me, he's bloody wrong, Chas. Nice big purple van, I'll have. Red lips on each side, name of the business will be Impressions. I'm not finished, nowhere near. Anyway, there you have it as far as the shop is concerned. It could be either fish and chips or a bakery, and nothing to do with me. Some shopkeepers prefer a lock-up and won't want the flat.'

'Oh. Right.' Chas wondered how Fullers Walk would react to the stench of chip fat, though he was prepared to listen. 'So why is it either or, mate?'

Paul shrugged. 'I've a friend who's a baker, another who wants to set up a chippy. He was brought up dipped in batter – family business. His dad would probably put up money for fittings, so that shouldn't be a problem. Would we be allowed a chip shop here?'

'I don't see why not,' said Chas. 'But I reckon a bakery would do better. Would the cooking be done on the premises? I'd have to get the fire advice people out to check if we're having ovens or deep fryers.'

'No. My friend's dad has a few shops dotted about, and he told Joey he could find another one if he wanted to. As long as it's in a good place, his dad will do the baking at the unit in Bolton and deliver stock to Joey's shop. Joey's OK. He's honest. I might be a partner whether it's chips or cakes. And Mo will just have to buy me out.'

Chas liked Mo. 'So Mo's going to be short of a hairdresser?'

Paul raised his shoulders for a second. 'He told me to get out, and I've got out. He'll not find another like me in a hurry, and that's for sure. I'm not stopping there, Chas. He knows I love him, but I realize now there's definitely no chance for me. I thought ... well, I always hoped he'd come to his senses and pick me over her, but it seems he's not gay after all.'

Chas didn't know what to say, so he stuck to business. 'Look. Let me make this a bit easier for you. You don't have to be a partner in any shop next door. If you can find somebody who wants number three as a lock-up, I can separate the two issues – you rent the flat, and the other person rents the shop. For a kick-off, there's this purple van you're on about. That's not going to come cheap even if you get it second-hand. You'll need some kind of storage system for your hair stuff, manicures, false nails – all that palaver.'

Paul nodded. 'Yes, and I don't use cheap products. But just think – with a wedding, I could do a demo a few weeks earlier, get all the ladies together with a few glasses of wine – one wedding could make a bomb on the grooming front.' He counted on his fingers. 'Bride, her mother, groom's mother, bridesmaids, anyone else who wants to look good . . .' He would show Mo Jones, by God he would.

'Don't get carried away yet,' Chas advised. 'And are you sure you want to punish yourself by living so close to Mo?'

Paul had no intention of punishing himself. His intention was to undercut prices, to leaflet the new estates and to preclude Mo when it came to picking up new business. The bridal idea would be his exclusively, and Mo would come to realize after a while that Paul was the true star of the show.

'What about the drag act?' Chas was asking now.

'He can drag off,' replied Paul tersely. 'He can manage without me.'

'And *Britain's Got Talent*?' Chas knew that Paul wanted to be recognized, wanted that spot on TV. 'You'd be good together.'

'No chance,' Paul snapped, standing up. 'That's all over and done with. I'll get back to you, Chas, when I've spoken to Joey and his dad. The sooner I get out of that guest house the better.'

'You'll need other stuff as well as the van,' the landlord reminded him. 'The flats are all let unfurnished, as you know.'

'Mo will buy me out,' came the answer. 'And he'll be sorry.'

Chas was sitting alone with his thoughts when Eve came in. She studied him for a moment. 'Is this you thinking and brooding? Well, forget it, because we're buying that house even if it's falling down. Don't start coming over all I'm-not-sure.'

Chas looked at her. 'I don't like what's going on, Eve. Paul wants to move next door.'

'Gay Paul? Moving to number three?'

Chas nodded.

'Bloody hell. So the partnership is definitely dissolved, eh? I mean, he must have known he had no chance with Mo. We thought Sally was the lodger in the small bedroom, but they fooled us all. Did he really believe he could turn Mo gay?'

'Love's blind,' said Chas.

'That's what I keep telling myself whenever I look at you,' she said, her eyes laughing. 'But seriously, Paul has to be centre stage. He's always thought he was God's gift to Pour Les Dames and that Mo was there just to make up the numbers. As for poor Sally – how must she have felt with everybody thinking her husband was gay? They say they did it for the sake of the business, but Paul must have twisted Mo's arm.'

'Right up his back,' muttered Chas. 'Oh God, Eve – I told him he could go ahead. What have I done?'

'Not much. Just started a turf war, that's all. Never mind. We'll just buy bullet-proof vests, eh?'

Dave Barker and Philomena Gallagher had more in common than either had expected. They enjoyed reading, crosswords, jigsaw puzzles, gardening and some television programmes. Most of all, both liked to cook and eat. While Philly was not slim, she was by no means obese, yet they studied together determinedly in order to come up with an eating plan that would benefit both without leaving stomachs feeling hollow. The idea arose out of Dave's sudden decision to lose his spare tyre, though Philly was only too pleased to try to lose a few pounds of her own. They raided the Reading Room for books on the subject, discussed likes and dislikes, arrived at compromises and one or two split decisions.

Their routine established itself without any real effort. Both rose early and, since Dave no longer had to look after Enid, they went to the shop together. Breakfast was taken in the Reading Room, then Philly prepared the day's snacks while Dave sorted newspapers. He vacuumed, she dusted. He ordered books, she checked till receipts. Like a well-oiled machine, they ran the business and their home life in perfect harmony. It was as if they had always been together, as each seemed to be aware of the other's unspoken requirements.

Dave was so blissfully happy that he waited for it all to end, because life so far hadn't been like this. If he'd enjoyed school, his mother always spoiled the day for him as soon as he arrived home. If someone called and asked him out to play, she would say he was too busy. He would never be able to count the times when Enid had stopped him reading, when she had torn a book from his hands and thrown it into the fire, when she had screamed at him because reading was for lazy people.

Philly, too, was happy. She had someone to talk to, someone to cook for, someone who liked to cook for her. There was no embarrassment, because they made room for each other. It was almost as if they followed some unwritten timetable regarding the bathroom, as they seldom clashed. The job she had always loved now stretched across the full day, though she sometimes went home for a rest at lunchtime. Despite the fact that she begged him repeatedly to do the same in turn, Dave seldom left the shop. He was happy among books, was keen to order and obtain for customers even the most remote of subjects and titles. Philly admired him greatly, because he was a dedicated man.

The Reading Room continued as busy as ever, though the heat meant that a couple of tables were set outside the shop, and people sat there quite happily with newspapers, books and magazines, most of which had been purchased inside. Dave, always with an eye to business, turned blind when the occasional customer arrived with a book obtained elsewhere. Such items were often exchanged, but Dave maintained his silence. Like Chas Boswell, his knowledge of human nature stretched beyond the breaking of small rules. As long as his business survived, Dave would fail to notice the odd sin or two.

The arrival of the new computer was much appreciated, particularly by the older clientele. Youngsters came to help, and many Eagletonians were suddenly in touch with relatives all over the globe. 'I made the right decision,' Dave whispered to his assistant one sunny afternoon. Screams of glee had spilled out all over the place when an old man had finally contacted a nephew in New Zealand. 'Life gets better, Philly.' Since his mother's exit from the lower floor, Dave's shop had become the chief meeting place for folk of all ages. At last, he felt that his life might just be a success after all. 'Yes, Philly, it gets better.'

'It does,' she replied, though she realized immediately that she had spoken too soon.

When the car hit the dog, Dave was sitting outside while Philly, who was learning how to use Microsoft Word, lingered in the back of the shop until all hell broke loose. She ran out quickly, overturning a stack of newly arrived novels in her haste. Dave had picked up the animal and was beginning to run towards the vet's house across the way. She joined him, noticing that his shirt was soaked in blood, and that the dog's tongue hung out of the side of its mouth. 'I'm coming with you,' she told her employer. Then she looked over her shoulder. 'Look after the shop,' she told no one in particular. One of the dog's hind legs looked crushed. A trickle of blood escaped from between strong white teeth.

It was a long afternoon. Philly and Dave sat together in the vet's waiting room. They scarcely noticed that they were holding hands, as both found themselves near to tears. Dave had always loved dogs, though he had never been allowed to have one. Philly, too, was a lover of animals. The reason for not having a dog of her own was a simple one – she went to work, and dogs liked company. 'It has to live,' she said repeatedly. It wasn't an old dog; wasn't ready to shuffle off just yet.

At last, Tim Mellor came through from the treatment room. 'I had to amputate the left rear leg,' he told them sadly. 'It was too mangled to save. Monitors appear to be saying I've stopped all internal bleeding, but it's still a waiting game. She isn't chipped.'

'What?' asked Dave.

'I have a little machine that tells me whether the dog has a microchip in a shoulder – it's a sign of a caring owner. There isn't a chip. She's about two years old, mostly Labrador, and she's a fighter. I'll have to keep her here for a day or two, but if we don't find the owner I won't get paid. That's a risk a vet has to take from time to time.'

Philly and Dave looked at each other. 'We'll have her,' they said in unison. 'I'll pay,' Dave added.

The vet smiled. 'Do you realize what you'd be taking on? Labs eat anything and everything. They're dedicated thieves and good at their job. On the plus side, a bitch is very faithful, and a Labrador bitch is the best animal on earth. She'll love you unconditionally for her whole life.'

Philly sniffed back a tear. 'And the leg?'

'She'll manage. If arthritis sets in later on, we fit her with wheels. While she's young, she'll hop along quite happily. They accept the loss of a limb and take it in their stride – excuse the pun. Now.' He sat at the desk. 'I have to try to find the owner, since I am legally obliged to do that. But I have to say I hope you don't lose her to someone who didn't care enough to have her chipped.' He smiled. 'If you pay, it'll be five hundred. For anyone else, it's double.' He liked these people, had always liked them. If anyone deserved the love of a Lab, it was Dave from the Reading Room. 'Go home. Any change in her condition, and I'll let you know right away. I promise.'

They returned to the shop. A grizzled old man gave them their takings, apologized for not being able to use the till, and asked about the dog.

'She's fighting and doing well,' Philly told him. 'When she's better, if no one claims her, she'll live at my house. But she's lost a leg.'

The old man tutted. 'It was Derek Boswell who knocked her down – he's gone home in bits. I'll let him know on the way past that she looks as if she might pull through. Nice lad for a Scouser.'

Alone in the shop, Dave and Philly had coffee laced with brandy. 'We can't do anything,' she moaned. 'I wish I could have stayed with her. She needs to know someone wants her alive.'

Dave patted her hand. 'You think Tim Mellor'll leave her? I've known him stop with a pet rat until he was sure he'd won. It'll be all right, love. And we'll have a grand dog. Pity we can't call her Cassidy after Hopalong Cassidy. Babs's daughter's Cassie, so we need another name.'

'Skippy?' suggested Philly.

'The bush kangaroo? Excellent. Let's drink to that.'

Neither realized that love was claiming them, that the accident with the dog had sealed their fate. They were just two good friends drinking coffee together. Weren't they?

Paul made sure that the salon was busy before he came to claim his property. He banged about in the room behind the shop, throwing things into boxes and bags, enjoying every moment of his self-indulgent tantrum.

'Don't worry,' Mo advised Paul's customers. 'I'll see to all of you, and there'll be another stylist here as soon as poss.'

Sally apologized to a woman whose head she was massaging, then took herself off behind the scenes.

'You're behaving like a child,' she told Paul. 'Stop stamping about and try behaving like an adult for a change.'

With a hand on his hip, he stood still and looked her up and down. 'Are you sure you know where he's been?' he asked loudly. 'I think he swings both ways, love. Best get yourself a blood test, make sure you're not HIV positive. Be on the safe side.' The silence from the salon was total.

She crossed the small space between them and swiped him across the face with the flat of her hand. 'He's a dozen times the man you are, you big stupid girl. You're not needed and you won't be missed. Someone is being trained as we speak – well, as we quarrel.'

Mo dashed in. 'You all right?' he asked his wife.

Sally laughed, though the sound was hollow. 'I've taken on bigger women than this one, Mo. He's a mean-spirited, nasty bit of near-human dross.' She addressed the culprit again. 'Get out,' she roared. 'Clear off before I really lose my rag.'

Paul straightened his spine. 'I'll be living at number three,' he said menacingly. 'And plenty of my customers will want their hair done at home, because I have always been the better stylist.' He turned to Mo. 'Without me, you'd be nowhere. I want my investment back.'

Mo reached into the pocket of his white overall and passed a cheque and a sheet of paper to Paul. 'There you are – every penny and with interest. Sign here.'

Paul obeyed silently, then threw the signed document at Mo's feet. 'Traitor,' he hissed.

Mo smiled coldly. 'I've heard on the grapevine that Mr Clegg doesn't want a shop here. Joey's looking over a place in Bromley Cross as an outlet for his bakery. Unless your chip fryer turns up trumps, there's a good chance that Tim Mellor will take the shop unit and the flat. He'll use the upstairs as business premises, because he wants to use his house as a home – number three would suit him down to the ground.'

'And up to the flat,' Sally added. 'Storage, operating rooms, waiting areas – he's very keen. It's a good place for a vet.'

Paul's jaw dropped. He snapped it back into its rightful place, then left the premises by the rear door.

Mo looked at his tearful wife. 'Come on, love. You know you've always said that massage is good for the giver as well as for the receiver.' He led her back into the shop. 'As you were,' he told his silent customers. 'Show's over.'

But the show had moved to the off-licence. 'Is it true?' Paul asked Chas, who was standing behind safety glass.

'Is what true?'

'That Tim Mellor is after number three?'

Chas cleared his throat. 'Well, if it's not going to be your bakery or your chip shop, he'll be having it. I hear Clegg's not interested, so where do you stand on the fish-and-chip front?'

Paul felt his shoulders sagging. 'They don't want it,' he said reluctantly. 'So can I still have the flat while you find someone who needs a lock-up?'

Chas shook his head. 'It's stood empty ever since Greenhalgh's closed down. I'm losing rent, Paul. And I'd rather let it all to one person whether they live in or not. The vet needs all the space. It was only as a favour that I said you could rent the flat if you found someone for downstairs.'

'And I can't open as a hairdresser?'

'No.'

'Since when has Tim Mellor been interested?'

'No idea. You'd have to ask him.'

Nothing loath, Paul crossed the road and knocked on the vet's door. He pleaded for the flat, then for a room in the flat, but was turned down straight away. 'Why?' he asked.

'Because there will be someone living upstairs, and that someone will be caring for sick animals while I reclaim my home. The second bedroom at number three will be for storage. There's no room for you.'

Paul thought about the job. 'I could do it. I'd be there every night to keep an eye on things.'

The vet was not going to be fooled. He didn't like this man, didn't expect him to have feelings for animals or for his fellow humans. 'No,' he replied firmly. 'The person living in will be a qualified veterinary nurse. Sorry.'

Paul found himself standing at the wrong side of a closed door. He was furious and had to force himself not to kick the gate as he stormed out. There was definitely a plot on. Well. There was only one thing to do, and that was to advertise for lodgings. Someone in one of the villages would take him in. The property would have to provide parking for his Impressions van, but there must be someone somewhere who wanted a clean, tidy lodger.

Back at Pour Les Dames, he sneaked in the back way and continued to pack up his belongings. No longer in a position of power, he had lost the urge to make a point through noise. There was a lump in his throat. He had given his all to this shop and his heart to Maurice Jones. There had been a suggestion that the place should be called Alias Smith and Jones, but Mo had insisted on the French rubbish.

Depleted and deflated, he left quietly and packed his property in his old van. It wasn't over. It was never over till the fat lady sang, and from now on Mo would be singing alone. Paul would miss the drag shows, but he had to admit that his partner had been the stronger performer. But Paul had been the mover and shaker, the power behind the act. He had not been appreciated, and that was why he felt so injured.

It wasn't fair. None of it was fair. But he would find a way to get even. If it took him years, he would bloody well show them all.

The dog went home with Philly and Dave, her new would-be owners. No one had responded to advertisements and flyers, so Skippy was theirs by default, though for a while they were concerned in case the neglectful owner turned up and tried to claim her. Derek Boswell came to visit several times. He was terribly upset at first, but he was finally convinced by Dave that there was little he might have done, because Skippy had come from nowhere, and all the witnesses sitting outside the Reading Room had verified that fact.

According to her new family, the dog had really come from heaven. They doted on her, used a towel as a sling to help her walk until all the stitches had been removed, fed her on the best cuts of meat and spoiled her thoroughly. She adapted quickly, and was soon chasing a ball up and down the back garden of Philly's cottage. A natural lunatic, she was even funnier without her fourth leg, and many a happy hour was spent laughing at her antics.

The pair sat with Derek and watched her as she adjusted to life on three legs. 'She's a tripod,' said Dave.

'Though I doubt she'd stay still long enough to be any use as a camera stand. Hey – Derek?'

'What?'

'The vet said Labradors are special. You could put two hundred dogs in a field, and the Labs would find each other. They aren't like most dogs.'

'Canadian wolves,' Derek told them. 'Trained themselves to bring in fishermen's nets, got fed by the fishermen, got tame. They volunteered. Supposed to be sensible, but this one looks daft enough to me.' He stood up. 'I looked Labs up on the Internet after the accident. If I ever have a dog, it'll be one of these. Oh, and thanks. I'd never have lived with myself if you hadn't let me pay the vet.'

'Are you going?' Philly asked.

But Derek lingered, his face colouring as he asked, 'How's that florist getting on?'

Philly frowned slightly. Here was another one who was interested in the newcomer. The vet had asked after her, this young accountant was clearly interested, while the parish priest, sworn to celibacy, came over rather strange whenever Lily Latimer was in view. 'She's all right,' she answered. 'Buying the presbytery – aren't your parents buying the cottage at the other side of the church?'

'Yes. Anyway, thanks again for letting me pay. It makes me feel … not better, but more satisfied with myself.'

'We know,' said Philly. He was a decent chap who seemed to care about what his car had done to the animal. 'See you later, Derek.'

The gate closed. Like a long-married couple, Philly

and Dave sat until the sun began to sink. 'Am I cooking or are you?' Dave asked.

'Your turn. Spaghetti, I think you said. Use the wholemeal – that's better for us than the usual stuff.' She could scarcely remember life before Dave. He was like a longed-for drink of water that had been presented to her after weeks in the Sahara. 'We'll try to finish that jigsaw later, if you like.'

Dave stopped in his tracks. 'The five-thousand-piecer?'

'Yes. Why?'

'Because there're about eight bits missing. Skippy ate them.' He went indoors to prepare supper.

Philly sat for a while with Skippy, who lay on a blanket next to the chair. In this moment, woman and beast were truly content. 'I can't imagine life without you and your dad,' she said absently. After delivering the words, they seemed to echo in her brain for several seconds until she noticed them. Happiness was not something she had expected or sought, but it was wonderful. She was a Catholic, while he used to be a Methodist. Did any of it matter?

The house was finally hers. Lily started painting, carrying swatches of material into various rooms, buying bits and pieces for the kitchen. She felt like a child who had been given free rein with blank paper, because this place was hers and only hers. Onto a blank canvas, she could paint her own life – her own future. Nothing could be done about the past, but her house would be another bandage for wounds that should begin to heal, in part at least.

Because it had been a home for priests, there had not

been a great deal of attention paid to decor and furniture. Everything was basic, adequate and terribly plain, so she decided to go mad with colour. With the same neutral carpet throughout the whole house, she achieved continuity at floor level, then brought into various equations a portfolio she had used years ago, when she had been something else and someone else. Having kept up with trends, Lily knew what was in, what was out, what was for ever.

Babs was delighted to join in. She left Cassie with Philly, Dave and their three-legged friend so that she could come across in the early evenings and splash a bit of paint about. The splashing had to be minimal, though, because although the new carpets were covered in film used by professional decorators, paint was an item that had to be tamed.

'What do you think of the red?' Lily asked. She was standing in the dining room, scarf tied around her hair, a large blob of paint on her right cheek.

'Suits you,' declared Babs, dabbing ineffectually at her friend's red face. 'And I love that huge black flower on the white paper.' This was Lily's true forte. She could probably have thrown a few stones on the floor and still made the place look fabulous. 'Curtains?' Babs asked.

'Muslin floating in the breeze when the French window's open. I'll get thicker ones for the winter. No double glazing, because to destroy these windows would be a capital offence. Reclaimed wood for the table, chairs with full, padded backs, black and white crockery, chandelier low over the table.'

'Sideboard?'

'Will be just that – a board to the side – reclaimed wood again. Just a long table on which to place dishes and so forth. I'll store everything in the kitchen – it's big enough.'

'Will you be giving dinner parties?'

Lily shrugged. 'Perhaps.' She knew only that she was enjoying doing a job she had loved for years, a hobby she could now pursue exclusively behind closed doors. There would be no photographs in magazines, no interviews, no TV people asking her to help with a makeover programme. All her talent must be hidden in here, so she was making the most of it. 'We're losing daylight,' she advised her companion. 'Time to tidy up and go home.' She didn't want to go, but she couldn't stay here yet, because she was waiting for her bed. It was to have a circular wrought-metal headpiece that would emphasize the window against which she planned to place it.

'Hello? Can I come in?'

Babs noticed the slight flush on her friend's unpainted cheek. There was something going on here, because Father Walsh's face was similarly stained when he entered the dining room. 'My goodness,' he said when he saw the paint. 'What are you making here? A bordello?'

'He knows nothing about decor,' said Lily in a deliberately sad tone. 'Such a sheltered life these men of God lead.'

'But red?' he asked.

'This is to be the room for flagellation,' Lily told him. 'We have enough space to cater for the needs of most men.'

She was laughing at him. Inside, where it hid its face, her humour was planning to escape from prison. 'Oh dear,' he responded mournfully. 'Shall I look for lodgings elsewhere?'

Lily wanted to say yes, but she couldn't. If she did answer in the affirmative, he might guess the reason for her reluctance to share a roof with him, albeit on a part-time basis. By ignoring his silly question, she was laying herself open to ... To what? He was a nice man, a good man. He had a cleft in his chin that put her in mind of Kirk Douglas, though the rest of his face was less rugged than the film star's. He still had untidy hair, the sort of hair she wanted to comb— She ordered herself to stop it. This was a priest, and nothing would happen, because nothing could happen. He could comb his own bloody hair if he wanted to look human – he was a grown man, after all.

She stared through the window. Blackbirds were making their nightly arrangements, quarrelling over who slept where and who had let the kids fly away. The scent of honeysuckle tickled her nose, and she experienced a swell of emotion when she looked out at the beginning of dusk. 'Reminds me of my grandfather's house,' she said quietly. 'He had apple trees.'

Michael heard the sadness and decided to lighten the mood. 'First meeting of FADS next week,' he announced. 'You'll do the stage for us, won't you? Lily?'

She turned slowly. 'Why?'

'Your forte,' he answered lamely.

'How do you know I'm not a budding Vanessa Redgrave?'

The priest shrugged. 'Because Redgraves don't bud – they're delivered from the womb with microphones and clapperboards. Do you want to act?'

'I don't know. When I do know, Philly will know.'

Realizing that he had been dismissed, Father Michael Walsh left the room.

'What's up?' Babs asked.

'Don't ask.'

'I have asked. What do you want me to do? Take back my words, put them on toast and have them for supper?'

Lily simply lowered her head and shook it.

'There's stuff happening, isn't there?' Babs whispered. 'He looks like a lovelorn lion – too much hair. And you're acting like a teenager waiting to be asked out for a date. It's chemistry. Like you noticed between me and Pete.'

'It can't be.'

'Cupid doesn't know the difference between priests and mere mortals. Look, you'd better tell him to stay elsewhere when he's in Eagleton.'

'Can't.'

'Can't or won't?'

'I don't know.' That, at least, was the truth.

Outside the church, Michael clutched to his chest the Holy Eucharist, the small circle of unleavened bread that incorporated the sacrifice made by Jesus for all mankind. He was taking it and Unction oils to a dying parishioner, was about to send a blessed soul back to its Maker. He patted a pocket, made sure that he had the purple stole.

She was lovely. He was smitten. This was a very dangerous world.

They found Arthur Moss hanging this morning. Sheet or something round his neck, tongue hanging out like the pendulum on a grandfather clock according to Brian Short. Clock. Time ticking away, but not much I can do about it yet. She disappeared. They both did – three of them if you count the kid.

Arthur's is one way of getting out of this place, I suppose.

Plain pine box, no mourners, one less crim to cater for. The minute they shut the door on you in a place like this, you don't exist any more. They have to feed you, keep you warm and fed and safe, but that's because they're jobsworths. The way they look at me, I know they'd kill me given half a chance.

Ho ho ho. Just watch this space. I'll find them, by Christ I will.

Five

Babs, Pete and Cassie were having a day out on the town. He was on a week's leave, and they had decided to make the most of it. The pair seemed a perfect match, but Babs, the more seriously wounded of the two, had been persuaded by Lily to take her time. 'He's a widower, yes,' Lily had said. 'And he's been through a tragic loss that resulted in his having to rear kids all by himself. Not easy. But your history is nastier. Be careful, hon. Like I said before – don't jump. It's better to walk in or out with your eyes wide open and your ears pinned back.' Lily talked a lot of sense, and that fact was sometimes annoying.

Babs was about to hand over her child to the tender mercies of Valda Turnbull. Valda had five of her own, and three of them were at school. She was a registered child-minder and an excellent mother. Little Cassie, an only child, was going to learn to interact with her peers, because Babs was returning to work with Maurice Jones. Maurice had trained under Herbert of Liverpool, a character, a hard taskmaster and a stickler for detail. Babs had much to learn, and she had decided to enjoy these last few days as a full-time mother.

A little fair had been set up on the Town Hall square:

rides for children, Punch and Judy, some jugglers and a few clowns on stilts. An old-fashioned barrel organ made a splendid noise, while a monkey in a bright red suit tumbled happily on top of the instrument. The place was bustling with people who had taken a rest from shopping in order to watch the fun and games. Babs, a people-watcher, was more interested in the crowd than in the entertainment. It was good to see so many people laughing and enjoying the sunny day.

Cassie had a wonderful time, but she began to tire after a couple of hours of enthusiastic cavorting and was fast asleep in her pushchair by four o'clock. The two adults ate sandwiches and drank tea from a flask. Sitting across from the civic buildings, Babs commented on their undeniable beauty. 'I think I love Bolton,' she remarked.

'People imagine dark satanic mills when referring to northern towns,' Pete told her. 'But Le Mans Crescent was built by factory workers during the cotton famine ages ago. It reminds me of Bath.'

Babs nodded her agreement. Bolton had been both a shock and a surprise, the former because the accent was so different from her own, and the latter because the area was extraordinarily beautiful. 'I like the moors as well,' she said. 'It's all a lot prettier than I expected. Of course, I had to get used to the way the natives talk – so did Lily. I suppose you find our accent odd.'

'Reminds me of the servant in that film – *Ladies in Lavender*. That was set in your neck of the woods.'

She remembered it well. 'Judi Dench was in it. Lily likes it – she has the DVD. Young lad nearly drowned, and he turned out to be a whiz on the violin. I cried buckets because Dame Judi played an old woman who had never been loved by a man. Sad. In her heart, she was eighteen.'

'Like you.'

She dug him in the ribs. 'I'll let you know when I'm old, my lover. I'll send you a telegram.'

Pete knew that 'my lover' didn't mean anything, yet the phrase struck his heart with a soft, warm pain. Babs and Lily might not have survived all that had befallen them in recent years. Twin monuments to the strength and power of womankind, they had relocated, had made lives for themselves and were battling memories and fears that were known only to the unfortunate few. Unfortunate? He shook his head. Terrified might have been nearer the mark.

'Why shake your head?' she asked.

'Thinking,' he replied. 'About you and Lily and Cassie.'

Babs pondered for a moment. 'Cassie knew nothing. In time, I expect she will be told. As for Lily – well, there's a lot more to her than meets the eye at present. I never in all my life met such anger, strength, kindness – she's not always been quiet. Not that I knew her, of course. Until . . .'

'Until Clive Chalmers.'

Babs nodded. 'That's the pig, yes. Though Lily loved her grandad's pigs, so I apologize to the pig world. He brought us together, you might say. She'd go mad if she knew I was talking about her. She still feels trapped, you know. She's started to peep through the bars of her prison, but she has a fair way to go yet.'

The policeman cleared his throat of a mixture of emotions. 'I'm a copper, love. I know most of it already.

The details are yours and hers. But.' He wiped his eyes to remove what might have been perspiration, might have been a couple of tears. 'But you're great women, both of you.'

Babs lowered her head. 'If I'm great, it's because some of her must have rubbed off on me. I've never been what you might call a bad person, but she altered me. I was having a rare old time – hairdresser during the week, mad as a hatter at weekends. Expecting Cassie stopped me drinking right off, I can tell you that for nothing. Then I met Lily. She was cross with me at first, and then–'

'Then it happened.'

She sniffed. 'Yes. I happened and he happened. The rest of it was all over the newspapers, wasn't it? When she was away, I prayed for her day and night. Not in church – I'm not the churchified kind. But anything I did, like someone's hair or a bit of cleaning, I sort of offered up as what the Catholics call penance. The harder I worked, the better were her chances of coming home. Daft.'

'She came home, though.'

Babs laughed. 'She would have come home anyway, Pete. Her survival was nothing to do with the way I handled a difficult customer or scrubbed a floor. I can't explain.' She stopped for a few seconds. 'Some people have a kind of light in them, a burning centre that doesn't always show. Like the middle of the earth – white heat. Nowadays, it's sometimes there in her eyes, like when she's doing up that rambling place she bought. I think the light is the child we all used to be. Growing up completely isn't a good idea. The Lily-child is on its way back. At least, I hope it is.'

Pete placed an arm across the back of the bench and

rested his hand on her shoulder. '"Go forever children, hand in hand." Wilfred Owen, I think. You're right. Never grow up.'

Then he kissed her lightly on the lips, not caring where he was, not worrying about the world and his wife's witnessing a police sergeant loving a woman on the Town Hall square. 'You should write poetry,' he told her.

'I already do,' she answered.

He was not surprised. Nothing she did would surprise him. For the first time in well over a decade, Sergeant Peter Haywood was in love.

'That Babs one is going to retrain as a hairdresser.' Mary Turnbull placed her shopping on the table. 'And yon chap she's hanging around with is a Sergeant Haywood with the police. Widower, or so I heard. Anyway, he seems to like Babs well enough and it looks as though she likes him.'

'Hmph.' Enid peered through her binoculars. 'Lily Latimer's looking set to move across the road any minute. She'll be rattling about like a pea on a drum, because it's big enough for a family of six or more.' She placed the binoculars on a table and looked at her new flatmate. 'Did you see him?'

Enid nodded. 'Downstairs with her and that three-legged dog. It's getting well behaved, I have to say that. It begs for food, like, and it mithers the old folk a bit. But . . . er . . .'

'But-er what?'

'They keep smiling at one another. I've noticed that a fair few times. Always smiling.'

'Him and the dog?'

'No. Him and her.'

Enid delivered another of her famous snorts. 'Who'd look at him? Can you imagine Dave with a woman?'

Mary shrugged. Dave was a bit overweight, but he wasn't ugly, and he was a lovely man. 'They've always got on,' she ventured tentatively. 'He's not a bad bloke, Enid.'

'Nor should he be. I raised him, didn't I? But he's chapel, and chapel doesn't mix with Roman. Anyway, she's no bloody oil painting either. She's not what you'd call a beauty, Philly Gallagher. Her mam was plain, and her grandma, too.'

Mary decided to shut up. Compared to Enid, Mary judged herself to be a gentle soul, though everyone knew she was capable of giving as good as she got. She'd never met anyone quite like Enid Barker. Enid seemed to hate just about every soul in the village, and her own son looked to be top of her list. 'Will I make a brew?' she asked.

'Aye. And I'll have a couple of arrowroot biscuits – they aren't too bad on my sugar. I'm bad with melegs today, have to be careful what I eat. Bloody diabetes. Type one, I am – had it nearly all my life.'

While Mary made tea, she wondered whether Enid had ever used the words please, thank you or sorry. Mary wasn't renowned for politeness, especially when it came to her opinion of her daughter-in-law, but she'd never been as nasty as Enid seemed to be. Had she done the right thing by deciding to move in here? Reluctantly, she had to believe that she had, because the grand-children were too many, too noisy and too near her bedroom in her son's house. But Enid was a big pill to swallow. She moaned all the time, and never had a good word for anybody.

They sat drinking tea. 'When's the drama kicking off?' Enid asked. 'This stupid society they're supposed to be starting.'

'In a couple of days, I think. Why?'

'You should go.'

'Me?' cried Mary. 'What the bloody hell could I do in drama? Can you see me as Lady Macbeth or the back end of a pantomime horse? I'm well past all that.'

Enid nodded. 'They want people as can sew and make costumes. Then some poor bugger has to sit at the side with the book in case they forget their lines. There's all kinds of jobs. You could keep an eye out for me. You'd hear all the latest in that school hall.'

Mary sighed. The sooner that wheelchair turned up, the better. Though Mary would have to push the damned thing, she supposed. Weren't there chairs with motors? With one of those, Enid Barker might be able to do her own spying. 'I'll go, then. But if I don't like it, I'll not go again. I don't like shoving myself in where I'm not needed.'

Something in Mary's tone told Enid to shut up, so she shut up. People were not as easily manipulated as they used to be. They didn't listen to sense any more, were no longer open to ideas or suggestions. Used to her placid son, the old woman was not pleased about having to moderate her demands. This was her flat, and Mary Turnbull should be doing as she was asked, but there was no point in over-labouring the drama society thing.

The main problem for Enid was that things just weren't the same any more. She needed her son, though she would never admit that to herself. It had been more fun with him around, because he was vulnerable. On the outside, he was a strong, stocky man, but she had been able to get to him. Even when he made no reply or pretended not to hear her, she could tell by his stance, by the back of his neck or the curl of a hand, that she was affecting him. Mary was different. She was a woman and she was stronger. More than anything, Enid wanted Dave back. He would come back. Wouldn't he?

'That cuppa all right for you, love?' Mary asked.

'Lovely.' Her flatmate would go to the initial meeting. For now, that would have to be enough. 'I wish that wheelchair would hurry up.'

Mary nodded. 'I was just thinking the same thing myself. And I wondered about them motorised ones – you'd have to keep it downstairs, but you could get anywhere you wanted with one of those.'

'We'll see,' snapped Enid. 'Now that my own son's abandoned me, I suppose I'm going to need all the help I can get.'

Mary sipped her tea. The only thing that amazed her was the fact that Dave had stayed for so long. Would she stay? Could she tolerate the drip, drip, drip of something caustic on a daily basis? Time would tell, she supposed. Meanwhile, when her tea was finished, she would go downstairs in search of more pleasant company.

Dave's clothes were hanging quite loosely. At last, he was losing weight, because Skippy needed to be walked. In spite of the loss of a limb, the young bitch loved her daily exercise. She also liked the shop and all the people who visited it, especially those who slipped her a bit of sandwich or scone on the sly. She was hard to resist when it came to looking hungry, but Tim Mellor had stressed that she must not put on weight. 'You'll be on a diet soon,' Dave advised his pet. Then he told Philly, 'I'll have to be going for some new things soon, though I don't want to spend a lot, because I'm not halfway there yet.'

She smiled to herself. She, too, was losing weight, and it was amazing, since neither of them seemed to be suffering any great pangs of hunger. 'Bolton Market,' she told him. 'Couple of shirts, a pair of trousers – you'll get by until you've lost the rest. You don't need to go mad, and I may be able to alter some of the stuff you already have.'

He chuckled. 'We're doing great, aren't we, Philly?'

'We are. Come on – Skippy wants her evening walk. We'll take her behind the church, because it looks like it's thinking about raining, so we don't want to go up into the hills.' Exercise was vital, because the young Lab ate like a horse and would soon be the size of one if care wasn't taken.

Moving as one person, they swapped slippers for shoes, put on lightweight, waterproof jackets, called the dog. She stood in front of them, tongue extended and quivering as she panted her excitement. Philly fastened lead to collar, stood straight and found herself looking into Dave Barker's eyes.

'You all right?' he asked. Her face was flushed, while frown lines between her eyes told him that something or other was afoot.

'Yes.' Of course she was all right. Or was something showing in her face – did she look guilty? She hadn't done anything, not really. Like Dave, she needed new clothes; unlike Dave, she had allowed herself to be persuaded in the direction of fashion, but he hadn't seen any of the catalogue things. And she could send them back to the company if she changed her mind. Some of the items were ... not exactly racy, but a far cry from anything she had ever bought in her whole life. She was forty-three. She was still blushing. 'Come on,' she said. 'Before it starts to rain.' Busying herself with the excited animal, she opened the door and stepped out.

They crossed the village green, each aware that the eyes of Enid Barker were boring into them. If looks could kill, Dave thought, he and his companion would be pools of grease on the path. 'She never leaves that window,' he said. 'Sitting there taking the mickey out of everybody – and that's on a good day. Mostly, she moans and curses us all. I've wondered all my life what the hell it is she gets out of hurting people – mostly me.'

'Take no notice of her,' ordered Philly. 'We're doing nothing wrong.'

Behind the presbytery, they heard banter passing from Father Walsh to Lily Latimer and back again. They were clearing part of the garden, and he was obviously the labourer, while she was acting foreman.

'If you lop any more off, it'll be a bush, not a tree,' cried the female voice. 'I'd like to see you making chips – I bet there's more peel than potato when you're let loose with a knife.'

'Rubbish,' he called. 'And if a job's worth doing–' This reply was cut short.

'You're going to fall if you don't stop playing the fool,' Lily shouted. 'Just be careful, because my insurance doesn't cover mad clergymen.'

'I am not playing the fool – I am a fool. Or I wouldn't be up here trying to be the Texas chainsaw massacre-ist.

This isn't easy, you know. The ground is very uneven just here.'

'Just don't saw the bough your ladder's leaning on,' was Lily's answer. 'You're getting more like a Buster Keaton film by the minute. Forget the Texas thing, you're definitely Keystone Cops.' A door slammed.

'Well,' muttered Dave. 'They seem to be getting on like a house afire.'

Philly was of the same opinion, though she found nothing to say on the subject. If her parish priest had decided to stray, it was none of her business, and he would have to deal with his soul via his own confessor. He and Lily Latimer would have been well suited had he not taken Holy Orders.

Skippy had spotted a rabbit and was hopping along behind the frightened animal. Philly called her name, and the dog came back immediately. Skippy was well fed, and therefore obedient.

The rain began very suddenly, pouring from a leaden sky, huge drops at first, then a steady stream that soaked them both right through to the skin. 'Waterproof?' scoffed Dave. 'Ridiculous. I'm fair witchered.'

Philly smiled. The old Lancashire word probably came from 'wet-shod', and it was certainly appropriate on this occasion. She re-fastened lead to collar, then began to run past the back of the presbytery, the graveyard and the end of Rose Cottage's garden.

When they reached home, Dave panting slightly from unusual exertion, each started to laugh at the other. Philly's hair, which had been newly coiffed and coloured at Pour Les Dames, dripped all over her face like lengths of dark, soggy string. Dave took off his jacket, opened the front door and wrung the item out in the fashion of an old washerwoman from days long gone. 'There's rain and there's rain,' he commented. 'But this rain is filled with bad intentions. God's emptying His watering can. Why does it always have to be Lancashire?'

Philly went off to dry the dog and set the kettle to boil, while Dave climbed the stairs and changed into pyjamas and dressing gown. There was no point in wearing proper clothes, as he had no plans to set foot outside on a night as determinedly bad as this one had decided to become.

When Philly had taken her turn upstairs and Dave had poured the tea, they sat in armchairs near the fireplace. Philly turned on a little halogen heater that she used in summertime when the weather turned inclement – it was not worth lighting a real fire, as she explained to her lodger.

Dave drank his tea. 'You know, Philly, this is the first time in my life that I've been happy.'

'Me too.'

The following few minutes were spent trying to avoid each other's eyes. Neither was used to announcing feelings; neither was used to having anyone who cared about those feelings. Dave washed dishes in the kitchen while Philly talked to the dog. She wanted Dave to stay for ever, and she wanted him to be more than just a lodger. That was a frightening realization. She stood up and hung wet clothes on a maiden near the heater.

He came in. 'Philly?'

'What?'

Dave sat down in his chair. It was his chair. Right from the start, each had known where to place him or herself in relation to the other. It was as if they had been together for twenty years or more. 'I don't know how to put it,' he began. He was afraid that she would throw him out, because the words he needed to use might well offend her Catholic sensitivities beyond endurance.

'Just say it,' she said. 'No matter what, just say it.'

So he did. It all tumbled out of him in a disorganized, stupid mess, possessing neither rhyme nor reason, no framework, no boundaries, no finesse. And she was fighting a smile. He couldn't be a Catholic, but they might marry mixed, and any child would be reared within her faith. He wasn't a good-looking chap, but he loved her. She might be too old to have children, anyway, and that would be all right, too. They got on well and they both loved the shop and they both loved Skippy. He'd never thought of himself as fit for marriage, and his mother hadn't helped. 'I'm certainly no Heathcliff,' he finished.

Philly nodded and tried hard not to look pleased. As well read as he was, she denounced in moments three of the greatest heroes in English literature. 'Heathcliff was a sociopath,' she said, 'and Rochester a fool. Why try to marry an innocent governess when you've a killer wife locked in the roof? As for Darcy – well, he was socially inept, ill-mannered to the point of boorishness and, if Colin Firth was anything to go by, needed a damned good wash, a haircut and a shave.'

'Right,' said Dave.

Philly stood up. 'I'm going to bed now,' she said. 'And I'll think about all this. I don't want to spoil our friendship by saying yes or no just yet. At my age, marriage is a big step.'

He understood, and he said so.

Philly ran upstairs like an eighteen-year-old. She lay on her bed and stared at the ceiling. Dave was a lovely man, one of the best people she had ever met. He was kind, generous, thoughtful and intelligent. She was happy working in his shop, was even happier sharing her home with him and Skippy. He'd looked so worried when he'd said all that – could she leave him lying awake all night and wondering what she would say, what she would do?

At just before midnight, she slipped out of bed, walked past the bathroom door and let herself into Dave's bedroom. Even in the darkness, she knew he was awake, because his breathing quickened as soon as she went in.

'Philly?' he whispered.

'Who else lives here? It would have to be me or the dog, you daft thing.'

Neither would ever be able to account for what followed. She was standing, then she was sitting, then she was in the bed beside him. There was no question about it – Philomena Gallagher was not her usual self on this occasion. She was alive, abandoned, liberated. And she cried. The weeping happened not afterwards, but during, because she realized what she had been missing for the past two decades. Sex was beautiful; sex with a man who was loved and loving was something that defied description.

They lay together in the single bed. 'I've got cramp,' announced Dave, 'but it was worth it. You've gone quiet.'

She had been extremely noisy. Fortunately, the walls were of thick stone, the woman next door was as deaf as a post, and Philly's house was an end of terrace. 'It's a sin,' she said.

'We're all born of sin, Philly.'

'Yes, so we are. And we need a bigger bed.' She kissed him on the forehead and went back to her own room.

The next morning, Dave woke with a smile on his face. He looked into Philly's bedroom, but she was not there, so he went to find her downstairs. She wasn't there, either. Skippy, too, had disappeared, so Dave assumed that Philly was doing the first of the dog's walks. He made tea, went back up to get showered and dressed, came down again to an empty house.

It was time to get to the Reading Room, because the newspapers would need sorting. He and Philly breakfasted there almost every day. On Sundays and some holy days, Dave would be alone, but this was neither Sunday nor a holy day, because she would have informed him had she needed to attend church to celebrate the life of some long-dead saint.

An uneasiness crept over him, chilling his body right through to the bone. She was ashamed, and could not look him in the eye. Desperation had driven her to have one sexual encounter in her life, and he had happened to be there when she'd needed a man – any man. The mirror told the truth. Dave Barker was not handsome. Not desirable. Where was she?

At the shop, he sorted papers and set them out on stands. Breakfast was out of the question, since his stomach seemed to have moved north and was threatening to heave. What had he done? Why hadn't he kept his bloody mouth shut, just as he had when sharing space with his mother? He couldn't go back there, wouldn't go back to the flat above the shop.

Why hadn't he been satisfied with what he'd already had at Philly's house? There had been no quarrel, no holding on to the rising tide of temper, no dread of going home. Where was she? And why hadn't she left a note? Perhaps he should have searched her bedroom to see if she had taken any clothes, but no, Philly would never leave a house that had been in her family for three generations.

The door opened, and there she was, complete with a smile and a happy dog. 'Did you get my note?' she asked.

'What note?'

'You see?' she cried. 'It's as if you're already family. I expect you to know that we always leave messages next to the clock.' She kissed him on the cheek. 'I'd better get moving. Sandwiches don't make themselves.' She went through to the Reading Room, dog and employer hot on her heels.

'Where were you?' Dave asked.

'Oh ... yes ... sorry. I had to wait for Father Walsh. There's a funeral this morning, so I knew he'd be here. Before that, I went for a walk to clear my head. Anyway, the short story is that he knows.'

Dave's spine was suddenly rigid.

'It's a sin,' she advised him. 'Though Father Walsh said – what did he say? It's not that big a deal – something like that. He'll sort it all out and marry us. After that, it won't be a sin. Oh, and I told him I was a bit old for having babies, but that any children would be raised Catholic.'

Dave dropped into a chair. 'Do you tell these priests everything? Like what you had for breakfast and what you watch on TV?'

'No.' Philly studied the man she loved. 'There's more to it, Dave. There's a lot more. You know how some folk have to go and see psychiatrists because they're not well?'

He nodded. 'Came close enough myself when I lived with...' He pointed to the ceiling.

'Sometimes, when I go into the confessional box, I haven't a lot to say. You can go through the Commandments and decide that your problems are on a different list. Little sins like wishing you had a baby or a partner or even a friend. A bit like jealousy, but not that strong. And he listens. You get a blessing and come out feeling a stone lighter.'

'So it's therapy?'

'Definitely. I didn't go into the box this morning. I told him face to face. And I could tell he was pleased for me. He went on a bit about sex not being the worst thing unless it was rape. Then he wished us happiness and told me you're one of the best men he's met in his life.'

'So we're all right?'

'Better than that, because he approves.'

Dave nodded. 'And if he hadn't?'

Philly shrugged. 'Never mind if. Open that door, because Bert and Sam will be here for breakfast and a newspaper in about two minutes. Oh – one thing, Dave Barker.'

'What's that?'

'No more shenanigans till we're married.'

'All right.' With a big fat grin on his face, Dave went to invite the day to enter his shop. Philly was very Victorian. Dave, who had studied the enigmatic queen, knew that her composed exterior had hidden a multitude of passions. No more shenanigans, indeed. Philly was the one who'd come to him in the night. In that moment, he was the happiest man on earth. For the first time ever, someone valued him.

Lily, who had received all monies from the sale of her home and the business premises in Somerset, paid off the bridging loan and took possession of the deeds to her latest acquisition. She owned the huge house, and that meant something. The pile of bricks and mortar was testament to a past that had not been wasted; it stood proud and tall in memory of Leanne Chalmers, the most successful interior designer in three or four west country counties. In part, it belonged to her grandfather, who had left a small fortune for Lily in his will. He would have approved, she thought. He would have loved that wild garden with its meanders, sundial and orchard, and the broken-down summerhouse. 'Make money work for you, Leanne.'

Leanne was not dead. It was she who dictated to Lily what must be done, she who colour-coded and themed the rooms, who chose drapes, cushions, rugs, and bartered for fireplaces reclaimed from purveyors of architectural antiques. Was this Lily's happiness? Or were she and her previous self merely papering over cracks with materials that cost an arm and both legs? 'Oh, Leanne,' she breathed on the evening of the first FADS meeting. 'Name this house for me, will you? Come on, you know you can do it.'

The name Chalmers could never come into it – didn't deserve to be used. Latimer had been her grandmother's maiden name, and she was tempted to use it as the replacement for St Faith's Presbytery, but the need not to be discovered dictated that Latimer was rendered unsuitable. She had deemed it safe to have as an adopted name for herself, but she didn't want it chipped into stone near the front door. 'You're silly,' she told herself sharply. 'You have it as a surname, but you don't want to advertise? Per-lease!'

Who knew her grandmother's maiden name, anyway? Probably no one, yet she must leave no trail, no solid evidence on which people might work in order to find her. The church was St Faith's. St Faith had been a martyr in the fifth century, or even earlier, and her death had been nasty – grilled over an open fire, then beheaded. Oh, joy. She wasn't going to use that. 'Faith, hope and charity,' Lily said aloud. 'And the greatest of these is charity.' That wouldn't do, either, or she might have every tramp in the district begging for food at the door. Charity House? No.

Hope seemed just about right. Hope House. Where there was life, there was hope, and that was another little riddle solved. 'Thanks, Leanne,' she breathed. It was almost seven o'clock. Tonight, after the meeting in the church hall, Lily would be sleeping for the first time in Hope House. The room with the circular window was ready. Excitement did battle with trepidation, and Lily forced the former to win. She would not be afraid. Fear had belonged to Leanne, who was doing a good job on the house, since her soul lived on in Lily Latimer. But this was Lily's house, and she would claim it right away.

In her best jeans and a T-shirt, she made her way for the first time to the St Faith's school hall. Unlike the church, this was partly modern, with cheap, almost pre-fabricated classrooms fastened on to the original building. Inside, every centimetre of wall was covered in posters and the work of children, bright colours clashing joyfully on walls panelled in plasterboard. It felt happy and busy, exactly as a primary school should.

The first person she met was Michael Walsh, and this time he was not attached to the supposedly less dangerous end of a motorized tree-trimmer. He wore a dark shirt, black trousers and no dog collar. His hair looked as if it had taken a walk on the wild side, so there was no improvement in that area.

'We're starting off with a pantomime,' he advised her. 'For January. That gives us plenty of time to write it, learn it and get dressed up for it. Though one of us is dressed up already.' He led her into the hall.

Maurice Jones, having heard that it was to be pantomime, had arrived to claim his place as dame. He staggered about on red high-heeled shoes wearing a terrible dress with false boobs clearly straining towards freedom, while his face was a multi-coloured mess. Topped by an incredible red wig and some huge hooped earrings in scarlet plastic, he looked marvellous.

His wife touched Lily's arm. 'I couldn't stop him,' she whispered. 'Look at the state of him – ever the exhibitionist.'

'Nor should you stop him,' said the priest. 'He's got it, so he should blooming well flaunt it. Unfortunately, there is no dame in *Cinderella*, but he can be one of the ugly sisters.'

When Mike Walsh had left them, Sally sat down with Lily at the back of the hall. 'He's nothing like a priest, is he? I thought they were dead serious miserable creatures.'

Lily shook her head. 'Not this one. But if you ever get a garden and he offers to help, say no. He tramples. He cuts shrubs back at the wrong time of year, and he rescues things like foxes and rabbits. I let him loose and am beginning to regret it.'

'He's nice, though,' remarked Sally.

'Yes, he's very nice.'

The very nice man was clearing his throat and welcoming all to FADS. The pantomime was to be *Cinderella*, and he would write it. Philomena Gallagher was in charge of meetings and money, Lily Latimer would do sets and props, others would be acting, making refreshments, selling tickets, keeping order in the hall – this was a school, so they had to leave it as they found it. Costumes needed to be sewn and fitted, strong men would be required for scene-shifting, and he would produce and direct. Next time, someone else could have the hard job of keeping everyone up to scratch.

'He's doing a lot,' said Sally quietly.

'He does,' answered Lily. 'And he's lumbered me with sets, even though I never quite agreed.'

'Is there dissent in the ranks at the back?' he called.

Sally shook her head, but Lily stood up. 'Thanks for volunteering me without my permission,' she said loudly.

'No problem,' came the reply. 'Always happy to help. You'll make a very fine job of it, Lily.'

She sat down again. There had been quite a good response to Philly's leaflets, and Lily recognized only about half of the faces. She poked Sally's arm. 'Isn't that Valda's mother? Over there, near the front.'

'It is. She's staying with Enid Barker, isn't she?'

Lily nodded. 'And God help her.'

Philly was there with Dave and the Boswells, and Babs had dragged Pete along. He was holding Cassie, who would be late to bed tonight. 'They look cosy,' Sally commented. 'Philly and Dave, I mean. Do you think there's something going on?'

'No idea.' Tim Mellor was present, as was Derek Boswell. Both had begun to buy rather a lot of flowers. Lily, whose radar was powerful, awarded no more than a glance to Dave and his landlady, because she was suddenly aware that the two men were not looking at her. The vet's eyes were temporarily fixed on the priest, while Derek's gaze was wandering about like a dog released from its lead. She could have done without this. All she needed now were complications in the form of interested males.

'She'll go mad.' Sally was whispering now.

'What? Who?'

'Mrs Barker. She can't stand Philly, because she's a devout Catholic and she can cook. Mrs Barker's cakes were designed to break teeth, and she knows we were all glad when she retired to the first floor.'

Lily looked at Philomena Gallagher and her lodger. 'You may be right,' she said. 'And if we can see it, so can Mrs Turnbull.'

'I like Dave and Philly,' said Sally. 'They're looking like a couple already. It'll be handbags at dawn.'

Michael Walsh brought the inaugural meeting to a close. 'I've nearly finished writing,' he informed the room. 'We'll meet again next week for casting. Come even if you don't want an audition, because we need a lot of help.'

Maurice stood up in his finery. 'Mike?'

'Yes, my love?'

The hairdresser waited until the ensuing laughter died. 'I'm not ugly,' he said in a very effeminate voice.

134

'People would die for looks like mine. Is it all right if I read for Cinderella?'

'Do what you like,' replied the man in charge. 'But save yourself for me, ducky. I'll meet you later behind the bike sheds. Any other business?'

Had anyone in the room still considered the parish priest to be a dry stick, they would have altered their opinion immediately. He was just a bloke with tatty hair, and he wanted to do something for the community.

Maurice hadn't finished. 'Free haircut for you, young man. It's time we tidied you up. You look like a string mop parked the wrong way up.'

The any other business part of the meeting went completely downhill after that. Lily, anxious to get out as quickly as possible, slipped through the door and into the corridor. But men have notoriously long legs, and the vet caught up with her almost immediately. 'Fancy a drink?' he asked, his tone engineered to be casual.

'No thanks, Tim. I've stuff to do at home.'

'So you've finally made the move?'

'Yes.'

'I'm moving,' he said. 'Business, not house. I'll have a nurse on stand-by in case we get something serious in, but number three will be largely work premises.'

'Right. Good luck with that.'

'Thank you.'

After bidding him good night, Lily walked home. On the long path that led to the front door, she found herself almost running. She was supposed to have stopped doing that. Her vow to have nothing whatsoever to do with men still stood. Neither Leanne nor Lily needed courtship, but there was no need to run. 'This is a safe place,' she said as she entered the house.

Inside, she leaned against the door. The building was so big, so silent. Had she done the right thing? Time would tell, she supposed – and she could sell it on if necessary. There was someone at the other side of the door. Its thickness meant that she heard nothing, yet some sixth sense warned her that she was not alone. Was Michael Walsh thinking of sleeping here tonight? Would she feel safer if he did?

The someone tapped quietly on the knocker.

'Who is it?'

'Derek. Derek Boswell. Wondered if you might come for a drink or two.'

Lily sagged against the wall. 'Not tonight, Derek.'

'Oh. OK, then. Another time, perhaps?'

She made no reply. In the kitchen, she sat at a white deal table that looked as if it had been there since the house was built. Something was missing. She closed her eyes and took herself back to the farm. Carbolic. The table had always been scrubbed with that harsh soap. Another scent she recalled was new bread in an oven. She remembered blue-rimmed enamel bowls left near the fireplace while their contents proved; the sight of her mother kneading, breaking dough and shaping loaves. Plaits, oven-bottom bread, cobs, pound loaves still hot from baking, butter dripping after it was spread.

So safe, she had been in those days. Nothing could touch any of the family, or so she had believed. Innocence. People dying, no more bread, kitchen table no longer as clean as it had always been. Cows sent to market, fields left fallow, living with an aunt, going to college, growing up, meeting him.

Her eyes flew open. How had she failed to see what was hidden behind the sparkling eyes and handsome

136

face? Suddenly, she was weeping. It wasn't an ordinary weep, wasn't just a few tears and a bit of sniffing; this was a full-blown event, loud, painful and draining. Nothing had changed since yesterday. There had been no new trauma, no earth-shattering event that had altered irrevocably the course of her life. One of the doctors had warned her about flashbacks, but she hadn't been thinking about the night when it had all gone–

'Lily?'

She almost jumped out of her skin. 'Father–'

'Mike. When I'm not in uniform, I'm Mike. Makes me feel human.' She had been breaking her heart, and she didn't need a witness. 'Do you want the keys back? You can kick me out and change the locks – I won't be offended. I'm intruding.'

The shock made her stop in her tracks. 'No. I said you could stay, and you can. I'm just ... just remembering.' She dabbed at her face.

'Can I help?'

'Of course not. You weren't there. How can you help me remember?'

'Perhaps forgetting would be better.' He sat opposite her. 'Talk to me. Did I upset you by lumbering you with the stage dressing?'

'No. Well, yes, but that isn't anything to do with ... with anything.'

'Right. Where do we stand on the cuppa front? Do I bring in my own, do I pay you, or do you drink strange herbal stuff?'

'Tetley's,' she answered. 'Just get on with it.'

While he pottered about, Lily repaired to a ground-floor bathroom in order to compose herself. The poor man was only trying to help, but he couldn't. No one could. There was just Babs. Babs would probably be spending the night in bed with Pete, because Cassie now had her own room. Lucky Babs. She had found a man who seemed solid and strong, someone who would take care of her and her little girl. Would they take Cassie away?

She splashed water on her face. Her distance from Cassie was greater than ever, because it had to be. Cassie could never be her daughter. She stared into the mirror and scarcely knew herself. The weight she had shed had not returned, and the round-cheeked Leanne was unrecognizable. There had been no need for plastic surgery, because she looked completely different. After all this time, she should have grown used to the blonde hair, but she felt she never would. She missed herself, mourned the woman she had been before ... before Clive Chalmers. Even thinking the name made her want to vomit.

'Tea,' Mike shouted.

Lily re-entered the kitchen. 'Sorry about that,' she said, her voice still shaky. 'I don't know what came over me.'

'Yes, you do. You know perfectly well, and I'm sorry to have invaded your space. Goodness knows you paid enough for this house. If you like, I will go and make other arrangements, but you must unburden yourself to someone, so why not me?'

'I don't have the answer.'

He poured tea and handed her a mug. 'Now that was Father O'Hara's very own drinking vessel. I nearly put it into the grave with him, because he went ape if anyone else used it. But he's dead, so enjoy.'

Lily stared into the mug. 'I suppose he must be dead if you buried him.'

He nodded sadly. 'Yes, but I was sorely tempted on many an occasion to have the burial before the death. He was into his eighties, deaf as a post, and I think he went to the same charm school as Adolf Hitler. I was a young priest and scared to the bones of him. Then I realized that he was actually stupid, and stupidity must be forgiven. He couldn't have been academically unsound, as a priest has to learn some difficult stuff, but he–'

'Like joined-up writing? Did you learn that?'

'Yes.'

'And pantomime?'

'All right, all right. Stopped you crying, anyway, didn't I? But he'd no common sense. He needed the simplest things doing for him, and his personal hygiene was questionable–'

'And this is his cup?'

'It's been washed.'

Lily got up from the table and brought her own mug. Mike filled it for her. 'Better now?'

'It comes and goes.' She didn't want to look at him, wished he would go into another room. 'It will be some time before I can talk sensibly. But I'll tell you now that it was serious enough for me to change my name, give up a promising career, consider cosmetic surgery and come up here.'

'And Babs?'

'Part of the same package. You don't ask her about me, either. Understood?'

'Yes. Now, I'll take myself off and think very seriously about the threat made tonight. Maurice Jones is a decent enough chap, but he should leave my hair out of things.'

'Out of your eyes would be a start.'

She was calmer. He knew that he could leave her now. Michael Walsh was a man of the world. Priesthood had not diminished him; on the contrary, it had served him well, because he now knew more about human nature than most psychiatrists ever managed to learn. His inner core was attracted to the sad female at the table. It wasn't the first time he had felt physical desire, though he had seldom experienced anything deeper. But now he was on the brink of something or other that could alter his life for ever. Falling in love? No. It wouldn't happen.

Lily washed the cups and left them to dry. She walked out into her massive garden and sat on a flagged patio just outside the dining room and kitchen. A security light turned itself on as she settled herself on a broken-down chair at a decaying table. She looked at the wilderness that was freehold and hers. It was a big undertaking, and she needed a better gardener than the one upstairs. Her heart skipped a beat when she reminded herself of his kindness, his gentle, forgiving nature, his acceptance and understanding. It was a pity that many religious figures seemed not to learn from those who toiled at the coalface of life.

The magic happened then, while she sat and surveyed her extensive domain. Unafraid of the light, they stepped out of shadow and stood staring at her – the father, the mother and the two cubs. When she rose from her seat, they did not move; when she returned with meat on a plate, they were still waiting. She placed the food at the edge of the paving stones, then went inside.

In darkness, Lily Latimer stood at her kitchen window and watched the foxes. Babies scuffled and took what the parents gave them. Never before had Lily been so close to a fox. Grandpa had shot them, because they killed chickens. She could not do that, no matter what. Nevertheless, she would keep no hens. Tears flowed again, but she was smiling through them. The fox family walked away, one of the parents stopping to look over a shoulder, as if saying thanks.

Life went on. No matter what, day became night, dawn broke the dark, evening brought longer shadows. 'Accept, just like the foxes do,' she said softly. One day, she would talk to him. One day, she would need his help.

Six

Enid Barker sat in her usual bird's eye position, turning to look over her shoulder only when her flatmate walked in. 'I missed them coming out of the meeting,' she moaned. 'The school's at a funny angle, anyway, but I had to go to the bathroom, and even with the walker melegs were all over the ... What's up with you, Mary? Have you swallowed a gobstopper or something?'

Mary sank into the armchair nearest the door. She couldn't just say nothing at all, because somebody else would say something when Enid decided to become well enough to sit listening on the stairs, and it had to be dealt with sooner rather than later. So she let it all pour out in a steady stream, her voice flattened to the point where no emotion showed. When she had finished, she closed her eyes and leaned back in her seat. It was like waiting for the wrath of God to descend upon her, and she wished that she had never gone to the flaming meeting of FADS. This business was nothing to do with her, and she regretted her change of address yet again. She'd seen Tommy and Valda, and they'd talked about building a small granny flat at the back of their house ... Enid had turned a funny colour, and her mouth was hanging wide open.

It hung open for quite a while. 'Mary?' she cried when her lips finally met each other again. 'What the bloody hell are you telling me? Hand in hand? Dave walked back to her house holding hands? With that blinking Gallagher woman of all people? And everybody watching? The whole bloody village finding out before me?'

When Mary looked properly at her companion, she noticed a further change in the colour of Enid's skin. It had turned an interesting tone bordering on pale puce, if such a shade existed. 'I could be wrong,' she said sheepishly. 'It's possible, you know.' But she knew that other villagers had commented on the new closeness between Dave and Philomena. 'Enid, I don't think I should be responsible for telling you—'

'No. You're not wrong, Mary. You weren't wrong about Valda not being good enough for your lad, and you've stuck to your guns right from the off. Give you your due, love, you're like me. You're a woman of very strong instinct. There's something going on all right.'

Mary didn't want to think of herself as being like Enid. Enid Barker might well have a degree in nasty – even a doctorate – because she did nothing but find fault with everything and everybody. 'Calm down, Enid,' she pleaded. 'No sense in making yourself ill over it, is there?' It was time to make peace with Valda, because the alternative might be to end up like this crazy harridan. She had to get out of here. Whatever the cost to her pride, Mary needed to go home to her own little room or to the extension currently under discussion. Noisy grandchildren? Stupid daughter-in-law? They were infinitely preferable to this way of so-called life.

But Enid was past the point of no return. 'Hand in hand? I'll give him hand in hand when I get hold of him.

He's had it drummed into him since he was a lad. No Roman Catholics. So what does he do? He starts walking out with a saint who's not dead yet. It must be like courting one of them daft holy pictures they carry round in their prayer books.' She shivered. 'This has got to be put a stop to. I can't let it happen, Mary. Everything in me screams that I have to do something straight away before he goes too far. Hand in bloody hand?'

Mary nodded.

'She's RC.'

Here came the bigotry again. Enid Barker seemed to enjoy repeating herself, as if she chose to underline in red ink every opinion she expressed. Mary needed to scream, wanted to tell her companion to shut up about the Catholic thing, but she dared not. 'I know.' She sighed. 'But it's the twenty-first century and folk don't seem to—'

'Too old for kids, she is. All they'll have for family is that bloody daft dog, and that's only three-quarters furnished in the leg department, never mind daft as a brush in its head.'

Mary knew that Enid was completely legless at the moment, because she had tried to stand seconds earlier and had failed miserably. She was probably in some sort of shock, yet Mary Turnbull could not quite manage to worry about her hostess. 'Shop's being run by Valda and two of the old blokes tomorrow. I heard Sam Hardcastle telling Bert Thompson that Dave and Philly are going out somewhere, probably to town.' She wondered whether they might be going to buy a ring, but she dared not air that possibility, or Enid Barker might literally have a fit.

Enid's heart, pushed along by a great surge of adrenalin, was well into overdrive. 'Get that bloody wheelchair sorted – I saw it being delivered, so I expect it's in the store room at the back of the Reading Room – and help me down them bloody stairs. Well? What are you waiting for? The three-fifteen to Manchester?'

'You're going nowhere,' replied Mary with as much determination as she could muster. 'I saw you trying to stand before you got really worked up. I'm no spring chicken, Enid. I can't get you down below while your legs aren't working. We'd both break our necks. Sorry.'

Enid managed not to scream. 'How can I stop them, then? But I'm having a stairlift put in, and I'll see if I can afford a motorized scooter or some such item. Then I won't need help from you or anybody else. But I can't get them things by tomorrow, can I? Fetch me that phone. If I can't get there in person, I can speak my mind, at least.'

Mary experienced a sudden desire to be elsewhere – preferably in the southern hemisphere. If Enid phoned Dave and Philly, they would know that she had gone back to the flat and started tittle-tattling to his mother. 'Why don't you wait till you feel a bit calmer?' she suggested.

'Because I'm not going to feel any calmer. If I let this go till morning, they'll be at Preston's of Bolton and she'll be wearing a diamond set in platinum. Philomena Gallagher's out for what she can get. I mean, look at him. Fat as a pig, does no exercise – when I'm out of the way and he drops dead, she'll get the business.'

'But it's half past nine, Enid. A bit late for a phone call–'

'Thank you, speaking clock. If I'd wanted the time, I'd have looked at my watch. Get me the phone.'

Mary brought the instrument, handed it to Enid, then walked into her own bedroom. She didn't want to hear any more, but she heard it anyway. She had a strong suspicion that Manchester might have heard it. She turned on her television, and managed not to listen to the ranting from the next room.

Philly answered the phone.

'Is my son there?'

'Yes. Just a moment, please, Mrs Barker.'

He came to the phone. 'Mother?'

'You're carrying on with that fat Catholic, are you? Going to marry somebody whose life runs according to the Roman calendar, all holy water and plaster statues, who can rob a bank on Monday and get forgiven by a priest by Friday?'

'That's right.'

Enid gritted her teeth before wading in again. 'Then you can buy me out.'

'Whatever you wish, Mother.'

Taken aback, Enid was silent for a couple of seconds. Her pension was pennies. The bit of income that floated into her bank from the shop once a month was the only bright spot in her life. A diabetic needed good food. An old woman needed good food. As she listed herself in both categories, she was twice as needful as most people. 'Are you marrying her?'

'Yes.'

'Why? Is she pregnant?'

'No.'

'What have I told you all your life, eh? We don't mix with Romans. They're not right in the head if they think a bit of bread turns into flesh. Whispering confessions to a bloke who carries on like he's big enough to talk to

God at a different level from the rest of us, carrying pictures of saints in their handbags—'

'I promise not to carry saints in my handbag, Mother. The rest of it is none of your business. Philly's a Catholic, and that's an end to it.'

'It should be the end. And where are you going to-morrow?'

'Why? Do you want to come along for the ride?'

'No, I bloody don't.'

'Birmingham,' he said.

'Birmingham? Why?'

'Jewellery quarter. Anything else? Are we playing twenty questions?'

'You can't marry her,' she screamed.

'Better that than coming back to you, Mother. Better to get married than carry on like you used to, selling yourself for a few quid shoved behind the clock on the mantelpiece. I'm grown up now. You can't whip me, can't lock me under the stairs, can't frighten me any more. You've done your worst. It's my turn now, and I am doing my best for myself and for Philly.'

'How dare you?'

'Because I am talking to an ex-whore who doesn't even know who my father was. Because Philly is a good, God-fearing woman who wants to marry the ugly son you bore. And I dare because you have pulled to bits every decent body in this village and the residents of at least another five. So bugger off. I can't be bothered with you, Mother.'

She heard the phone as he threw it into its base. Her fingers shook when she dropped her own handset. From a pocket, she took a glucose lozenge and placed it on her tongue. The shock had pushed her towards a hypo.

Dave had a lot to answer for. Then, as if presenting the last straw, Mary Turnbull emerged from her bedroom and stood near the stairway door, a suitcase in her hand. 'What ...? Where are you ...?' For once in her life, Enid ran out of words.

'I've had too much of this,' Mary announced. 'I can't do it any more, Enid. God knows I'm bad enough, but you're in a class of your own. Even my telly couldn't drown out your screaming just now. I can't be your yes-woman. Things aren't right here, so I'm going. I'll send for the bigger stuff in a day or two.'

'Who'll look after me?'

Mary lowered her chin for a second. After counting to three, she raised her head and looked Enid Barker straight in the eye. 'The devil will mind you. He's your best mate, anyway. For now, I'm off to throw myself on the mercy of your lovely son and the nice woman he's been lucky enough to find. My grandchildren will be asleep, and I don't want to disturb them, so I'll crawl back to Valda tomorrow. Because I've learned something while living here, love. I'm not as bad as I thought I was, and I am prepared to apologize. You'll never do that.' She left the flat, closing the door softly.

Enid gulped, almost choking on fizzing glucose. There was nobody here. For the first time ever, she was completely alone. She could phone Dave again, she supposed, but he'd know in a few minutes that Mary had left her, so there was no point. Who would see to her now? Who would make a cuppa when melegs got worse, sit with her when she needed company, help her when she wanted a shower? Where could she apply for help? The Catholics had it sorted, of course. There were so many of them hereabouts that Father Walsh had made a rota for the elderly and disabled, and he didn't stick just to Catholics. But Enid would die before she'd beg at his door.

Reaching out for her walker, she managed to stand. Fear made her weak. The knowledge that no one would come if she fell terrified her, but she was determined. She could walk and she would walk. Given a stairlift and a scooter with a motor, she could do anything she liked. Couldn't she?

Philly, who had clearly been crying, opened the door. Dave had shot upstairs after the call from his mother, and Philly was giving him a chance to recover. 'Hello, Mrs Turnbull,' she said. 'Come in. You look upset.'

Mary entered the cottage. 'I am upset, love, and so are you. But can I borrow your sofa for the night? Only I don't want to wake my grandchildren, you see. I don't know what sort of reception I'll get from Valda, and if there's a row when I turn up—'

'She'll be all right. Valda's a good woman. You're both good women, Mary, but you're going to have to make space for each other. And I don't mean separate living rooms – I mean inside, in your heads. If you do that, she'll be fine with you.'

'Better than what I've been living with, and that's for sure.'

Philly went into the kitchen to make Lancashire's universal cure, a cup of tea. She popped her head through the doorway and asked whether Mary would care for a biscuit. 'No thanks,' was the reply. 'I couldn't stomach anything after what's gone on. Sorry I told her. But it's all round the village anyway—'

'Don't worry. It'll be all right.'

Mary sniffed, dried her eyes and wiped her nose. 'Will Enid be all right, though? Her legs are terrible today.'

'That's our problem now. I know what she's like and I know what she thinks of me. What's had me in tears is finding out about how she's treated her son. She gave him a terrible life, and she intends to carry on doing just that. But I'll sort her out, don't you worry.'

'You?' Mary failed to keep the shock from her face. Philly was a gentle soul, far too kind to survive more than a couple of rounds with Enid Barker.

Philly nodded, and a watery smile appeared on her lips. 'I'm stronger now.' She didn't know why she was suddenly confident, though she nursed a suspicion that her new status owed something to the fact that she now considered herself a complete woman. 'We won't be here tomorrow.'

'I know.'

'So I'm going to fetch Valda now.' Philly raised her hand. 'She won't be in bed yet. The meeting finished only just over half an hour ago. Don't try to stop me, because I've made up my mind.' She left an open-mouthed Mary with a cup of tea and no company except for Skippy, who was begging for food again.

Until Dave came down. When she saw her master, the dog laid herself across the hearth rug. There were no biscuits anyway, so she might as well pretend to be obedient.

'Where's Philly gone?' Dave asked.

'For Valda.'

'That's the ticket. I'll get myself some cocoa.' He went into the kitchen.

Before he returned with his drink, Philly and Valda

150

arrived. The latter approached her mother-in-law without any hesitation. 'You're coming home,' she said. 'I know we haven't always got along, but we're going to – and that's a threat, madam. Your son loves you and wants to look after you. When we've finished the extension, you'll share our kitchen, but you'll have your own bedsit and bathroom. You'll be able to bring friends home to your own part of the house, and the kids won't come into your bit unless you say so.'

Mary burst into tears. She didn't deserve it. She'd been a bad mother, too possessive, and she'd been horrible to Valda. These statements emerged crippled by tears.

'Oh, shut up,' Valda said. 'You're coming back with me, and that's an end to it. If you start being difficult, we'll lock you in the shed with a crossword and a pot of tea. Every mother thinks no woman is good enough for her son. God alone knows what I'll be like when my kids start bringing folk home. I'll be on to Babs Cookson's policeman to ask if any of them have criminal records. Just get back to our house and stop whingeing.'

'What now?' Philly asked when she and Dave were alone.

Dave raised his shoulders and spread out his hands. 'I don't know. I've never known what to do about a mother who switched from prostitute to saint as soon as her looks went. Not a Catholic saint, mind. She'd have to be a Methodist one.'

'Are there any? I think most saints are Catholic, created by a pope.'

Dave was suddenly deep in thought. 'The problem is, we have an ageing diabetic who needs help. Everybody's sick to the back teeth with her, but the fact remains that I'm her son. As she has alienated just about everyone within a ten-mile radius, who's going to want to help her?'

Philly swallowed hard. 'I'll do it. You'll do it. We'll do it together.'

'But what—'

'Never mind that what-ing and iffing. It has to be done. Since ... since you and I got together, I've changed. I can do the water-off-a-duck's-back thing. She'll not frighten me. Now, if she's ill while we're at the shop, she can ring a bell – get an electric one fitted. If we're at home, it's only a couple of minutes away, and she has a phone.'

Relief made him smile. 'Thanks, Philly.'

'You're welcome. Now, off to bed with you. I've never been to Birmingham before. What shall I wear?'

'Clothes?'

'Ha-ha.'

'All right. Clogs and shawl, then they'll know where we come from ...'

Eve Boswell was in her element. Rose Cottage was theirs, though the mortgage was considerable – and she was going to have a party before moving in. She had invited so many people that caterers were involved, and there would be no furniture to speak of until after the cele-bration. She'd no intention of filling the house with nice stuff just for people to abuse it while drunk.

'Where will they all sit?' Chas asked.

'A sensible question for once,' Eve said. 'They can bring deckchairs, garden seats, tea chests, bean bags – three-piece suites – I don't care. They're not messing it up with booze and food after I've decorated and fur-nished. And it's a massive garden. If the weather holds, I might let you loose with a bit of charcoal and a packet of sausages. Tomato sauce, too, if you behave.'

'Gee, thanks,' was the enthusiastic reply. Chas wasn't keen on the garden. He called it the Devil's Jungle, and had been overheard on many occasions stating his determination that he wasn't going out there alone, as there might be tigers and other large beasts secreted within its depths. Whenever gardening was mentioned, he said he wanted a guide, a gun, a compass and a tent.

As far as the inside of the house was concerned, Chas quite liked the oak beams, though he expressed a desire to skim over the rough plasterwork. He survived the ensuing barrage from his wife, who accused him of planning quite deliberately to be obtuse, ignorant and downright daft, though he knew she could tell from his face that he understood the value of Rose Cottage's original features. 'Can we have some proper glass in the windows? The world out there's distorted,' was another cause for argument, so he stopped teasing her, because Eve had a swarm of bees in her bonnet when it came to history and conservation.

'That glass was hand-made in a sweatshop hundreds of years ago, probably by children.'

'No,' he contradicted her. 'The kids were all up chimneys, weren't they?' However, if he heard her yelling once more, 'It's seventeenth century, you soft lad,' he might well get a headache, so he tried not to mention draughts, bumpy walls, uneven floors and doors that didn't quite fill the gaps for which they had been constructed.

The party was to be a double celebration, because the engagement of Philomena Gallagher and Dave Barker was to be announced. Dave's mother had been invited.

She had neither accepted nor declined, but no one expected her to turn up. 'She'd put the best of us off our vols-au-vent, anyway,' said Derek.

Derek, who had taken a liking to Rose Cottage, had changed his mind about remaining in the flat over the shop, to the consternation of his father, as Chas had wanted Derek to keep an eye on things at number one. Now he would have to make do with Paul Smith, the hairdresser who had gone mobile in a big purple van. Nobody seemed to like Paul, but beggars couldn't be choosers. Chas was desperate, as was Paul, so that was an end of the matter. The importation of illicit goods for special customers might well have to cease.

The trees nearest the house were decked out in fairy lights of many colours. As the weather held, food was spread on trestle tables on a paved area outside the dining room. Philly, who had been a great help, fussed about with various covers in an effort to keep insects away. She overused her left hand, smiling when the half-carat diamond reflected light from the decorated trees.

Dave arrived by her side. 'Well?' she asked.

'Spitting bile, as usual. Going on about Valda swapping sex for clothes. And that's coming from somebody who bartered with her body until I was about ten years old. She's got this wonderfully selective memory. Her life started the day she put on a dowdy coat and walked down to the Methodist chapel. Everything before that never happened. I think she's had her hard drive surgically removed.'

Philly shook her head. 'She's not coming.' It was not a question.

'No. And when I explained to her that Tommy and Valda had always wanted a big family, and that he buys her an outfit once her pregnancy's confirmed, she shut down. She didn't shut up, though. Wanted the price of your ring and to know had we bought anything else. When I told her about the matching wedding ring, she went a funny colour. But at least poor Valda got a rest for a while.'

Philly stopped messing about with food for a few minutes. 'I think you should stay away for a week or so. Let me deal with her.'

Dave stared blankly at his fiancée for a few seconds. 'She'll eat you alive. You know how rotten she was with you when you took up her elevenses. Philly, you're too nice for her.'

She smiled. 'Am I? Watch this space, David. Just you wait. She's seventy, and I'm a stripling of only forty-three. Anyway, I'm different now.'

It was his turn to grin. 'I wonder why?'

People began to arrive in serious numbers, many in possession of fold-away chairs, large cushions, stools and, of course, the obligatory bottle. As most of the booze had been bought from Chas's shop, he decided to enjoy himself after all. Although he wasn't exactly built to specification for al fresco parties, he threw himself into the event quite literally, and was dragged out of a small pond by villagers who were finding the occasion every bit as hilarious as they had expected. Scousers were guaranteed to be amusing, and Chas was certainly up to standard.

He stood there dripping. When the laughter faded, Eve approached him with a small paper napkin. 'Dry yourself,' she ordered as she handed him the flimsy item. 'And don't forget behind your ears, you big wet nelly.'

'What's a wet nelly?' Valda asked.

'Him,' replied Eve. 'It's also yesterday's cake gone stale. It sits in the shop window, only drenched in syrup to jazz it up a bit. You serve it with custard.' She cast a disdainful eye over her beloved husband. 'Yes. Looks a lot like that,' she said before stepping away to see to her guests.

Chas walked home to change his clothes. He squelched across the road and almost collided with Babs Cookson and her policeman boyfriend. 'Oh. Hiya,' he managed. 'I fell in the pond.'

'We'd never have guessed, would we, Pete?'

'I'd have to look at the evidence and get forensics on to it.'

Chas was allergic to policemen, so he walked on. Babs shouted, 'Is Lily there yet?'

'No.'

Pete and Babs stopped at the gate to Rose Cottage. 'I'm going to have a look at her,' Babs announced. 'Sorry, but I need to know if she's OK.'

'What if she's not ready? What if she doesn't want to be in a crowd? Babs, think of what she's been through. People take different lengths of time to recover.'

'Wait there. I know what I'm doing.' The determined little woman marched off past the church to Lily's house. At the front door, she paused and waited for a while. There were voices coming from within, and she didn't know whether to listen or make a hasty retreat. The voices became clearer. 'You can't hide in here.' It was the priest.

'Mike, leave me alone. I'll come along when I'm ready.'

There followed a long pause during which Babs pinned her ear against the letter box.

'You have to talk to me.' The man's voice rose in pitch. 'Whatever has happened to you, unburden yourself and leave it all in the past where it belongs. Allow this village to keep you safe. It's that kind of place – we'll help you.'

The door was not locked. Babs walked into the house, stood with hands on hips in front of Father Walsh, and gave him both barrels. 'Listen, you,' she said, her colour heightening. 'I don't care who you are – priest, rabbi, vicar or some lunatic sitting in a nappy on top of a hill until he dies. Leave her alone. You've no idea what she's been through, no knowledge of what she suffered. Pete's a cop, and he knows enough to leave it be. If she wants to come to the party, she'll come. It's nothing to do with you, so bugger off.'

He opened his mouth to speak, thought better of it, and buggered off as ordered.

Lily sank into a chair. 'Babs, you shouldn't have done that.'

'Why? Have you not had enough browbeating from a bloke who thought he knew better than the rest? Just tell him to sod off, Lee. Pick up speed when you're ready. Stay in, or go out when you want to, not when someone pushes you.'

'It's just—'

'It's just in case somebody who saw you on TV recognizes you. You don't do crowds. If you don't do crowds, stay where you are. And there's the vet and Derek sniffing after you, so make up your own mind. Don't be listening to him just because he sometimes wears his shirt collar back to front.'

Lily shook her head. At the ripe old age of twenty-seven, Babs sometimes managed to sound like somebody's grandmother. She was wise and silly at the same time, was a good friend in spite of the inauspicious way in which the two of them had met. 'He's a nice man, Babs. He means well.'

Babs threw herself onto a stool. 'They're all after you, missus – even the priest. There's that Derek – far too young–'

'Four years,' said Lily. 'I'm twenty-eight, he's twenty-four–'

'A middle-aged vet, that man who delivers flowers, the milkman, the postman, even the priest.' She shook her head in mock-despair. 'Look, stay here if you want to. I'll get back to Pete.' She waited for a few beats of time to pass. 'I'll stop here with you if you want, my lover.'

Lily bowed her head and sighed. 'I'm tired, Babs. I've been tired ever since it happened, and I'm sick of trying to grow eyes in the back of my head.' She groaned softly. 'They've moved him to Walton jail in Liverpool.'

'Where Charlie Bronson threw all the tiles off the roof?'

'I don't know. Probably.' Lily stood up. 'Only forty-odd miles away. Sometimes, I think I can hear him breathing in the next room. His asthma often gave him away.'

'And the cops know you're here?'

Lily nodded.

'But they still . . . Where's the sense? Look what you've given up, from a job that paid a fortune to your beautiful hair. When will they learn? I'll talk to Pete about this. Something's got to be done.'

'No.' There was vehemence in Lily's tone. 'Look, I trust Pete and I know you do, but who will he talk to? Leave it, Babs. Promise me you'll do nothing. Pete can't change this – he can only make it worse by inadvertently talking to a bent cop or probation officer. Silence is best.'

Babs ran a hand through a tangle of dark auburn curls. After all their efforts to leave the past behind, it was following them. Would they have to move again?

Lily answered the unspoken question. 'No more running. We stay, and we keep quiet. All right?'

Babs nodded. 'It's Cassie I worry about.'

'Me too.'

'Are you coming to this party or not? He's not even drunk yet, but Chas Boswell's already managed to baptize himself in that ornamental pond. Lily, if you're scared, I understand. But you run a shop. People come and go in there all week, and there's easily as much danger of you getting recognized while you're behind the counter as there is at a party. A party's just all the customers coming at the same time and refusing to form an orderly queue.'

'He'll be there.'

'Who?'

'Mike. He won't let me call him Father. I can't look at him. It's as if I owe him a confession, a list of sins. He looks straight through me.'

Babs tutted her impatience. 'He's a man, babe. You are still one extraordinarily good-looking woman. Remember that chap from the telly? He was going to leave his job, his wife, his kids and his brain behind just to sit at your feet. And now that the light's started to come back in your eyes, you're giving out signals without knowing it. Pete reckons you should be in Hollywood.'

Lily shook her head. 'If I went to California, he'd find me, or get someone else to do it for me.'

'We're not talking about Father Wotsisname or Pete now?'

'Of course not. Babs, Clive's got money hidden at his mother's house. He's got friends on the outside. The planet ain't big enough.'

Babs sat for a while, then excused herself to go off and find Pete. Her babysitter, a young girl from a nearby estate, had to be home by midnight, so Babs would need to leave the celebrations relatively early. And Pete didn't deserve to be left standing for too long.

Lily stared into an empty grate. Although she was enjoying doing the work on Hope House, she could never be completely happy while Clive Chalmers lived. Everything had been spoilt or killed by him, the man in whom she had placed all trust. Forty miles away, he would be on a landing or a wing with men who, like him, had attacked the most vulnerable members of society. His companions, with whom he might never mix, would be paedophiles, child-killers and rapists. If he was still on 43, that was. Should he be moved to an ordinary wing, he'd be meeting all kinds of people who— No. She mustn't think about him employing someone to make matters worse. Lily sighed. Wormwood Scrubs had seemed far enough away, but it hadn't been. Mars might have been OK, but only just.

Why had they moved him, though? And why up here? His mother, who had been completely shocked and incredulous when he had been arrested, would have difficulty travelling to see him, and that was a shame, because she was a nice woman. Perhaps that was the reason; perhaps the authorities were moving him to a place where he would have few contacts.

But she knew him. There was an evil streak in him,

broad as a motorway, complicated as Spaghetti Junction, and he would find her. It would be by proxy, because it would have to be, but there was no real hiding place.

It was nine o'clock. She checked her make-up to be sure that her mascara hadn't taken a trip down her cheeks, dragged a comb through her blonde, carefully streaked hair, and walked down the hall. In spite of all she was going through, she smiled when she remembered Maurice Jones and the advice he had given. 'Don't be all blonde, sweetheart. Let's throw in some low-lights. After all, we need to be convincing, don't we?'

What had he meant by that, she wondered as she locked her front door. It didn't matter, because Maurice was a gentleman, which was more than could be said for his ex-partner. Paul was doing his best to pull the rug from under the feet of Mo and Sally by undercutting them, by trying to blacken Mo's name, by working twelve hours a day. Lily knew how it felt when the ground became unsteady, when a person to whom one had been close suddenly turned into a monster.

She reached Rose Cottage, took a deep breath, then walked round to the back of the house. It was chaos. Chas was playing the mouth organ very badly, while Derek, who had probably been commandeered against his better judgement, accompanied his father on the spoons. Eve, having taken rather a large amount of Chardonnay, could not find the right notes on her accordion. The resulting noise had sent most of the party fleeing to the far end of the garden. Only the stalwarts and the tone deaf had the guts to remain and face this poor excuse for music.

Derek's eyes were immediately on Lily. He put down his spoons, which were, unfortunately, the least offensive of all the murdered instruments, and made a beeline for her. Eve ceased playing for a few blessed seconds and nudged her husband. 'He's setting his cap at her,' she whispered.

Chas stopped blowing into his mouth organ. He shook it, muttered something about the bugger being full of spit and beer, then continued the torture. It was arrested abruptly when his wife's words finally registered after negotiating a route to his brain past Stella Artois and red wine. 'Well, he won't get her. Nobody will. She's built a wall the size of Hadrian's around herself.' He started to play again, after shaking more moisture out of his harmonica.

Eve watched her son. The enthusiasm had gone out of her playing, while Chas, whose mouth organ was still delivering all the wrong notes in the wrong order, also gave up. 'Where is everybody?' he asked.

'In the jungle,' his wife replied. 'They made a dash when you started the assassination of "Amazing Grace".'

'I never played "Amazing Grace",' he said, his tone reflecting deep injury. 'It was "Knees Up Mother Brown".' Chas armed himself with a yard brush and another can of ale before venturing forth to rescue friends and neighbours from wild animals, killer insects and dangerous snakes.

Ghostly figures began to emerge from the depths of Rose Cottage's not inconsiderable acreage. Lily saw Valda and Tommy, Philly and Dave, Maurice with Sally, Babs and Pete. There were many others whose names she didn't know, but the main problem was Derek, who had taken up a nonchalant position against a wall. One look at Lily's face had told him to stay away. Tim Mellor was approaching her, but he was easily fifty, so he didn't count in Derek's inexperienced book.

'How are you?' asked the notoriously cheerful vet.

'Fine,' she answered. 'I shan't stay long, though. I'm not a great drinker.'

'Me neither.' He took a long draught of beer, covered a belch with a polite hand. 'We should get to know each other better,' he continued. 'You must come for dinner one night. Mind, I'm not the best of cooks, so it would be takeaway. There's been nothing decent cooked in my kitchen since the wife ran off with the rep for a company which manufactured diet food for dogs. She's on the Isle of Wight now. I suppose someone has to live there.'

For a non-drinker, he was terribly drunk. Lily excused herself and went to talk to Babs and Pete.

Just on the edge of her vision, Mike Walsh stood, drink in one hand, Skippy's lead in the other. He had probably taken charge of the dog so that Dave and Philly could cut their engagement cake. There were speeches, followed by applause, then ABBA blared out all over the garden. It was clear that Skippy was not an ABBA fan, because she bolted just as 'Waterloo' began, the priest hanging on to the lead for dear life. Lily smiled. The dog had lost a leg, but she could shift, while many people here were more legless than Skippy would ever be.

Mike regained his composure and handed Skippy back to her grateful owners. He approached Lily, a hand beating his breast. 'Mea maxima culpa,' he said.

'Can't you get ointment for that?' Lily asked.

He made a remark about people who didn't know Latin, so she reeled off a list of plants with names that were inches long.

'Touché,' he said before wandering off.

Lily sat alone for a while, just watching other people having fun. This was how ridiculous the inebriated seemed to the sober, then. Chas was standing on a chair. For some reason best known to himself, he was reading out the American Declaration of Independence. His wife, the lovely Eve, had decided to show everyone her curtain swatches, some of which had ended up in the pond. Dave and Philly were sober, as were Babs, Pete, Valda, Tommy and Sally, but the rest of the company were in a state of sore disrepair.

Tim Mellor had attached himself to a piece of eye-candy from the other end of the village, while Maurice was making a collection of garden gnomes, strays left behind by a previous owner. He was lining them up under the dining-room window, and he seemed to have plans for them. 'He's going to drown them in Fullers Brook,' a voice said. 'There will be a suitable service conducted by himself in a frock.'

It was Derek. If he asked her to go out for dinner again, she would have to make herself clear. It was no, had always been no, would always be no. He must have seen the expression in her eyes, because he staggered off without further comment or request.

Lily decided that she was a miserable cow, and went to put that right. Eve, having eaten enough to soak up the wine, was one of the least tired and emotional revellers present. She greeted Lily with enthusiasm. 'Good to see you, Lily. Glad you decided to come.'

Lily smiled. 'If you'd like to stop by my house one evening, I have a portfolio that belonged to a friend of mine. She was in interior design, and she had a way of making the truly modern work without spoiling the history of a house. It's all Belfast sinks and brushed steel, but it works given the right colours and textures.'

Eve was delighted. 'Oh, ta, love,' she gushed. 'Here, have a prawn vol-au-vent. I'd say I made them myself, but it would be a lie. Yes, I'd be glad to look at your porto – what was it?'

'Portfolio.'

'Like an artist has when he goes to college?'

'Yes.' Lily pulled Eve to one side. 'You won't be offended if I go home, will you? It's a headache.'

'You go, sweetheart. I'll see you tomorrow, if that's all right.'

Lily took herself off. She couldn't drink more than a couple of glasses of wine, because she had seen first-hand what happened when people over-imbibed. Sober, Clive had been evil; drunk, he had always become the devil incarnate. Alcohol changed people, and seldom for the better.

At home once more, she wondered whether she was now doomed to be a mere spectator, an outsider like Mrs Barker who sat all day at a window and watched a life in which she no longer took an active part. She had been reduced to this by marrying too young, by marrying the wrong man. He would have been wrong for just about anyone.

In the dining room, she stood in darkness, because the outside security light was on, and she knew it was announcing the presence of her little fox family. They had begun to allow her into their lives, because domestic food was palatable and they were becoming unnaturally tame. Was that a good thing? Had they managed to make a friend of the one animal that had always been their greatest enemy?

Out of the shadows, a human figure stepped, and Lily's heart began to crash about until it seemed to threaten her ribs. But it wasn't a stranger. It was Mike. He sat down carefully at the edge of the paved area and reached out a hand, and one of the adult foxes came and took food from him. It was unutterably touching. Here, in a dark garden, a man trusted by timorous beasts seemed to portray all that Lily had lost. He was no threat. He removed nothing, gave everything, was full of love for all around him.

Lily's heart slowed to its normal pace, and she retreated from the window to sit on a dining chair. She could still see him, could tell that he was talking to the creatures. The babies, growing older and more sensible, skittered about less enthusiastically now that wisdom was colouring their behaviour. But they didn't run away. Nothing and no one ran away from him. Except Lily Latimer, of course.

He came into the house, and she was drawn to join him. At the kitchen sink, he washed his hands, turned, saw her standing there. 'Lily?'

'They're so tame now.'

He nodded. 'And you are in charge when I'm not here. On the one hand, we have upset the balance of nature, but on the other we are privileged beyond measure.'

'They'll be inside the house soon,' she said.

'Perhaps. But keep them away from your Chippendales.'

'Imitation Chippendales. I'm not that wealthy.'

He hung up the towel. 'What now, party girl? Scrabble, dominoes, Monopoly?'

'I hate Monopoly.'

'Cards?'

'No. I think bed is the best place for me.'

He lowered his head for a few seconds. 'Lily, this isn't the first time.'

'What? First time for what?'

'I've fallen in love before. Never did anything about it, but it's more frightening this time.'

She didn't ask why, because she already knew.

'This ... feeling is travelling in more than one direction. Isn't it? That's why I have the courage to speak to you. Emotion as strong as this couldn't exist in a cul-de-sac, could it?'

With anyone else in the world, Lily would have shrugged it off. She might have called the man foolish, stupid, deluded, would probably have advised him to go away and play with the other infants in the school yard. But with Michael Walsh, there had to be absolute truth at all times and at whatever cost. She whispered, 'No,' then sat at the table. 'But nothing will be done this time, either, Mike. Not just because of your position in the world, but because I'm not suitable. Too damaged.'

'I need to find somewhere else to stay.'

'No. We're adults and we are in control.'

He sat opposite her. 'I'm glad you feel like that. But sometimes, if I wake in the night, I am sorely tempted to climb that second flight of stairs. Just to look at you, just to hold you ... but we both know it wouldn't stop there. I should have more sense at my age – I'll be forty in a couple of years – but I'm like a teenager whose hormones are just kicking in.'

In spite of herself, she smiled at him. Then, with a more serious expression on her face, she gave him a part of her past. 'There is a possibility that I may not be able to ...' Oh, God, how could she put this? 'There was physical hurt, you see. I was very badly injured, in and out of hospital for eight months, in a coma for the first couple of weeks. I had some extremely fancy embroidery done on my ... abdomen. None of the blood in my body was my own. They started me on O neg, did the tests, gave me the right group. I owe a lot to the hospital, everything to blood donors. I should have died.' There was no need to tell him that she had wanted to die at the start, when she had woken from the long sleep.

'God,' he breathed.

'No, it wasn't God – it was a surgeon named Myers. He put me together again. I was luckier than Humpty-Dumpty, you see.'

He reached across the table and took her hand. 'I'm sorry you went through all that, Lily, but I'm so glad that you survived it. I don't care what you can or can't do – this is more than sexual. That's why it's different.' It was powerful and dangerous. It was true that he had been attracted to women in the past, but this was the first time he had been afraid. Beyond the fear loomed excitement, adventure and the loss of his job. But she shone more brightly than anyone he had ever known, and he would sacrifice anything at all to be with her. He squeezed her hand. 'Your face was dead when you arrived here. Now, you're coming to life.'

Her hand tingled as if hit by a bolt of lightning. She didn't believe in any of it, had never set much store by the concept of chemical love, as she termed this kind of attraction. The idea of love at first sight was similarly alien to her mind. Yet the fact remained that she was shaking inwardly, that she wanted to dash round the table and hold him in her arms. But Lily was an adult. 'It will be all right,' she said, her voice slightly unsteady.

'How can it be all right?'

She looked straight into his eyes. 'It can be all right because it isn't hell. I've been there, so almost everything is easy after that.'

'Who did it?'

'A man.'

'Lily—'

'Go to bed,' she told him. 'Go and sleep in the room that was always yours, and I shall go to my room. I'm not ready for any great changes, and I don't know whether I shall ever be ready. You are a priest, and I don't need to tell you what that means. You're a good man, and these villages round here need you. Not just for church, but for—'

'Pantomime, last rites, rotas for loving thy neighbour. Most of all, for pantomime.'

'For the community, yes. It's not just the Catholics, you see. Apart from Mrs Barker, who hates almost every-one, this whole area values and loves you. Can you imagine how they would feel if you gave up all that for me, abandoned them for me? Or for any woman, come to that. We have to act our age and just carry on carrying on.'

'And without carrying on in the other sense of the word.' He held on to her hand as if it were a lifebelt. 'Who are you, Lily? Who sent you here?'

She shrugged. 'I came all by myself. Stuck a pin in the upper part of the map, and here I am.'

'Like a piece of magic.'

'No, Mike. Like a wounded animal that daren't trust its own kind. I may be ten years younger than you, yet I am half a century older, because what happened to me made me old.'

'Was Babs part of it?'

She nodded.

'But she wasn't injured.'

'Her heart was broken, but her physical hurt healed. And she has Cassie. Cassie is the only good thing to have emerged from the whole sordid mess.' She freed her hand and stood up. 'If you are truly tortured in my house, find another place. But I like having you here. You're the closest I've come to trust. Apart from Babs. She and I have needed to believe in each other. Good night, Mike.'

It was lonely upstairs. Even the circular window didn't cheer her. Nor did the crisp sheets, the mirrored French furniture, the beautiful curtains. He was suffering, and she hated that. She was used to pain, physical and mental, but he had never asked to be dragged into this, whatever 'this' was.

On the floor below, Mike undressed, showered, said his prayers. He was a priest. Priests could overcome just about anything, because God was on their side. He groaned. Sexual attraction he might have dismissed as a feeble effort by Satan to get him on board. After all, hadn't Christ Himself been tempted by the devil?

Neither slept well that night. Each was tormented by the knowledge that comfort and understanding were just a few steps away. Each was wise enough not to take those steps.

The trouble with screws is that the government pays peanuts and gets monkeys. Give a monkey a nut to chew on, and he'll follow you home.

Some following has to be done. We follow the money. Her house is sold and her shop, too, has changed hands.

Those places were sold by Leanne Chalmers. Even if she has changed her name, there are people in banks and solicitors' offices who are open to suggestion. So. We need to know the area to which the money was sent, the bank into which it has been paid, the name under which it is making interest.

Walton's OK. It's not the Ritz, but the locals are amusing. Bright, too. Scallies, as Liverpool calls its fallen ones, are not without brains. That quick-fire humour conceals nothing, and it shows intelligence behind such wit.

I know a man who'll pay a man who'll pay another man. Leanne, I'm on my way, babe.

Seven

'Right. You can eat it or leave it, Mrs Barker. I'm not going to stand here worrying like Dave used to. If you don't eat, the insulin you've injected will be too much for you, and you'll get confused, fall over and may go into a hypoglycaemic coma. That'll be you in hospital for several days at least.'

Enid's hands closed into fists. Here was another one who'd swallowed a bloody dictionary. Between them, Dave and his fiancée knew English inside out, and they used it as weaponry. If only she had her health and strength, she'd send this one back downstairs at a faster than normal rate. There again, if she had her health and strength, she wouldn't need to be in the same room as Philomena Gallagher, because she'd be fending for herself. Determined not to talk to this madam, Enid allowed only a small grunt to punctuate the ensuing silence.

'Well? Shall I get the doctor to come? Shall I tell him you're sulking and making yourself ill by refusing food? Because he'll put his foot behind you, mark my words. Acting like a child, refusing food—'

Enid picked up a fork, stabbed half an egg and transferred it to her mouth. Who the bloody hell did Philomena Gallagher think she was talking to?

'Good decision,' said Philly before rushing back down-stairs. She was in a state worse than Russia, and she had to deal with a certain matter immediately.

It was a computer day. Bert and Sam, a pair of recidi-vists who couldn't go a day without the Reading Room, were fighting over a woman they'd both met online. Bert, who walked with the aid of a stick, was a few years older than Sam. 'I'll be bloody dead in a few months,' he cried. 'You can have her when I'm gone and buried. The way your arthritis is thriving, I'll leave you my stick and all.'

Sam snorted his disgust. 'What is this? Pass the parcel? Leave a girlfriend in your will? She likes me, not you.'

'Children, children,' Philly shouted. 'Stop the fighting, will you? I've trouble enough upstairs without you two kicking off. Skippy, who gave you that scone?' She looked round the Reading Room. 'Stop feeding the dog,' she ordered. 'In case you haven't noticed, she's one leg missing and we have to keep her thin.'

'Don't get your corsets in a twist,' said Sam. 'You've gone all . . . what's the word, Bert?'

'Religious?'

'No, is it heck. You've gone all . . . wotsit since you got engaged, Philly.'

She gave him the word. 'Bolshie,' she snapped. 'I've gone difficult.' She smiled, then reminded herself that she shouldn't be smiling. Because there was a question that needed to be answered right away.

Nevertheless, she was proud of herself. For years, she'd never said boo to a goose, but now she could tackle a gaggle or a skein, because she had Dave to back her up. Feeling powerful, she clicked the computer off line. 'Now,' she said, a finger wagging at the two old

173

men. 'Stop courting and fighting in here, because we've no licence for entertainment.'

Bert made a rude sign, while Sam stuck out his tongue.

Philly, referring to the latter protrusion, expressed the opinion that its owner should leave the object to medical science, as it owned more coats than most women's winter wardrobes.

'Clever,' said Sam.

Philly picked up her handbag and went through to the washroom. She locked the door, sat on the lid of the lavatory and tried to get her mind in order. It shouldn't have happened. It couldn't have happened. Knowing her luck, it probably had happened. She followed instructions to the letter, stood, and stared in the mirror while waiting for her fate to be decided.

Several minutes later, she shot through the shop like a deer with a dozen stalkers on its heels. Where had he gone? She dashed back into the shop. 'Where did Dave go?' she asked.

'Memory's buggered,' was Sam's delivered opinion.

'Market – for trousers,' said Bert. 'He's going to slide down the bath plughole if you keep starving him.'

Philly blinked, then backed away. 'You're in charge,' she told the two elderly men as she moved. 'Bert – books and papers. Sam – Reading Room teas, coffees and whatevers.'

'We want bloody paying this time,' yelled one of them as she disappeared altogether.

Philly stood on Fullers Walk wondering what she was supposed to do next. She couldn't do next, because Dave was supposed to be next. He was the father, so she should talk to him first. She felt sick. Feeling sick was probably part and parcel of the situation in which she found herself. Unable to keep still, she marched up and down outside the florist's and the salon. 'Stop it,' she said under her breath. 'He'll be here in a minute.'

'Philly?'

She turned to find Lily Latimer behind her. 'Oh. Hello.' Their names rhymed. Was this an omen? 'Can we go inside?' she asked. 'Only I'm not myself today.'

They entered the flower shop and Lily shut the door, turning the sign to CLOSED. 'What's the matter?' she asked.

Philly pointed to the ceiling. 'I told Dave I'd see to her, because she whips the rug from under his feet every time he visits. So I decided to stop her. She hurts him. She's been hurting him since the day he was born.'

Lily nodded encouragingly. 'You've done a lot for him. He's even had a proper haircut, hasn't he? No more plastering down the long bits to cover the baldness. And he's a lot thinner.'

'Yes.' Philly looked round the shop. 'Has Babs started next door?'

'Maurice has begun to re-educate her. Cassie's with Valda.' Lily paused. 'What is it?' There was definitely more than the old hag behind all this. 'Are you ill? Is Dave ill?'

Philly shook her head. 'No, no, we're fine. I want Dave, but he's gone into Bolton again to get trousers from the market. He'll have three different sizes now. All he needed was a bit of love and encouragement.'

Lily stared hard at her visitor. 'You have to tell him first?'

Philly nodded.

'A baby?'

Philly stayed very still.

175

'You haven't told me. You haven't said anything, my lovely.' Lily ordered herself to fight the jealousy. It was normal, but it was ugly. It was probably impossible for Lily to ever go full term, but she must not resent this lovely woman who had to fight her own guilt. The Catholic Church thrived on guilt, nurtured it, drummed rules into the heads of infants, some of whom then grew up with a distorted view of life. If the worst thing a woman ever did was to get pregnant before wearing a wedding ring, that was a small crime. In fact, it wasn't a crime at all, and Lily said so.

'But we have to get married.'

'You are getting married.'

Philly began to pace about the shop. 'It has to be quick. Father Walsh is arranging it, because we're a mixed couple, but it has to be now.'

'This minute?'

'Almost. Only I can't speak to my priest before telling Dave, can I?

Lily supposed not. 'Stop marching, Philly. You'll be wearing out the floor if you carry on like this.'

'Sorry.'

'And don't panic. If you are carrying a child, you don't want to make yourself ill.' Why were men never where they should be when you needed them most? Did they follow a different clock, or a calendar women hadn't heard of yet? 'When did he go?'

'Don't know. Can't remember.'

'When did you buy the test kit? I'm assuming you've done a test?'

Philly nodded. 'Nine o'clock, when the chemist opened.' She coloured. 'I told a lie, said it was for some young girl.'

'And Dave had already left for town?'

'Yes.'

'So you do know. You know he left before nine. Sit down.'

Philly sat while Lily opened the door and stood waiting. Feeling as if she carried someone's proxy vote, Lily lingered in the doorway,

coming inside only to serve three customers who arrived at roughly ten-minute intervals. 'His van's coming now. Look. I'll go upstairs and you get him in here. Go through to the back. If I get a customer, let me know. You can't tell him in his own shop – it's full of computer loonies. Do it here among the flowers.'

So, after announcing that he was now the proud owner of two more pairs of trousers, Dave Barker was standing alongside buckets of summer blooms when he learned that he was to be a father. He blinked stupidly as if waking from a long sleep, then wept a few tears of happiness. 'We'd better track your Father Walsh down,' he said when he regained some composure. 'I've never been happier, Phil. Thank you so much for loving me.'

Lily sat at the top of the stairs, skirt held tightly to her ankles, head bowed onto her knees. She was empty. There was a part of her that was so empty that sometimes she wanted to die. Not now, not at this moment. She was happy for Philly and Dave, because they were wonderful people who deserved to be fulfilled. Nevertheless, Lily's pain was almost physical.

But she was an adult and she would cope. She would sell flowers, make wreaths for the dead and bouquets for the hopeful. She would sleep in a house where a beautiful man sometimes stayed, and she would be sensible, as would he. The wheel of life turned daily, and she had to carry on.

'Feather it.' Maurice Jones stood back and cast a critical eye on the workmanship of his new trainee. 'What did they use in Devonshire?' he asked. 'A flaming plough-share?' He stepped forward and demonstrated again, explaining to the model that the styling was free, that she was a guinea pig, that she would be all right once he had put Babs's small mistake to rights.

'I think I'll give up,' Babs moaned.

'No, you won't. You've got promise.'

Babs laughed. 'Well, God help any bad hairdresser who comes your way. I've not had any praise from you at all, and I was very well thought of down south.'

He grinned at her. 'You think I'm difficult? The bloke who trained me's a tartar, but he gets results.'

'Was Paul better than me?' she asked.

'Of course he was, because I trained him all over again, didn't I? Also, what you're doing isn't necessarily wrong – it's just not what we do at Pour Les Dames. Right. Come here, madam, and do this bit. Round the ear – shape it back. Now, we want a couple of tendrils feathered down – that's right. See? You're not as daft as you look.'

'I couldn't be.'

Sally drifted in. She was having what she described as a sleepy pregnancy, because she could scarcely keep her eyes open for more than an hour at a time. 'I'll go and heat my wax,' she told her husband. 'And I'd love a cuppa, if anyone's offering.'

Babs went to brew the tea while Maurice finished off the model. Up to now, Babs had been allowed to wash and put finishing touches to hair, but Maurice's style of cutting was a whole new world for her, and she was enjoying learning in spite of the exchanges of words and the heavily applied advice.

Sally returned from her little space next to the store room. 'Mo?'

'What, love?'

'I've no wax, the trolley's been taken apart, the clients' couch is slashed to shreds, and everything's in a right mess.'

Maurice paused and laid down his implements. 'What?'

'Somebody's broken in and ruined everything. There's acrylic nails everywhere, nail polish poured all over the place, towels soaked in God knows what. I can't do manicures, pedicures or waxing. All I can do is Indian head massage on your clients in here.'

Maurice stormed into the back of the shop. Babs looked at Sally. 'Who do you think did it?' she asked.

'Paul, of course.'

Babs went to finish off the tea-making. Paul was a nightmare. Keen to wipe his ex-partner off the face of the earth, he had set up Impressions and had over-booked himself, failing to account for travelling time between appointments, and ignoring the fact that some clients needed more attention than others. Paul Smith was an extremely angry and aggressive man. If he had done this, he needed dealing with, and pronto.

Maurice looked grim when he returned. 'Stay out of there, love,' he told his wife. 'It's a crime scene. Let's get the police.'

Babs's head was suddenly filled with a scenario that might damage Maurice and Sally. 'Just a minute,' she

179

said before drawing the two into the rear end of the shop, well away from today's guinea pig. 'He can make things worse,' she advised. 'From what I've heard, he was head over heels with you, Mo.'

Maurice shook his head. 'If you want to meet a real bitch, choose a jealous and furious gay. If he'd loved me, he wouldn't have done all this to Sally. This isn't love.'

'No,' Babs agreed, 'it isn't love – it's territory. Mo, if this goes to court, he can call you a stinking good-for-nothing bisexual man who hurt him. They won't know the truth. Why did you let it come to this? Why did you allow the world to think of you and him as partners in the closer sense?'

Mo hung his head. 'We were already well known as a drag act. Some on the circuit knew we weren't a couple, and those who came on to me were aware that I was straight. I just drifted into it, Babs. Psychology. A woman likes a hairdresser she can talk to. Women talk to gays rather than to other women or straight men.'

'Sally?'

Sally answered Babs. 'I hated it. We were man and wife upstairs, but Mo was a caricature down here. Everyone thought I was the lodger, and yes, I was unhappy about all of it. Now that I'm pregnant, Paul is as mad as a frog in a box.'

'Then don't let him tear you to pieces in court. I'll deal with it. Well, Pete will.'

Mo stared at his new recruit for several seconds. 'Thanks, Babs,' he said.

Babs was only too pleased to help. 'I can't promise anything,' she said. 'But I'll do my very best.' She wished she could do the same for Lily. But the threat to Lily's well-being was not visible, was more than a slashed

couch and some spilt polish. If Chalmers ever got to her
. . . She shivered.

'Are you cold?' Sally asked.

'No,' she replied. 'Something just stepped on my
grave.'

Eve Boswell and her husband were in their forties, yet
they seemed to have retained a youthful and open
attitude to life. Eve, especially, was a lively soul, and
every time she visited Lily in Hope House she arrived
overflowing with ideas, material swatches, paint charts
and photographs of furniture. These offerings were often
a mixed bag, so Lily guided her through the portfolio,
explained about direction of light, where to place the
first length of wallpaper, how to best enhance crudely
plastered walls and bare stonework.

'There's only one room for wallpaper,' Eve explained.
'Some soft sod skimmed over the original walls, like my
husband suggested.'

'Chas? He didn't.'

'He was joking. He knew it would be a capital
offence.'

'Ah.' Lily opened one of her files. 'Look at this one.
Same shades from front to back, lighter colour in the same
group on curtains and cushions, darker for the carpet,
take the carpet through to the rest and you have continuity without boredom.'

'Let me have a study of this lot, then.'

While Eve did her studying, Lily set the kettle to boil.
She was grateful to this Liverpudlian woman, because she
had not expected to make close friends at this end of the
country. But Eve was amazing and amusing. She carried
her own mental portfolio filled with pictures of her youth

in Liverpool, word sketches that she drew in her own inimitable manner.

Her husband, she had explained, was in women's underwear. Lily smiled as she remembered how confused she had been – wasn't he in wines and spirits? But Eve had returned a ready answer. Chas's brother and Chas had been a pair of knickers, though the K had been dropped from the front of the garment. Nickers were thieves, so the point became clear eventually.

There had been generations of nickers in the Boswell family, and one of the more famous had been hanged for accidentally killing a chap during a theft from the docks. The Boswells spoke of their deceased ancestor with pride, because he had paid the ultimate price for his chosen vocation. Chas and his brother had been luckier, though Robbo had been caught robbing – there sat another pun that was not allowed to pass unnoticed – while Chas was a lucky bugger and had avoided a criminal record by the skin of his teeth. Had he been caught, he would never have obtained the licence to sell alcohol and tobacco. 'He's going to have to let his special customers down,' Eve said now. For some reason she could never explain completely, she trusted Lily Latimer. Lily knew all about bother – it was written on her face.

'Special customers?' Lily passed a mug to her visitor.

'Boswell business,' replied Eve. 'They still manage to release the odd case of spirits from prison in a bonded warehouse, and Chas sells the stuff round the back of the shop – from the garage. There's ciggies as well. That'll have to stop now, because Paul Smith's moving in.'

'Oh.' Lily didn't like Paul, but she said nothing.

'My Chas is a good man, Lily. You can be a villain and still be a good man.'

'I know.' Lily also knew a villain who was so bad that he was not allowed to mix with normal, decent criminals. At least, she hoped he was still segregated … 'Have a look at this second folder, Eve. Notice how magnolia doesn't need to be a cop-out.'

Eve stared steadily at her hostess and guru. She knew an awful lot about interior design, so why was she in flowers? The new file, which depicted the interior of a country cottage, rang a muffled bell in the deepest recesses of Eve's mind. She experienced a déjà vu moment, but everyone had those. 'Lily?'

'Yes?'

'Do you mind if I ask you what you did before you came here?' There were secrets. Most people had one or two of those, but Lily's careful guardianship of her past was not typical. There was something big there, the sort of event that left emotional scars.

Lily tried not to look afraid. 'This and that. Some party planning, wedding flowers and so forth.' Her heart raced. This should not be happening. She was a fool to think she could use Leanne's portfolio and get away with it.

'And Babs?'

'Was a hairdresser.' Well, that was the truth.

'Ah.' Eve leafed through the pile. She had seen the photographed house before, but she couldn't quite place her finger on where. Then it crashed into her mind like a jackknifed articulated vehicle on the East Lancs. 'Leanne?' she said quietly.

Lily staggered back a couple of paces. She swallowed painfully and looked through the window.

'Leanne Chalmers? Dark hair, dirty laugh, the interior version of Wotserface Dimmock that did gardens with her bouncy boobs?'

Lily remained silent.

'Not that Leanne Chalmers had bouncy boobs, but she was every man's idea of feisty high-class crumpet.' Eve paused for a few beats of time. 'I'm right, aren't I? You're Leanne Chalmers off *Makeover Madness*. Your catchphrase was we do the impossible, miracles only if pressed. You're so thin, so changed . . .'

Lily nodded. Eve Boswell was an all right person; Eve Boswell would not let her down.

Eve covered her face with her hands. 'Shit, shit, shit,' she whispered. 'They put it about that you'd moved abroad, but that was because of . . . Oh, Lily. Oh, my God. And here am I sitting and saying that criminals aren't all bad. I am so sorry, queen.' She was. 'You're smaller, blonde . . .'

'It's all right.' Lily sat at the table.

Eve was weeping openly. 'Who knows?'

'Just you. Babs does, of course. No one else. Oh – Pete has access to details. Mike can tell there's something major wrong with me, but he hasn't placed me yet. He probably never watched the programme. Don't cry, Eve.'

Eve saw the headlines, read them all over again. Jill Dando, God love her, had died. But this wonderful, vibrant, cheeky and opinionated woman had survived. Hadn't she? Had she? It had been so horrible when it was printed. Seeing something written down was somehow far worse than hearing it. Lily was a shadow now. 'You don't look right with blonde hair,' was all Eve could manage.

'It had to be done, Eve. He has friends – well, he knows a lot of criminals who aren't doing time.'

Eve could see Leanne strutting about, ripping off

wallpaper, consigning a householder's belongings to a skip on the path. 'Where is he?'

'Walton. Just been moved from the Scrubs.'

Eve jumped up and began to pace about. It was like Philly all over again, back and forth, stop and think, back and forth like a quickened pendulum.

'Keep still,' said Lily. 'And dry your eyes. I don't want tears all over my bits and pieces, thanks.'

Eve sat down. 'I know people in Walton. Chas even knows a couple of the screws who've been good to their Robbo in the past—'

'Don't waste your breath. He might well be segregated.'

The little Liverpool woman placed a hand on Lily's arm. 'The segregated can be dealt with – remember the Yorkshire Ripper lost an eye? What you went through, babe, was just beyond anything normal. He should be bloody well shot. I'm supposed to be a good Catholic, but I'd kill him as soon as look at him. Christ, I'm angry.'

Lily nodded. 'As was I. I'm still angry, I suppose. For a while, the anger turned inward, because I should have got away before the situation became so horrible. The depression was awful.'

'Must have been, love. Look, I won't say a word.'

Lily smiled. 'You can tell Chas, because I know this is too big a thing to keep inside. You're so close to him, and I'd rather he knew what's affecting your mood. I know it must hurt, because we've become good friends.'

'We have,' said Eve emphatically.

'But don't tell Derek. It's not a matter of trust, it's that I can't stand to be pitied. Pity is painful to receive.'

Eve lost interest in interior decor. She pushed away the files and drank her cooling tea. 'Lily?'

'What?'

'You frightened?'

'Yes.'

'There's ways,' Eve said. 'Say the word, and I'll do my best to get him dealt with. You wouldn't be afraid if he got killed.'

Lily nodded thoughtfully. 'The difference between me and Chalmers is that I can't commit murder. I couldn't help anyone else do it, either. Leave it, Eve. Tell Chas the same. And if your parish priest asks about me, say nothing.'

'He's taken a shine to you, hasn't he?' Eve noticed a slight flush on Lily's cheeks after the words had been delivered.

'He's a friend, Eve.'

Eve, having been raised in a city full of life, bustle, gossip and interesting characters, was astute when it came to instinct. Father Walsh had a way of looking at Lily that gave him away. Sometimes, he didn't look at her. Those were the occasions on which he thoroughly betrayed himself, because he could not bear to expose his true feelings. So. Eve cleared her throat. So it looked as if Madam here had gone from frying pan to fire. No, he wasn't a fire, he was just a bloke in a dog collar. But was Lily moving from one impossible situation into another? 'Lily?'

'What?'

'Have you told him nothing?'

'Who?'

'Our parish priest, that's who. I'm a good judge of

character, love. You have to be when you live among vagabonds like my Chas's lot. And there's something.'

Lily shrugged. 'Eve, no way.'

'What do you mean by no way? Did you never see that programme about the Irish priest who had a kid by his housekeeper?'

'No.'

'The priest's dead, the housekeeper's dead, and the kid's out in the cold, because nobody wants him. His dad was forever on *The Late Show* about contraception and should priests marry – he was famous. He was there when the Pope arrived in Ireland, there when somebody wanted him to sing. And all the time, this bloke the Irish worshipped was having his leg over. They do have relationships.'

'Not in my house.'

Something in Lily's tone made her visitor quiet. There was still an air of authority about her, a small remnant left behind by the woman who had chased decorators across the television screen, who had put together impossible marriages of colour and made them work, who had changed the nation's ideas on home decor. 'Hey, Lily?'

'Yes?'

'Do you remember the chap who reckoned to know everything about ergonomic furniture?'

Lily smiled. 'God, yes – that pompous prat.'

'And you told him his 1950s retro chair was good for hitting him on the head with?'

'And he walked off the set?' Lily giggled. 'You meet some fools in that game, Eve. I mean, I'm all for retro stuff – we should mark every development in architecture and furniture by keeping or imitating great examples. But I wasn't having a lump of red plastic in a room filled with French pieces.'

Eve was laughing. 'And you said about bringing the garden into the house, so they played a trick on you.'

'Oh, yes. Ten rolls of turf carpeting a conservatory – that was funny.'

'You miss it. You miss the tricks they played most of all.' It wasn't a question.

'I do.'

Eve gazed at her new-found friend. 'You'd still have all that if it wasn't for him.'

'I'd have a lot more,' Lily said. 'I'd have everything.'

Eve burst into tears again. She was determined to go to the central library and read the newspapers on microfiche. The framework was still in her mind, but she'd forgotten some of the details and she needed to know. To ask Lily to fill in the blanks would be cruel, so— 'What are they for?' She fixed her eyes on two items Lily had just placed on the table in front of her.

Lily sat down. 'If you're going all watery, you can peel my onions.'

Sometimes, thought Eve, Leanne Chalmers came back. She peeled the onions.

Sergeant Peter Haywood sat in his car outside the flower shop. Lily was tidying up in preparation for closing, while Babs and Cassie had gone upstairs to the flat. Peter had seen the mess at the back of Pour Les Dames and was waiting now for the alleged perpetrator to come home in his purple van. Babs's boss didn't want to go to court. His wife was pregnant, and he was worried about how

188

far Paul Smith was prepared to go in his search for revenge.

Pete sucked on a Polo mint. He didn't like being involved at this level, as he believed that matters should be dealt with in a proper fashion – forensics, statements, court – but he would do just about anything for Babs. She was a character. She pulled no punches, was humorous, affectionate and devoted to her daughter, so Pete was about to break his own mould, and that worried the policeman in him.

The beautician arrived eventually. His purple van swung left behind the row of shops, presumably to be stored in the alarmed garage at the rear of the off-licence. Pete waited for five minutes, then locked up his car and went to ring the bell at the back of number one. The garage was closed, so Paul Smith was probably inside the flat.

The door to the private stairs was flung open, and Paul presented himself. He carried a rolling pin, and was clearly ready to do battle with the man whose premises he had burgled the night before. 'Oh.' The weapon was suddenly hidden behind his back. 'Aren't you . . . ?'

'I'm Sergeant Peter Haywood, Greater Manchester Police.'

Paul tried and failed to produce a convincing smile. 'No uniform?'

'Not today. I thought you'd rather I did this in mufti. We need to talk. May I come in?'

Paul led the way up to the flat. He was still living out of boxes and bags, and he was forced to move a few items so that his visitor could sit. 'Well?'

Pete cleared his throat. 'There was a break-in at the

hairdresser's,' he said. 'Someone destroyed everything Sally Jones needs to do her job. They know it was your way of punishing Mo.'

Paul gulped audibly. 'They know wrong, then, because it wasn't me. You've no right to go about maligning–'

'Who were you expecting just now?' Pete asked. 'You seemed to be looking for trouble with your rolling pin – what was all that about? I can't see any pastry hanging about waiting to be rolled. Were you expecting Maurice Jones to come round and give you a good hiding for upsetting his pregnant wife? He won't descend to that level, mate. So. Come on – I'm waiting. Why answer the door with a rolling pin in your hand?'

'Well – I just thought–'

'You just thought you'd arm yourself for the fun of it? Now, listen to me. I'm doing you a favour by volunteering to come here. My colleagues have been to the shop,' he lied, 'and they found prints. Forensic evidence seldom lies.'

'I was in and out of there every day for months on end–'

'Fresh prints. Where the window was forced.'

Paul scoffed. 'Rubbish, because I was wear . . .' His voice died.

'Wearing gloves?'

'No. I wasn't there. I didn't do it.'

The large policeman leaned back in his chair. 'If this comes to court, you'd be better pleading guilty. If you say not guilty and are found guilty, it could mean a custodial sentence.'

'And?'

'And what Maurice wants is reassurance that you

won't do anything like this again. If you give me that reassurance, there is a possibility that charges may not be brought.'

Paul Smith was fed up to the back teeth. Even when Maurice had married that girl, Paul had still clung to the hope that the man would appreciate that Paul loved him more than any woman possibly could. Then, when Mo had stood by Sally, Paul's fairy tale had fallen apart at the seams.

Happy ending? The van had cost an arm and a leg, beauty equipment wasn't cheap these days, and the circumstances in which he worked were often far from ideal. Doing a set of acrylic nails took an hour, and he dared not charge more than twenty-five quid. Then there was the petrol—

'Well?' Pete was losing patience.

'All right.'

A corner of Pete's mind felt sorry for the lad. He was clearly gay, was jealous of Sally and Mo, and was out on his ear. He would probably have loved to be in the pantomime, too. 'Why don't you go to the next FADS meeting? Mo isn't the type to bear a grudge, and that daft priest is having to play the other ugly sister. You and Mo could do your drag act. Between the two of you, you might well turn that panto into something the village would never forget.'

Paul shrugged. He and Mo could have done 'Big Spender'. And 'Diamonds are a Girl's Best Friend'. They'd have stolen the show between them.

'Swallow your pride, lad. Pride's worth nowt a pound. You'll meet somebody soon enough. And Babs can only do part time at Pour Les Dames. You could do the other part and still have your own customers for Impressions.'

Paul eyed his supposed adversary. 'I'm not crawling.'

'No. But I can get Mo to come and visit you.'

'After ... after what's happened?'

Pete shrugged. 'What do you have to lose apart from stubborn pride, Paul? The job you're doing isn't easy.'

'No.' The beautician pictured himself at some old lady's kitchen sink, the only rinsing implement available a Pyrex jug, the only certainty to hand the knowledge that he was already half an hour late for his next client. 'I work in difficult conditions.' The word impossible would have been nearer the mark.

Pete thought for a moment. 'How do you feel about elderly folk?'

The younger man smiled. 'They make me laugh and I enjoy helping them feel good. And I enjoy their stories and their memories. But it's difficult. They tend not to have the right facilities.'

'It would be different under contract to an old people's home with a proper room for hairdressing.'

'It would.'

'Leave it with me. I have a relative involved in caring for the aged. And I'm going to send Mo to see you.' The policeman smiled. 'I know what it's like to be thwarted in love, mate. We all feel pain, gay or hetero.'

'Thanks.'

'Listen. It's one thing being a gay hairdresser – imagine what a homosexual cop has to face. Even in this age of protected minorities and positive discrimination, comments are made. Cheer up and stop hurting folk. At the end of the line, it's yourself that gets damaged.'

When Pete had left, Paul stood at the window and looked out. Dave and Philly were running across the road again. They'd been knocking at Lily Latimer's door for a while. He wondered where the fire was, before going to grill a few fish fingers and warm a can of beans.

He shouldn't have done it. Mo would never love him. Even if the marriage broke down, Mo would be looking for female company. 'The bloody wedding nearly killed me,' he told the grill pan. 'Best man? I was a spare part.' To Maurice, he would never be more than another well-trained hair stylist, a partner on stage, a bloke who could dance in five-inch heels and a strappy frock. The dream had never been more than that, just a fantasy, one-sided and doomed to die.

The fish fingers were overdone, while the baked beans were cool. In number seven, he, Sally and Mo had shared the cooking. Yes, there had been some strange meals, but there had been company and laughter and fun. And the greatest of those had been fun. 'Right,' he told the mess on his plate. 'Canal Street, here I come.'

Lily brought them into the house. They had been back and forth all day like a pair of ping-pong balls involved in a bizarre doubles match, twin spheres under pressure, their consciences acting as the bats that drove them over the net with a frequency that had become monotonous. 'Sit,' she ordered.

They sat on a sofa, clutching each other's hand. 'Are you sure he's in Eagleton tonight, Lily?' Dave asked. 'Only she's getting herself in a right state here. I mean, I don't know what he can do to hurry things up, because we're a mixed marriage and there are things—'

'Protocols,' interposed Philly. 'But I have to tell him.'

'She has to tell him,' said Dave.

Lily had prepared a few nibbles, because she knew the couple would be back. She set these offerings and a pot of coffee on a low table in front of the sofa. 'Help your-selves. Nobody refuses coffee out of my Susie Cooper original pot. I save this for special people.'

'All matching,' remarked Philly. 'And a different col-our inside each cup. Where is he?' The question was added seamlessly to the previous remark.

'Funeral in Edgworth,' replied Lily. 'Huge Irish family. The relatives have invaded, so it'll probably go on until quite late. But you can wait.' God forbid that she should be the one to send them home to a sleepless and worried night. 'I don't mind – honestly. But I want to say that you're lucky. Some people try for years and never have a child.'

'Just the once for us.' Dave's cheeks were stained with embarrassment. 'But we have to get married, Lily. And it has to be in the Catholic church, otherwise it doesn't count.'

'Doesn't count,' Philly echoed.

Lily covered a smile and left the room. They were already behaving like a long-married couple, one repeat-ing what the other said, each aware of the other's ways, both open, simple in the best sense of the word, and very honest. Where was he? She'd waited until the ser-vice would have been over then phoned him on his mobile, had left a message that the business in hand was not urgent, though it was important.

She was learning that Mike was not just a priest. He was a man who liked people, who loved a good laugh, who was at his best in company. If what she had heard about Irish wakes was true, the event he was attending might well go on until about Thursday. Or did they have the wake before the burial? Wasn't there something about having the deceased present in an open coffin?

Lily shivered. The idea of a corpse being guest of honour was hardly palatable.

She used her phone again. He was sorry that he could not take her call at the moment, but if she left a message, he would contact her at the earliest opportunity. 'Mike,' she snapped. 'This is becoming ridiculous. I've two people here waiting for you. If this carries on much longer, I'll get on my broomstick and fly round till I find you.'

Lily sat in an armchair and thought about Eve. Scousers were supposed to be alert, and Eve had gone a long way towards proving the legend. It was inevitable that she must pass on to Chas all she had learned about Lily, because they shared everything, and Eve's new knowledge was too burdensome to be kept inside. Lily kept it hidden, and therein lurked the danger. Perhaps she should speak to Dr Clarke about getting some more help. She was managing in the physical sense, but her nerves were beginning to fray slightly.

They were whispering in the next room. Lily closed her eyes and pictured them clinging together for dear life. It must be wonderful to have someone dependable like Dave. He wasn't the best-looking man in the world, but he cared. He would work hard for his wife and child; he would even make sure that his terrible mother would be safe and fed.

Where was Mike? She felt like the proverbial wife waiting behind the door on a Saturday night, poker in hand, list of questions printed in upper case on the front of her mind. Where have you been? Are you drunk again? Who is she? Why are you never here when I need you?

Giving up smoking had seemed a good idea at the time, but Lily found herself longing for just one drag on a Superking – low tar, of course. For how much longer could a two-o'clock funeral last? Why wouldn't he answer his phone? He seldom obeyed orders, was still at odds with the hierarchy about contraception, hadn't even had his hair cut. He was probably considered to be something of a maverick, but she was glad about the hair. It was the tatty head that made him human, she had decided.

She closed her eyes and tried to relax. Mr Darcy, with his square chin, fierce eyes and proud expression, had been completely let down by his hair. How could Elizabeth Bennet have taken seriously the supposed coldness of a man whose hair had been that of an unruly child? Mike had Firth hair. No matter what he did with it, the stuff went its own way, and to hell with whatever the world thought. With short hair, Colin Firth wasn't as pretty. With short hair, Mike would look too . . . ordinary.

It would soon be ten o'clock. She had an early start tomorrow: flowers to be received at seven, shop to be spick and span by nine, another wedding to organize, contracts to fulfil for shops in Bolton. A grand place called the Last Drop wanted quotes for guest bedrooms, public areas and restaurants that needed fresh blooms arranged and delivered on a regular basis. Even as a florist, she was becoming famous locally.

Five minutes to ten. Were they building a mausoleum? Had guests been merry enough to fall into the grave with the coffin? Worse still, had Mike been involved in an accident? She shifted in the chair. The thought of him lying in a hospital bed was horrible. The idea of life without him was a killer. Life with him? If she stole a priest from a number of parishes, would she ever be forgiven? He wanted her. She wanted him. For the moment, she needed him to act normally, switch on his bloody phone and re-join the human race. It was OK to cut oneself off from the world during a Requiem, but the service had to have been over hours ago. Even allowing time for burial and ham sandwiches, he should have been back by six at the latest.

A car coughed. She recognized the congested breathing of Mike's geriatric Volvo. Relief flooded her veins, but it was contaminated by impatience and anger. He should not have put her through this. She now understood the moaning and groaning of so many neglected pub widows.

The door opened, and she was there in a flash. 'Where the bloody hell have you been? Where's your phone?'

He steadied himself against a wall. 'Hospital,' he managed. 'Heart attack. Don't start on me, Lily – I've had more than enough today.' Today? He felt as if he had been gone for two or three weeks.

'Oh, God. Are you all right? Why have they let you out after a heart attack? Shouldn't you be plugged into the mains with about fifteen wires?'

'Eh?'

'Heart attack?'

'Not me, woman. The dead man's mother. She keeled over in the cemetery and I followed the ambulance to town. Phones had to be switched off, and I forgot to turn mine on again. I managed to get the necessary from St Pat's, so I did Extreme Unction. She lived only four hours, bless her.'

'I'm sorry.'

'Not as sorry as I am. She was good fun, a down-to-earth Dubliner, full of Irish jokes and a laugh that would

197

curdle skimmed milk. I liked her, and she died holding my hand. Burying her only son was simply the last straw for her.' He shook his head wearily. 'Some days are just plain nasty.'

'Sorry,' Lily repeated. 'But Philly and Dave have been coming and going all day. She's in a terrible state, and he's worried about her being in a terrible state. You'd better go through – they're in the second sitting room. I'll make myself scarce.' She went upstairs in order to be out of their way. She knew what was going to be said, but they still required a semblance of privacy.

He walked into the room and saw Philly's face. 'Before you start,' he said, 'I'm pinching a drop of whisky. Just don't ask me about today, Philly.'

They waited until he had furnished himself with the required medication.

'We only did it that once,' Philly began, hands twisting in her lap.

'Just once,' said Dave.

Mike grinned. 'And you've made a baby? That's the greatest news I've had in a while. Leave it to me. I'll talk to the bish and we'll get it over and done with before you can say wedding cake.'

'How did you guess?' Dave asked.

The priest continued to smile. 'What else might it have been? Just look at the state of you, Philomena Gallagher, soon to be Barker. Anyone would think you'd bogged off to Wales and emptied the Royal Mint. There's a new life inside you, a precious child–'

'He'll be Catholic,' said Dave.

'He'll be fine,' pronounced Mike. 'So stop looking as if you're responsible for the state of Iraq. To be perfectly honest, I wouldn't care if he or she was Jewish or Muslim.'

Philly frowned. He was certainly unlike any other priest she had met, was a thousand miles apart from the clerics who had populated her childhood. What would Mam have thought if she had heard him saying it was all right to be Muslim or Jewish? And he was one for the ladies – she knew that well enough. He was kinder to women, and he listened to them very attentively. She thought about Lily, who was more beautiful than many film stars – they lived together here for some of the time . . .

Mike was going on about the rules, mentioning consanguinity, affinity and spiritual relationship as barriers to marriage. 'That's it, then,' he finished with the air of one dismissing an audience. 'Please, let me sleep. Today was a month long.'

They left. Mike finished his whisky, poured another, prayed for the lovely Mrs Maguire who had departed this life on the day of her precious son's funeral. Her levity had been the cloak she had worn to disguise her grief, but the grief had killed her. How many people died because they had simply given up, because their reason for continued existence had been eradicated? Mrs Maguire had been fiercely alive. It was she who used to drag the family across the Irish Sea every time Liverpool FC played some special match, she who had organized the funeral, the wake, the flowers. No one had attended the wake, because they had all been at the hospital praying that she would live.

'Mike?'

She was behind him. She was behind every thought,

every step, every waking moment. Perhaps it was time to run, to start again at the other end of the country – just as she had. Was she an emissary from Satan, a messenger sent to tempt him? Never. 'What?'

'Sorry I was angry with you.'

He drained his glass. 'No matter. I should have checked my messages, but the whole thing became a bit fraught.'

'It would. Will she be shipped home, or will she be buried with her son?'

'Dublin, I imagine. She was a beautiful woman. A widow. Five daughters, one son. She'll go home, I think. The majority vote will carry her back.'

Lily came to stand next to him. The feelings she was experiencing in the presence of this man were supposed to be dead. They had died on the end of a far-reaching knife, words that had cut, fear that had turned her into a near-murderer. While she had fought for life in an intensive care unit, her lawyers had also borne arms, and charges against her had been dismissed. But this was her real sin. Her brain knew full well that there was no future with Father Michael Walsh, but her heart would not be quiet.

'Difficult?' he asked.

'Yes.' How did he manage to know what she thought and how she felt? What had he said? Something about feelings as strong as these moving in two directions? This was not a one-way street – it was a ring road, round and round the edge, don't turn left or right, do not pass Go, do not collect . . .

'I'm falling in love with you, Lily Latimer. It isn't your fault.'

'Is it yours?'

He shrugged. 'I should know better. When I see the bishop about Philly and Dave, I should talk to him about this, too. What normally happens in such situations is that the priest gets transferred. I ought to move on to a different place.'

'I want you to stay.' Feeling desperate, yet brave, she slipped her hand into his. 'Never in my life have I felt like this, Mike. Like you, I know it's wrong.'

'Wrong?' He laughed mirthlessly. 'It's normal. We were created to create. And beyond the merely physical, I have this urge to protect and guard you, while—'

'While I want to touch your hair. Don't cut it. Don't you dare.'

This time, his laughter was real. 'No, I should get it cropped. If you can't love me with short hair, the problem is solved.'

It would never be solved. By some strange quirk of fate, the newly created Lily had travelled from the outskirts of Taunton – well, from the centre of Taunton if she counted her business premises – to a largeish village in the north-west of England. Here lived a man for whom she was forbidden fruit, and she had become his Eve. Was this meant to happen? Could she have been sent to release him and to free herself of past nightmares? 'What are we going to do?' she asked.

'You know perfectly well. Unless you really are too injured for such activity.'

Lily swallowed her fear. 'I don't know. But I was left in a mess. I have healed, but—'

'But you may still have pain?'

She nodded. 'I don't care.' She wasn't a reckless woman, not any more. Since the incident … since the series of incidents that had ended in near-death, she had become protective of herself. But she wanted this man. Did she want him because she shouldn't have him? Was the old Leanne still alive and kicking, still wanting to cock a snook at the world and his wife? 'I'm not afraid of you,' she said.

'Nor should you be.'

The first kiss lasted for several minutes. Each was completely lost in desire for the other; it was so right that Lily concluded it had to be wrong. But her heart won the battle, just as she had expected. The whole thing was inevitable. Neither could make a decision about the future until after the event. So, when the kiss ended, she allowed herself to be led to the stairs.

In her room at the top of the house and on a three-quarter bed, Mike and Lily became lovers. There was no pain for her. Sometime in the future she might well find herself wishing that there had been some discomfort – it might help when options were discussed. But, for the present, she was deliriously happy. Lying in the arms of her man, she was too content to worry about the future. He was a priest, yet that no longer mattered.

Remembered reading Charlie Bronson's Good Prison Guide. *He was quite kind to Walton, as he had done thousands of pounds' worth of damage to the roof, and he had a whale of a time. People can say what they like about Charlie, but he definitely has a sense of humour.*

He was right about the Scousers. They are humorous almost to the point of being completely mad. I like them. They don't suffer fools.

Am off 43, keeping my head down, just making chit-chat and listening to jokes. Bloke called Lofty came to see me. He's under five feet tall, and very useful when it comes to burglary, because he knows alarms. Dan and I have got a solicitor's clerk in our back pockets, and Leanne's money is being traced. I bet a pound to a penny she changed her name.

See, the trouble with this country is that nobody gets paid enough. Bent screws are ten a penny, because their take-home pay is peanuts. Within a couple of weeks, you can get a screw interested in earning a few bob. Drugs, info, booze – whatever – you can get it all in here. All you need is cash – that would have been a better title for the Beatles' song.

Same with solicitors' clerks. All he has to do is find his boss's password and I'll be on to Leanne. Well, somebody will. Just a matter of time. Have to be patient. Am making boxes out of matchsticks. The excitement is killing me.

Eight

There was no embarrassment.

Lily woke the next morning to find her lover standing by the bed, a breakfast tray in his hands, a yellow rose stolen from her garden clamped between his teeth. With a flourish, he produced a tea towel, and when she had raised herself into a sitting position, he spread this rather less than clean item across her legs and placed the tray on top of it. The rose was handed to her with all due ceremony, then he sat down and poured tea. 'Breakfast, madam. No orange juice, so no Buck's Fizz.' He stood back and bowed. 'Should Modom require anything further, room service will provide anything within reason. Except, of course, we do not have the aforementioned Buck's Fizz.'

'Pity. But thank you all the same.' She was strangely hungry. Having expected to find the morning after extremely difficult, she discovered herself to be completely at ease with him. Had this been casual sex and no more? She found herself hoping not. Last night had not been his first experience with a woman; he was adventurous, uninhibited, gentle, yet powerful. 'Have you eaten?' she asked.

'Music is the food of love, so I listened to Lonnie Donegan.'

'Who?'

'"My Old Man's a Dustman".' He sang a few bars for her, then mopped up spilt tea. 'It's a very romantic piece, and you should not be laughing – it betrays a lack of soul,' he said. 'If your spirit can't share the moment with me, don't spit tea, I beg you. Would you have preferred "Does Your Chewing Gum Lose its Flavour on the Bedpost Overnight?"? It lacks a certain romanticism–'

'Stop it, or I'll choke. You're killing me, Mike.'

He stretched out beside her. The instinct that had drawn him to Lily in the first place was in no way diminished. He needed to make her happy; he wanted to make her laugh. There was, he knew, a lively woman buried deep under layers imposed by life, and he longed for her to tell him her secret fears. But he now knew that he must not push for disclosure, because she would tell him when she chose. He yawned loudly. 'The good thing about you is that a man could never get truly bored. There's always an alternative, you see.'

'Really?'

He nodded solemnly. 'When sex loses its appeal – as if it ever would – there's always noughts and crosses.'

'What?'

'The scars. If you had a small tattoo to lengthen one side, you have the grid on your belly. Bags me being the X, though. I'm always X.'

He displayed none of the misplaced respect syndrome that might have inhibited any other man. The scars were a part of her, so he embraced them and tried to find a silly use for them. Mike Walsh was almost unbearably lovable. He took hold of life, bit down hard and got on with it. He was doing the same with her toast. 'Get your own,' she advised him. 'I'm starving.'

'Now, that's a compliment,' he said, rising from the bed. 'I am going shortly to do my job.' He stared through the beautiful, multicoloured window. 'Don't be afraid,' he whispered. 'Whatever happens, I'll be here for you – or somewhere for you. The somewhere I have to be today is with the Bishop of Salford. The wedding – Dave and Philly – plus a couple more diocesan matters, like how the hell can I run three churches single-handedly. Everyone expects miracles these days.'

'Oh, yes. The wedding. She was frightened to death, poor Philly.'

'I wonder if they'll have a three-legged Labrador bridesmaid?' he mused aloud. 'There's a possibility that I may mention another small matter to the bishop. Because I don't want an affair with you, Lily. I want more. He'll have to be told. Dishonesty is not an option.'

She touched his arm. 'Mike, don't do anything in a hurry. We may burn out, then you will have gone to a lot of trouble for nothing. Please wait.'

'No. I've waited long enough, and I didn't even know I was waiting. It has to be done, with or without you. Not something that can be taken lightly, I grant you, but the Church and I parted company somewhere between Spaghetti Junction and contraception. I have given absolution to several Catholic women whose pregnancies have been terminated for a plethora of reasons. I can't condone abortion, but I uphold their right to make that terrible, often life-shattering decision. However, I have gone where no good priest should tread – off the map drawn by Rome. Until we get a pope under the age of seventy, priests like me will always be at odds with our bosses.'

Lily didn't know what to say to him. He loved people,

206

enjoyed his work, was at ease with himself and with God. 'They used to marry, didn't they? Priests, I mean. I think they should, then they'd have a better idea of their parishioners' lives.'

He nodded. 'True enough, they were married. Then some medieval anal retentive, who was probably impotent, decreed that celibacy was the flavour of his particular month. It stuck. We're now running out of clergy, the seminaries are empty, and no pope has budged. I can live with what I have done, as can my God. But the bish will have to be told. Many priests go to him only when their women become pregnant. They keep quiet for as long as possible and hope they'll get away with it.'

'What happens when there's a pregnancy?' Lily asked.

He sighed heavily. 'You won't like the answer. Suffice to say that bishops, too, are human. Churches need to be staffed, so priests are encouraged to remain on board whatever the human cost.'

'And their babies?'

'Sometimes adopted. Often, the woman is left to her own devices. Husbands rear children who aren't their own. When a woman is abandoned to her fate, she frequently makes a certain decision. In the eyes of the Church, the sin is hers and hers alone.' He turned from the window and smiled down on her. 'The hands of the hierarchy remain clean wherever possible. The women are allowed to pay the price on their behalf.'

'And your paedophiles?'

'Don't make me angry, Lily. Oh, not with you – I didn't mean angry with you. They hide behind their cassocks for as long as possible. When the stories break, they run to senior clergy and weep, blame the drink, blame a terrible childhood. Historically, they've got away with it. Some months away on retreat within a monastery, then back to work in a different place. But it's also back to square one, because there is no cure. Recently, though, successful prosecution has begun. I think America and Ireland led the way. So we'll lose more clergy again.'

'Thank God,' she breathed.

Mike smiled sadly. 'We're not perfect, you see. Life is full of mistakes, and my church is a part of life.' He kissed her forehead, then went off to begin another of his flawed days. 'See you later for noughts and crosses,' he called up the stairwell.

Lily knew that the flower man would have left her order in the back yard – he had a key. She also accepted that the shop would open a few minutes late today, and she could not manage to worry about it. She felt lighter this morning, steadier and healthier, almost optimistic.

Before stepping into the shower, she paused for a few seconds, because she didn't want to wash his scent from her skin. That, she informed herself, was the reaction of an animal. Mike didn't wear perfume. The aroma he had left was warm and embracing, but she had to be clean. 'At least I won't need an abortion,' she said aloud as she stepped into the cubicle. The words of her surgeon were engraved on her soul – 'It is unlikely that you will carry a child to full term. Pregnancy might even threaten your life. However, you are not going to find conception easy.' Fair enough. She began to weep. It wasn't fair at all, was it? Cassie. She was doing so well in her effort to avoid the child – Auntie Lee was probably guilty of neglect.

The tears dried. Lily could not continue unhappy today, because the night had been wonderful. She could love again in the physical sense. Even if that was all she had learned, it had been worth it. But, like him, she wanted more. Life with him was what she longed for. He would not be able to live without work. But Mike was one of the bright sparks who had used his brain before embarking on years in a seminary. He was a fully qualified psychologist, so, if he did quit the church, he would soon find employment. But could he be happy without his flock?

She applied make-up to a face that looked different this time, as if a cloud had moved away from the sun to allow light through. People would notice; Babs would certainly comment. Babs would be in Pour Les Dames now, because Mo was going to see Po. If those two daft creatures could mend a few bridges, Mike's winter pantomime promised to be brilliant.

'You're still you,' she told her reflection. 'You're still Leanne Chalmers, whichever wrapping paper you use.' A legally changed name could never alter the past. The husband she had divorced continued to exist in a crowded jail just a few miles away. All that separated them was the East Lancashire Road – or a couple of motorways – and while he lived, Lily's life was in danger. But she had to forget about all that, had to move onward like a good Christian soldier. Well, perhaps not, because this Christian soldier had bedded a priest, so she was rather less than good.

She walked out of the house and across the road. Mike might also become a target if the relationship endured. Clive's jealousy had driven him and her wild, because it was so angry and uncontrollable. Scissors, curtain material, knife, blood. Lily shivered. When she relived the event, it moved in slow motion across her mind, his face twisted by hatred, her heart pounding with fear. In truth, that final attack had probably been over in seconds. She had to pay for a lifetime; he would probably be free in under ten years. Nevertheless, Lily achieved a smile. Noughts and crosses, indeed. Where was the respect in that suggestion?

For Clive, Leanne had been perfection. A brunette with cornflower blue eyes, good posture, remarkable figure – he was in his element. Until she became success-ful. Until other members of the human race had the ability to watch her chasing decorators and carpet-fitters on TV, until she had become so popular that anyone who was anyone used her to furnish their home. He hated her spreads in the glossies, couldn't bear her to talk to any other man about any subject whatsoever.

Mike was completely different from Clive. He had stopped asking questions, was not afraid of her supposed beauty, made fun of imperfections he had discovered in intimate moments. He loved her, and not just because she was attractive. Her abdomen was a mess, yet he had embraced those criss-cross scars as an integral part of the woman he happened to love. Did the fact that he would need to change his job matter? Many people altered direction, moving to the other side of the world, giving up a career for children – why should he be different? Because his was a vocation rather than a job? Because he needed to remain at the helm in order to push for reform within the faith?

There was a part of Mike that would be forever priest, she supposed. But first and foremost, he was a man. He was the man she wanted and needed. Yet the decision must be his alone, since he was the one who was disobeying mortals who considered themselves to be in authority over him.

She rescued her stock from a very hot back yard. The sun was beating fiercely, and the flowers needed to cool. Her phone buzzed in the pocket of the tabard she wore for dirty work. The message made her smile again. *Remember I am X. U R O. Have bought indelible pen, forget tattoo. X.*

Maurice Jones perched on the edge of a sofa and leaned against a black bag filled with his ex-partner's clothes. The position was not exactly comfortable. 'Aren't you going to unpack?' he asked. 'The place looks like a bomb hit it.'

Paul explained that he would sort himself out eventually. He was busy; he had a lot of work.

'I know you're working hard,' Mo replied. 'But there's not enough time in a day to do all that travelling. Keep your best clients, then work part time for me. We'll forget what happened. Your old dears in particular miss you. They ask for you all the time, and can't get you through Impressions, because you're always fully booked. And the little girls miss you, too.'

'I'm over-booked.' Paul Smith was thoroughly ashamed of himself. He was bitchy, and he knew it. Jealousy was a terrible burden, and he had to get rid of it. 'Pete the Plod's trying to get me an old people's home. I'm sorry, Mo. Poor Sal. But I always loved you, and because you act more camp than I do, I really believed that you'd turn to me in the end.'

'It ain't gonna happen, mate. We should never have lived the lie in the first place.' Mo glanced at his watch.

'Look, I'll have to go, because Lily's coming in for colouring, and I'm not used to her hair yet.'

'Right.' Paul dabbed at a tear. 'On your way back, pop into her place and tell her if she'll wait till tomorrow, I'll do her. If she needs it done today, I have her file here.' He pointed to a box on the coffee table. 'Her colour charts are on top, list of treatments below. She needs a lot of conditioner, because I use some fierce stuff. But try to hold her off until tomorrow, because I can do her then.'

'In the shop?'

Paul nodded. 'Yes, I'll go half and half. Half Impressions, half the real thing. Sort out the hours with Babs – that little girl needs her mam.'

Maurice stared at the floor. The other sad thing about Paul was that he loved kiddies. With children and oldies, the man was in his element. Paul would have made a great dad. 'Thanks, Paul,' he said. 'So Mo and Po ride again, eh? Two bundles of trouble in one small shop.' He paused. 'I know you've been an angry bitch, but I also know you're not all bad. We've not seen the best of you yet, mate. Come home, and we'll soon be those two bundles of mischief and magic again.'

'Three, shortly to be four,' Paul answered. 'Well, five if we count Babs. I reckon she could start a war in a phone booth. Now, get gone while I sort out my schedule. Some of us have to work.'

Skippy had a job. There had been no forms to fill in, no interview and no trial period, as she had created her own area of expertise and was definitely the best dog for the post. There was no travelling involved, lunch was provided by her employer, and no tools were required.

Skippy had appointed herself receptionist, welcoming committee and keeper of order in number three, Fullers Walk. Perhaps she remembered that Tim Mellor had saved her life; perhaps she had become fed up with newspapers, books and old men fighting over computer dating. For whatever reason, Skippy turned up for work on the day the newly located practice began to function.

Mornings were open surgeries, and the waiting room was often congested. With a professionalism seldom displayed among humans, Skippy disposed of all negative feelings. Dogs, cats, rabbits, birds and rodents were all treated with respect, though she continued to chase anything that moved when she was taken out for exercise by Philly or Dave.

Everyone was amazed. She woofed a quiet welcome to all who arrived, led people to their chairs, and always knew whose turn it was to go into the treatment area. She hopped about on her three remaining legs, led the next victim to the business end of the shop, and was in receipt of many pats and cuddles of praise.

The veterinary nurse was astounded. She had seen many dogs in her lifetime, but she had never met an animal with so much sense. The first few days were peppered by her exclamations. 'She's done it again – are you sure you're the next to go in?' and 'Who trained her to do this?'

Skippy lapped up the praise. She was a different dog, a special dog, and she made sure that everyone knew it.

Philly and Dave were nonplussed at first. Didn't she want to live with them any longer? Had she chosen the vet over them? But she came back to the Reading Room after lunch each day, and made no effort to attend evening surgeries. They decided that Skippy, like Babs, wanted to work part time and, once they were sure that she was in no danger, accepted that she was simply a mornings-only workaholic. The dog made no attempt to enter the vet's premises on Sundays, even if an emergency arose. Skippy, they concluded, was a people-pleaser, and they were bursting with pride.

They were also on pins as they waited for Father Walsh to call them. The baby, according to a book Philly had borrowed from the shop, was now the size of a very small pea. She wanted to protect that tiny person from the disgrace of illegitimacy, and her nerves were fraying. When Dave's mobile finally rang, Philly almost jumped out of her skin. She dragged her man out into the back yard. 'Answer it now,' she begged. 'Come on, come on!'

After a few yeses and a couple of thank yous, Dave smiled at her. 'Two weeks,' he said as he turned off the phone. 'He'll do us in two weeks.'

The baby might be the size of a mature marrowfat by then. Philly's hands were twisting. 'Not enough time to get ready,' she gasped. Yet they must be ready, because the baby needed them to be ready. 'Wedding clothes, a party for our friends—'

'Stop.' Dave stepped forward and grabbed her anxious hands. 'No party. Get a smart suit and two witnesses – in that order.' He inhaled deeply. 'We have to tell her upstairs.' Both raised their eyes to an upper window. 'She'll hit the roof. Knowing her, she'll just bounce off and land in a bed of roses. She's always right, you see, always falls on her feet. Well, she would if it weren't for melegs.'

Philly's mouth set itself in a firm line. 'We do it together,' she said. 'You're not going up there on your own, but I can't do it by myself, either. She's your mother—'

'I don't need reminding about that—'

'She's your mother, so you tell her, but with me there. She's more wary of me, because I'm a woman.' Philly entered the shop and asked a couple of old stalwarts to keep an eye on the place. 'No fighting,' was her parting shot.

'What?' Dave's eyebrows moved north. 'Right now? Do we have to do it this minute?'

'No time like the present,' replied Philly. 'But your mother won't like the present we're taking with us.'

When they entered the flat, Enid Barker was in her usual place. 'That Lily one seems right pleased with herself today,' she said. 'I heard her singing in the yard before while she tiptoed through her tulips or whatever she's selling these days.'

Well, at least Madam was speaking.

The old woman turned and saw them standing hand in hand. 'Oh, both of you,' she exclaimed. 'Whatever have I done to deserve a full state visit? Will I get my best cups and spoons out? Is my hair good enough for royalty?'

Sarcasm. On a good day, Enid Barker used that instead of head-on abuse. Was this a good day, then? Dave opened his mouth, but the words emerged from Philly. 'We're getting married in two weeks,' she said. 'Not quite sure of the date yet, but Father Walsh has had permission from the Bishop of Salford. He phoned just now and told Dave.'

Enid blanched. 'Are you in the club?' she yelled.

'I'm pregnant, yes.' Philly surprised herself. Even a few weeks ago, she could not have stood there and made that statement. The strength Dave had given her was beyond measure; he, too, had gained in confidence, and it showed in several ways, including the new haircut and a flatter belly.

'And what's that to do with the bloody bishop? My son needs no bishop to tell him what he can do and when. We're Methodists. We don't run round breaking rules just because we can get forgiven by some jumped-up Irish priest with—'

'He's not Irish,' Dave said. 'He's of Irish descent.'

'A quick descent to hell is what you'll get, David Barker. What have I told you all your life? Keep away from bloody Catholics.'

Dave stood his ground. 'Mixed marriage,' he said, 'and Philly needs permission to marry me. I have to promise that the child will be reared Catholic.'

Enid inhaled sharply. 'You're a disgrace,' she told her son.

He had taken enough. He approached the woman who had birthed him. 'My child will have a father on his birth certificate. He'll know who his father is. That's where he'll have the advantage over me, Mother. Why can't you be pleased? For once in your life, why can't you be normal? Even pretending to be normal would do for now.'

She turned her back on both visitors. 'I won't be at your wedding,' she snapped.

'Good.' Dave returned to Philly's side. 'Because you wouldn't be welcome. We don't need any miserable old women to come and spoil our special day. Anyway, we've told you what you need to know. If you want anything, ring the bell. Philly will be up later with some food.'

Outside on the stairs, Dave remembered how often he had shaken when standing on this very spot, how much she had upset him, how great a job she had done of undermining him. 'My kid will have a proper mother,' he said softly. And he wasn't shaking any more.

It took a few days for Eve to take on board all she had learned about Lily Latimer. Several times, she found herself on the brink of talking to Chas, but the fact that she alone was in possession of the details made her cautious. Chas was not a gossip, but his mouth sometimes ran away with him, coasting along like a car out of gear on a slope. Unless his wife happened to be around to apply the handbrake, he sometimes sped along like a ship in full sail. Yet she needed to tell someone, since the burden was a heavy one, and it was affecting her performance in the shop and at home.

The cottage was coming along, because Lily, true to her word, had helped greatly with searches for pieces rescued by builders and sold through architectural reclamation yards. But Eve was not at ease, would never be comfortable until she had talked to Chas. No matter how pleasing the ring-turned legs on her table, she couldn't enjoy anything until she had offloaded some of the worry.

On an evening in August, the pair sat in their rear living room. Derek was minding the shop, and Eve was glad that her son was out of the house. 'The fewer people who hear this, the better,' she told her husband. They hadn't switched on lights, because this was the loveliest time of day. Through open windows, the scent of stock and honeysuckle drifted on a summer breeze. Blackbirds fussed, while a lone nightingale began a prelude from the uppermost branches of one of the trees.

Eve simply said it all, allowing it to pour from her lips in one solid section, no tears, no emotion at all. It was like a work of fiction, so vicious had the crime been. She could have wept over a story in a book, yet what she was saying now was too bad for tears, because it was real. When she had finished, she leaned back in her rocking chair, closed her eyes and waited for him to react. But he remained silent. 'Chas?' She raised her eyelids and looked at his outline against the frugal light of dusk. 'Chas?'

'What?'

'Did you hear what I just told you?'

'I did.'

'And?'

'And bloody what? What do you expect me to say? Slime like that – I'm not wasting energy on him. Anybody who treats a woman so badly wants hanging. I'm going.'

'Where?'

'To clear that flaming mess outside is where.'

She heard him, felt his fury as he stamped about and banged into his workbench. He stumbled round in the little brick-built lean-to, clattering tools in an ancient slopstone, cursing after tripping over something metallic. He was in a temper. This didn't happen often, but when it did he needed a clear deck to manage his anger, and she should leave him to it. Dared she do that? His red-hot temper was one thing, but this white heat advertised a fury that matched for temperature the magma vomiting from a volcano. It was just too hot, and it was burning him on the inside. In such a state, he would hurt only one person, and that was himself.

Then he walked down into the Devil's Jungle, and began slashing and cutting at anything and everything in his path. It was almost dark, and he would injure himself if he didn't slow down. She shouldn't have told him. His dad used to hit his mam, and stories like this one probably picked scabs off wounds that would never heal completely. 'I shouldn't have said anything,' she announced to a watercolour next to the fireplace. Poor Chas. Poor Lily ... 'I need to be stronger and keep things to myself.'

'Get back, you bastard,' Chas was shouting now.

Eve ran out. He had reached a tangled mass of brambles and bindweed, and he was in a very dark mood. 'Chas? Stop it. Stop it now, or I'm going to fetch our Derek. What the bloody hell do you think you're doing at this time of night? Them thorny bushes will have your eyes out – show a bit of sense, lad. You'll have the village coming round here en masse any minute. Give it up, Chas. This is something you do during the day.'

He stopped, but was still breathing heavily. 'Where's Capability Brown when you need him?' he asked, before bursting into tears.

Eve held the weeping man in her arms. 'Shush,' she whispered. 'Can you hear him? Our nightingale. He's done his overture, and he's coming over all Mozart.'

They clung together and listened to Nature's court musician while he poured out his soul to a darkening sky. 'How many in Toxteth have heard a nightingale so close? Or in Berkeley Square, for that matter?' she asked. 'We're lucky, babe. Just try to calm down a bit. I know it's a terrible story, and perhaps I should have kept my gob shut–'

'I'm your husband, damn it.'

'And you're upset.'

He nodded, then wiped his nose on the sleeve of his shirt. 'There's something else, love. Our Robbo's been framed. Some job at the back end of Bootle. He never done it. The one time he's absolutely innocent, and it looks like he'll get a stretch, because some guard got a bang on the head.'

'Are you sure he didn't do it?'

Chas nodded fiercely. 'But he bought some of the stuff off them that did do it, so he's banged up. Magistrate Monday for referral to Crown. No way will he sidestep this one, Eve. I'll have to go over and see him. It's not fair.'

'I know, love.'

'See, we've never damaged people, have we? We might have pinched a few bobs' worth of booze and stuff off the bleeders who pretend to run the country, but our Rob would never hurt a fly. He's like me, isn't he?'

Eve offered no reply.

'It's all wrong,' Chas continued. 'Take that lovely girl – Lily. She had a smashing job and a good life and look what happened. He's in jail. In jail? I'd have him drawn and bloody quartered in the middle of London. He's gone and ruined her life. Now, he should never come out of prison, but I bet you anything you like he'll be free in a few years. Things like that shouldn't be allowed to walk about, but our Rob? He could get a three stretch for something he never done in the first place.'

'Yes, it's wrong. But come in, Chas. No point putting yourself in hospital. This garden wants somebody with the proper stuff to have a go. You know – big machines that rip everything out and turn the ground over. Then we grow spuds.'

'Eh?'

'Spuds. First year is potatoes. They help the soil.'

'Have you been reading books again?'

She nodded.

'I'm going to get drunk,' he announced, leaving her to tidy away his tools. 'If anybody wants me, I'll be in the pub,' he called through the window.

Eve picked up all the bits and pieces, carried them into the little workshop and stood for a while looking round the lean-to, one of many additions made to the cottage since the original build. It had a low sink called a slopstone, and she pictured women long dead who had stood at sinks like this one, rubbing and scrubbing till their hands were red raw and stung by carbolic. This must have been a very small wash house. It would have held just one slave at a time, she guessed. Life was so easy now. Except for people like Lily.

The cottage was taking shape. Lily had told her to go incongruous and enjoy it, so Eve had looked up the word and taken her friend's advice. Among dressers that took up whole walls and next to doors made from vertical planks, Eve had placed her washing machine, dishwasher, dryer and cooker. But she had hung on to the black grate with its open fire, drop-down hob and swinging kettle-hook because it was beautiful. The old oven, too, remained. One day in winter, Eve would make bread in it. She would do it because the oven deserved to be used, and because bread made in these primitive appliances was supposed to taste better than any other.

She hoped he wouldn't get too drunk. She hoped his

mouth wouldn't run away with him, because the last thing Lily needed was sympathetic attention from her neighbours. In fact, Eve would go and join him, in case he needed someone to stop his gob before it got away from him. She combed her hair, grabbed a cardigan and stepped out into the cool evening air.

Halfway to the Reaper and Scythe, which was her husband's favourite hostelry, Eve stopped for a moment. An unusually short man was standing outside Pour Les Dames. He dropped a cigarette end and ground it to death with a foot. Slowly, he melted away into the darkness up the side of Fullers Walk. Was he waiting for Chas? Did he have something questionable to sell? Was it Lofty? Lofty, who had gained his nickname because he was about three inches short of five feet, was a Liverpudlian who would do just about anything for money. No. Lofty would have gone to the shop, and Derek would have sent him on to Rose Cottage.

Eve stood still for a few moments before pulling herself together. She was a woman on a mission, and she had to keep Chas quiet, so men with cheap booze for the shop were low on her agenda. The main thing was to get to the pub as quickly as possible.

All thoughts of the undersized man were deleted from her mind when she walked into the bar. Chas was doing his darts show, so he was all right. Blindfolded, he scored double top twice. Bending down and throwing the dart between his legs, he managed a near bull's eye. He wouldn't talk tonight, because humour was his own therapy and he was using it well.

She sat with Babs and Pete, trying hard not to feel like a gooseberry. But she wasn't uncomfortable for long, because these two lovely people were not a closed shop. 'Hey,' whispered Babs.

'What?' Eve grinned at the copper-headed southerner.

'Lily's up to something.'

'Is she?'

'Take no notice,' said Pete. 'There's nothing wrong with Lily – she's just that bit happier, that's all.'

Babs dug him in the ribs. 'Listen, Plod. I know that girl better than anyone round here, and I'm telling you, she's changed.'

'Into what?' Eve asked. 'A pumpkin?'

Babs blew a raspberry. 'Shut up, ye of little faith. If she's happy, something's happened. I know stuff you two don't know.'

Eve knew enough, but she kept her counsel. 'It's time she cheered up,' she said. Chas was still in his element. With his sleeves rolled up and his forehead furrowed, he concentrated on acting the clown. As long as he didn't actually kill anyone with a dart, he would be OK. 'I'm going,' she said. 'And, if I were you, I'd have an ambulance on stand-by, because he gets dafter by the minute when he's showing off.'

Outside, Eve breathed in the scents of the countryside. She remembered wanting to remain in Liverpool, remembered feeling that she would never be at home anywhere else. She was still congratulating herself when she entered her newly acquired home. Rose Cottage reminded her of a patchwork quilt, since so many extra bits had been added over the years since it was built. But it all fitted; it was all good.

She was staring at the bellows on the kitchen hearth when a tremendous pain arrived in the back of her head.

Staggering, she fell awkwardly onto her rocking chair and turned slightly. This time, she saw the weapon as it descended. This time, she slipped gratefully into unconsciousness.

Eve didn't hear the small noises made by men rifling their way through the house in search of treasures; nor did she hear the criminals leaving. She simply lay there in a beautiful house on a perfect summer evening. The nightingale did not wake her, nor did the owl. Her sleep was too deep to be disturbed.

Skippy was fooling around again. Good as gold when helping to run the vet's surgeries, she remained a puppy when out on her walks. After almost getting stuck down a rabbit hole, she was now tethered to her master and on her way home to the cottage. But she wasn't exactly behaving herself.

Dave and Philly had taken her down to a place known as the Dell, a steep dip in the land behind church and graveyard. She had paddled about in the brook, had chased a frog, and was now dripping her way homeward. Dave hung on to the lead. 'She's powerful. With an extra leg, she could have pulled a dray from here to Manchester. Something in the Dell upset her – did you see her messing about and whining near the water?'

'I did. She's never done that before. Be a good dog,' Philly chided. But the animal seemed to be distracted.

When they reached Eagleton's main street, the bitch began to whimper again. 'She gets like that if I try to stop her going into the vet's place in a morning,' said Dave. 'Are we giving her too much of her own way? They're like kids, you know. They can be spoilt.'

'She's not herself.' Philly stopped walking and spoke to Skippy. 'What's the matter?'

The dog whined.

'Is she in pain?' Philly wondered. 'Shall we go and knock at Mr Mellor's door?' She bent down and patted Skippy's head. 'Come on – let's go and get your dinner. You've got chicken and lamb's liver . . .'

The word 'dinner' might have been designed for this greedy Labrador, but on this occasion it had no effect on her. The whining grew louder, dropped in timbre and became a near-growl. She wasn't going home. She had no immediate interest in food. She knew where she wanted to go.

Dave removed the lead. Since her accident, Skippy had needed next to no constraint, since she had learned the hard way that vehicles were bigger and faster than she was. Released, she dashed through the gate of Rose Cottage, her owners hot on her heels.

Dave slowed down and grabbed his fiancée's arm. 'Remember, you've a passenger on board, love. Slow down a bit.' He looked round, and the dog had disappeared. The front door was open, and an old armoire had toppled across the opening. Skippy had clearly run underneath this angled furniture, but Dave had to set it upright again before entering the house. 'Chas?' he called. 'You there, Eve?' But the place remained silent until Skippy howled. This time, she sounded like a wolf baying at the sky. 'Stay where you are, Philly,' Dave called.

He entered the hell that had been Eve's kitchen, where Skippy sat beside the still form of Eve. Although there was little light, Dave saw blood seeping from the woman's head into a folk-weave rug in front of an upturned rocking chair. He dropped to the floor and felt for a pulse. 'Phil?' he cried. 'Ambulance and police. Do it now. Don't come in here.'

He listened and waited until she had made the call. 'Go to the shop and get Chas,' he ordered. 'Right away, love.' When her footfalls were no longer within earshot, Dave continued to search for signs of life. A faint, thready pulse faltered in a wrist. Eve's breathing was shallow, so he turned her into the recovery position, thanking God for the Red Cross and the course he had done with them. She gurgled, and more blood came from her mouth. 'Dead men don't bleed,' he whispered. 'Stay with me, Eve. It's Dave from the Reading Room. Philly's gone for Chas.' The blood in her throat might have choked her had she remained on her back, but that hadn't been the greatest of her problems. Her skull had been battered at the back and on the left temple. 'Eve, you're going to be all right. Stay with us, lass. Don't you dare leave me, don't you dare.'

Derek entered the room at a run. 'What's wrong?' was his first question. Then he saw his mother. Shocked, he slid down the wall and sat on the floor. 'Oh, my God,' he repeated continuously. Then, thickly, he uttered, 'Get Dad – try the Reaper and Scythe.'

Dave called out to Philly and sent her on a second errand as soon as she entered the hallway.

By the time Chas arrived from the pub, the siren of an approaching ambulance was growing louder. Chas crouched beside his wife while Dave went to switch on the lights. There was a great deal of blood. Her head was no longer the right shape, but the bleeding had slowed.

'Who?' asked Chas, his voice thickened by fear and grief.

'No idea.' Dave placed a hand on Chas's shoulder. 'Looks like a burglary gone wrong. The door wasn't closed, there was furniture tipped over – the dog came in, I followed, and found...' He waved a hand in Eve's direction. 'The parameds are here now, Chas,' he said, gently pulling him away. 'Let them get to her. Come on, we're only in the way. They have to take her to hospital and get her sorted.'

From the hallway, Chas, Derek and Dave listened to commands about fluids, bags, stats, ventilation, defibrillation. It was a while before Eve was stable enough to be moved. She was carried out on a stretcher, a spinal board beneath her, a collar round her neck. Only then did the dog return to her master. 'Good girl,' whispered Dave. 'Whatever happens, Skip, you did your job.'

Philly was in the front garden when Eve was placed in the ambulance. She expected Chas to accompany his wife, but the vehicle screamed away at speed before he was given the option. Eve wasn't dead, Philly kept reminding herself. Had she been dead, the paramedics would have driven at a slower pace. She ventured into the house.

Dave shook his head and placed a finger to his lips. On the floor beside him, propped up by the walls, sat the husband and son of Eve Boswell. Not a sound was uttered by either of them. It was eerie. Neither was reacting, and Dave realized that they were in deep shock. 'We can't go in the kitchen,' he told his wife. 'It's a crime scene and we've already contaminated it. Open the shop and make sweet tea for these two.' He gave her a bunch of keys.

The village had arrived outside in the street. It seemed that someone from every house in the immediate vicinity had put in an appearance, while both pubs had spilled out customers in various stages of bonhomie that died immediately when they realized what had happened. Some tried to talk to Philly, but she pushed her way through, because she was focused on her mission. Sugar for shock, she kept telling herself. She glanced upward, saw Dave's mother at the window as usual. But the old woman was standing, so perhaps she had seen something?

While waiting for the water to boil, Philly went upstairs. 'Mrs Barker?'

'Three of them,' came the reply. 'The cops are there now – send them up here, will you? And make me a hot drink. Please.'

Philly paused for a split second. Please? But there was no time to lose. She dashed out, took tea across the road, told a policeman that Mrs Barker had something to say, then returned to her side.

'What happened to Eve Boswell?' asked Enid.

'Somebody beat her halfway to death, Mrs Barker. She's gone in the ambulance. The house looks as if it's been burgled, and Eve's been hit about the head. Dave's with Chas and Derek – neither of them can move for shock.'

Enid shook her head. 'One of the men was less than five feet tall, I swear. The other two were normal size, dark clothes all three of them. I think the little fellow hid behind a bush in the front garden while the other two followed her in. But I can't be sure where the small chap went – I can only say what I saw and what I think went on. They waited for her. For a burglary, they'd have gone in while the place was empty. It's her they were after, I'm sure.'

Philly sat down. She felt sick, and she wanted Dave, but she couldn't leave his mother on her own at a time like this.

'Philly?'

'What?'

Enid bowed her head. 'Stuff like this makes you think. I'll never alter, but this has shook me to the bones. I'm sorry. I'll tell Dave I'm sorry, too. Life's too bloody short, isn't it?'

Philly burst into tears. Eve's almost lifeless body had been the bridge across which Enid had walked to make her first attempt at peace. Was Mrs B intending to join the human race?

'Don't start skriking. We've enough on without all that. Go. Go on – get out and send me a policeman. And tell Dave to get that man and his son to the hospital. She'll need them there when she wakes up.' Enid shook her head. 'If she wakes up, God help her.'

Philly felt as if she had been running up the steepest bit of Everest. She found Dave, Derek and Chas in the hall of Rose Cottage, but the Boswells were mobile now, and clearly preparing to leave. 'I've told the police to talk to your mam,' she whispered to her husband. 'She saw a lot. And she apologized to me.'

Dave grunted, his eyes fixed on Chas.

'Come on, Dad,' begged Derek. 'The taxi's waiting.'

Chas allowed himself to be led out of the house. He looked like an improbable cross between a child and a very old man. Skippy remained on guard at the door. She wasn't sure about these police people, but her master and mistress seemed to trust them, so they deserved the benefit of the doubt.

After their interviews, Philly and Dave repaired to his

mother's flat. She made no comment about her canine visitor, but she spoke very clearly to her son. 'She'll have told you what I said, eh?'

Dave nodded.

'Well, same goes for you. I likely won't improve, but I'm saying sorry anyway. Give that dog a drink, it looks parched. And there's some bits of ham in the fridge – keep her going till she gets home.'

Dave stared at the floor while Philly fed the dog. He owned too gentle and reasonable a nature to react badly to his mother's words, but had she no concept of the harm she had done for forty-seven years? Was it all over and forgiven because she had finally climbed down from her high horse?

'I know what you're thinking,' Enid said. 'And I can't say I blame you. What can I do or say, Dave?'

'Nothing.'

'Exactly. Just wait till the police come, then leave me. I'll remember better on my own.' She looked at the dog. 'She's all right for one with a leg missing, isn't she?'

Philly almost smiled. 'She came up from the Dell and went straight to Eve's house – we couldn't do a thing with her till she got to Eve.'

Enid nodded. 'That's because whoever was in Rose Cottage tonight must have got away across the brook. You were probably only about two minutes away from them on your walk. They didn't come out through the front door. Your dog will have picked up the scent of something bad down in the Dell. They definitely went the back way.'

'That's true,' said Dave. 'They shoved a cupboard across the front door. There could be evidence in or near the water.' He walked across the room and threw open a window. 'Officer? My mother says she thinks they escaped the back way. If they went through that garden, they'll be scratched and nettle-stung. I dare say they climbed over into the graveyard. You'd better come soon and talk to her.'

'They could be covered in poor Eve's blood as well,' said Philly.

'Well, they've got police dogs out there now.' Dave closed the window. 'They should have borrowed Skippy.'

Enid sighed. 'I've never liked Scousers. But it doesn't do to feel like that just because somebody talks different. Happen I've learned my lesson.'

Dave let a detective into the flat. 'My mother's seen a fair bit tonight,' he explained, 'but we'll leave you to it. You've a better chance of getting details if she's got no distractions.' He led his fiancée out and down the stairs.

In the shop, they sat with their dog and stared across the road at Rose Cottage. 'Eve never did anybody any harm, I'm sure,' said Dave. 'So why her? Why did they have to pick on her? Mam's sure it wasn't a burglary. Stands to sense they would have robbed the house while it was empty instead of waiting for somebody to come home.'

'Chas knows some funny folk, Dave. His brother's been in and out of prison since his teens. But Eve? She's a lovely woman. I'm sure she'd never break the law.'

Dave held her hand. 'Stay calm, love.'

She sniffed away a tear. 'Can I sleep in your bed tonight? Just for comfort and company?'

'Course you can, Phil.'

They took their precious dog and walked home. They

would never forget tonight; Dave, in particular, would carry with him the picture of Eve Boswell's injuries. He needed Philly as much as she needed him.

Like I said, nobody gets paid enough in this bloody country. It's going to the dogs, and I'm probably best off in here. All kinds of asylum-seekers and Europeans coming in, undercutting our working men, bringing British folk to their knees.

Anyway, the solicitor's clerk, who remains anonymous, traced the money through his employer's records. She's a florist in a place called Eagleton, pronounced Eggleton. All her mail goes to the shop, but she doesn't live there. Seems she bought a house across the road. Calling herself Lily Latimer, bloody daft name.

Taunton and Liverpool are in cahoots. Money's come from Taunton, but the workers up here will be paid. She has it coming. Right from the start, wherever she went, men's eyes lit up and followed her every move. What did she do? She went on TV so that more of them could ogle her. Makeover Madness? Lunacy, more like. Even pregnancy didn't stop her. If anything, she was more beautiful when carrying the kid, though I never fancied her then, did I?

It'll be soon. I suppose they'll have someone keeping watch while it happens. Can't be done in the shop, has to be in the house. Seems she's doing well enough with her buttercups and daisies. There'll be men after her, but that won't last, because she'll be either dead or disfigured – I hope she'll be dead. When I know she's not out there showing herself off, I'll be OK.

And all I have to do is lie here and wait...

Nine

Mike's idea of a romantic evening was, at best, hilarious.
Lily was beginning to grow used to his sense of adventure, so she was hardly surprised when she found herself
in the Canal Street district of Manchester. Here, the gay
community lived its life to the full, and Mike was clearly
no stranger to the area, since he was on first-name terms
with many of the people who sought entertainment in
the bars and clubs. 'They need spiritual guidance just
like everyone else,' he told Lily. 'And there's still a lot of
prejudice. Apart from all of which, they cook the best
food in England, so that's as good a reason as any to
come here. I do enjoy a well-presented meal.'

They finished their tour in a restaurant cum nightclub
named Sisters. Their dinner was superb and they were
served by cross-dressers. All waitresses were men; all
waiters were women; and, on the whole, they were a
handsome crowd. A band played, and several people
were making use of the dance floor.

'We're here for a reason,' Mike announced as they ate
a delicious crème caramel. 'Mo and Po are performing
tonight, and I wanted you to see how good they are. I
asked them what they were doing, and it's quite a
mixture. You should know that your hairdressers are

a great deal more than simple crimpers. They are stars in the making. As long as Paul hangs on to sense and doesn't collapse into one of those black holes. He does love Maurice, you know. It's sad when love is one-sided, but there's nothing can be done. I always thought they were daft for not telling the truth in the first place.'

'Right.'

'The real reason we're here is because I have decided to go very PC with the panto. It's time certain social problems were addressed. No more of the same old same-old. It's time for the revolution.'

'Oh, yes? Shall I make a banner?'

He smiled benignly and, for a moment or two, looked rather like a priest. 'Why Cinderella?' he asked. 'Every damned fool seems to worry about her with her rags and her sweeping brush and her hard life. What kind of a role model is she for today's women? The concept of a human female accepting such treatment is positively Victorian. We must move on.'

'I thought her poverty and ill-treatment were the point of the story. Virtue reaps its own reward and all that jazz.'

He drained his glass and ordered another double orange juice on the rocks. As he was driving, he could not drink wine, but he still liked to display the air of a man living dangerously. He was living dangerously. She was lovely, she was his, and she was definitely forbidden fruit. 'Cinderella's got the looks, kid,' he said. 'And we all know that a pretty woman has a head start in life. Why the hell did suffragettes bother throwing themselves under horses, chaining themselves to railings and getting force-fed in jail if Cinders is going to carry on unliberated in the hearth every winter? What about her two unfortunate stepsisters? Has no one ever given a thought to their situation?'

'They're ugly,' said Lily.

'Exactly. Ugly and in the bin just because of unfortunate faces. Now, why should they suffer because they look like the back of a crashed bus? Just picture this. Buttons is a surgeon. OK? All in white, even has to sing through a mask.'

'I'm trying to imagine that. It's not easy.'

He motored on. 'So Salmonella and Pneumonia are as ugly as mortal sin: warts, bottle-bottom spectacles, manky hair, big feet and fat bellies. They're so hideous that no man will ever give them a second glance – or a first, for that matter. People have dropped dead of heart attacks after looking at these two.'

'And they're played by Mo and Po? They're working together again, so I guess they'll play together.'

'Yup.'

Lily leaned forward, as the place was becoming noisy. 'They're beautiful men, Maurice and Paul. You'll never make them ugly.'

'We can soon change that. I'll duff them up behind the bike sheds – I was a terrible bully at school, so I know how to break a man's nose. And we'll have a make-up box, of course.'

Lily laughed. He was in his element.

'The Fairy Godmother is on their side, because she's a Communist and all for the underdog. And believe me, they are definitely dogs. So the uglies get the tickets to the ball – plus a special offer of reduced-rate facelifts as long as they buy four hundred boxes of cornflakes. Oh, and there's liposuction available at sale prices via the *Daily Mail*. Fairy Godmother's also Mafia, therefore she can be bribed, so all that wand-waving will serve to iron out any residual wrinkles after the fat has been hoovered off. You see? I cover every eventuality. Buttons does the plastic surgery, then Salmonella and Pneumonia cop off with a couple of princes and—'

'Where's Cinderella?' she asked through laughter. Could a Communist be a member of the Mafia? Weren't Mafia folk Catholics? But Lily kept these questions to herself, because Mike was in full flood.

'Cinders is a theatre nurse. We all know how much surgeons make, so Buttons will do for her. See? It all dovetails together wonderfully. This fairy tale has been waiting to be written.'

Lily thought about it. 'Buttons?' she asked.

'What about him?'

'I hope he used stitches and staples instead—'

'Instead of buttons? I am ahead of you, girl. When the ugly sisters first appear, they'll be ghastly. We'll need vomit buckets for the first few rows of audience. Then two pretty girls in similar clothes will come out of the wings and meet their bridegrooms once the swellings have died down. Damage from surgery, I mean. A much better story, isn't it?'

Lily wasn't sure. But it didn't matter what she said – he would go ahead anyway. Loving him was so easy. He had the imagination of a child and the brains of a professor, so he was a rare creature. On the brink of leaving a career for which he had endured years of training, his main aim in life seemed to be to replace himself, thereby saving the bishop a job. He had a friend returning from Africa, and he would suggest him to the bishop as a suitable candidate to take over the parishes. Mike wasn't giving up; he was moving on.

'I'm not an ugly sister any more,' was his next line. 'Not a priest, not an ugly sister – there's no place for me.'

'You should carry on being a priest.'

'With a mistress?'

'Possibly.'

It wasn't just her. He needed to get out anyway before he exploded, before he lost his patience and took issue with the bishop, the cardinal, even the Pope. If the Church didn't grow up, it would die in its cradle. Two thousand years was a relatively short lifespan, and there would be no chance of resuscitation once the grass roots had stopped providing oxygen. Places of worship were emptying; people congregated instead at football and concerts, raising their voices to heaven in praise of a team or a pop group. If Catholicism was not prepared to get real, it would cease to exist.

'You've gone quiet,' Lily complained.

'Enjoy. It happens very rarely.'

She studied him. He was an amazing man with excellent looks and a way with people – any people. His charm could probably get him just about anywhere, yet he seemed to have chosen a florist from a small shop in a large village. 'Mike?'

'What?'

'Don't give up the priesthood for me, will you?'

'No. You're just one face on the dice, Lily. There are at least five others, all stamped with a reason for me to quit. Stop worrying. You're not guilty, whatever the outcome.'

A fanfare ripped through the air and the MC, a very butch girl in top hat and tails, announced Maurice et Paul. The latter was dressed as a very handsome woman.

His costume was Spanish and red all the way from patent shoes right up to the scarlet mantilla and comb. A recording of traditional Spanish music was played, and Paul danced as well as any female performer of flamenco. He played the castanets, executed brilliantly the steps made famous by gypsies of Andalucia, and took away the corporate breath of a very large audience.

Maurice emerged with his cape. It was red on one side, gold on the other. Like Paul, he was a true professional, and his body was the perfect vessel from which to pour the passion expressed in a matador's cloak. 'Nice bum,' whispered Lily to Mike.

'It'll be a good pantomime,' was the quiet reply. 'What a pity he'll be wearing a skirt. With a backside like that, he'd certainly please the ladies.'

The set ended with a standing ovation, and the pair of triumphant performers left the stage to prepare for their next piece. In the meantime, a small jazz band filled the gap, and Mike ordered coffee. 'There's true talent in those two,' he pronounced. 'They don't need me. They don't need anyone, because they could fill the school hall ten times over. But I'll write the script.'

'You'd better. No one else would think of something so original. What's the title?'

'*Never Mind Cinderella, What About the Rest?*' he suggested.

'Bad title. Too wordy.'

'Then you choose one. I didn't realize I was going to marry my chief critic.'

Several beats of time passed before Lily absorbed what he had just said. Her hand shook when she picked up the coffee cup. It had been like this last time. Clive had made all the decisions, and she had found herself engaged, then married. This man was nothing like Clive, yet the speed at which he travelled still managed to frighten her. Did she want to re-marry? Did she need to? It occurred to her that she might feel safer in an alliance with a priest, as there could never be a marriage while he remained in his post.

'Lily?'

She looked at him. 'I may not want to be married,' she said.

'Then we shall live in glorious sin. Over the brush, they call it in these parts.' He knew he shouldn't have said anything, but it wasn't the type of statement that could be changed easily into an amusing aside. He wondered whether she understood that she had been a final decider, certainly not a catalyst or a vehicle to transport him out of the clergy. 'Lily, it doesn't matter what we do afterwards.' He paused. 'That's not true, because I'd like to marry you. But I was going to quit anyway. Although I've received absolution from my father confessors, the way I treat my parishioners is not in line with many of the edicts emerging from Rome. I am not forgivable.'

'You are,' she replied. 'And that's the problem – my problem. But you must realize that I have fallen head over heels in the past and the relationship didn't work out. In fact, it was damaging. I've known you just a few weeks—'

'A couple of months.'

'All right, a couple of months. And you're wonderful. You make me laugh, you're clever and handsome and very beguiling. It all terrifies me. Speed frightens me, Mike.'

'Then I'll slow down.'

A smile played on her lips. Slow down? He had several speeds, and the lowest was overdrive, while the fastest broke the sound barrier. Mike didn't know how to go slowly, except in a car. Strangely, his quickness was one of the main factors that contributed to his charm. He had not allowed adulthood to contaminate the inner child, had never permitted sense to interfere with his goals. Yet he remained one of the cleverest people she had met in her life. And oh, how tempted she was!

'Sorry,' he said.

'It's OK. As long as you don't take me for granted, Mike. Remember, I've been through ... hell.'

'How can I remember what you won't tell me?'

'I'll tell you when I'm ready.'

The MC was back.

This time, Mo and Po had a bash at the overdone piece 'I Will Survive'. But this was survival with a difference, because it ended with a punch-up that involved flying wigs and torn dresses out of which false breasts fell to litter the small stage. The MC rang a bell, the contestants retired to their corners, seconds appeared, gum shields were inserted, and boxing gloves entered the fray. As did towels when both were counted out. At the end, Mo and Po were carried off on a pair of stretchers, lifeless hands trailing on the boards.

Lily found herself weeping with laughter. She stood with the rest of the audience to salute a performance in which timing had been perfect, singing excellent until punches had landed, and costumes glorious. It was no wonder that they were going up for *Britain's Got Talent*. They had the special magic born of true individuality.

'Shall we go?' Mike asked.

'All right.' She was feeling tired. This was her first real night out since she had recovered, and the exhaustion she experienced was almost total. Something called ME had been mentioned after a blood test, but she had ignored it. No way was her working life going to finish when she was not yet thirty. In Lily's opinion, sixty was rather young for retirement.

He drove slowly, and that was another point in his favour. And he didn't return to Eagleton right away, because he wanted to show Lily more of the beauty that belonged to Lancashire. They went up hills and down dales, past remote farms and tiny hamlets, while the route became steeper. 'This is the way to the Pennines,' he said. 'The backbone of England. It's stunning on this side, but we must go to Yorkshire at some stage, because West Yorkshire is nothing short of magnificent.' Even in near-darkness, the landscape was amazing.

After another drive, they landed at the foot of Rivington Pike, where Mike delivered a lecture on history. This was not the Sermon on the Mount, he explained; this was the sermon before the mount was climbed. The pike, he told her, was twelve hundred feet above sea level, and on a clear day, landmarks for miles around were visible. 'You can see the Isle of Man, Blackpool Tower, the hills of Wales and the Cumbrian fells. You could see Ashurst Beacon, which was lit as a warning during wars, but they've moved it now to the Last Drop Village.'

'I do the flowers for that place.'

'Good for you. They use only the best.'

'Of course. What was Rivington Pike for?' she asked.

He told her about hunting parties using the tower, about roaring fires and mulled wine. 'But it's no longer enjoyed. All boarded up, no windows, no way in. Sad. Everything of note has to be protected from the very people who are supposed to appreciate it.'

'They're too busy collecting ASBOs to take an interest in an eighteenth-century folly,' said Lily. 'Do you mind if I ask to go home? It's been my first night out since … since my last night out.'

'Which was a long time ago?'

She nodded. 'A couple of years. But I've enjoyed myself. Thanks for Manchester and thanks for this lovely countryside.'

'Thank God, not me,' he answered. 'He made this lot. Mind you,' the car came to life, 'I'm not sure He made Manchester. No, we mustn't blame Him for that …' Before taking off the handbrake, he stroked her cheek. 'Keep me on the list, Lily.'

'List? What list?'

'Of potential suitors.'

'I'll think about it,' she promised.

Skippy wouldn't settle. They tried her downstairs, upstairs, on the landing, even at the foot of their bed. 'She wouldn't fit in with us, anyway,' moaned Philly. 'This is only a three-quarter bed, and you take up two-thirds of it.'

'Is that a complaint?'

'Yes.'

'Then do it in triplicate and send it to management.'

'Who's management?'

'The dog is,' he replied wearily. He sat up. 'It's no good, I'll have to take her out again. I can't sleep, any-way. I keep seeing that poor woman every time I close my eyes.'

Philly agreed. She hadn't seen Eve in the kitchen, but the memory of her almost lifeless body on the stretcher was enough. Poor Dave had been witness to everything. 'We may as well give up and get dressed,' she said.

'You're pregnant,' he protested. 'You can't be running about half the night.'

'Pregnant, but not ill,' she reminded him. 'And I'm stopping nowhere on my own while there's somebody out there attacking folk.'

'You heard my mam, Philly. What she saw more or less proves that Eve was targeted. They'll be miles away by this time – it's coming up eleven o'clock. Stay where you are.'

'No. I won't,' she replied. 'I feel safer with you and Skippy. That's a compliment, in case you hadn't noticed. Till we get over this – if we ever get over it – we stick together.'

'Yes, Sarge.' Dave performed a comical salute.

Once outside, the dog dragged Dave along until she was almost choking. She displayed no interest in Rose Cottage, preferring to struggle onward past Fullers Walk until she reached the end of the block. She stopped suddenly, and Dave managed, only just, not to fall over her. 'She's got good brakes,' he said. 'Nearly had me on the floor then.'

Philly took a torch from her pocket and shone it on the tarmac that led to the rear of the shops and all the garages. 'Dave?'

'What?'

'I can't be sure, but I think it's these two cigarette ends.' She shone the light on Skippy's spine. 'See? She's got her hackles up.'

Dave agreed. Skippy was doing a fair imitation of a

Rhodesian ridgeback. 'Don't touch anything, Phil. The cops are still across the road – I'll fetch somebody.'

A nervous Philly waited with Skippy until Dave returned with a policeman. The dog was growling again. It was clear that she had no affection for the person whose scent she had pursued so avidly. The officer stopped and pulled on a pair of purple surgical gloves, picked up the cigarette butts and placed them in a small transparent bag. 'Is this the famous three-legged dog that led us to the crime scene?' he asked.

'Yes,' Dave answered proudly. 'She was a stray, but we took her in after she lost her leg. Anyway, we were walking her behind the church and she set off whining. She was very fretful near the brook, yet she wanted to turn back. There was nothing else for it – she had to go to Rose Cottage, and you know the rest. She wouldn't sleep. The way she's carrying on, there may be a chance that one of the criminals smoked those cigarettes. Before you go, can we ask how Mrs Boswell is?'

'Not sure,' said the policeman. 'Last I heard, they were trying to stabilize her to make her fit for surgery. You may get good news in the morning, please God. Tell you what, though. We've a vanload of dogs out there, but we'd make room for this one. If it turns out that these fag ends are connected to the crime, yon dog will be declared a genius.'

'She is a genius.' Philly's voice trembled with pride mixed with many other emotions. If Eve Boswell lived, it would be because of Skippy; if the poor woman died, Skippy had done her best. 'Come on, Dave. Let's get Madam home.'

*

'She's still not in.' Babs glanced over her shoulder at Pete, who was lying on a sofa and trying to recover some energy. 'She never goes out. If she did go out, she'd tell me where she was going and what she was doing.'

Pete groaned. He'd had a hard time tonight, and he genuinely needed rest. 'Come away from the window, love. She'll not get home any faster if you stand there worrying. Put the kettle on.'

Babs felt like screaming. If she drank one more cup of tea or coffee, she would drown. And there had definitely been a change in Lily of late. It had been quite sudden, too, and joy connected to the house she had bought was not wholly responsible for it. There was a new lightness in her step, and her skin, which had become dull in recent months, had started to glow again. 'I can't stand this,' Babs moaned. 'The hospital tells me nothing about Eve, Lily's gone missing—'

'And I'm tired after helping out across the road. You'll be ill next if you carry on like this, lady.'

But Babs remained where she was. When the news had reached the pub, she and Pete had spilled out with the rest. After Eve had been taken away in the ambulance, Babs had gone straight to Lily's house. But Lily had been nowhere and was still nowhere. Well, she was probably somewhere, but she wasn't at the somewhere she was supposed to be. 'She'd never, ever go out without telling me,' she insisted.

'You'll drive yourself mad,' Pete said. 'You're getting your knickers in a twist over nothing – Lily's a grown woman. She doesn't need to sign a late book or ask permission – she's not on probation. If you like, I can get her an ASBO and she'll be on curfew with a fancy tag bracelet round her ankle.'

Babs tutted. 'The minute she comes home, I'm going over there. You stay here in case Cassie wakes. I have to be the one to tell Lily what's happened. She'd grown quite close to Eve. In fact, I'm ashamed to say I was a bit jealous, which isn't fair, because I've got you and Lily's got no one.'

'Glad to hear I'm better than nobody,' he said.

Babs stamped a foot. 'Stop twisting my words, Plod. You know what I mean, and you know I really care about you, so shut up. Where would she go on her own, though?'

'How do you know she's on her own? She might be talking about flowers with a bride-to-be, or perhaps she's gone to see a film or a play.' He closed his eyes and tried to rest. It had been a dreadful couple of hours, and the police dogs were still out there in the hollow behind the church. They would have to give up soon, because officers might be needed elsewhere, there was no light, and little could be done until forensics had tackled the bits of evidence that had been recovered.

'Pete?'

'What?'

'Come here. Come on – hurry up – she's back. And look who's with her! Blood and Carter's Little Liver Pills, I don't believe it.'

Pete joined Babs at the window. 'So what? They share a house from time to time, so why shouldn't they go out for a meal or something?'

'It's the or something I'm wondering about. I mean, he's a priest, and—'

'Hey – are you in training to become the next biggest

246

Lancashire gossip? You'll be overtaking Mrs Wotserface soon.'

'Mrs Barker. And I'm a south-westerner, thanks. Pete?'

'Yes?'

'He's holding her hand. See? He's pushed her into the house and he's running past the church to Rose Cottage—'

'Or you could become the new commentator for the Grand National. Give over, Babs. You're getting on my nerves now.'

Exasperated, she abandoned him to his own devices and ran downstairs. Poor Lily. She'd probably had a nice night out, albeit with a Catholic priest, and she was returning to this. It was plain to anyone arriving that something serious had happened, because Rose Cottage was cordoned off by the familiar blue and white police tape. And the priest had gone and left her on her own in that massive place . . .

Babs knocked at the door, and it was opened immediately.

'What's going on?' Lily asked.

Babs led her friend through to the kitchen and sat her down. 'Now, don't panic. We don't want you back on the don't-jump-off-the-roof pills, do we? Eve's been attacked. She's unconscious in hospital, her husband and son are with her, and the cops are still at the cottage.'

Lily's face blanched. 'Who did it?'

Babs shook her head. 'No bloody idea, my lovely. One minute we were in the pub, Chas was doing tricks with darts, and Eve was sitting with me and Pete. She went home. Then Philly came in, Chas disappeared like a magician's rabbit, someone shouted about an attack, and we all came to see what was going on. Next thing was the ambulance, then the police, then everyone was interviewed.'

Lily began to rock back and forth.

'Don't start that, Lee. You'll have me seasick.'

'Is she going to live?'

Babs raised her shoulders. 'They won't say anything at the hospital, except they told me the doctors were with her. I don't like to keep telephoning, because those nurses are busy enough without me making things worse. The short story is we'd be better waiting till morning.'

Lily remembered those very words. 'Wait till morning,' the nurses had said repeatedly. Friends had come, friends had gone and, many times, she had wanted to shout, 'I'm here – look.' But she hadn't been able to. Nurses had told people to try again tomorrow, that there was always the chance that she would wake at any minute. She hoped that Eve wasn't in that condition. Hearing the voices of those around her, needing to talk, wanting to answer questions, trying to prise open her eyelids – it had been so hard. Eventually, Lily had woken properly, but the nightmare had been true. It had all happened; it hadn't been just a bad dream.

'Lily?'

'What?'

'You don't think . . . ?'

'Think what?'

'Never mind,' said Babs. 'Forget it.'

'I won't forget any of it, Babs. She's in a condition similar to mine, right?'

'No. She got bashed on the head.'

'So she's unconscious. The method isn't important –

the result remains the same. I was out of it for a couple of weeks.'

Time ticked by while Babs allowed the possibilities to enter her mind. She didn't want to ask the question, yet she knew she must. 'Him?' was all she said.

Lily bowed her head and thought. 'Yes. Definitely. I'd bet my life it's him.'

'From prison?'

'Yes. He's in the ideal place for it, because the old lags will know people on the outside, and this isn't far from Liverpool.'

Babs pondered for a while. 'But your name's changed. Where you live's changed. All letters and stuff are addressed to Lily Latimer—'

'At the shop. The shop is still my address. No mail comes here. Haven't even had my driving licence altered. It's changed to Lily Latimer, but the address is number seven Fullers Walk. How he found me I don't know and may never know. But Eve has dark hair like mine used to be, and I've lost an awful lot of weight. To someone with a description of Leanne Chalmers, Eve would be the nearer match. I know she's older, but she's dark-haired and about my height.'

'So someone's found you for him? But presumably they've seen you in the shop and know you're blonde. So why would they attack someone else? They must have looked at the village. Don't they case the joint first?'

Lily shrugged. 'I don't know how he worked it out. Perhaps he paid off solicitors – I've no idea. The shop's too busy, anyway, so they'd want to do it away from Fullers Walk. And the blonde in the shop could be Lily's assistant. Clive knew I had money from my family as well as from my own job before I became Lily. And there was the compensation fund – I'm wealthy, Babs. I could afford an assistant.'

'Yes.'

They sat in silence for a few moments, then Lily shot from her seat in one swift move. She ran to the dining room, only to return seconds later with a cardboard box. 'You see?' she said, her tone desperate. 'It's my fault – I should have changed it.'

Babs said nothing.

'Look!' Lily opened the package and took out a wooden sign. 'Hope House,' she cried. 'Outside, this is still St Faith's presbytery. Right. Listen to me. Say nasty people came to find me after he'd traced my new location by some means. And say they saw me in the shop, but I'm blonde.'

'OK.'

'Leanne Chalmers is brunette. So the woman in the flower shop would be Leanne's assistant.'

'All right.'

'So if a man – or a woman, for that matter – wanted to know where I lived, anyone in the village might have said I'd bought the house across the road next to the church.'

'Still with you so far, Lee.'

'In the past, Rose Cottage would have suited me better than this place. I don't know how much the attackers know about me, but I always had a cottage in Somerset, didn't I?'

'You did.'

'So, these unknown criminals cross the road and check out the houses near the church. This one has St Faith's Presbytery on the sign. It's a priest's home. No one would look twice at it if they were looking for a woman. Rose Cottage still has FOR SALE outside, but with SOLD plastered across the middle of the board. Which house would you choose? Eve dyes her hair dark brown to hide her grey—'

'And they got her by mistake.'

'Yes.'

'Oh, my God.'

It had nothing to do with God, Lily told herself inwardly. Poor Eve had been attacked by servants of Satan himself, and they had gone for the wrong target. They might come back; they might carry on picking off women until they got the right one. 'It's my fault,' she whispered. 'If I hadn't come here, Eve would still be staining that beautiful staircase in her cottage.'

'Stop it, because—'

'And I never saw a happier marriage. Even when she's telling him off for being daft, you can see how much they love each other. If she dies, he'll die inside. Just perfect together, those two.'

'You can't blame yourself.'

'Can't I? Oh, I know I've done nothing – but neither has poor Eve. Babs, if I'd stayed away, none of this would have happened.'

'And if wishes were horses, beggars would ride.'

'My gran used to say that.'

'And mine.' Babs busied herself with tea-making, because she felt she had to do something that appeared sensible. It had been her experience in life so far that doing ordinary things meant staying inwardly sane and outwardly calm, and she had to be both. Lily was terrified all over again; someone had to give the impression of level-headedness. She set a tray with cups, saucers, milk jug and sugar bowl. Lee wasn't a sweet-tooth, but she was in shock.

Lily stared unseeing at the tray when it arrived on the table. 'He's put a curse on me, Babs.' A thought struck. 'And what if he comes after you and little Cassie? He sees you as part of his downfall, and we know he doesn't care about children.'

Babs swallowed hard. 'I'll get Pete to stay with us.'

'Twenty-four seven? He does have a job.'

Babs gulped again. 'What are we going to do, Lily?'

'We're going to run.'

'What? I've got Pete and a job. I've got Cassie settled with Valda and her kids. I like it here.'

Lily nodded. 'So do I. I like it very much. But after what's happened here tonight, I don't trust anyone – not even the police. We're two hundred miles from Somerset, yet we've been found. Think about Cassie and only Cassie. Babs, we know he'd kill anyone.'

'Tell the cops that he's organized this from jail. Tell them he needs sending to Siberia or somewhere.'

'Proof?' Lily asked.

Babs poured the tea. 'You're having sugar, because you need it. We both do.' She sat down. 'You're right, it's down to proof. They'll need to catch the people who did this and make them talk. And what are they going to do to him? Give him a longer sentence? He'll still be there. He'll still be able to pay people to come after us. And, at the end of the day, it could have been a simple burglary.'

'It wasn't. Lord, I hate sweet tea. You think there's no hiding place? So do I, but we can play for time. Babs, we're going. I'll sell up here, then—'

'No. If we go away, it's just for a short break, to give them time to find the attackers and get them to confess.

We can't let him dictate our lives from now on. We belong here. You have to learn to compromise.' She lowered her eyelids and glanced through the lashes at her friend. 'Lily?'

'What?'

Babs paused and took a sip from her cup. 'What's going on with Mike?'

Lily stared stonily across the table. 'Shut up and drink your tea. Now, nothing will happen tonight. The offenders are on the run, and this village is too hot for them. Send Pete home. If he's asleep, get rid of him as early as you can in the morning. Order a taxi to pick you up behind the shop, not at the front. I'll be outside the village on the top road – near the telephone kiosk. Transfer your luggage from the taxi to my car, and we'll bugger off for a few days. Or weeks. I'll be there from about seven o'clock.'

'If you insist.'

'Bring Cassie's child seat and clothing. We'll buy her some toys when we get there.'

'When we get where?'

Lily sighed. 'To the end of whichever bloody road. I don't know.'

The front door opened. 'It's Mike,' said Babs.

'Yes. Go now. Not a word to Pete.'

'What about the shop?' Babs whispered, standing up.

'Closed till further notice. Can't be helped.'

Mike entered the room. 'Lily? Babs? Are you all right?'

Neither replied.

'I'll stay tonight,' he said. 'Though I'm expected in Harwood tomorrow morning. This is a terrible business, isn't it?'

Babs, who was standing uneasily in the line of Lily's penetrating stare, made her farewell and left the house.

Mike sat in the chair she had vacated. 'Eve's still alive,' he said. 'They're trying to stabilize her for surgery, something to do with bloods and gases – I don't understand medical jargon.'

Lily sighed. 'I do. I've been there. I've been in Eve's position and I know she could die on the table if they took her in now. They have to get her body as balanced as possible before taking a proper look at the wounds. She's already in shock, and the trauma of surgery might kill her. They'll be working damned hard to save her.'

He looked steadily at Lily's face and decided once again that he must ask no more questions about her own past crises. All he wanted was to comfort her, but she wasn't here any more. The woman who had laughed herself silly just a few hours ago, who had enjoyed his tour of the countryside outside Bolton, had disappeared. In her place sat an animal as terrified as the rescued rabbit had been after its long containment under the tree. If anything, she looked worse than she had in the first few weeks after arriving in the north. 'Go to Harwood now,' she told him. 'I need to be by myself.'

Mike leaned back in the chair. 'Aren't you afraid?'

'It's already happened, hasn't it? They aren't likely to come back tonight, because they'll be too busy putting as much space as possible between themselves and this village.'

'You don't need me?'

Lily paused before speaking. 'In the last couple of years, I've made sure I don't need anyone. And I like my own space.' She did need him, but she didn't want him to get involved with the dreadful truth – not yet, not until she had decided what to do in the long term.

'Plenty of space for you here, then. This house was built to contain more than one priest – and their housekeeper – so you'll have plenty of room to rattle around.' She wasn't telling him anything. Instinct and experience informed him that what had occurred tonight in Eagleton impinged on her in some way. It was a great pity, because she had been making progress in leaps and bounds. 'Eve and you have become friends,' he said.

'Yes. I like Eve. Chas is a good man, too.

'I'm praying for them, Lily.'

'Oh, good. Everything will be all right, then. I'm sure God will listen to one of his ministers who's been breaking every rule in the book.'

'Sarcasm doesn't suit you.'

'Sorry, Mike. But nor does the knowledge that someone I care about is in hospital with her head bashed in. Mike, will you please leave? I have to be alone tonight.'

'Will you visit Eve tomorrow if she's better?' he asked.

'Not sure. Now, I am exhausted. Please go. Go now.'

He rose from his chair, opened his mouth to speak, thought better of it and went upstairs to collect some of his things. When he came down, he stood for a few seconds in the hall, but the whole place was silent and dark. Whilst every instinct prompted him to stay, he realized that he had to go. This was her house, and she didn't want him here at present.

In the kitchen, Lily sat in complete silence. The happy evening seemed to have taken place months ago, perhaps in some parallel universe she might never visit again. But he had gone, at least. She couldn't have packed with him there, would have been incapable of accepting comfort or love. After what had happened to Eve, she didn't want anyone coming close, because she was perilously near to tears.

The front door opened – he must have left it on the latch. 'Lily?'

'Who is it?'

'Paul.' He ran in. 'What the hell's been happening while we were in Manchester? Thrilled to bits to see you and Mike in the audience at Sisters, but– What's the matter, love? Oh, bugger, I didn't mean to upset you.'

'It should have been me,' she said, her defences suddenly flattened. Emotion came crashing in. Oh God, poor Eve. Lily had held herself together in the company of Mike, but she was too tired, too bone-weary, to keep up the act. 'Eve might die, and it should have happened to someone else . . .'

'What should?'

'They got Eve.' In a voice that was on the brink of cracking, Lily gave an account of what had befallen her friend. 'That's all I know,' she said. 'Because I wasn't here, either. They were looking for me, those murderers.'

'What makes you believe that?'

She sniffed back a disobedient tear. 'There was a load of folk in the pub. Chas was messing about, and Eve was sitting at the table with Babs and Pete. She went home, and the attack happened then. Not a burglary, you see. Burglars like an empty house. They were looking for me, Paul.'

'Never!'

'I'm sure of it. Babs and I are going away for a while tomorrow. We're on a hit list. Oh, I know it sounds a bit

Chicago, but it's true – all connected with stuff that happened before we came up here. No one knows about this – except for Babs, of course.' And Eve ... 'We have to keep Cassie safe, Paul.' These were the words she ought to have said to the man she loved.

'God, yes, that lovely little girl. I'll tell Mo that Babs's absence couldn't be avoided. I'll say she's sorry to let him down. I'll have to do more hours.'

In spite of everything, Lily found herself almost smiling, because Paul had failed to remove all his make-up. 'You look like a doll in a shop window,' she said. 'Thanks, Paul. I don't know why I've allowed you to come near to the truth, but ... oh, you look ridiculous, man.'

'We were good, though – weren't we?'

'Brilliant.'

He sat and held both her hands. 'Look, keep in touch with me and only me. I'll give you a card with my mobile number. I'll try to take full notice of what's happening round here, and—'

'Thanks, Paul—'

'And it should be in the newspapers, so you'll get the bigger picture wherever you go. You know what? I'm so glad that you told me some of it. Makes me feel a bit special. How do you know you can trust me? Is it the gay thing?'

She shrugged. 'Not entirely sure, but it could be. Because you treat us like people, you see. It's easier for a woman with a gay man, because she doesn't have to dress up and pretend to be anything she isn't. But the other thing is that you're a family sort of person, Paul. Like a brother? Oh, I'm not sure why I'm sure, but I trust you.' Why hadn't she been able to tell Mike? Paul was a long way from perfect, yet her instinct was to lean on him.

'I'll leave you to do what needs doing,' Paul said. He kissed her on the cheek and left the house.

Mike loved her, and the truth would hurt and anger him. Telling Eve all of it and Paul some of it had been easy, because she had no plans that included either of them. But she could imagine Mike's reaction, and she wasn't ready for it, not yet. She was going to miss him. Apart from her family, she had never missed anyone as badly as she was going to miss Mike. He was so ... unusual, so gentle and understanding, funny, different, uninhibited. 'I love him,' she told a very old mirror.

It was time to start packing. In the hall, she noticed that the answering machine showed a green light, so she clicked to hear her messages. There was just one, but it was enough to prove that she was doing the right thing. A clerk from the Taunton solicitor's office had disappeared. He had broken every confidentiality rule in the book, and it was not her bank's fault. The clerk had managed to crack a cipher and had contacted a junior executive at her branch in Bolton, whom he had persuaded to 'confirm' her name and business address. He had probably sold the details to someone connected with her ex-husband. 'I thought I should let you know, because there could be something sinister behind all this. I'm sorry, Miss Latimer,' said the disembodied lawyerly voice. 'The manager of your bank is mortified, but the damage has been done.'

So. There it was. Clive was at the back of everything again, and was controlling her life just as he had since the day of her wedding. She picked up her mobile phone and sent a text to Babs. *Solicitor proved me right. Should have been me, not Eve. It's Clive. See you in the morning.*

In her special room with the beautiful circular window, Lily packed a suitcase. She couldn't take much, because she needed to leave space in the boot for Babs's stuff. And Cassie's. She looked down at the pair of sensible shoes she was taking with her. Cassie. 'If anything happens to her, I'll find a way of killing him myself,' she announced to the suddenly lifeless room. Street lighting illuminated the coloured glass, but it needed sun to make it truly effective. She didn't want to go. Mike's reaction to her disappearance would give him away – the whole village could guess the truth.

At a table, she penned a note to him.

My darling Mike,

   Please try not to be too upset by my sudden disappearance. Babs and Cassie will be with me, and there is a very good reason for running away. Don't look for us. I shall find you when I feel strong enough to come back.

   Please know that I am falling in love with you and I want to see you again as soon as possible. Suffice to say that I now have proof that Eve was mistaken for me. I am taking the only action that seems possible at the moment. Cassie is in danger, too.

   I didn't mean the nasty things I said tonight. Sometimes, we hurt so badly that we turn on those we love. Please carry on praying for Eve and for Chas. Talk to God about yourself, too. He loves you. So do I.

   Lily x

She re-read it several times, then lay on her bed. She had always believed that she could never love again, but he had wandered into her life with a rabbit and some foxes ... The foxes. She jumped up and added a PS that advised Mike to watch out for her pets, as they were becoming too tame. They liked Pedigree Chum, though she didn't know whether it was good for them, and the babies loved eggs.

Sleep proved elusive. She tossed and turned, finally dropping into a restless doze after three in the morning. Clive was in the dream again. There was the knife, and she saw those black-handled scissors, blood soaking through the material in her lap. Twenty pounds a metre, she remembered. Good value, heavy fabric with years of wear in it. She stood, he staggered, she screamed and the neighbour came.

Lily's eyes opened. It was dark, almost as dark as those weeks had been. Coming out of the coma had been frightening ... She switched on a lamp. It was a quarter past three. The dream that had lasted for ever had, in reality, spanned just a few minutes. Would she be fit to drive? More to the point, would Eve Boswell ever be well again?

By seven o'clock, Lily was sitting in her vehicle near the telephone kiosk on Ashford Road. There was very little traffic, as the road led only to a few farms, so she was reasonably sure that no one would spot her. Time crawled. Babs and Cassie arrived at ten minutes to eight. 'Sorry,' said Babs. 'Pete stayed the night and didn't leave till gone seven.'

The taxi driver transferred luggage and child seat from his cab to Lily's estate car. Lily paid him, and he drove off. 'We're doing the right thing,' she advised Babs. 'The solicitor said his clerk had disappeared because he knew he had been found out. He provided the information for Clive. Whoever hit Eve thought she was me.'

Babs fastened Cassie into her seat, then placed herself next to the driver. 'Where are we going?'

'Not far today. I've had too little sleep.'

'Blackpool?' suggested Babs.

'It'll be busy.'

'Exactly. We'll be just three more tourists looking for a good time on the Golden Mile.'

Blackpool wasn't too far. Lily switched on her satnav and turned the vehicle round. 'We're going for a holiday, Cassie. We'll get you a bucket and spade, then you can bury Mummy up to her neck in Blackpool sand.'

'Thanks, Lee,' said Babs. 'I always knew you were on my side.'

Got the signal that it's all going ahead. The golden makeover girl will be finished, and I can sit out my sentence at Her Majesty's pleasure, no stress, ignore the useless screws, get what I need out of the others.

Sit back and wait now. Lofty'll let me know as soon as he can. Patience is a virtue I'm trying to develop, because I've a long sentence. All kinds of fights in here, but I try to stay out of that sort of stuff. Reformed character. Never lose my temper any more, don't get into arguments, become a model prisoner.

Models. We make a lot of those in here with matchsticks. You can buy matchsticks, but they don't strike, because they're made just for us. Some soft swine are making the Titanic *and* Concorde *– just as well they're serving life, otherwise they'd never finish.*

I read a lot. She used to read a lot, thought she was a

cut above. It's not a bad life if you keep your head down, though the food is gross. When we get salad, it sometimes walks off the plate. Prison cats can't keep the rat population down. If they could, we'd have a few loose screws, ha-ha.

Yes, I'm keeping my head down. I wonder how Leanne's getting on? I hope they do her slowly. I hope she realizes I'm at the back of it . . .

Ten

While Lily and Babs were making their escape from Eagleton, Chas, Derek and Mike remained prisoners in the hospital. Mike, who had arrived shortly after midnight, telephoned Monsignor Davies and arranged for another priest to attend a recently bereaved family in Harwood. There was no chance that he would leave the Boswell clan in their current state. Chas, who was speechless for the most part, was the more worrisome of the pair. Derek, once the initial shock had begun to evaporate, was agitated but talkative; Chas, however, seemed to be existing in a state of trauma far too deep to be reached.

'I'm worried about my dad,' Derek said.

'So am I. Has he said anything at all?'

Derek took the priest into the next corridor. 'Something about Lofty. Lofty's under five feet tall and he comes from Liverpool – Dad knows him. But then he said it wasn't Lofty, it was his twin – there's about an inch difference in their heights if I remember rightly. Mam and Dad used to joke about Lofty and Titch when we lived in Liverpool. They're Scallies. Lofty would have recognized Dad if he was near enough, but whoever it was just walked away. I don't think Dad's ever met Titch. He'd know him by sight, but–'

'What's a Scally?'

'Scouser gone bad. The twins get used a lot, because they can fit through small windows when there's a robbery. I don't know what Dad was on about. I asked him when and where he'd seen Lofty's twin, and he just said the man had walked away. Then he started that terrible staring into thin air again. I might as well not have been there. He's sitting and waiting, but I'm not sure he knows what he's waiting for. It's as if he's gone missing, but his body's still warm and with us.' Derek swallowed hard. 'He won't manage if she ... He can't manage without Mam.'

'Let's pray for the best, Derek.'

They returned and sat with Chas, who had refused all sustenance since arriving at the hospital. Cups of tea had been left to cool, a ham sandwich was curling on a paper plate, while the man for whom these items had been purchased sat with his head bowed.

Mike tried again. 'You should eat and drink, Chas. You'll be no use to anyone if you don't make an effort.'

Chas raised his head. 'I think it was Titch,' he said clearly. 'Not Lofty. They couldn't use Lofty as a look-out, because he's as blind as a bat when it comes to distance. I thought he hadn't seen me properly with his eyes being buggered, but I'm sure now it wasn't him. Lofty can read the phone book without specs, but he'd mix up a double-decker with an elephant unless they were parked under his nose. I was close enough to be recognized, though. It was Titch, deffo.'

'Deffo' was Liverpool-speak for definitely, Mike guessed. He glanced at Derek. All this time, Chas had been concentrating, it seemed. 'Titch?' he asked.

'Twins. Titch is shorter than Lofty. I know Lofty. He's

264

visited me in Eagleton, but I've never seen his brother round there. Till I was on my way to the pub. I nearly shouted out to him, then I saw the ciggy. Lofty doesn't smoke. Titch is a chain smoker. I realize now he was keeping watch for whoever did this to Eve. Never gave it a second thought at the time.'

'So it was deliberate?'

'Oh, yes. But I think they got the wrong house.'

'Why?'

'I just know it. Eve...' Chas gulped hard. 'Eve told me there's somebody nearby in a lot of bother. She spilled it all out before I went to the pub.' He swallowed again. 'I was messing about with the arrows when she came, doing my blindfold tricks, the upside-down darts, arsing around as bloody usual. Never even spoke to my old woman. She went. Next time I saw her, she was ... a mess.'

Mike asked Chas for the identity of the person in 'bother', but Chas closed down as suddenly as he had come to life just minutes earlier. 'Derek?'

'What, Father?'

'What's he on about?'

Derek had no idea. 'First thing I knew, Philly Gallagher came running into the shop and told me to get home quick. She didn't give me any details, because she hadn't seen Mam. I don't know what happened, but I do know my dad. He's working something out, and when he does work it out, God help whoever clobbered my mam. I thought he'd gone into shock, but he's thinking hard. Nobody gets away with hurting my mother.'

A door opened and a tall figure entered the corridor: Mr Hislop, Eve's surgeon. 'How's the husband doing?' he asked Mike.

'Strangely lucid, then back to square one. He's concentrating his energy on working out what happened and why – still not completely with us.'

Chas stood up. 'I can talk for myself, thanks. What's going on with my wife?'

'Sit down, Mr Boswell.' The surgeon dragged a chair into position and sat opposite his patient's husband. 'We've done the scan. Strange to say, but the person who hit your wife did her a favour. As long as there's no damage we've missed, that is, and we're ever hopeful in my job. What's your first name?'

'Chas.'

'I'm Richard, but that's a heavy name to carry – Richard the Third and all that – so I'm Rick to my friends. The bleeding has stopped, and we have managed to release blood that had collected in her skull. She's had transfusions, so we've topped up her tank. There's a growth, Chas. Knowing Eve's history – now that we've read her notes – we looked for malignancy, but the path lab's initial findings point to a benign tumour.'

'In her head?'

'Yes. We've exposed the bugger right down to its roots. Benign it may be, but it could have grown to a size that might have precluded surgical intervention. It could have affected her life in many ways, so we've stopped it in its tracks.' He smiled reassuringly. 'There'll be a steel plate in her head. That is one tough little lady, Chas. She'll need a wig when she gets home.'

A lone tear tracked its way down Chas's right cheek. 'She will come home, then?'

'Let's take one step at a time, shall we? I have to go and do my work on Eve, but I'm pretty confident about the operation. There's no denying the brain is something we still don't fully understand, but she shows every sign of coming out in one piece. You cross your fingers, and get your priest to pray. She'll be in intensive care for a while, but she's steady for now.' He patted Chas's shoulder, and left the scene.

Chas seemed to have come back to life. 'I'm going outside,' he said. 'I want to use my mobile. This means war, Derek. I'll get the bastard who did this if it takes me what's left of my days.'

Mike shook his head. 'Revenge isn't worth the price you pay, Chas.'

'Oh yes? I'll play the game with my rules, thanks, Father. And the less you know about that, the better. Go home. Me and our Derek can manage now. Thanks for coming.' Chas picked up the stale sandwich and bit into it. After ordering his son to find him something more palatable, he went outside.

Mike sighed heavily. 'Law of the jungle?'

'Law of the Dingle,' replied Derek. 'That's where he was born – the Dingle in Liverpool. Keep out of it, please. My dad's a tank with no brakes now, so don't be thinking you can stand in his way and stop him, because he'll run you down as soon as look at you. It's a matter of honour. Read your Old Testament – the Israelites knew a lot about justice. Our faith concentrates on the New Testament. But remember, the Commandments were given to Moses, and the Red Sea was parted for him and it drowned his enemies. Plagues and all sorts came down on Egypt – it was bloody rough.'

'I suppose it was.'

Derek half smiled. 'I did RE at A level. Seems daft for

an accountant, but it was interesting. If we had Moses and Solomon and a couple more of that lot back, there'd be no ASBOs.'

'No, but there'd be a lot of brutally punished people, Derek.'

'Exactly. So look on my dad as a junior Moses. And again, stay out of it. You'll be safer that way.' Derek went in search of food for his father.

Mike stretched his legs. He walked up and down the corridor for several minutes before deciding to take Derek's advice. He had learned over the years that people made up their own minds when it came to the serious areas of life, and little difference could be made by intervention when a man was in a blind rage. Perhaps Chas would cool down after a few days. And perhaps he wouldn't. Whatever, Mike needed a shower and a change of clothing, so he set off towards Eagleton, his mind still reeling about the Lofty and Titch twins. He'd lost track and forgotten who was who . . . 'I hope Lily's all right,' he said aloud. 'And Eve, too, of course, God keep her.'

He drove like a bat out of hell all the way back to the old presbytery. She wasn't there. The panic hit him immediately – he couldn't lose her, wouldn't lose her, panicked at the idea that the criminals had got to her while he'd been at the hospital. He went into her bedroom, interpreted piles of clothing and a rejected suitcase as evidence of recent packing, even went so far as to peep inside her two wardrobes. The summer one was almost empty. So Lily was definitely the person in trouble; she had run, because the crime committed against Eve had really been meant for her. A powerful dart of fear pierced his chest; he had to find her, had to protect her from whatever was out there. Where was she? Like something from a Disney cartoon, he ran stupidly from room to room, knowing that she wasn't there, yet managing to hope that she might be.

He found the note, read it, re-read it, ran across to the flower shop. CLOSED UNTIL FURTHER NOTICE was the message on the door. No one answered when he rang the bell connected to Babs's flat. Would Pete know? How could he find Pete? Entering Pour Les Dames, he asked Mo whether Babs was supposed to be in today.

'Yes, she is, but Paul's filling in for her. Paul?' yelled Mo.

Mo's partner entered, face rather flushed. In his left hand was clasped a big lie in the form of a mobile phone. He had just received a message from Lily, who had used a new SIM card. He alone had her phone number. 'Babs has gone away with Lily,' he said lamely. 'No idea what it's about, but I suspect it's some sort of family trouble in the south. Or a friend in difficulty,' he added, his voice rising slightly in pitch. 'Babs told me because I have to fill in for her.' He busied himself at a washbasin, his cheeks darkening even further.

Mike was used to lies, could spot them from a great distance. Paul knew more than he was saying, but he had probably given his word to Lily and her friend. 'Thanks,' he said before leaving the salon. If necessary, he would work on Paul later, though he suspected that Paul just might be a person who didn't break promises. In which case, he was a better man than most, and should be forgiven for recent behaviour.

Outside, he stood helplessly on the Walk and wondered what the hell to do next. Then he remembered the eyes and ears of the world. She hated Catholics, but Mrs

Barker missed next to nothing. The Reading Room was open, and Mike stepped inside. Dave had begun organizing daily newspapers and some magazines. He stopped when he saw Mike. 'You're the early bird today,' he said. 'We didn't get much sleep, either. How's Eve?'

Philly, abandoning her scones and sandwiches, ran through from the back room, Skippy hot on her heels. 'How's Eve?' she echoed.

'She's being operated on now,' Mike said. 'And it looks hopeful, although we have to wait for her to regain consciousness. The surgeon is very optimistic, but it's still a waiting game for the rest of us.'

'God love her,' breathed Philly. 'I'm praying, Father. I'm even offering up my work as prayer.'

Mike smiled at the good woman. 'But have you any idea where Lily is? Or Babs?' he asked, his tone deliberately light.

Dave offered no explanation.

Philly sat down. She was full of tears, but she managed, just about, to stem the tide. Journalists were coming to ask about their clever dog, and she didn't know what to say because she was too upset. 'They're calling Skippy a heroine, and I'm proud, but I can't stop thinking about Eve and Chas,' she said. 'Father, are you sure she's going to be all right? I mean, when I saw her on that stretcher, mask on, bloody bandages, big collar round her neck – well – I wondered if she'd ever be Eve again.'

Mike told her again what the surgeon had said, and decided that Philly was in no fit state to hear any more about the disappearance from the village of two further women. 'May I go up and see your mother?' he asked Dave.

'Have you got your hard hat?' Dave asked. 'No, I'd better re-phrase that, because she's decided to start being nice. I'm warning you, Father, because it may come as a shock to your constitution. She's mending her ways. Now, I don't think she'll mend them all at once – nobody has a long enough darning needle for that job. But you may not need a gun or an anti-stab vest. Good luck with her, anyway.'

Mike ascended the stairs and knocked.

'Come in,' called a disembodied voice.

The priest entered Enid Barker's personal arena. Prepared to find himself in the modern equivalent of a lions' den, he was surprised when her only comment was, 'Oh, it's you.'

'It is indeed, Mrs Barker. How are you?'

She sighed audibly. 'Get in if you're coming in – I can't be doing with hoverers. How am I? Different. Angry. Tired. That Liverpool woman never did anybody any harm as far as I can work out. Makes you think, doesn't it? I've not slept. Well, I might have dozed off a time or two, but I've kept my eyes and binoculars pinned to this bloody window nearly all night. They've not been back, them bad beggars.'

'They won't come again, Mrs B. The place is too dangerous for them. Shall I make a brew?'

'Aye, go on, lad.'

This was progress indeed. He had gone from 'that holy Roman' to 'lad' in a matter of minutes, so she must be on the mend. It was strange how the worst for some people brought out the best in others. Until this moment, few would have believed that Mrs Barker had a better side, but he could see it now. He brought her a cup of tea. 'You should sleep,' he said. 'A full night awake's bad for the constitution – I should know. Get your head down.'

'I can't yet, but I'm sure I will soon. I just need to know she's all right. I phoned the hospital, said I was her auntie, and they told me she was in theatre. How's her husband taking this?'

Mike couldn't tell the truth, dared not say that Chas was bent on vengeance. 'Eating at last, walking about a bit. I'd say furious and afraid.'

Enid nodded. 'See, till it lands on your own doorstep, you don't think, do you? Any road, your landlady's gone. She was up before seven and planting luggage in the back of her car. Later on, her friend took the little girl in a taxi from the back – I saw them through my other window. It looked as if they didn't want to be seen leaving together. Babs had luggage, too. None of them's come back.'

'I know,' he said carefully. 'I don't suppose you've any idea where they've gone?'

'Not a clue, son. Fetch me a digestive, will you? No sleep means my diabetes is up the pole.'

He handed her the packet of biscuits and his card. 'Any time you need me, Mrs B.'

'Thanks. Go on now, off with you. I'll have to catch a few minutes' sleep before I start seeing things. They'll be parking me in the funny farm if I have one of my hypos.'

Taking this as his dismissal, he walked to the door.

'Hang on a minute,' she ordered. 'That Lily one likes you, doesn't she?'

He nodded.

'And you like her?'

Again, Mike simply bowed his head.

'Well, bloody good luck to you. Time priests got flaming well wed and found out how the rest of folk suffer.'

'Priests can't marry yet,' he told her.

'Oh, aye? What will you do?'

'The priesthood is not imprisonment, Enid. May I call you Enid?'

'It's my name.'

'I'm Mike.' He left the flat. Should he have denied 'liking' Lily? Should he have insisted that there was nothing going on? No. That might have seemed like protesting too much.

Enid watched him as he walked across the road. It was as if his shoulders had become heavy, because he looked shorter. He was a good-looking bloke. That Lily was a pretty woman if she'd just liven herself up a bit. They'd look good together, that pair, and they'd probably have handsome kids. She wondered for a moment what her grandchild might look like, because neither Dave nor Philly was much to look at. Ah, well. It couldn't be helped, she supposed. She had to try to like Philly, must make an attempt at peace with her son. It wasn't easy, because her nature was angry.

So. She had a secret. And it was time she learned to keep such information to herself, because folk expected her to talk behind their backs. The priest and the florist – it sounded like some Victorian never-darken-my-door-again kind of story.

Enid closed her eyes and slept fitfully. In her dream, everything was her fault. She woke in a lather, sweat running into her eyes. Dave was right. She had been a bad mother and there could never be an excuse for it.

Old dogs and new tricks? 'I can only do my best,' she told herself before dropping off again. This time, there was no dream.

While Derek went off to buy essentials for his mother, Chas stayed at her bedside. Apart from breaks to eat and visit the lavatory, he did not move. Nurses in the unit were impressed by him, as he talked almost constantly, reminding his sick wife of how they had met, their wedding day, holidays, getting the shop, moving to Rose Cottage. Almost every tale he told was funny. 'And I'm not staying there without you,' he told her. 'So you'd best buck up, because it's your bloody choice, not mine. The state of that flaming garden for a kick-off – OK, I haven't found a tiger yet, but the missing link's living in a hole near the privets. Says he wants a telly, a washing machine and a fridge. Oh, and double pay on Sundays.'

Members of staff were fascinated, many lingering for a minute or two after completing necessary tasks, since this man was a born teller of stories.

'Remember when your red high heel got stuck down the grid? And the lads pulled the whole thing up, and you had to carry the grating home so that your dad could get your shoe out? Hey? You were well pissed that night, babe. I mean, standing there screaming at the Liver Birds because the shoes had cost a tenner? I think that was when I knew I'd marry you. If you'd have me, like. I'm glad you did, girl.'

Rick Hislop, Eve's surgeon, was checking something on Eve's chart. He smiled encouragingly at Chas. 'That's good,' he said. 'Sometimes, patients can hear you. I've known them come out of coma and talk about what was happening around them before they woke. Carry on with the good work, Chas.'

Chas was worn out. His shop was shut, but he managed not to care a fig about that, because his wife was shut, too. There were machines bleeping and drawing lines on a screen; there were tubes and plasters and all kinds of things stuck to her. In fact, the more he looked at her, the more she looked like a re-sized aerial photo of a plate of spaghetti. Or, if he concentrated on her head, an Egyptian mummy. 'Eve?'

There wasn't even a flicker.

'Eve? If you don't talk to me soon, I'm going to cut up your Barclaycard. And your chequebook.'

Nothing.

'And your American Express. It's time we cleared out some of your mess, too, kid. You keep saying things'll come back in fashion – when? After the next Preston Guild?'

Was he mistaken, or had that left eyelid flickered?

He took hold of her hand carefully, keen to avoid interfering with her wiring. 'I'll sing to you,' he threatened. 'I'll sing till all these intensive care buggers wake up and run away. Would you like "You'll Never Walk Alone"?'

The eyelid definitely twitched.

'Or I could have a go at "Bright Eyes". Remember? *Watership Down*?'

Both eyelids moved.

Chas pressed the buzzer, and a nurse appeared. 'She flickered,' he said. 'Left eyelid, then both. If I sing, she'll do it again, I'm sure. My singing's so good, it makes all the dogs for miles around howl. She's going to be all right, isn't she?'

The nurse looked at the readings, then shone a torch in Eve's eyes.

'She won't like that,' said Chas.

'Pupils equal and reacting,' said the young woman.

'Eh?'

'She may well wake up soon. Now, you come with me.' She almost had to drag him into the office. After pushing him into a chair, she delivered her lecture. 'Don't be afraid if she appears to have forgotten things when you get her to wake. Her brain's been shaken up, so it may take a while for her to get her memory back.'

'You don't know my Eve.'

She sighed. 'All I'm asking is that you be patient with her. I know you love her – we can all see that. But she might not respond properly for a while, and we don't want you getting downhearted.'

He nodded, then leaned forward. 'Listen, love. She was made in Liverpool. She's a twenty-four-carat piece of Scouse, my wife. She's coming to because I threatened to cut up her credit cards and get rid of all the clothes she's collected over the years. As for shoes – Imelda Marcos has nothing on my wife. She once went out and bought eight pairs. Eight pairs in one shop.' He shook his head. 'If she'd just wake up, I'd buy her every bloody pair of shoes and boots in Bolton. Mind, I'd get no thanks, because she'd still want something different, even if I'd bought the whole lot.'

The nurse couldn't help laughing. 'All right. Go back and keep talking.'

'I've only just started,' he replied. 'Wait till I tell her I'm selling her house.'

'She'll have a stroke!' she said.

'As if.'

'Just be careful. You might frighten her.'

'No, I won't. She'll get out of that bed and tear a strip off all of us.' He gulped. 'God willing.'

'Mr Boswell?'

'Yes, love?'

'You're doing a grand job.'

'Ta.' He rushed back to his wife.

When Derek arrived with toiletries and nightdresses, he found his father fast asleep in an armchair while his mother, who was supposed to be the comatose one, was wide awake and glaring at Chas. 'Thank God,' Derek breathed. 'Mam, we've been so worried about you.' He blinked away a few tears.

His mother fixed him with a steely stare. 'Where've you been?'

'Buying things. We can't get back in the house yet, because it's a crime scene. So I got you some nighties and stuff. I hope they're the right size.' He unwrapped one of his purchases. His mother was alive, and he no longer cared about his shopping being wrong or right. 'There's this blue one, and there's a—'

'Where did you go for that article?' asked the head injury in the bed. 'Rent-a-Tent?'

'It is a bit on the large side,' admitted Derek. 'The woman said it was medium, but she was about the size of the *Titanic*. I suppose it's all relative.'

Eve decided to give her attention to her snoring husband. 'Typical. I wake up and he drops off. He's going to destroy my credit cards and sell the house. I had to come round to stop him.' She winced. 'I've got a terrible headache.'

Chas woke. A huge smile crept across his face, while his eyes filled with saline. 'Hello, love.' He grabbed her hand. 'Oh, God, oh, God—'

'Oh, shut up,' ordered the patient. 'And leave my bloody credit cards alone.'

Chas wiped away a tear and pressed the buzzer.

The cheeky young nurse appeared. 'Mrs Boswell. Hiya. I'm Sarah. Good to see you looking so well.'

'Well?' She looked at Chas. 'She calls this well? Have you seen the state of me? Tell her I'm in pain. I want three aspirin and a boiled egg.'

Sarah folded her arms and tapped a foot. 'Right,' she said. 'Shall I send the wine waiter and the à la carte?'

'I don't want a cart, or a horse, for that matter. Just a four-minute egg and some soldiers. Grenadiers will do. I like their hats.'

Chas laughed through the tears. 'See? What did I tell you? Twenty-four-carat Liverpool, my wife.' He gazed steadily at Eve. She was the most beautiful thing on God's earth. 'They found something in your head.'

'Oh, good. If it had been you, they'd have come across a few bits of fluff and a sea breeze.'

'But Eve—'

'I heard them. Benign growth, frontal lobe, lucky woman. If I hadn't been walloped, I'd have been in trouble.'

'You can have a drink of water,' Sarah said.

'Gee, thanks, babe. Can I have drugs? My head's like a busy soup kitchen just before payday. And perfume. I want my perfume.'

Sarah threw up her hands in mock despair and went off to ask Mr Hislop whether Eve's hunger might be appeased.

'I'm not wearing that,' Eve told her son. 'Go and ask for your money back, then get yourself to our house. Tell those police buggers I want my stuff. I'm not lying here without my perfume and my own knickers.'

'And the mail,' Chas added. 'I'm expecting something by courier, so bring all the letters.'

Derek kissed his mother and left.

Eve opened her mouth to say something, but Chas had pursued his son. 'Derek?'

'Hiya, Dad. Now, stop crying. Come on, she'll be all right.'

But a sudden surge of emotion drove the father to hug his son. Chas hung on to the boy as if life depended on this moment, and held him uncomfortably close. 'Derek,' he managed when the sobs subsided. 'I don't mean to use you as a bring-me, fetch-me, carry-me, but I need that letter. There's a VO in it.'

'Eh?'

'A visiting order.'

Derek processed the information. 'But Uncle Rob's not in jail yet.'

'That's right.' Chas swallowed a stream of sad and angry words. He would not break down completely, because he was the man of the family, and he had better remember that. 'Derek, I just want to say I'm proud of you, lad. I know I rag the arse off you, but it's only in fun.'

'I know.'

'And I wanted you to have brothers and sisters – we both did. You must have been lonely.' Chas told himself to shut up, but he couldn't.

'You what? Lonely? With Mam and you? It's been more like a bloody three-ring circus ever since I was born. No worries, Dad. I know she lost her womb and it can't be helped – I'm fine.'

'Get me that VO, son. And make them hand over your mam's stuff – nighties, knickers, perfume – you know the score.'

Derek paused for a moment. 'Why the VO, Dad? What the hell are you going to do with one of those things?'

'Don't ask, lad. It's better if you don't know. Just remember we love you.'

The younger man turned to leave, then came back to face his father again. He knew Chas very well, realized there was something grossly amiss. 'Dad, they saved her life in a way.'

Chas nodded. 'They didn't set out to do that, though, did they? The fact that your mam has a thick skull is just a piece of luck. And they haven't finished. Oh, they may not go for my Evie again, but they've not done. The buggers'll be back, lad.'

'Dad, this isn't nicking a few boxes of Scotch or betting on a horse. You can't do anything here without risk. This is the big lads, the ones who play to win.'

Chas straightened his spine. 'Ah, well. I played to win when I put my last five grand on an accumulator and won enough to get us where we are today. And where my family's concerned I'm in the big boys' class too, Derek, and I'm not just the milk monitor. I know people. I know people who know people. This is going to be nipped in the bud before somebody else gets hurt.' He glanced up and down the corridor. 'They weren't after Eve, son. Your mam was a mistake, and yes, I know the mistake saved her a lot of bother with that thing in her head. But they're out to get somebody else we know. They didn't do any of this out of Christian charity. Now, bugger off out of it and do as you're told.'

'But Dad—'

'Now, Derek. My mind's made up. It was made up last night when I saw the state of her. Nobody does that to one of mine. And nobody does it to a good friend of one of mine, either. See you later.' He walked back into intensive care.

'You'll have to get me out of here,' complained the love of Chas's life. Some of her wiring had been disconnected, and she looked well, if rather pale.

'That's right, girl. I'll put you somewhere private.'

'No. I didn't mean that. If I'm forced to stay in jail, an ordinary ward'll do for me. Looking at these poor people around me does nobody any good, God love the poor souls. I need somewhere among the living. But I'm not going private.'

Eve was another who refused to be shifted once her decision had been made. He smiled at her and hoped she couldn't see that he'd been weeping again. 'There's two cops in reception,' he told her. 'They've been hovering like a pair of bluebottles over a pile of shite ever since you were brought in. I suppose they'll be wanting to talk to you.'

'Are they good-looking?'

He shrugged. 'I wouldn't know.'

'Well, I want something to eat first, then a good wash, get my hair done and then ... Ah. I've been shaved, haven't I?' She touched her heavily bandaged head. 'Bugger. And I've spent a fortune on that colour, too. Lovely, my hair was.'

'Yes, but you're still lovely, babe.'

'Right. Get me a wig catalogue. I can have a different colour every day of the week.'

Chas groaned. It was going to be like the shoes all over again, but at the other end. Seven wigs? One for each day of the week? 'You can have anything you like, Eve. Now, shall we put these coppers out of their misery?'

'All right, then.'

Out in the corridors once more, Chas found himself leaping about and punching the air like a kid at his first football match. He hadn't wanted to go overboard in front of his wife, because she'd just had brain surgery, but he certainly needed to let off steam. And, he decided when he caught a whiff of body odour, he could do with a shower as well.

The constables followed him back to the intensive care unit. They were given five minutes, and they learned nothing except that Eve saw a large item dropping through the air just before she was hit the second time.

When they had finished, Chas followed them out into the corridor. 'Any idea who it was?' he asked as casually as he could manage.

'Three people are being interviewed, Mr Boswell. We're hoping they'll be charged sometime soon, but we have to be sure. There's lab work going on. DNA's brilliant, but it doesn't work overnight. Though we're quietly confident that the men in question should be of some help with inquiries. One's squealing like a stuck pig already.'

Chas breathed an audible sigh of relief. He didn't

want to ask any questions, because he had plans, and it was best to keep quiet.

'Mr Boswell?'

'Yes?'

'Two women have disappeared from Eagleton overnight. One's left a new job and taken her young daughter, while the other seems to have abandoned a nice little business. Any ideas? It seems strange that they should go so soon after your wife's attack. And we're told that Miss Latimer and your wife are good friends.'

Chas knew why they'd gone. Poor Lily was on the run, and she'd taken her hairdresser friend with her. 'No idea,' he replied, fingers crossed childishly behind his back. 'But your seniors might know – something to do with Miss Latimer needing to get away from the south. Is it all right if I get back to Eve now? Only she's not been awake long.'

They gave their permission, said they would talk to Eve again as soon as she was better, then walked away.

Chas sat on a chair in the corridor for a few minutes. So much had been packed into the past few hours. Eve had told him about Lily before the attack, he had lost his rag and gone to the pub, Eve had followed. 'I should have stopped messing about. I should have gone home with her,' he whispered into space. But they might have hit him too; they might have killed him, and what would have happened to Eve then?

A stop should be put to all this before it went any further. Chas had been an opportunist, though he had never set out to do any real harm. Luck had got him where he was today, but a man sometimes had to create his own good fortune. Eve was everything to him, and he had to ensure her safety. Somewhere out there, either on the loose or in a police cell, lay the answer. The men who had hurt Eve were the tools of someone else's trade, and that someone was probably in jail. Chas knew folk. He knew those who kept company with the big boys. He was well respected, because he had helped many an old lag to survive in a cold, cruel world.

This situation could arise again. Next time, Eve might be visiting her new friend in intensive care or at some funeral parlour. No wonder Lily had fled; no wonder the poor woman had been scared halfway to death when she had first arrived in the village. For Eve's sake, Lily Latimer had to be safe. Eve had taken a shine to the woman, and that friendship needed to be nurtured.

When he got back to the unit, Eve had fallen asleep again. Visitors were kept to a minimum in intensive care, so he crept out and asked Sarah to tell Eve that he'd gone home for a shower. Surely the cops would have finished by this time? 'Shall I bring you a corned beef butty when I come back?' he asked the nurse.

She grinned. 'I'll be off duty soon,' she said. 'And I can't stand corned beef.'

Chas could. For the first time, he felt really hungry, and his mouth watered at the thought of two big door-steps of very unhealthy white bread with a quarter of corned beef between them and half a bottle of ketchup dripping down the sides. He was fine. His wife was going to be fine, and his son was a good lad. Or he might get a bag of chips. Chips and corned beef – he was going to heaven. Above all, he wanted to get his mitts on that visiting order. The process of finding the true perpetrator would begin very soon.

*

Eagleton had been turned into a circus. Clowns took several forms, some carrying boom mikes, others hiding behind cameras, while the precious few stood in front of the cameras, make-up exaggerated, clothes perfect, script scrolling up electronic idiot boards. Chas was of the Princess Anne school of thought when it came to journalists, so he told a few to bog off while he went inside his own house and begged permission to take a shower. Fortunately, the sergeant in attendance was Peter Haywood. 'We'll be out of your hair any minute,' he said. 'And we've lost Lily and Babs.'

'I know,' replied Chas. 'And I know why as well.'

'Yes.' The policeman took Chas to one side while white-covered SOCOs left the house for the final time. 'I think we've got the men who did this. They're from your neck of the woods.'

'Yes.'

'He's in Walton.'

Chas pretended to be ignorant. 'Who is?'

'Lily's husband.'

That was good news. Chas prayed that the authorities would not move him on just yet. 'Really?'

'Really. We all know who's to blame for this, you know.'

Chas could say nothing to Babs's Pete. Cops were not the enemy, but they were to be avoided when it came to certain aspects of life. 'I'll grab a shower,' he said. 'Is our Derek still here?'

Pete shook his head. 'No. He collected his mother's things, then went back through the graveyard. He was meeting a taxi on the top road, because he wanted to avoid that lot outside.'

'What do they want, all them flaming paparazzi?'

'The dog. It's a hero. Look, have your shower, then I'll take you back to the hospital. That way, you can avoid the crowd outside.'

While Pete waited, Chas took his much-needed shower in Eve's almost completed en suite. According to the lady, a house was nothing until the master bedroom had its own facilities. She knew it was a cottage, was aware that plumbing was primitive at the time it was built, but she was going incongruous. Never mind, because this was a very powerful shower, and Chas was glad of it.

He dried himself in the bedroom. The police were aware, then. They probably knew that Lily's ex had ordered the hit, that he had found a way to pay the hired assassins, that Chalmers was the real culprit. 'Keep him where he is,' Chas begged the air as he dressed. 'Keep him in Walton.' For now, the danger was over. Eagleton was a hot-spot. No one would try again for a while, and Lily was safely out of the way.

When Chas went downstairs, he was surprised to find Derek and a taxi driver waiting with Pete. 'I thought you were avoiding that lot outside,' Chas told his son.

Derek pointed to the driver. 'Tell them,' he said.

Thus Chas and Pete learned that Lily and Babs had probably gone to Blackpool. 'I'm Eric Johnson,' said the man. 'The woman told her little daughter she'd like Blackpool, and then they got in another woman's car. This was the second time I'd been to that phone box today, you see, once to drop off, once to pick up, and I just mentioned it to this young chap here. It was a red-haired woman I drove, the one who talked about Blackpool.'

'Aye, it would be her,' commented Pete. 'She's a right blabbermouth.'

'Wise enough move, Blackpool,' said Chas. 'Busy place, especially at this time of year. Half of Glasgow'll be there for a start.' He thanked the taxi driver and asked him to take himself and Derek back to the hospital. 'Save you a trip,' he told Pete. 'And see if you can locate Lily and Babs. Just to be on the safe side, like.'

The three men had to push their way through a gaggle of reporters with microphones. Derek and Chas climbed into the rear seat while their driver fought to get behind the wheel. 'Nosy buggers,' he yelled at the intruders. 'Leave them alone. They have to get to the hospital.' The car edged its way forward inch by inch until it cleared the crowd.

Chas exhaled loudly. 'Tell you what, Derek. If that's our fifteen minutes of fame, I could have done without it.'

Derek agreed. 'I hope I've got all my mam's stuff,' he said anxiously. 'I don't want her kicking off again. For somebody who's just had brain surgery, she looks like a very good candidate for the Olympics.'

'Naw,' replied Chas. 'They don't do mithering. If they did, she'd take gold. There'd be no contest.'

Stupid bleeding bastards. I've been questioned by police. Pleaded ignorance, of course, but the chances of them believing me aren't good.

They got the wrong woman. I'm sure my face would have changed when the cops told me that. Wrong house, wrong target, wrong everything. And there's something going on in here. Took a punch to my right kidney this morning, can't go to the gym any more. No real loss, because the gym's full of gorillas on steroids – don't know how they get them, but they do.

Even the screws are looking at me funny. When I was hit, one of the two lags holding me still said the blow was a gift from a man called Boswell. The other told me the screws will turn a blind eye, because Boswell helped a few repeat offenders on their way to the straight and narrow.

I should have used my own people. Messages can be sent just about anywhere; all it takes is careful planning. Bloody Scousers. They might be quick and funny, but they don't know their arses from their patio doors. Have to keep my wits about me now, because I could be in real danger. Boswell's wife's in hospital – I wish I was.

They were supposed to have cased the joint. I described her well enough, but now I wonder whether she's changed her appearance. She's got enough bloody money, I know that. The fact is that Leanne's a tart. Some of the letters she got from men who watched her on TV were filthy, and she just laughed at them.

'Beautiful and feisty' was one of the descriptions of her in the gutter papers. She loves being looked at, likes the thought of men panting after her, never gave a shit for the one that married her. What are my chances of getting her done in now? Will I be charged again? Will the Scouse canaries sing so loudly that I'll have no chance? I hope they move me. I hope they move me soon...

Eleven

Blackpool had developed a rather pleasing split person-ality. Neither Lily nor Babs had seen it before, but they had read about the most popular resort in England, how it had burgeoned, how people had flocked there during the first half of the twentieth century. Now it embraced bistros and taco bars, upmarket restaurants and some extremely grand hotels. Nevertheless, in spite of all the renovations and spectacular improvements, the soul of the town remained untouched. Although it probably had its fair share of crime, it was a place to which a family might come to feel safe and embraced, because it was friendly, welcoming and lacking in pomposity.

Fortunately, it did not yet boast the huge casino with which it had been threatened, so the town was not overrun by dedicated gamblers and nervy females addicted to one-armed bandits. It was a lively place, though, and Babs took to it immediately. Lily, aware of Babs's good-time-girl past, rented a flat well away from the centre. It wasn't that she wanted to extinguish com-pletely her friend's fire; the fact was that she preferred to keep Babs where she could see her. 'We are supposedly in hiding,' Lily repeated at least twice a day. 'So stay in during the evenings and shut up.' For the most part,

Babs did as she was advised, though she still insisted on talking to strangers, since she was a self-described collector of folk.

Lily too rather liked Blackpool. Alongside all the recent developments, stalwarts upheld tradition by clinging to the glorious past like limpets to a ship. Seven glorious miles of pure golden sand ran alongside housing estates and newer commercial premises. But in the centre, the Golden Mile was still punctuated by all the old stalls selling candyfloss, kiss-me-quick hats and the inevitable Blackpool rock and naughty postcards. Here and there, fortunes were told by large ladies in flowing skirts and red headscarves, while fish and chip shops thrived among elegant and newer feeding troughs. All these factors proved to Lily that the past mattered, and that the real Blackpool lived on.

Cassie loved it. Armed with bucket and spade, she copied the actions of older children and concentrated hard on giving birth to her first intact sandcastle. Several abortive efforts were accompanied by unhappy weeping, but she finally mastered the art, leaving Mummy and Auntie Lee to bask in sunshine while they could. Like the rest of Lancashire, Blackpool occupied space west of the Pennines, so it enjoyed a better climate than Yorkshire, but wetter weather. Avoiding the showers was a skill that the two women were learning fast. Rules were simple. No matter what the temperature or how blue the sky, always carry collapsible umbrellas, raincoats and proper shoes. Wrap picnics properly unless you don't mind sandwiches turned to soup, and take a towel with you. Once the law was formulated and complied with, life in Blackpool was easy.

'I could stay here for always,' sighed Babs. She was

coated in cream of a factor so high that the sun needed to apply in triplicate for permission to kiss her skin. Like many redheads, Babs could not take too much ultraviolet.

'Could you?' breathed Lily sleepily. 'Without Pete? Could you really live anywhere without the love of your life?'

Babs shrugged. 'He may be the love of my life, or perhaps he isn't.'

'Fickle.' Lily laughed.

'He could get a transfer.' Babs stuck out her tongue, but Lily, whose eyes were closed, did not see the action. 'I'm going to phone him, Lily,' Babs went on. 'I can't bear the thought of him worrying.'

'So he is the love of your life, then?'

'Probably. But I'm not allowed to phone him, am I?'

Lily sat up and looked at her friend. 'He'll tell the police where we are, just as we had to when we first moved to Eagleton. The top brass will be asking about us already, but there are bent cops, Babs. Pete could tell the wrong chap, and we'd be found when that wrong chap sold the information. Do you want me dead?' She felt mean after Babs's last question, because she had been phoning Paul Smith without mentioning it to Babs.

'So we stay here incognito for the rest of our lives? Shall I put my daughter's name down for a Blackpool school? This has to end sometime, Lily. We've already run almost the length of England – do we try Wales or Scotland next?'

'No. We wait. According to the newspapers, three men are being questioned. If they sing – isn't that the word criminals use for confessing? – the authorities will be on to Clive. Hopefully, he'll be stopped.'

Babs threw the remains of a sandwich at her friend. A

brave gull swooped and snatched it away before Lily could wrap it for disposal. 'He'll be stopped,' Lily repeated.

But Babs, a lover of lurid fiction, had other ideas. 'There's a whole network, you know. Anyone in prison can find someone to do their dirty work. He can try again as soon as he likes.'

'There you go, then,' said Lily. 'All the more reason to stay here for now. Hoist by your own petard, Babs.'

'What?'

'Never mind. Be quiet and eat your choc ice.'

Babs groaned. The trouble with Lily was that she had rather too much common sense. For someone with an enormous gift for artistry and decoration, she displayed a total lack of imagination when it came to other areas of life. Babs liked to take chances, but Lily always weighed the odds. When it came to the prospect of being murdered, Babs had to admit that only Lily could act as maker of decisions. Nevertheless, she felt trapped and contained, her natural energy forced into a straitjacket of Clive Chalmers's making.

'I'd like to visit the Lakes,' was Lily's next statement.

'Not yet,' groaned Babs. 'Just a few more days in Blackpool, please. Cassie loves the sand and the sea.'

Lily smiled. Babs had played the trump card. Where Cassie was concerned, Lily was a walkover. 'All right,' she said. 'But your ice cream's dripped all over your T-shirt.'

Babs mopped her front with a baby wipe. 'Anyway, you,' she said, her tone engineered to sound cross. 'You always ask the questions like a teacher, while I have to be the good girl and produce the right answers. So it's my turn now. I get to ask a question. OK?'

'Goody,' said Lily. 'I can scarcely wait.'

Babs took a deep breath. 'You and Mike,' she said quickly, as if spitting out medicine that tasted bad. As soon as she had said the words, she wanted to take them back, because they were even nastier out than they had been inside. 'Sorry. But there's something, isn't there?' She half dreaded the answer, since Lily's love life had been spectacularly awful thus far, and the poor girl needed more trouble like she needed a hole in her head.

Lily nodded. 'There's something, but God knows what.'

'What do you mean?'

'What I mean is I don't know what I mean.' But she did know . . .

A breeze, made cooler by the sea over which it had passed, made both women shiver. They packed their bags, placed Cassie in her pushchair and began the difficult walk through sand back to the car. Halfway, Babs stopped, released the child and folded the chair – it was easier to carry than to push. 'Lily?'

'What?'

'It won't be long now, will it? Until we can go home, I mean.'

Lily frowned and concentrated. 'I shouldn't think so, but I'm not sure. If those three men crack, they'll still go down for the attack, but Clive will be charged as having instigated it. He'll be in court, and perhaps that will teach him a lesson.' She didn't believe the words she had just framed and expelled. She knew him. Once he got the knife in, he twisted it. Sometimes, she believed that the sexual jealousy that was the cause of all the trouble had literally sent him mad.

'Will we be safe after that?'

Lily was certain about nothing. 'Like you said, Babs – anyone can find anyone if they're determined. But, you know, I do rather like living in Eagleton. Once this particular issue is resolved, we'll think about what to do next.'

'I really do miss Pete.'

'I know.'

Babs piled bags and pushchair into the back of the estate car. 'And you miss Mike.'

'Yes.'

'Bloody hell, Lee. We are a pair of idiots, aren't we? Falling in love within five minutes of relocating, hearts on our sleeves, forever teenagers.'

Both women stood on the pavement and laughed helplessly. Neither was completely sure why she was amused, but glee took over and rendered them useless. Cassie joined in. She giggled until she got the hiccups, and the hysteria started all over again.

Once settled in the car, Lily mopped her eyes. 'He loves me, Babs.'

'Right.'

'And he's amazing.'

'Right.'

'Stop saying right.'

'OK. Wrong, then. He's a priest, my lovely. They have to be – what's it called? Celibate. They can't have a wife or a mistress.'

'But they do. It's quite common.'

'Common as in cheap and nasty?' Babs turned and looked at her daughter, who had already fallen asleep. 'Is he any good in bed?' she asked in a stage whisper.

Lily closed her eyes, opened them, looked up to heaven. 'Don't go all vulgar on me, Babs.'

'Is he?'

'Is Pete?'

'Yes.'

'Good. I'm very pleased for you.' Lily started the car. She pulled into the traffic and aimed the car in the direction of their rented holiday flat. Babs's question hung large in the air like a balloon that hadn't lost all its helium. The subject would be raised again later, of that Lily was certain. So she bit the bullet. 'He's very good. End of.'

Babs giggled. 'Well, you certainly take the whole Ryvita, don't you? Nothing as ordinary as a custard cream, because you're too keen on your figure – but Lily, how can a Catholic priest be part of your daily diet?'

'He isn't. It happened just once. And if it doesn't happen again, I'll be very sad, but I dare say I'll survive. Don't tell anyone – not even Pete. Mike has issues with his faith, and I'm not a part of that. If he leaves the Church, it won't be for me. It'll be for himself.'

Babs was suddenly sober. 'If he leaves the Church, the village will blame you. They love him. Even the non-Catholics think he's an asset. Look at what he does – arranging for the elderly to be fed and helped, going out of his way for the panto – they'll say it's your fault, kid.'

'Perhaps. Just don't ask your horse to jump before you reach the gate, Barbara Cookson. Now shut up and let me concentrate. There's a tram behind us and a horse and cart in front.' She edged out to overtake, trying hard to avoid startling the placid animal, although its stolid plodding seemed to indicate that it had long come to terms with the nuisance of the internal combustion engine.

They drove the rest of the way in silence, and Lily was relieved. Back at the flat, she made supper while Babs bathed her daughter. It was an undeniable fact that they couldn't stay here for ever. Apart from anything else, Babs had started to work again and was enjoying it, while Lily had been forced to pass a couple of weddings to another florist. The business had to be dependable, or it would fail.

Then there was Mike. Yes. Father Michael Walsh, who wanted to quit the priesthood and spend his life with a woman he scarcely knew. This should be the time during which they could become better acquainted ... A smile played on her lips and she stood still, a fork in one hand, a plate in the other. The wondrous thing was that neither she nor Mike needed to know more about each other, because it was already there. Whatever 'it' was ... Hadn't Prince Charles used something like that line when trying to define the term 'in love'? But whatever existed between Lily and Mike was overpowering, and it had to be love. Real love. She placed the cutlery on the table and crossed her fingers. 'This time, let it be real, God,' she whispered.

'Are you setting that table or dreaming about bedtime with Mike?'

'Shut up, Babs. Did she eat her banana?'

'Yes.'

'Have you cleaned her teeth?'

'Yes. Honestly, Lee, anyone would think she was yours— Sorry, love. You know I didn't mean—'

'It's all right. It's always been all right.' It would never be all right, yet it had to be.

Babs sat down and awaited the arrival of the gourmet meal – fish fingers and baked beans followed by fruit salad from a tin. 'Sometimes, I could cut out my tongue. After all you've done for me, after what I did to you, I should know better.'

'Stop it, Babs. You did nothing to me. You're my best friend, so be quiet or I'll hit you with this serving spoon.'

They spent the rest of the meal fighting about which bit of the town they might visit tomorrow. Babs wanted to go to the top of the tower, which was, as she reminded her friend yet again, a grade one listed building and a piece of history. 'It's a half-scale version of the Eiffel,' she said.

'And I go dizzy on a thick carpet, so you can go on your own.' Lily longed to visit the Grundy Art Gallery, but she realized that both Babs and Cassie would be bored, so a compromise was reached. They would go to Blackpool Sea Life Centre and watch all the weird creatures that lived there. She had already half promised Cassie, anyway, so that was an end to the argument. The Grundy would be a solo trip, and— Lily glanced through the window to the opposite side of the rather broad avenue on which the flats stood. 'Babs?'

'Yes, ma'am?'

'That car. It's come back again – it was there last night.'

Babs peered out. 'Yes. And there's a man sitting in it.'

Lily swallowed a mouthful of fear. Not yet, surely? Weren't people being charged, wasn't Eve only just out of hospital, hadn't Clive been interviewed by police? And no one knew about Blackpool – no one except Paul. Even after the trick he had played on Mo's wife, Lily believed in him. Paul knew what it was to be hurt and disappointed; Paul would never tell a soul where she was. 'Did you tell anyone?' she asked.

'No.' Babs was cross. If Lily didn't trust her now, she never would. 'I haven't even phoned Pete. I promise you, Lee, I—'

'All right. You pack, I'll watch.'

'But where are we going?'

Lily turned and looked at her best friend. 'No bloody idea. But I have our passports, took yours with me by mistake when I moved across the road, because they were both in one envelope.'

'No, Lee.'

'It may be the only way.'

'No. I'm not going abroad. My daughter is English and she'll remain English.'

'Who said anything about emigration?'

Babs had taken enough. She raised her voice and both hands in order to emphasize her words. 'It's inevitable. Blackpool for a week, not far enough. We can't go back to Somerset, so where do we go? When will we be safe – in five years, ten? Might as well go the whole hog and shift to Canada, because at this rate you're going to be running for the rest of your life.' She stilled her arms by folding them. 'Sorry. You're on your own, sweetie. I'm taking Cassie back to Eagleton. There are two of me, you see.'

'Yes.' Lily blinked away some tears.

'I know that hurts, but I still need to emphasize it, love.'

'I understand.'

'She needs a proper and predictable life. I'm not dragging that poor child from pillar to post. I want her settled. I want her to have friends, school, college, university.' She caught her breath. 'And I need Pete. I think he's the one, Lee.'

Lily sat down, her eyes fixed on the car outside. She asked Babs to turn off the lights before coming to sit nearby, and, in near-darkness, they ate a little of the fruit salad Lily had served. Everything Babs had said made sense, but it didn't eliminate the fear. Clive was crazy enough to try almost anything, because he had no fear of a longer sentence, didn't care about anything beyond his ideas for revenge. She reached out a hand and touched Babs. 'Do what you have to do,' she said.

'You know I can't leave you on your own. You know I won't abandon you.'

Lily stared at a wall and looked into the past. She opened a door in her mind, plus a door in the house she had shared with Clive Chalmers. At the other side stood an angry, russet-haired woman. The uninvited guest asked to see Clive . . .

'Lee?'

'What?'

'Don't go there. Don't think about that.'

This was how well Babs knew her now. Their first contact had been made at that front door, and it had involved a slap from Lily that had left the slighter woman reeling and in tears. These days, Babs knew what Lily was thinking about, understood her better than anyone. Lily blinked. She could hear the screams now behind the door she had slammed. 'I'm pregnant,' the little woman had yelled. Down the years those words echoed, as clear now as they had been on the evening of their birth.

'Stop thinking about it, Lee,' repeated Babs softly.

Lily stabbed a bit of pineapple and forced herself to eat. She needed energy, because she had to do this thing, and she had to do it right away. It was time to stop running, and perhaps Babs was right. Returning to Eagleton had to be an inevitability.

'Where are you going?' Tired of eating in the dark, Babs switched on a lamp and closed the curtains. The man in the car was still sitting there. 'Lee? What the devil are you up to now? Good God – Eve was nearly killed! What if he's come from Liverpool like the first lot did? Lee!'

Lily draped a cardigan across her shoulders. 'I'm going to ask him why he's there. If I can't get a straight answer, I'll tell the police to shift him. There are houses everywhere, and it isn't completely dark yet. It's time I faced my demons. He's loitering with intent.'

Babs stood by the window and peeped past the edge of a green curtain. Lily didn't often lose her rag, but when she did it was as well to be in residence somewhere at a distance. Like Jupiter or Saturn. Babs bit her lip, flinched when the downstairs front door slammed, watched round-eyed as Lily approached the parked vehicle.

She marched across the road and hammered on the windscreen of the silver-grey Vauxhall. She walked round to the pavement, standing with her arms folded until he opened the passenger door. 'You're being watched from many windows,' she warned. 'So don't do anything stupid. Who the hell are you, why are you here, and when do you plan to bog off into the bloody sunset? Because I am sick of the sight of your damned car, mister.'

The man left the vehicle and came to stand next to her. 'Miss Latimer?'

Shivering slightly, she stood her ground. 'Who wants to know?'

'I do.'

That wasn't good enough, and she told him so. If he had come on behalf of Clive Chalmers, guest of Her Majesty the Queen, he could bugger off and tell said Clive Chalmers that she wasn't afraid any more. Furthermore, loitering in a decent neighbourhood was never a bright idea, and the neighbours were all up in arms, especially those who were permanent residents of Blackpool. 'I can die only once,' she added. 'So get it over with, because I don't mind missing *Coronation Street* this time.'

He shook his head. 'No wonder that priest's going out of his mind,' he said. 'Have you any idea of the trouble you caused by buggering off without a word? People miss you.'

'What?'

'And Pete Haywood's fretting like mad about your mate.'

'What?' she repeated stupidly. 'Look,' she said, drawing herself to her full height. 'Lock that flaming car and come into the flat.' She looked him up and down. 'You look about as dangerous as a fish supper without vinegar. Get inside and I'll put the kettle on.'

The man stood for a few moments before doing as he had been ordered. His cover was blown, just as Pete had predicted, so what was the point in worrying? After securing his vehicle, he followed Lily up to the flat. Like a man being led to the gallows, he hung his head, because he had some idea of what was coming to him.

Babs was waiting, rolling pin at the ready. 'Unless you've come over all domesticated, put that away,' ordered Lily. 'He's harmless. You can tell just by looking at him that he couldn't crush a grape.'

The man edged in and sat at the uncleared dining table.

'Who sent you?' Babs asked. 'I suppose it's us you're watching.'

'Yes – sorry.' He went on to explain that he was a retired police sergeant, that Pete Haywood had tracked the pair of them to Blackpool and that he was here for their own good. 'My name's Alan Burke,' he informed them. 'I'm in charge of you.'

'God help us,' uttered Babs.

'How did they know we were in Blackpool?' Lily asked.

'Something Miss Cookson said to the child when they were in the taxi. I think she said she hoped it would be Blackpool.'

'Sorry,' Babs mouthed to her friend.

He continued. 'It was just a matter of Pete getting some young PC to phone all the letting agents and find out where you were staying. I'm a private eye now. Pete and that priest are paying my fees. So I've been doing my job, no more than that.'

Lily sat opposite the detective. 'We've been reading the papers. Is there anything we don't know?'

He nodded. 'Chalmers will be charged. All three sang like thrushes once they got going. It's attempted murder for them, and Chalmers will get done for arranging the attack. Incidentally, I've met Mrs Boswell – she's home, and she wants to see the pair of you. She needs her friends after what she went through.'

Lily asked after Eve's health and was told that the steel plate in her head allowed her to pick up Radio Four as long as she stood at the top of the stairs, that she could change channels on satellite TV by wiggling her ears, and that her magnetic personality was interfering with reception on her mobile phone.

'That's Eve,' said the two women in unison before laughing out loud.

He read out a list of all who missed them, reminding them that their presence at the wedding of Dave and Philly was compulsory and that Mo and Paul wanted Babs back. 'They say it's too much without you and there's nothing to laugh at,' he concluded.

Lily went to make the promised tea.

Babs asked about Pete and was told he was well, though unhappy. She shot a quick look over her shoulder. 'What about Father Walsh?' she murmured.

Alan too made sure that Lily was not within earshot. 'He's going to marry Dave and Philly, then he'll tell the congregation on the following Sunday that he's opting out. He wants her back. If you could see the state of him – he worships the ground she stands on.'

'Oh, bugger,' whispered Babs.

'She's not the reason,' he said. 'I was asked to stress that if you accosted me. It's all tied up with human rights and contraception and other stuff. But he's resigning whether she'll have him or not.'

Lily came in with the tea. 'You can sleep on the sofa tonight,' she told him. 'And we can't come straight home, because I promised Cassie she could see the funny fishes at some stage. We'll leave tomorrow afternoon.'

Alan Burke stirred his tea. 'Is Cassie Clive Chalmers's child?' he asked.

'Yes,' snapped Babs. 'Charming Chalmers fooled me into believing he was a single man. Then I met Lily, and she marked my card for me. We've been close ever since he ... ever since what happened to her.'

Alan Burke looked at Lily and wondered at her calm facade. After all that had happened, he would not have been surprised if she'd finished up in a psychiatric unit. 'It's good that you have each other, and better still that I don't have to sleep in that car. Thank you, ladies.'

They put him right on that one, because they weren't ladies, they were women. He was invited to eat anything he could find that didn't smell strange, and then Lily and Babs went off to bed. It was early, but tomorrow would be busy.

Lily was settled with a book when Babs came in. She listened while Babs told her about Mike's intentions, about how he needed Lily by his side. 'He's doing it whatever you say,' Babs concluded.

'I know. Good night, then.'

Alone, Lily turned to the wall and waited for sleep to come. 'I know,' she had said so glibly, so easily. But was he sure? Or was Lily a part of the mix that had finally made him decide to give up, to stop looking after Catholics in three or four parishes?

The real worry about what the villagers might say was compounded by the fact that she was an incomer, a stranger from a part of England many of them had never seen. It might all be blamed on her, and she would need to be strong.

'Am I recovered enough for that?' she asked the darkening room. She didn't know the answer, wasn't even sure of the question, because the kind of decision he was making might well stretch her beyond anything she had experienced so far. He was a good priest … Itwould take a very special kind of strength, but she would find it. Wouldn't she?

Whatever, Babs was right. Two women and a child

could not run for ever. Cassie needed stability, while her mother should be working in order to gain a degree of independence. And the flower shop was important; perhaps, given time, the business could become part of a wedding-planning consortium. There was even a chance that Leanne Chalmers might return to her old job, the career she had really loved. Could *Makeover Madness* ride again? Could Clive be contained in a unit so solitary that he would never meet another soul?

Lily gave up after an hour and crept into the kitchen. To her surprise, she met Alan Burke, who was making cocoa. 'Want some?' he asked.

'Yes, please.'

They sat on the sofa that had become his makeshift bed. 'Lily?'

'What?'

'Eve Boswell needs you.'

'Oh?'

He nodded sadly. 'She's all right, and she begged me not to tell you, but I think I should. She had a fit the day she came home. Because she pleaded and cried when it was over, Chas let her stay at home, though he spoke to the doctor when she was asleep. The doc said it could be a one-off. But then the second one happened. Eve has epilepsy. Chas is selling the off-licence and hanging over her all the time. She wants you to take him in hand.'

'Right. Bit of a mess, isn't it?'

Alan sighed. 'Yes, but better to go home and face the music.'

Eve was sick to the back teeth, and she made sure that everyone in her household was aware of it. She got her new wigs, was indulged completely by her doting husband, was forced to have daily help in the house, and was generally treated like a total invalid. The tablets were great. As long as she remembered to take them, she was perfectly all right except for the odd headache and slightly blurred vision. But she was fed up with Chas, and was tired of telling him to go away and leave a bit of oxygen just for herself. 'I can't breathe,' she told him accusingly. 'You keep panicking. If you panic, I panic, and we all know what might happen if I end up in bits. So go away, buzz off, make yourself scarce, because you are ruining my nerves and I can't take any more!'

Chas stood his ground. He was getting rid of the off-licence, and that was the end of it. She could mither till the cows, goats, hens and geese came home, but her working life was over, as was his. 'Do as you're told,' he said.

She folded her arms and straightened her spine. 'I'm not in my dotage yet, Chas, and if you think I'm—'

'Don't get worked up. The doc says you haven't to get worked up.'

Her foot tapped the floor. 'Not get worked up? With you hanging round me twenty-four hours a day? Impossible. If I sneeze wrong, you're like an old mother hen hovering over me, do I feel all right, should you get a cushion, do I need the doctor? I can't be me any more! Now bugger off and take that shop off the market before I do us both some damage.' The foot tapped again. 'I mean it, Chas. This is the closest I've come to wishing I could be single again. You've got our Derek daft as well – he keeps looking at me to make sure my head's not fallen off. The bloody village grinds to a halt every time I step out. I was thinking of getting some squirty cream and putting it round my mouth so they can all say they saw me in a fit and get it over with. After all, I'm the cabaret and we don't want to disappoint our neighbours, do we?'

Chas ran a hand through already tousled hair. 'I'm trying to be sensible.'

'Well, there's a novel idea if ever I heard one. Charles Boswell and sense? That's a new partnership. Please, please don't go all sensible on me. I'm alive. Yes, there's a bit of brain damage, a loose wire or something, but these pills will stop it, Chas. Once they've found the right dosage, I'll be fine. Go to the shop. Don't sell it. If I don't have a fit for two years, they might even let me drive again. The best way to put me back on my feet is to bugger off and let me be.' She nodded angrily. 'Sell the shop, and I'll leave you. I'll go and live with our Vera.'

'You can't stand your Vera since she moved to Crosby and started putting her aitches in the wrong places.'

'Blundellsands,' said Eve. 'I have to correct you there, because our Vera's living on the bit where the posh Vikings landed, the ones who took off their horned helmets before raping and pillaging. It's nice up there. Like the seaside.'

'It's the River bloody Mersey.'

'I like the bloody Mersey – it runs in my veins. Lovely bungalow on Mariners Road, stand at the front gate when the tall ships come and go – did I tell you the river's visible from our Vera's gate?'

'Only about three hundred times, yes.'

'And the kiddies come past to go to the swimming baths or play on the beach – it's great. Hi shall heven put my haitches where they hought to be. Just because hit's Blundellsands, like.'

Chas left the room. It was difficult to know what to do for the best, as he could never tell when she was serious. They'd been engaged three times because she'd kept saying she was joking. Now, she was having epileptic fits, and he was flummoxed. He loved his shop. Even these days, when he was turning down cheap booze and other ill-gotten goods, he made a fair living. And he would miss it, since he enjoyed the comings and goings, looked forward to meeting people and forging friendships across the counter.

She didn't like having a home help, didn't like not being allowed to drive, was fed up with being watched and cared for. The trouble with females these days was that they didn't know how to lean on a bloke, had no idea of how to make him feel needed.

As he perched on the end of the marital bed, he admitted to himself that he probably needed her more than she needed him. Epilepsy could cause added damage with each episode, and therefore the fits had to be stopped, because he couldn't face the concept of life without her. The tablets could go some way towards achieving that goal, but Eve needed to be calm. She wasn't calm with him around. It had never been a peaceful marriage, because it had been filled with laughter, rows, practical jokes and some hard work. He and Eve ignited each other even now, after all these years of wedlock. Chas grinned. Would he swap her? Would he hell as like.

Compromise. That was a big word. Eve needed to be forced to accept help in the house, yet had to be allowed to continue planning and decorating the place. He had to watch over her, but he must keep the shop in case the selling of it upset her too much. 'I've heard of folk going to some lengths to get their own way,' he told the wall, 'but she's in a class of her own.'

He would give in to her yet again. It was the easiest course, as it involved little or no decision making and no effort whatsoever. If she had a lot of fits, he would set his foot in concrete and there'd be no discussion about the matter. Yes. If she carried on having bad attacks, he would ... Would what? He was kidding himself all over again. Unless she went completely doolally, Eve was always going to win. That had been the unspoken arrangement from the very start.

He stood up and took a deep breath. Northern women were a tough breed. If fielded in the arena of battle, they would be tanks with huge guns in their turrets. Yorkshire and Lancashire had produced a legion of war mares that were supposed to have died out a century ago, but no. They were here, they were well and they were cunning. As for the females from Liverpool – they defied description. And he had married one.

Downstairs, Eve was experiencing a similar period of introspection. She was scared, but she daren't let him see it. The loss of control had terrified her, and she didn't like the idea of waking repeatedly after a fit with no idea of what had happened to her, no concept of what those around her had seen. The doc had been positive enough. Epilepsy like hers, which had happened after trauma to the brain, was potentially manageable. He had ordered her to rest, just as she had already been told by the hospital, and to give her grey matter time to settle. 'It could all stop of its own accord,' he had said. 'But, to be on the safe side, I'll write a prescription . . .'

She had the pills. She had her son, and she had her

wonderful husband. But Chas was useless when in the vicinity of illness. He fussed too much, worried himself halfway to death, couldn't control his fear. Chas needed to go back to work, while she wanted to tackle her situation in her own way. Her own way. She would have it, or he would suffer . . .

Like many other villages, Eagleton was in possession of a process whereby gossip travelled silently, because no one would ever admit to starting the process. When Lily and Babs had been gone just a few days, a form of osmosis took over, and messages were passed chemically, almost of their own accord.

Father Walsh was giving up the priesthood. Father Walsh loved Lily Latimer. Father Walsh had already been struggling with his conscience long before Lily had moved to the village. He believed in contraception and the right of individuals to make decisions regarding their own bodily functions. He had absolved people of sin when he should not have done so; his relationship with God was too personal to be affected by the dictates of Rome. So he disagreed with the Pope, and he had to leave. He would remain Catholic, as the faith was closest to his basic beliefs, but he would no longer be a member of the clergy. It seemed fair enough, and all but a few rigidly bigoted people remained on his side.

Pour Les Dames had metamorphosed into a whispering gallery. Paul, who was lighter of foot since meeting a new man at Sisters, wanted to scream and tell them to mind their own business, but he managed, just about, to keep his counsel. People should be left alone to get on with life, and he longed to yell that message until he learned, from the little he overheard, that most folk were supportive of the prospective changes.

Today, the gossip was audible, since Mo had announced to a fascinated audience that a new client would be arriving at any moment.

Valda almost dropped her cup. She couldn't wait to rush back and tell her mother-in-law what was happening. Things were much better now that she and Mary had made their peace. Mary watched the kids while Valda had a break, and today's break was special, because everyone was getting hair styled for the forthcoming wedding of Philly and Dave. 'Never,' said Valda after saving her coffee. 'Can Sally do my nails in here, Mo?' She didn't want to miss anything.

'Sorry,' replied Mo. 'Standing room only in the salon, and you're nearly done. But you can leave the door open if you like when you go through for your manicure.'

The congregation stilled itself when the door was thrown inward. 'Well?' shouted the newcomer. 'Are you going to help me in or not?'

Paul rushed to handle the unwieldy contraption. He wheeled in Enid Barker and helped her across to one of the sinks. She leaned heavily, and he was almost gasping for air when he deposited her in position. 'I'll ... I'll get you a gown,' he said.

Enid looked at all the silent people while Mo pushed her wheelchair out of the way. 'What's up with you lot?' she asked. 'Never seen the mother of the groom coming to get her hair done? Paul would have done it at home, but I fancied a trip out.' She knew what they thought of her, but they were just a little bit wrong this time, because she was trying her best to be decent. Ever since poor Eve Boswell's tragedy, Enid had kept her mouth shut. Well, nearly shut. She still went on a bit when her son was around, but that was an old habit that would take some murdering.

'I want a bit of colour,' she told Paul. 'And cut it. It's neither one thing nor the other at this length.' She looked at all the starers. 'You can put your eyes back in your heads, because I only talk behind your backs, not to your faces.' She winked at Paul. 'Oh, there is one thing, though. Lily and her friend are on their way back. I found that out this morning when I trolleyed over to see Eve. She won't let him get rid of the business, by the way. Now, if you don't mind, I'm getting my hair done.'

The room buzzed once more and, for the first time, most people were glad that Enid was among them. Because of melegs, she missed nothing, and everyone listened carefully when she told them about the night of the attack. 'Two of them were big bruisers,' she said. The fact was that Eve's attackers grew several inches with each telling of the tale. 'But it was a little fellow that was watching. He wasn't what you might call a dwarf, because he was all in proportion, just shorter than any man I've seen. He smoked a lot. Happen that stunted his growth.'

'That's a clever dog,' said Valda as she made her way towards the rear room. 'Skippy – she's bright.'

'My Dave's clever and all,' answered Enid. 'I know he does himself down, but he reads a lot, doesn't need a fancy degree and letters at the back of his name. He'll have that dog trained to deliver the newspapers soon.'

There followed a short silence while the audience digested that, as Enid was known for giving her son a hard time.

'What's Philly wearing?' enquired Paul.

Enid laughed. 'Don't ask, because I'm sworn to secrecy. There was near blue murder before I came, because he came into my flat without knocking and she had to dive behind the sofa so's he wouldn't see her suit. Still, never mind. It'll all be over tomorrow.'

Paul went out to the back in order to pick up some products for Enid's hair. Sally was doubled over behind the door when he and Valda went in. 'Bloody hell,' said Mo's wife. 'Who's been cheering her up?'

Paul put a finger to his lips. 'Sally, miracles happen,' he whispered. 'Shut up, or we might frighten her away.'

But Enid was clearly in her element. She was speaking to a small crowd. People were listening to her at last.

Philly was what Dave termed 'in a tizz', because getting married had proved to be slightly more complicated than she had at first expected. Dave, who was of the opinion that new suits and two witnesses were enough, had been forced to give in to Philly's wishes, and the whole thing had escalated beyond even her expectations.

Everyone wanted to come. Both bride and groom were well respected, and people from Eagleton and several of the smaller satellite villages had promised to come to the church, many protesting that they didn't expect to be fed. 'We just want to be there for you,' was the statement made by most. 'What you and Dave have done for us all – that Reading Room – is brilliant. It's somewhere to go for a cuppa, and it's nice for the old folk since our libraries got closed. Oh, we'll be there.'

Philly had been cooking and baking for days. Every freezer in Eagleton was full, because she was parking her food wherever she could, and lists were getting out of hand. As the school was closed for the summer holidays, Father Walsh and a few other men had turned the hall into a reception area with full-sized tables and chairs. Philly had hired glassware, cutlery and crockery, but the guest lists were in such a muddle that the seating plan had to be scrapped. Now, she had a huge hall with tables against walls, and the whole thing was a confused sort of buffet with a dance floor in the centre.

Philly and Dave stood in the middle of chaos. 'Where's the cake going?' he asked. Philly had made her own wedding cake. It had two layers and no chance of feeding all the guests unless some didn't mind just a few crumbs and a bit of icing. 'And people have to sit somewhere,' he added. So they pulled out the tables and began the task of lining the walls with chairs. 'They'll be stuck behind the tables now,' he protested.

Philly awarded him a withering glance. 'They can please themselves,' she said rather sharply. 'I don't know what's happened, Dave. The whole thing ran away with me. I never wanted all this.'

'Yes, you did. Right at the start you carried on about feeding folk. I told you we didn't need all this business.' He grasped both her hands. 'They just want to see you happy, Phil. If they only get a pie and a pint, they'll be happy.'

She burst into tears.

'Right,' he said, 'that's it. Enough is enough, Mrs Nearly-Barker. Hairdresser, then home. Leave all this to me.'

'But I—'

'Go.' He pointed to the door. 'Get out before one of us bursts a blood vessel. Think of the baby.' He kissed her forehead and gave her a gentle push in the direction of the exit.

When she had gone, he looked at his watch. Surely they would be here soon? It was all very eleventh hour, but he would give his lovely bride the party she deserved even if it killed him. He walked outside and began his vigil. When Lily's estate car finally hove into view, it was four o'clock. Lily was a miracle worker; Lily would sort it out.

She didn't even get the chance to visit poor Eve, because Dave was on her like a ton of bricks the minute she stepped out of the car. 'Lily,' he pleaded. 'She's my princess and my saviour. I want her to have the best. The wedding's at three, and I'll keep her away from the hall. Women all over the place have the food, and they'll bring it across tonight and in the morning, because it needs time to thaw. All that cloth you have, all those lights and silk flowers and ... oh, I don't know. Make it fit for a princess.'

'Is it all right if I breathe first? Babs, go and see Eve – take Cassie with you – you can phone Pete from Eve's house. Tell Eve that Dave's on my case, it's his fault, and I'll see her as soon as possible.' Lily paused and leaned against the car for a moment. 'Listen, you,' she said to Dave. 'Dig up every man you can find – get them out of their graves if needs be. I've an attic full of wedding bling and tat, but I'm doing no carrying.' She looked closely at Dave. 'Are the arrangements a mess?'

He nodded wordlessly.

'Leave it to me. I do the impossible every day of the week, but this miracle is going to take all night.'

'She's worth it,' he said.

'Of course she is. Right. Find me six men, then buzz off for a pint. I don't want you there, and Philly is banned.'

'Thanks, Lily.'

She smiled. She was home.

Mike wrapped his arms round Lily and lifted her up in the air as soon as she entered her house. 'Thank God,' he repeated several times.

After a long kiss, she cried, 'No time, no time. Unhand me, varlet, and get up those stairs immediately.'

He grinned. 'I thought you'd never ask.'

But she wasn't asking, she was commanding. 'Attic. Boxes marked wedding. Fetch. Don't ask me to fill in the missing words—' The door shot inward, and Dave marched in with Valda's husband Tom, Chas, Derek, Tim Mellor and a couple of men whose names Lily didn't know. She sent them off upstairs in pursuit of Mike before going to change into overalls and an old shirt. Weddings usually looked beautiful, but those who planned and furnished such occasions were invariably reduced to wreckage.

When Dave had been sent to the pub, Lily sat for several minutes in the centre of the school hall, which she considered to be a disaster zone. Mike, complete with silly grin, kept his eyes on her. If he thought said silly grin would get him out of helping, he could think again, since this was a matter of dire urgency. In less than twenty-four hours, the mess had to become beautiful for Philly, who deserved only the best. So the best had to be made of an appalling job. 'Should I be getting jetlag after travelling from Blackpool?' she asked of no one in particular.

The school hall was not the perfect venue for a reception. It had huge windows, plasterboard walls and harsh lighting. But Lily refused to be daunted. Yard after yard of cream muslin was pinned by helpers to walls and windows while Lily worked on a gigantic chandelier made from wire, crystals and large fairy lights. Silk roses were pinned here and there to break the muslin monotony, and every wall was lit by tiny fairy lights just strong enough to show through the sheer drapery.

'It's like fairyland,' Mike declared when the room was almost finished.

'I'm glad you're so easy to please,' said Lily. 'Now, open the curtains on the stage and put a small table up there – I've brought some Irish linen cloths. Tim – you cover these terrible buffet tables and the smaller one for the stage. They can cut their cake up there. I'll do napkins and decorate the stage tomorrow.' She waited until her orders had been obeyed.

'Right – sit,' she said.

The men were fed up. 'We need a drink,' Chas complained. 'I've a sick wife at home, and–'

'Oh, shut up,' snapped the woman in charge. 'Favours.'

'I'm doing no more favours for anyone,' said Chas.

Lily threw a pile of net circles on a table. 'Fifty should be enough, as they're just for women. So do a few each.' She demonstrated with a handful of sugared almonds, one of the net circles and a piece of satin ribbon. 'Chas,' she said, 'you are excused. Go to your shop and take beer to my house. You and the rest of these reprobates can get your reward there. I'll pay you later.'

'No need,' said Chas gratefully. He was glad to escape the making of favours, and he needed to check the shop anyway, as it was still unattended and closed.

The vet looked at Lily. 'I can sew up a cat and I can probably neuter an elephant at a push, but when it comes to sugared almonds—'

'And I'm OK with baptisms and weddings—'

Lily glared at the man she adored. 'Get on with it. Anybody with less than ten out of ten stays in after school and does extra arithmetic.'

She smiled as she watched large fingers trying to do the work usually apportioned to women. After a few minutes, she sat with them and helped, because they were remarkably slow learners. Just after eleven o'clock, Lily declared herself satisfied with their labours. 'Take this lot of favour-makers to my house,' she told Chas, who had reappeared sometime before. 'I'll go and see if Eve's still up.'

While the men made their way to the ex-presbytery, Lily walked past the church and into Rose Cottage. Cassie was asleep on a sofa, while her mother dozed in a chair. 'Don't get up,' whispered Lily to Eve. 'I am absolutely exhausted. How are you?'

Eve smiled. 'Good to see you, girl. He's not getting rid of the business, so that's a start. And I've decided not to have epilepsy, because it brings him out in a rash, and we can't have that.'

Lily sank into an armchair. 'I am so, so sorry. It was meant for me. I believe Clive's being charged with something or other, and they've got the men who did the crime for him. I shouldn't have run away. What sort of friend runs when she's needed most?'

'A frightened one with a child to save. Stop it, Lily. What happened saved me from paralysis or some such thing – they didn't know what that cyst thing might have done to me. I could have ended up talking broken

318

biscuits and walking like a ruptured duck. Look on the bright side.'

Lily exhaled slowly. 'I am so tired. But we've got the hall almost ready, and all the men are at my house chilling out with beer. I suppose I'd better go and supervise before they wreck the place.' She stood up and planted a kiss on Eve's forehead. 'Send Babs home when she wakes,' she whispered. 'See you at the wedding.'

Lily walked slowly past the church that had owned Mike for many years. He was about to turn his back on many parishioners in the cluster of villages, and she would be seen as one of his reasons. It always came back to this, she told herself silently; it always reached the point where she worried about herself and what folk would think of her. It wasn't about her at all. Mike was the one who was going to suffer most.

Her house was as silent as the graveyard next door. Standing at the French windows, she saw a few glimmers of light in the orchard, and deduced that her favour-makers and curtain-hangers were enjoying their reward al fresco and were using her storm lamps as illumination.

'Lily?'

She shivered when his hands crept round her waist.

'Thanks for telling Paul to let me know you were all right.'

She turned to receive his kiss before clinging to him as if she might never let go. 'I was so afraid,' she said. 'Terrified, in fact. There was Cassie, there was Babs, there was me. I had to make sure we were safe.'

'It was reaction,' he said. 'Is Cassie his?'

Lily nodded mutely. After a short silence, she continued. 'Babs came to our house because she was angry and afraid of being a lone parent. He had seduced her

319

and she was a couple of months into the pregnancy.' She paused. 'That was when everything started to go completely haywire.'

He stroked her hair as if comforting a child. 'You're exhausted.'

'And you're sober.'

He laughed. 'Two pints is my limit. If I have any more, I either defy the law of gravity or succumb to it completely. I had an uncle the same. He fell asleep in Liverpool and woke next morning on the Isle of Man.'

'No!'

'Yes. The trouble was, he was getting married that day.'

'Good Lord. What happened?'

Mike shrugged. 'She married a Protestant, I think, decided he was the safer bet.'

'And Uncle?'

'The crew liked him so well that he joined them and spent the rest of his days ferrying folk from dock to dock.'

'Liar.'

'Yes. Go on. You're too tired for my anecdotes.'

She nodded. 'I need a bath. A couple of hours in a car followed by the school hall frenzy is just too much. I am forbidden to get tired. Doctor's orders. Are you staying tonight?'

'Yes. Go and have your bath while I get rid of the fairies at the bottom of your garden. It's a big day tomorrow.' He turned to leave the house. 'By the way, I love you.'

'And I love you.'

It was as simple as that. He was just a man, albeit a rather wonderful specimen. He was an adult who was about to change the course of his life, and she would be there to comfort him when the Church showed its impatience with him. The love between Lily and Mike had come suddenly and unbidden, but that was the nature of love. It homed in and focused on the bull's eye and to hell with all the outer rings on the target. Love was not controllable. She went to have her bath.

They lay together that night in a bed that was far too small, and apart from a few kisses, there was no love-making. Tomorrow would be Mike's last wedding, and they shared the unspoken knowledge that he had to be at his best in the morning. Lily turned to the wall, and he fitted himself behind her like a spoon against its twin. They slept for ten hours, and when she woke, Lily knew that she had definitely arrived home. She would hang her hat in Eagleton. As would he.

Sudden silences, then mutterings when they think I'm out of earshot. Those who spoke to me before now ignore me completely. I should have used someone who knew her, or somebody with the sense to find out properly before wading in.

The name Boswell has come up a few times. From the little I've heard, he's been good to cons on the outside. He's well thought of. There's something going on, and I've asked for a move. Even the screws won't look at me. They tell me I'll be moved when the governor's ready, and not before.

Whisperings again this morning. Not content with see- ing me dragged out of prison and into court, they want more from me. This is frightening. The worst was last night just after lights out. When the screws had checked after lockdown, the lags whispered in unison. It hissed along the landing till it reached my cell at the end. The word sounded like 'Chazzer', but I'm not sure.

Escape from here's impossible. This morning, I told a screw about the whispering. He said nobody heard a thing. Well, I heard it…

Twelve

The day started well. Some runt called Walter spat in my breakfast, so had to do without. Threw the plate in his face and got marched out by screws. If some old con tells you he got beaten up by prison staff, don't assume he's lying. Some of these officers are psychos. Others are so ugly, they're probably sexually frustrated, so they hit us instead of clobbering their women. If they have women, that is.

No breakfast? No problem. The food in here is in breach of the Trade Descriptions Act, because there'd probably be more nourishment in the crockery. Even the water tastes bad, as if the purification works is leaving in half the sewage and most of the bog roll. I'm told I'm too picky and that some prisoners even enjoy the food. Well, they must have been living out of dustbins before they got here, then. Seems some folk will eat anything.

I'm on laundry. It's exciting work if you like other people's pyjamas and underpants. Got punched in the gut. Hard. Two held me behind a skip while the third waded in. 'That's from Chazzer,' they said. It's this chap Boswell. Walter the Spitter's brother got helped out by this Chazzer, runs a stall now on some market or other. Chazzer is the good egg who gets reformed crooks stalls on markets and I am the bad bastard. There's an ill wind blowing in my direction and it's coming not just from the inmates. Even the decent screws don't talk to me any more. As long as they don't put me back on 43 ...

Lunch. Gravy like congealed blood floating a raft of fat, mutton dressed as lamb with watery mint sauce, spuds lumpy with that greenish taste they get when they're seriously diseased and unfit for human consumption. Losing weight now. Talk, talk, talk. Jabber, jabber, mutter. It was Chazzer's wife who got the bang on the head. Yeah, yeah, I knew that. Daren't say anything. Daren't say it was bone-headed Scousers who got it wrong. It wasn't me. I was curled up with Len Deighton when the job went down. Went wrong.

They're building up to something and I'm the target. Bleeders know I've been in court, know I sent the loonies to do the job even if I did plead not guilty. Need eyes in the back of my head, but no money would buy them. So I'm stuck here waiting to be crippled while they go on about Chas/Chazzer Boswell, sainted man who helps old lags to walk the narrow when they get out of the big house. I suppose I am scared. Acting laid back is one thing, but feeling it is impossible.

More news. Seems Chazzer's coming in to visit Walter the Spitter. He visits him a couple of times a year, according to the whispers and mutters. Chas has done well for himself, owns a row of shops and an off-licence. Leanne got away and Chazzer's missus copped it and she's gone epileptic or some such tragic thing. Anyway, I'm in everybody's bad books, so things have taken a turn for the even worse.

Thinking of a half-attempt at suicide, make sure they find me and move me to a hospital. Or I could just act *crazy and start spitting in food, I suppose. But they wouldn't notice. See, what most people fail to understand is that the screws can be as bad as the cons.*

It's all wrong. The system's gone to pot and I'm going to get done over while the screws go deaf and blind. Still. As long as they leave me alive, I'll get out of this bloody dump. Survived the day. Another day in paradise. Get my head down, try not to think about tomorrow.

The rain was torrential. Philly jumped out of bed and ran to the window, hoping against hope that the lashing sound had happened in a dream, but the noise didn't stop. Today was the day of her wedding, and the heavens had opened. She shivered and hugged herself – was this a bad omen? Was God punishing her for getting pregnant before being married? She prayed inwardly for it to stop, but it showed no signs of abating.

'Shut up,' she said aloud. 'Anyone would think you'd considered becoming a nun, all this praying and penance.' She almost smiled when she remembered the shy, silly girl who had gone as a postulant to the Poor Clares. St Clare, a favourite with many impressionable teenage girls, had given up a privileged lifestyle to live in prayer and contemplation, and had been a contemporary of St Francis of Assisi. 'And I thought I could exist like a Franciscan,' murmured Philly. The sisters made altar breads for distribution throughout Britain, and their days were spent in communion with Christ. 'Not for me,' she concluded. She enjoyed the good things in life; loved cooking, reading, theatre and concerts. 'I wasn't holy enough,' she said gratefully as she took her wedding outfit from the wardrobe. And it was still raining malevolently. 'Please, God, help me to be good enough for Dave and for my child. Oh, and I'd be delighted if You'd stop raining on us.' Would He listen? Should she stop begging and act normal? Rain was rain, and life went on even when dripping wet.

There was a French saying that translated roughly into 'rainy wedding means a happy marriage'. All well and good, but rain as heavy as this also made for straggly hair, damaged clothes and ruined shoes. Women were already arriving at the school hall with food for the reception, and Philly watched them for a few minutes before going to draw a bath. They were scuttering about with bags and umbrellas, and every one of them had probably paid for a decent hairdo. Dave wasn't here. He had spent the night at Eve's house, as Chas was to be his best man. He hadn't to see his bride before church, but Philly wished he could be here. He was such a comfort, such a gentle, caring man. Skippy whimpered a little, because she missed her master. A bone quietened her while the bride gathered her thoughts and tried to look on the bright side. Better a wet wedding to Dave than a sunny one to someone who didn't care for her . . .

Lily had been up to something, but the bride had been ordered to stay away. There had been activity in the hall last night, and it meant that she probably didn't need to worry about the reception, because Lily was a genius with weddings. Everyone had been so kind. Instead of wedding gifts, Dave had asked for DIY vouchers, as he intended to put a new kitchen and a new bathroom in Philly's house. Up to now, they had received enough for everything except flooring, so they were lucky people.

'I'm fortunate,' she said. 'I've got a really good man.'

Lying in the bath, Philly thought about poverty, chastity and obedience lived in a world that was completely enclosed, a place where the laughter of children would never be heard. At the time, it had seemed to be the right thing, and her Irish family had been thrilled, as there were no boys to become priests. But Philly had failed them. Now they were all dead, or still in Ireland. She had invited none of the Mayo clan, because a mixed marriage would not be good news for them. Better to tell them after the event than to listen now to the moans and pleas of aunts and uncles who still stuck to the old mores of Catholicism. His mother had relented and would be at the church. That, in itself, was miracle enough.

It was going to be Father Walsh's last wedding. The Church was losing a valuable man, yet Philly understood him. Her one experience of the physical aspect of love had proved surprisingly pleasurable, and it was only normal for such a handsome man to fall for a beautiful woman like Lily. It was rumoured that his real reason for quitting went deeper than that, but Philly was sure that he would soon be married, and that finding a true soulmate had given him the courage to depart. Newer gossip divulged his intention to lecture in psychology – he was supposed to have had a successful interview. Or was it philosophy? It didn't matter. As long as he was happy, Philly and Dave would be pleased, as would most of his congregation.

Having gone overboard with perfumed bath oil, she decided to finish with a shower, because she had never been a fan of strong scents. Her hair, held in a net under a shower cap, was protected from the ablutions. Paul had done it yesterday, and had refused payment. Everyone was so good. She was marrying the loveliest man and would continue to live in Lancashire's best ever village. After drying herself, she went down to make coffee. Her stomach was all over the place, so she decided to postpone breakfast for a while.

The phone rang. It was Lily. 'Oh, I am so glad you came back. How are you? How are Cassie and Babs?'

'Tell you when I get there.'

'Get where?'

'I'm coming to do your make-up. And, before you start, you won't look like something that's patrolled the streets of Soho for five years. Tell me the colour of your outfit.'

Philly described her suit. She wanted to ask whether Mike had stayed the night at the presbytery, longed to discover the truth about the relationship, but she did not own Dave's mother's cheek. Instead, she thanked Lily for volunteering, then drank her coffee. Several hours stood between now and the wedding. It was going to be a very long day.

Then the rain stopped. Philly ran through to the kitchen and looked at the sky. There was a brilliant rainbow with a paler echo in the distance. God was smiling after all, and blackbirds were singing His anthems.

Just lying with him was simply wonderful. He touched her face a lot, tracing cheekbones with tender fingers, stroking her hair and neck, planting small kisses on her flesh. There had been no sexual contact. Lily knew he was holding back because he wanted to give all of himself to today's service. It was probable that they would not make love again until after he had left the priesthood, but it didn't matter. Just having him near her was almost, but not quite, enough. He was kind, he was fun and he was clever. And she loved him with all her being.

Lily pushed a few curls from his forehead.

'I didn't get a proper haircut,' he said.

'Yes, I can see it's still highly improper. And you're breathing in my ear.'

'But I did build an ironing board.'

It was on such ridiculously misplaced remarks that their relationship had been founded. The rabbit, the foxes, the ironing board – these were all part of something she had never known before. Her marriage, built on a highly volatile foundation of physical desire, jealousy, anger and cruelty, had allowed no space for the smaller and more important signals of love like ironing boards, cups of tea and cold beans on burnt toast. 'What's wrong with the old one?' she asked.

'Erm ... Well.' He cleared his throat. 'One of your programmes – I think it was in Plymouth or some such foreign-sounding place–'

'You know who I am?'

'Of course I do. I've bought the DVDs of series one. You were giving grief to some poor kitchen fitter who was stuck under the sink with cramp in an arm. You shouldn't have laughed at him, sweetheart. Anyway, they had this fancy contraption that fell out of the wall and became an ironing board.'

'How long have you known?'

'Eh?'

'How long?'

'About four and a half feet with a heat-resistant bit for the iron. It's sheets, you see. Ironing boards need to be longer for the sheets. Especially when we get a bigger bed. I must have got it a bit wrong, though, because–'

'Mike?'

'Shut up, woman. Just don't use it. I nearly got

concussion in my hip bone. Can one have concussion in a hip? Anyway, it hurt like hell, so don't use the board till I find some hydraulic system – oh, and it brought down a bit of the wall, just some plaster, five tiles and a couple of loose bricks. Also, you should stop bleaching your hair, because I have photographs now. You are even prettier as a brunette.'

Lily got out of bed and put the phone back on its charger. She had to finish the hall, help Philly prepare for the big day, get herself showered and changed, summon some other willing company because the bride was too nervy to be left to her own devices, and he knew she was Leanne Chalmers. 'Secrets in this village don't survive long, do they?'

'It's in the old scullery that you're making into a utility room. It'll be a good idea when I get it right.'

He was impossible. The recipe from which he had been made was unworkable, yet it did work – perfectly. He was near-genius wed to silliness, generosity with an added pinch of common sense, naughtiness bonded with a respect for a God in whom he placed his full trust. 'You're a madman,' she said. 'A lunatic. Why can't you leave things alone?'

He winked. 'I am deliberately leaving some things alone, madam, and most of those things are fastened to you. The puritan in me tells me to be chaste, so I use up my energy on ironing boards. You were the one who buggered off to Blackpool. I had to do something. My boss was cross with me, and my woman had gone missing.'

'Bishop not pleased?'

He shook his head and wiped away an imaginary tear.

330

'Wanted me to go on retreat for a couple of months to think about things. He made me feel thoroughly guilty, said that many priests have to answer to their consciences when it comes to certain sins like contraception – he didn't listen, and I listened with just half an ear. It was a draw. Or he may have won on points.'

'I'm sorry.'

'Well, I can't have it both ways. Do you have an electric drill?'

Lily clouted him with a pillow. 'Shall we ever have a sensible conversation?'

'I hope not,' he replied. 'There's concrete in that pillow. And I see we are to have paper napkins.'

'Listen, Nancy Mitford. For a wedding, I would normally hire linen. The tables are covered with my own emergency stuff, but I don't happen to have a hundred napkins, so yes, paper will have to do. You can come and help me fold them.'

'Bugger that – I have to put my best frock on. It was sewn by nuns and there's real gold in it. But I don't know whether to go for the peep-toe sandals or those sequined Indian mules. I shan't wear heels this time – they throw me off balance. Bad enough falling over at a wedding. Christenings can be a minefield in my Jimmy Choos.'

Lily lowered her head and refused to look at him. She wouldn't laugh. If she started to giggle, there'd be no napkins and no make-up for the bride. He knew who she was. He knew she'd buried a pair of sewing scissors in her husband's side after he'd ... She mustn't think about after or before, not today. She thanked God that Clive had lost his temper in court, because he had tried to make the jury believe that she had stabbed him first. That day in court had been the one time when she'd been glad about his short fuse–

'Stop it, Lily.'

Like Babs, he could get into her head. 'Who told you?'

'Chas. After Eve was injured. Not the full story at first, but I wheedled the rest out of him when you were in Blackpool, then I went to the library.' He jumped out of bed. 'May I borrow your heated rollers?'

'No.'

He flounced out of the room like an injured Paul Smith, arms akimbo, nose in the air. Lily heard him as he stumbled over something on the landing. The words he uttered when responding to pain should never come from the mouth of a man of God. Seated on the bed, Lily tried to compose herself. A wedding planner cum interior decorator cum florist cum Jill-of-all-trades needed her wits about her. She pulled on some ragged clothes and went to find napkins. Philly would like swags and bows, so she rooted out a few for the cake table before going to find Mike.

He came in from the garden and sat at the dining table. 'By the way,' he said, his tone casual. 'Will you marry me?'

Lily pretended to think about it. 'Only this once,' she said eventually. 'I don't want to start making a habit of it.' She saw the tears in his eyes. This clever man needed her. 'I love you,' she said. 'But stop the home improvements, yes? Remember, I'm the *Makeover Madness* girl.'

He bit his lip. 'Ah. So you don't want me to triple-glaze the windows?'

'Er . . . no. The windows here are precious.'

'Draughty.'

'No, Mike.' It wasn't going to be easy. He had a little devil in him, some sweet, childlike imp that allowed him to continue being a young offender. His nickname should be Asbo. She knew he would never touch the windows. She also knew that she would never find him predictable. 'I'm going,' she said. 'See you in church.' Yes, he would carry on being predictably unpredictable. He was wonderful.

Dave was thrilled to bits. The rain had stopped, he was getting married, Philly was delighted, and he had lost even more weight, because he could get his fingers down the waistband of his new suit, and it had been completed according to measurements taken just three weeks ago. He wasn't fat any more and he was happy at last.

Eve walked round him in a slow circle. 'Shoulders back,' she commanded. 'You're the groom, not some little altar boy who doesn't want to be noticed. Don't twitch.'

He felt as if he was back at school with the headmistress giving him gyp. 'You'll be asking have I done my homework next,' he grumbled.

'Oh, you've done your homework all right.' Eve grinned at him. 'She's pregnant, so eleven out of ten for that. And get that pocket hanky straight— Chas? I hope you're ready. And I hope you're not going to show me up by pushing your finger down the collar of that shirt all the time.' She cast an eye over the groom. 'My husband is allergic to suits,' she said. 'Chas?' The tone was firm.

'What?' came the reply from the hall.

Eve found her husband fiddling with his mobile

phone. 'Right. What's going on? Did you say something about going over to Liverpool on Monday?'

He cleared his throat. 'I thought I'd go and see our Jack. Their Tracey's got herself up the duff by some loonie druggie from Kirkby, and our Jack wants me to talk some sense into her.' It was nearly the truth. It was the truth, though it wasn't the whole truth, not the absolute version of—

'You're clearing your throat and holding your head to one side. How long have I known you, eh? And what are you hiding from me? You always tilt your head when you're hiding something or other.' She tapped a foot. 'Out with it.'

'It's nothing.'

Eve opened a small bureau and took an envelope from one of the internal drawers. 'A visiting order from Wally Willie.'

'I've not seen Walter Wilson in a while, and he's due out soon. I thought I'd call in, because our Jack's house isn't far from Walton.'

Eve sighed and folded her arms. She was supposed to be going across to sit with a nervous bride. She'd just promised Lily on the phone that she'd go and keep Philly company. 'Why now?' she asked.

'Why not?'

'You always tell me what's going on, Chas. But first you get a manager in the shop without mentioning a dicky bird to me, and now you're gallivanting off to Liverpool – which I'd never have known except for our Derek.'

'I just want you to rest,' he said.

'I could rest at our Vera's. It's nice in Crosby this time of year.'

334

'Blundellsands,' he corrected her, his accent very clipped.

Eve nodded. She was using her special cleverness. She had discovered over the years that when she tackled him head-on, the result was more satisfactory if she distracted him for a few seconds in the middle of the attack. Vera had served her purpose, as had Crosby and Blundellsands, and it was now time to move in with the big guns. 'Is he still in Walton?'

'Walter Wilson? Course he is – he got a three stretch and he's served nearly all of it for causing bother. Always kicking off, is Wally. No time off for good behaviour, so I don't know how I'll help him when he gets out. But Mrs Wilson was good to us, so I feel as if I should—'

'Clive Chalmers, I mean.'

Chas stopped in his tracks. 'Eh? Who?'

'Don't make me repeat myself, lad. You know what I'm on about. Wedding or no wedding, I'll clobber you if I think you're up to something. Then you can have a black eye while you make your best man's speech.'

Chas took the letter from her and folded it carefully before placing it in an inside pocket. He straightened his spine. 'Eve, leave it.' There was a steely edge to his tone.

She looked hard at him. His head was erect, and there was no more throat-clearing. Two or three times during the marriage, he had put his foot down so hard that it would have taken a JCB to shift him. He met her gaze, did not flinch when she continued to stare. There was no need for words, because she knew full well that nothing she could say would alter the course of imminent events. 'You've feelers out, I take it?' she asked.

'I'm not walking blind, girl.'

The joking, teasing and threatening would not work,

335

because her Chas had made up his mind. He was a clown and a mischief, but he was also a man. 'Are you safe?'

He nodded.

'Is Walton Wally Willie safe?'

'Yes. Well, as safe as any daft sod can be in that dump.'

Eve blinked back some saline. There was to be a wedding, and she must not weep. 'But Lily isn't safe.'

He made no reply.

'And Cassie isn't. Because Cassie's his daughter, right?'

'Yes.'

She clung to him. 'Promise me you'll be careful. If you went inside, I'd die. You know I can't live without you.'

He clenched his fists. 'Same here, kid. Don't worry. I've picked a good team. The score'll be one-nil and there'll be no comeback. Now, stop this, or the pills won't work.'

Eve nodded. 'I'm taking the medicine and I feel ... different. As if something's clicked back in place. In my head, I mean. I really believe I've had my last fit, but I'll take no chances.'

'Good.'

'And I don't want you taking chances, either. So mind what I said.'

'I won't take any chances. Nobody will connect anything to me. Just stop your mithering, woman.'

'I'll do my best. But if you do to him what he did to me – by proxy – you'll be as bad as he is.'

'Will I?' He inhaled deeply. 'Whatever I've done in my life has been for us, Evie. For you, Derek and me. But

I've never killed a child. Nobody I know would stoop that far. Now, you know you're not going to get round me on this one, so go over to Philly's and make sure she's still in one piece. Tell her everything in the school hall's lovely.'

'Is it lovely?'

He almost growled, then laughed. 'It was all right last night, but Lily's in charge today and we're all banned. Tell Philly it's all absolutely beautiful, or she'll be in pieces.'

'All right.' She kissed him, wished Dave all the best, then left the house.

Chas stood for a while watching her crossing the road. He could not help nursing the terrible fear that she would collapse outside and get run over. Whenever Eve was out of his reach, he felt terrified, since he lost control every time she went out. He had some idea of how to deal with a fit, but not everyone could cope. It should never have happened to her, should never happen to anyone. With luck and a following wind, it would not happen again.

She went into Philly's house, and Chas returned to the groom. As best man, he had a duty to perform. Monday must not overshadow today, because Dave and Philly deserved the best from everybody. Monday was just another fly that would land in the ointment named life. And flies should be exterminated . . .

Philly and Valda were weeping with laughter. Dressed only in their best underwear, they could not quite manage to pull themselves together.

Lily, who was wearing old jeans, a T-shirt and one of her more determined expressions, stood over the pair and tutted. 'What's got into you now?' she asked. 'Aren't you supposed to be having a civilized game of whist while we wait for the main event?'

Valda could not speak, while the bride simply bowed down and placed her forehead on the table among a tumble of playing cards. If she laughed any more, she wouldn't be able to walk.

'Some kind of wedding this is going to be,' said Lily despairingly. 'There was nothing else for it, Valda. I couldn't have you sitting here in your new frock till three o'clock. As for Philly – think of her amazing suit. It would have been wrinkled past saving by now.'

Eve entered after leaving her new clothes upstairs. She was wearing a bathrobe, and she threw a couple of dressing gowns at the other two women. 'It's playing whist in their knickers that got them reduced to melted butter,' she told Lily. 'Come on, put these on and let Lily do our faces.'

Lily began with Eve, who was the least hysterical of the trio. Napkins and cake table were done, but Lily needed to make up the women before going home to prepare herself. She was proud of the bride, because Philly had been so incredibly brave with her wedding suit. A nice, sensible blue-grey three-piece had been returned to the shop, because Philly had made a decision.

The decision was oyster satin, the skirt full length but with a kick at the back. This item was paired with a long-sleeved blouse buttoned high to the throat, and an Edwardian style hat with an open-weave veil. Because she wasn't tall, Philly had opted for heeled shoes, and she was going to look spectacular. The village would be taken aback when they saw that the butterfly had emerged from its chrysalis. She had surprised even Lily, who had not expected such self-confidence from the quiet little woman. And she was decidedly sleek, since she seemed to have lost most of her extra weight. 'There won't be a dry eye in the church,' she promised. 'You are going to look stunning. The Edwardian look is so right for you. We're all proud of you, lovely.'

When Eve's make-up had been perfected, Lily started on Valda. Valda was more up to date than the other two, so the job was easy except for mascara that had run during the whist-in-knickers session.

Then it was the important person's turn. She had amazing skin that had suffered no contact with heavy make-up, and Lily stuck to browns and beiges, finishing with a flourish of a lipstick named fourteen carat, because it had a sheen over a pink-brown base. The bride was ready. 'You're done and dusted,' Lily announced. 'I'll leave you the lipstick, but no cups of tea, no eating, and none of you is to get dressed before half past two. All right?'

'Yes, miss,' Eve replied, the other two echoing her words. 'You'd better do something about yourself,' Eve continued. 'Unless you're coming as the lucky chimney sweep. You look like you've stepped out of a pigsty.'

Lily ignored her friend. 'No make-up on clothes. Try not to pull anything over your head while dressing.' She looked at the three of them, told them they looked well prepared but gormless, then went home. Was gormless a Lancashire word? Oh well, she thought as she opened her gate, perhaps if she hung round for thirty years, she might be accepted as a Lancastrian . . .

He was in the front drawing room, and he looked so beautiful, so right. Lily stood in the doorway and gasped, because he was almost as pretty as the bride. 'Hello,' she whispered.

He turned, and was suddenly a prince dressed in splendour so magnificent that he was clearly prepared to pay homage to a king. 'Hello,' he replied. 'This is my best frock. I had to come back from the vestry, because I'd forgotten my grandmother's missal. Even though it's in Latin, I always carry it during a sacrament.'

'They should have kept the Latin,' said Lily. 'It was a universal language that worked no matter which country you were in.'

'True.'

'And your shoes?' she asked.

'Alas, black and sensible.'

Lily sat in an armchair. 'Tell me about the clothes.' He would lose the ability to dress in splendour, to baptize and marry people, to administer the last rites, to bury the dead.

'Well, there's the alb, the white undergarment that goes from neck to feet. It symbolizes innocence. The maniple – here on my left forearm – is a sign of endurance. My matching stole is supposed to mean patience, while the gorgeous chasuble represents charity. Pretty, eh? And very, very hot in this weather.'

She smiled. 'Mike, you must have regrets.'

'Of course. Don't you?'

'Yes.'

He sat opposite her. 'Don't be impressed by the vestments – there's just a man underneath all this cloth and embroidery. It's a man who is sure he wants to leave the priesthood because it isn't right for him any more. Your arrival on the scene is not significant.'

'Thanks.'

'You know what I mean.'

She had known from the start what he meant, had recognized a traveller whose company she might enjoy on the journey through life. Friendship had turned to love and need in so short a time that it had taken her breath away. 'And tomorrow, you leave the Church.'

'Right. I shall announce it, but they know already. They probably knew before I did. I stayed because of Philly. Even she has accepted my decision, and she was as old-fashioned as they come. Some of the elderly people are taken aback, but we soldier on, you and I.'

Lily voiced a worry that had sat with her for some time. 'And we can't be married in your church, since I am divorced.'

He turned and looked through the window. 'Lily, I can give you a list of wealthy people who have been granted annulment even after they have had a full marriage – including children.'

'So Rome is purchasable?'

'Yes,' he breathed so softly that he was scarcely audible. 'Everything has a price.' He looked at her again. 'My God will marry us out there in the orchard, at the top of Rivington Pike, or on the number thirty-two bus from Moor Lane. My God forgives, and He doesn't need money.'

He had decided. She'd already known that, but seeing him in his uniform had made her wonder yet again.

'Are you going to a wedding like that?' he asked.

She looked down at her wrecked clothes. 'Would your God mind?'

'He wouldn't even get off His horse to look at you. But I think Philly might have something to say about jeans full of holes and a shirt that looks like a dishrag.'

'OK, I'll get changed.' She went upstairs, stood on the landing and listened while he left the house. A quick shower was followed by a rush to get dressed, and she applied a bit of make-up just before leaving for the church. She closed her gate and stepped onto the pavement. After a very wet start, the day had become promising, and the sun was trying to shine through a layer of white cloud.

'Lily?'

She turned. It was Mrs Barker in her wheelchair, and she had clearly taken care with her appearance. At long last, she had made an effort for the son she had never valued before. 'You look great,' Lily said.

'I waited for you, because I didn't want to be a pest. Everybody thinks I'm a pest, but you don't know me, so I thought you'd do. A few offered to come for me, but they're all up to their eyes in flans and vols-au-vent and God knows what else, so I told them I'd made my own arrangements. You push me. And take me to the front, because I'm his mam.'

'Yes, you are.'

They began the short journey. 'When is he leaving?' Enid asked. 'The priest, I mean.'

'Tomorrow.'

'Well, he's a nice enough man, I suppose. Just be careful – you haven't known him for more than five minutes. Don't be rushing into anything, because you can't keep changing your mind and getting divorced, can you?'

'No.' Lily pushed Enid to the front and left her in the first pew on the right. She didn't look at Mike – didn't dare. If he winked or grinned, the whole thing could turn into a fiasco.

342

But it didn't. The service was short, as there was no nuptial mass because it was a mixed marriage, and Philly had not asked for a dispensation in the matter. Dave's mother had been anti-Catholic for a very long time, so the ceremony was simple.

Philly almost wept when she saw the decorations in the school hall, but she managed to remain dignified. Lily watched bride and groom and knew that Dave had played a part in the strengthening of his wife. The expected child, too, would be a factor in Philly's improvement.

Mike, after changing into a suit, arrived when an hour had passed. He took Lily to one side and informed her that he had spoken again to the bishop and would be released from Holy Orders in just over twenty-four hours. 'I'm still doing all the other stuff,' he said. 'Including the pantom–' The sentence was curtailed when a very tall and well-muscled black man picked him up with no apparent effort.

'What's going on?' Mike asked helplessly when his captor flung him into the fireman's lift position.

'Nothing, really,' replied the assailant pleasantly. 'Just kidnap, that's all.'

They left. Lily found herself standing open-mouthed until she noticed that Maurice and Paul had also disappeared. The stranger was probably Paul's new partner, and they were definitely up to something. She went to the door and looked across the road. Five men were entering Pour Les Dames, and Sally was ushering them inside as quickly as she could. They were gone for over an hour, and Lily could scarcely wait to see what they had managed to dream up. There was definitely a plot on, but she kept it to herself.

It was a rare treat. The tall black man, Maurice, Paul, Mike and a man in his eighties were all in female attire, and they sang 'Sisters', a piece they had been practising for the pantomime. There wasn't a dry eye in the hall, as everyone found the act ridiculous to the point of tears. The rendition might have offended Irving Berlin and a host of stars from some ancient movie, but it was hilarious.

Lily held a tissue to her face. Then she stopped laughing, because a thought had popped into her mind. It was all just clothes. A couple of hours earlier, Mike had been the celebrant at a wedding; now, he was an extremely ugly woman in fishnet stockings and a basque that did nothing to enhance his masculine shape. Blacked-out teeth contributed to his comic appearance, and he was clearly enjoying himself.

The song neared its conclusion with a well-staged fight that had obviously been rehearsed for *The Ugly Sisters*, as the pantomime was now called, and the old man, complete with Zimmer frame, was appointed referee of the fracas. It was the perfect mad celebration of a wonderful day, and Philly was doubled over with laughter. Dave climbed onto the stage and thanked the participants, giving each of the 'women' a peck on the cheek. He raised a hand and waited for quiet. 'Thank you all for coming, and thanks to Philly for marrying me and saving me from becoming a hopeless case.' He cleared his throat. 'A very special thank you to my mother, who made us a wedding gift of her share in the Reading Room. We both promise to take care of it.' He looked directly at Enid. 'Thanks, Mam,' he said.

The silence in the room was heavy at this point. Everyone knew Enid Barker; almost all had been vilified by her at some point in their lives. Had she made a grand gesture just in order to be forgiven by a village whose memory was notoriously long? Or had her conscience finally surfaced from beneath layers of acid bitterness and acrimony? Only time would tell, many thought as the whispering started.

'Carry on eating, drinking and enjoying yourselves,' commanded the groom before stepping down.

Before the guests had time to obey Dave's orders, the vet stepped out of the wings. He raised a hand and asked for silence. 'Right, you lot,' he said. 'You've seen two of today's stars, but what about the really important one? She runs my surgery waiting room and is becoming an excellent secretary. She also helped save the life of someone special to us all. Skippy, come.'

The dog hopped her way onto the little stage, while Chas brought on a table, then a chair, then a large box.

Tim Mellor sat down and set the scene. When all was prepared, his mobile phone rang. Skippy picked it up and passed it to her boss. When the applause subsided, the more intricate trick practised by man and dog began. He set a bin and a wire basket on the floor before starting to open envelopes. Anything rejected was squashed and given to Skippy with the spoken word 'Bin', and she tossed the offending item into the rubbish. The command 'File' meant that she placed the page in the wire basket.

The vet screwed up many pages and threw them out of the dog's reach, and she fetched and binned the lot. But when given a ruined page and told to file, she froze until the order was corrected. Similarly, she refused to bin anything that remained flat. When the act speeded up, she made no mistakes, and the audience continued enraptured.

The finale involved the phone again, but this time Tim answered it and held it to the dog's ear. 'It's for you,' he said.

She woofed politely into the instrument, then followed her employer and took a bow.

Eve was trying not to weep. This Labrador bitch had persevered until her owners had followed her into the cottage. There were some terrible things in this world, and then there were animals. She vowed there and then to rescue an unwanted dog as a tribute to Skippy.

Lily and Enid were both watching Eve. She didn't stand up when most people started to dance. 'She was near tears while that dog did its tricks,' remarked Enid. 'She's still a long way from right.'

Lily knew that Eve wasn't right. None of it was right, because she shouldn't have suffered in Lily's place. Anger rose in Lily's chest until she thought it would choke her. If she'd changed the name of the house, if she'd never met Clive Chalmers, if pigs could fly . . .

Enid turned to Lily. 'They don't believe I can change,' she said.

Lily snapped out of her reverie. 'Mike does. He has a great deal of faith in you.'

'And in you as well. I'm sat up there at that window on my own a lot.'

'I know.'

'And I mouth off. I've always had a runaway gob. But I see people. And I see the way he smiles at you and teases you, and I wish some man had loved me like that. Look after him and make sure he does the same for you.' She sniffed, then stuffed a vol-au-vent in her mouth.

Lily grinned. Enid Barker didn't get emotional, so she would never weep, would she? 'That was a nice gesture – giving Dave and Philly your share in the business.'

The older woman swallowed. 'Not as daft as I look, see. They'll be grateful and they'll look after me.'

'And that was your only reason, of course.'

'Aye. And if anybody says different, refer them to me.'

Mike arrived. He had thrown someone's raincoat over his costume, so he looked slightly less drag artist, though still rather deficient in the dental department. 'That's a very smart suit, Enid,' he said.

'Bloody sight better than yours. And you'll get a few bob off the tooth fairy tonight.'

He rubbed at his teeth, but made little impression on the mess Sally had made. 'I'm going home,' he told Lily. 'Are you staying or coming?'

'I'll come.' She made her decision then, while everyone could see her. He was reaching out, so she placed a hand in his, and called goodbye to bride and groom before stepping out for the first time with her man. Let them all see, she thought. Let them know that he is loved, that he will be cared for. It had been a long day, and her back was aching. 'I have to get my tens,' she said as they entered the house. 'It helps with the pain.'

His eyes narrowed as he watched her climbing the stairs. He had read the old newspapers, had trawled through microfiche at the library, but he still wanted the story from her. Pain? She had never mentioned that before. He followed her up and watched as she manoeuvred pads and wires across her lower back.

'Sciatic nerve,' she said.

Mike sat on the bed. 'He did that?'

'I think so. I also lost my spleen and some of my intestine.'

'And the baby.'

'Yes.' She placed herself next to him and took his hand again. 'Sorry about the wires, but this is preferable to drugs.' She waited for a reply, but none was forthcoming. 'Mike?'

He sniffed and dragged the sleeve of someone else's coat across his face.

'Don't cry,' she begged.

'How could a man . . .'

'Please, love. We're both tired, and it's better to go through all that when we're in better shape. Just don't cry, or I'll start. Go and get that ridiculous stuff off your teeth, then come to bed.'

He left the room and went down to his own part of the ex-presbytery. Kneeling on his hassock, he poured out grief and anger to the man on the crucifix. Tomorrow, Mike would not say Mass, but he would act as server for his friend, the priest who would take over the parishes. The tears came not as goodbye to the Church, but as a greeting for the woman he hoped to make his wife. Her past had to be faced by him; she needed to go through it again as half of a couple, because he wanted to know her properly, and she must let go before taking on the future. 'Between us, let us conquer this, dear Lord. We will conquer it with Your help.'

He went down, locked doors and windows, looked for foxes but saw none. Bearing two cups of cocoa, he walked back up to Lily's bedroom and saw that she was fast asleep. Quietly, he placed the cups on a table and went to stand over her. She was wearing one of his T-shirts. In a loosely curled hand on her pillow, she held the plastic box enclosing batteries that would help with her pain. She bore it well, he decided. And he, too, must bear it all with fortitude.

Trying hard not to disturb her, he pushed a paper napkin under her pillow. It contained a piece of Philly's wedding cake, and folklore decreed that Lily would dream tonight of the man she would marry. 'Dream about me,' he whispered. She was not well. In spite of that, she worked hard and seldom complained. And this stabbing in his chest was hatred. He had never experienced it before, and it came as a great shock. At last, he understood Chas Boswell. The need for revenge was not a primary factor; Chas just wanted to make sure that it would never happen again.

Sleep proved elusive. Mike found his foxes, put down food for them, heard music emanating even now from the school hall. The sky had clouded over, so there was no star on which he might wish. So he did what he knew best and prayed to his Father, to the Son who had perished on the cross, to the Holy Ghost who mended souls and distributed gifts of charity, joy, peace and benignity. 'Help me, great Spirit,' he begged. 'Help me not to help Chas . . .'

Thirteen

Eve had been doing her best to ignore Chas when it came down to her greatest worry. If she asked him about his visit to Walton jail, he put his foot down hard and refused to discuss the matter. She had to wait for him to open up, but he didn't. So, when Sunday evening arrived, she felt time slipping through her fingers like water from a tap. She had to try again, because Chas might well end up in more trouble than he was bargaining for.

She decided to tackle him after the evening meal, when Derek had left to lend a hand in the shop. Patrons liked to see a member of the family behind the counter, though the temporary manager was a pleasant enough man. But Eagleton wanted familiarity, and Chas would have to get back to his work sooner rather than later.

Eve dabbed her lips with a napkin. She needed to go softly, because she had only just got Chas to agree to the purchase of a set of banisters with special knops that had been hand-carved in the eighteenth century. By the time it had been adapted to fit the staircase of Rose Cottage, the item was going to cost a fair amount. Chas had already complained rather loudly that it would leave him with no legs to stand on, so he wouldn't be needing stairs with or without fancy hand-carvings on the spindles. 'Chas,' she began. 'I just wondered whether—'

'No. Don't start, love. I'm telling you – don't go there.'

'I haven't started, have I? But I'm about to. Somebody has to do it.'

He grunted, but offered no intelligible reply.

'Wasn't yesterday lovely?' she breathed quietly. 'A perfect, perfect wedding.'

The response was another grunt, this time accompanied by a frown.

'The thing about epileptic fits,' she said in a tone designed to be neutral, 'is that you have to let your feelings out. If I don't let them out, I could have a bad turn. They told me that at the hospital.'

At last, he spoke. 'And they told me you hadn't to get upset.'

'I don't want a fit.' She paused for a few seconds. 'Wasn't yesterday lovely?' she asked again. 'See, we have to think about the Middlers.' The Middlers were those who lived in the centre of Eagleton, which had always housed a close community. 'Dave and Philly – so happy,' she said. 'As for Pete and Babs – I know they're not real Middlers, and I know they've been together only a couple of months, but they're like a pair of socks that got separated in the wash – they belong together. I reckon they've always belonged together, so fate made them meet.'

Chas raised a suspicious eyebrow. 'What's that to do with the price of fish on Bolton Market? What's your point, Evie?'

'Then Lily and Mike,' she continued seamlessly. 'They're happening people. They remind me of the flower power days when everybody buggered off to San Francisco with flowers in their hair.'

'And not just their hair – they had flowers painted on their passion wagons in psychedelic colours,' muttered Chas. 'Bloody vans with daisies on them and daisies inside them as well. I saw a programme about that rubbish. All drugs and no knickers.'

Eve was not going to be dragged into unnecessary discussion. She had tailored this conversation and was building up towards a big finish, and the Love Children of the sixties would not be allowed a starring role. 'Valda's getting on all right with her mother-in-law – even Enid Barker looks as if she might take a turn for the better. It's all nice and settled.'

'And?'

'And you're going to bugger it up by arranging to kill the man who saved my life.' There, she had said it. Well, she had said most of it. 'When Eagleton has a murderer in its midst, how are they all going to feel? And just when everything's getting nicely sorted out. Even Paul's OK now he's stopped hankering after Mo.'

Chas jumped to his feet. 'Clive Chalmers didn't have you clobbered to save your life, Evie. He had you nearly murdered instead of Lily Latimer. What happens to your happening people when she happens to get killed, eh? What about when he rings the bell for round two and sends some other bruisers to kill Lily? How will you feel at her funeral? Who'll do the flowers? Because she'll be in no fit state for making floral tributes and pretty wreaths.'

Eve shook her head. 'He won't do it again,' she said.

'Oh, well, I'm glad you did your doctorate in psychology. He's focused on Lily, obsessed with her. One of the psychiatrists at the trial said he should be in a secure facility for the insane – he's not right in the bloody head, girl. The chances are that he'll keep trying till he's dead, or till he runs out of cash. He wants her dead, Evie. He's got money somewhere, and there's plenty of folk about that would do anything for a bit of brass.'

A weighty silence followed. 'So you'll not stop at home tomorrow and look after me?'

Chas laughed, though there was no humour in the sound. 'You've lost your place in the hymn book, Eve. Usually, you tell me to bugger off and let you get on with it, but now that I'm doing something you don't want me to do, you decide to be ill enough to need watching. Look. What happened to you is headline news in Walton – and not just there. Every prisoner in Britain knows what was done to you. It's already started. The grapevine's spread beyond my reach. It's already too late, love. But I can try to make sure Wally Willie stays safe.'

'How?' she asked.

'I don't bloody know till I bloody get there, do I?' Chas left the room. He prayed that she wouldn't start crying. If she wept, he would go back to her and promise her the earth, but Eve was not manipulative. She wouldn't cry for effect, or to get her own way. Eve was a good woman. She was the best. Anyway, Valda was coming round soon, so Evie would hold herself together.

Eve fiddled with her napkin. Since the incident, she seemed to have changed. She saw things differently, more clearly. It was as if a thin veil had moved away, and her inner vision had improved as a result.

But. The world was going mad, and most of the madness was man-made. There were bad females, but it was the male who never grew up, who wanted to be

353

cock of the walk, who needed to be the one who could piss highest up the wall, get the best woman, drive the fastest car, start and win every war. 'I am sick and fed up,' she told her reclaimed fireplace. It had been a good buy, thanks to Lily.

Lily. Could Eve really live with the knowledge that her new best friend's life would be on the line for ever? Would Mike on his own be strong enough, wily enough, to stop the next invasion of Eagleton? 'I don't know, do I?' she whispered. 'It's out of my hands.'

Then the doorbell sounded.

They sat in the Man and Scythe, Chas with a pint, Mike with a St Clement's. He was driving, so he was the one who had to remain sober. He needed to have a clear head anyway, because Lily was in pain and he was learning how to massage her lower spine. He couldn't leave her for too long, yet he wanted to speak to Chas. 'Sorry to drag you all the way to town,' he said.

Chas shook his head. 'No. I was glad to hear that doorbell. My Evie was coming to the boil.'

Mike grinned ruefully. 'If we'd gone to a pub in Eagleton, I'd have been plagued, because they'd all have been asking about the new priest and my plans as a layman. So. You go tomorrow, then?'

'Yes.'

'To see Walter?'

'That's right.'

Mike could see that his friend had taken an ear-bashing already, and the ear-basher was probably Eve. 'Is she giving you a hard time?'

Chas nodded. 'I've left her waiting for Valda. Valda's expecting her umpteenth child, so that should give them

354

enough to talk about. Evie will be wielding her crochet hooks and patterns – it'll keep her occupied for an hour or two.'

'Right. What are you going to say to Walter?'

'I don't know, do I? I mean, the jail network knows everything as we speak, so it's past the stage where I can call a halt. I admit I was angry at first and I put pressure on for a visiting order. Yes, I regret that. But prisoners have their own way of dealing with this kind of crap, and they would have found out eventually.'

'Especially now the men have pleaded guilty and dropped Chalmers in the soup.'

'Exactly.'

Mike looked round the pub. He had never been here before, though he had read about Ye Olde Man and Scythe, first mentioned in 1251 in a market charter, and the oldest premises in the town. 'This place was partially rebuilt in the seventeenth century,' he told his companion, 'though the vault is original.'

Chas offered no comment.

'And over there's the famous chair where the Earl of Derby sat before the Roundheads chopped his head off. We're in one of the ten oldest pubs in Britain.'

At last Chas broke his reverie. 'The poor bugger who lost his head owned the pub,' he said. 'But Bolton was famous for wanting royalty dead, buried and disinherited.' He took a long draught of ale. 'I hate Chalmers,' he announced.

'So do I. And neither of us has met him. But Eve's right, Chas.'

'I can't stop it now. It'd be like trying to stop this lot beheading the Earl. Prison's a machine with its own engine. Once it starts running, nobody can stop it – they seem to have built the bugger without brakes. All I can do now is see what's what.'

'You've helped a few ex-cons, haven't you?'

Chas nodded.

'Then surely you can pass some sense down the line?'

'Depends what you mean by sense. You should listen to our Derek and his Old Testament stuff – he reckons folk were violent as hell before Jesus came along. The wrath of God, he calls it. Mike, I don't know what they intend to do, but they won't stop Chalmers this side of death. In his mind, Lily belongs to him. If he can't have her, nobody can, so he sounds very Old Testament to me.'

Both men stared into their drinks for a few minutes. Chas could hear Eve going on about how peaceful the village was, about the vet having transferred his affections from Lily to a glamorous new veterinary nurse, about how even their Derek had started courting an office temp, about everything in the village being lovely except ... except for the fact that Lily's life was still in danger. 'He could kill her yet, Mike.'

'I know.'

'And you can live with that?'

Mike raised his arms. 'I don't know. We could move.'

'There's no hiding place. Unless you want to emigrate.'

'I don't. This country might be in a bloody mess, but it's our bloody mess.'

The conversation circled for a few more minutes before dying of natural causes. They finished their drinks and left the pub.

On the way home, they continued to talk, though nothing changed. Mike's lecture on revenge fell on deaf ears, while Chas simply sat in the passenger seat and offered the same arguments as before. It was too late. The machinery was in gear, and nothing short of a miracle would close it down.

Fourteen

Although Chas had paid many visits over the years to Her Majesty's Prison, Liverpool, the sight of the building never failed to upset him. The sheer size of the fort from which no man could escape was overwhelming, as were the perimeter walls that seemed to reach higher towards the heavens each year. Most places seemed to grow smaller when a person reached adulthood, but this was the exception.

There were worse prisons, he supposed, jails with tiny rooms into which two or three men were sandwiched for twenty-three hours out of the twenty-four, but Walton was a forbidding and evil-looking place that seemed to bleed all residual hope from the soul of any newly arrived observer. But he had to go in. Soon, his brother might be an inmate, and Chas shivered when that thought hit the front of his mind.

He parked his car and glanced at nearby council houses, ordinary homes containing ordinary families. The people who lived cheek by jowl with Walton probably scarcely noticed it after a while. It was here the way St George's Hall was in town, the way the Liver Birds sat on the shore watching out for returning sailors, the way the pub was down the road and the church was round the corner. But Chas saw it sporadically, so he feared it. Yes, his brother might be here soon, but that problem was not to be on today's agenda. This was the day on which Chas might learn what was about to happen to the man who had tried, albeit by proxy, to kill a woman. Eve. It should not have been Eve, yet it had been Eve. A shiver travelled the length of his spine, causing him to grind to a halt near the gate through which visitors were beginning to walk.

He could hear her, could hear Mike asking him not to cause any more trouble, but what could he do but go on? He couldn't change anything. If Walton had decided on the fate of Lily's ex-husband, nothing would stop the march of the contained. In prison, everything was magnified, because life was small, restricted and edgy. An imagined slight could result in a broken arm, while even a dirty look could begin a war between landings. Old lags remembered the Boswell family. Their mother had been kind, while Chas's brothers had earned the respect of many who lived on that delicate cusp between lawfulness and criminality. Chas had helped some who had been determined to reform, so the Boswells were a kind of royalty. Eve, a Boswell by marriage, had to be defended at all costs by the folk behind these walls.

Chas didn't know what to hope for. Wally Willie was known by friends and enemies alike as a mad bastard, but he wasn't a killer. Wally knew killers; killers knew and respected Wally, because he kept the jail alive and amused through long, grey stretches of time filled with little beyond model-making and banter. God. Chas neared the gate and swallowed. He would never get used to this dump. Those inside made delicate boxes out of matchsticks, sewed together tobacco pouches for friends at home, used any method available to plod their way through days that seemed endless.

While queuing, he concentrated on what he had read in Charlie Bronson's *Good Prison Guide*. Charlie had awarded Walton five stars out of ten, because Scousers had made him laugh, while his destruction of the roof had cost the government over a quarter of a million pounds. Guards had allegedly beaten Bronson senseless after the event, but who would listen to a crim with a bad habit of kidnapping people and refusing to be subdued? It took up to ten screws to shift Bronson when he didn't want shifting, so they had punished him for making them look inadequate.

There was a new rumour about inmates getting together to prepare suits against guards, civil actions to be mounted after release, but it would be a waste of time, Chas believed. Anyway, most of the warders here were OK. But the few bad men who concentrated on torturing those with long sentences made a mockery of the whole system by becoming criminals themselves. So. He tapped a nervous foot. His wandering thoughts had passed several minutes while he got inside, and he handed over his visiting order. Yes, he was inside, and that knowledge made him shiver anew.

'Chas?' said the guard.

'Oh – hiya, Mr Martin. How are you doing?'

'Seen better days, lad. I'm getting past it now. Come to see old Wally again?'

'That's right. How's he getting on?'

Mr Martin laughed. 'He's more trouble than a pimp at a Methodist Sunday school picnic – he'll never learn. Still causing bother. Some don't improve with age.' He leaned forward and lowered his tone. 'There's been a bit of trouble. Go careful, lad.' Immediately, he drew back and reverted to normal. 'Enjoy your visit. Wally's in fine form. There's a rumour he's caught a mouse and started to train it, God help us.' He moved on to the next in line.

Chas placed his coat in a locker before sitting in the visitors' lounge. A bit of trouble? Martin was a man who could be trusted, a screw who had always been more than fair. He had a reputation for kindness, since he often carried sweets for prisoners and, when he found time, would even listen to their grievances and worries. A bit of trouble. Chas went though the search, walked past a couple of sniffer dogs, stood by while his personal belongings went through a scanner. When he had retrieved his money and bits of jewellery, he stood among the rest and waited for the automatic doors to open.

Immediately, he sensed the atmosphere. Guards who usually stood around the walls were dotted about among prisoners' tables, while those behind glass at mezzanine level stood to attention, eyes scanning the room below. Inmates sat very still and quiet, though a low buzz of conversation began when relatives greeted loved ones. This was a tough prison and it allowed for no nonsense. Rumours abounded about the availability of drugs, but, at this moment, Chas could not imagine any quarter being given by the currently rigid, sour-faced staff. They appeared to be in shock; something of moment had happened, and it had happened today. They were on red alert, and it would be better not to breathe too deeply just now . . .

Wally Wilson was at the far end. His bib sported the number nineteen, and Chas hastened to greet the old reprobate. Guards hovered. They seemed to be steering themselves away from families and towards those who had just one male visitor. As Wally and Chas fell into the latter category, they were plagued. After the exchange of pleasantries, Chas went to buy drinks and biscuits from machines. Following the prison code, he left the lid on Wally's drink before handing it over. A removed lid could mean drugs concealed in the cup, so it remained sealed.

They discussed prison food, the length of time Wally still had to serve, football, the Iraq war. Wally eyed the hovering guard. 'If you come any closer, we'll have to get married,' he snapped. Then he turned and nodded almost imperceptibly in the direction of a group at another table.

Pandemonium erupted, though it seemed to be a harmless enough chaos. While prisoners banged on their tables, everyone in the room sang Happy Birthday to someone or other. Under the weight of this noise, Wally finally managed to convey a message. 'It's happened,' he said. 'Over half an hour ago. Fazakerley Hospital.' He joined in the singing and banging. Whistles blew, guards brought the room to order, and Wally ordered Chas to stay where he was.

Chas understood. If he tried to leave too early, the guards would suspect that Wally might be connected to whatever had happened. Clive Chalmers was in hospital. Beyond that certainty, Chas knew nothing and would discover little while the wardens remained on red alert. They talked about Wally's brother, about Derek and his new girlfriend, about Liverpool's year as Capital of Culture. 'They should come in here if they want culture,' said Wally, his voice deliberately amplified. 'There's all kinds growing in that shower block. Oh, and we're training our cockroaches to do the military two-step.' He winked at his companion. 'Some of these screws are talented, too.'

'Really?' asked Chas. 'What can they do?'

'They can make three years feel like ten.'

The man near their table stood and glared at Wally. There'd been a reason for the sudden singing, and he suspected that Wally might well be at the back of it, but there was nothing he could do when it came to proof. Chas looked up and winked at the guard. 'Turned out nice again,' he said in the manner of George Formby.

'You're becoming a Woollyback,' pronounced Wally.

There were many things worse than Lancastrians, Chas thought. Woollybacks were long-ago miners with sheepskins stretched over their bodies as protection. Underneath the slower-than-Scouse speech, they were solid folk. The hour dragged, but he was finally liberated and breathing air that was not fresh, but it was free. Fazakerley. Bloody hell. He didn't know what to do next . . .

Chas spent several hours not knowing what to do next. He ordered a meal in a city centre bar, scarcely tasted it, could not have described what he had eaten. After four pints of beer, he shut himself in his car on the dock road and waited to get sober. To that end, he consumed over a litre of water and a full pack of biscuits rescued from the glove compartment. The biscuits made him sick, and he deposited the contents of his stomach as neatly as he could in a roadside drain. There was no point in contacting the hospital, because Chalmers would be under guard and Fazakerley might well refuse to admit that he was housed under their roof. He didn't phone Eve, didn't speak to anyone, since he had no idea what to say.

After sleeping himself sober, he woke to a darker Liverpool. A small idea popped into his head, and he drove to a newsagent to pick up the *Echo*. Nothing. He looked in the stop-press column, found no late report about the condition of a prisoner, decided that the authorities had actually managed to keep this juicy item from the press. The paper would be filled to the centre when Robbo and his cronies got sent down for receiving stolen goods, yet the murderer attracted no attention.

It hadn't been just Eve. His first murder attempt had been against Lily, and he would try again if Satan spared him. Was he alive? Was he crippled or dead? Chas tossed aside the newspaper. He sat on Crosby Road North and wondered about driving up to see Vera, but Eve's sister would be full of questions, and there were no answers. Going to see his brothers was not advisable, either, not if there was huge trouble afoot. He had better travel homeward. Eve could be worried sick by now. He sent her a text – *hope you get this babe bad reception round here see you later.* That should keep her quiet for a couple of hours. He really could not go home while his brain was in such turmoil . . .

Then his phone rang. 'Hello?'

'Chas?'

'Yes?'

'It's Bill Martin from Walton. Got your mobile number from Wally. I took your visiting order off you this morning – remember? I'm off duty now. Are you still in Liverpool?'

'I am.'

'Then meet me at the town end of Stanley Road, Bootle.'

'What's going on, Mr Martin?'

'Not on the phone, lad. See you in a few minutes.'

Chas drove to Stanley Road. Bill Martin, still in uniform, got into the car. 'Where've you been since one o'clock, Chas?'

'Pub, dock road, asleep in the car.'

'For over seven hours?'

Chas shrugged. 'Time flies when you're having fun. Anyway, what's going on?'

Bill Martin fastened his seat belt. 'Drive,' he said. 'Turn left at the bottom. I'll tell you as we go.'

It was just clothes. But beyond that was the clear fact that Michael Walsh didn't seem to give a fig about how he looked. He could be a priest in gilded vestments, a drag artist in a corset, or a tramp in torn jeans. Lily wasn't sure what he was supposed to be at the moment, though he definitely didn't care. How many men could sit at a kitchen table in Bolton Wanderers underpants and a pink silk dressing gown? His face sported shadow far denser than the famous five o'clock stuff, while his hair, which had grown wilder than ever, was a mess. And he was still beautiful. In the bedroom, he had been all soft words and tender touch, and Lily knew that he was in love with her. Yet in the kitchen he began to play the fool again, because that was his gift. This was when he loved her best, because he laid himself completely open, warts and all. There would be no lies, no cunning plans, no threats.

Now was the moment he had chosen to persuade her

to tell the truth. He didn't need to know what had happened, as he had discovered all that for himself, but he wanted to know how she felt today, how she had felt in the past, and whether he could help her move on.

'You look ridiculous,' she advised him. 'And I shall have a rash from your beard. Pink is not your colour.'

'It was the only thing to hand when we got out of your bed,' he replied smartly. 'Which item of furniture is still too small. If you will drag me off to have your wicked way with me when I am wearing only underpants, what am I supposed to do when I have ceased to be of use? Wander about naked? Shall I go and change?'

'No.'

'Then get on with it. I have an ironing board to invent.'

She sat opposite him and took a deep breath. 'You realize I've been through all this stuff with doctors and head-shrinks, most of whom were dafter than I was.'

'Yes.'

'And it's not easy.'

Mike smiled. 'Nothing's easy. Just thank God that you met someone wonderful who can help absorb your pain.' He stood up, lifted her hand to his lips and kissed it. 'Come on outside. I have put together our upholstered garden swing, and it was built for two.'

Lily prayed that he had done a better job with the swing than he had with his famous ironing board, but she followed him as bidden. They sat in the swing and held hands like a pair of teenagers, away from phones, from doorbell, from the rest of the world.

She told her story exactly as it had happened, beginning with her grandparents' farm, the move to Taunton, schooldays, college, meeting Clive. 'He was spectacular,' she said. 'So handsome and funny. Of course, I didn't notice at first that he couldn't laugh at himself, or that his car was rather better than it ought to have been – he was just a salesman for windows and conservatories. Then I allowed myself to be dragged into the conservatories – I did blinds, floors, furniture and so forth. I curtained the plastic windows he sold, tried to make them look decent. We were a team. He bought me a two-carat diamond, and we were suddenly engaged.'

Yes, it had been sudden. She supposed that the term 'swept off her feet' was applicable in her case, because she couldn't recall a proper courtship. Her gaze slid sideways to the man of the moment – had this been a proper courtship? She thought not, but he was the right one.

'Was he a criminal?' Mike asked.

'Yes. An entrepreneur was how he described himself latterly. Anyway, the owners of conservatories and plastic window frames liked my work, and I got commissioned to do whole rooms – sometimes, a whole house. So he married me.'

'Because?'

'He needed to own me. The penny didn't drop until the glossies began to follow me around. There'd be Linda Barker on one page, me on the next. But the straw that really broke his back was *Makeover Madness*. He thought I was having affairs with every craftsman from Dundee to Paignton. The programmes he recorded were played over and over while he decided which man had bedded me, which one was planning on bedding me – it was a nightmare. I was away from home for days at a time, so he gave up his legitimate work and began to travel with me. But he still had money. When we were at home, some less than savoury characters called at the house – I knew he was up to no good. He got phone calls at all hours of the day and night. Some of his conservatories fell off lorries, I think.'

'But not the glass?'

Lily grinned. No matter what, Mike managed to winkle out the ridiculous option. 'I worked out that he was acquiring materials and that the visitors to our house were building conservatories and fitting windows while Clive followed me all over the country. He had his cake and was eating it.'

'And he still wasn't content?'

'No – far from it. So he made me pregnant.' Lily stopped and shivered, though the evening was warm. 'I have a DVD of my baby – one of those special ones. It shows his face. He was a thumb-sucker and a mover.'

Mike gripped her hand tightly. 'You can stop for a while if you like.'

She sighed. It was now or never, so it had better be now. 'How did I feel? That was what you wanted to know. Trapped. Contained. If I didn't speak, I was sulking. If I spoke, I said the wrong thing.' She paused for a few seconds. 'Life picked up a bit when I became too big for work and he started to go out alone at night. He hated my appearance when I was heavily pregnant, but I didn't care. My face was prettier, he said, but he wasn't keen on my shape. I was happy on my own. I was nesting. Then, when I was nine months along, Babs arrived at the door. She had discovered where he lived, and wanted to talk to him about her pregnancy. She thought he was single. Everything negative went into the blow I gave her. I can still hear the scream she gave when my hand crashed into her cheek.'

'It's all right,' Mike whispered.

'It isn't. Well, it wasn't. I couldn't hit him, so I hit her. He came home, found her crying outside and threw her into the road.' Lily smiled sadly and shook her head. 'When I woke in hospital about twelve days later, she was sitting there reading a magazine. I'd been hearing her droning on about Leanne Chalmers and her interiors, but I hadn't been able to answer, because I was still semi-comatose. She looked at me, put down the magazine and told me that he'd almost thrown her under a Ford transit van. This had offended her sensibilities, because she would have preferred a Merc or a Rolls. "I have my standards," she said.'

'That's Babs,' Mike said.

Yes, that was definitely Babs. She had become almost a sister to Lily. Cassie would have been a sister to Daniel, but Daniel had never been born.

'Lily?'

'He killed my son. He deliberately put the knife through my abdomen and . . . and I felt . . .'

'You felt his death?'

She nodded. 'I lost a kidney, a piece of intestine, and pints and pints of blood. I almost lost my mind. But the biggest loss was, of course, Daniel.'

'Yes. Lily, look at me.'

She obeyed.

'I love you.'

'I know you do.'

They sat in silence for a while before she continued. 'He said I'd stabbed him first, but, when questioned in court, he lost his temper and the truth came out. I was making curtains. I buried my scissors deep in his side to stop him stabbing again. But I missed all the vital organs and, as far as I know, he was back on his feet in a week.' Lily turned and looked at her man. 'My womb was cut through. Even my spine was damaged. They stapled me together again as best they could. There's a chance that I cannot have children.'

'Yes.'

'You don't mind?'

He put his arm across her shoulders. 'I mind. I hate hating the man, and I know you wanted that baby. But for myself, I am happy to have just you. We'll be all right as long as I find my own dressing gown. You may cry now. I'm here, and I'll always be here.'

Lily didn't want to cry, didn't need to produce tears. She had handed herself over into the care of this wonderful man, and she had a future with him. He had been right all along, because she had needed to share the past with him. Being right all the time might become annoying, but—

'I can't help it,' he said.

'What?'

'Being right all the time.'

Lily shook her head before hitting him with a cushion. He was clearly a mind-reader, and he—

'Lily? Lily? Where the bloody hell are you?' Eve rushed along the side of the house and into the rear garden. 'I've been phoning and phoning and I've rung the doorbell—' Eve stopped and blinked. Even in the dim light of evening, she could tell that there was something wrong with Mike Walsh's clothes, but she didn't have time to work it out. 'You have to come,' she told him. 'Have you got satnav?'

'Yes, we have,' he replied.

'Hurry up,' urged Eve. 'Fazakerley Hospital near Aintree in Liverpool. I can find my way if I'm in Liverpool, but not if I'm here.'

Mike, who had grown used to the demands of parishioners, dashed into the house.

'You and all,' said Eve to Lily. 'You've got to come.'

'Me? Is Chas all right?'

Eve nodded frantically. 'It's a woman called Diane.' She placed herself next to Lily on the swing. 'She wants you to come. She says she can't do what needs doing until she's spoken to you.'

Lily swallowed hard. 'Diane Chalmers?'

'Yes.' Eve grabbed her friend's hand. 'She's your mother-in-law?'

'She was. She's in Somerset.'

'Not any more. The police brought her to Liverpool. It took hours for her to get there, and she's in a terrible state. Look at me, Lily. I know it's gone dark, but I want you to look at me.'

Lily looked. 'Yes?'

'Your husband – I mean, your ex – is in a critical condition. His mother's terrified and all on her own – she won't speak to anyone until she's seen you.'

Lily felt the blood draining away from her head. She didn't want to go anywhere near him, didn't want to be on the same planet, let alone—

'I'll be with you. Mike'll be with you. Chas is already there. Nothing can happen while the man's ill and you have friends around you. It's for Diane, love. My Chas says she's a lovely woman.'

She was a lovely woman. Too afraid to visit her daughter-in-law in hospital, she had made herself scarce since the attack. Clive had always been able to pull the wool over his mother's eyes, because she had adored him. An only child, he had been smothered by the love of his single parent. She had probably handed over money to pay Eve's attackers, though she would not have been aware of its purpose. Always, she had tried to believe the best when it came to her son. She was a mother first, last and always. 'All right,' said Lily. 'But Mike mustn't leave my side for an instant.'

Relieved, Eve exhaled and took Lily's arm. 'Come on, babe,' she said. 'Let's get it over and done with.'

For Lily, the journey was a blank. She didn't notice the motorway, the East Lancashire Road, the flattening of the landscape as the Pennine foothills petered out to make way for the Mersey plain. The first thing she recorded consciously was a sign for Aintree Racecourse, famous for its steeplechases, including the Grand National. She didn't like the jumps, because horses died or became winded for the rest of their lives. This was a killing place, and her killer was nearby.

Mike, who had attempted conversation at the beginning of the journey, gave up. He caught a glimpse of the florist who had arrived in Eagleton just a few months earlier, saw the pale, drawn face, the absence of life in features that had been so mobile just an hour ago. This was the woman whose negligee he had worn to make her laugh, whose body he had touched and loved, who had unburdened herself only for the nightmare to start all over again.

Eve, in a rear seat, had her own worries. Did Chas know what had happened in the prison, was he part of it, would the police come looking for him? When would life revert to normal? When would Lily be able to walk about free and happy? It wasn't fair. From the sound of things, a third woman was suffering untold agony at this very moment in Fazakerley Hospital. When would this business end?

The hospital was a huge, ugly place. Parking cost two pounds, payable on exit, and Eve wondered how poor people managed to visit relatives. If they had a car, their visits would be few; if they had no vehicle, bus fares cost more than a meal for a household. Perhaps they lived in their old bangers on the car park and paid just the once? Life had gone crazy.

Lost and mistaken, the three entered the main reception area of A and E, looked at the seated and wounded, read the board that pronounced a three-hour wait. Mike went and stood in a queue only to be told in the fullness of time that he was in the wrong building. 'I can see that,' he told the lacklustre receptionist. 'It should be condemned.'

Under direction from a sympathetic visitor, they followed various paths until they reached neurology. 'It's supposed to be the bee's knees for neurological stuff,' announced Eve. 'But you should go and look at the main building where the wards are, Mike. It's a ghetto. It should be called a stalag or something. It looks like one of those terrible blocks of flats they built in Russia.' She took Lily's arm. 'You'll be all right. I promise you.'

Would she be all right? At last, she asked the question. 'Is he hurt?'

'Yes,' Eve replied.

'Who did it?'

'Does it matter?' Eve held on to her friend. 'No idea, love. Now, it's Diane who needs you. After what he did to you – and to me – the details are what you might call irrelevant.'

The neurological centre was spick and span, carpeted, comfortable and so unlike the main body of the hospital that Eve felt she was entering the foyer of some five-star hotel. 'Is this still National Health?' she asked Chas after greeting him.

'Yes. It's Aintree Trust's special area of expertise, babe – they 'copter people in from all over the place.' He nodded towards Lily. 'Looks like she's not of this world, just like when she first came to the village.'

Lily stood as still as stone in front of the seated figure of her ex-mother-in-law. Diane Chalmers was small, round and grey-haired. Her clothes were creased, while a battered hat lay on the carpet at her feet. On the seat next to hers sat the statutory handbag and a photograph album. She looked as if she had got past tired ages ago – her face was devoid of emotion and drained of all colour. Lily recognized the shell, because she had lived in a similar cocoon for long enough before getting to know Mike and some of the other villagers. 'Hello, Mum,' she said softly. It was like looking into a mirror and seeing an older version of herself – sad, confused and in shock. But Lily was better now. As soon as she returned to Eagleton, she would be whole once more. 'Mum?'

At last, Diane reacted. 'Leanne?'

'Yes.' Lily squatted on her haunches.

'They've got a lot of lavatories,' said the older woman. 'Every one of them's big so they can get the wheelchairs in. See, this place is for those who can't get about properly.'

'I know.'

'And computers to play on while you wait, and a lovely cafeteria, and nice people … Oh, Leanne, I'm sorry. It was opened by Princess Anne.'

374

'Right.'

'Centre of Excellence. I never went to see you, did I? Just left you there, I did. So ashamed of myself. I was scared of seeing you in that other hospital where they put you, because—'

'It's all right, Mum.'

'Because he killed my grandchild and he nearly killed you.' Coming to terms with the real character of a much-loved son had not been an easy process; the deepening lines in her face were proof enough of that.

There was nothing she could say, Lily thought. How might she comfort the mother of a killer? How could anything be done for Diane Chalmers now? The poor woman looked as if she belonged nowhere, and Lily knew exactly how that felt, too.

'I swear to God, Leanne, I didn't know what the money was for. That man – Chas – his wife got hurt.'

'Yes. Yes, she did.'

'And it's all my fault.'

'No.'

Diane jumped up. 'I raised him. I spoilt him. I let him explain everything away and sometimes I knew he wasn't right, that he was up to no good—'

Lily stood up. 'You did your best. No one can do more than that.'

Diane picked up the album. Inside, treasured photographs of her little boy preceded pictures of his wedding, of the honeymoon, of high days and holidays enjoyed by Clive and her daughter-in-law before the world had ended. She had lived for and through her son, had bragged about his cleverness, had boasted to neighbours about his wife in the fancy magazines and on the television. The album was all she had left.

A doctor appeared. 'Mrs Chalmers?'

Both women turned to look at him. Old habits did die hard, decided Lily, because some part of her still responded to the old name. She noticed Chas, Eve and Mike in the corner with a uniformed man, possibly a prison guard. There was blue carpet on the floor. Leanne Chalmers would have chosen a different shade.

'Is it done, all that scanning?' the older Mrs Chalmers asked.

'Yes. I'm sorry, but there's no sign of improvement.'

Diane drew herself up to full height, achieving all of five feet and two inches when her spine was straightened. 'Then we do what needs doing. I waited for my daughter-in-law, you see.' She grasped Lily's hand. 'Come with me. Be with me when ... when ... They can't use any of his stuff. There was something wrong with him – he wouldn't have lived long anyway.'

The room moved. Lily remained completely still while the world shifted around her. Mike caught her just before she fell. But she hadn't been falling, had she? 'This is Diane,' she managed before being pushed into a padded chair. Seated, she regained her equilibrium. Where was the joy? He wasn't going to live, and all she felt was a terrible, cold sadness. Didn't it say somewhere that Mike's God suffered when a sparrow died? Clive had been a person – a terrible person, but ... Poor Diane.

Mike knelt in front of the woman he adored. 'Sweetheart,' he began. 'Clive's had several tests and scans, and he's not alive any more. Diane could have had the support turned off an hour ago, but she waited for you because she needs you to be here. Meanwhile she made them test again just to be sure there was no brain activity. Can you help her? Can you do this one last thing for her?'

The doctor hovered and expressed concern, but Lily shook her head. 'It was just the shock,' she said quietly. 'I'm all right, no need to worry about me.' He was gone. Clive had left the world, had been dying before the incident at the prison. 'What was wrong with him?' she asked the doctor.

'He fell in jail,' came the reply. 'Probably because he had a heart condition that had somehow managed to remain undetected.'

'So he wasn't killed or pushed by another prisoner?'

'There's no evidence to suggest that he was. It was an accident, we believe.' The medic looked at the two women and sent Chas for cups of tea. The patient's mother was in shock, while the newly arrived ex-wife also seemed to be suffering. Clive Chalmers had given little to the world and had taken much out of it, including an unborn child. Even his organs were not usable, so he had died exactly as he had lived – without sympathy and without generosity. 'I'll be upstairs when you're ready,' he told Mike. 'Give these two the time they need.'

Diane managed to drink some tea before finding some words for the woman she knew as Leanne. Clive had fallen down some stairs, and his back had been broken in two places. The hospital staff had now declared him to be brain-dead, but Diane, as the only living relative, had to give permission for life support to be withdrawn. 'He looks like he's breathing, but he's not,' she said sadly. 'Such a good little boy, he was.'

'I know,' said Lily.

'Drew pictures for me, brought me breakfast in bed,

picked flowers and tried to help with jobs round the house.' She smiled wanly. 'Course, the flowers were probably stolen. What happened, Leanne? What went wrong?'

'I don't know.'

'All that hatred. All that nastiness – where did it come from?'

Lily offered no reply.

'Come with me,' Diane begged.

Lily looked at her love. 'You have to come, too,' she told him. 'He's a priest,' she advised Diane Chalmers. 'He can say a prayer.'

They went up in a lift and walked along corridors that led to wards. Mike held Lily firmly, while she clung to Diane's hand. Music was playing somewhere. It was soft, gentle music that reminded Lily of birdsong travelling on a summer breeze. The walls were cream. Machinery bleeped and stuttered. He was in a white bed. The nurse who had accompanied the group in the lift melted away into the background.

Lily looked at the man she had feared, and he was still beautiful. With no lines on his face, no hard eyes fixed on her, he was just an ordinary man with extra-ordinary good looks.

Diane pulled herself away from Lily and went to straighten her son's hair. She placed on the bed a photograph of a small boy before nodding to the doctor. A switch was pushed, and the machinery grumbled until the classic flat line appeared on a screen. Mike walked to the bed and placed a hand on Clive's forehead. He prayed for a man who had murdered a baby, who had almost killed the child's mother, who had ordered the attack on Eve.

Diane turned to Lily. 'I have to take him home.'

Lily brushed away a tear and hugged the little woman. 'Not tonight,' she said gently. 'And not on your own. Mike and I will go with you to Taunton.'

The ex-priest followed the pair out of the room towards the lift that would return them to the ground floor. He knew why he loved Lily. She had a generosity of soul that was far more valuable than her obvious assets. Lily, or Leanne as she might now choose to be called, was a real woman, a good person who would always try to do the right thing.

As they drove back to Eagleton, he listened to the two women in the rear seat. Lily was telling Diane that she could stay with her in Eagleton, perhaps for a holiday, perhaps for ever. 'Don't decide now,' she said. 'But Lancashire worked for me.'

It occurred to Mike that there was irony in today's situation, a grim sense of fairness about what had occurred. Clive had killed his son; Clive's mother had turned off machines that had kept the man alive in the technical sense. The difference was, of course, that Diane's actions had been born of kindness, whereas— He didn't want to complete the thought. Sometimes, thinking was not a good idea.

Fifteen

She still sat upstairs for most of the day, though she had moved slightly to the right and was occupying a different window. Enid had a lodger, and there had been a reboot on the bedroom front, but she was just one of the people who had endured change. In Eagleton, 2008 became known as the Year of the Shuffle, because people moved around like men on a chessboard, hither and yon, a few pauses for calculation, some stalemates and the knocking down of several walls.

But Enid remained *in situ*, as did the village stocks and a couple of Ice Age boulders around which fences had been erected. However, Enid's place of residence was now above the re-named and re-located Lily's Bloomers, and the Reading Room occupied two units, one of which had ceased to sell flowers, while the other no longer operated as Pour Les Dames. Fullers Walk currently housed the off-licence, a veterinary practice and a florist, while the extended Reading Room took up the last pair of shops.

Maurice and Paul, having reached the final of a national talent show, were currently working in Las Vegas, though Sally, mother of a newborn, had stayed in the village. She was happy, her marriage remained solid, and she waited patiently for her husband to return from cruises and tours all over the world. Blessed with a temperament that was placid and accepting, she carried on her life away from the glitz and noise that surrounded her talented partner. Wealth neither worried nor excited her, because she lived for her son and for the day when her man would come home from his latest tour.

The invasion of Eagleton had begun in the autumn of the previous year. Like Holmfirth in Yorkshire, the village became famous, though for different reasons. No Compo or Foggy had wandered its streets, yet hundreds had come, in the wake of Clive Chalmers's exit from the world, to catch a glimpse of the Leanne they remembered from TV and magazines, the poor woman who had suffered greatly at the hands of a terrible husband.

She gave few interviews, wrote no book, accepted no payment from editors who wanted to hear 'her side of the story'. Her ex-mother-in-law took over the flower shop, and she, too, developed a way of coping with intrusion – she simply closed the shop until questioners gave up and went home.

Diane Chalmers had been absorbed into Eagleton and was fast becoming one of its fixtures. There were two chairs at Enid's bedroom window, and the pair of old women often looked down to watch the world and his wife (and his children) on the green below. Enid was frail, and she preferred to eat in her room. Diane coaxed her out as frequently as she could, but resistance was sometimes tiring, and the immigrant from Taunton was no spring chicken.

However, they got on like the proverbial burning house. They sat now side by side, cups of tea on small tables, biscuits spread on a plate, each leaning forward to study the Mothers' Union as it assembled on the grass. Valda was there with her youngest son. She had named him Patrick, and he had a shock of red curls inherited – or so it was said – from a great-grandmother. Valda's husband had been heard joking about the milkman or the window cleaner, but all remained well in the Turnbull house.

'There's your Philly,' cried Diane.

Philly looked up and waved, turning the pram so that Dave's mother could see Simon.

'He's a little belter.' Enid smiled. 'Pity I never loved his dad like I love him. I was a selfish, good-for-nothing, cruel young woman, Di.'

Diane patted her companion's arm. 'We were both useless, my lovely. You can love a child too much. You can love him too blindly. My son did more damage than yours ever would or could. They never did find out for sure whether his death was an accident. It doesn't matter. What sort of mother can say that? It should matter.'

'Oh, you're all right, you are. Take my word for it – I know all about bad, because I was no better than a bloody prostitute.' Enid shook her head sadly. 'Till I got past it and became a Methodist instead.'

Unfortunately, Diane's mouth was full of tea, and she almost choked on it when she heard that. Enid didn't know how amusing she was; she took life too seriously and blamed herself for everyone's ills these days. 'God, I wish you wouldn't do that, Enid.'

'What?'

'Make me laugh when I'm eating or drinking.'

Enid sniffed. 'Come forth with that stargazey pie thing

again, and there'll be no more eating in this house. I don't care about your Cornish mam and her recipes – I'll never look another sardine in the eye as long as I live. Bloody heads poking out of the pie crust – whatever were you thinking of?'

'Home.'

'Do you miss it?'

'No. I'm all right here, thanks all the same.'

'Then shut up and fettle with yon teapot. See – there's young Sally arrived now with little Jonathan. All boys, eh? Not a one of them with a little lass to dress up nice and pretty. Still. As long as they're happy, eh?'

'They'll be happier still this afternoon, Enid.'

'They will. And so will you, pet.' In a rare gesture of true affection, Enid grasped her lodger's hand. 'Aye, by tonight, it'll all be great. And if anyone deserves great, you do.' The wetness in her eyes was because she had a cold, Enid told herself. Because she never wept . . .

People had flocked to see Lily/Leanne, but they continued to come in droves long after her tale melted into history, and Dave was due some of the credit for that. His double unit served several purposes, and he used both levels to maximum advantage. After long discussion with Health and Safety – most particularly with the fire service – he and his staff manned a ground-floor restaurant with permission for corkage and a menu that stretched as far as Philly's imagination would allow. As mother of a tiny child, she functioned in a supervisory capacity only, working on recipes and doling out orders from her modest home.

Dave got the glory. The whole village felt that he deserved it, because he had worked like a dog since time immemorial. Then there was the actual dog. The eccentricities of Skippy, along with several other factors, meant that people continued to think of Eagleton as a place to be enjoyed. Bed and breakfasts sprang up out of nowhere and, in spite of financial recession, visitors continued to come. The scenery was magnificent, the village friendly and pleasant, so outsiders arrived all year round, and there was even talk of a Christmas meal in the Reading Room.

Dave's cleverness meant that his Reading Room was always busy. Those who used the place as an Internet café grew younger, while those of the clientele who liked to eat out brought their own wine in the evening and enjoyed a decent meal, live music at weekends and good service at all times.

Until the dog got in. With the passage of time, Skippy developed skills that might have been admirable in a foreign diplomat, because she granted herself full immunity and nowhere was verboten. She went where she damn well pleased, was happily disobedient and extremely well fed. Her proper job was with Tim Mellor, and she was very serious about her chosen career in the area of veterinary science. But once the surgery was closed, Skippy entered a twilight zone created by and for herself, a dimension in which rules were no longer applicable. She could get through the smallest of holes, was not averse to creating and improving such apertures, and, as a result, attracted dog lovers from miles away. When she entered the restaurant, applause was sometimes deafening, and staff who had once chased the three-legged Labrador learned not to try, because Skippy's public needed her.

The bookshop thrived. Even now, in a period of recession, folk wanted to buy *The Story of Skippy*, a hardback coffee-table book without which no home could be considered complete. The large, slender publication was filled with photographs, and each copy of the book was signed by the author, David Barker, and by the subject. Her signature was smudged, usually in purple, and no issue of the work could be regarded as complete without that paw mark. This was a dog whose life had been saved, who had gone on to save a human life before leading detectives to damning forensic evidence. She had been national news, and her fame continued to be impressive.

At the beginning of summer 2008, Skippy adopted a paper boy. His name was Mark, and he had a tendency to fall off his bike, so the bitch took him under her wing and went with him each morning to take papers from bike to houses. As a result, Mark's round was extended, since people seemed extra pleased when Skippy hopped her way to their doors with a *Guardian* or a *Mail* between her teeth.

But Dave's true genius lay in his love for and his treatment of good literature. Twice a month, a book club met in the ground-floor shop. Authors came to read and sell their work, and when no writer was available Dave would do the reading. On alternate weeks, amateur critics gathered in the same place to discuss their homework, a book they had all read, or pieces they had written. Dave was over the moon. Anything that encouraged people to read and compose in an age filled by easier entertainments was worthwhile. His clientele grew, with people driving in from Manchester, Cheshire and even from Yorkshire. The Wars of the Roses were put to bed while reds and whites came together to read, criticize and write. It was a triumph.

Dave Barker stood with his dog in the doorway of his and Philly's little empire. Philly was on the green with two other new mothers; visitors were walking up and down, some in footwear heavy enough to proclaim their intention to do some serious tramping over moorland. Life was almost perfect; by this afternoon, the picture would be complete. He nodded to himself. This was the day on which the jigsaw could be finished.

Diane nudged her companion. 'Wake up,' she admonished. 'I think we're under starter's orders.'

After a small snore, Enid opened her eyes and sat up. 'Look at the state of him,' she said, pointing a finger at Mike Walsh. He was dashing from the church in his altarboy uniform, hair all over the place, legs going nineteen to the dozen. 'To think he used to be the priest,' she said, her head shaking. 'He favours a man what nobody owns.'

'He's looked after Leanne,' whispered Diane.

'I know, love. I know he has.'

The man stumbled, righted himself against the graveyard wall, slipped off a shoe and emptied from it some foreign object.

'He is funny,' Diane admitted.

Enid nodded. 'You should see him in a corset.'

A streak of humanity shot onto the green. When it ground to a halt, it was seen to own auburn curls and a small girl. 'Babs and Cassie,' remarked Diane unnecessarily. 'Is Pete at work?'

'I suppose so. Look at her.' Babs left Cassie with Valda, Philly and Sally, ran towards Hope House, came back with a colouring book, ran again, stopped, returned with Cassie's juice. Enid sighed. 'It'll be a rum do with her,

Eve and Chas in charge. They couldn't organize a riot in Strangeways. Where's he gone?'

'Mike?' Diane shrugged. 'He's in the house. I suppose I'd better get ready.'

'A cardy will do,' Enid called to her disappearing friend. 'Too hot for a coat. And don't start skriking.' She paused. 'That's Lancashire for crying.'

Diane presented herself for inspection. 'Will I do?'

Enid nodded. 'Aye, you'll pass muster. Go on. Get gone with you. I'll still be here when you get back.'

The door closed behind Diane, and Enid wiped her face. She wasn't weeping. It was sweat, wasn't it? She watched while her lodger crossed the road and entered Hope House. After a few moments Diane and Mike emerged, got into Mike's car and drove off in the direction of Bolton.

Then it all began. Sally was left to mind three babies in prams and one small girl who was trying to colour the village green red. Wax crayons made little impression, so there was no danger of too much change in that area. But the rest of Eagleton was a flurry of poorly coordinated activity.

Chas, Eve, Babs, Philly, Valda and Dave struggled with bunting, strings of coloured lights and home-made signs. Chas had to do all the climbing up ladders, and he made a poor fist of fastening items to street lights and telegraph poles, but it was fun to watch. Enid's laugh made its way up rusty pipes before bursting out of her body and into the room. She hadn't howled like this in years; the scene below was funnier than anything ever produced by Buster Keaton or the Keystone Cops.

They had to be quick, because the people for whom

387

the surprise was being arranged were no more than five miles away. On a whim, Enid picked up her phone. She nursed not the smallest hope of preparations being completed satisfactorily, so she stepped in. 'Listen, love, you keep them there for as long as you can,' she begged. 'Because they're making a right pig's breakfast here.' She paused. 'Well, I don't know what you must do, do I? Just ... oh ... give them some advice, some lists about how to do stuff ...' Chas Boswell was wrapped in flex and light bulbs. 'Look, there's a bloke here going to be electrified if we don't shape. Right. Right. That's the ticket. Thanks.'

She put down the instrument and leaned through the open window. 'Oi!' she yelled. 'You've an extra ten minutes, so buck up. It's like watching a bloody Charlie Chaplin film. And that sign's not straight.'

She leaned back and closed her eyes. If she didn't stare at them, they might do better. And the above-mentioned pig might fly to its breakfast ...

As soon as Diane Chalmers entered the room, Leanne passed Matthew to her. 'There you go, Grandma,' she said softly. 'He won't break.'

'So tiny,' remarked Diane. A tear ploughed a lonely furrow down a careworn cheek.

'Tiny?' Leanne pretended to frown. 'He was a bag and a half of sugar when he was born. He's huge now. Aren't you, Matthew?'

Mike lingered in the doorway and surveyed the scene. Only his beloved wife could hand her child over to a woman whose son had killed this baby's half-brother. Only Leanne seemed blessed with sufficient generosity of heart to blame no one for anything. He swallowed hard and walked to the window.

It had been hell. Leanne had spent months in the unit, monitors and drips attached, blood pressure gauge always *in situ*, people forbidding her to worry, sometimes not allowing her to walk, always watching, taking blood, testing, scanning, listening to her belly. Had he heard the word placenta one more time, he would have screamed.

They had delivered Matthew by section at thirty-three weeks. Leanne had refused to leave him, and had remained with the Augustinian sisters until this very day. She was brave, strong, wonderful and adorable. As for his son – well – he was definitely a fighter. Right from the start, the baby had gripped his father's finger every time it had made its way into the incubator.

'Mike?'

He turned to look at her. 'Yes?'

'Will you carry my bags, please?'

A nun rushed in. She stared hard at her little upside-down watch and began to gabble in a thick Irish brogue. 'Now, you know not to overfeed, don't you?'

Leanne nodded.

'And,' continued Sister Bridget seamlessly, 'we've written down a few bits and bobs and found some interesting items that say about development and suchlike and so forth.' She looked at the watch once more. 'Now, you're to treat him just like any other baby, but a few weeks younger than he actually is when it comes to the picking and choosing of clothing and what have you, and he may wean a bit later than usual. Now, I had a thought, and—'

Leanne wondered whether Bridget was going to start every sentence with the word 'now'.

'—don't be wrapping him up too tight, for he's better upholstered in himself than most prems at this stage.'

Mike raised an eyebrow and Leanne fought a giggle. Had their son just been compared to part of a three-piece suite?

'Out of the sun, of course,' the nun continued. 'And ... er ...' She glanced at the watch once more. 'I wonder would Mrs Chalmers bring him to the office so we can all say goodbye? He's been such a blessing and a treasure, and we'll miss him sorely, so we will ...' The voice faded into the corridor as nun and adoptive grandmother left the room.

Mike sank into a chair while Leanne stretched out on her bed. She would be glad to leave behind all this clinical whiteness, found herself longing for colour, sound and texture out there in the real world.

'You all right, darling?' he asked.

'Fine. I just want to get the hell out of here.'

Mike smiled. He knew what they were all up to back in Eagleton. Chas had been flustered for two days, bunting had disappeared from beneath the school hall stage, and there wasn't a coloured bulb to be found in the whole village. Would Leanne want a fuss? He looked at her. She wouldn't mind as long as she got a decent cup of tea. Her gifts were many, yet her needs were few and simple. The nun was in on the surprise; she was stalling them because someone had phoned to request it.

At last, they made their escape. When the baby was in his safety harness and the grandmother had settled next to him, the new mother and father got into the front of the car. Leanne found herself almost overwhelmed by the outside – so many shades of green along the road to Eagleton, so many different colours of cars, doors, flowers in gardens. Everything was bright and beautiful, but Matthew would soon be hungry.

WELCOME HOME signs stretched across shop fronts, while almost every resident had crowded onto the green to welcome home the youngest member of their community. As soon as the car came round the corner, applause rang out. Skippy, with a blue bow on her collar, waited at the gate of Hope House.

It had all been leaked, of course. A news crew approached Leanne as soon as she stepped out of the car. Diane took the baby indoors while Mike remained on hand if his wife should need him.

'How are you?' asked a journalist. 'How's the baby?'

'Fine,' she answered, looking not at them but at Enid in her wheelchair, her son and daughter-in-law by her side. She smiled at Eve and Chas, at Babs, at the vet and at a very happy Labrador. 'It's good to be home,' she said into the mike.

'And Mr Walsh?' came the next question.

Leanne sighed. 'As well as can be expected. Now that the baby's born, we have the full grid for noughts and crosses.' She tried not to smile when the man looked puzzled. 'But I have to tell you this,' she said. With the air of one looking for interlopers, she glanced over her shoulder. 'There is no such thing as a perfect man. He is absolutely hopeless with ironing boards.' With that, Mrs Leanne Walsh turned on her heel and walked into the house.

Mike followed her. 'You shouldn't have said that,' he told her.

'Why?'

'Because I fixed it.'

She stared very hard at the man she adored. '*You* fixed it?'

'Yes. Well, sort of. There was a bit of plastering, so I had to get an expert in after the brickie had mended the wall. Then the tiler did his bit. Oh, a painter made good, and . . .'

'And?'

He shrugged. 'Well, I bought you a new ironing board.'

She hit him with her handbag and pushed him into the kitchen.

Acknowledgements

I thank Gill Currie, who keeps my household ticking over – she has the common sense with which I was never endowed.

Also cheers to a certain young man who spent some weeks at Her Majesty's pleasure in Walton, our local prison, where the guards are nowhere near as cruel as they are painted herein.

Thanks to Billy Guy, Cassie, Tilly, Fudge and Treacle. Billy is not a Labrador, but the rest are.

Special gratitude to Avril, my captive audience, who listens to every plot-line and absorbs every developing character. She would escape, but MS keeps her contained.

Readers – thanks yet again.